TRESPASSERS

GARY STAPP

BROTHERS

One, a scholar and a dreamer, the other
a lover and a fighter.
In 1979, they are the heirs to a ranching legacy.
In 1878, they are surviving as

TRESPASSERS

Playing cowboys and Indians was a childhood game for JT Tescott and his brother Dent while growing up in the 1960s on a Kansas ranch. But in the infancy of their adulthood, fantasy becomes reality when the power of an arcane talisman summons an ancient race and opens an aphelion portal, transporting the brothers and four of their friends into the Wild West of 1878, an era renown for devouring boys and birthing men.

Trespassing into the alternate dimension with the Tescott brothers are life-time friends, Blaine and Sam, as well as outcast Kival and resident bully Oleander. As the six of them piece together the truth of their alien abduction, they find themselves still present in their native Kansas but navigating life 101 years back in the past, a time wholly absent of any other human souls previously known to them.

But fate adventurously leads them to the historic frontier town of Hays City and the rustic environs beyond, accelerating them into the maturity of young men. There on the High Plains, they experience life and death as danger looms in the expansive shadow of a vile, narcissistic, 20th century presidential assassin, while amid their inescapable jeopardy, love spins tangled webs in a time that was not meant to be repeated. And linking them all together are the mysterious and supernatural Burmano-Ku-Partika, waiting to be called upon to reopen the time portal and return the transient visitors through the archway of the Smoky Hill Pyramids.

FOR MY GRANDSON, LUKE

So that you might know a part of who I am.

DEDICATED TO MY FAMILY

With special appreciation for my wife, Kim, and daughter, Lacey. Thank you for the love and encouragement you've shown me as we, together, adventured through the writing of this story.

PROLOGUE

I sat nervously upon the front half of a thinly padded chair in the dim corner of the hospital room, fidgeting with the ring on my left hand.

And feeling helpless.

My eyes were aimed at the floor, staring at the intersecting lines separating the squares of polished tile, but my mind cared little about the surface, even less about its details of geometry. Instead, my thoughts were preoccupied with the inevitability of an affair that was moments away from unfolding in my presence. Yet my sight was also distracted by a profound sadness that had cruelly overwhelmed me, then before I was able to deflect it, another uncontrollable stab of sorrow pierced my heart as a spasm of despondent breath wheezed from the shallows of my lungs.

Damn me, I silently scolded myself, my brain commanding my throat to be quiet and unobtrusive.

A few feet away from me, unconscious upon the rigid mattress of an ICU bed, lay a little girl, her tiny, broken body shrouded by a cold, sterile sheet.

A daughter.

Her parents were my friends, each of them holding onto a small hand, the mother sitting next to a child who would always be her baby, the father standing opposite, knowing his little girl had only precious minutes of time before she would be gone. Earlier, they had fully surrendered their grief, their eyes releasing rivulets of tears that traced wet pathways down their cheeks and dripped silently, melting into the crisp linen shroud. It was then I had dropped my gaze and had willingly abandoned my watch.

In my twenty-six years, I had witnessed more death and dying than I cared to dwell upon. But here I was again, with a front row seat.

Yet, so far, I, myself, had never killed anyone, though I would be lying if I said I had not considered it before. There had been one man whose life I could have ended. I had possessed the motive, a weapon, and the opportunity, a prosecutor's hat trick. But my conscience had stopped me, though I had imagined the help of an accomplice. Even in this moment, I recalled the sense of an intervening hand. But that mattered little, not now, not in this place, not in this time of heartbreak.

My lungs ached. I did not know how much longer I could force them to contain my sobs of despair. At once, a wave of nausea overcame me, reminding me that I was weak and that I was scared. It had been a battle, one where my choice of weapon had been willpower, but it had already let me down at least once. But soon, very soon, I would have to be strong. I would have to be resilient.

For them.

They would need my strength, my resolve. They were counting on it. I had a promise to keep, but I was terrified that I would not have the courage to uphold that conceivably impossible vow. I cursed silently, hearing the profanity rise again in my mind as I thought of the reckless man who had caused us to be here in this place, in this situation. The idiot had been driving far too fast. And in a school zone no less. He was a thirty-five-year-old father with two children of his own. What was he thinking? He should have known better!

I was angry. And when life support had been removed, I had been, for a moment, livid.

I fought to suppress the volatility of emotion that pulsed through my mind. And it was imperative that I win that fight. I had a job to do. A task that required focus and expediency, and action without hesitation. One, two, maybe three fleeting minutes were all that remained between now and the event I hoped would prove to be miraculous. And upon the stage of this hospital room, I had a leading role to play that was critically important. I knew that I would have to act with logic but even more so, with faith. Yet, to fulfill my commitment, I would have to forsake the morality of my soul.

At present, the four of us were alone. The apologetic doctor had left the room, the nurses had followed him. Privacy had been requested. A time for intimacy between a father, a mother, and a child had been sympathetically granted.

But more importantly, we required secrecy. We needed time without interruption. Little did the hospital staff know that my presence there had a purpose beyond the provision of consolation. I was there because my friends had begged me to be. I was there because I had agreed to do as they had asked. I was there and I was ready. Inside my jacket, within easy reach of my hand was a Glock 17, loaded.

Without a flicker of forewarning, the soft beeping sounds of the

VIII

electronic monitor abruptly began to ebb, and I looked up to see a father kiss the forehead of a child he would perhaps never see again, though the three of us adults believed and hoped otherwise. Either way, if they came for the child, there would be no choice except to follow through with the plan.

But we were also intelligent enough to know that despite our experience, there was no absolute certainty. Our understanding was minimal at best. Something different could happen this time. It was entirely possible they would not come for any of them, or perhaps not take all three. And if one of them were left behind, I was going to be in serious trouble.

I listened as the beeps steadily slowed, the intervals between the sounds widening with each audible timbre. And then a wrathful tone, jarring and unrelentless, filled the room. The machine had signaled death.

As premeditated, I quickly stood and scrambled to the door, lodging a large rubber doorstop between its bottom edge and the threshold of the entry. Suddenly the temperature of the room turned cold, and I was instantly relieved.

They had come after all.

I turned and watched with awe as gray ghostly figures began to appear, churning as if in a soft wind, camouflaging the child. Their actions were neither alarming, nor were they unexpected. Two of us had seen them before. And we had convinced ourselves that we understood their purpose and their motive.

Then the young father, a man who had unexpectedly become one of my best friends, crossed to me, his eyes replenished with tears, his chin quivering. Briefly, our eyes locked, and we exchanged the acknowledgment of the brotherly love that had bonded us, then we shared a firm, but hurried embrace before he quickly stepped past me. Once behind me, I knew he was setting the backside of his torso heavily against the door, firmly planting his feet and pressing his weight backward, and then applying an unrelenting death grip upon the cold, metal handle.

And then she was there in front of me, a wife and mother, her eyes clear and brave. The time had come to initiate a sequence of events, an idea that she, herself, had conceived as their only alternative.

"Now, Jermyn," Anja nodded. "Do it now!" Then her hands reached for my face, and I felt her warm fingertips press protectively into the cavities of my ears.

IX

Time had become an enemy, so I did not hesitate. I slid the gun from inside my jacket, placed the barrel against the swell of her left breast and fired the weapon into her heart. A muffled explosion sounded in my head, then instantly, her petite body convulsed. Instinctively, I caught her in my arms, and felt the warmth of her blood trickling over my hands. Gently, I eased her to the floor as the sting of a cold, icy breath of wind enveloped us. I stared at her, knowing I had just taken her life, but also realizing my innocence as a killer had just been forfeited. But I could not dwell upon guilt. Not now. Time was of the essence. I could not spare even a single second.

"Hurry!" The voice behind me quivered with anguish. Quickly I rose and crossed to him, and then just as we had prepared and practiced, I pushed him forcefully against the door, pressing my chest into his, and resting my chin upon his shoulder, knowing that in just moments my one-hundred seventy-five pounds and his dead weight would be all that would keep the medical team from interfering with our plan.

I cried out as I fired a second bullet, this time into my friend's heart.

The gunshot burst against my eardrums, deafening my perception of all other sounds. But the assault did not spare me from the punch of his wretched flinch against me. Then his body fell limp and I let him slide to the floor, his blood and that of Anja's dripping from my fingers.

At once, beyond the door, voices sounded, first with concern, then with escalating alarm. I leaned powerfully forward, pressing my bloodied hands and perspiring forehead against the door. Instantly the air around me turned frigid and I felt the windy movement of the apparitions swirling below my waist. Then a swish of a three-fingered hand crossed near my face, an appendage with substance and physicality that lasted only a second but used that fraction of the clock to touch me. I looked to where I had felt its caress and realized the thing had cleansed the blood from my hands. With guarded awe, I glanced downward and watched as the alien band of docile spirits swarmed and enveloped the lifeless body beneath me, stealing him from my sight.

For a moment, time seemed to have stalled, even though movement and shadow blurred my vision. Then within mere seconds my friend disappeared before my eyes.

Suddenly the tangible movement of a whirlwind swooshed over me, then instantly all was still.

X

Quickly, I turned and pressed my back to the door, and braced my feet before me, praying that the traction of the rubber soles of my shoes would afford me the leverage of a few more seconds. Then once again, my eyes were locked upon the floor between my legs, although this time my focus was not on the intersecting lines of the tiles. Instead, I stared at the shimmer of ice crystals glistening softly in the dim light of the room. Then my gaze crossed to where I had laid the body of my friend's wife. Like him, she had also vanished. In her place was a faint glimmer of moisture in the vague shape of her form. Already, the last signs of her presence had begun to evaporate.

Gone, too, was the child. Moments earlier, four human souls had occupied the room. But three had been taken away. I, alone, had been left behind.

Alone, but no longer afraid. And though my heart was pounding heavily within my chest, I felt no remorse.

No guilt.

Instead, I simply embraced relief. As we had expected, just as we had hoped for, the gentle thieves had come and had performed their unfathomable duty. I was neither angry with them, nor resentful. The shadowy beings were transporters of the lost. They were escorts for those who had cheated time. And this family of three had, after all, trespassed into the dimension of an existence in which they did not belong. And trespassers were not allowed a finite death in a time that was not their own.

Or so we believed.

PART ONE

Time and Time Again

CHAPTER 1

JULY 1979

In the corner of my bedroom, I sat at a vintage oak desk that was one half of an identical pair my mother had bought at a local garage sale for fifteen dollars each.

It was a simple square-legged piece of furniture that for most students would have been more than adequate for doing homework. But as far as I was concerned, the surface area could barely accommodate an opened textbook partnered with a folded spiral notepad, and my TI-30 pocket calculator, while hardly sparing room enough for the essential trio of study aids: A package of black licorice twists, a bag of potato chips, and a can of Shasta orange soda.

Still, I managed to reserve space to oblige my collection of vintage cameras, which at the age of seventeen I had assembled a total number of three that included a Brownie Target 6-16 and an Ansco Shur Shot, both of which were classic box cameras, and a Univex Twin Flex given to me by my recently deceased grandmother.

Granny Evelie Tescott was a do-er more than a reader, and it was she who had suggested that I get a hobby that might occasionally distract me from my books. But her influence in my life began many years earlier. By her example I learned at the age of four to drink coffee. As a nine-year-old we would take walks along the Smoky Hill River and share dreams of traveling to exotic places. Later, as a teenager, she taught me the pleasure of plug tobacco, if one could claim the habit a satisfying vice.

Upon the desktop and squeezed within a narrow gap between a green glass Mason jar I used as a pencil holder and the precarious edge of the desk, I had managed to display a picture of my girlfriend, Laurie. I had taped her printed image to a seven-inch square chunk of native limestone commonly found on the land of my family's ranch, a rock I had decided when I was thirteen would make a great paper weight, though I had never once used it to anchor anything down. And now, it encroached upon precious square inches of desktop real estate, but at least the rock had become useful. Besides, Laurie's picture needed to be displayed prominently, not simply pinned among the miscellaneous items of a bulletin board.

The photo was tiny, an exchange-size print included in the annual school picture packet. Most parents, mine included, bought the standard set of photos, keeping the signature eight-by-ten for themselves, gifting the two five-by-sevens to the grandparents, with the remaining photo sheet populated with a dozen miniature pictures to share with friends, though any number greater than three was overkill as far as I was concerned. But for outgoing and popular teens like Laurie, twelve was a laughable quantity that could not begin to meet the demand.

I studied Laurie's face, sky blue eyes delightfully competing with a smile formed of rose-tinted lips that framed movie-star white teeth, and a nose that had, at the age of fifteen, lost the prominence of the freckles I remembered from when she was a grade school kid. I cherished that little photo. It had given me an assurance that I was liked. Liked by a girl. And any teenage boy will tell you, being liked by a girl can be a big thing. Especially, if by nature, the boy is shy and self-conscious, which were two unfortunate traits puberty had fostered me to embrace. But I was at last beginning to grow out of my awkwardness, and because Laurie had asked to trade pictures with me, her request had given me the nudge I needed to ask her out on a date to the local movie theatre. Three weeks later, I had mustered the courage to suggest we go steady, not just because I hoped that status might discourage competition, but also because I had never learned to share well. And now, seven months down the road, my shyness was a fading thing of the past.

The two of us had kissed.

A lot.

In fact, we had gotten to second base, frequently. But no further than that. Mostly because our two sets of parents had their own high school history, and were still to this day, best friends who continued to regularly socialize in each other's homes, sharing a meal, a few drinks, and playing the prerequisite card game of gin rummy. Allegedly one time, this being a story my mom, Clair, delighted in telling far too often, while our family was visiting at the Edwards home, Laurie and I had disappeared from the living room only to be discovered in a bedroom, hiding within the narrow space between bed and wall, and kissing like, well, like a three-year-old and a five-year-old would kiss.

Cute and innocent.

Not at all like our make-out sessions had developed into now. Months earlier, we had nervously talked about third base, and I had secretly dreamed of what a homerun might be like with her. But Laurie's dad, who happened to be our town's number one police officer, had not been at all bashful with his threat to cut off my dick if I even thought about having sex with his little girl. And why his warning had been made in the presence of my dad and my brother, I never quite understood or appreciated, but still, I took his words seriously.

Very seriously.

Luckily for me, Laurie's dad, Chief Edwards, was unable to read my mind. Even now, my thoughts drifted. Images filled my imagination. I closed my eyes, stretched the length of my legs out before me, and—

"Hey bro!"

Instantly I blushed as my eyes flew open and I racked my knees on the underside of my desk, completely startled, again. My brother seemed to like nothing better than to barge into my room, unannounced and unwelcome. The thought of knocking was a completely foreign concept to him. And locks on either of our bedroom doors were forbidden. Parental rule number seventeen, or seventy. Or somewhere in between.

Dent laughed. "What ya doing there, Germ?"

"Nothing."

"Did I see a boner?" he teased as he strode toward me.

"No," I denied, pulling my notebook into my lap, and wishing that I had not changed out of my blue jeans and into a pair of revealing gym shorts. I met his eyes and then saw him glance at Laurie's picture.

"Thinkin' about your girlfriend, weren't you?" he grinned, as he curled his arms upward at his sides, hands forming into fists, biceps bulging, his hips vulgarly thrusting. "Or maybe daydreaming about Farrah," Dent suggested with a double-bounce of his eyebrows as he nodded at the poster on my wall depicting a sexy Farrah Fawcett in a provocative red swimsuit that had frequently made the fifteen-year-old me blush with appreciation.

"You're such a perv."

"Ain't I though?!"

"What do you want?" I demanded, quickly changing the subject.

"That ain't no way to talk to your big brother, especially since I'm planning your birthday party."

"No thanks. I don't want a party," I informed him adamantly. "And I especially don't want one planned by you," I added, as I scanned the array of books lining the shelves attached to the wall above my desk.

"Man, that cuts me. Cuts me deep."

"Right." I replied, sending my brother the message that I was clearly doubtful.

"Look, Germ, tomorrow you turn eighteen."

"Yeah, I know, Denton," I said, emphasizing the second syllable of his name. As I chose a book from my collection of studies of American History, I wondered if I had managed to push the right button. I looked at him and saw that he was, in fact, annoyed. I smiled at my success.

He was pointing his finger at me, a finger I had often felt punching into my chest. "Don't call me that."

Immediately a movie reel of memories flashed through my mind, times when I had called him Denton and he had beaten the hell out of me, intentionally bruising me in places that would be conveniently hidden by my clothes. But one time, I had fought back, my blows had been unexpected, savage. I had finally had enough. But I had also been shaken and ashamed, fearing I had perhaps unleashed a monster within me that might become something impossible to control.

Dent, though, had been stunned by the violence of my defense, both of us wondering how his normally wimpy brother had embarrassingly bested him. But I had no desire to brag about my triumph. Besides, we were forbidden to fight one another, and I didn't want additional guilt or punishment. Instead, Dent chose to craft a story to explain his bumps and bruises: He had been thrown from his horse landing on the corral fence.

We were never quite sure Dad had bought the explanation, after all Dent was a skilled equestrian, learning to ride at a time when I had barely learned to walk. Regardless, I had not offered the truth. But from that point on, Dent had shown me a modest increase of respect and had become less tempted to exercise his dominance over me. However, my brother had a temper and occasionally it would push him over the line of restraint. Still, since that time, physical fights between us had been few and far between.

"Don't call me Germ," I said to him, and watched his eyebrows arch. Because we were brothers, we were very aware of the weaknesses in each other's psyche. Those emotionally tender wounds that could be picked at by either of us, at any time. Though most often, those incidences were initiated by him. But, coincidentally, one sore spot that bothered each of us was our respective given names. My birth certificate read Jermyn Thomas Tescott. Thomas, being that it was my mother's maiden name as well as a common first name, did not bother me. Jermyn, however, had often caused me grief.

More than my fair share, in my opinion.

Mom had chosen Jermyn, pronounced like German, and bestowed

upon me in honor of her great grandfather. But at an early age, kindergarten to be exact, my first name quickly evolved into the nickname "Germ," and being a sensitive child of five, I had cried a lot from the teasing, and had subsequently begged my parents to rename me something else: Joe or Troy or Mike. Anything was better than Jermyn.

Before I had aged into double digits, my nickname morphed into "The Germ," and eventually in Junior High, a select few kids began to call me "Germ Worm" because of my love for books. All were monikers my brother Denton had first been responsible for pinning on me.

Even now, thirteen years later, I still remember my dad calling me a sissy, demanding that I suck it up and act like a little man worthy of the Tescott family name, expounding on some diatribe that the surname was most important anyway. But Mom, at least, had been more sympathetic, wiping the tears from my eyes, yet encouraging me to ignore the kids, and always ending with *"it's a good name, Jermyn. A family name. Your great-great grandfather was named Jermyn. You should be proud."*

I was not, and I doubted that my ancestor who was doubly great had been very fond of his name either.

My brother's official first name was Denton, conferred as an honorary nod for Dad's older brother who had been killed in action in the Korean War. But his middle name was Dean, named after Dad. And given my brother's penchant for getting into trouble when just a youngster, he was often called Denton Dean when being scolded by Mom.

One evening as the family had gathered for dinner, the opinionated eight-year-old declared he was *"not gonna eat no more damn green beans."* Then two more unbecoming remarks followed, and Denton Dean had been paddled for back-talk and sent to bed. But ten minutes later, he had defiantly returned to the kitchen, and he had failed to clothe himself in his pajamas. Instead, he was decked out in blue jeans and size five cowboy boots and wearing our dad's battered and sweat-stained cowboy hat, arguably dressed as a miniature version of the man of the house.

With his arms folded, my brother had announced that he no longer had two names and would only answer when called Denton. And if that had not been ballsy enough, he had informed the woman who had carried him in her womb for nine months that she might want to write that down.

I still remember Mom, angrier than I had ever seen her, looking down at my older brother and enlightening Denton Dean that she would call him whatever she wanted. He retaliated with a hard kick to the refrigerator door. Dad had apparently found this tantrum amusing and had sat my brother upon his knee and made an announcement to him, to me, and to our mother. *"Tell you, what, little man,"* Dad had said, pointing to the damaged appliance. *"From now on, I'm just gonna call you Dent."*

And there sitting in our father's lap, a place that was easily the equivalent of a king's throne, Dad had laughed and roughed up Dent's hair, the two of them relishing their individual proclamations of how it was going to be. I had realized then, for the first time, that my dad had a favorite son, and it was not me.

A few years would pass before I found the courage to likewise suggest an alternative name for myself, but I did so with far less bravado. I had decided that I would adopt my initials as my name. In fact, my best friend, Sam Chambers, had been the one to suggest it and he had immediately begun to call me JT. Mom protested. Dad was indifferent, though later I would learn that he had not cared much for my first name either.

"Look, JT," Dent addressed me with sarcasm etching the pronunciation of my abbreviated name. "It's your eighteenth birthday. It's a milestone. You become a man. Well, maybe not a man in your case, but old enough to drink beer. Legally!"

"I don't need to drink beer. Legally or otherwise."

"Jeez, you're such a puss."

"And that means so much coming from you," I added, as I thumbed through the pages of an encyclopedic volume of Reader's Digest's *The American West*.

"Like it or not, you're getting a party. With a keg. Dad's even paying."

"Dad is not paying for a keg for me, not for my eighteenth birthday. Not for any occasion. So, Dent, stop with the lying, okay?"

"I'm not bullshittin' ya. It's Dad's idea. Like me, he thinks you need to grow up. Pull off those little boy panties and get drunk and get laid."

I jerked my head toward him and read the honesty in his eyes. "Tell Dad to keep his money. Save it for a few more months and buy you the keg. You're the beer-drinker. You're the party-guy. Not me."

"That's what I told the ole man. But you know him."

I looked away. "Yeah, I know him. Obviously, he doesn't know me."

Dent crossed over and flopped down onto the top of my bed, crossing his sock feet at his ankles, and folding his hands behind his head as he made himself comfortable with my pillow.

"You know what your problem is?"

"Oh, God. Just leave, okay?"

"You are a momma's boy."

"And there it is … again."

"It's true. But then you are Mom's favorite."

I glared at him. "No more, or less, than you are Dad's favorite son." I turned away from him, anxious to change the subject before I unintentionally admitted to my brother that I harbored strong feelings of jealousy toward him that went beyond parental favoritism. And I had a practical list of things to be envious about, but two specific items strongly competed for the top position.

Dent was as exceptional athlete, his skills easily eclipsing mine. We both had participated in team sports, he as a starter while I watched from the bench. And he was socially popular, naturally endowed with confidence, charisma, and charm. Girls had always been attracted to him. Rarely did I seem to get a second glance even though we shared similar physical characteristics. We had the same build, medium-frame, slender, though I was an unnoticeable half inch taller.

We also shared the same nose, something between Dad's Roman beak and Mom's Welsh button. And the shape of our eyes, and the way we smiled was nearly identical. But to that end our differences were more obvious. Like Dad, Dent had hair the color of strong coffee and he was genetically gifted with a dark skin tone that spared him from an easy sunburn, not to mention he was blessed with azure blue eyes that could quickly wreck a somber mood with unabashed frivolity.

On the other hand, I had a sandy version of Mom's golden locks, and if I allowed my hair to grow for more than a few inches in length I would begin to have the portents of curls, which I passionately despised. And I had my mother's eyes, orbs that mirrored the humility and compassion of her hazel irises, but I was also favored with Mom's fair complexion, for which she often argued was the reason I had managed to get through puberty with relatively minor bouts of acne. I had my doubts, but it was hardly worth a debate.

But personality-wise, Dent and I could not be more different. He said what he thought, did not worry about hurting someone's feelings, and did not give a shit when other people refused to agree with him. And like Dad, Dent was quick-tempered, tough, outspoken, outgoing, and reckless. He was afraid of nothing. All balls and all in with every aspect of his life.

And I was simply the opposite.

Even as toddlers, our polar personalities were apparently quite clear even though our physical statures as kindergarteners were nearly identical. Strangers often mistook us as twins. But we were not. I was seven months younger. And yes, to this day that unusually short gap between our ages continues to raise an eyebrow or two.

Interestingly, we were both born on holidays. Dent made his grand appearance on Thanksgiving in 1960, and in my opinion that fact alone was why he often acted like a real turkey. I, on the other hand, entered this world on Independence Day, but I was far from being thought of by anyone as a firecracker.

Conceived roughly six weeks after the birth of my big brother, my debut into this world had been three months ahead of my due date. Apparently, it was touch and go as far as my doctors had been concerned, giving me a solid fifty-fifty chance of surviving. I had spent several weeks in a hospital in Hays, a railroad city birthed in the days of the Old West and steeped in the lore of notorious gunfighters and Indian raids and range wars.

Named for the Western Kansas outpost of historic Fort Hays, the town of nearly sixteen thousand souls rose up from the grassy plains nearly eighty miles east of our hometown of Custer. Because of the hour and a half drive between the ranch and Hadley Memorial Hospital, Mom had spent nearly a month with me, night and day, while Dad and Granny Evelie took care of little Denton and the business of the ranch.

Knowing my mom, though, I knew it had to have been hard for her to be away from baby Dent. But even after my dismissal from the hospital, my circumstances undoubtedly persisted in robbing my brother of his fair share of motherly attention. I suspected Dad had gladly picked up the slack, and his relationship with my older brother had naturally become more special. And in relatively rare moments when I fell victim to the melancholy of being second best, I would remind myself of the situation that had given Dent the advantage of a closer relationship with our father.

But amusingly, the relativity of our births, mine more so than Dent's, had thrust our little family into the spotlight, the four of us temporarily achieving small-town celebrity status. Custer's local newspaper, *The Monument Telegraph,* had documented our story, prolonging the Tescott family as a popular topic among the gossip circles of diners and beauty shops. But before my brother and I were out of diapers, we had finally become old news.

Though despite my weak start, I had grown and developed quickly, catching up to the size of my brother by the time we were both ready to set upon the path of a structured formal education. And because of our respective birthdays, we both had entered kindergarten at the age of five.

"So, the party will of course be at the Pyramids," Dent continued.

"Why tell me? I won't be there."

Ignoring me, he kept talking. "Gotta keep your party legit, so we can't have anybody there that's not legal, even though the Pyramids are on our land. Nobody under eighteen. Gotta keep Dad out of trouble with the county gunslingers. So obviously you can't bring Laurie, you know, because of her age and her ole man, Barney Fife. Not that he'd probably shut us down since he's best buds with Dad, but the deputy Barney Fifes might. So, definitely no hard stuff either, even though Olly says he's bringing— "

"Sedgwick?"

"Yeah. Look, I know you don't like him— "

"Damn right, I don't. Oleander Sedgwick and I are like Batman and the Joker. We don't get along. Period. Why would he want to come anyway?"

"I invited him. Besides, it doesn't matter to him that you are the guest of honor. As far as he's concerned it's just a party."

"Yeah. That's what I thought. Just a party. An excuse for you and your friends to get shit-faced."

"Yeah. So?"

"Forget it. Like I said, I won't be there."

"Look, JT, you can invite your nerdy friends. I don't give a rat's ass."

"Really? Thanks for your permission. So, Blaine can come?"

Dent glared at me, then sat up and threw his legs over the side of the bed and said, "Whatever."

Throughout our elementary years, Paul Blaine Wallace, Jr., as he was known then, was a year ahead of us, but in high school he and Dent had been solid teammates, both excelling on the football field and the basketball court, and until recently they had seemingly been best friends. But a couple of months earlier, just before Senior Prom, something significant had ruffled the feathers of one, or both, and neither Blaine nor my brother had shared more than three words of explanation between them.

"Dent, I don't get it. What happened between you two?"

"Not a damn thing," Dent said with a disinterested shrug, then he stood and immediately crossed to the door. "We've got pinkeye duty tomorrow. Don't forget."

And as quickly as Dent had entered my room, he had exited just as fast. Surprisingly, he shut the door behind him.

In less than twenty-four hours the passageway back could be entered, the escorts could be summoned.

CHAPTER 2

The summer had so far been a blistering one. Above normal temperatures combined with long, full days of glaring hot sunshine had been a model precursor for the all-too-common affliction in cattle called pinkeye. And the white-faced Herefords that were the bread and butter of the Tescott family ranch were especially vulnerable to the intense summer climate that exacerbated the development of the disease.

Dent and I had ridden our horses east, trotting along the ranch's northernmost boundary, searching among the grazing livestock for any animal with an acute infection of the ailment, characterized by the staining of their checks by excessive tearing of their bloodshot eyes. Like Dent, I thoroughly enjoyed being on horseback, though my appreciation for the equine creature was not realized until I had turned fourteen, a good ten years behind Dent.

In the formative years of my adolescence, I had been, frankly, fearful of horses, and cows for that matter. But Dad, surprisingly, had been patient, never pushing too hard to force me to confront my nervousness with the two species of ranch animals. Yet, he still encouraged me, taking the time to explain the nuances of animal behavior, and his gift of that information helped me to understand the necessary balance of respect between man and beast. Caution, he had said, was a good thing, and I appreciated that he had never belittled mine.

Dent, too, had encouraged me, in his own brotherly way, to join him and become more interactive with the working particulars of the ranch, though, more often than not, he did so by endeavoring to shame me for my refusal to cowboy-up, as he would call it. But eventually, and relatively on my own, I did at last cowboy-up, and my motivation had been almost instantaneous. That incentive was a thousand pounds of bone and muscle, and hide and hair that now moved powerfully and obediently beneath me.

My horse.

The day before my fourteenth birthday, Dad had left on an overnight trip to neighboring Colorado where he had traveled to finalize a transaction he had been negotiating via the telephone to procure an addition to the ranch's remuda. He, of course, had taken Dent with him. Left behind, I had been assigned the temporary duties of man-in-charge, which primarily meant I was to keep Mom company. The next morning, they returned, their arrival uncharacteristically announced by the distant sound of the tinny horn of Dad's Chevy half-ton blaring unapologetically as it rolled exuberantly upon the graveled road.

I had been in my room, flipping through the pages of a pictorial book populated by intriguing illustrations explaining the science behind how things fly, when the white pick-up entered the ranch yard, skirting along the circle of driveway that separated the house from the outbuildings, its horn being orchestrated to the tune of a cavalry charge, a sound that had impatiently begged that my curiosity be abated. I had hurried to my window half expecting to see Dad arriving in tow with an elaborately decorated grand marshal float primed and ready for the next Logan County fair parade. But instead, the truck returned with what it had left in tow; a matching white horse trailer hitched to its rear bumper.

However, something was afoot, and because it was my birthday, I was suddenly suspicious. I left my room and raced down the hallway and dashed from the house to see what the excitement was all about, arriving in time to find Dad, and Dent, both grinning from ear to ear. Then Mom was there beside me, draping her arm across my shoulders, her face, too, beaming. I still remember being overwhelmed with curiosity while simultaneously feeling an intense degree of anticipation that had fully taken my breath hostage. Then Dad opened the trailer gate, and from inside stepped what I could only then describe as a show horse, radiant and handsome.

"Happy birthday, Son," Dad had exclaimed, his own excitement as genuine as mine.

I had glanced at my mother, completely stunned. "For me?" I had asked with an arch of one eyebrow.

"Well, don't just stand here with your mouth hanging open. Go get acquainted," she had urged me. And I had not needed a second nudge. I had then crossed to the horse, moving calmly as I had been taught, and was instantly in awe of the shimmering red of the gelding's blood bay coat and the flashing of white that encased the lower eight inches of his two stamping hind feet. I had gently touched him, my hands roaming along the animal's side, feeling the sleekness of his hair and the power of muscle that flexed and quivered from rump to shoulder. I had patted his neck, then had taken the lead rope offered by Dad and had let the horse nuzzle at my hand before I had reached up to stroke the crooked white blaze that ran down the length of his finely chiseled head. I felt an instant bond with the animal and realized in that moment that Winston Churchill had been right.

There's something about the outside of a horse that is good for the inside of a man.

A quote my father had often recited, though one I didn't fully appreciate until that moment.

"What do you think?" Dad had asked.

"He's the best thing ever," had been my reply. And now, four years later, Jericho was still my favorite thing about the ranch.

I leaned across the thick leathered horn of my Dick Heye crafted saddle and gave my beloved steed a firm pat on his neck. "Good boy," I said, smiling at the familiar warmth and softness of his glistening crimson coat. I glanced over at my brother, astride his own Quarter Horse, a golden sorrel gelding he named Copper, but my eyes lingered on the pair for just a moment before my gaze unavoidably passed beyond them to the landscape that swept southward beyond us.

My view was almost entirely dominated by land that was my legacy, and also that of my brother. The vast acreage was an assemblage of real estate contributed by both sides of our family tree. Mom's great-grandfather, my namesake, had founded his portion of the sprawling ranch by enjoining a handful of failed 1880s homesteads he had shrewdly acquired by trading dispensable livestock for land deeds, and subsequently merging them with his own initial one-hundred-sixty-acre claim. Shortly afterward, the English pioneer allegedly acquiesced to a suggestion made by his new bride that the collective land be given a name. Her recommendation was to call the ranch Sweetwater, an appellation that served as a venerating nod to a meandering stream that traversed the gently rolling landscape, its languid course flowing west to east.

My father's side of the family, the Tescotts, had occupied two thousand acres beginning in 1946 when my grandparents, Vernon and Evelie, purchased three sections of land just after World War II had ended, then moved there from Alabama with their two young sons. The transplanted family had struggled, barely able to scratch out a sustainable livelihood. Their home had been little more than a shack, but Dad had often pointed out in the presence of his mother, that there had always been the best home-cooked food on the table and the warmest of beds for sleeping, both of which, according to my grandmother, was a determined result of hard work and unshakable love.

Then later, a war in Southeast Asia, tragically robbed them of their eldest son, and shortly afterward my grandfather, Vernon, had died suddenly, and the passing of these men had thrust the youngest son, a thirteen-year-old going on thirty, into the responsibility of keeping the small ranch afloat. Eventually, the boy, who would become my father, realized the need to contribute to the family income and so he sought a part-time job by asking a neighboring landowner, a third-generation occupant of the ranching Thomas family, if he might have any odd-jobs he could do for him in his spare time on weekends and after school.

As it turned out, the compassionate rancher was immediately convinced he did, in fact, need help, especially since he had just one daughter and no sons. Little did either of them know at the time that a romance would ultimately develop between his teenage girl and the hired boy. My dad often relished telling his version of how their affair had blossomed. He claimed it was because of his irresistible charm, wooing my mother before he had even begun to shave, though my mother would straightaway argue that she was little more than a child-bride of an arranged marriage. If Mom would have ever countered Dad without failing to smile and blush, I might have believed her.

Following graduation, the pair of high school sweethearts became not just a matrimonial merger of a young man and woman, but their marriage was also a precursor to the joining of the two adjacent ranches.

At nearly six-thousand acres, the present Sweetwater Ranch was approaching a centennial celebration of its original founding by my ancestor Jermyn Thomas. However, this relatively flat part of the Western Kansas prairie was more than just my home. It had been my playground of sorts, a vast nine square miles of natural rangeland, stippled with sunflowers, scrub sage, prickly pear cactus, and the broad spiny leaves and pale-yellow blooms of yucca, all vegetative companions of the short, but nutritious buffalo grass that was the life source of a variety of herbivores, both domesticated and wild. An environmental biome nearly unchanged for centuries.

Or more.

Most certainly more.

In the few short years of my own modern cowboy days, Jericho and I had explored every acre of Sweetwater, enjoying our adventures, both real and imagined.

Inspired by the Western storyteller, Louis L'Amour, I would often pretend to be his William Tell Sackett, a favorite character of mine, combing distant horizons for evidence of potential enemies and trail-hunting for signs of a lost friend among the random thickets of elm and willow that had sprouted along the lazy meander of the Smoky Hill River. And when time allowed, Jericho and I would usually begin our adventure from the westernmost edge of Sweetwater, just as the two of us, horse and rider, exited from the corral of the ranch headquarters. We would almost always end up being drawn to the far northeast corner of the property, steering our way among the unique landforms known officially as Monument Rocks, referred to semi-formally as the Chalk Pyramids of the Smoky Hills, though locally we simply called them the Pyramids.

As my gaze drifted eastward, the flattened crests of the natural collection of rocky landmarks poked above a lowly knoll, inviting my sense of adventure to revisit their place. Even now, I was able to easily imagine how our ranch had once been a part of a greater land, untamed, unsettled, and largely unexplored.

A romanticized American West.

A legendary place of wild horses and savage Indians. Of cowboys, gunfighters, and outlaws. A wide, open vista where great herds of bison would have lumbered carefree, undulating like blankets of umber shadow beneath pillars of towering clouds.

"Hey, Wild Bill!" Dent called out to me, snapping my attention to the present. He knew of my penchant for the Old West and so he would on occasion call me Wild Bill in honor of the legendary Hickok, though Dent intended no flattery with the nickname. Neither could he identify with my appreciation for the paperback literature of popular Western storytellers.

Thankfully, however, I could credit my dad for introducing me first and foremost to the quality writing of L'Amour, and so cementing our common admiration for the great author's Western stories. Those particular novels were among a select few things Dad and I could pleasurably discuss within the parameters of casual conversation. And that was something that meant far more to me than he probably realized.

"Quit your daydreaming. You just passed a patient."

I looked to where he was pointing and saw the calf, one of the larger ones that had likely been born in early February, its white cheeks dingy and damp, with eyes fiery red and watery.

Suddenly Dent spurred his horse toward the unsuspecting adolescent bull, startling him and his nearby bovine mother into a frenzied combination of eight legs going fifteen different directions, one animal lunging left, the other springing to the right. Separated by the horse and its rider, the calf, now frantic, began to sprint in full panic mode. And Dent and Copper were immediately behind him, guiding the frightened animal away from the herd as my brother, in poetic chorus, began to loosen his rope, forming it into a lasso, while expertly clinging to his saddle. I watched as puffs of dust and divots of grass kicked up from the heels of the galloping horse, the big sorrel chasing the Hereford calf as it dodged across the camouflage of the brown-green flora of the parched summer pasture.

Knowing the routine, Jericho took off after them, needing little more than the feel of my bootheels pressing into the upper edge of his belly. As we raced along, closing the gap between us and our cohorts, I watched as my brother reined his horse to the left rear side of his prey, twirling the loop of his lariat above his head as he expertly positioned himself and Copper for the desired perfect throw. At once, the lasso snaked out from Dent's grasp, flying forward, the loophole settling over the white head of the calf, and then within the expanse of a split second, Dent was dallying his end of the rope around the saddle horn. Simultaneously, he tugged on the reins of Copper's bridle, bringing the three of them, including the calf, to a near sudden stop.

Captured, the young Hereford had leapt into an airborne about-face, snared by the taunt trap of rope that had snapped him around, his feet shifting horizontal and sending the four-hundred-pound suckling calf thudding instantly to the ground. Seemingly unfazed, the calf scrambled to his feet, bawling, and fighting against the pull of its captor. My turn to play cowboy had arrived.

And I was ready. Even before my brother had scored his catch.

Having expertly crafted my own lasso, a substantially larger loop than the size Dent had used, I began the propeller-like motion of the rope above my head, steering Jericho toward the calf. Dent had turned Copper around and with the rope tethered about twenty feet between the two animals, he had begun leading, if you could call it that, the agitated calf away from me, its hind legs shuffling defiantly forward, the spindly pair of appendages being the target of my attention.

Jericho instinctively trotted along behind, positioning me for my own flawless throw. I let my lasso whistle in the air above me for three seconds longer, then I swung my arm outward into a wide arc, released the rope and watched as it fell, as planned, precisely in front of the calf's rear limbs, setting the snare for its feet. I jerked my end of the rope upward toward my right shoulder, drawing the loop tight around the ankles of the legs, heeling the calf.

Immediately I pulled on the reins, carefully backing Jericho a few steps while remaining watchful as the rope patiently stretched the young Hereford's back legs outward behind him before quickly robbing the animal of its center of balance. At once the calf tipped over. Again, it lay on the ground. Only this time it would stay there, anchored in opposite directions by a pair of ropes held firmly in place by a duo of well-trained and disciplined members of the equine species. I glanced at the heavy breathing of the calf, then shared a nod of affirmation with my brother.

"Nice catch, bro," Dent called over to me as we both dismounted. He strode to our captive, gliding his gloved hand along the taunt rope, while I pulled at the zipper of the leather pouch tied to the back of my saddle.

"Thanks," I replied, genuinely appreciating his recognition of my own positional skill. Calf-roping required teamwork. A header and a healer. A ying and a yang, working in tandem as we both contributed to a necessary part of the operation of running a modern-day ranch. "You weren't so bad yourself," I replied, genuinely awed by his natural ability with a lariat.

From inside the pouch, I gathered two needled syringes and a plastic bottle containing milky-white penicillin. For a moment I reflected upon how well my brother and I worked together. Despite our regular bickering throughout most other times in our daily lives, when it came to the responsibilities our dad had assigned to us regarding the business of the family ranch, we completely put our personal rivalries aside. Here, working at a job we both loved, we were teammates.

Partners.

Forgetting our differences.

Instead, we focused on the one commonality either of us was quick to admit; a profound sense of pride in Sweetwater, the ranch that had been our home and would one day, hopefully, be jointly owned and occupied by both of us. Arguably, we were also grateful for being part of a family industry that was sadly, but steadily, shrinking away from its hey-day just decades earlier. Among our friends and classmates, we were two of perhaps just a half dozen other kids whose livelihoods were directly attached to ranching.

"This poor guy has it bad," Dent spoke as I crossed to join him. He held his knee in a firm, but gentle position of rest upon the calf's neck as the tips of his fingers examined the swollen, irritated eye that rolled about warily watching us.

"Looks like. But hopefully we're catching it in time," I said, as I inserted the needle of the syringe into the rubber stopper of the medicine bottle. I siphoned the appropriate number of CCs of the antibiotic into the syringe then knelt on the ground opposite Dent. I frowned at the tear-stained cheek of the white-faced calf as I noted the hot pink abscesses crowding the corners of the young animal's eye. It was a textbook example of the blinding disease. One that had been particularly infectious due to the summer's scorching sun which typically contributed to a high number of infected animals, mostly calves, this one included.

"Okay, hold him still," I said, giving Dent the heads up that I had traded proverbial hats, and was about to play veterinarian. Gently, I lifted the eyelid and inverted it outward exposing the veined, fleshy membrane of the underside of the lid. "Here goes," I announced, just as I inserted the needle into the inner surface of the inflamed tissue and slowly dispensed the medicine.

"Man, what's this make, JT? The seventeenth, eighteenth one today?"

I did not have to look at Dent to know his head was turned away, his eyes averting the specifics of my actions and focusing instead on the chest of the little red and white animal, watching intently as its furry sides expanded and contracted like a blacksmith's bellows.

"Eighteen, I think," I replied, knowing that he did not really care about the number. I glanced at him and smiled, not because I found this feebleness of his funny, but instead because I felt a twinge of compassion for my brother. Beneath the shade of his woven-straw Stetson, I knew queasiness was bleaching his cheeks of the redness caused by the heat of the afternoon sun. His otherwise, rough, tough, and ready demeanor was instantly erased at the sight of a needle.

And it was a weakness he hated.

Dent could shoot a coyote, or skin a jackrabbit, or castrate a bull calf, and never once blink, or be swayed into a bout of dizziness. Blood never bothered him. But a needle could turn his stomach inside out. At times, I admit, I enjoyed the humility of his Achilles' heel. After all, it was perhaps the only aspect that made me tougher than my brother. At least, in my mind, it was a win. However, I wisely never teased him about it. If I had, he would have probably beat my ass.

"Are you done yet?"

"Yeah. Just finished. Now for the other eye."

We rolled the calf over and repositioned ourselves accordingly, then repeated the medicinal procedure.

"Okay, all that's left is the general." I then loaded the second and largest of the two syringes with the penicillin, then leaned over the animal, patting the large muscle of his up-turned thigh for a few taps before sticking the needle through the soft hide and discharging the antibiotic. "He's good to go," I said as I stood up.

Our treatment of the animal completed, Dent removed the noose from around the calf's neck as I quickly trotted over to Jericho and loosened the end of the rope from my saddle and dropped it to the ground. Dent nudged the calf with the toe of his leather Justin brand boot and the animal scrambled to his feet, kicking the rope loose from around its heels. Immediately he ran off, loping away for a distance of roughly thirty yards before stopping and turning to glare at us with admonition. He stood for a moment, posing with his white head held high as though he dared us to try that again. Then just as quickly, he shifted gears and galloped away, enthusiastically bawling for his momma.

"He sounds kinda like you, JT," Dent goaded with a laugh.

"Kiss my ass," I said turning away and smiling.

CHAPTER 3

Declaring that we had undoubtably notched an above average day of ranch work, Dent had insisted we resign from our cowboy duties earlier than normal since we both needed to cleanup for the beer fest he had planned for the Pyramids later in the evening. Again, I reminded him that I had no intention of attending the get-shit-faced shindig he was clearly masquerading as the celebration of my eighteenth birthday, but neither was I going to argue with him about quitting early. I had my own plans. I had a date with Laurie.

Just the two of us. Beer party be damned.

Thus far, I had been relatively successful in conquering peer pressure when it came to brews and booze. Not that I was a completely virgin teetotaler. When I was nine, I had ignored my Grandpa Jake Thomas's warning to stay away from his drinking glass and had naively sampled Jim Beam bourbon, which I promptly spat out and vowed never again to drink any more of Grampa's water.

Then as a high school junior, I had been impressed by a Miller Lite commercial featuring Bubba Smith who first pitched the low-calorie beer as *less filling and great tasting,* then bare-handedly ripped off the top third of the aluminum beer container proclaiming that he also loved the easy opening can. So, when my brother had prompted me to give the touted beverage a try, I succumbed to the influence of both him and the Super Bowl-winning defensive end. I managed to drink down three-quarters of it before my taste buds persuaded me to throw in the towel upon which I gave the beer two solid thumbs down.

But in my early teens, I confess, I had even taken a drink from a bottle of Johnnie Walker Red Label, but from where I had gotten the whiskey and with whom I had shared a sip of the hard stuff would be a secret taken with me to the grave, as promised. That said, I was certain I had been tricked into drinking what had to have been horse piss.

Collectively, Jim and Miller and Johnnie, had ultimately convinced me that I was not cut out to be a consumer of alcohol, and despite the relative popularity of the drinking song, "One Bourbon, One Scotch, One Beer," I was able to say that I literally identified with the song, though in title only. For now, I was more than content to commemorate my crossing into the realm of legal adulthood without the indulgence of alcoholic libation.

Pizza and a movie at the modest but appreciated Arrowhead Theater on Main Street was good enough celebration for me. And besides, Laurie seemed genuinely interested in seeing *Moonraker,* even though she admitted she had little knowledge of the James Bond series of films but knew enough to erroneously assume that Sean Connery still portrayed the British MI6 agent.

It was mid-week, and because our father also worked a daytime shift as a foreman at the Sedgwick Window Company, he would not get home until after six. That would allow me just enough time to give him a report of what Dent and I had accomplished for the day before I headed into Custer for my dinner engagement at the locally popular Pizza Shack.

Showered and clad in my newest pair of button-fly Levi 501s, the only pair of jeans I owned that did not have the faded tell-tale ring in the back left pocket that proved I had once had a vice: Skoal tobacco. But I had abandoned that two-year-old habit for Laurie, though Mom assumed that it had been she, herself, who had convinced me to go cold-turkey and give up dipping snuff.

I hurriedly slipped on my favorite green-plaid Western shirt though I chose to delay the fastening of the pearl snap buttons. Instead, I plopped down on the edge of my bed and quickly pulled onto my feet my new pair of size ten-and-a-half, black Nocona shark-skin cowboy boots I had recently bought myself from wages Dad had paid me for helping on the ranch.

Neither Dent nor I had ever asked for an allowance, much less a salary, but Dad had been in our shoes himself as a high school teen, and he knew our social life came with expenses. A hundred dollars a month to each of us was worth it to him to keep us invested in the ranch and away from an hourly two-buck-ninety after-school job in town. He did, however, expect us to put aside twenty-five to thirty percent of our wages as savings for a rainy day.

I stood up from the bed and glanced down at the pointed toes of my exotic boots and nodded approvingly. Although, in my father's opinion, a boot vamped in anything other than cow hide was an unnecessary extravagance. But I had the rest of my life to be practical. Still, Dad's comments had almost made me feel guilty for buying them.

Almost.

But having recently embarked upon a day trip to nearby Hays, I had seen the Noconas displayed in the window of a Western outfitters store, and I had unexpectedly found myself coveting them, regardless of their impracticality for the daily toils of the ranch. But then I had no plans to slide these boots into stirrups. These were my dress boots. And besides, we Tescott brothers had been given the latitude to spend those earned dollars at our personal discretion. Dent typically bought beer. I invested in footwear. We were, after all, proverbially cut from different bolts of cloth.

Boots on, I returned my attention to my shirt and snapped the faux-pearl buttons together. Then I retrieved my watch, a timepiece that had been my granddad's, and given to me by my mother upon my high school graduation six weeks earlier. Its hands informed me the time was 6:18.

The earth was in position, the passageway could be opened.

I replaced the watch inside the top drawer of the bureau, maintaining my personal philosophy that I was too carefree to keep a vigilant tab on time. Tucking the tails of my shirt into the waist of my jeans, I hustled down the narrow hallway that primarily accessed two bedrooms and a bathroom, the boys wing of our sprawling ranch home, and met Mom as she stepped from the utility room, packing clean towels in her arms.

"You're in a hurry, Jermyn."

"Running a little late. Laurie and I have a date."

"I know. And as much as I like her, I don't especially appreciate having to share you with her on your birthday."

"Mom, we agreed I could do the family thing this weekend. I mean honestly, I'm not a little boy. I don't need a birthday cake. I don't need candles. I'm eighteen, and now," I began, affixing myself with a playful smirk I knew would gently annoy her, "I'm legally a grown man. I can do what I want."

"Don't get smart with me. We both know you're full of …"

"Full of what?"

"Crap."

"I did sound like Dent, didn't I?"

"Little bit," she said, smiling. "And for the record, I dislike being a minority in a houseful of men."

"Hate to be you," I chuckled, then began to move past her.

"Hold up there, sonny boy. You're not too old yet to give your mother a kiss before you leave."

I backed up until I was even with her and bent my chin down to give her a peck on the cheek. "I'll probably be late. Don't wait up."

"Of course, I'll wait up," she replied, disappearing into the bathroom I shared with my brother.

"Of course," I said, trotting onward, the footfalls of my prized boots tapping along the hardwood floor. As I neared the end of the wide passage that connected to the kitchen, I heard Dent's voice.

"He said he ain't going."

I entered the kitchen to find Dent sitting at the table, his sock feet propped up on the chair next to him, his head craned toward my father who was leaning against the edge of the countertop, his hand wrapped around a bottle of Budweiser.

"Ask him yourself," Dent prodded, shifting his glace toward me.

"JT, Dent says you're not gonna celebrate your birthday. Why the hell not?"

"I am celebrating my birthday. With Laurie."

"But what about your party out at the Pyramids?" Dad goaded me with a second question.

"That's Dent's party, not mine."

"Look, son, I want you to celebrate turning eighteen like most other boys do. Like I did, and like Dent."

"Dad, you know that drinking beer is not a big thing to me. I don't understand why you have to ride me about it."

"I ain't riding you, JT. I—I just want you to experience life. Live it up a little. Be more normal."

"Normal?"

"Yeah. More like me. More like your brother. More like a man."

"Thanks, Dad," I said, shaking my head.

I was angry, and worse, I was gut-punched. It sucked that my own dad could not find value in what was, or was not, important to me. But that was nothing new. And I did not want to rehash an old conversation. In my mind, I knew it would be best to say nothing, and just leave.

Silently, I crossed the kitchen and threw open the back door, intent upon expressing my angst without using words. But then a second later I changed my mind and opened my big mouth and spoke over my shoulder, "I'm sorry I'm such a disappointment to you, Dad."

Then before he had a chance to argue otherwise, I pivoted to face my pair of manly role models. "Honestly, I'm damn glad I'm not like you. Or him." Then I turned and stepped through the door, leaving it open behind me. Instantly, I regretted my words, but I was not ready to apologize for them.

Not yet.

I had a date. But not just with Laurie. I would later discover that I also had a predestined appointment for an unexpected journey with unimaginable escorts.

And had I only known of those unpredictable details, I would have turned around, then and there, and walked back into that house gladly expressing my honest regrets for saying those words to my father.

But then how was I to know what was soon to become of me?

In less than three hours the passageway would close.

I sat silently on one bench of the cafe booth, barely noticing that the jukebox had switched from playing reggae artist Johnny Nash's "I Can See Clearly Now" to "Ring of Fire", a Johnny Cash country song that had first became a hit in the early 60s when I was still in diapers. I was, however, aware enough to wonder if someone in the Pizza Shack was reading my mind and messing with me.

But I didn't dwell on that possibility for very long. I was too heavily absorbed by a mood of regret and was disquietly wrestling with twinges of remorse for the words I had spewed at my father little more than an hour earlier. Before me was my dinner I had barely touched. One slice of pizza had only two bites hewn from its triangular shape, the other slice remained cold and whole.

"You're like a million miles away, JT," Laurie commented as she stared warily at me from across the table, her hand hesitantly reaching out to touch my arm. Her cautionary eyes and the timidity of her touch had not been entirely lost on me, but then Laurie had, herself, been uncharacteristically quiet since the moment I had picked her up at her house. In fact, she had offered an apology for not feeling well, and had been quick to inform me that she would probably not be the best company for the celebration of my birthday.

Preoccupied with my own demons, I had not been as perceptive of her comments as I would otherwise have been, and so I had not pressed her for an explanation of her somber mood. Instead, I insisted we at least go eat, skipping the movie if she did not feel like going. And here we were, thirty minutes into a date that had been nearly devoid of any significant conversation.

"Sorry," I said, glancing guiltily into her sparkling blue eyes. "I'm being crappy company. And trust me, this mood I'm in has nothing to do with you."

"It doesn't?"

"No. Why would you think that it did?"

"Oh!" Laurie exclaimed with a flash of apparent relief. "Well, you know how people like to talk and, and spread lies and rumors, you know, just to stir things up. I just thought maybe…"

For a long moment she stared at me, her eyes unable to hide her struggle for words.

"I like you JT," she said finally. "I like you a lot."

"And I like you a lot, too," I replied, squelching my impulse to simply respond with ditto.

I did like Laurie. She was fun to be with, though if I were to admit it to myself, my feelings were relatively superficial. She had become my steady girlfriend, and with her I was unavoidably testing the waters of hormonal stimuli and trying my best to navigate the turbulence of adolescence without setting either of us up with impulsive long-term expectations or permanent commitment. Afterall, we were just teenagers.

But one thing I was becoming more cognizant of in the past few weeks was that I was learning to distinguish between infatuation and love. And one thing I was increasingly sure about was that I was not in love. Not with Laurie. Not with anyone. And I hoped she was not too emotionally invested in me either. Especially since I would be leaving for college in less than two months.

A couple of minutes ticked by, neither of us speaking, the silence between us neither uncomfortable nor unusual. We did not necessarily share many similar interests. Just two high school kids whose parents were friends. That was about it. Except for making out, our time together had not been especially conversational. But for high school couples that was probably pretty normal, I guessed.

"JT, you're obviously bummed about something. If it's not me—"

"I told you, it's not you," I snapped. Her eyes flared for a moment, then seemed to settle with relief more than forgiveness.

"Sorry," I said quietly. "It's—my issue is with my dad."

"Uhgg!" Laurie exclaimed. "Dads are the worst. I know mine is. I finally get to have a car and he won't even let me drive it out of town. It's ridiculous!"

"He just doesn't want you getting hurt."

"Oh, so you're on his side?"

"I didn't pick a side. Just offering an explanation."

Laurie subtly rolled her eyes and looked away, then emitted a sigh that was her signature notification that she was bored. She glanced back at me and smiled. "Since you're not hungry, let's go park somewhere."

"What about the movie?"

"James Bond?" she said, with a more demonstrative roll of her eyes. "That's a double 'O' no."

"Fine."

"Wait. Sorry, it's your birthday. I forgot," she added without sounding genuinely apologetic. "You know … maybe," she looked at me, intently reading my eyes, "maybe you'd like something else … for your birthday."

I studied her for a moment, realizing the suggestion of her words, and I felt the instant heat of both panic and excitement warm my face.

"We could go out to the Pyramids. Watch the sunset and … and stuff."

Her inuendo was intriguing. But the thought of her badge-wearing father thumped its neuron finger against the inside of my head reminding me that I had certain valuables currently stowed away in my BVDs of which I wanted to keep safe and intact.

"I don't think that's a good idea," I responded, giving her a look that was meant to prompt her into recalling the threat her dad had made to me. Suddenly the bell that hung at the entrance door jingled, and my eyes darted past Laurie and I saw Sam Chambers enter the pizza café.

"JT," Laurie said, giving me the smile that matched the one in her picture on my desk, "it's not against the law, you know."

At once, I realized a painful truth. "Well, as of today, it is," I informed her, certain she was not intentionally trying to set me up for a possible felony charge. Thankfully, my head with a brain in it was in control of my conscience.

Ignoring my comment, or more likely ignorant of its meaning, Laurie pushed again.

"Then let's just drive out to the Pyramids and take this pizza with us and just talk."

"I'm not going to the Pyramids. Not tonight."

"Hey Buddy!"

My eyes shot back at Sam, and I watched as the grinning young man crossed to us, his gangly frame topped by a disappointing imitation of a real cowboy hat, and his feet shod in fashionable square-toed Dingo boots. A definitive fan of hall-of-fame rodeo champion and country music singer, Chris LeDoux, Sam was, from head to toe, a drugstore cowboy, openly wishful that he owned a horse, and regularly lamenting that it was his misfortune that his home was located smack dab in the center of town instead of situated somewhere out on the range, like mine. But to be honest, his horseback riding skills were sub-par at best.

And I had told him that truth. When it came to one's best friend, honesty was important.

"Great," Laurie scowled. "I hope he's not going to be a third wheel."

"What the hell?" Sam asked.

"What the hell what?" I countered, giving my life-long friend a perplexed stare.

"I thought you'd already be at the Pyramids by now."

"Pyramids?" Laurie asked, suddenly interested and obviously suspicious.

"I'm not going to the Pyramids."

"But JT, it's *your* party."

"There's a birthday party for you at the Pyramids?" Laurie asked.

"No."

"Well, sure there is, Buddy," Sam corrected.

"Oh, I get it. You just want to party without me, right?"

Her accusation instantly annoyed me. "Laurie, I didn't ask you because I'm not going. It's really Dent's party. He's just using my birthday as an excuse." I threw Sam a condemning glare. "I'm surprised you're going."

"Your brother just stopped by and invited me. He even gave me a bona fide thirty bucks to pick up the pizza. And besides, I'd be a douchebag if it didn't go celebrate the birthday of my best friend."

"Maybe I'll just go the Pyramid party on my own," Laurie interrupted.

"You can't go, Laurie. There's going to be beer and no telling what else."

"So?"

"You're sixteen. You're a minor. You can't drink."

"I could if I wanted to."

"Then you shouldn't. What would your dad say?"

"He wouldn't have to know."

"But he'd find out. And he trusts me to keep you away from that sort of stuff."

"Sometimes, JT, you're such a nerd."

"I can live with that," I replied, not exactly sure why being smart was a bad thing.

"And clueless," Laurie added. "You know, maybe I don't need you to keep me away from anything. And for certain, I don't need another old man."

"Maybe I should take you home," I suggested, both my voice and my eyebrows rising. Immediately I regretted my suggestion, adding it to the other words of regret that had fallen out of my mouth in the last hour or so.

Abruptly Laurie slid along the bench and slipped out of the booth and sprang to her feet. "No thank you, JT Tescott. I'll walk!" Quickly she crossed to the door but turned back toward me. "Happy Birthday, Jerk," she quipped, her sentiment clearly absent of anything happy.

CHAPTER 4

Two seconds after Laurie had walked out on our doomed date of celebration, Sam looked down at me with an embarrassed grimace. "Well, that … sucks."

"No shit."

"You could do better, you know?"

"Shut up, Sam."

"Ten-four," he replied with a grin. "I promise, I'll never, never, ever say another negative thing about your girlfriend again. Ever."

"Right."

"Come on, let's get a move on. I'll drive."

"I said—"

"I heard ya, JT. Loud and clear. But I'm still taking you to that party."

Often, throughout the years of our friendship, Sam had pushed me into stepping outside my comfort zone where I was often content to be a bystander instead of a participant. He had encouraged me to do and experience things first-hand, instead of relying on a safe and vicarious way of life.

I had refused to learn to swim but absent of caution he had pushed me into the deep end of the city swimming pool. And later he pushed me into Golf, and Choir, and Drama Club, of all things. Reluctantly, I had given those activities a shot, though I quickly found out I could not act, could not carry a tune in a bucket, and could swing a Five Iron only slightly better than I could dribble a basketball, which wasn't saying much. But I did learn to swim, and for that, I was grateful.

"Fine. But I'm not drinking."

"I wouldn't expect you to."

"Guess I'll meet you out there," I said to Sam as I began to shift my butt across the vinyl seat.

"Ha!" Sam coughed. "Nice try. You're not driving. Like I said, you're riding with me."

"My truck is just—"

"Nope," Sam spoke, cutting me off. "Cinderella didn't drive herself to the ball, did she?"

"Funny."

"And I'll even make sure you get home by midnight if that's what you want. But listen, first I gotta pick up Alex, then we'll stop at Sonic and get some cherry limeades or something. Sugar-free for me, of course." Sam was a diabetic, a condition he had been managing since he was just six years old, but never complained about it.

"Whatever."

"Alrighty then. Hang on a sec while I get the pizza ordered."

Thirty minutes later, I grudgingly found myself being chauffeured by Sam, while the two of us listened to his newest 8-track purchase of *Waylon Jennings Greatest Hits.* In the following half-hour later, we were a trio riding in Sam's '68 Ford pickup, but without any serenading from the outlaw county music star. With Alex, Sam's girlfriend, sandwiched between us, we crossed the city limits of Custer, a jurisdictional boundary marked by a sign that bore a somewhat cartoonish image of General George Armstrong Custer, and the phrase "Come back, again!"

I glanced over my shoulder to the reverse side of the sign, with a twin of the general declaring "Welcome to Custer!" but with a notation at the bottom that read "Population 912." I shook my head, wondering what had possessed the founding fathers of my hometown to name the place after such a despicable human being, albeit an illustrious man.

"What's wrong?" Sam asked. I glanced at him and met the chastising look of his eyes.

"You know."

"Do you shake your head at him every time you leave town?"

I nodded. "Pretty much."

"Shake your head at who?" Alex asked.

"Custer," Sam replied with a grin. "As in George. JT doesn't like him."

"Who does? He was practically a pathological killer."

"Thank you, Alex. See, I'm not the only one."

Sam laughed. And I smiled back at him. Though we had been best friends for years, we rarely disagreed with one another. But one exception was GAC.

George Armstrong Custer.

Sam considered the man a legend of the Old West. A *bona fide legend* as he put it, but I had long since given up arguing with him that being a legend did not make him a good person. But Custer had too often been portrayed as a hero in the history books found in American high schools, and therefore Sam considered it cool that the town had the renowned cavalry colonel as its worthy namesake.

I did not share that feeling with Sam. My study of a few unflattering biographies written about Custer proved that a dozen paragraphs in a fundamental textbook were an inadequate representation of the real personality of the army officer, and that supplemental knowledge I had of the arrogant brute kept me from placing him on a pedestal of admiration.

But still, Custer was my hometown. A place that had sprouted as a stagecoach stop for the historic Butterfield Overland Dispatch, or the B.O.D. as it was known back in the 1860s. But despite the failing of the B.O.D., both wise and gambling men had laid foundations and roots for a community to grow upon. And for a while Custer had relatively flourished, riding high upon an agrarian economy.

A central community park had been developed, complete with tennis courts, an outdoor basketball venue, and a unique circular public swimming pool. And though the economy had eventually dwindled, Custer still boasted of having a thriving main street, complete with its own movie theater, a bowling alley, a drug store with a soda fountain, a five and dime retail outlet, a pair of retail clothing stores, several cafes, and a barber shop located conveniently under the same roof as a beauty shop that advertised haircuts for "He and She".

And anchoring one end of the town's shopping boulevard stood a one-story hospital complex, while at the other end towered the white skyscrapers of the rural Midwest: Tubular-designed grain storage structures referred to simply as elevators, a lasting nod to the still-thriving agricultural landscape that spanned in every direction.

Custer was also the place of my elementary school, where I, as an awkward and shy Kindergartener, found myself frequently paired with a goofy eyeglass-wearing kid who had staunchly proclaimed that he was going to be my best friend. And he had been right.

Sam and I had easily bonded, first as five-year-old members of an imaginary pit crew who raced tiny Hot Wheels cars upon flexible tracks of orange plastic, then later we endured friendly competitions of bicycle marathons, exhausting ourselves by regularly trying to set personal-best records as we sped around the semi-circular perimeter of town. Eventually we graduated to engine-driven vehicles during our freshman year of high school, and we relished the small-town pastime of dragging Main Street in our very own pickup trucks.

Other than Sam, there was another guy I considered a good friend, a second-best friend as Sam would remind him, but Blaine never once seemed offended by the subordinate ranking. As opposed to Sam, my friendship with Blaine was relatively new.

Growing up in a small town and attending a high school that typically registered no more than a hundred and twenty kids in its student body census, I had known Blaine by sight but not much more than that since he had always been a grade level ahead of me. But then troubles at home had caused him to miss a lot of classroom hours in the second half of his Senior year and he was forced to repeat the last grade of high school in order to graduate.

As a star running back, the football coach was tickled pink to get Blaine Wallace returning to the team roster, and coincidentally Sam had also managed to persuade me to join the football team in a now-or-never pitch to once again drag me outside the perimeter of my comfort zone.

And it was there in that atmosphere of pigskin and jockstrap camaraderie that Blaine had chosen to take me, the less athletic Tescott, under his wing. As a first-year player, and unsurprisingly a third-string running back, I had yet to truly experience the genuine glory of being a member of a sports team. But in a singular game against our rival school, Blaine had orchestrated an opportunity for me to shine upon the gridiron and my gratitude for his intervention had bonded us on the playing field, cementing a new friendship and elevating me with a sense of pride in representing the Fighting Indians that was our mascot.

No, the irony had not escaped me.

In forty-three minutes, the passageway would close.

We traveled north on US 83 for a distance of three miles beyond the city limits of Custer. At the intersection of the highway and our exit road, stood another prominent billboard depicting our locally dubbed Pyramids. Multiple sheets of plywood formed the canvas of the artwork designed and executed by none other than our high school science teacher, Mr. Cleon Lattimer, nicknamed Professor Neutron by some of his wayward students. However, the bespectacled man with blonde and unruly hair had proved he was as adept with paints and brushes as he was with Bunsen burners and beakers.

The previous year, the county commissioners had decided that it was paramount that a fresh, new sign be created to replace the weathered and nearly illegible one that advertised the area's most notable tourist attraction. Officially branded as Monument Rocks, it was a striking place and worthy of being inducted as the first National Natural Landmark in Kansas by the Department of Interior a decade earlier.

After a tedious month of bitter arguments among commissioners as to whom should get the distinguished artistic honor, a contest was agreed upon whereas any interested person, regardless of age or walk-of-life, could submit his or her vision of the signage that should grace the highway exit advertising the chalky landforms' location.

Only five entries had been tendered. One in particular was an anonymous submission fervently rumored to have been a vulgar version of the town's welcome sign featuring a naked and prostrate legendary general with a skyline of obelisk limestone towers rising from the crack of his derrière.

It was unanimously disqualified.

Excepting the debarred contestant, only one other person besides the commissioners knew the confidential details. And this person had been solely responsible for spreading the rumor of the comical submission, though he had deliberately kept the artist's identity a secret. Like I said, Sam and I were best friends.

Steering his truck sharply right, Sam exited the busy, paved highway, trading it for a dusty road of sand and gravel, upon which he skillfully dodged an occasional washboard of roadway while still managing to keep the vehicle between the bar ditches. Lumbering eastward for two miles, we drove along the hard-pack strip of ground and crossed the Logan-Gove County line, where the same dust plumed from behind us regardless of jurisdiction.

Alex, without the patience to inhale a full breath to re-charge her lungs, chattered non-stop about this, that, or another thing she thought important regarding high school gossip. I did not bother with trying to appear interested. Instead, I stared out the side window and tried to tune the Chatty Cathy out of my mind.

After an additional distance of two more miles, the road veered to the right and up ahead I could see someone walking along the grassy shoulder. Sam slowed down then steered the vehicle to the left, giving a wide berth to the pedestrian, whom I at once recognized.

"Hey, that's Kival."

"Yeah, it looks like," Sam agreed as he drove past the road-trekker.

"Stop. Let's ask him if he wants a ride," I suggested, not at all in a hurry to get to the party that was allegedly being hosted in my honor.

"Seriously?" Alex asked. "He's like the weirdest kid in our school. Nobody likes him. I say we just leave him alone." But Sam ignored her and braked to a stop. I smiled, appreciating that despite his girlfriend, he still had a mind of his own.

"Seriously?" she repeated, folding her arms, and pursing her lips into pouting mode. Without a word, Sam shifted the pickup into reverse and backed up until my opened window was adjacent to the strolling teen.

"Sup Kival?" I spoke. "Can we give you a ride?"

"Naw, I'm almost there. But thanks."

"Almost where?" Sam asked.

"Uh, the rocks … you know…"

"The Pyramids? That's where we're going," I said.

"Oh. Well, uh, I didn't know," he replied, glancing hesitantly in the direction of his destination. "Sorry." He turned away and reversed his bearing of travel. I wondered if he knew that the Pyramids, though open to the public per an agreement with the DOI, were actually situated on private land.

Tescott land.

And I wondered if it was because of that fact that he felt apologetic for his intended trespass? At any rate, Kival did not appear to be aware of the gathering of his peers at the place that was often used as a party venue.

"Wait," I called out to Kival. "Don't go back to town just because we're all going to the same place. You know, anyone is allowed to be there."

Kival stopped, dropped his eyes to the ground and spoke toward his feet. "Uh, thanks, but I kinda like to go there when … when it's like, you know, just quiet."

"I get that. But all the same, you're welcome to go with us."

"Uh … yeah, I don't … well … maybe another time."

"Dude, we're having a birthday party at the Pyramids for my boy JT, here."

"Oh." He looked up and glanced at me before looking away again. "Uh … I'm sorry. I didn't know."

"Probably because you weren't invited," Alex chimed in.

"Okay. Well …," Kival trailed off as he glanced in the direction of what he knew now to be our mutual destination. "Uh, well … happy birthday, JT," he added before taking another step in the direction of Custer.

"Wait," I said again, my voice stopping him. "I would—I'd really like for you to come with us. To the party."

"Uh … like she said. I'm not invited."

"You are now."

Alex coughed a dramatic sigh of protest. "And just where is he going to sit? There's not enough room here in the cab for all four of us. And I am not sitting on anyone's lap!"

I shifted the stack of boxed pizza from my lap to hers and opened my door and stepped out, then closed it shut. I peered at Alex through the open window. "Don't worry. I wouldn't dream of inconveniencing you." I glanced at Sam, who apologetically shook his head.

It was understood that neither of us was very fond of the other's girlfriend.

"Come on, Kival," I said patting the side of the pickup. "I'll ride back here with you."

"Well, okay … but I—well, I don't want to cause any problems, or anything. I don't mind at all, you know, walking back into town," he added with a nod to the west.

"It's no problem," I said as I stepped up onto the bumper and clambered my way into the pickup bed. "Here," I added, extending him my hand. He hesitated for a second, then accepted my offer and I helped him up and over. We settled down onto the hard, metal floor-bed, our backs to the window, then over my shoulder I tapped the cab and called out, "Okay!"

Sam put the vehicle in gear and punched the gas and we ambled forward, jostling along the rutted road that was in dire need of the maintenance of a road grader. Kival and I sat with our knees folded, balancing upon our posteriors, and watching the dust from the road boil up from the tires beneath us.

"Thanks," Kival said after a few moments, glancing at me briefly before ducking his head to stare at his high-top Converse sneakers that at one time had been pristine white, but were now more beige than alabaster, the canvas cloth mottled with penetrating remnants of road dust. Unlike his shoes, his denim jeans were notably older, well-worn, and faded, and his t-shirt, royal blue and sporting the iconic image of the original Mickey Mouse, loosely draped his torso from shoulders that were almost too broad for his boney frame. Though by all appearances clean, the shirt was obviously a full size too big, and it was losing its hem along the left side.

"I'm more of a Pluto guy, myself," I said to him, raising the volume of my voice in an attempt to be heard over the roar of a faulty muffler.

"What?" Kival asked, turning to look at me, his eyes displaying an absence of understanding, not the necessity of repeating myself because of his lack of audibility.

"Mickey," I replied clarifying my statement and pointing to his shirt. I used to have a shirt with Pluto on it instead." The operative phrase being 'used to.' I had given up wearing t-shirts emblazoned with cartoon characters at least five years ago. "You know, his dog," I added, realizing I had not shed any additional light for him regarding the subject of Disney icons.

"Oh. Yeah," Kival nodded, then looked down at his chest. "It's a mouse," he said objectively.

As much as I hated to admit it, Alex was right. Kival was the weird kid in our school.

Seemingly friendless and extremely introverted, he was painfully anti-social, but that trait was in part the fault of the kids in our school, most of whom lived in circumstances that had not taught them an appreciation for being recipients of compassion, therefore they had not learned how to show and share that kindness with others. But as I matured, I had begun to notice that many people avoided those who were different, those who did not conform to the identity of the masses.

And even I had been one of them. At least, for a while. But then my perspective on this outcast who was my classmate changed once I had learned from my mother what she knew of Kival's life story. Still, she admitted to having very limited information regarding him or his family.

As a five-year-old child, he and his mother had been abandoned upon an isolated road and left to the ferocity of the elements of a cold January night. Desperate for food and shelter, they had appeared on our own doorstep and my parents had welcomed them in from the night. But even with that knowledge, I had taken no initiative to get to know him better. But that was going to change, starting now.

"Hey, I'm—I'm sorry about your mom," I said, mustering a sympathetic smile.

"Thanks," he replied with a nod, keeping his eyes fixed on the road as strands of his hair whiffed about his face. As far as anyone knew, he had never been to a barber, his hair being regularly, and unprofessionally, cut by his mother.

And she had died nearly six months ago.

Her death had made him an orphan, albeit an eighteen-year-old orphan.

No one knew anything of his father, neither past nor present. For that matter, hardly anyone knew much about his mother, other than her name was Kitty Freeman, but even the authenticity of her name was questionable. It was known that Kitty spoke very little English, and judging by her features she was arguably Native American, though of what tribe no one seemed to know for certain, but many speculated she was of Apache or Navajo descent.

It was rumored, however, that during the last several days of her illness, representatives from the Pawnee Indian Nation had come and taken Kitty to Oklahoma where she could die among her own people. Kival, though, did not make that journey with his mother and had stayed behind so that he might finish school at Custer High.

Unlike his mother, Kival's features were more subtle in terms of exhibiting an ancestral lineage of Native American. His complexion was lighter than his mother's, and his bright blue eyes were a striking contrast to those of Kitty's mahogany brown irises. Though not quite Hippy in style, Kival's dark, almost black, hair was relatively long, at least lengthy compared to his male counterparts in high school.

Kival was also an only child, and the family of two were poor, at best. They lived in what could only be described as a shack. It was a rough, unpainted, four-room house crowded just inside the city's limits of town, and luckily for them, it at least boasted of indoor plumbing. His mother had a job with the local feedlot, working as a cook and housekeeper for Ray Ackerman, owner of the cattle feeding operation and adjacent ranch.

Unable to afford a car, she walked three miles one-way, every morning, to prepare a breakfast and a noonday meal for the half dozen feedlot cowboys who loyally worked for the enterprising businessman. Ray, a long-time friend of my dad's, was a good man, and had insisted that conditional to her employment, he, or one of his employees, would at least give her a ride home each day. But on frigid winter mornings, Ray himself could be found outside the Freeman abode insisting she ride with him to work.

Through Dad, I knew how Ray had been good to her. And, also, how he had been good to Kival. Dad and Mom both greatly admired Ray, and like him, they too were philanthropic in practice, pitching in to help others in need, and in the process teaching Dent and me a valuable lesson in humanity. My parents had instilled in us boys a fervent belief to help others. To never weigh down those less fortunate, but instead strive to lift up people whose circumstance made it difficult or impossible for them to help themselves.

Since Kival was legally an adult, seemingly no one gave the surviving boy much thought. My parents, however, had invited Kival to live with us, but he had declined saying he would be fine on his own. Ray, too, had encouraged him to live at his ranch, and bunk with the pair of single cowhands who worked for him. But Kival had also refused his hospitality, content to stay in the house he had shared with his mother. But I had been impressed that he had been determined to ride out the remainder of his Senior year of high school, when I knew of several kids who had dropped out for lesser reasons.

But Kival had, however, accepted a job offer from Ray, working weekends at the feedlot doing the odd chores of cleaning equipment, mucking out livestock barns, and other tasks the feedlot cowboys preferred not to do. He worked enough to buy the groceries he needed. Though I had learned from my dad, that Ray took care of the utility bills for the dilapidated cottage that was Kival's home and had paid the ad-valorem property taxes though that amount was relatively minimal. Additionally, Ray had cleared the outstanding balance of a small bank loan that had been secured with his co-signature to pay for repairs to windows that had been broken in a hailstorm the previous summer.

Having learned those things about Kival had made me realize how fortunate my life had been. How jaded was my childhood, where I had never known what it meant to be truly hungry, or what it was like to wake up morning after morning to a cold and drafty house.

Neither had I ever felt unsafe, or unimportant, or hopeless. I wondered if Kival had grown up experiencing those painful feelings.

I hoped not.

At once, I felt the pickup lean as Sam bent the wheels of his truck to the right, continuing upon the southward stretch of the dusty road that was flanked on both sides by barbed wire and studded steel T-posts. When we had covered half of this two-mile leg of the journey, a jet stream of dust billowing behind a speeding vehicle caught my eye.

"Idiot," I said just loud enough to be a whisper. The east-west road we had just traveled, was not the Indianapolis 500. I shook my head, recognizing the unique color combination of the expensive orange and white pickup truck, and automatically I frowned at the identity of its driver.

Oleander Sedgwick.

I watched as the vehicle launched into a reckless skid as it swerved around the corner and onto the road behind us. I cursed, then turned to the window behind me and slapped my palm against the glass to get Sam's attention.

"Look out, Sam! There's an asshole coming up fast behind you!"

I saw Sam glance at his side mirror and like me, he also shook his head. Immediately he steered his pickup from his fair share of road, pulling to a stop onto a narrow shoulder where its tires crunched upon stems of sage brush and the meaty leaves of prickly pear cactus. Within moments of having hopefully secured the old Ford from the danger posed by the approaching driver, I could see that the daredevil classmate, and renown bully, was nearly upon us, and for a moment the imbecile had even aimed his vehicular missile toward us.

In the cab with him were two others. One a girl, whose face was a portrait of screaming fear, and whose genuine shrieks of terror still spilled from her seconds after Oleander jerked the wheel, missing us by mere inches. Snaking wildly past us, the horn of his custom Dodge Ram Charger began to blare like a war siren as I caught the reckless driver purposely flip me his signature F-U-bird. I scowled at him, knowing he wanted me to see his asinine gesture. Impulsively, I wanted nothing more than to reciprocate the same vulgar expression, but I resisted the urge. My momma had taught me better.

Oleander Sedgwick did not like me. And I certainly did not like him.

"PUSSIES!" Oleander yelled, his voice easily carried through the open windows of his vehicle. I glared at him, seeing red that wasn't just the fluttering tresses of his favored mullet hairstyle, but mostly because I was utterly pissed. At once, he paused the din of the blaring horn, then with a roar, he pressed the pickup into its most capable imitation of warp speed, burying us in a choking veil of dust.

"Asshole!" I heard Sam exclaim. We sat unmoving for two minutes as we waited for the airborne particles of prairie road to thin and settle. As the gap between Sedgwick and us expanded wider, the blaring of the new 1979 model Dodge continued to sound in the distance.

"I hate that guy!" Sam announced, then shifted his pickup into gear and pulled back into the roadway and drove leisurely toward our destination.

Though I shared Sam's feelings regarding Oleander Sedgwick, we had both decided years ago that neither of us would ever let the senseless, overbearing bully interfere with anything we chose to do. Nor would he stop us from being present at any place we also chose to be. Though I seethed at the prospect of being within hearing range of Oleander's obnoxiously grating voice, Sam knew better than to turn the truck around and head back home.

"Dick."

I glanced at Kival, his sudden and unexpected description of Oleander Sedgwick instantly amusing me. I laughed.

"Kival, you and I are going to be great friends!"

In Twenty-seven minutes, the passageway would close.

CHAPTER 5

Ahead of us stretched a barbed wire fence that spanned east and west and separated the land that was my birthright from that of our rural northern neighbors. At the perpendicular intersection of our road and the fence, there was a gap in the five horizontal rows of the twisted and prickly wire through which we could pass unimpeded. In this space, and embedded in the roadway, there was a cattle guard, a clever apparatus invented by someone who wanted a trouble-free means to get from one side of the division to the other without the inconvenience of getting in and out of his vehicle to open a gate and then repeating the procedure to close it behind him.

This particular cattle guard was installed specifically for the convenience of tourists who came to enjoy an exploration of Monument Rocks and was constructed fifteen years earlier by my dad. Of course, he had not built it by himself. He had the help of his sons, a pair of toddlers, both of whom had frequently begged for any opportunity to help their daddy even though, at that time, their enthusiasm greatly exceeded their abilities.

Gearing down his pickup, Sam slowed the Ford then meticulously eased the vehicle across the welded set of a dozen six-inch diameter metal pipes that were suspended above a relatively deep and shadowed trench and precisely spaced to allow for an unencumbered crossing of vehicular tires. However, by its intended design, the cattle guard discouraged almost any four-legged beast from attempting to tiptoe across the rounded surfaces of the cylindrical steel.

Within moments we had rumbled across the unassuming barrier and as a result, I had officially returned to my home turf. Guided by an innate desire to gaze, again, upon the Pyramids of which I had seen countless times before, I couldn't help but pivot my head and peer behind me through the back window and subsequent windshield and cast my eyes across the final mile of our journey marked by what had now turned into a distinct set of twin tire tracks worn across the surface of the prairie. At the end of this simple pasture road stood the lofty landforms that were our destination, remnants of the Cretaceous Period of the Mesozoic Era when a great body of water had inundated this central part of the continent.

Occasionally, I would reflect upon who had first thought to call this collection of rocks Chalk Pyramids, and why he or she had made such a correlation. In any event, the colloquial name had stuck, though from perhaps the perspective of an outsider, the term pyramid was a brazen example of false advertising. Absent the conical shape of the iconic structures of Egypt or the Mayan temples of Mexico, one had to engage an extreme amount of imagination and a heavy dose of forgiveness in order to think *pyramid.*

Arguably, the rock pillars could be more accurately described as having the likeness of a naturally occurring Stonehenge. However, to me, these God-created objects had instead always reminded me of giant loaves of bread setting out upon an expansive table of buffalo grass and sage brush prairie. But then Chalky Buns would have been a hard sell at the state's tourism office.

We followed the roadway as it made one last right-angle turn to the south and as we did, I glanced to my left and gave a respectful nod to the solitary landform locally dubbed Old Chief Smoky. Chief, however, was a noticeably shorter pinnacle of rock chalk than those natural towers that waited further ahead, but unique in that when viewed from the side, the wind-carved rock resembled a human face. And because of Monument Rocks' unofficial moniker as the Kansas Pyramids, Smoky had been associatively nicknamed the Kansas Sphinx.

A half mile later, Sam steered his pickup from the primitive road and into the realm of the northern-most cluster of the majestic sedimentary formations of Niobrara Chalk. My rocky loaves of bread were just yards ahead of us, rising as much as seventy feet skyward, only now they no longer resembled anything edible.

We skirted the western side of the Pyramids inching toward the south end of a jagged tower of rock that beheld the feature for which most people were drawn, and of which was also our specific terminus. It was an opening etched by eons of wind erosion and shaped much like the elongated pupil of a cat's eye, and roughly centered within the expanse of a six-story high wall of rock.

One visitor, who had written an article for a Kansas tourism magazine, had penned the opening as the keyhole. Another writer had referred to it as the eye of the needle and had photographed a blazing sunset piercing the landform just to emphasize his point and had ultimately included the image in a coffee table pictorial describing sights seen on the backroads of the nation. But as far as the local yokels were concerned, specifically my generation, we gave the opening a simpler name based upon what it looked like to us and without authoring an unnecessarily descriptive phrase.

The arch.

Although archway was probably a better term, the gap in the rock wall began with a floor eight feet across, and sides that mushroomed outward a few feet on each edge as it rose then narrowed again, converging at its ceiling to a width that mirrored the base. The vertical span of the perpendicular opening pushed upward nearly five stories in height and much like the cattle guard of the fence, it offered an expedient passageway between the landform's east and west sides.

Approaching the arch, I noted how the late beams of the falling sun sprayed across the western face of the towering rock pinnacle and brilliantly painted the striated surface with glowing hues of ochre. However, parked immodestly before this wonderous landscape was an orange and white pickup truck, a thing that was an insult to the natural beauty of the setting, though I was undeniably biased because I loathed its owner. At the very least, the vehicle was a conspicuous obstruction of our view of the foot of the penned keyhole that was certain to be the ground-zero location of the impending party.

Wisely, Sam chose to avoid parking beside the carriage of Oleander Sedgwick, and instead steered his Ford around the end of the rock wall into the darkening shadow of the celebrated landmark. He skirted the edge of the hardened surface that sloped gently away in all directions from the wind-hewn monolith. It was here upon these slopes of residual erosion that was the place of high school parties.

And tonight, the party was mine.

Hypothetically.

But several things were certain. One, Oleander, was here. And, in addition to that fact, was the truth that I both dreaded and resented his presence. He was someone whom I unapologetically preferred to shun. By the time I had become a teenager, I had realized the value of surrounding myself with positive-minded people, of whom Sedgwick was not a member. Conversely, I avoided the company of those with inherent negative attitudes and conceited feelings of entitlement and cruelly judgmental behaviors, which was an apt set of traits that perfectly described the class bully.

But at once Oleander's attendance at this place was unexpectedly less important as my attention shifted to the presence of two other vehicles parked somewhat intimately next to each other. Dent's blue Chevy C-10, and beside it, a red Mustang. I winced in disbelief.

The sports car belonged to Laurie.

Instantly I was wary and pissed. In my gut, I knew things were destined to go south and the mayhem would likely develop quickly. Not just because of Laurie, but because of my brother. He did have, after all, a sordid reputation concerning a fair sample of girls from our school.

Sam backed his Ford into a spot next to Dent's pickup then quickly put the transmission into park and got out and glanced up at me. I had risen to my feet, surveying the small group that had gathered upon the mounded earth. From my perch, the others appeared as silhouettes, framed within the natural arch, the golden sky their backdrop. And around them and between them, beams of horizontal sunlight spilled through the aperture aiding in the attempt to disguise their identities.

"Oh, boy," Sam whispered, nodding toward the little red car.

"Yeah," I said succinctly.

"Laurie's here!" Alex informed me with a smile and a giggle as she gleefully pounced from the cab of the pickup and slammed its door.

"Looks that way."

"Whoo-hoo!" Alex called out as she skipped across to the gathering. Then I watched as Oleander Sedgwick, his business-in-the-front-party-in-the-back mullet crowning the redhead's six-foot two-inch bulk as he lorded over the heights of those beside him, twisted his head to glance over his shoulder before raising a bottle into the air.

"Hey, hey, pussies! Refreshment is here!" he announced, before taking a swig of what I assumed to be some brand of hard whiskey. In spite of myself, I was almost impressed. I never imagined Oleander had a vocabulary consisting of any words exceeding eight letters in length.

Oleander Sedgwick was called Olly by his friends, which by most accounts totaled three, one of those inexplicably being my brother. Secondly, he was also Olly to his girlfriend, Consuela Alvarez, short and petite, the Mutt to his Jeff, standing next to him as though she were glued to his side. What she saw in the big oaf was beyond my understanding. Consuela was otherwise a super nice girl, fun, outgoing, a drama star on the high school stage, easy to talk to and certainly easy to look at. Conversely, Oleander was nothing like her. Sam interrupted my thoughts.

"Remember, JT, it's your party."

"And I'll cry if I want to," I replied, impulsively quoting the famous lyric popularized by the vocal artist, Leslie Gore. Instantly, I concluded that I had spent too much of my youth listening to Mom's teenage collection of 45's.

"Well, I hope the hell you don't do that."

I did not respond. Sam knew of my tendency to get overly sentimental, but I was pages away from feeling soppy. I was, however, on the unstable cusp of a tantrum.

I observantly glanced around. The party had hardly yet begun. But I knew that as soon as darkness swallowed the sky, others would begin to arrive and a drunk fest would ensue and continue well past midnight, upon which most of those present would have already forgotten the initial reason for the celebration. At any rate, I would be gone long before then. But first, I had a matter to deal with and I preferred to do it with as little scrutiny as possible.

Alex returned to us, moving again in a childlike gait. "I'm hungry."

I ignored her and watched as a figure who had been crouching beyond the odd duo of paramours suddenly stood and stepped aside and spoke into Oleander's ear. His profile, highlighted by his trademark backwards ball cap and his typically shirtless torso, was clear and expected.

Perry Hutchinson.

He was the third of Olly's so-called friends, though I suspected their definition of friendship would not match mine. Perry was a virtual delinquent who flagrantly professed of a regular habit of smoking pot, and who was suspected of breaking into Jeanette's Tops 'n Bottoms, stripping a half dozen female mannequins and posing them in a variety of lewd and lascivious positions. He had also become an obvious yes-man answering to Oleander Sedgwick's every bark.

At once, my attention was drawn to yet another figure, one revealed by Perry when he had moved. Somewhat camouflaged by the slender, bare legs of Consuela, I could now see my brother squatting before a small ring of concrete blocks that served as a makeshift fire pit.

Dent was leaning over the cache of dried twigs and parched wads of buffalo grass, cupping his hands into a shield against the soft southerly breeze and watching as the infant flame quickly began to mature. Beside him was a meager armload of cottonwood limbs and elm branches, fuel of which I was sure he had gathered from the yard of our ranch home. Out here, at the Pyramids, there were no nearby trees from which to gather dropped limbs that could be used to fuel a campfire.

For a long blistering minute, I stared into the dancing flames, my anger swelling, though I was not sure, in that moment, exactly why my feelings toward my brother were so incensed. But I was ninety-nine-point-nine percent positive I would have a good reason sooner than later.

Laurie, however, was who had caused my initial upset, though my annoyance with her had not yet elevated my ire to a level that currently matched that which I felt for Dent. And I hoped those measures would remain several degrees apart. I did not want to be angry with her. But why had she come here? I had explicitly told her not to. Her dad was the chief of police. His anger would easily supplant mine. Even Dent had discouraged me from bringing her here, though I assumed he had done so to keep Dad and Chief Edwards from locking horns.

Yet Laurie's car was here, and if it was here, then ….

"Hey, hey, hey!" Dent's baritone echoed from the wall of the towering rock façade.

Drawn to his voice, I caught him peering between the legs of the others, his focus upon me, his eyes already glistening with evidence of inebriation. "Hot damn! The guest of honor showed up after all!" He stood up and Oleander and Consuela stepped aside as though Dent had parted them in the same way Moses had divided the Red Sea. And there was Laurie, unsuccessfully attempting to hide a large red Solo cup behind her back.

Subconsciously I noted that my brother wore his "prowling" shirt, as Dent liked to call it; its billowy tails untucked and the front held closed by just the two lower snaps, purposely revealing a modest thatch of dark chest hair. It was, he claimed, his favorite Western shirt, hand-sewn for him by our mother, which she had cut from a gauzy fabric and then embroidered upon each yoke a matching design of an un-coiled lasso woven among red roses with green vines spiked with thorns. Often, Dent had bragged to me when wearing it, that it was the shirt he had worn when he had voluntarily surrendered his virginity.

If Mom only knew.

Then, as if the shirt had made him do it, he slid next to Laurie and wrapped his arms around her shoulders. "And this little—little gal, here—said you weren't coming."

With purpose, I strode toward the small group.

"Get your hands off her."

I blurted those words with an unmistakable edge of challenge, though I was not sure why. I was not inclined to physically fight my brother. History proved I generally came in second place. At best.

"Calm down bro. No big deal," Dent replied, dropping his hand behind her back, and purposely taking from her the container she had hidden. Grinning, he took the cup and chugged the entirety of its malted liquid.

"You're drinking."

"Course," Dent confirmed, rolling his beer-soaked tongue down over his lower lip before shaking his head like some rabid dog.

"Not you. Her."

"I'm not, JT, I —," she hesitated. "I was just holding it for him."

I wanted to believe her, but the look on my brother's face said otherwise. Laurie had lied. And though I was annoyingly peeved before, now I was pissed.

Proverbially, I bit my tongue, shook my head, then turned and walked back to find Alex spreading pizza boxes out across the opened tailgate of the Ford. At once the vocals of Waylon Jennings began to reverberate from inside the pickup. Then I noticed that our hitchhiker was not among us. I looked around.

"Where's Kival?" I asked Sam as he stepped out of the cab.

"Dunno," Sam said, shrugging his shoulders.

"Take me back to town."

"Hold on, JT —"

"I wasn't asking."

"We just got here."

"Fine. I can walk home from here," nodding westward across three miles of pastureland of which I was intimately familiar.

"Don't let Dent get to you. You know, if you leave now, you'll regret it tomorrow."

"I've already got regret blowing out my ass."

"Gross," Alex scowled, but I ignored her. Then from around the end of the arch wall, a dingy black El Camino eased into view.

"Forget it," I said. "Blaine is here. I'll ask him to take me back, since my best friend is determined to keep me here."

"Come on, JT," Sam countered. "Don't take your frustration with your brother out on me."

"It's not just him."

Then Alex chimed in with her unsolicited two cents.

"You can do better than Laurie, JT."

I shook my head. "I thought I knew her. Thought she was—," I sighed, "—like me."

"JT," Alex said, trying to be soothing. "She's not like you anymore. Not since—"

"Alex," Sam said, stopping her.

"Since what, Alex?"

"Don't." Sam spoke, his tone pleading.

I looked at him, and I could see in his eyes that he knew something. Something that I would not like.

"Since Dent."

"Alex, not today."

"JT's gotta find out sooner or later. You said so yourself. Might as well be now," Alex said turning to look at me with a vindictive glint in her eye.

"Hey guys," Blaine said as he joined our trio, but none of us acknowledged him. I, for one, kept my eyes locked on Alex.

"What is it, Alex?" my voice demanding.

"Well, let's just say that as far as the goody-two-shoes couple that you and Laurie pretend to be—"

"Oh, shit," I heard Blaine mutter under his breath, though his subtle interruption did not stop Alex from completing her declaration.

"You, JT, are the only virgin between you."

Her words rocked me, nearly taking my breath. Their meaning hammering home a truth I knew was entirely possible, even probable. I knew my brother.

In my head, I began to count.

One.

Two.

From the time Dent and I were little boys, Mom had coached me to slowly count to ten before beginning a fight with my brother. Sometimes it helped, the numbers diminishing my temper with the enumeration of each digit.

Three.

I turned and behind me the musical lyric *'mammas don't let your babies grow up to be cowboys'* touched my ears just seconds before I rushed toward the party, my eyes burning, my mind abandoning the plan to wait for the subsequent number four.

Sometimes counting did not help at all.

I plowed between Oleander and Perry, knocking the cup of beer from the hands of the half-naked doper, and leaped over the fire and drove my shoulder into Dent, angrily wrapping him in my arms as we tumbled to the ground.

"Fight! Fight! Fight!" I heard Oleander cry out. And he was one hundred percent correct. I punched my right fist hard against my brother's ribs. Dent recoiled, cursed, and between the profanities I faintly heard Laurie pleading for us to stop. Suddenly I felt strong hands gripping my arms, pulling me up from the leech I had pinned beneath me. I tried to wretch free, but Sam and Blaine held tight and pulled me further away from the jackass that was my brother.

"What the hell is wrong with you?!" Dent cried out, though there was a glint of a smile in his blue eyes.

Spittle frothed from my mouth as I glared at him, aggravated that my assault seemed to amuse him. "What the hell is wrong with you?!" I echoed the same words, in no mood to embellish the demand with my own spin on what was already a flawless question.

At once Laurie was at my side. "JT?"

I peered down at her, expecting to find an expression of concern or compassion. Instead, what I read in her eyes was fear.

And guilt.

"Leave me alone," I spat at her, disappointment and disbelief electrifying my words.

"JT, I—"

"GET — AWAY!" I ordered my so-called girlfriend, then I returned the focus of my eyes upon my adversary. "JUST. GO. HOME." I pleaded, determined to keep my anger and disappointment with her in check, assuring myself that she was a victim of a selfish seduction instigated by my amoral brother.

Laurie hesitated for a second, then from the corner of my eye I watched and waited as she moved away and hurried toward her car, my ears perceiving the sniffling sound of what I assumed to be weeping.

In front of me, Dent proceeded to rise to his feet. Then around me others began to move about, and within my peripheral vision, I knew that the other two girls, Consuela and Alex, had followed Laurie to her car.

Good.

It was best that this ungentlemanly business was left to the men.

Or boys.

It was fifty-fifty what any of us aspired to be at this moment.

A garble of feminine voices softly cooed both consolations and admonitions. Then a car door slammed shut. Then another. The Mustang's engine roared to life, then it charged backwards before peeling away in a cloud of dust.

But throughout the commotion, my eyes did not waver. I had kept the contempt of my gaze anchored on Dent.

My brother.

My betrayer.

On this day of the year when the earth was at its furthest from the sun, a mere three minutes remained to engage the passageway.

"How could you?" I asked him openly, though in my mind, it was a rhetorical question.

"How could I what, bro?"

"Don't," I snarled. "Do not act innocent with me."

"Oh, you mean Laurie?" He caved with a shrug, then snickered. "I can't help it," he continued, his eyes glancing past me and seeming to focus specifically on one of the other guys. "What can I say, I like girls."

"Woof! Woof! Woof!" Oleander began to chant.

"Damn straight!" Dent exclaimed, again, not speaking to me, but to Oleander or to Perry or to all of those who waited behind me, I was not sure. And did not care. Apparently, he had suddenly found it difficult to look me in the eye.

"You're a coward, Dent."

A pronounced moment of silence laid a sober clarity upon the declaration of my statement.

"What did you say?"

Good. I had now gained my brother's full attention.

"And you're scum. Just like Sedgwick," I added, the two of them tormenting my thoughts because of their disrespect for the virtues of Laurie and Consuela, and who knew how many others. "Neither of you care about anyone but yourselves. Turning innocent girls—"

"JT," Sam calmly cautioned, as he appeared beside me, his hand clasping my shoulder. I jerked away. He was too late. An inevitable moment had arrived.

I was mad and disgusted.

And I was beyond remaining quietly outraged.

But Sam's hand was again on my shoulder, his grip firmer than before, relaying his understanding, and fear, of what I might say next. Then unexpectedly, I was grievously overwhelmed with shame.

Who was I to judge any of them?

At once, my eyes began to well, but I was determined not to let anyone notice. I was not Leslie Gore.

I abruptly turned from Dent and stepped away, passing by Blaine, then Perry, crossing toward the arch where Kival had suddenly appeared from the shadows of the other side as though he had been lurking there, watching and eavesdropping.

I stopped beside him, the pair of us within the center of the great gap of the millennially layered chalk wall. I paused for a moment, my moist eyes drawn to the ground, peering along the elongated shape of my shadow cast by the last vestige of the setting sun. Then I heard a rush of footsteps followed immediately by a clamoring of urgent voices.

"Kick his ass!" Oleander's words rang loudest above the vocal din.

Just as I began to lift my eyes toward the commotion, the momentum of a strong, powerful body propelled me painfully onto the ground as though I were little more than a tackling dummy on the practice field. Dent scrambled on top of me, then straddled me, pinning me down upon the solid surface of impacted limestone residue. He grabbed the front of my shirt and lifted me up and punched my face in a quick succession of three fierce blows.

Fireworks exploded in my head as I felt my lip split and my blood spurt into the enormous cavity positioned behind my two rows of teeth.

I had said more than I should have. I had poked the bear. And I was about to pay for it. Dent was the fighter; I was the thinker. As Dad had often pointed out to me, my alligator mouth had a habit of overloading my hummingbird ass.

Dent hit me again, his hard fist landing fiercely upon the brow of my left eye. For a moment, lightening burst within my skull, momentarily blinding me. I lifted my arms defensively, managing the deflection of another intended blow to my head. Through my crossed arms, I caught a glimpse of the fury in my brother's eyes. Then using what I knew to be his weapon of choice, a right hook circumvented my limbed shield, and I felt a powerful fist crack against my jaw as a wet blanket of darkness began to engulf my sight.

A chorus of shouting voices echoed all around me, and I felt someone forcing himself between me and my brother, his body undoubtably absorbing the wrath of Dent's attack. I reached out to push my rescuer away, my hand pressing against a jawline before sliding downward along his neck, my fingers unwittingly becoming entangled with what felt like a thin chain. Abruptly, my avenger was ripped away from me, though within the snare of my grasp I still had entwined between my fingers what I perceived to be a necklace, its chain snapped apart.

Soft links of metal dropped against my knuckles, and within my palm I realized I held an unfamiliar object.

Small. Smooth. Circular.

Suddenly I felt the weight of Dent lift from me as he was pulled and dragged away, the sound of his boots scuffing across the ground. I rolled to my side, my jaw throbbing, my lips and chin blood-soaked. I struggled to my knees, my aching face bowing toward the dying sun.

Behind me I could hear bellows of profanities overlapping with grunts of determination that were presumably being abated by the successful efforts of others to cease and desist. It was a melee of shouting, a verbal and physical contest between those struggling to stop the fighting between two brothers and those who wanted the battle to continue.

"Perry, get my gun!"

Though I clearly heard Oleander's command, in the haze of my weakening consciousness, the implication made no sense to me. Then, despite my delirium, I remembered the thing I still clutched. I opened my bloodied palm to get a better look, but my fingers cast a veiled shadow courtesy of the setting sun, and I could barely see what was at rest in my hand. Squinting to improve my focus, I flipped my hand over, allowing the object to dangle from the chain entwined between my knuckles, and I lifted it up into the last rays of sunlight.

Spontaneously, an explosion of light enveloped me.

Blindingly white, a thief of any discernible detail, the intensity of the light was pure and hot, but not painful, though in my mind I wondered if I had just been struck by a bolt of lightning. Defensively, I squeezed my eyes shut guarding them against what I perceived to be potentially irreversible blindness.

Suddenly, an abrupt Arctic coldness assaulted my senses and cut at my exposed skin like the metal spines of a welder's brush.

Seconds later, a weightlessness overwhelmed me.

And then I felt the hands.

At least, I sensed they were hands. But in the gulf of sightlessness, I was certain I was being touched. Or more specifically, I felt that I was being caressed by the energy of hundreds of imagined fingertips pulsing against my bare skin, gliding along the contours of my face, across the physical conformation of my arms and my legs, exploring what I believed to be an inexplicable nakedness of my torso.

I shuddered.

At once I felt vulnerable and threatened by an imminent violation of the physicality of my body. My mind was screaming that something unnatural was upon me. Then in the next second, I felt the most excruciating pain imaginable, as if I was being skinned alive, my flesh stripped and shredded from my bones. As though my skeleton was being incinerated into searing pebbles of ash.

As if I were being cremated.

I screamed.

But an eerie deafness shielded me from the agony of my own voice. And then the vacuum of a black hole devoured my observance of time as an indeterminable expanse of minutes, or perhaps hours, elapsed beyond my sensibilities, but at last I began to selectively hear again.

Sounds that I believed to be emanating from others, only one or two wails at first, but then joined by others until they crescendoed into a chorus of cries that rung with fear, and helplessness, and were humanly masculine. At once, I felt exceedingly faint, overwhelmed by fatigue.

Then darkness devoured me.

And the door of the passageway closed shut.

CHAPTER 6

A flickering of consciousness tugged at me, pulling me into a vague realm of awareness. I lay still, or at least I sensed that I was prostrate, curled up like a fetus, seemingly frozen in place, unable to move.

Or not wanting to.

Minutes passed. Perhaps even hours had lapsed as I quietly listened to the hollow rasping of my breaths, and the loud, exaggerated beating of my heart that seemed to echo like a drum in an empty auditorium. Suddenly, a long and violent shiver crossed over me and after the calm had returned, I began to perceive the coldness creeping away, replaced by a tingling, pleasurable warmth that pulsed through my veins, gradually and steadily intensifying. Then a strange acuity stabbed at my growing consciousness.

I was thawing.

Suspended in unmeasurable time, I simply lay quiet, save my breathing. Unmoving, though I felt the shifting of my eyes behind my closed lids. For a moment I remembered the agony of immense suffering, but at present, I felt no pain, and wondered if I had only been dreaming.

At last, I intuited something else. Something different, yet familiar.

A presence.

I compelled my left eye to open to a mere slit, fearing what a full view might reveal to me. Light, though dim, pierced the tenderness of my pupil, and involuntarily my lid closed shut. I waited, counting to ten, then fifteen, twenty. With my second effort, I narrowly opened both eyes, peering through the veil of my lashes, adjusting to the haunting illumination of an ethereal fog. Then I witnessed a collective movement. A mingling of vaporous shapes among those with finite substance having legs, arms, and torsos.

And large, domed heads.

For a brief moment, I discerned one of the more physical beings seemingly floating toward me. At once a shadow of someone or something crossed before my eyes, stealing my view. But after it had passed, a face appeared before me, inches away. I caught my breath and held it.

The visage was boney and malformed, its skin speckled, but colorless, neither light nor dark. And its eyes were large and ice blue and they affably peered at me. Overwhelmed by wonder, I returned the creature's gaze, feeling no trepidation, but instead a spiritual peace. It lingered for a moment, its ghostly eyes reaching into my soul.

I blinked.

When I next opened my eyes, I found myself lying on my back, a tepid darkness surrounding me. Looking upward, I could see a sprinkling of stars hovering above and the sliver of a pale moon peaking from behind a vague silhouette of a suspended bridge of stone.

The arch.

The Pyramids.

I had returned.

But to return, implied that I had gone away. But surely, I had not gone anywhere. Why I had deduced that I had been someplace else made no sense to me. I was here, at the very place I had been just seconds before the explosion.

Explosion?

I contemplated the term as I sleuthed through the bank of my neural images seeking a memory that had triggered that perception. I closed my eyes and remembered the brilliance of a blinding white light. But an explosion? That was surely an illogical conclusion. I was aware. I was alive. I appeared to be in possession of all my parts and my faculties seemed to be operating on all cylinders, therefore nothing catastrophic was plausible. I was not hurt. I felt fine, almost euphoric. Then suddenly I remembered the others.

I rolled to my side and propped myself upon an elbow and looked around. But the reflection of the moon was weak, and thus my field of sight was minimal. Then at once I heard a movement near me accompanied by an awakening moan. I shifted to my hands and knees and crawled toward the sound, discovering that the body was just feet away from me. Relieved that I was not alone, I reached out, my hands blindly touching a head, feeling long strands of hair.

"Kival?" I whispered.

"Yeah."

"Are you okay?"

"Yeah," Kival repeated, his succinctness a reasonable sign that he was not interested in participating in a conversation.

"Good," I said, patting his chest before finding his arm and helping him to maneuver into a seated position. The backside of my hand brushed against a familiar surface, so with the pressure of my touch I encouraged him to lean backward and rest against the wall of rock just inches behind him. I pushed myself up onto my knees, then managed to scoot my feet underneath me and lift myself onto the pillars of my legs.

At once, an acute awareness tapped within my skull, shifting my attention to the object still entwined among the crevices that were formed within my hand. Blindly, I felt its shape, massaging it between my fingers, untangling its chain from between my knuckles. Suddenly, a click sounded in the haze of darkness and instinctively I tucked the necklace into the front pocket of my Levi's.

The click sounded again, and I peered around me, searching in the dark for its source. A dozen feet or so away, Dent was sitting upright, a Bic lighter in his hand warmly illuminating his face. Immediately our fight flooded my mind and I glared at him, though he seemed unaware of my stare. Instead, he shifted the cigarette lighter around him, casting its flickering light upon the prostrate forms of three others, their postures essentially fetal. At once one of the three moved, lifting his head to look around. I waited for our eyes to meet.

Blaine.

He stared at me for a moment, his eyes wide and wary.

"JT?"

"Yeah?"

"What the hell was that?"

I shook my head gently. To voice a reply of *'I don't know'* seemed inadequate, so I said nothing. Then, to the right of Dent, a large-limbed form stirred and eventually established himself upon the foundation of his buttocks, then immediately muttered a pair of colorful expletives. There was no question of his identity.

As Dent's miniature torch continued to glow, I gazed between us at the stillness of the third body. At once, I was alarmed. I cautiously padded toward Sam, dreading that I might discover an absence of life in him, but regardless, I rolled his corpse-like body over onto his back.

"Sam!" I cried, urgently patting both sides of his face with my hands as though I was performing the naïvely universal method of reviving an unconscious human being. His eyes opened, and I exhaled a sight of relief. "Sam, are you okay?"

"Think so," he breathed. Then he looked at me as the glimmer of a smile etched across his face. "Wow," he whispered.

"Wow?" I replied, not expecting such an enthralled reaction to whatever had happened to us.

"Yeah. Wow," he repeated.

"Why don't you pussies get a room," Oleander snarled.

"And I'm good, too, brother," Dent spat, emphasizing his relationship to me. "Thanks for asking," his sarcasm continuing. He stood up, smiling without any sincerity of joy, and with the snap of his thumb, he extinguished the lighter, recasting our group into an understated obscurity of night.

"Damn, it's darker than shit!" Oleander exclaimed. "What happened to our fire?"

At once, Dent relit the igniter he had used to start the evening's miniature bonfire, and stepped around aiming it first one direction, then another, searching within the reaches of its limited glow. "What the hell?" he muttered.

I knew at once what my brother alluded to, so I crossed near to him and joined him in his search for the ring of concrete blocks and its expected containment of an active fire. Or at least, its remains. Nothing. Not a block, not an ember or even the presence of ash.

"The fire! The whole damn thing is gone," Dent announced as much to himself as to the rest of our group of six. But in the next instant, I realized there should be seven of us. One other had remained behind post the departure of the girls.

Perry Hutchinson was, for the moment, missing.

"Where's Perry?" I asked, specifically expecting a reply from Oleander. He did not disappoint.

"How the hell should I know?" Oleander boomed.

Suddenly a recollection of an unsettling statement sounded in my mind, a command voiced by Oleander that had risen above the mêlée of the fight.

"Perry, get my gun." I echoed his statement, though with far less enthusiasm.

"What?" Oleander glared at me, ignorantly unaware of my point.

"That's what you said, Sedgwick. Perry, get my gun."

He hesitated and then scoffed.

"No, I didn't."

"Yes, you did," said Sam, stepping next to me.

"We all heard you," said Blaine, flanking my other side.

"Bullshit!" Oleander declared, shifting his eyes to my brother, obviously seeking his support, because without it, he would be a team of one.

"I heard you too, Olly," Dent countered, then stepped boldly into Oleander's personal space, fiercely tapping his finger into the bigger man's chest. "Just what the hell were you going to do with a gun, Jackass?!"

Oleander swung his hands up in front of him, pushing away the challenge of Dent's prodding digit. "I don't have to listen to any more of this bullshit!" Then he stepped past Dent heading for the gap of the arch, belligerently shouldering his way between Sam and me.

A click sounded, and darkness enshrouded us once again.

"Hey, dick-wad! I can't see where I'm going!"

Dent clicked the cigarette lighter, and its flame faintly re-illuminated our surroundings. "Call me another name like that, and you'll be back in the dark digging this out of your ass."

I laughed, though it sounded nearly like a giggle. And despite my impassioned feelings toward my brother earlier in the evening, it was hard not to argue in favor of a partial pardon for him after having witnessed his dominance over Oleander as the alpha male. Maybe Dent considered Oleander a friend and maybe he didn't. But my brother was certainly not going to take any bullshit from the physically intimidating peer.

"Screw you, cowboy!" Oleander remarked, though I did not know if he meant me or my brother. I watched as he disappeared through the arch and into the darkness beyond the rock wall, but not before spitting on the ground next to where Kival lethargically reclined.

I glanced at the remaining four young men, a part of me eager to talk about what had just happened. Anxious to know if they had shared an experience identical to mine. Or had I just been hallucinating? But if delusions were the cause, Sam, at least, had been seriously impressed by something.

Suddenly, Oleander reappeared at the keyhole.

"I can't find my damn truck! I need your lighter!" He could have said please but that word was likely nonexistent in his vocabulary.

"Piss off," Dent responded, dousing the miniature torch.

Again, we were pitched into the shadowy darkness of a crescent-moon night, forcing my eyes to adapt to seeing with minimal illumination. I listened, hearing Oleander trudging around on the far side of the arch, stomping about with his orange and white Style 38 Vans, skater sneakers he had ordered custom made to match his swanky Dodge Ram. "Where the hell?!" he bellowed, as the sound of his exploratory footsteps tapped upon the ground, scratching through the dismal blackness that engulfed us, demonstrating his determination to find the pickup he claimed was not where he had expected it to be.

Suddenly it occurred to me that at no time during Dent's examination of our immediate surroundings had his truck, or any of the other vehicles parked here on this side of the arch, been exposed by the weak flickering of the cigarette lighter.

"Dent," I said.

"What?" he asked pointedly.

"Where's your truck?"

Suddenly the Bic flicked to life in Dent's hand, and he turned eastward, using the lighter to steal away a layer of obscurity from the night. Able to illuminate only a short distance before him, Dent walked forward, treading down the gentle slope of chalky sediment. He stepped further away, aiming the lighter left, then right, then back again as he walked.

Nothing.

Gone were Dent's Chevy, Sam's Ford, and the decade-old coupe-utility muscle car that Blaine had driven here.

"Sonofabitch! We've been jacked!" Dent exclaimed, his words supplying a logical, though unconvincing explanation. "All of us!"

Then Blaine was suddenly brushing past me. "Oh, no!" he exclaimed as he, too, shuffled across the ground, frantically glancing about into the empty space where the vehicles should have been. Nowhere was his father's prized '68 El Camino. "No, no, no, no, no...."

"Yep, he's as good as dead," Sam woefully whispered, both of us knowing that Blaine's alcoholic father would surely beat him for this. The senior Paul Blaine Wallace had physically abused his son countless times before and with far less provocation.

"Well, it looks like we're going to have to wait for a ride. Or walk," Sam added, the theft of his own vehicle neither alarming nor agitating him. But that was Sam. Calm, rational. The opposite of my brother.

"I'm going to castrate every last jackass that pranked us and left us out here without wheels!" Dent announced, proving my comparison of his disposition to that of Sam.

"Not to mention the beer," I pointed out in jest.

"Hell, I didn't even think of that! The beer's gone too!" Dent wailed as he marched toward the arch, his miniature butane torch guiding his way.

Then ahead of him, Oleander's voice exploded, ranting, and swearing even more colorfully than usual. In the gap of the arch, Oleander appeared from the far side, meeting my brother in the same place where Dent had beaten me a short while earlier. I glanced their way, and saw that in the glow of the lighter, Oleander's eyes furiously bulged within the plane of his pale face, and with the help of his fiery and unruly red hair, he looked maniacal, an Irish version of Mr. Hyde or Dr. Frankenstein.

Then my attention fell to the area occupied by Oleander's feet. Seemingly unconcerned by the angry, towering presence next to him, Kival squatted within the base of the arch, his hands busy skimming across the ground as though he were searching for something. At once, the object I had secreted in my pocket flickered in my mind. But then another expletive erupted as Oleander stormed past Kival, shoving him over and out of his way.

Bypassing my brother, Oleander powered toward me, like the star athlete that he was, and within seconds he was in my face.

"Some ass-wipe has stoled my truck!"

For a brief second, I thought about correcting his grammar, but decided I did not need any more damage to my face than that which Dent had already dealt me. "Hold up a sec—"

"Yeah, hit the brakes douche-bag," my brother spouted, promptly acting as a mediator but not until he had first given Oleander a firm shove against his thick, muscular shoulder. "Open your eyes, dipshit! We've all been ripped off! All of our vehicles are gone! Mine … Sam's … his," Dent added thumbing at Blaine.

Oleander paused for a moment, glaring down at Dent. For a moment I believed Oleander was going to punch him, but as already demonstrated, if anyone could reprimand Oleander Sedgwick, it would be Dent. I doubted if Perry Hutchinson would have escaped unscathed if he had delivered those same words to his so-called buddy.

Perry.

His absence puzzled me, and I took a step away, peering into the darkness, pondering an explanation.

"That don't make any sense!" Oleander countered, "Asthma guy's old truck is a piece of shit. Who would wanna take it?"

"Perry."

I spoke aloud, but not as an answer to Oleander. But instead, more as a question.

"Hutchinson? No way!" Oleander barked. "And just where is that pussy?"

"Exactly."

I shared a glance with the others. "Did Perry leave with the girls?"

Sam shook his head.

"That pot-muncher better not of stoled my truck."

"Stolen," I corrected, appreciating that measurable yards of distance now separated us, thus improving my odds of escaping a heated jab of Oleander's wrath. Ignoring me, he spoke to the others.

"I'm going after him. Who's with me?"

"It's darker than a bitch out here," Dent countered. "Without my lighter, you'd barely be able to see your hand in front of you. Besides, have you guys forgotten? This is a party, remember? There's going to be tons of other people coming here any minute. Then we'll get rides back into town with them, and then get to the bottom of this bullshit."

It was a persuasive speech, but the thoughts that had been pinging in my mind were telling me that something else had happened. Something bigger than a hijacking of four automobiles. But still, I could not disagree with Dent. A stroll in the night would be a blind walk in the dark. And I said as much. But Oleander was determined to argue. I gave up and moved to the arch. Promptly, I sat down and pressed my back against the face of the rock wall, near to where I had been when I had awakened from—from whatever it had been.

Dream? Hallucination? A bizarre out-of-body experience?

Sam and Blaine, and then my brother, joined me, finding their own resting spot along the striated wall of eroded sediment. But Oleander stood his ground, deciding to isolate himself from the rest of us before plopping his butt down upon the hard surface of the ground. Then Dent doused the light, once again casting us into the confines of midnight, while also purging our desire to converse. For a long while, we held our voices quiet, though I could hear the breathing of the others, the sounds of their grunts and shifting movements, and could, on occasion, catch a vague glimpse of Oleander as he caught a subtle reflection of the light from the waning sliver of the moon.

Nearby sat Kival, who had barely moved away from the arch. He had been completely silent, even with or without the activation of the lighter, neither adding to the conversation nor seemingly interested in processing the information spoken among the rest of us. Instead, the irrefutable introvert seemed preoccupied with his own private thoughts and was correspondingly obsessed with an exploration of the ground around him. Even now, I could hear what sounded like the scooping of dirt and the sifting of the finely textured soil through his fingers. I moved my hand to my pocket, briefly thinking I should share with Kival what I had put there, confident that it was the thing he was searching for.

But what was it? And why was it important? If I gave it to Kival, I might never find out. And that would not work well for me. I had an inquiring mind that hungered for answers and thrived on knowledge.

Suddenly, the Bic lighter flicked back on, and I impulsively moved my hand away from my pocket. I could not think of a good reason to reveal my possession of it, at least not for now.

"Screw this," Oleander hissed, as if the spark of light had reasserted his right to speak out loud. "I'm leaving," he said, scampering to his feet.

But Dent responded with his original argument that he should stay put and wait for the imminent rescue by those who he adamantly insisted would be arriving soon to join our so-called party. But Oleander would not buy it.

In spite of hearing an additional five minutes of persuasive debate advising against leaving, Oleander chose to ignore reason, and instead acted upon the right of his own discretion, and boldly stepped through the darkened passageway and into the deepest shadows of the night.

"Watch out for rattlesnakes," Dent calmly warned, though I could detect a subtle laugh in his throat. Then he flicked the lighter off and thrust all of us into darkness.

"Rattlesnakes?!" Oleander exclaimed. "Oh, shit, why did you have to tell me that?!" But still he continued to walk away, the sound of his sneakers padding softly upon the ground. None of us who remained followed him.

As though captured by the entertainment of a radio, we listened to the sounds made by Oleander's departure, and heard him searching for the presence of the track of road that had led him here to the Pyramids, while cursing his audience of listeners. It was impossible not to be amused by his antics.

After a few moments it became clear that the prodigal young man had abandoned the direction of the roadway and was instead blindly manipulating his way into the flora of sagebrush and yucca that encompassed the landforms that I suspected would ultimately provide for us a night-long shelter. With focus, I could hear the sound of his blue jeans brushing against the stiff branches of the aromatic plants, mixed with the exhalation of huffs and puffs as he slowly threaded his way through the inky night.

He should have kept to the road, I thought, but knowing him, I imagined that he had opted for the misconception of a more convenient shortcut. At once, his voice, edged with fright, carried across the dark summer air.

"Shit!" Oleander shouted. "Shit, shit, shit, shit, shit!" We listened as his pace quickened and drew nearer but not before he tripped and tumbled to the ground.

Dent laughed out loud. I, however, simply grinned, shamelessly pleased with Oleander's struggle. Moments later, the reckless adventurer re-entered the archway of the giant rock. "I heard something!"

"What was it?" Dent asked, flicking on the lighter to reveal Oleander peering intently into the direction from whence he had come.

"How the goddamned hell should I know?"

Several chuckles echoed among us, and even I could not help but laugh. Oleander returned to the line of our group and sat down at the end, as far from me as he could get.

I sat immobile, suddenly feeling very tired, but my mind was still busy pondering. At first, I found myself thinking about the Hollywood legend, John Wayne, who had passed away just weeks earlier. Then without warning, an image appeared in my mind.

A face. Unworldly. With eyes that were pools of translucent sapphire.

My imagination? Or had the others also seen this Martian-esque creature? And what of the pain? My fugue had almost erased that experience from my memory. But had the others also suffered through a similar torment? I obviously had questions. Perhaps my companions had answers.

"So," I spoke aloud, having decided I lacked the patience to wait any longer, "Did any of the rest of you see the alien dude with the bright blue eyes?"

Silence met my ears. And that, I decided, spoke volumes.

The six of us had much to talk about. Already, in my mind, I had created a checklist of things almost forgotten, even though they were items and events that were just hours old.

The explosion of light.

The ethereal quiet.

The cold.

The pain.

The ice blue eyes.

A snore lifted into the quiet, but I could not tell if it was genuine or fake.

Morning. I could wait until morning for their responses. Unless someone intervened by showing up and delivering us back to our respective homes. It was possible Dad might arrive within the next few hours, wondering why his boys had not returned as expected.

But my gut told me that when morning came, we would still be inexplicably alone.

CHAPTER 7

orning arrived, its faint promise of light birthing quietly upon the Western Kansas landscape. I had been fully awake for upwards of what I estimated to be an hour, although I could not be sure without a watch.

Though within those sixty-some minutes I had been waiting.

And thinking.

But mostly wrestling with emotions, especially those concerning my brother.

And Laurie.

My anger and my anguish had waned. My mother had taught repeatedly of the healing power of forgiveness, and I had paid attention. I wondered, however, if my brother had learned anything from her about remorse or consequence. Regardless, at some point during the night, I had made up my mind to move on. Yet, moving on did not necessarily partner with resolution. And in my heart, I knew of the closure I needed.

Aside from my personal feelings, my thoughts had also been dominated by questions. Questions plagued with answers and explanations that either defied logic or were too spectacular to rapidly win over my sense of reason.

Yet what had been prominently reeling freshly in my mind were two things that had been created for purposes of entertainment, but throughout the night they had held hostage my imagination. A few months earlier, I had taken Laurie to our little town's movie venue, and we had watched a terrific, yet disturbing, film called *Invasion of the Body Snatchers*. A year earlier, Sam and I had met at the Arrowhead Theater and had been riveted by the storyline of the movie, *Close Encounters of the Third Kind*. I could not help but wonder if I, and the other five of us, had hours ago lived through a real-life sequel of either one, or perhaps both, of those science fiction films. If so, then those Hollywood motion pictures were not completely fictional after all.

And with that hypothesis pinballing around in my mind, I was as much dumbfoundedly giddy as I was scared shitless.

Had there been a sudden appearance of a spacecraft? That could explain the intense white light. Had I actually seen genuine beings of a third kind? Been touched by them? Abducted by them? I closed my eyes, and immediately the translucent face with the luminous liquid blue eyes clearly materialized in my mind, quarrelling with my rationality that I had, in fact, been in the presence of a supernatural being.

I shivered. But I was not the least bit cold.

Hours earlier I had confessed to the others about the thing that I had seen, or believed that I had seen, and had done so with an air of absurdity though I had been relatively serious. But no one had taken the bait.

Yet.

Still, I could not let go of the feeling that the six of us had been taken, perhaps transported somewhere, but, by all accounts, we had been safely returned. Most of us, at least.

Perry Hutchinson was missing.

Also vanished were four vehicles. To an alien with a spaceship, I suspected our modern modes of transportation were at best primitive, so it was unlikely the blue-eyed, shapeshifting beings would have given them a second glance. Then of course, last, and certainly least, was the absence of the concrete blocks and burning remnants of our campfire. Separated and considered individually, Perry, the automobiles, and the campfire could be explained as simply a desertion, a theft, and a prank. Collectively, their disappearances painted an alternative picture, causing me to revisit, again and again, a possibility that if I accepted it, the dots would all connect into what I knew to be an unnatural, ultra-imaginative, and, if I were honest, a thrilling revelation. My conclusion was that none of those things were missing at all. They were where we had left them.

Where we ... left ... them.

Suddenly, but quietly in his cowboy way, Dent rose and disappeared through the arch, an act, I presumed, to discreetly relieve his bladder.

I sat still for a moment, looking at the perceptible breaking of daylight in the eastern sky, though too early yet for sunlight to peek over the horizon. I shook my head, dreading the conversation I needed to have with my brother. I let a minute pass, then I stood up and followed him through the arch and onto the western side of the monolith beside which the six of us stranded teens had taken refuge for the night. Several yards away, I saw him standing, gazing westward.

Apprehension weighted my feet, but I moved toward him anyway. And then he, also, began to walk onward, though he gave no indication that he knew I was behind him. I followed him for thirty yards, not thinking much about where I stepped or what my boots treaded upon or around, much less noticing what was not there that should have been. My focus was upon him, my brother, the back of his head as it owlishly pivoted from left to right. At once he stopped and posed with his hands resting on his hips. I caught up with him and stood at his side.

Dent glanced at me, then looked away, but stayed his ground. I waited a moment giving him the chance to break ice. And then to my surprise, he did.

"I'm sorry," Dent said, his voice slightly above a whisper. And I knew to what his words of apology were referred. What and whom.

"Why, Dent?" I asked, suddenly emotional. "Why, Laurie?"

For a long minute, he said nothing, the two of us standing next to each other but staring ahead as though we were two strangers aligned in front of a bathroom urinal.

"I have demons, JT," he said, turning to me. I peered at him, trying to study his countenance, but the shadow of dawn was barely sharing any detail of his face. "I have demons," he repeated, and I could tell by the regret in his voice that he had tears in his eyes.

I did not understand what he meant, but knowing him, I was not expecting any additional particulars. Dent was a young man who did things his way, and in his time. I knew better than to push. But his apology had been heartfelt. Perhaps he, too, had learned something from Mom, despite himself. So, I offered him my words that were essential for own my healing.

"I forgive you."

Dent inhaled a sharp gasp of breath, the capturing of what I suspected would have been a sob if it had gotten away from him. At once, he turned and strode away, moving north and parallel to the western line of the monuments, their flat tops beginning to be unveiled by the dawn of the eastern sky.

Around us, daylight was beginning to crack, and I welcomed it. I had something I needed to get a better look at. Something that had also been weighing on my mind, strumming the guitar strings of my curiosity. I slipped my fingers into the fold of my jeans pocket and carefully pulled at the two ends of broken chain. I turned toward the direction of the impending sunrise and peered at the peculiar object as I dangled it in front of my eyes. I noticed then that the chain itself was otherwise ordinary, its string of fine links threading easily through one of three small holes seemingly drilled at equidistant points around its perimeter.

Mesmerized, I studied the pendant. It was round, but disc-like. A nickel could cover its entirety. And metallic, though it appeared to be neither gold nor silver, but a color of something in between. And it was thick, with a large, dark hole in its center, and instantly it reminded me of a Lifesaver candy, albeit an unappealing flavor.

With the illumination of dawn, it became easier to conduct a more thorough examination, and so I spent several minutes intently peering at its details. The first things I focused upon were the etchings of minute lines and the impressions of tiny dots that covered both sides. Resembling a haphazard imprinting of Morse code, I could not discern a particular pattern in the symbology. At least nothing that appeared obvious to me.

Second, and the most extraordinary subject of my inspection, was the pendant's center, a dark hole that appeared to be solid, yet simultaneously there was an essence of liquidity about it that challenged what I knew about the basics of matter and its various physical states. Easing the object down into the palm of my hand, I touched the murky center with the tip of a finger, expecting hardness, or at least some degree of tension, only to discover that I could feel nothing at all.

"Whatcha doin?"

Sam's sudden appearance behind me nearly caused me to piss myself, and I wondered how the hell he had managed such a stealthy approach.

"Shit!" I exclaimed, whirling around to face him. "Sam, you nearly scared the be-gee-bees out of me!"

"More than nearly," he replied with a mischievous grin. "What's that you got?" Sam asked, obviously more observant than I preferred him to be.

"Nothing," I replied, suddenly engulfed by an overwhelming desire to safeguard the thing in my hand. Quickly I turned away, trying my best to furtively return the mysterious object to my pocket.

"Didn't look like nothing."

"I was just taking a leak," I countered, as I immediately feigned closing the buttons of my Levi 501s. I was not sure why I had lied to my best friend, but I sensed that I needed to be careful. To be protective of the object that had inadvertently fallen into my secretive possession. To avoid another lie, I sought to change the subject.

"So, Sam, how'd you sleep?"

"I suppose as well as I could with a rock pile for a bed. Honestly, I feel super tired," Sam informed me as he stepped away a few yards and began to immodestly relieve himself while simultaneously watering the ground where a sunflower stood, its yellow-wreathed face still pointing west where the setting sun had led it. "And I'm hungry," he added.

"How do pancakes sound?"

"Bona fide perfect. I'll take a stack of 'em. But hold the syrup."

I chuckled at him, then politely waited for him to finish his business.

"So, JT," he added, his bladder capable of functioning in tandem with his jaws, "how's your head this morning?"

"My head?" I asked.

"Yeah. I mean, man, Dent sure gave you a beating. Your face has to be sore as hell."

"Not really," I responded, ready to add scout's honor if he decided to doubt me. Curiously, I glanced toward the Pyramids, wondering when the others would be waking. "Rest of the guys still sleeping?"

"Sedgwick is sawing logs like there's no tomorrow. Man, he infuriates me even in his sleep. Blaine slipped off that away," he said, waving toward the southern group of pyramids clustered a quarter of a mile away.

"Why?"

"Dunno. Didn't ask," Sam replied, zipping up. "Number two maybe?"

"And Kival?"

"He's over there scratching in the dirt. Like I said before, he's one weird dude." Stretching his arms upward, he twisted his head around and looked eastward. "Any idea what time it is?" Sam asked me, tagging a yawn onto the end of his question.

"You're asking me?" I replied. "You know I don't wear a watch."

"I know, I know. Some bullshit about not caring what hour of the day it is during the summer cuz ya got plenty to do on the ranch without worrying about the time."

"Something like that."

"Wish I could be so lackadaisical about time."

I laughed. "That's a pretty big word for you, Sam."

"Kiss my ass," Sam chortled. "Comes from hanging around you all the time. Point is, my watch—it's crapped out," he added, lifting his wrist to show me his timepiece. "There's no tick. Winding it up doesn't do a damn thing."

I noticed the arrangement of the hands read 9:14. It certainly wasn't that late in the a.m.

At once, Sam shifted around, crossing into my personal space, and squared himself boldly before me, his eyes roaming the front of my head. Then he curiously squinted at my face, his brow furrowing likewise.

"Okay. That's weird," he said.

"What's weird?"

"Your face."

"Funny."

"I'm serious."

"I'll bite. What's wrong with my face?"

"Nothing. And that's the problem."

Instinctively, I cupped my cheeks with one palm then trailed my fingers across the corner of my mouth and over my chin, wondering what practical joke Sam might be setting up for me. Then suddenly I realized that my lips were neither sore, nor bleeding. I sent my touch upward and palpated my forehead. The cut made from Dent's iron fist upon my brow, a laceration that had profusely masked the side of my face with my blood, was not there. I lowered my eyes, wondering and subsequently discovering that neither was my shirt bloodied.

"Never saw anyone heal so damn fast," Sam said, barely above a whisper.

Suddenly, I heard my name being called, and I looked to see Dent waving toward us, motioning for me, or Sam, or both, to join him in a meeting. Accepting his invitation, we began to walk toward him, and in those first hurried steps it hit me like a brick as I realized there was another thing to add to the list of the missing. Automobiles, injuries, and Perry Hutchinson were, granted, inexplicable, for now. But this was different.

Gone was the roadway that should have been underfoot and encircling the Pyramids.

I braked for a moment and glanced around to confirm its absence, then hastily crossed what was close to the length of a football field, Sam trotting at my heels. We joined Dent where he stood waiting.

"So, JT, where the hell is the road?"

I was not surprised by his question. I only wondered if he had made the observation before or after his stroll to this point. Probably before. Dent knew this place as well as I did.

"And the fences," he continued, confirming that his question about the road had been rhetorical. "There should be a barbed wire fence just over there," he added, with a subtle bounce of his head. "But it ain't there." I looked in the direction of his nod, and then added my own, silently agreeing with him. I had already been postulating what had happened to us, and considering the absence of other things, this newest revelation fit perfectly into my theory.

"And take a good, long gander over there, little brother," Dent said, pointing to the east, the cusp of the sun just breaking the horizon, pouring a soft light upon the land that rolled for miles in the direction of the rising golden globe. "See those brown spots?"

"I see them," I replied, and I was instantly awed.

"They're moving," Sam observed.

"That they are, Sambo. That they are."

"Cows," Sam suggested.

"Them ain't cows."

"They're buffalo," I said, wonder filling my eyes.

"Something else, too, boys."

"What?" Sam asked, still processing the bison.

"Don't look just yet, but over there behind Old Chief Smoky, I saw something. Something hiding. And sure as there's a hell, it's been watching us."

From the corner of my eye, I saw Sam's head swivel.

"I said, don't look. Don't want it to know we know about him."

"Is he bullshitting me?" Sam asked.

I shook my head. My brother was many things, but he was not a storyteller. And although the lonely pilon bearing the likeness of an Indian stood close to a thousand feet away, I knew that Dent had the keen eyes to spot a coyote at least that far away, so I did not doubt his words. But I did have a question.

"What was it?" Sam asked, beating me to it.

"Not was," Dent replied. "Still is."

"An animal?" I asked, stealing a glance in the direction of the face-shaped landform. "Or a man?" I looked again.

"Could be," Dent answered.

"Perry?"

"I don't think so."

"Should we go find out?"

"I don't think so," Dent repeated. "Not now. It might be…" he trailed away.

"Might be who?" Sam asked impatiently.

"One of … them."

Instantly I knew of whom he meant. "You saw them, too?"

He turned to me, and a careful grin etched across his face. "I saw them," Dent replied acknowledging my question. "Ghosty-looking bastards with ice-blue eyes."

"Sonofabitch! So that wasn't a dream?!," Sam spouted, his bewilderment sounding genuine. I looked at Sam, his face was a puzzle, or a facsimile of one.

"Last night, before you even said anything, I knew, JT, I knew you had to have seen them, too. I just knew it," Dent continued. "And I bet you've been pondering like shit to make sense of this whole thing, too, haven't you, brother?"

"A little," I admitted, but Dent knew that I was understating the truth.

When it came to knowledge and understanding, I was, as Sam often called me, a bona fide nerd, though I preferred the label of intellectual.

I loved books, loved to read, had my own eclectic library of textbooks and novels stored and organized in shallow boxes beneath my bed, not to mention my collection of L'Amour Westerns. But there were others, books that I doubted a normal American teen would own, much less read, but Miss Younce, our high school librarian, had helped nurture my hunger for knowledge, pointing me to works I might not have otherwise discovered. Among those that earned a place in my personal library were copies of *Mere Christianity* by C.S. Lewis, Sun Tzu's *The Art of War*, and Shakespeare's *The Tempest*.

Mom, however, had been my strongest supporter when it came to learning, and because of her I developed a thirst for reading at an early age. She had likewise tried to be as influential with Dent, but he had always been more like Dad, preferring to pave his own way rather than reading what others had gleaned from their personal experience of exploring and engaging in life.

But, indwelled within me was an old soul, something my mother would often remind me of. A maturity, she said, that was far beyond my years, though I suspected that phrase might have been her way of telling me I was a boring, unadventurous kid.

Still, I could spend hours playing Pong on my Atari.

"Whatever," Dent mused at my attempt to minimize my contemplation. "The other guys may have thought you were just pouting and licking your wounds, but you've been thinking. Thinking about every damn minute and every damn detail that's happened since that—thing—last night. I'm right, right?"

"You're right."

"Then tell me. Tell me what you're thinking!"

I was silent, pausing to reflect upon the things that were factual, as well as the experience of the explosion of light, the visions of blue-eyed ultra-terrestrials, the sensations of extreme pain and intense cold.

Additionally, I considered the injuries I had sustained to my face, a busted and swollen lip, a cut and blood-clotted gash in my brow, results of a very real ass-whupping I had blatantly received from my hot-tempered brother. But, as Sam had pointed out, the injuries had vanished.

Admittedly, I had developed a suspicion. An idea far from logical. Conceivably, biblical. Supernatural for certain. I had been healed.

Healed by Them.

"Straight up?" I asked, breaking my silence.

"Straight up."

"I suspect," I began, though I could not keep from inserting a seriously pregnant pause for dramatic effect, "somehow, some way, we have traveled through time."

"Sonofabitch! I knew it!" Dent cussed, moving away a few steps from Sam and me.

"Time traveled?" Sam asked as though he had not clearly understood me.

"Yeah," I replied. "I think we have traveled back into a time before—well obviously, before this place had roads or fences. A time when buffalo still roamed freely across the plains," I added, nodding toward the beasts that grazed distantly in the east.

"But," Sam stammered, "but, how?"

"Yeah, JT," Dent said, turning toward us, "how did it happen?"

I did not know the answer, but I did have a suggestion.

"I think we got here with help."

"You mean, the blue-eyed dude-things?"

"Yes," I replied succinctly, but my thoughts also leapt into my pocket, wondering exactly what the thing was that I had hidden there. Had it played a role? Had it been the catalyst that had initiated this previously unimaginable event? I surreptitiously shrugged at those private thoughts, guiltlessly deciding that my silence was my best answer. Though, even now, I pondered upon it.

And upon the identity of our spy.

Was it one of them, as Dent surmised? Or someone else?

My money was on someone else.

CHAPTER 8

inutes later, Dent and Sam returned to the arch to gather the others. As a group of six, we had a serious subject to discuss, and to speculate upon.

I was anxious, though, wondering how receptive Blaine and Kival would be to my hypothesis. Oleander's reaction would be no surprise. He would scoff, bellow about how stupid he thought I was, and of course he would call me something other than my name. But I would not hear their initial reactions, as I had stayed behind, suggesting that I should remain as a nonchalant sentinel watching for any sign of the unidentified one who Dent had scrupulously observed to be watching us. However, I kept my face poised on the roaming herd of buffalo that had steadily migrated toward the Pyramids, an effort to avoid raising the spy's suspicions that we were on to him.

But my ulterior motive to seclude myself from the others hinged on the fact that I wanted another chance to study the necklace. And once I was alone, I would do just that.

Patiently, I waited until my brother and my best friend had disappeared, crossing through the arch. Abruptly, I slipped the object from my pocket and began to examine it a second time. Only now my focus was entirely upon its enigmatic center.

In full daylight, the miniscule abyss was astonishingly strange and ominously black.

It appeared as though it had a depth that was infinite, limitless, but for a fraction of a second it seemed to glimmer as if it were a pool of unrefined oil. Again, I touched the ebony core with the tip of my smallest finger, wishing that my pinkie was half its size so that I could fully insert the tip into the heart of the object. Again, I felt nothing. It was as if it were a black hole, empty, without mass. Suddenly I had an idea.

Pinching the thick rim of the disc between my thumb and index finger, I took one end of the broken chain and held it above the circular object, then slowly I lowered it toward the aperture of the disc and inserted it into the black orifice. I watched as the chain disappeared into the nothingness of the dark dot. Then I tilted my head to get a view of the underside of the pendant, expecting the metal chain to have exited through the identical circle of black on the opposite side. But though I had fed several inches of the string of tight metal links into the dark cavity of the disc, the chain had not appeared. Nothing was there.

I was stunned.

If only Mr. Lattimer were here. I'd ask him to scientifically explain the phenomenon.

I spent a full minute analyzing the diminutive void, before opting to pull the chain from inside out, noting that my fingertips felt no resistance, no friction. The chain simply moved freely, as if through air, or liquid. Touching the portion of the necklace that I had fed into the disc's center, I had thought that I might feel something that would prove that there was, in fact, a tangible substance within the illusion of oblivion.

But as before, there was nothing, no matter, no trace, no evidence of anything whatsoever. At once my mind considered a fantastical alternative.

"A magical talisman," I whispered aloud, my imagination conjuring images of powerful amulets and enchanted jewelry from the stories of Merlin and Bilbo Baggins. Hearing my own words spoken out loud, I knew then that I had a name for this thing.

"Give it to me!"

The voracious command had come from behind me, a snarling of four words that would have felt like thorns if they had been endowed with a physical property. Startled for a second time while being captivated by the talisman, I turned and found Kival glaring at me. Fear, more than anger, seemed to flash within his blue eyes. He reached for the necklace, his hand swift and determined.

But he had not been quick enough. I pulled back, and shoved my free hand against his chest, pushing him away.

"GIVE IT TO ME!" Kival cried out, his voice intense and demanding, desperate for the return of his precious. "It's mine!"

I stared at him, incredulous that he was acting in a manner that was borderline psychotic. I had never known him to be hostile or belligerent, or to act anything other than complacent and passive. Then, in the next instant, that perception of him changed.

Permanently.

In his hand he produced a knife.

From where it came, I did not see. But the blade was moderately long, five inches at least, its hilt equally as long and held in a fierce grip, the veins of Kival's arm swelling beneath the surface of his coppery skin. I was stunned that he stood before me, brandishing a knife, threatening me with bodily harm. Or worse.

"PLEASE!" He begged, though his voice was like a growl. "Don't make me—I don't want to hurt you."

"Okay," I said. "Okay, Kival. Just calm down." Then I slowly relinquished the object of his desire.

Kival snatched it from me, gathering the chain and talisman into his hand, cupping the charmed necklace defensively against his chest, concealing and protecting it. Slowly, he backed away a few feet, then three yards further, then more until we were separated by a distance too great for me to rush him. He turned and raced away toward the north end of the landform cluster, disappearing beyond the far side. And with him he carried the magical amulet.

A mystical thing that engendered ambiguous abilities.

As to how, and from where, it had come to be in my possession instantly began to cut through the fog of my memory. And from whose neck I had pulled it free was now conclusive. The talisman belonged to Kival.

Or at least he asserted himself as its owner. Clearly, he intended to retain its guardianship.

But how had he acquired it?

Fifteen minutes later, five of the six of us had gathered at the place where Dent had apologized to me and had confessed of his affliction with demons. He had taken the lead, pointing out the absence of the road and the fence. I noticed that he frequently glanced toward Old Chief Smoky, his concern about what or who he had seen there was obviously genuine.

Kival was not among us. I had not seen him since he had vanished beyond to the east side of the monolithic rocks. The others had not seen him either and did not appear to care as much about Kival as they did about the meaning behind my brothers' pointed demonstration.

"Just because this egg-head brother of yours says that's what happened, doesn't make it true!" Oleander argued, his head wavering as though he had spoken a profound truth.

"Doesn't make it false, either," Blaine countered. "JT is our class Valedictorian."

"Big whoop," Oleander said with a roll of his eyes.

"He knows a shitload of stuff."

"You pussies can buy his horseshit, but I'll keep my money!" Oleander shouted, challenging Dent. "Deducted by aliens?!" he added with a scoff.

"Abducted, dipshit, not deducted," Dent corrected. "But it's a possibility."

"Whatever. So, yeah, my truck is gone, stoled by that pussy, Hutchinson. Couldn't be anyone else. Anybody with half a brain can figure that out! And somehow, he stoled the road too, to trick us."

"Olly, you dumbass," Dent blurted. "How can anybody take a road?"

"Well, it ain't there, is it? Perry must of done it! And where the hell is he?" Oleander questioned then marched along a grassy expanse that had yesterday been a two-track roadway. "HUTCHINSON!" he bellowed as if he believed Perry was close enough to hear him.

"He's an idiot," Blaine spoke aloud, voicing what the rest of us were thinking.

Sam, like me, had been unusually quiet. He seemed to be accepting the time travel scenario, but he neither joined in support of the proposition, nor argued against the bizarre suggestion. I was, however, deeply distracted by what had happened earlier between me and Kival. I glanced back to where I had last seen him, and a sight met my eyes that caused me to gasp.

"Guys," I said, my voice guarded, but also edged with veneration. "Look."

"Holy crap!" Blaine exclaimed, his words an excited whisper. "Should we run?"

"No," Dent barked softly. "Just stand still."

From within the midst of our cluster of vertical chalky pyramid rocks, three adult bull buffalo had emerged, the massiveness of their heads and forequarters mantled with coarse fur. I watched them walk, their powerful shoulders rising mightily above the sway of their enormous skulls, attributes that were an anatomical contrast to their sleek and almost dainty posteriors. From each side of their shaggy heads a pair of menacing black horns jutted outward from their temples, their points sharp and shiny, angling upward toward a mat of curly hair resembling a bad toupee. These animals which I had seen earlier as distant brown dots, were here before me, wild representations of specimens I had only been acquainted with when stout, wire-netted fences had separated us. I was both awed and nervous as hell.

The American Bison was known for having an unexpected and unforgivable temper.

So far, the trio of native beasts ambled along, unconcerned, and seemingly unaware of our nearby presence. But that did not last for long. Behind me, I heard heavy footsteps and then his loud voice.

"Whoa!" Oleander exclaimed, apparently as impressed as I was, though his actions demonstrated his ignorance of the dangers posed by wildlife.

"Shut up!" Dent ordered, but it was too late.

As if in response to the demanding consequence of Oleander's word, the buffalo, in unison stopped and turned their bearded faces toward us and lifted their heads. They were close enough that I could see their small dark eyes, though buried in fur, staring at us, glistening and wary.

"Oh, shit," Dent exhaled.

I had thought the same thing, fearing that my pants were seconds from becoming soiled from the inside out.

"All of you, slowly, do like me and crouch as low as you can."

"No thanks," Oleander replied. "I'm gonna run like hell."

"You dumb ass, you can't outrun them," Dent whispered with anxiety. And from the corner of my eye, I saw him begin to lower his body, diminishing his size, reducing the threat the bison might perceive in us. I reciprocated my brother's actions. Sam and Blaine followed, then finally Oleander's survival instinct overpowered his stupidity and he, likewise, crouched with the rest of us.

I held my breath, watching.

And praying.

After what had to have been a record number of seconds in the expanse of a single minute, the lead buffalo lost interest in us, and refocused his attention forward and recommenced with his leisurely stroll. The second bull duplicated the action of his leader, though the one that was their caboose cast toward us a taunting eye followed by a displeased shake of his head, then issued a snort of warning before falling in behind his comrades. We held our positions, watching them as they trod southward. In the nearby distance just beyond the pilons of chalky rock, a bison herd of perhaps fifty head, cows, calves, and a handful of yearling-sized buffalo floated across the short grass prairie, their destination seemingly the same as the three older males that had instead chosen their route through the maze of my Pyramids. Without a doubt, they were all headed for water.

And suddenly, I too, felt thirsty.

South of us, for a short distance of perhaps a mile, the gentle meander of the Smoky Hill River flowed easterly. The absence of a

Sonic Drive-In, or even a watering trough at the base of a windmill forced us to realize that our best and most convenient source of water would have to be shared with these monarchs of this western prairie. Unfortunately for us, those animals would not only drink from the river, but they would also bathe and defecate in it.

Feeling as though we had dodged a bullet, the five of us returned to the arch and waited while keeping tabs on the small band of buffalo. With the others, I watched as they loitered about in the topographically low area where the river flowed, until finally moving away, southward, grazing peacefully beneath what had now become a mid-morning sky.

"Okay, pussies," Oleander prodded. "Let's go!"

We had decided that once the buffalo were gone, we too, would go to the river to drink. All of us were ready to cave to our thirst, even if it meant drinking from a natural stream of water hopefully free of any life-threatening impurities.

And we were also getting hungrier by the minute. Blaine was the first to complain of the gnawing in his stomach. But what exactly we had planned to eat was a whole other issue.

Oleander had suggested we chase and tackle one of the smaller buffalo, slaughter it, and flame roast its flesh on skewers held above an open flame. Apparently, he was channeling a scene from an episode of television's *Wagon Train*, underestimating what it would take to accomplish such a task. Running down a buffalo would be virtually impossible without a horse, not to mention the only universally known weapon in our collective possession was Dent's pocketknife. Mister Boy Scout was never without the small foldable blade, a gift from our grandfather. Of course, I had been given one like it. However, too many accidental launderings in Mom's washing machine had reduced mine to a rusty item of sentimentality.

But Dent's pocketknife was not the only weapon in the armory of our stranded troupe. Kival had a knife. A big one. And it was certainly capable of fatally wounding one of the younger meaty herbivores. But for now, I planned to keep that fact to myself, as well as the circumstance that had led me to the knowledge of Kival's persuasive blade.

At once, I recalled the feral anxiety I had witnessed in Kival's eyes, the desperate tone of his voice. Though I may have harbored uncertainties before, I was now convinced his social skills were in serious need of refinement, but if I were to reveal to the others what had transpired between the two of us, I doubted that any of them would embrace an opportunity to get to know him better. And despite his threatening behavior, the last thing I wanted was for him to feel further ostracized from our group, although the detail of his current absence was entirely his own doing.

Even now, I wondered where he had gone. Covertly, I explored the surrounding pillars of rock seeking a glimpse of Kival hiding among the chalky monoliths, but I spied no sign of him anywhere. Surely, he had not abandoned us for a solitary journey back to Custer, a place I was convinced did not yet exist in this time.

Stepping through the gap of the archway, Dent acted as the point man for the excursion of our assembled company of five and began to lead us southwesterly away from the Pyramids. He had wisely insisted that we seek a part of the river that lay further away upstream from where the buffalo had congregated, educating the city boys of our group of the upside of drinking from a place untainted by animal urine and feces. No one had objected. Not even Oleander.

I did not immediately fall into the march. Instead, I waited an additional minute to see if Kival would make an appearance, and perhaps join us. I called out his name. My voice echoed within the labyrinth of the landform, then silence laid its feathery head upon the pillow of the warm air around me. With disappointment, I turned and followed the others.

Within a few minutes, I had caught up with Sam. He slugged along, moving slower than the others, seemingly unhurried or even unworried about his next meal. I had sensed that there was something else weighing on his mind and I wondered if he was just feeling unsettled by what had surely happened to us.

"Hey, Sam," I said, stepping beside him, and slowing my gait to match his pace. "Are you processing all of this, okay? I mean, I know it's like right out of a *Doctor Who* episode minus the Tardis and without the black and white guardians, but I don't know what else it could be, you know?"

"I know," he solemnly replied.

Obviously, Sam was preoccupied. Perhaps a little bit scared as surely all of us were. But he was my best friend, and I intended to lift him from his funk.

"You know, Sam, this could be a terrific adventure. Most guys our age are preparing to go to college in a few weeks. Or joining the army or entering the work force. Think about it. We are on the brink of an unheard-of opportunity to live in a time that is not our own. I mean, you've always wanted the chance to be a cowboy. This could be it, to get a horse like you've always wished for. Honestly, I'm excited about it."

"Good for you, JT," Sam replied softly. "I get it. This is your chance to actually live out one of your Louis L'Amour novels."

"That's true. But the best part is we get to do this together. You and me."

"Not me," Sam corrected. "We're not in Kansas anymore."

I glanced at him, his eyes forward and serious.

"Yeah, well maybe not the Kansas we know," I said, offering a degree of understanding.

"It's not the Kansas I need to be in," Sam countered, then after a heavy pause he added, "I'm a dead man walking, JT."

I reached my arm out in front of him, stopping him without needing much effort to do so. He turned to me, and I to him and I gazed curiously into his eyes. Eyes that had lost the flicker of fun that I had always seen in them before. Instantly, I knew something was wrong. Seriously wrong.

"What is it, Sam? Tell me."

"I'm a diabetic, JT. I need insulin," he replied, with a shrug of defeat. "I can't live without it."

Sam might as well have smacked my head with the thick heel of a golf club. His revelation jolted my vacationing brain and instantly throttled me with a shudder of panic and fear. Then guilt rushed at me from all corners of my heart. I had not even thought of Sam's medical predicament. Since the previous night, I had brooded and mulled over a dozen or more aspects of what had happened to us, but not once, not one single time, had I thought of what any of this might mean to Sam.

"Sam—I—oh, shit," I stuttered, my chin quivering. I knew enough about diabetes to know the lifesaving importance of insulin. I had learned from Sam, growing up with him, that his condition precariously set him upon the constant edge of catastrophe. For years, his regimen of insulin necessitated three daily injections of the substance. A supply that he always kept at his disposal, whether at his home, or safely stored in his pickup truck. I immediately realized that he was already two doses behind.

Sam also required a regimented diet to assist in maintaining the proper levels of his blood sugar. I doubted he had taken any time to sneak a slice of pizza before my chaos had ruptured the party, and other than the sugar-free Sonic limeade, he had drunk nothing in what was approaching thirteen or fourteen hours.

Too long for a diabetic.

Lost for words, I reached for him, pulling him into my arms, trying hard not to let a sob escape me. But it punched through anyway, sending the façade of my manhood into a tailspin. I did not care. I loved this guy.

"I'm …. I'm such an idiot, Sam," I whispered over his shoulder. "A bona fide idiot." Then I cursed silently to myself, instantly and almost irrationally angry. I pulled away from him, locking his elbows in the palms of my hands, a resolve building within me. "There has to be a way—"

"No," Sam spoke firmly. "There is nothing. There is no way. Even if there was a doctor or a hospital, it would only postpone the inevitable. It's only been maybe fifty years since they even came up with a treatment for my disease. This," he added with a glance around, "is way further back than that."

I let go of him so that I could wipe the tears from my eyes. And while my fingers brushed away the wetness that had slipped down my cheeks, I suddenly realized that I had to be strong for him. I had to man up. I gazed at him and could not help but admire his bravery. I expelled a deep, hard breath, then mustered a smile.

"You're not alone," I said with a shake of my head. "I won't leave you alone."

Sam looked at me and smiled.

"For the record, I couldn't have asked for a better friend," he said, nodding his head, his own eyes weakening with emotion.

I choked back a sob. I was shitty at manning up.

"One thing, though, JT. I don't want the others to know. I don't want their pity. I don't want to hear them tell me I'll be okay. We both know I won't be."

I promised Sam that I would be discrete, though I knew it would likely be short-lived. At some point, be it hours or days, he would slip into a diabetic coma. And then … then I would have to break my promise. We started walking again. Silence between us. But an idea occurred to me, and a spark of hope began to arc through the network of biological electricity that pulsed in my brain.

The talisman.

If, by some kind of magical power, it had been the cause of our time travel, then perhaps it could be used to get us back to 1979 where we belonged. A time that made life possible for my friend.

I had to get the talisman back.

And time was of the essence.

But Kival had it. Would he give it back to me to save Sam?

In my gut, I doubted it.

And if that were the case, I would just have to take it from him. But I had to find him first.

CHAPTER 9

Sam and I arrived at the narrow waterway a full five minutes after the others. Dent met us twenty yards out.

"Don't get mad," he said.

I studied him suspiciously. He conceded a sidestep to the left and I glanced past him and saw Blaine looking apprehensive, disgusted, and apologetic. He, too, stepped aside revealing Oleander on his knees near the water's edge, his legs astraddle something that was growling and groaning. Then I saw a pair of high-top canvas sneakers thrashing, then a pelvis heaving upward in a futile attempt to throw his captor. His jeans were wet, torn, and muddy, and my first thought was that our pot-head classmate Perry Hutchinson had been located. Oleander looked over his shoulder at me, sneering.

"Looky who I found!" he laughed impishly. And then he lifted his hand, waving a knife. I recognized it immediately, and in a split second I explosively panicked.

I rushed over to them and found Kival, his wrists mercilessly pinned to the ground beneath the crushing, boney knees of the snickering bully. His face cringing, Kival looked toward me, and though his hair was a mess of dark, wet strands lying in thick slices across his face, I could see that his eyes were desperate and pleading. Ignoring my brother's pointless request, I instantly succumbed to my volatile emotion, and I did not need to deliberate the matter before getting to that point. I lunged at Oleander, my hands pummeling against the mass of his shoulder.

"Get the hell off of him!" I yelled, pushing him with as much force as I could muster. My assault caught Oleander off-guard, propelling him from his abusive position of power and toppling him into the water. I landed across Kival, my body unintentionally replacing that of the stout, aggressive tormentor. Kival scrambled from underneath me, scooting away, the heels of his sneakers plowing furrows into the soft dirt. I lifted myself up onto my elbows and caught his eyes. "It's okay, Kival. It's okay," I said with genuine assurance.

"You—little—pencil-dicked prick!" Oleander gasped through spits and coughs as he resurrected his head above the surface of the shallow river, his David Bowie inspired hair-do granting him the suitable appearance of a drowned rat. In a fit of rage, he flailed his arms about, splashing water in every direction of the compass. He spewed and roared as he crawled onto the embankment. A malfeasance radiated from his eyes and for a moment, I thought I was doomed. But then Dent and Blaine were suddenly beside me, seizing my arms and lifting me up, pulling me from the threat of Oleander's immediate reach.

"That's enough!" Dent bellowed, pushing his way past me, confronting my imminent assailant. Though my brother was a good forty pounds lighter than Sedgwick, he was powerful. And quick. And he possessed a pair of fists that could shell out significant pain and damage and do so swiftly, with neither pause, nor mercy. I, for one, knew of those fierce merits first-hand.

And so did Oleander.

"One day," he spat at me, his face as red as his river-soaked hair, water dripping over the ridge of his neanderthal brow and from the underside of his square chin. "One day," Oleander repeated with a snarl, his nostrils flaring, "when your big brother isn't around … your ass is mine!"

I saw the hatred in his eyes, and though I knew better, I could not help but deliver him a verbal jab.

"Sorry, Sedgwick, but I don't swing that way."

Oleander growled and tore himself free from the grasp Dent held on his shirt. He stepped past me, his broad shoulder knocking against my lesser one. I looked across at Dent, giving him both a nod of appreciation and another of affirmation.

"I told you not to get mad," he said to me.

I glanced at Kival, reclining backwards, his elbows propping him up from the ground in a deceitful position of leisure. His legs were splayed before him, and my eyes confirmed that he had not moved, though his breathing was rapid and labored. He looked genuinely beat, though there were not any perceptible cuts or abrasions on his face or arms. He was, however, thoroughly soaked, as though he had been through a baptism or two.

Or three.

Then I noticed his knife lying near my feet. Apparently, I had knocked it loose from the careless grip of Oleander Sedgwick. I leaned over and picked up the weapon, and crossing to Kival I offered it to him hilt first, my fingers carefully pinching the end of the blade.

"Uh, that's not a good idea, brother," Dent warned. "The dude acted like he wanted to gut us with that pig sticker."

I ignored Dent and continued to offer the knife. Kival reached out and gently took it from my hand. I smiled at him. I wanted, and needed, to secure his trust. Sam's life depended on it.

I turned and looked for Sam, finding him seated on the ground a mere half-dozen steps away from where my hair had theatrically caught on fire causing my urgent departure from his side. I walked toward him, with Blaine suddenly on my heels.

"I'm sorry, JT. When we got here, we sort of caught the dude by surprise. Next thing I know he has that knife out. Then Sedgwick just grabbed him and in two seconds he had the knife. And that was even more scary. I was afraid if I got in the middle of the two of them, that big idiot was sure to lash out and hurt someone."

"I get it, Blaine. Don't worry about it."

We reached Sam, and I offered him my hand.

"Can I buy you a drink?" I asked, with as much of a smile as I could manage. He accepted my offer, and I helped him to his feet.

"Man, Sam," Blaine spoke, "You're starting to look like crap."

"Feel that way, too," Sam replied, then he tepidly walked toward the water.

Blaine glanced at me, his brow furrowing.

"Is he okay?"

"Flu," I said, lying. Then I followed Sam.

The two of us knelt at the edge of the stream, and without hesitation, I cupped my hands into the cool water and drank from the vessel of my palms. The water felt good in my mouth. More than good. And, thankfully, it tasted normal. I drank again, several times. I had not realized just how thirsty I had become.

Sam mimicked my actions, though he only drank twice. He then sat back, and I saw a grimace appear on his face. He turned his head and vomited. I helped him back to the water's edge, and he drank again. This time he managed to keep the water in his stomach. Then he lay back upon the ground, his head settling into a subtle niche in the grass and closed his eyes. I looked at him for a moment, my heart clamoring for my big boy pants.

Time was running out.

Then I stood and moved a few feet from Sam, my eyes searching for the others. Dent stood furthest away, looking back toward the Pyramids. I assumed he was diligently being watchful. Upstream, and nearly as far away as my brother, was Oleander. He had stripped himself of his muddied blue jeans and white sleeveless muscle shirt that, wet or dry, had clung to him like a secondary skin, and was squatting at the edge of the bank, rinsing his clothes.

Between him and me stood Blaine, the star running back of our Custer Fighting Indians '78 football season, stretching his arms skyward as I had often seen him do in preparation for a game on the gridirons. From a distance of about three first downs, I watched as Blaine dropped his arms and began to pivot his torso upon his hips, stretching his back first left, then right, then left again, a repetition performed to help relax the body before the physicality of a big game. He then bent at his waist to touch his heels, then rising he pointed his arms upward again, extending them in another calisthenics exercise.

Blaine had plans to eventually be a teacher and coach. He would be great at both. He had personality, compassion, and discipline. And kids, young or old, would love him for all three.

In that moment, a memory surfaced. One that was treasured and still very vivid in my mind. It was the last regular season game of our senior year, a contest between our Custer football team and our rivals, the Oakley Plainsmen. At stake was a chance to compete in the state playoffs, and a win would give us that opportunity.

Less than a minute remained in a game dominated by both offenses, but my Fighting Indians had managed to be in possession of the ball at the Plainsmen one yard line, thanks to the agility and speed of our team's go-to running back, Blaine Wallace, Jr. From the sidelines, I had essentially watched the entire game, participating in only a single play, so far, as the backup to Blaine. And that moment of my gametime contribution had only occurred because Blaine had thrown a shoe on a prior scramble, and I had been sent in to replace him while he re-laced.

Oleander Sedgwick was the team's quarterback, and though I was loathe to admit it, he was a talented athlete. But he lacked genuine sportsmanship to be an effective team leader. Even as a grade-schooler, he was more about the "I", and seemed to care less that the letter was missing from TEAM.

With the game literally on the line, Coach relayed to Oleander to signal a running play, but instead, the quarterback chose to throw the ball, the perfectly spinning pigskin slipping through the hands of his receiver and was nearly intercepted in the endzone. Furious, our coach had called a time out and at the sidelines, he had gotten squarely into Oleander's face.

"Sedgwick! You will hand off the ball to Wallace! Do I make myself clear?" I remembered him shouting, his finger punching into the top of the red number nine that was emblazoned upon Oleander's jersey.

I was behind the sideline huddle, but in front of me was Blaine. And just as the offense began to return to the field, I happened to look down to see him abruptly move the toe of his left cleat to the heel of his right and pull his foot free.

"Coach!" Blaine had called out. "I've lost my shoe!"

"Are you shitting me?! Now what?"

"Put JT in," Blaine promptly suggested, and I shot him a gawk of disbelief and caught him wink at me.

Coach had shaken his head, knowing he was running out of time. Without the benefit of a better option, he had looked at me and said, "You're in, Tescott."

"Yes, sir!" I had replied, giving Blaine a perplexed glance before I rushed out onto the field.

"Same play!" Coach had called out to me.

I entered the huddle.

"You?!" Oleander had hissed.

"Coach says same play," I hurriedly reported.

"No way," Oleander had blurted, then he rebelliously exclaimed "Torpedo One!"

The substitute play was a quarterback sneak. A good one, actually. Or should have been if Oleander had not fumbled the football. But in the melee of twenty-two guys scrambling for the lost pigskin, I had been the one to recover it and had somehow managed to move the ball within inches of the goal line.

An immediate timeout was again called from our side of the field, resulting in a defiant display of exactly who was running the show. With only seconds remaining, the last play of the game had Blaine under center and Oleander on the bench, putting a bewildered me in a do-or-die situation as the replacement ball carrier. Following the coach's original play call, I received the handoff and squeezed myself between the wall of linemen and secured the game-winning touchdown.

I had been elated.

Even Dent, our team's pre-eminent linebacker who had in his sophomore year secured a school record for quarterback sacks, was bear-hugging me and zealously lifting me off my feet.

It had been a surreal moment, one that had resulted in my teammates surrounding me with vociferous enthusiasm and uncountable taps upon my helmet, my shoulder pads, and my back. But not Oleander Sedgwick. He had been livid, plying his way angrily through the joyous crowd of our peers, pushing them aside before unexpectedly shoving me backward, sending me to the ground.

"I am not going to be showed up by a second-string pussy!"

Immediately, Dent and several others were in Oleander's face, they, like him, were fuming, though for different reasons.

Then Coach was suddenly there, lambasting Oleander, furious at his quarterback's conduct.

"You're off the team, Sedgwick!"

"Whatever," Oleander had scoffed. "I got the playoffs, now."

"Turn your gear in," Coach had retorted, and he had meant it.

Oleander did not play again, but neither did we end up advancing in the state bracket. But that moment, that gift that Blaine had unpredictably given to me, had become a defining point in my relationship with him and, for that matter, with Oleander.

I shook my head, tossing aside the recollection of that memory, and turned to look behind me, fearing for a moment that I had let Kival disappear, again. But there he was, standing, just yards beyond where Sam lay, staring into the mud-churned water.

I crossed to him, and I laid my hand on his shoulder.

"Thanks for staying with us," I said.

"Not … not much, choice … out here in the middle of … of nowhere."

"Look, Kival, I want to apologize. I didn't mean to take your—your necklace thing. I think in the fight, I just accidentally found my hand tangled up with it, and then there was the blinding light, and … well, you know."

"Doesn't matter anymore."

"Thanks, I'm glad you understand. I really do want to be friends."

"That's … not what I meant," he corrected me, his eyes still glued to the shimmering surface of the stream.

"What then?"

"Don't have it anymore," he said, nodding at the water.

Instantly I realized what he meant, and my heart sank from the implication that the item I most desired had been stolen by nature's lifeblood.

I stared across the top of the glistening thief, more of a stream than a river, but still deeper than it had been even the day before when Dent and I had watered our horses. But we were now in a time that was God knows how many years earlier, a year when the rains of June had apparently been more generous.

"Kival!" I shouted, louder than I had intended. "Come on, I'll help you look for it!"

He shook his head, his face an expression of helplessness.

"I—I can't swim," he confessed.

I glared at him. In this day and age, how could he not know how to swim? But now was neither convenient nor imperative that I ask him that question. But knowing how desperate Kival had been to get the talisman back into his possession, I had to accept the fact that he was being truthful, for otherwise I was sure he would have already been doing what I was about to do.

"Where?!" I asked him, hoping he could at least give me an idea. He pointed to a place several yards out, near center, across from the edge of the bank where I had found him pinned by Oleander. Quickly, I pulled my beloved boots from my feet and leapt into the water. Where I jumped, the river was only waist deep, though I knew that several feet further in, the surface might rise as far up as my chest.

But probably no deeper.

As a child, I had grown up exploring this water, wading barefooted, catching minnows and tadpoles in the places where our cattle had stomped their cloven hooves into the mud and pressed out miniature ponds at the river's edge. Further downstream, though, at the easternmost end of our ranch was a small place in the river that had greater depth, carved out at the foot of an old cottonwood. It was a pool within a pool that was deeper and colder, and ideal for Dent and me to play and laugh together, taking turns dropping from the tree branches as we competed for the biggest splash. As youngsters, pushing slowly into adolescence, we had often skinny dipped there together, our immodesty not yet reined in by puberty.

I took a balanced step forward and felt my foot sink into the soft sediment of the riverbed. I looked down and watched as putty-colored swirls of liquid silt spun within the water, still relatively murky from the dispersion of inundated soil that had been churned from the bath I had given Oleander.

The movement of my foot on the squashy bottom of the stream instantly caused the water to become even more cloudy. I took another step, and the clarity diminished again. I leaned down, sticking my arm as deep into the water as I could, my fingers reaching and feeling for the muddy bottom, my chin dipping into the surface of the stream.

I felt nothing. Then I dove, immersing my head below the surface, my hands scratching across the soupy bottom, my fingers raking into mud. My effort was at once reminiscent of a search for the clichéd needle in a haystack.

I was wasting my time. But I was reluctant to completely abandon hope.

I lifted myself up and wiped the water from my face. I methodically glanced around me looking desperately into the water, internally screaming for a sign of the thing that I was seeking. Moments passed, then it became clear that it would be useless to continue the search, for my efforts would only strangle the water with more sediment, eventually reducing visibility to near zero. Until the natural movement of the water resettled the liquid dirt, there was no way to thoroughly explore the riverbed with my eyes. And even then, it would be a crapshoot. Chances were, the talisman had already been pushed into soft mud, buried by my own invasion or that of Oleander.

Or perhaps lost within moments of the unprovoked skirmish that had apparently taken place here.

"What the hell, Wild Bill?"

I turned toward the bank and found my brother glaring at me.

"Are you actually washing your nasty ass in our drinking glass?"

Like a wet dog, I shook my head, flinging droplets of water. Then I shot Kival a defeated glance and shook my head again, but with more subtlety. I watched as he lowered himself to the ground, staring into the gentle stream of water that had apparently robbed him of what I wondered was perhaps his most prized possession. I waded forward to the bank's edge where Dent offered me a hand of assistance. I took it, and he pulled me up and out.

"What the hell were you doing?

"Nothing," I lied. Then silently I cursed. I was not one who normally held secrets.

"Just decided to go for a swim? With your clothes on?"

"Something like that," I replied, looking away.

"Uh-huh. So, JT, what's with Sam?" he asked as if reading my mind. I looked to where he had nodded and saw that Blaine was sitting beside the prostrate form of my dying friend. I ignored his question, just as I had ignored his earlier plea that I refrain from getting mad.

"Dent, we need food. Him, more than the rest of us."

"Yeah, well, we're all hungry. What I wouldn't give for nice juicy burger from the Butterfield Café."

At once, a thought pinged in my head. I began to mentally thumb through the pages of words and information that I had banked in my mind from the reading of books and essays of history I had innately stored in my brain. And I had read a lot of books. Many of them historic, specifically related to this region of my home state. I was, undeniably, a nerd.

A bookworm.

Germ Worm, as coined by my brother, was an unappreciated nickname, but it was unintentionally accurate. And then the thought pinged again.

The Butterfield Overland Dispatch.

Along this very river, perhaps even where we stood, a stagecoach service had been, or would be eventually established. A route that had linked Kansas City to Denver, though abandoned because of the railroad. But Custer grew from a place that had been a stopping point for the passengers of the BOD. A place to water and replace horses. A relatively isolated homestead that had been created to provide a traveling customer with a place to rest and to eat.

"Dent," I spoke, my words sounding more urgent than I would have liked. "We need to head for Custer."

He scowled at me.

"Do you think it even exists? You know, here, in whatever the hell the year is?"

"I don't know. I honestly don't. But Custer was founded on the trail of the BOD."

"Yeah, I know. So?"

"There's a chance that's exactly where the Butterfield Café was built, the original owner might be there now. Or somebody else. I don't know. It's a long shot. I know it was there a hundred years ago. More than that. But for all I know we might also be standing in a place where a dinosaur or a mammoth might show up here for drink, and in that case, well— "

"We're screwed."

"Yeah. But we might not be either."

"JT, you don't have to convince me. I'll gladly walk to Custer. I ain't got anything better to do. And on our way, we could stop by the house and say hi to Mom and Dad."

I looked at him and saw that his eyes were without the sarcasm that could have been interpreted from his words. He smiled.

"What about the rest of them?" he asked.

"Ideally, we stick together. We'll just have to persuade them to join us."

Dent wrinkled his nose. "Including that asshole?"

"Don't give me that. It was you who had invited him in the first place."

Dent thought for a moment, then shook his head.

"You got me there," he agreed. "Don't know if I can get Olly to buy into an afternoon hike but surely I didn't lose the ole Tescott charm while zipping around through time and into other worldly dimensions."

"Right. So, let's get going," I said.

CHAPTER 10

For a solid twenty minutes, our group could have resembled a Fortune 500 company board meeting, though without the privacy of corporate walls, or a grand conference table, or chairs to sit on, genuine leather or otherwise. Neither did we have enough money in our pockets to even pretend to be wizards of Wallstreet. But we were engaged in a hullabaloo of distrust and disorganization. Unsurprisingly, heated arguments had arisen between the predictably argumentative.

Oleander and Dent.

But also, there had been unequivocal, though not unprecedented, silence from the characteristically withdrawn.

Kival.

And yet a somewhat rational discussion was effectively shared among those of us occupying the central section of the bell curve.

Me and Blaine.

And Sam.

He had awakened easily from his nap but was intensely thirsty. I had helped him to the river but scooped into my own hands the water for him to drink. Nausea had hit him again, but he managed to keep the vomiting at bay. When he had been refreshed, we stayed put at the water's edge, and I had imploringly motioned for Blaine and Kival to join us. And then I laid out to them my idea, the business I optimistically hung my hope upon. Blaine was on board, and though he was weak, Sam was willing. Kival, though, had hesitated. He had openly confessed that he felt disconnected from our group, that he was unimportant, and had suggested we go without him.

But I did not intend to leave Kival here, out in the middle of who-knew-when, alone.

Further away from the place where Oleander had stripped and then redressed, Dent and he stood sparring, each one trying to trump the other with the loudest expletive. After an excruciating five minutes, the arguing had ceased, and judging by the owner of the closing remarks of their debate, Dent had allowed his vociferous opponent to have the last word. In the next moment, I heard my brother call for me and I angled my eyes to look in his direction and saw him gesturing for us to come.

Beyond him, Oleander was trudging westward along the river, with or without the rest of us. Apparently, he had decided that he would do the leading. And knowing him, he had likely appointed himself the trailblazer with me and the others assigned to be his entourage of time-lost castaways.

Minutes later, the remaining five of us were in a compact caravan, two-legged and single-file, bunched together, me bringing up the rear position immediately behind Sam. For most of a half-hour, we walked steadily, but not too fast, as Sam was determined to keep pace with the rest of us. At once, Dent began to trot away, distancing himself as the lead pedestrian of our sub-group and quickly closed the gap between him and Oleander. Though the boisterous jackass stayed with the river, both of us Tescott boys doubted he had the acumen to guide us to our destination or even recognize it once we got there. To be honest, I was not even certain I would know.

Two more minutes ticked by, and I looked and saw that Dent and Oleander had stopped and together they were waiting for us. And in that pair of minutes, fatigue had ambushed Sam. Both Blaine and I had offered to assist him, but Sam waved us aside and lugged onward. By the time we had arrived at the rendezvous point, I was confident that Sam could not possibly make it further on his own.

"So," Dent said to me, directly. "Look familiar?"

I glanced about our immediate surroundings seeing nothing I recognized. Then I shifted my eyes and peered into the distance, and a spark of detection captured my consciousness. I maintained the same discerning gaze, but I pivoted circularly, as though I were the life-size equivalent of the little ballerina that danced in a pink jewelry box where Laurie had once revealed to me as the hiding place of my love notes, mementos of our developing romantic relationship. I had secretly winced when I had learned she had kept them. God knows the embarrassment they would cause me if those juvenile expressions of adoration were ever made public.

Sans a tutu and a tiara, I completed my three-hundred-sixty-degree visual reconnaissance and I realized we were standing where our home should have been. In fact, I had concluded that we were likely occupying the place of our kitchen if there had been walls.

"I'll be damned," I said, suddenly feeling homesick. For a brief moment, I felt a flash of panic, wondering if I would ever see my mom and my dad again.

"Home sweet home," Dent spoke, "but hard to get too excited over the views. Amazing though how even with the house and the barns gone, nothing much is really different."

"Except the trees," I offered, my gaze leading Dent's eyes to the river that lay a short distance from where our horse barn and cattle pens would one day be built.

"Yeah," Dent agreed. "They are different looking. And there's a lot more of them and they're bigger. I would have expected saplings you know, sprigs that would grow to become our trees. Odd, isn't it? But I suppose Great-Great Grandpa Thomas probably chopped them down for firewood."

"Or for building," I suggested, though for now there was no way of knowing if those trees would be in his time, or from a time much, much further in the past. I hoped for all of us, especially Sam, that the past these trees were a part of was just a modest one hundred years or so from our time of 1979.

Suddenly the sound of dry heaving touched my ears, and I immediately went to the source. Sam was on his hands and knees, painfully retching, stomach bile and saliva dripping from his gaping mouth, his eyes, barely moist, were sunken. He was rapidly going downhill, his health precariously declining faster than I would have expected. It was obvious then just how seriously Sam's body depended on regular injections of insulin. Without the supplemental hormone, his life was unsustainable. I bent down to Sam and did my best to comfort him.

"I am ... so ... thirsty," Sam spoke, his voice barely above a whisper.

The agonizing tonality of his voice made my chin quiver, but otherwise, I kept my countenance rigid and focused. I motioned to Blaine to help me, and we escorted Sam to the river's edge. As before, Sam drank from my hands, but little more than a sip passed his lips, and he shook his head inexplicably adverse to ingesting more of what he sensed he craved.

Blaine and I hoisted Sam up from the ground and carried him between our shoulders to a relatively large cottonwood that stood a few paces from the water, the dry summer breeze stirring its crop of green leaves. We eased him down, and he leaned his back against the tree and closed his eyes. Then I felt a tap on my shoulder and turned to find Dent staring down at me. For a count of ten, he studied my forlorn eyes, then silently instructed me to follow him. So, I did. He waited for me a few pickup lengths away.

"Sambo's not just fighting a bug, is he?" Dent asked, as though he were making an accusation.

"No," I whispered, shaking my head, desperate to blink back tears of grief I could feel being pressed by my eyes. I was clearly on the cusp of allowing my brother the opportunity to witness the softer side of me. Again.

"His diabetes?" Dent asked, and I nodded. "Then, this is serious, isn't it?"

I nodded a second time.

"Shit."

I looked at Dent, determined to keep my chin steady, and in his eyes, I saw that he had reached an obvious and regrettable conclusion, the result of a frightening experience we had previously shared with Sam.

Six years earlier, before we were old enough to have earned a driver's license, Sam had come to our ranch to spend a day in fun exploration of the Pyramids. And since Sam was not yet comfortable with a horse, the three of us had decided to walk the breadth of the ranch to get there and had ultimately spent more than five hours playing Cowboys and Indians among the inspiring monuments.

We had missed lunch, having immersed ourselves in an overly active game induced by our imaginations, hiding and chasing and ambushing each other from every crook and cranny of the towering complex of rocks. At one point, our citified friend had eluded us longer than normal, and when Dent and I had found him, Sam had lapsed into a convulsive physical state. He had apparently sensed the onset of a diabetic episode, for in his hand he clutched an unopened Hershey chocolate bar, soft and melted.

Dent had raced the three miles back to our house to get help, while I had tried to feed Sam as much of the dark sugary goo that I could dip onto my fingers and into his mouth. I had known for a few years Sam's habit of carrying a candy bar with him in the event he might begin feeling unexpectedly weak and needing an immediate boost of energy. How lucky for him, I had often thought. Sam could have candy seemingly whenever he wanted it. Whereas my brother and I, our enjoyment of sweets was promised as an incentive if we had managed to get through a week without fighting. Needless to say, as kids we rarely experienced a sugary reward.

But on that day, I learned that Sam was not as lucky as I had thought. But fortunately, Dent and Mom, followed by an ambulance, arrived in time, and from our mother, we boys learned of the exact precariousness of our young friend's condition.

And now, here we were again. No longer naïve youngsters but learned young men. But in a far worse circumstance. This time, there was no candy, no ambulance, no hope.

"Dent," I began, "It probably won't matter, but if you find a Hershey bar at the Butterfield station—"

In less than two minutes, Dent had barked orders, and he and Blaine and Oleander were trotting away, disappearing beyond the low knoll that girded the west edge of this place that would become the Sweetwater Ranch, the home and enterprise of the Dean Tescott family.

Dent did not need to ask; he knew that I would not leave Sam. Kival stayed behind with me, neither being told to follow my brother, nor voluntarily doing so. But I was glad he had chosen to remain with me and Sam. If something were to happen, something that was at present unspeakable, I did not want to be alone.

The afternoon waned into early evening, and I had spent the bulk of two hours propped against the cottonwood next to Sam, his head resting against my shoulder. He had slept most of that time, though he had awakened with a gasp as a sharp pain assaulted his abdomen and had caused him to slump sideways against the tree. Luckily, the discomfort did not last long, and the incident had stimulated him enough to want to talk for a few minutes, though he was obviously exhausted.

"JT," he whispered, "remember the first time I … came out to your ranch and … you showed me the cows and the horses?"

"Yeah, I remember."

Sam laughed softly, weakly.

"Saw that old cow, a Hereford, I think—"

"Yeah, that's right, she was a Hereford," I confirmed, knowing what memory he was about to revisit.

"She was out there," he said, raising his hand and indiscriminately pointing at a place on the dry landscape, "… in the pasture … back hunched … tail straight … in the air…"

"Peeing," I said, remembering with a smile, Sam's surprise at what position the animal had to get herself into just to urinate.

"So … weird … to me."

"Yeah, well, you were just a town boy, then."

"Bona … fide," Sam breathed in agreement. "But … you taught me … stuff …"

"I tried," I said, reminiscing. "Took you forever to learn to rope. But I made you start with the basics before letting you throw from a horse. We would spend hours out in my yard, throwing lassos at those stick cows my dad made from scrap lumber. We practiced and practiced until our arms wore out."

"It was fun … throwing lassos—"

"Yes, it was fun," I responded as moisture began to blur my sight.

"That … dog—what was his … name? The one that … always … tried to hump … my leg?"

"Oh, yeah," I said, blinking back my tears. "That was Dad's ole Australian Shepherd he called Whiskey."

"No…," Sam whispered with a gentle shake of his head.

"Well, Dent and I called him Frisky, for obvious reasons."

"Yeah … Frisky—I hated that … dog—"

Instantly, my face collapsed. "Yeah, me too," I whispered as tears streamed down my cheeks, droplets falling and staining the front of my shirt.

"Yeah … bona fide … uh …," he said weakly, his words trailing.

And then Sam was quiet. His breathing noticeably shallow. Moments later, Kival joined us, sitting on the opposite side of Sam. Reverently, he lifted from the dusty ground the limp hand of my sleeping friend and repositioned it into the comfort of Sam's lap. I smiled at Kival, nodding an expression of appreciation for his thoughtfulness.

I sat there for a long time, thinking about friendship. Against me leaned a kid, a buddy, who I had often leaned on when I needed to vent about Dent, or Dad, and to whom I had confessed the pubescent crushes I had developed for various girls during our years in grade school. Then in an unexpected moment of clarity, I felt incredibly grateful for knowing Sam. Thankful for the friendship we had shared year-in and year-out, from our first meeting in kindergarten and then through to the end of high school. And then, without intending to, I wondered who I might lean on and confide in later … when—

I shook my head, attempting to clear from it the foreboding that I preferred not to think about. I reached my hand under his chin and cupped the side of his face and pulled him gently into the cradle of my chest and shoulder, then compassionately I began to caress the hair on the backside of his head.

I would not realize until later that Sam and I had already shared our last conversation.

Dent and his two companions returned just as dusk began to close upon us. They had been gone much longer than I had expected, since their destination had been only about three miles away. However, when they arrived, they brought with them tension and disunity.

And a snake.

"Asshole," Dent muttered as he walked by where I knelt assembling dry grass, and sticks and scraps of fallen tree branches in preparation for a fire. I was not Boy-Scout enough to coax a blaze without the help of a manufactured ignitor, but I would not have to worry or cuss the absence of that skill, now that my brother had returned with his faithful Bic lighter. Then a dozen steps behind him strode Oleander, a headless rattlesnake dangling from an outstretched hand.

"We got dinner!" Oleander announced, then tossed the dead reptile toward me, its tubular body landing with a thump just a few feet from the arrangement of my hopeful campfire. If Sedgwick expected me to jump and scream like a girl, I had thoroughly disappointed him. Rattlesnakes were commonplace on our ranch, and I had often dealt with them, dead or alive.

"Man, you should have seen that fearless brother yours! He's got balls, I'll tell you that!" Oleander gushed. "It was far out, like I never saw nothin' like it! Dumb-ass Hollywood Wallace here," he continued with a nod toward Blaine, who stepped past the jabbering baboon angling to join Dent at the river. "The pussy nearly stepped right in the middle of that bad-ass snake. It goes to buzzin' its tail and Wallace hollers like a whore in a church house! Practically pisses himself! Then Double-D jumps right in! Seriously, that crazy-ass cowboy jumps in feet first, his bootheels poundin' and smashin' the shit out that snake. Unbelievable!"

"Is that all you've got?" I asked, hiding my admiration for my brother. I had seen Dent do the same action several times before. He did have balls; I could not deny it. But as far as I was concerned, my brother was also a brazen imbecile.

"Yeah, that's it," Oleander replied. "We got there, and the place was a shithole. And the dude that lived there, was dead. And the shack was ransacked, and shit scattered everywhere."

"Dead?" I asked.

"Yep. Dead as a frickin' doorknob. The dude looked like week-old roadkill. It was gross as shit."

"No food?" I asked, expecting to be disappointed.

"Not to speak of. A bunch of jars of beans and shit busted up into a pile of broken glass. Maggots having a heyday with it and with the dude. It was disgusting."

"I'll tell you what was disgusting," Dent growled, walking up to us bare-chested while using his shirt to dry the river water from his face. "That piece of shit," he continued, pointing his finger at Oleander, "he found the one GOOD, UN-damaged jar of sweet plums and he ate it all. Every last bit of it."

"It was one jar," Oleander shrugged. "Wasn't enough for all of us. And besides, I found it."

"Yeah, you found it. While Wallace and I did the burial."

"I told you pussies to just leave him. No way was I going to get within ten feet of that rotting corpse."

"Just," Dent hissed, "just get out of my sight before I decide to kick your ass after all."

"Fine," Oleander sneered as he headed to the water. "I want to wash all that nastiness off of me anyway."

"A dead man?" I asked Dent.

"Yeah," Dent replied. "But first, how's Sam doing?" he asked, glancing toward the tree where Sam lay curled up in the long shadow of its trunk. "He's not dead, is he?"

"No," I said. "Just sleeping. That's mostly all he's done since you left."

"I'm sorry, JT. When I saw the place from the distance, I just knew I'd be bringing something back for him, for all of us."

"What happened?"

"We got there, and it was just an old shack with a small corral, empty. Stuff was scattered about in the yard, an overturned buckboard wagon, wheels busted apart, a couple of old books, and some old newspapers blowing around everywhere. The door was hanging open and right away we smelled him. Walked in and found him all strewn out on the floor. Dunno if strewn is the right word, but anyway, he'd been dead for a couple of weeks I would guess. Animals, probably rats and coyotes had been eating on him."

"How did he die?"

"No idea. I ain't no Quincy M.E. And I wasn't about to try to figure out how either. A few chairs were lying about like they had been flung around, an eating table was tipped over, a tiny little cupboard was picked clean, and other crap just scattered all over. There was an old dugout behind the house, guessing it was used as a cellar or something. Found a shitty-ass little shovel in there. Figured the man deserved to be buried, so that's what I did. Blaine helped me get what was left of the dude outside and we took turns digging a hole to put him in. Wasn't easy. That shovel was almost useless for grave digging, might as well have used a spoon. But between us, we got it done. That's why it took us so long to get back."

"And Oleander?"

"That lazy-assed prick. He didn't do blessed thing, other than snoop around in that dugout while Blaine and I did grave-digging duty. After we finished getting the body covered up in the hole, we looked over and there was Olly, sitting in a chair he had carried outside from the shack, his legs crossed at the knee, looking at a newspaper and licking his fingers of the last bit of fruit from a jar he had found in the dugout."

"I guess Norman Rockwell missed his chance," I replied with surrendering sarcasm.

"God, I hope Olly gets food poisoning! A full-on rectal blow-out! The selfish bastard," Dent exclaimed, without validating my nod to the famous cover-illustrator of *The Saturday Evening Post* of which many were included in a collection compiled by our mother.

Suddenly a thought occurred to me.

"Newspaper?"

"Oh, yeah. I looked. It was dated April twenty-second, *eighteen—seventy—four*.

"Eighteen Seventy-four?"

"Yeah, but they weren't brand new. Old, yellowed, and tattered. But the newspaper was a *Hays Sentinel*.

"Wow," I said, as a rush of excitement pulsed through me, though simultaneously I was feeling relatively relieved that the past we had stumbled into was perhaps only a century, instead of two-hundred or three-hundred years. Or more.

"Right. At least we don't have to worry about dinosaurs."

"Dent," I said, feeling the need to share with him something else that had been weighing on my mind. "I'm worried about Mom. And Dad. We've been gone for a full day now. To them we are missing. Vanished." I added.

Both of them would have been calling other parents, and undoubtably learning that four others had also disappeared without a trace. Maybe five, depending on which side of the time leap Perry Hutchinson might be found. Chief Edwards would certainly be looking for us, and perhaps the KBI. Dad would be combing every inch of the ranch. Mom would be waiting for us. And praying.

Then in another day or two, the media would be harassing the parents, and once again, the Tescott brothers would be front page news. Though this time, eighteen-years later, our unusual age-difference would be mundane compared to our disappearance from the universe that was 1979.

"I can't imagine what they think has happened to us."

"I know, JT. I've been thinking about them too. And, if you're right about everything, then they have found my pickup, and the other vehicles, abandoned. The keg is probably still sitting in the back of my truck, practically full."

"True. And that alone will tell Dad that something serious must have happened to you."

Dent chuckled, but his laugh was melancholy.

"And he would be right, my brother. He would be right."

CHAPTER 11

Five of us sat around the fire, our hunger temporarily abated by a portion of barbequed rattlesnake meat.

With finesse, Dent had gutted and skinned the snake with his pocketknife, then had filleted it from its elongated rack of vertebrae and spiny ribs, after which he had sliced the three-foot length into a pile of bitesize nuggets. My contribution had been the gathering and sharpening of the cooking utensils. From a place a quarter mile downstream, I had plucked slender willow branches from a modest cluster of the river-hugging brush that fringed a short stretch of the waterway. Having distributed the green and flexible sticks to the others, we were each responsible for skewering and cooking our own meal.

I had also volunteered to wash dishes, but that attempt to elevate the somberness of our collective mood fell flat. I had forgotten that my brother was the resident comedian, not me.

Blaine and Kival had stepped right up, willing, and apparently eager to get something in their stomachs. Oleander had balked at eating the snake, even though he had earlier boasted that it was the entrée of our evening menu. Whether he ate the viper or instead chose to fast, I did not much care, and doubted if the others did either. But after watching the rest of us and seeing and smelling the meat that had been fire-cooked and flame-broiled, his primordial sense of survival persuaded him to partake in our simple meal. Though our roasted reptile was not the meat and potatoes we could have been enjoying had we, instead, on this night, been gathered around the dinner table at our respective homes, it was far more food than many around the world would be getting. And for that, I silently recited grace.

Dent and I were no strangers to rattlesnake meat. My brother considered it a delicacy, although I often found the taste too gamey for my pallet, at least when eating it without a liberal dressing of assorted herbs and spices. Dad would periodically bring home one of the slithering creatures and would prepare half-inch pieces in a skillet, frying the exotic meat with slices of bacon and a generous sprinkling of dried chilis, adding chopped sweet peppers and onions. That was a recipe I could tolerate, though Mom refused to eat it, and never cooked it.

The first time Dad had served it at our dinner table, the snake had been breaded and fried, the coating golden and crispy. Still, I had pushed my plate away. Dent, though, picked up his fork, and like Dad, devoured it like it was a ribeye steak.

"Gotta learn to live off the land, boy," Dad had said to me. "Pick up your fork and man-up like your brother."

Shamed into trying it, I had reluctantly followed his instructions and had speared the smallest morsel lying unappealingly upon my plate. My expectations had been low, and I had doubted that I would successfully manage to chew and ultimately swallow the reptilian cutlet. But it had been a necessary risk if I were to be one of the men at the kitchen table. Admittedly, it had not tasted as bad as I had anticipated. It was white meat, a little rubbery in texture, but otherwise comparable enough to chicken.

Over the years, I had decided that I liked rattlesnake best when deep fried and wrapped in one of mom's homemade tortillas, and with lots, and lots, of spicey salsa. Tonight though, there was no salsa, no flatbread. But crouching before the fire, I executed the next best alternative: I embedded the skewered meat into the broiling flames and grilled the hell out of it, blackening the exterior into a nice crunch.

After I had finished eating, I straightened my knees and crossed to where Sam lay sleeping. I watched for a moment the rise and fall of his chest, relieved that he was still with us, though earlier I had been unable to awaken him. In my hand, I held a pair of the barbecued nuggets, hoping I could coax him into eating a bite of our rationed dinner. But he continued to cling to sleep.

I sat with Sam for a while wondering what the next few days would be like for him and for the rest of us. I thought about the wide, open expanse of untamed land that surrounded our makeshift camp, isolating the six of us from communities that would take several days of walking just to get to. Because of the newspaper that had been discovered a few hours earlier, the town of Hays was clearly our most logical bet if we decided our next move should be transplanting ourselves to a place that had at least some of the necessities and conveniences of which we were accustomed.

But Sam's physical condition rendered him incapable of making a journey on foot, though carrying him was an alternative, but not an appealing undertaking. Hays was roughly seventy-five miles, as the crow flies, to quote my Grampa Jake. And at least that distance as the man walks, to coin my own derivative of the phrase. But I doubted I would have to carry him alone. Dent would help. And Blaine. Probably Kival, too, but knowing Oleander as I did, it was practically a sure bet he would scoff and hold up his hands and say something like "not my problem, pussies."

Quietly, I cursed. Damn this place. Or more appropriately, damn this time that had placed Sam's life in peril and separated us from the lives we had naively been taking for granted. Then, once again I questioned the reality of what I had decided was true. That I and the others had genuinely traveled back into time. And pairing with that doubt was the alternative explanation that I was just dreaming. That all that had happened in the last twenty-four hours was simply a figment of my unconscious imagination. That any minute I would awaken from this fate that threatened Sam, and I would find myself in my own bed, safe and sound.

If only …

Sam shifted his head slightly and murmured a brief string of unintelligible words. I moved my face close to his and leaned my left ear toward his mouth hoping for a clearer auditory reception. I waited for a full minute to pass, but within that time Sam remained silent. However, because of the intimate proximity of my face, I had detected that his breath exuded a sweet, fruity smell.

Odd, I thought.

I laid my palm against his forehead checking for a fever, which made no sense, but I could think of nothing else to do. My touch found his skin balmy and cool, a diagnosis that was, for the moment, reassuring. Reluctantly, I returned to the group and sat down and rejoined the post dinner-time conversation.

We had been hashing over the revelation of the newspaper, and what it meant to be here in the time of the American Old West. An era before automobiles and highways, airplanes and space exploration. Before fast food, stereos and televisions, and the common use of the telephone, perhaps not yet invented by Alexander Graham Bell. So many modern conveniences that had always been part of our daily lives but were now gone. Maybe not gone, exactly. Just not here. Yet.

We also discussed the perils of living in a time of the historic westward expansion that had aggressively emerged across the Great Plains. Of lawlessness and outlaws, of Indian fights and cavalry rescues. Of scarcity, hardship, and adventure. My input had been more exuberant than I had intended.

"That doesn't sound so great, if you ask me," Blaine chimed in. "Take Sam over there. This is a rough place to be with no medicine, no doctors, or hospitals. I mean, JT, you and Dent, well you guys are cut out for this way of life, growing up on a ranch, but the rest of us, we're way out of our element. We haven't exactly been groomed to live like this."

"Hey, Hollywood, you pussy. You don't speak for me. I could easily dig it out here. If I just had some radical transportation, I'd be set."

"What's with this Hollywood crap you keep calling me?" Blaine asked. I had even wondered what had triggered Sedgwick to give Blaine a label that was surprisingly not a contemptuous slur, but I had not cared enough to engage Oleander in any unnecessary conversation.

"Dude, you're a pretty boy, like Travolta. None of us here match your looks, even if you are still a dork. Besides, I like giving nicknames to those of you who reside on the lower rungs of my social ladder."

That explanation, then, helped answer my apathetic speculation, though still I listened to Oleander with utter amazement. There was no way he had contrived that last statement all on his own. He had to have heard it from someone else. His parents, perhaps. In any event, it was obvious he believed in his social superiority.

"Okay," Dent interrupted. "Let's get back to the issue at hand. We are now apparently gallivanting around in a time that is a frickin' hundred years or more counterclockwise from 1979. What are we going to do? We got nothing! No money, no jobs."

"No McDonalds," Oleander offered.

"Right, dipshit. Ronald hasn't served one single burger yet, much less a million," Dent added sarcastically. "Guys, we gotta make a plan. Where are we gonna go? Cuz we can't stay here."

"East," Blaine suggested. "Civilization lies east."

"No, west," Oleander offered in rebuttal.

"Why west?" Blaine asked.

"Ain't that where the gold mines are? Think about it, man. We could capitalize on finding those big caches in California. Get there before them 49crs get their hands on it. Get rich! And with Germ Worm here with us, he's bound to know the who, and the what, and the where to get us there."

"The California Gold Rush began in the 1840s and lasted about ten years," I offered matter-of-factly.

"See, what did I tell you? With this nerd, we can't miss."

"The gold rush is over you dumb shit. Didn't you just hear him?" Dent scolded. "We've already missed it, by thirty years."

"Maybe. Maybe not," Oleander countered. "I ain't seen any positive proof that we've actually split from reality. Hell, as far as I know, I'm just high on that shit Perry Hutchinson talked me into woofing down with the hooch. Or maybe all this bullshit is just some wild-ass dream that's messin' with my brain."

"Olly, you don't have a brain," Dent proposed, triggering Oleander to flip him off.

"Okay, I'm on board with needing to make a plan," I said, deflecting the tangent Oleander had taken. "Dent is right, we can't stay here and do nothing. But, instead of trying to assimilate ourselves here, why don't we figure out how to get back home instead?"

"How do you suggest we do that, JT?" Blaine asked, adding "we don't even know how we got here."

"Any more ideas on that, brother?" Dent chimed.

For an instant, I directed my eyes toward the silent Kival. He caught my glance, then immediately fumbled it. He knew something, I was sure of it. And it all kept coming back to the thing I had begun to call a talisman. An object now lost in the murky depths of the Smoky Hill River.

"Nothing," I said, "except ..."

"Except, what?" Dent questioned.

"Except that we got here at the Pyramids. I'm thinking the arch functioned as a time portal, somehow. I can't help but think that there is where we get back through. I just don't know how to re-open it."

Again, I glanced at Kival. He had leaned back onto his elbows, his eyes peering upward into the starry night sky. What did he know that he was not sharing? And if he did know something, would he ever reveal it to any of us? And if not, then why not?

"Well, you guys figure it out. I need to go pee," Blaine announced as he rose and sauntered away, politely distancing himself from the site of our meager camp.

"Hey," Oleander called out to Blaine, "wait up!"

"What?" Blaine asking stopping to glance back at Oleander.

"I'm going with you."

"Sedgwick, we are not girls. We don't have to go to the bathroom in pairs."

"But there might be, you know, ass-munching wild animals out there, or scalp-huntin' Injuns. Ain't that right, Worm? Besides, what are you worried about, Hollywood? You ain't got nothin' we ain't all already seen in the locker room."

Blaine shook his head and continued to walk away. "I happen to have a shy bladder. So, stay at least ten feet away from me, okay?"

They stopped a short distance away, remaining barely visible within the faint edge of the firelight, and surprisingly Oleander respected Blaine's privacy by standing several yards apart from him.

Suddenly Kival scrambled to his feet, looking toward me, though his eyes were locked on something beyond where I sat. But his face embodied a manifestation of fear.

"Shit," Dent whispered, his expression duplicating Kival, his eyes alarmed and staring into the space behind me. Although sometimes ignorance was indeed bliss, I did not really want to know what had made the two of them instantly distraught, but neither could I keep from looking. I turned my head and peered over my shoulder.

Two men, athletically slim and shirtless, were poised there within the light of our fire, daringly staring at us, their faces painted and culturally familiar. Inexplicably, my eyes were drawn to the garlands of animal teeth that draped from around their necks, their white and pointed shapes contrasting boldly against the dark skin of lean and hairless chests. My scrutiny then shifted to their legs which were covered by soiled grey trousers that appeared to be rudimentarily manufactured yet were juxtaposed with the other elements of their costuming including the foot-protection of deerskin moccasins that were clearly hand-made. But most disconcerting was the fact that they were armed. With knives.

Large and sharp.

Appearing to be twenty-something, barely older than me, their eyes were dark and fierce, and framed by hair that was black, long, and stringy, and glowering at us from faces masked with streaks of ebony and crimson, designs that radiated from a broad nose with artistic precision.

Indians.

Honest to God, Indians.

And they did not look pleased to see us. Consciously, my thoughts flew backward to the concern Oleander had voiced just moments earlier, and a phrase unpredictably leapt into my mind.

Speak of the devil and he doth appear.

Then from the darker side of our camp where Blaine and Oleander had been relieving themselves, I heard their exclamations of surprise and trepidation.

I looked their way and saw them being impelled forward, Blaine tumbling to the ground, his assault coming from a knife-wielding Indian similar in physical appearance as the first two. He, however, wore a black derby hat, its rounded shape accented with an eagle feather and a bullet hole. Additionally, this Indian was dressed differently from the pair behind me. Instead of pants, he wore a navy-colored loin cloth fashioned from a remnant of what appeared to be a military uniform. But more opposite, was his footwear, a pair of near-emaculate cavalry boots that rose tightly over his calves, causing a mental twitch in my grey matter that brought Nancy Sinatra to mind. But that thought lasted no more than a second as I watched Blaine rise to his hands and knees, only to receive a savage kick from a booted foot that sent him sprawling to the ground a second time.

Oleander, though he had also been shoved toward us, managed to maintain his balance, allowing him to turn and face his attacker.

"That all you got?!" Oleander spat, his words heavy with both anger and apprehension.

"Sedgwick," I whispered as loud as I dared. "Shut—up!"

Then from the shadows, a tall, powerfully muscular man emerged into the light of the fire. His appearance literally robbed me of my breath.

A furred coyote skull, its ears intact and erect, crowned the top of his head, its tan-grey pelt draping downward onto the warrior's broad shoulders, its long snout rigid and fiercely baring the fangs of the dead animal, their white points pressing into the dark forehead of its bearer as though it were biting into him except without the mate of a lower jaw. Entwined within the narrow strips of the boneless legs of the carcass were feathers and claws of various birds of prey, grotesquely framing a face almost entirely masked in white except for a black band painted across the space that contained his wild, tempestuous eyes.

Unlike the others, this Indian wore what had to have recently been the uniform of a cavalry officer. It displayed the accoutrements of embroidered bars of gold that shone like burnished wings upon each shoulder of the long coat and a multitude of brass buttons garnished its opened front from collar to tail and was tied securely by a leather belt displaying a cache of large bullets and an axe that had been wedged between it and a smooth, bare stomach. His trousers were a match to the color of the coat and the length below the knee of their textile legs was wrapped with bands of thin, leather cord, accentuating the muscularity of the man's lower appendages. Lapping at the cuffs of the pants, were large, fur-fringed moccasins adorned with tufts of hair that appeared human in color and texture, leaving me to believe the wispy decorations were remnants of scalps. Apparently, the boots worn by his companion had not been his size.

He stood for an extended moment studying each one of us individually, seemingly boasting of the trophies he wore atop his head and over his shoulders, and upon his feet. In his hands he held a rifle, and his posture made it clear that he was the man in charge.

I thought then, how he and his comrades looked nothing like the Indians portrayed by Hollywood and television. Recently, I had been engrossed in the TV series, *How the West Was Won*. Not once had James Arness's character, Zeb Macahan, ever tangled with the likes of these men. Instead, they appeared as a fragmented mishmash of Native American, and Cavalryman, and Fur Trapper all wildly blended together, the result almost hideous, certainly terrifying. Their leader, clearly a Frankenstein of the West.

At once, the coyote-hooded CEO barked words that were decidedly of his native tongue. Promptly, his comrade who dauntingly posed next to him, bent over Blaine, his knife drawn and primed for laceration. He grabbed Blaine by the back of his hair and with immense strength, he hoisted my friend and gridiron teammate to his feet, as easily as if he were posing a life-size rag doll. Helplessly, I watched as Blaine rolled his eyes sideways, anguish forming upon his face. For a moment, I feared I was about to witness his murder, but instead, the Indian brought him to where Dent and I still crouched at the fire and threw him brutally onto the ground beside me.

The man, having now viewed him up close, was by American standards, moderately handsome and superbly muscular, with biceps and thighs bulging with thick knots of flesh. Then, like a lion, he turned and pounced upon Kival and seized him by his hair and began to drag him toward us.

Kival struggled against the Indian's grasp, but without a misstep the Native Adonis hurled Kival downward and kneed him viciously in the face. Kival's nose cracked from the blow and his body flipped backward, landing with a thud upon the ground. He moaned and rolled into a fetal posture, his arms shielding his head. Fiendishly, his assailant bent and gripped the back of Kival's Mickey Mouse t-shirt and the waistband of his worn, denim jeans, then lifted and tossed him into the dust at Dent's feet, as though he were merely handling a lightweight bale of straw. Kival rolled his head toward me, and I could see his face was smeared with blood, spital, and dirt, his eyes wide and wary, fretfully waiting for a subsequent blow.

The next anticipated assault did not come. Not to Kival.

The Indian had headed for Sam. Abandoning caution, I spontaneously propelled myself to my feet. Instantly, I felt the sharp point of a blade pricking into my back. I halted, praying that the knife would not be mortally plunged into my flesh, its tip protruding from the wall of my stomach. I glanced at my brother and saw that the other guardsman was behind him, and I guessed that Dent was also experiencing the threat of a weapon.

Powerlessly, I watched as the muscular Indian kicked Sam in the gut with the blunt, square toe of a boot that had once belonged to someone more civil. When Sam did not respond, he kicked him again, but with greater determination. I winced at what sounded like the snap of a rib. But no utterance or gasp came from Sam. He seemed stoic, unaware.

Perhaps, mercifully, he was dead.

The Indian squatted beside him, removed his derby, and pressed an ear near Sam's mouth. He stood and turned to his superior and uttered a phrase that was naturally unintelligible. The chief grunted then strode charismatically to him.

From the corner of my eye, I saw movement and looked to see Oleander backing away, considering an escape. After a step, his eyes looked my way and I subtly shook my head, begging him to stop. Abruptly he halted, although I suspected it was the eyes of the man behind me that had anchored his feet.

I returned my attention to where Sam lay and watched as the pelt-domed Indian circled Sam, as though he were a winged scavenger that had discovered unclaimed carrion. Nearly imperceptible in the black band of his makeup, an animated sense of wonder widened the lids of the Indian's eyes, exposing the yellowly gleam of their whites. Suddenly, he squatted beside Sam's head, and then plucked a pinch of fur from the hide of the coyote headdress and held it to Sam's nose. It was obvious what the Indian was assessing, but from where I stood, I could not tell if the animal hair was moved by Sam's breath, or not.

In the next instant, the chieftain stood and returned his attention to Oleander.

Standing grounded just a few paces away from him, the commanding Indian studied Oleander, as though he were speculating or analyzing the statuesque young man. I wondered, because of Sedgwick's superior size, if there was an assumption being developed that Oleander was, likewise, our group leader. Loudly, he spoke again in his native language, only this time he directed his words to Oleander. The Indian in the loin cloth cackled, and behind me I heard a breathy laugh.

Wisely, Oleander kept silent. But unwisely, perhaps because his fear had pricked his ever-reckless bravado, his left hand rose as though he were about to salute, but instead Oleander displayed a gesture of contempt.

The idiot flipped him the bird.

After a moment, the painted man who bore a visage that was part animal, boldly crossed to Oleander, confronting him with a slow, but steadfast lean into the face of Oleander. With their noses barely inches apart, Oleander decisively began to arch his back, modestly distancing himself from the intrusion of his personal space.

"Dude, ya ever hear of mouthwash?" Sedwick sneered, though there was a chord of fear underlying the stupidity of his insult. Hopefully, neither his gesture nor his words were comprehended.

For a moment, the costumed Indian formed a smile, but seconds later he was caterwauling then shrieking with a repetitive bird-like pitch. Startled, Oleander stepped backwards, but instantly the Indian wearing the derby hat leapt forward, his muscular arms locking around Sedgwick's torso, pinning his hands behind him. Vicious anticipation shaped the Indian's expression as he forcefully steered Oleander toward the great cottonwood and lodged him against the trunk of the tree. Then, as though I were involuntarily mesmerized by a Vegas illusionist, I watched as the Indian's hands seemingly appeared from nowhere, captured Oleander's skull, and brutally slammed his forehead into the unforgiving surface of bark. Oleander cried out and I saw his knees buckle. But with reactive instinct, the wickedly impassioned warrior pressed against him, trapping Sedgwick against the tree.

A sense of foreboding immediately overwhelmed me. Then within the next few seconds, I watched as the Indian yanked Oleander's left arm upward, fiercely bending Oleander's middle finger from within the clutch of his fist and forced it flatly along the surface of the Cottonwood's trunk.

At once, the chief Indian crossed to them and withdrew the hatchet from behind the ammunition belt.

Without thinking, I stepped forward and yelled from the depths of my lungs.

"NO!" I cried out, and immediately I felt the grasp of hard, boney fingers entangling into my hair, pulling my head sharply backward, my chin thrusting upward. And then suddenly the edge of a knife caressed my throat. I held deathly still, moving only my eyes to glance at Dent, ascertaining that he, too, was similarly restrained, complete with a blade pressed below the bulge of his Adam's apple. Then I heard the horrific whack of the hatchet as it sunk into the bark of the tree, and I listened to the wretched scream of pain escape from the lips of the one whom I had considered to be my nemesis. Yet, sorrow gripped my throat.

Reluctantly, I switched my eyes toward Oleander just as the barbaric men stepped away from him. With anguish, I watched as Sedgwick slumped to the ground, his searing cries shuddering his body, his intact hand clutching the one maimed by an unconscionable act of savagery.

The inscrutably hostile man then sauntered toward us, halting next to our fire. Then to his lips he lifted Oleander's severed finger and sucked the blood from it before tossing it into the flames.

Surely, the arrival of these Indians and the scene that had horrendously unfolded upon this century-old stage to which we had been delivered by alien beings, had been nothing more than just a dream. A nightmare. Something from which I could awaken and be gratefully relieved that none of it had been real.

But I knew better.

In that moment, my romanticized and nostalgic notion of living in the untamed era of the Old West had wholly evaporated. Gone, as if up in smoke.

CHAPTER 12

Hours had passed.

And in that time, I had witnessed horrific tortures perpetrated by savages. The term was racist, I realized, and dim-witted and moronic, and under normal circumstances I would not have referenced the typical American Indian in such a way. I had been reared by parents who professed to believing in the concept that all men are created equal. Mom and Dad not only talked the talk, but when it came to condemning discrimination and prejudice, they walked the walk and taught Dent and I, by example, the importance of acceptance.

But these four were not typical Indians. This historic time that I had been transported into was certainly not a normal circumstance. Though I am sure that my mother, if she had been here with me, would have also considered these violent men to be savage. She may even have added a certain expletive as an adjective. Admittedly, more than once, I had thought it.

Now, as I lay on my stomach, my hands tied behind my back, and my feet likewise bound in strong bands of leather ties, I fought to keep my eyes open. I was physically, mentally, and perhaps worse, emotionally exhausted. But I did not want to rest. I needed to be alert, vigilant, ready to seize an opportunity to escape, though I could not imagine how I might manage to free myself and save my brother and my friends. But there had been moments when my fatigue conquered my willpower, and I had closed my eyes, but visions would instantly haunt me, anxiously goading me awake.

In the darkness of my respite, I relived what the savages had done.

To Sam.

Their commander, the evil one with a dead animal for a hat, had been irresistibly intrigued by Sam. With ghoulish curiosity, the Indian had almost scientifically entertained himself, and the others, as he experimented with various approaches to rouse Sam from his inexplicable sleep. He had cut him. Burned and branded him. I had witnessed him piercing Sam's eyes with the long needles of cactus. Other atrocities may have been endured by my seemingly insentient friend, but my heart had screamed that I had seen enough, too much, and I had forced my eyes away from the macabre spectacle. And I had wept.

Only when I had finally understood why Sam could not be awakened, did I feel some degree of relief. Sam had mercifully slipped into a diabetic coma.

But the liberation that is often brought by unconsciousness had not, likewise, been gifted to Oleander Sedgwick.

At least, not a permanent unconsciousness.

Having already had a finger brutally severed from his hand, he had later been stripped naked and strapped backwards against the rough bark of the thick, mature cottonwood tree, forced to kneel upon its surfaced roots, his bare feet splayed awkwardly behind him. His arms had likewise been twisted and pulled behind him and tautly stretched along the circumference of the trunk, one bound hand reaching for the other on the far side of the tree, yet too far apart to ever touch. But humiliation had not been enough for these purveyors of pain and suffering.

With callous glee, they had taken the willow branches we had used as cooking skewers for the rattlesnake meat and had beaten the sensitive arches of Oleander's feet and had lashed at his stomach and groin, cackling with delight at his cries of agony. The worst, though, had been the cactus.

Resembling the shape and size of an open palm, flat, thick, and spiny, the leaves of nearby prickly pear had been harvested by the Indian garbed in the loin cloth of cavalry blue and wearing the derby hat vented by a bullet. He had carefully, yet sadistically, placed a wedge of the cactus in the hollows of Oleander's armpits, in the space between his chin and throat, and beneath the sagging of his scrotal sack. With any movement of his legs, or the tensing of his arms, or the relaxation of his head, the spiny needles would further pierce his skin and flex painfully within the depths of Oleander's flesh. That cruelty had been fathomably unbearable, and Oleander had cursed his tormentor. And he had sobbed woefully.

I too, had also cried. For Oleander's suffering and for the inhumanity I pessimistically expected to likewise receive. At least, I had assumed that at some point the rest of us would get our turn to be the victim of their horrific entertainment.

My mind drifted. Perhaps empathetically, so that I would not dwell on the acts of torture I had witnessed with both my eyes and my ears. But still, my thoughts were focused on these men who held us captive. This race of human beings that were not acting human at all. What had made them this way? Was it their culture, their religion? Their circumstance?

I wish I had understood their words. I wished that I knew what had motivated them to behave with such cruelty and violence. That knowledge might definitively explain my simplistic question of why? But deep down, I did know. At least in part. I was well-read, self-educated beyond the norm of public schooling, generally knowledgeable of a substantial array of subjects regarding the history of the settlement of this country. My United States of America.

We, the collective white man, invaders and destroyers, had struck first. Therefore, it bears to be asked, were we not to blame for the creation of these savages? Should our ancestors, the pioneers of westward expansion, not take responsibility? The authors of Manifest Destiny were surely guilty. And neither could fault be dodged by the politicians of the time.

One could argue it had been a conspiracy by all of them, whether they were willing players or simply pawns in a game that was far bigger than themselves as individuals. Most had been civilized Europeans, fleeing homelands fractured by war or collapsing under the weight and strain of tyranny and the unfettered disappearance of resources. Some arrived upon the promising soil of this new, civilly unclaimed land seeking an escape from religious persecution and hoping to find the freedom to worship as they wished. Adversely, others had been motivated by the evils of greed and power.

But many were like my great-great-grandfather, relatively innocent, or at best, naive, buying into the propaganda that land was free for the taking, that unlimited opportunity awaited those who were willing to work hard to build new lives for themselves.

The cost? Only the livelihoods, and homes, and cultures of an Indigenous people who were clearly incapable, or unwilling, to exploit the innate riches of an untamed and unsettled continent. It was no wonder the Native American people had fought back.

They were driven from their homelands by the encroachment of immigrants. They had witnessed the mass, and senseless, slaughter of multitudes of wildlife that had plunged hundreds of tribes into starvation and poverty. Homes were taken, villages razed, men killed and imprisoned, and women and children massacred because they were different and were of lessor importance in the ideal society of the white man.

I would have fought back, too. To defend what was now mine, and that which belonged to my family. Yes, it was a hypocritical irony. Perhaps, under the same circumstances, I would be no different than the Indian men who held me captive. But, I hoped, and prayed, that if

I were to follow their destiny, I would not—would never—resort to their savagery.

Earlier, the pair of obvious underlings had vanished into the night, but not for long. They had returned mounted on horses and each leading a second Indian pony, all four tacked out with woolen blankets instead of saddles, braided ropes in place of bitted bridles, their manes garnished with strips of colorful cloth and feathers that shined white with tips of black.

As soon as they had dismounted, they came for the five of us who were not crucified to a tree. Using their knives, they had herded us away from the fire just far enough to be relieved of the heat, but visible at the edge of its circle of light. There, they had bound us individually, then positioned us in an orderly manner, side by side, head next to head, like wooden ducks in a carnival booth, waiting for our turn to be the next target of their games. When they had finished our arrangement, they had joined the others who had made themselves at home around our fire.

Then Blaine had whispered to me, but his voice had carried too loudly. Immediately one of the younger, athletic Indians shuffled lithely to his horse and retrieved his bow. When he returned, he played us as he would a piñata, delivering to the four of us who were conscious enough to talk, multiple blows with the blunt end the weapon. Several of his strikes were directed at the back of my head, a punishment that caused a burst of fireflies to throb through my skull.

The message had been clear. We were to be seen, not heard.

Hours had passed, but how many I could only guess. Unable to force myself to be vigilantly awake, I lapsed in and out of a tormented slumber. But now, as I regained a sense of awareness, I realized that the light around me had changed. The yellow hues of the fire were gone. The smokey haze of the approaching daybreak teased my vision. Hesitantly, I lifted my head and peered over the dark form that separated me from being the first in our lineup of hostages. If only I could conjure a way to free myself of the bindings, disarm our captors, mount the six of us on the four horses, and race away and return to our own time, and to be free of this nightmare. But I knew it was only a fantasy.

I carefully returned my head to the ground, my eyes falling upon the body next to me, identically bound and positioned as I was, as all of us were. Only he had no awareness of the hopelessness of our situation. He would have no memory of the physical abuse that had been inflicted upon him. Perhaps Sam's unconsciousness had made him the luckiest of us all.

At least, that is what I hoped, for upon the length of his arms the soft and early light of dawn revealed blistered wounds that had been branded into him by the flat tip of a hot knife. I grimaced at the recollection of what the cavalry-jacketed savage had done to him.

Then, suddenly and without expectation, Sam moved. It had been little more than a subtle convulsion, but still the movement had startled me, and I had gasped before calling out his name.

My voice had instantly alerted the Indians. I heard the shuffle of their booted and moccasined feet padding toward us, but then suddenly the footfalls stopped. I lifted my head just enough to peer over Sam, and saw their gloomy silhouettes aligned several yards away, frozen in place as though they were statues lining a palatial garden. Then suddenly I could hardly see them at all.

Grey whisps, like thick clouds of mist, had swarmed Sam's body, masking the Indians from my sight.

And the air.

Instantly it turned cold, almost arctic.

I shivered, not only because of the sudden drop in temperature, but mostly because I had discerned that within the icy swirl of fog, limbs and heads and faces had taken shape.

And I had seen them before.

Then suddenly familiar eyes, unworldly large, pulsating, and ice blue, appeared before me as though to say hello. Then just as sudden, the thing that claimed the pallid face melted into the abyss of a brighter shade of grey, and for a moment I thought I had glimpsed Sam, his body lifting.

As I questioned the vision of what I was surely hallucinating, I heard the bark and cackle of foreign words uttered between manly shrieks of fear. Then at once, the things that had frightened the Indians were gone.

As was Sam.

In his place, a shimmer of frost painted the ground.

Then I watched as the two younger braves turned and raced for the horses. Not to be left behind, the two that were most evil hastened after them, one with the pelt of his spirit animal bouncing upon the top of his head, and the other one running hard and fast, his black derby hat tumbling to the ground behind him.

With swift but graceful chaos, the four of them leapt to the backs of their horses and raced away, dust churning in the wake of their retreat.

And in the cool air of the breaking dawn, I listened to the staccato of alarm lifting from their throats, steadily diminishing as they distanced themselves from the bizarre phenomenon they had witnessed.

I lay still for a moment, wondering if I had indeed been dreaming. Then Dent's voice brought me back to what was regrettably my reality.

"They—they're gone!" he whispered with exclamation.

I rolled my head toward him and saw that he had shifted upon his side, staring past me. Blaine and Kival stirred between us, silent at first, both deliberately daring not to breathe.

"We're … we're free," Dent muttered, his tone hinting of disbelief.

"Are we?" I whispered back to him, my bound hands and feet, uncomfortably numb and rendering me nearly immobile.

At once, Dent began to thrash and stretch, twisting against the bindings that detained him as a prisoner. Then Blaine and Kival joined him in a struggle to end their own captivity. And though I knew I should do something to help myself, my mind instead was spinning a reel of memory film, seeing again the alien apparitions and their assumed kidnapping of my friend.

Then at once, I saw movement from behind the tree where Oleander was displayed, and I held my breath, fearing that one of the savages had doubled-back for a second look-see, scouting to learn if any of the ghostly beings still lurked about.

As if confirming my dread, a figure appeared, stealthily prowling and crouching. Then the form rose up onto his feet, a man, dark and subtly beguiling. But unlike the natives who had fled, he was attired in boots and a soft leather jacket, and an olive-green shirt tucked into the waist of tan trousers, and a Western hat molded from a light felt sat comfortably atop his head, and in a brief second, I had the strangest thought.

Did he also wear socks and underwear?

After a night spent in the company of the sadistic and the grotesque, I needed this man to be more like me. Civilized and compassionate. Then I saw what was in his hands, a gun clinched in his right palm, a knife in his left, and I feared that we had only traded one evil for another.

I then watched as he glanced quickly to the west where our captors had vanished beyond the horizon. Then he refocused and hurried toward us.

"Guys!" I yelled, trying to warn the others. But too late, the man was upon us.

"Do not be afraid," he spoke into my ear. "I am here to help."

Then he took his knife and severed the leather bindings around my hands and feet. I shook them loose and gingerly rolled to rest upon my backside and I sat staring at him.

"Who are you?" I asked, both amazed and bewildered. But he ignored my question.

"Here," he said, handing me the knife. "Free your friends."

He then trotted away thirty yards or more, surveying the western landscape. I did as I was instructed, quickly slashing the knots of the leather straps that held Blaine and Kival, leaving them to untangle themselves from the bindings. I finally moved to my brother, who had been laid furthest away from me, and I freed him. Dent stood, rubbing the numbness from his wrists and hands, and like me, he was stunned by the appearance of the Black cowboy. We stood next to each other and watched as our unknown rescuer trotted back to join us.

"Who the hell are you?" Dent asked, his voice bathed in wonder, his eyes an expression of genuine appreciation.

He precluded his reply by flashing us a smile that shined brightly from the dark pigment of his face. "Your savior," the man replied, whose age I guessed to be around that of Jesus at the time of his crucifixion. "Now, listen to me. Your friend, there," he said gesturing toward the tree, "he is still alive. All of you, gently remove the cactus. Perform that task first. Then cut away the bindings and ease him carefully to the ground. Address his wounds as best you can. Give him water and reclothe him."

I listened attentively to his instructions, but my ears lingered upon his voice. It was almost melodical, an English speech blended with the nuances of a Jamaican or Valencian accent.

"But leave his shoes from his feet, they are much too swollen. And do not waste time." Then at once he brushed past us, crossing toward the east.

"Wait!" I called after him. "Where are you going?"

"I'll be back," he promised. "Trust me."

Then he jogged away. We watched him for a moment then turned toward Oleander to begin our assigned tasks of aide.

"Hey!" Blaine exclaimed suddenly. "Where's Sam?!"

The others looked to where Sam should have been, my eyes looking there as well, discovering that the frost that he had left behind had also vanished. Dent turned to me.

"What happened? Where the hell is he?"

Kival glanced at me, his eyes revealing a vague sense of comprehension, but he kept silent.

"Where's Sam?" Blaine repeated.

"They took him," I replied.

"They?" Dent asked.

"The Indians?" Blaine questioned.

"No. Not the Indians." They looked at me, their eyes demanding further details, more explanation. "Later. I'll tell you what I saw later. Right now, we need to help Oleander."

I was the first to cross to the tree where the Indians had propped Oleander as though he were a discarded human puppet, tied and tortured, his appearance resembling a macabre sculpture of death, albeit he, at least, was still living and breathing.

For better or worse.

He had been repeatedly beaten and whipped. All four of the Indians had participated in that gruesome battering, each cackling with delight when Oleander would cry out with an agonizing litany of profanities. And I had heard it all. From beginning to end, helplessly privy of the onslaught from the prone position of my barely distant front row seat.

With a cursory glance, I could see that a few of the cuts and gashes Oleander had suffered were relatively severe, though luckily most seemed less acute. Up close, his face and chest and thighs were smeared and spattered in a color of red that was ominously darker than the rich auburn of his hair. His face was grotesquely swollen, as was the area of his groin, and over much of his torso he was raw with welts. Not once, in the most violent of movies, had I observed such vicious maiming.

I knew there would be blood, either dried or in various stages of coagulation, perhaps in places, still oozing. But I was not prepared for the immeasurable evidence of the life-sustaining fluid, nor was I mentally primed to imagine that the tally of his wounds would be so abundant, certainly uncountable given the limitation of our time.

For a moment I rocked my head left and right, stunned that he had endured such an assault. Still, I was doubtful he would ultimately survive, especially in the here and now of a time that was decades in the past, as far as my eighteenth birthday year was concerned.

His severed finger aside, the garish display of Oleander's injuries and wounds were astonishingly gruesome, and at once my stomach churned, but I summoned a deep, resolute breath and battled my queasiness and calmed it. Dent had not been as successful. Needles, be they man-made or natural, easily unsettled him and within seconds he retched at the sight of the tortured man. But, within the fleeting timespan of a single minute he recovered and refocused and with less hesitation than the rest of us, he began to work on our humanitarian assignment.

We did exactly as the mysterious cowboy had instructed us. And we did it with the efficiency of a laboratory team, simultaneously extracting the cactus from the four places the Indian had positioned them upon Oleander's body.

I started first, choosing to tackle the place I believed to be the most urgent, the one where a spiny chard of the cactus had become clinched between Oleander's swollen throat and chin. I gently lifted his jaw and grimaced as the spines glided effortlessly from the irritated, oozing, and stubbled skin of his lower jaw. I felt nauseated, thinking that I could have easily been in his shoes, and wondering how, or if, I could have summoned the fortitude to have possibly endured such torture.

Pushing those thoughts from my mind, I tugged at the thick, green pad of the prickly plant, myself getting poked several times by a few of its many sharp points. At last, I had it free and tossed it away. Miniscule droplets of blood began to appear from where the needles had been drawn, but quickly they became less stark as the sweat from his face and brow skimmed downward, merging with the red globules creating pinkish rivulets. A few smaller, less mature spines lay embedded in the skin at the hollow of his throat, and I tenderly picked at those, removing most of which I was able to get pinched between the edges of my fingernails.

Twice, Oleander stirred and expelled a grunting sigh, his cracked lips unsuccessfully forming any words that were intelligible. At once, I felt the need to reassure him, and so I did.

"You're going to be okay, Olly," I said, though I personally had never abbreviated his name so candidly.

Beneath me, Dent squatted next to Oleander, diligently working, as I had been, to remove the pads of cactus embedded within the tangle of the red hair of the left pit of his arm. Across the limp, naked body of our patient was Blaine flanking Oleander's right side, carefully pulling at a cluster of sharp needles that had broken away from the surface of the cacti, their ends protruding from the puncture points that seeped with blood.

With an injury of his own, Kival, his nose possibly broken but certainly swollen, knelt before Oleander, and knee to knee he attended to the spiny plant that had been positioned beneath Oleander's scrotum and within the cleft of his upper thighs. Kival had, without protest, assumed the responsibility of attending to the most intimate of

Oleander's anatomy, as neither Dent nor Blaine had volunteered to aid him in that place. Without a sign of timidity or so much as a word of disgust, Kival lifted Oleander's inflamed scrotum and gently pushed aside his flaccid penis, as though he were a veteran physician performing a routine examination.

In that moment, I felt an obscure sense of pride. Here was a young man, a loner and an outcast, a fresh recipient of Oleander's bullying, yet he had not argued against helping his offender. He had not shrugged his shoulders or shook his head to deny an obligation of assistance, as would have been the case if their fates had been reversed. Instead, Kival had, without hesitation, joined us in administering to the unlikable person we all knew Oleander to be.

Collectively, we had managed to remove the larger thorns and as many as was possible of the smaller, hair-like spikes from Oleander's flesh. If we had been blessed with the luxury of unlimited time, we would have certainly been more thorough, but the man who had rescued us would surely be returning anytime. Satisfied that we had remedially done the best we could, Dent, using the small pocketknife that had neither been found nor searched for by the Indians, cut away at the leather bindings. Then lifting him enough to first straighten his legs from behind him, the four of us carefully eased our wounded companion to the ground.

Lying on his back, Oleander's breathing began to deepen, though he looked like a corpse. The odds of his survival could not be good. Like Sam, Oleander was in a dire condition that required a hospital or trauma center. He needed doctors and nurses to attend to the countless wounds, raw and inflamed and likely, sooner than later, to fester with infection. I grimaced again at the lesions and bruises displayed across his abdomen. I winced at the sight of his feet, black, blue, and swollen. If it had not been for the rise and fall of his chest, he could easily be mistaken as a candidate for the morgue.

Again, Oleander stirred, this time opening his eyes, but barely wider than a slit. I was at his side, but his eyes seemed to focus on Dent, before shifting to Blaine, then me.

"You're going to make it, Olly. Just hang in there, okay?" Dent said, offering him reassurance, though I wondered if he would, in fact, live through the day. We were after all, stranded in the middle of nowhere and with nothing save the clothes on our backs.

Already this time and this place had essentially killed Sam. And I genuinely hoped that Oleander would not be next. But if he did succumb, I wondered would the alien apparitions also steal his body away?

"I'll get water," Kival announced, then left for the stream, though I doubted he would return with much in his hands. Dent stayed at Oleander's side as Blaine, and I scavenged about for his discarded clothing. I had found his white briefs lying crumpled on the ground and immediately I realized that they had been understandably soiled, thus perpetuating my executive decision that he would be going commando. Ultimately, the two of us decided that socks would be okay, agreeing with the analysis of our rescuer that his shoes should not, and probably could not be replaced upon his swollen, battered feet. I had, however, scooped up his pants, before rejoining the first-aid team.

"Let's just put these on him without the underwear," I said without graphically explaining the condition of Oleander's BVDs. "No sense in wrestling him around anymore than we need to."

The others agreed, then Kival was there beside us, topless, his own t-shirt soaked and dripping with the cool water of the river.

Brilliant, I had thought, then I held Oleander's head and parted his lips just wide enough for Kival to wring heavy droplets of water into his opened mouth. Oleander weakly suckled at the moisture, while Blaine and my brother dressed him in his jeans. Five minutes passed, each one marked by a dribble of water into his mouth and down into the welcoming gullet of his parched throat.

Oleander's sleeveless muscle shirt, which had been recovered by Blaine, was no longer pristine white, but speckled with dried splatterings of blood and vomit. It was hardly a suitable garment for a wounded man to be dressed in, but if Blaine, or my brother, or me, for that matter, would have been Oleander's size, any one of us would have gladly given him the shirt off our back. Without an option, we carefully eased his arms and his head into the corresponding openings of the sullied shirt, though we had considered cutting its length along the center of the front side from neck to hem before dressing him in it but abandoned the idea in favor of expediency over comfort.

However, the prominence of a dozen haphazard sites of swollen skin and flesh proved to be troublesome as we refitted him with a shirt that was much like a giant sausage casing that, now, completely failed with its normal flattery of his athletic physic. The only redeeming aspect of the shirt was that it would, at the very least, provide some degree of protection from the sun.

We had barely completed Oleander's re-dressing when the cowboy of assumed African ancestry returned on horseback, galloping into our midst before reining his transportation to an abrupt stop.

I watched as the agile man of mystery swung his leg over the high edge of the saddle's cantle and completed his dismount. Without hesitation, the expert rider dropped the reins trusting that his faithful horse would stay put, apparently trained to respect the ground-tie just as I had taught Jericho.

With no disrespect toward my own cowpony, the one now standing just feet away from me was magnificent. A specimen worthy of an equine magazine cover, and its retrieval from wherever it had been hidden was probably one reason why the man had scrammed with such urgency. I, too, would have been anxious to be reunited with such an exquisite animal. But given the brief period of the man's absence, his horse had not been secreted too far away. Certainly not the three-mile distance to the monument rock of Old Chief Smoky, where I surmised had been the man's earlier place of hiding.

The Black man shot me a quick intimate glance followed by a nod of his whiskered chin; a gesture that appeared to be given out of respect but was also borderline creepy. I reciprocated the nod as he promptly passed by me enroute to the others, but neither my eyes nor my thoughts lingered upon him, despite my silent gratitude that the cowboy had kept his promise to return. Instead, my attention was drawn elsewhere. I could not bring my eyes to wholly abandon their admiration of the genetically gifted creature that had carried the man back to us.

The stallion was an astounding beauty. My dad would call it a blue, though its color was commonly referred to as grullo. The sleek coat of the horse was a soft gunpowder grey with a bluish sheen, his mane coal black and frosted with rows of shimmering silver. Four socked feet, shaded in snowy alabaster, held up slender, sinewy legs, fronted with an ombre of blackened bars seamlessly melding into the rich neutral hue that replicated the animal's primary body color. Cleaving the horse's muscular rear quarters was a dark, dorsal stripe of dusky gray extending from beneath the rear skirt of the Western saddle and trailing to the thick, ebony strands of its dancing tail. Most striking was the mask of white that covered its face from forelock to nose with a breadth that encompassed both of his fiery blue eyes.

Having thoroughly appraised him, the grullo stallion cocked an eye in my direction then nodded his head as if to confirm that he knew he was a pretty boy. At once, I felt myself smile. Something I had not done since yesterday when Sam and I had reminisced of his discovery of the standard posture of a urinating cow.

"Good," the stranger spoke from behind me. I turned to see that he was assessing the condition of our patient, his eyes corroborating with his voice that he was pleased that we had accomplished our holistic task of tending to Oleander in what must have been a modest expanse of time lasting no longer than twenty minutes.

"Gently, please, place your friend up there, in the saddle."

Referring to Oleander as our friend was at best a stretch, though now was not the time for grievances and grudges, however I did feel an enormous amount of pity for him. Obediently, we followed the man's orders as though he were our captain, and we were a lowly band of sergeants.

Between the four of us, we carried Oleander to the horse and lifted him as delicately as we could and perched him upon the saddle, his body slumping forward. Dent and I had been paired on the right side of the horse and together we held Oleander balanced upon the calm and cooperative mount. Then quickly the stranger gathered the reins of the bridle as Blaine and Kival stepped aside, and with a firm grasp of the saddle horn, he gracefully swung his right leg over the back of the horse and settled behind Oleander, his thighs pressing beneath the hard, leather cantle of the saddle, itself a work of craftsmanship that paired nicely with the exquisiteness of the horse it was stationed upon.

"Where are you taking him?" I asked.

"To a woman. She is the only one I would trust to heal him."

"What about us?" Dent asked, vocalizing what the rest of us were all thinking.

"What if … what if *they* come back?" Blaine added, clearly apprehensive.

"Listen to my instructions," he began, implying a less than courteous response to the question. "Go east. Follow the river. But keep to low ground. Walk for two days, steady," he emphasized.

"Two days?" my brother interrupted.

"Two days, *if* you leave now. And *now* is when you should leave."

"What is at the end of two days?" I asked.

"Near to the river you will find a soddy built into a hill, surrounded by a field with rows of red golden grain. Two men live there. They are my friends. They will know you are coming. They will also provide you with shelter and a meal, maybe two. And later, I will come for you."

"Then what?" Dent questioned.

"Then we will disguise you from the boys that you are," he paused, then added "to the men you need to be."

"Disguise us? As what, exactly?" I asked pointedly.

"You don't belong here," he answered, avoiding my question. "We must try to hide that fact, Mr. Tescott."

His address of my name startled me.

"How—?"

"We do not have time for questions or explanations. I must get your companion to the woman."

"Who are you? What is your name?" I asked, pelting him with the pair of questions, ignoring his behest. Without a reply, he reined his picturesque horse around, turning it away toward the east, suggestively intent on dismissing my inquisitiveness for a second time.

"And all of you, leave this place. Now!" he shouted, spurring his steed into motion. The horse trotted for just a few steps before easing into a gentle canter. But in less time than I could count to ten, the cowboy reined the stallion to a gentle stop, and poised the animal perpendicular to our line of sight. With Oleander conscientiously cradled between his arms, the cowboy turned his dark face toward us and shouted.

"I, my friend, am Morgan!"

I stared at him, our eyes locking, my mind wondering why he had seemingly and inexplicably addressed me alone.

In time, I would find out.

PART TWO

For the Time Being

CHAPTER 13

After the horse and his two riders had distanced themselves beyond the rolling horizon of the Western Kansas prairie, Dent turned and looked at me and lifted an eyebrow.

"He acts like he knows you."

Kival glanced at me with equal suspicion, which begged me to silently question why? Or perhaps I was misinterpreting his expression. At any rate, I had thought the same thing. The fact that the man had called me by my surname had taken me completely by surprise. But prefacing Tescott with Mister was another thing entirely, as if he had felt naturally compelled to address me with an honorific courtesy, or because he thought I would expect the socially polite conveyance of respect. Either made no sense to me. But neither was his knowledge of my last name logically acceptable. The most plausible conclusion was that this Morgan guy had, at some point, surreptitiously maneuvered himself within eavesdropping range of our group.

And if true, what other details of our conversations had he heard?

"He can't know me," I emphatically replied. "He was just being, I don't know, nice."

Dent shrugged. "And I guess the rest of us are chopped liver." Then my brother turned his eyes back to the trail of dust dissipating in the warm, morning air. "I hope Olly makes it," he added sullenly, and the inflection of his words revealed that he was genuinely concerned.

"Me, too," Blaine said warmly, affirming that he reciprocated Dent's sentiment.

I shared their conviction as well. But, before I could impart my thoughts as words, my brother spoke an accusation that had also crossed my mind.

"I think he is the guy I saw," Dent added, pointing his finger.

"That's exactly what I was thinking," I said, agreeing that this Morgan person must have been who my brother had glimpsed spying on us at the Pyramids.

"You saw a guy, this guy?" Blaine asked. "Where?"

"I'll tell you while we're on our road trip," Dent offered. "And I expect my little brother will also be telling us about what happened to Sam," he added, glaring at me with determined eyes, a familiar expression I knew all too well how to interpret.

Cuz if you don't tell us, I'll kick your ass.

"I will tell you," I promised as I began to step around him. "Now let's get going."

Three strides in, I realized Kival was no longer standing among us. I panicked for a second, but quickly located him. My eyes found him thirty yards away, next to a clump of sage vegetation, stooping downward, his arm reaching for something, though with his back to me I could not see what it was he had picked up from the ground. He then stood and turned and hurried toward us. In his hand was the black derby hat.

Kival trotted up to us and I saw him accurately read my incredulous eyes.

"What are doing?" Dent asked, obviously reacting as dubiously as me.

"Dude," Blaine choked, "you can't take that!"

"I can. And I will," Kival replied with a tone of authority, as if the ache of his blackened eyes and tenderness of his inflated nose had gifted him the necessary battle scars to stand his own ground.

"But" Blaine cautiously countered, "it … it isn't yours."

"Wasn't his either," Kival responded, sticking a finger through the bullet hole in the crown of the hat that had a secret story of its own. Then he plucked the large feather from the band and flicked it to the ground as if discarding the butt of a cigarette. Then he casually affixed the hat upon his head, his long, stringy hair languidly limp and dangling from beneath the circumference of the rim. In the next instant, he began to walk defiantly eastward, making it clear to the three of us that he was not interested in a debate.

"I think," Dent spoke aloud, "that's the most I've ever heard him say—at one time." Then he shrugged and stepped in line behind the temporarily quasi-chatty Kival.

"I don't like it," Blaine whispered.

"Don't worry about it, Blaine," I said. "But I get you," I added, patting him on the shoulder. The two of us followed my brother, the three of us being led by the one I considered least likely to take the helm.

Across the native prairie of a Kansas a century past, we walked steadily along, our pace expeditious though hampered somewhat by the knee-high clumps of sage, but cautious enough to carefully step around the too frequent sprays of prickly pear. As instructed by the man who had minimally introduced himself as Morgan, we avoided displaying ourselves along the revealing rims of the low knolls of the prairie. Instead, our traveling hugged the waterway of the Smoky Hill River, tracking the direction of its easterly flow. Alert, though subconsciously antagonized by thoughts of Sam and Oleander, I systematically kept watch for any threat of endangerment.

Oleander had suffered greatly. But his arrogance and impudence had likely been his greatest enemies. If only he had kept his mouth shut and his hands in his pockets. But if he had not been so damningly idiotic, who knows if the Indians would have instead chosen me or one of the others to mutilate and torture.

And Sam.

If it had not been for his kidnappers … well, it was not difficult to imagine what fate had awaited me or my brother. Or Blaine and Kival. All of us owed the unworldly apparitions a debt of gratitude, though I understood little of their role in this bizarre adventure of our time travel. I just hoped that wherever Sam was taken, he was in a better place.

After crossing half the distance of what was futuristically my family ranch, Dent suddenly initiated a conversation, recounting with minimal detail, his chance glimpse of Morgan beyond the rocky outcrop of Old Chief Smoky.

"I—uh, I saw him, too," Kival concurred without turning around. His announcement surprised me, and I expected the revelation had also triggered a similar reaction from my brother. I was not wrong.

"You did?" Dent was quick to ask. "Where?"

"Over near the rock," Kival began as he continued to lead us on our first leg of an anticipated two-day journey. "The one that … that looks like a fist—with a thumb."

"Hitchhiker," Dent spoke with a nod.

Hitchhiker had been a name he and I had used to describe the formation that stood as part of, though slightly isolated from, the southern cluster of the pyramid group. It looked much like an upright hand with folded fingers and the bump of what could represent the end of a thumb. And near to it loomed a chalk monument that I had named Dog Rock for its resemblance of a pooch, its head held high on a tall thick neck with a wide bridge of rock connecting to a pointy teepee-shaped tail rising behind it. Dent, though, having burst into puberty a few years later, had renamed the two ends of the formation, calling the tallest Boner and the other Tittie.

"Why didn't you say something?" Dent added, noticeably peeved.

"Nobody asked," Kival replied with simplicity, but it drove home a truth that we had all been guilty of excluding him from our conversations, intentionally or because of innocent neglect. Kival's words were spot-on, though there had been no inkling of animosity in his tone.

We had not asked.

That was the truth. I had talked with him, but I could not recall any of my fellow time travelers speaking directly to Kival. Not even once. But to be fair, Kival was extremely standoffish and had, of his own accord, disappeared from our group for a while. But his curt answer was also descriptive of the entire student body at Custer High School.

Exclusionary.

Silently, I vowed that I would do better by him. To engage with him conversationally. To be more interested. To ask him things, though I imagined it would be like pulling teeth from a mule. Stubbornly difficult and potentially dangerous. I thought of the talisman, though gone, I still wanted to know things about it, and Kival was apparently my only source for that information.

"Okay," Dent said, breaking into my thoughts. "Let's hear about it. What happened with Sam?"

Good question, I thought, as I trailed behind the others.

What exactly did happen with Sam?

Silently, I walked for several yards, the last of our four-person, single-file caravan and thought of my friend. Truth be told, I was torn between wishing he were with us, and thankful that he was not. Immediately my eyes grew moist, and my lips caved into a frown.

I was relieved that the others were in front of me, glad that they were focused forward. As a pre-teen, when I had experienced those moments when I struggled to hold it together, Mom diagnosed that I was just soft-hearted and that I had nothing to be ashamed of. Yet, there had been many times when I had wished for more success when it came to hiding my emotions. Especially now that I was conceptionally a man. Or at least one from a legal standpoint. Though I wondered if the transformation from child to adult was essentially imperceptible or would that moment when I would unequivocally become a man be indelibly distinct?

Oddly, the last twenty-four hours had been marked by formidable experiences of death and resilience. If I had still been a boy before then, I did not feel that way now.

"Well?" Dent prodded.

With a set of finite specifics that challenged my vision as being purely hallucinatory, I told them what I had seen, describing in vivid detail what had been imprinted on my mind. Whether my recall had been authentic, or a delusion triggered by stress and anxiety was arguably anyone's guess.

"That's just crazy," Blaine said.

"I know."

"So, what do you think happened to him?" Dent asked.

"I don't know," I replied with honesty. And then, without really planning it, I acted upon the personal vow I had made only minutes earlier. "Kival," I said, "What do you think happened to Sam?"

Without a stumble of hesitation, he was ready with an answer.

"They took him back."

"Back to—where?" Blaine asked.

"Home."

The remaining three of us drew silent, only the shuffling sound of our feet across the ground disturbed our individual contemplation of Kival's words. But within just a few moments I found my thoughts completely surrendering to the equivalent conclusion, for I had already been wishfully, or naively, thinking the same thing. They, whoever or whatever they were, had taken Sam back home, to our time. And if they had, then at least Sam's body would surely be discovered. His family would have some degree of closure.

Overcome by introspection, we had silently walked less than three miles when we found ourselves at the place in the stream that had been the swimming hole I had often enjoyed on hot summer days while in the company of my brother. But that had been another time.

Far into the future.

Suddenly, I laughed. Not because I was happy or that reminiscing of playtimes in the river was funny. But because it had just occurred to me that I was an idiot. I had fallen for the bullshit of my own convictions. Because to actually believe that I had warped through time was ludicrous. To time travel simply wasn't a real thing. I had to be dreaming. That was the only plausible explanation.

I had subconsciously imagined the existence of an enchanted talisman. I had subliminally conjured aliens and Indians directly from the boob-tube TV. What would I dream of next? Dragons and sorcerers? Legions of pointy-eared goblins dropping from the sky like rain? Or maybe around the next bend of the river the four of us would discover a lollypop village populated with Munchkins singing hi-ho, hi-ho as they happily toiled in a shoe factory specializing in ruby slippers.

Yet …

I knew I was not dreaming. The evidence that surrounded me was too great, and the protracted experiences that had defined the previous three dozen hours of my life were far too detailed and precise to be anything except reality.

I laughed again. It was either that, or cry.

"What's so funny?" Dent asked me, his head and face twisting around to look at me with the curiosity of a cat.

"Just—just thinking that I've got to be dreaming all of this."

"This ain't no dream, little brother."

"Convince me," I uttered without expectation. But before I knew what he was doing, Dent reached for me and pinched the tender skin of my bicep. "OW!" I winced.

"Convinced now?" Dent asked with sincerity.

"Yeah," I said, rubbing my arm. "I guess I am."

"So," he added, nodding toward the water. "Wanna swim?" Dent asked, this time with obvious insincerity.

"Pass," I replied, moving away without a second glance at the water. We had ground to cover. Miles and miles of it.

We hiked for what must have been eight or nine hours, thinking that if we had a two-day journey, we should be hoofing it for at least that amount of time, plus another hour, or more.

But literal time was unknown to us. Neither Dent nor I were in the habit of wearing a watch, and though Sam had faithfully worn his due to the necessity of monitoring the time between his meals, it had quit working at some point during our escorted voyage back in time. Except for Sam, Blaine was the only other one of the six of us who wore a watch, and like Sam, he had discovered in the first daylight hours of this new, earlier century, that his timepiece was also a victim of whatever had happened to us at exactly 9:14. Some forty hours ago, give or take.

Both inoperative watches had been taken by the savage with the cavalry frock. He had placed them over his own wrists, imitating the owners he had thieved and mockingly wearing them as the newest additions to his collection of white-man trophies. And by fate, or by fortune, the joke was on the Indian who had decided, broken watch or otherwise, the time had come for him to vamoose.

Or perhaps the joke was on me and my comrades. Time, that measure of minutes ticking around the numbered face of a clock, had now become relatively inconsequential to us given it did not really matter what time of day or night we were currently experiencing. We had no place to be at any particular time. No appointments, no curfews. Just freedom, if one dared to call it that.

Time, as measured in years, would be far more affecting for us in the days and weeks to come. And that concept both thrilled and unnerved me.

The hot late-afternoon sun of the July sky shone from a position I guessed to be around five o'clock, if I were to be concerned with knowing the time. And we were all beyond tired, and unanimously hungry, and I assumed the others had feet that were hurting nearly as much as mine, and probably Dent's, as our cowboy boots were not designed for walking long distances. That said, our footwear saved our toes from the perils of the prickly pear cactus we regularly encountered. Blaine, shod in blue and yellow Nike Waffle Trainers, would be the first to advise a wayward pedestrian against traversing the wildlands of Western Kansas wearing sneakers, having twice needed a respite to clear his shoes of broken and penetrating spines of the wicked succulent.

Another hour of promenading under the beams of an unrelenting sun convinced us to stop for a rest on the bank of the river. We drank, then leaned into the water face-first, rinsing the sweat from our heads and necks. I, for one, enjoyed the refreshing wetness that dripped from my scalp and spread down my chest and back.

I stepped away from the water and scouted our surroundings, a habit I embraced hours earlier when we had left the place that was to one day be the site of our family home. Carefully, I studied the landscape from whence we had traveled, checking for any indications of overt pursuit.

I saw no sign of any sort of natives, vengeful or otherwise.

I sighed with relief, not realizing I had held my breath. The Indians who had been our nightmare, I hoped, had forthwith hightailed it for Nebraska and beyond without so much as a glance back.

Again, I thought of Sam.

His departure, and by all accounts his demise, had essentially saved the rest of us from what would have likely been our own deaths, though probably first preceded by a brutality mirroring the experience Oleander had suffered. I looked upward toward the heavens of God, imagining the star-studded night sky and the beckoning infinity of the universe beyond, and gave a nod to Sam.

And to the others.

Angels or aliens, either way, their appearance and their theft of Sam had saved our lives.

"Anything?" Dent asked, appearing suddenly at my side. How he could always manage to sneak up on me wearing his heavy cowboy boots was beyond my comprehension.

"All clear," I assured him.

"Alrighty then, let's click off a few more miles, shall we?"

The four of us moved out, but this time Dent was in the lead with me on his heels. We had not gone far when abruptly he stopped, then just as quickly he had begun a dance of sorts. After a few quick, exaggerated stomps, he bent and picked up a small snake and displayed its limp form, the viper no longer slithering but still loathsome. As Dad had often preached to my brother and me, "the only good rattlesnake is a dead rattlesnake."

"I'm going to need to get a pair of those boots," Blaine spoke stepping up beside me. "This is no place for these," he added, gesturing to the athletic shoes on his feet that were now long past looking bright and pristine. My own pair of black dress boots I had worn for my birthday date with Laurie had fared better, a credit to the leather material of their exterior. But they were scuffed and dusty, the rims of their soles holding remnants of dried mud picked up from the mucky edge of the stream. I could have easily been ticked-off at the condition that had befallen my normally immaculate boots if there had not been a dozen more important things I would have changed ahead of what footwear I had chosen to stick my feet into two days earlier.

"Sorry, boys," Dent called out. "Not worth the fire it would take to cook him." Then I watched as he slung the snake away. Prodded by my stomach, I sighed, but I could not argue with him. But neither did we have the time to camp. Besides, Morgan had assured us that his friends would feed us, though enduring the scarcity of attainable food continued to challenge me. I was spoiled by my three daily squares, and the snacks in between. But if our survival hinged on patience, we would need to exercise another day of fasting.

We journeyed for a few more hours when our caravan roused a jackrabbit from its hiding place. We paused for a moment to watch it zig and zag across the prairie as if it were being chased by a pack of greyhounds set loose on a coyote hunt. I smiled at the thought that there bounding swiftly before me, was the nineteenth century version of fast food, but only if you could catch it. I was familiar with the taste of wild rabbit meat, another item from Dad's "living off the land" menu. Similar to snake, it too, was gamey, but still the thought of it made my mouth water.

At last, when the sun finally pushed down upon the edge of the horizon, we stopped next to a negligible thicket of willows that had inexplicably flourished a hundred feet beyond the edge of the humble river. Dent suggested we camp for the night among the scant collection of wispy trees, and no one argued with him.

After a hasty drink from the stream, the four of us settled down for the night, tugging boots and shoes from our aching and blistered feet before curling up, side by side, on the hard, grassy ground. Too exhausted to think, much less talk, I endeavored, like the others, to fall asleep. But the Sand Man passed over me, attending first to Dent and Blaine and Kival.

Too fatigued to move, I lay silent, listening as a recuperative slumber overtook my time-traveling comrades. Then at once, and quite unexpectedly, I felt myself weeping, and realized that even though I was physically spent, my mind had wandered to Sam. In the stillness beneath a blanket of stars, I, at last, grieved for the loss of my friend.

CHAPTER 14

The sharp pitch of birds tweeting and flitting about in the leafy branches of the willows had awakened me from a slumber that had been less than restful. Opening my eyes, I found that the light of what was to be the second day of our grueling hike had snuck upon us. Gingerly and without enthusiasm, I slipped on my boots, then I rose and groaned as I stretched my arms over my head and contorted my torso in an unsuccessful effort to un-kink the soreness in my back.

I glanced about at my comrades and saw Kival's fingers crawl under the brim of his newly acquired hat and scratch at his head as he stretched his legs out across the ground.

I stepped away, walking about twenty yards off and parallel to the stream, and paused long enough to relieve myself. Then I moved to the water's edge, knelt, and rinsed my mouth before swallowing a few handfuls of the cool water. When I returned, my companions were awake and were accordingly refitting themselves of their boots or shoes. After everyone had likewise stretched, peed, and pretended to partake in a morning cup of coffee, we started again, walking east along the river.

We had not gone far when Dent spoke and pointed across the water. In the distance, was a herd of bison moving slowly westward, grazing contentedly in the relative coolness of the summer morning. We paused for a few moments to observe and admire them. Symbolic of the Old West of my books and movies, the beasts were neither too far, nor too close for comfort, and seeing them peculiarly lifted my heart and I felt immensely awed by their presence. They were living postcards of an era that had often been the setting of my daydreams where buffalo freely roamed the plains. Sadly, I knew that the utopia of their existence would be wiped away in the next decade or two. Hundreds of thousands senselessly slaughtered, most just for the fun-of-it, their all-you-can-eat carcasses astronomically exceeding the needs of natural scavengers.

The remainder of the morning passed surprisingly fast, perhaps because I was consumed by my thoughts that were primarily dominated by questions that began with what. What had really happened two nights ago when, within that mysterious explosion of light, we had been transported back in time? What exactly had happened to Sam? What was now happening with Oleander?

And what were Mom and Dad thinking, and doing, and fearing? My heart ached, wishing that I could somehow tell my mother that I was fine, that Dent and I were okay, and to tell my father that I was sorry. I fully regretted the last words I had spoken to him.

I'm damn glad I'm not like you.

Though, at the time, I had meant what I said, upon reflection I knew I had not been whole-heartedly sincere. There were a handful of interests and mannerisms and beliefs I had in common with my dad that I was proud to share with him. I hoped I would someday get to tell him that.

Occasionally, I abandoned the solitude of my personal thoughts and joined in a little light conversation with the others, but I was not compelled to be too chatty. As we walked, I noticed that Kival had interjected a comment or two and I wondered if he was beginning to discover and embrace some degree of camaraderie with our unique and intimate group of castaways. For certain, the four of us had, within the past sixty hours or so, shared experiences unlike anything we had seen or done before. Despite our differences or our similarities, we had been transported into a time that pitted us against a new world known to us only through the writings of history. And if for no other reason than that unique circumstance, we needed each other.

Dent, too, had softened. He now seemed to have either forgotten or forgiven Blaine for whatever reason had caused the rift between them. In fact, the two, who had been friends since early high school, had been carrying eighty percent of our group's conversation, and I was glad for them.

Later, the hours of afternoon travel passed by as we put more and more miles behind us. Occasionally, we found ourselves seemingly chaperoned by curious meadowlarks; their bright yellow chests bibbed with a black shield. As iconic symbols of the plains, they would flit by, then perch upon a sprig of sage or the thick stem of a sunflower and briefly serenade us with their flute-like chirping. Luckily, our midday journey had become slightly more bearable than yesterday due to an abundance of bulbous white clouds that had floated in and filled the sky, their presence restricting the heat and forbearance of the sun.

Twice, while secreted within the sailing shadows of the clouds, we had surprised small families of antelope which had come to drink at the river that was our fluid guide.

The first was a mixed herd of adults and young calves numbering at least three dozen, the contrast of their tan and white coats providing a fair attempt to camouflage themselves against the shaded landscape.

A male, his thick, dark, and erect set of horned prongs pointing stoutly upward from his head, was the first to notice us after we had gotten within a proximity equivalent to seventy-five yards or so. Initially, he seemed to be unalarmed, remaining stationary, though obviously curious as he cautiously held his head high and studied us. But by the time we had cut in half the distance that separated him from us, I heard the snort of alarm bleat from the paternal buck, and he dashed away, leading the others in a frenzied stampede.

The second group of pronghorns were seven in number, standing belly deep in the far side of the water. Simultaneously their group and ours had been surprised at the unexpected appearance by each. Instantly, they sprang out of the shallows of the stream and bopped and bounded swiftly away to the south, the flashes of the white fur of their rumps seeming to wave bye-bye to us as they disappeared over a low rise. Comparatively, the four of us stayed put and kept the flashing of our white backsides to ourselves.

Two hours later, only a smattering of cottony clouds remained floating in the sky above, teasing us with an occasional respite from a sun that still had two hours before it would sleep beyond the lonely horizon at our backs. By then, I had found myself in the lead, splitting my attention between where to place my feet, and looking forward and beyond at the landscape into which we were traveling. How poignant, I thought, noting that leading was often more difficult than following. Then suddenly it was there.

A field with rows of red golden wheat, just as Morgan had described.

We had made it.

I turned and planted my feet and faced northward as the others, one by one, stepped up and aligned themselves with me. The area of cultivation was just a few acres, three, or four, perhaps five. And peeking over the spiky heads of wheat stalks was a dwelling, or so it seemed. But within the midst of the field stood two men, initially unaware of us, their focus intent upon something they held in their palms.

"I'll be damned," Dent said with a mixture of amusement and relief. "Farmers. My kind of people."

I was also relieved to see them, for I carried high expectations that they would be friendly and civil. Polarly different, I hoped, from how the Indians had behaved. Then an odd thought flashed through my mind. The inhabitants of this new world, as we knew it, had suddenly more than doubled our original number of six. These two nineteenth-century farmers whom we were about to meet, four Native Americans of whom I wished to forget, and Morgan, whomever or whatever he might be. A population of thirteen souls. Twelve, given Sam was no longer among us. At least we were not alone.

Whether by coincidence or because he had a feeling he was being watched, one of the men looked up and saw us. Immediately he cocked his head and spoke to his companion, though we were not near enough to hear his voice. With prompt nods of agreement, they abandoned their intent examination and waved to us, gesturing with an invitation to join them, or so I thought.

But they had not waited for us. The hand signal had, instead, been a sign to follow them. We complied and moved from the natural vegetation of the prairie and stepped into and between the rows of foreign plants that had been seeded and cultivated by men of agriculture. Careful not to step upon or break the brittle stalks of grain, we followed them out of the field, and found ourselves in the yard of a small dugout home built into the side of a natural mound of earth and faced with relatively even rows of sun-dried prairie-sod bricks.

A small corral built of three horizontal rows of thin, warped poles stood at one side of the dugout, and standing in its center was a large horse, brown and clunky looking, with big hooves and a shaggy mane. The giant animal tilted its gentle head sideways and rolled an eye toward us that seemed to communicate a curiosity of *what the hell?*

The two men stood shoulder to shoulder smiling radiantly and offered handshakes to the four of us and we each took them, with our English words of hello, hi, howdy, and Dent's highly informal greeting of "sup?"

In unison, the two roved their eyes over us, top to bottom, surely wondering of the design and manufacture of our shirts and pants and shoes. The taller of the pair was especially interested in Kival's Mickey Mouse t-shirt and Blaine's extraordinarily flashy yellow and blue sneakers bearing the Swoosh logo of their manufacturer.

As different as our clothes appeared to them, their attire was just as unique, yet representative of several vintage photos I had seen while flipping through volumes of pictorial history books concerning the Great Plains of which I had discovered neglectfully residing on a top shelf in my high school library.

Likewise, I studied their garments, noting that their loose pants bloomed down just past their knees, disappearing into colorful thick socks that clung to their thick calves and were tied with crisscrossing bands of brown, flat laces. The shaft of their umber-colored leather boots appeared less than half the height of my own pair of Noconas, as the socks and their strappings had been doubled-over the boot tops, apparently less a fashion statement than a means of sealing the interior of the boots from the intrusion of bits of dirt or irritating scraps of grass or weed or grain.

Their crisp, white shirts, barred by a pair of braided suspenders, were clean, their shirttails tucked inside the waistband of their brown trousers. Deep, wide-brimmed felt hats of dusty black topped their heads that were faced with big eyes and bigger grins.

"Velcom," the shorter one said, though because of their attire, the two could practically be described as twins. He spoke again, as much to his partner as to the four of us, but I was at a complete loss to comprehend even a syllable of what he had said.

It dawned on me, in that moment, that the two of them were likely members of the Volga German community, settlers of the High Plains of Kansas whose families had first migrated to Russia in the 1700s seeking refuge offered by Catherine the Great who had ushered in the era of Russian Enlightenment. There, the German refugees had established new homes in the Volga River region of the multi-ethnic land that was part of the enormous Eurasian continent. Decades later, after having lost the protections made possible by the German princess, they had fled Russia in search of new, more hospitable lands.

Many of the Volga immigrants found themselves being drawn into the heart of the North American continent, to a land that had been named for the Kansa Indians, the People of the South Wind. There on the plains of a new, ethnically tolerant state, they discovered an environment nearly identical to that of their former European homeland, and with a landscape that resembled the flat plains of the Russian Steppes. Naturally, the German-speaking settlers began developing farms and establishing homes and businesses and building communities with names like Liebenthal, Pfeifer, and Schoenchen.

It was then I experienced a second revelation: Perhaps, as my brother often chided me, I did, indeed, read too much.

Despite a linguistic barrier, we managed to learn their names, but not until we had employed the intervention of basic sign language.

Abelard and Karl.

And they were bruders – brothers – just as Dent and I were. Though older, appearing to be in their early thirties, if I had to guess.

Following the introductions, Abelard and Karl led the four of us into the confines of their primitive home, our entrance requiring each of us to stoop in order to pass through the doorway. Inside, I discovered a cavernous space, deeper than I expected, and faintly illuminated by the shaft of late afternoon sunlight that passed through the doorway. The ceiling was low and earthy, the floor hard-packed soil that looked as though it had been, ironically, swept. On one side of the room was a pair of narrow beds, stacked in a tight vertical space, with barely enough room to lay upon the top cot and still have the breadth of a twelve-inch ruler between one's face and the ceiling of exposed subsoil.

Opposite the sleeping area was a small table, its slightly longer sides each flanked with a narrow wooden bench. Abelard, a jovial man with a penchant for manly giggles, directed us to the table while Karl, the quietest of the two, ladled water from an odd-looking bucket and filled four metal cups. From a box fitted with a loose flap of burlap, Abelard withdrew a rounded loaf of bread and laid it on the table in front of us. It was all I could do not to steal it away and claim it as my own before impolitely burying my teeth into it.

After the bread was cut, and our drinks placed before us, Karl retrieved from a simple shelf a jar that was nearly full of brownish yellow jam and sat it centrally upon the table. Thanks, I am sure, to our individual mothers, none of us made an immediate dive for the objects of nourishment that had been offered to us, but instead we mustered the patience to respectfully wait for permission to partake in the meal. Then, on que, the two German brothers bowed their heads and spoke a few soft words of what was apparently a blessing, made the sign of the cross with their fingertips flashing from their foreheads to their chests, then nodded at us.

"Eat," Abelard instructed. And like pigs at a feed trough, our hands scrambled for the bread and the jam and quickly we began shoveling mouthfuls down our hungry gullets. To me, though it was simple, it was more of a feast than was the plentiful Thanksgiving table I had always taken for granted. Karl waited on us with refills of water, and he seemed genuinely pleased that we were enjoying their meal.

During the next hour, I felt my guard relaxing as I sensed the peace that comes from feeling safe and cared for. These two men had, in a short time, made us feel like family.

With sincere and grateful hearts, we expressed our appreciation to the brothers for their hospitality, and shared with them a few more laughs, though we were clueless of what it was they thought was funny. And because our appearance at their farm had been obviously an expected visitation, it was naturally presumed that Morgan had been here earlier. And with him, Oleander, or so I assumed.

Again, with a language barrier between us, we incorporated a mixture of simple English and creative signing to convey to them a pair of questions.

Had Oleander been with Morgan?

Yes, a red-haired young man had arrived on horseback with the Black man.

Was Oleander doing okay?

No, he looked like shit.

At least that had been my interpretation.

However, both Abelard and Karl implied that Oleander had drank and ate before resting for the night. I was hopeful. Perhaps, despite the brutal punishment he had suffered at the hands of the Indians, Oleander would survive after all.

Increasingly I had realized the room had been growing darker, and at one point, Karl had ignited a kerosene lantern. But the brothers had not been especially eager to shoo us out of their house. Instead, they seemed to genuinely enjoy our company, even though it mattered little whether we understood their stories, or that the Volga-German brothers completely understood our tales of experience and adventure.

Dent, as befitting his personality, had been the most prolific talker and was a naturally charismatic and theatrical storyteller. He had easily captivated the two brothers as his audience, telling them of what had happened to us and leaving nothing out.

They understood his pantomime depicting our encounter with the trio of buffalo bulls, and the capture and barbeque of a rattlesnake, and were especially comprehensive of Dent's story of the Indians, though I wondered if Morgan had already given them a teaser of that experience. They were, however, noticeably puzzled by my brother's animated depiction of an alien encounter and our transport back into time. Though for their own peace of mind, it was probably a good thing they could not grasp the charade of the "who" and the "what" which Dent enthusiastically attempted to describe.

Later, the call of nature summoned me outside and I excused myself and exited from the heart of the earthen home. The light of day was nearly depleted, so with caution I stepped around the house and took care of my business, then I crossed to the corral where the big horse stoically rested upon the slender pillars of four legs, as though he had been waiting for me to engage with him before he could bed down for the night.

With the tips of my fingers, I scratched the animal behind his ears, stroked the hard plane of his face and caressed the stiff whiskers and soft fur of his nose. Within a few minutes, Dent was beside me, though this time I had perceived his approach. He took his turn to pet the animal, and as he caressed the horse, I looked across the hard-packed yard and saw Kival meandering along the edge of the field of wheat, the black derby topping his head. Then from somewhere, Blaine had joined him, and I could see them taking turns pointing and nodding toward the golden plants as if they were a pair of seasoned farmers discussing the current price of wheat.

Their interaction caused me to smile.

Shortly, Abelard's voice called to us, and we returned to the front entrance of his home. He motioned for our group of time-lost travelers to return inside, and we followed him through the doorway. At once my eyes fell to the floor next to their bunked single-sized beds and saw that they had laid out a crude sleeping pallet formed from a pair of patched quilts. That sight also brought a smile to my face. The room had become a Holiday Inn, and I was glad that I would get to sleep on something other than bare ground.

Immediately, the two brothers encouraged us to rest, and we did not need to be told twice. I was exhausted. And my belly had been satisfactorily filled. I was ready to sleep.

Blaine was the first to plop down on the hand-sewn blankets, and at once, Karl uttered words that had a distinct inflection of protest. With his Slavic baritone, he spoke directions in his native language accompanied by hand gestures that indicated to Blaine that he needed to remove his dirty shoes and soiled clothes before lying upon clean bedding and perhaps sentimental quilts crafted by a beloved mother or other close relative.

Karl then looked at me before his eyes switched to Kival and Dent, seeking confirmation that we understood and were willing to comply. We nodded at him, though Dent appeared to be uncomfortable with the idea of shucking down to his skivvies, which made little sense to me since he was hands-down the most immodest person I knew. Then, at once, the room went dark, due to Abelard dousing the flame of the lantern with a heavy blast of breath.

We might as well have been in the bowel of a cave as the darkness that had swallowed us was pure and misleadingly infinite. I removed my boots and undressed, blindly tossing the items on the floor at the edge of the pallet. I then crawled upon the soft layer of blankets, knocking with my knees and elbows as I searched for a clear place to stretch out and lay my head. It was a tight space that forced us into tighter quarters than the four of us had been the night before when he had slept out under the stars, but similar to the proximity we had shared the night we had been bound and tied as prisoners.

At least here, there were no Indians, so none of us had any room to complain.

I closed my eyes and for a moment I thought of the sleepovers Dent and I had hosted when we were younger. Our favorite had been those nights when Dad had let us stake out pup tents in the back yard, two boys per tent. Usually I shared mine with Sam, while by brother, who was alternatively more popular than I, shared his tent with a variety of different friends. And on a rare occasion, with Mom's approval and Dad's supervision, we would build a small, contained fire for the roasting of hotdogs and the burning of marshmallows, so long as we promised to douse the hot embers with the garden hose before going to sleep.

Marshmallows and hotdogs, I thought again, then smiling I fully surrendered myself to the imaginative and magical dusting of the Sleep Fairy.

CHAPTER 15

I awoke after what I expected to have been a solid six or seven hours of sleep, only to discover that a thin rectangle of dawn glowed in the center of a windowless wall. I blinked at the light that had seeped into the dugout through a space where the door had been propped ajar and realized that perhaps as many as eight or even nine hours had elapsed since I had fallen asleep. I sat up then carefully arranged my feet beneath me and rose from the narrow space of the bed where I had been shouldered between two of my fellow time-dispersed travelers. With one foot, I explored the place on the floor where I had dropped my clothes and laid my boots.

Nothing.

Then, because my eyes had grown more accustomed to the dim light of the room, I noticed the table where we had sat for our dinner. On it were what appeared to be short stacks of laundry and four things that, at a glance, looked like a collection of fist-sized rocks. I crossed to the table and found my pants, my shirt, and my socks folded upon one another, sitting in the place that had been mine the evening before, and in front of each stack was a roll of bread. And below, on the floor at the foot of the bench were my boots, paired upright, heel to toe.

I dressed as quietly as I could, and taking one of the allotments of bread, I stepped outside. Immediately I heard a swooshing sound that sang out in the company of the whoosh of a man's exhalation, and I turned to see a figure swinging a scythe, its long, slender blade sweeping downward, shaving the ground with practiced strokes of efficiency.

Then I noticed the second brother stooping over the ground gathering the fallen, cut stalks of wheat. I took a few bites of my bread and watched as he went about bunching and binding the dry plants into sheaves before stacking them in a manner that resembled a miniature teepee, its conical shape matching that of several others nearby.

A summer harvest had begun.

And the German brothers had barely swathed a dimple into the acreage.

I re-entered the dugout, stepped to where Dent had slept between me and the wall, and I nudged his bare foot with the toe of my boot.

"Dent," I spoke, my volume well above a whisper. "Guys," I added, rousing them all from their sleep. "Wake up."

They stirred, and sat up, looking at me, two of them with sleepy expressions of wonder, the other peering up at me with annoyance.

"What?" Dent asked, his hair mussed about like the feathers of a molting chicken.

"Get dressed," I said, trying to sound as though I meant it as a suggestion. "Guys, your clothes are over on the table," I said, nodding. "And something to eat." I left them and stepped back into the pale light of dawn and finished my breakfast. Within a few minutes, the three of them joined me outside and they studied the activity I had been watching.

"Looks like a harvest," Dent said, gazing at the two brothers as they worked.

"I think we should help," I said, and no one offered an opposing opinion.

At first, the Volga German bruders declined our offer of assistance, seeming to suggest that we were their guests without obligation to work alongside them in the field of golden-red wheat. And from the interpretation of their foreign words and universal gestures, neither did they expect us to repay them for their hospitality. Without hesitation, Dent immediately pretended to have no idea what they were saying to us, and for the most part, we didn't.

"No comprendo," he said, brushing past them and scooping the fallen stalks into haphazard heaps. Then Blaine, Kival, and I joined him, making it clear that we would not be dissuaded.

Abelard suddenly stepped among us waving his hands and stuttering a set of words that sounded much like *okay, okay, okay*! Then, he and Karl proceeded to demonstrate the proper technique to gather the stalks into bundles of a preferred size and showed us how to secure the sheaves using straws of wheat as a tie. With that lesson under our belts, the four of us gathered and tied, as we had been shown, proving to them that we were all good students and capable farmhands. Next was a brief tutorial on how to arrange the bound sheaves into stooks, as Karl called them, the conical stacks leaning upright against each other allowing for ideal air circulation to facilitate the final drying process.

For the first several hours, we followed behind Karl and Abelard, each of whom wielded their own long, curved stick fitted with two handles and a very sharp blade. Diligently, we toiled at building the stooks and keeping them aligned in an orderly fashion. It was hard work, and I could not remember ever sweating so much. It was also itchy labor, especially on my arms, and I was quick to understand why the two brothers wore shirts with long sleeves, and had bandanas wrapped around their necks in spite of the heat.

By the time the sun reached a noontime spot in the Kansas sky, Dent had grown bored, as I knew he would, and had begun trying to persuade first Karl, then Abelard, to allow him to take a crack at using the scythe. It had taken both effort and determination, but my brother had stubbornly chipped away at Abelard's resolve, and so after a brief lesson on how to correctly operate the scythe without beheading somebody, Dent was quick to fall into a rhythm that looked much like he was just practicing a golf swing.

Then Kival offered to relieve Karl, who was more than ready to rest his arms and shoulders. With slightly less demonstration, the taller brother had replicated a similar lesson on the handling of a scythe, and Kival proved to be an adaptive learner, cutting away at the spindly stalks, and felling them alongside the swath made my Dent. Neither Blaine nor I were inclined to tackle the task of skilled labor, so the two of us continued to gather, and to bundle, and to tie, and to stack.

The six of us took frequent breaks to drink from the pail of water that Karl brought from the river that was at least one hundred yards from the house. He had carried the water in two pails, balanced at each end of a long, curved bow. The buckets were odd looking, much wider at the bottom than the width of the opening at the top, and they were fixed with handles made from straps of braided leather looped over and into notches carved in the ends of the wooded limb.

Though we drank often to replenish the bodily fluids that we had been losing through a copious amount of sweating, we did not break for lunch. Instead, we persevered well into the evening until only an hour of daylight remained. Abelard and Karl gathered us at the edge of the field nearest the dugout and stood proudly among us, nodding and jabbering at the results of our day-long toil. The field before us had been made into a mostly baron expanse of stubble dotted with a profuse and nearly uncountable number of wheat stooks that had created a landscape of miniature straw teepees.

There still remained as much as a quarter of the field left to harvest, but the pair of brethren farmers made it clear that enough, more than enough, had been accomplished for the day and they were, themselves, ready and needful of rest. I had seconded their hand-signed motion, and reported to those who understood my English, that I was in dire need of an itch-relieving bath and then headed for the river.

Blaine and Kival, as well as my brother, followed me, all of them apparently suffering as I was from the irritation of wheat pollens and scratchy bits of chaff. We stripped and jumped into the cool, slow-moving water rinsing out our hair and washing away the paste of dust and sweat that had coated us from head to toe. Leaving the water, we reluctantly redressed in our dirty clothes, with me thinking that had I only known that I was taking an unplanned trip into the past, I would have packed an overnight bag and filled it with another pair of socks and a t-shirt or two, and several extra pair of underwear.

When we returned to the dugout home, light from a lantern invited us inside, and so we entered to find the table set as it was the previous night, though in addition to the bread and jam there were also salted cuts of ham. Tonight, we were to dine as kings.

We enjoyed our meal, but all of us, including Abelard and Karl, were too tired to waste time in idle chatter. Bedtime came early.

I awakened the next morning, coincidentally about the same time as the day before, judging by the level of light in the room. The two cots of the brothers were empty as they had been the previous morning, and with a quick glance around I discovered our clothes had again been gathered and cleaned and stacked upon the table, paired as well with a duplicate set of bread rolls. The only comparable difference with the dawn of this new day was that Kival had succeeded in being the first to rise and dress, and I could see him sitting on the bench, tying the laces of his well-worn canvas Chuck Taylors. He gave me a nod, then capped his derby upon his head, and ducked through the doorway.

I quickly dressed, deciding to let Blaine and my brother sleep as long as they wished, and stepped outside only to discover that there was, in fact, a second variation between this new morning and the one from yesterday. And it was a major difference.

Morgan.

But he was not alone. With him were four extra horses, saddled and ready.

"Good morning, Mr. Tescott," he greeted, his full lips stretched by a smile, his even teeth shining bright white upon a face that was the color of rich chocolate. For a second time, this stranger who had been our rescuer, had kept his word to return to us. I took a moment to glance around, but I found neither Kival, nor the brothers were nearby. Then I returned my eyes to Morgan and reciprocated his smile.

"Good morning to you, Morgan," I said, strolling toward him. When I reached him, I offered my hand.

"What do you want?" he asked me.

"To thank you," I said. Then he took my hand, and we shook and swapped discerning stares. "You came for us," I said, speaking the obvious.

"Yes," he said, releasing my hand. "Did you have doubts?"

"Of course," I replied, and I was serious. He laughed, then I asked him, "How is my … Oleander—how is he?"

"Happy to report he is on the mend, Mr. Tescott."

"Good," I replied with earnest. Then I wasted no time in steering our conversation. "Can I ask you something, Mr. Morgan?"

"Not mister. Just Morgan."

"Just Morgan?" I asked.

"Just Morgan," he assured me.

"Fine. So, Morgan, how did you manage to get close enough to us to learn my last name and do so without getting caught? And why were you there at the Pyramids in the first place? It's like out in the middle of, well, nowhere."

"First, I did not, and therefore I could not," Morgan began. "And second, the place of the landforms you call pyramids, I was there before you arrived. Waiting."

I hesitated, trying to wrap my head around the meaning of his ambiguous and seemingly elusive answers. Believing I had resolved the gist of his first reply, I returned to the answer he had given me in response to my second question.

"Waiting? For what?"

"Not what. Who."

"Then who? Who were you waiting for?"

"You, Mr. Tescott."

I looked at him dumbfounded, convinced he was playing a game with me.

"Sure," I said, ready to return to my friendly interrogation. "Look, Morgan, we know you were watching us, there at the Pyramids."

"I was," he stated factually, as if he had been sworn under oath to dutifully divulge only the most basic of personal stats, like name, rank, and serial number.

"So, you had to know there were originally six of us. Me and five others. But you have not once asked about our missing friend. Why not?"

"You have many questions for me, Mr. Tescott."

"Let's just say I like to be well-informed."

Morgan laughed again, the inflection of his chuckle pleasant and genuine.

"Yes, you do, Mr. Tescott. You most certainly do. And that is what I like about you."

I smiled, suddenly realizing that I rather enjoyed listening to the rhythmic cadence of his voice, his words clear and concise, absent of the distraction of slang or the impurity of contractions.

"You speak as if we've met before, but I know that's impossible."

"Impossible?" he asked rhetorically, displaying a gleam in his dark eyes. "You are incorrect, Mr. Tescott, we have met before. Well, not before for both of us, yet. Just before for me, but after for you."

I looked at him as if he were a living, breathing, blabbering bobble-head, concluding that I had no idea of the meaning of his statement. But I was curious, so I asked a follow-up question.

"After what?"

"After now," Morgan replied as though his answer had clearly and completely explained our entire conversation.

Before I could seek a more satisfactory clarification of his enigmatic responses, Dent and Blaine stepped from the doorway of the dugout. Then coincidentally, Kival appeared from behind the earthen home and together the three of them crossed toward us.

"Brothers!" Morgan exclaimed as they joined our meeting. "I bring you tidings of great joy!"

Dent sauntered boldly into Morgan's personal space, ducked his chin and peered at him, eye to eye.

"You're not from around these parts, are you?" my brother asked.

"And neither are you, Denton," he replied.

Dent quickly shot me a glance, but I was as surprised as he was. How did this man know the given name of my brother? Especially when none of us, I was sure, had ever addressed him as such, at least not since our extraordinary arrival here in the Wild West.

"I'm not what?" Dent asked, acting as though the vocalization of his given name, spoken by this man called Morgan, had passed by him unnoticed.

"You are not from around these parts, either" Morgan countered.

"Well, actually—"

"No. You are not," Morgan politely interrupted, his words spoken as a statement of fact.

Dent and I just looked at each other. I wasn't sure what he was thinking, but I, for one, was beginning to get annoyed by Morgan's evasive and intentionally perplexing answers. Then abruptly the man with a cryptic tongue changed the subject.

"Therefore," he continued, "each of you must be attired appropriately."

I watched Morgan as he crossed to where he had left the group of horses tethered together much like a train, with the grey stallion, the mighty engine, anchoring the subordinates just outside the edge of the yard. From the saddle of the fifth horse, he untied three bundles wrapped in burlap cloth, one being noticeably lumpier than the other two, and a fourth and smaller one that casually revealed the shape and size of what I assumed to be a Western hat. He brought them to us, handing individual packages first to me, then to Dent, then to Blaine and Kival.

It was as though Santa Clause had come to town.

"Please," Morgan said, nodding at the gifts in our hands.

I opened mine, one of the smoother and squarer bundles. Inside were a set of folded shirts, eight to be exact, in various colors, two that were stripped with fine, grey lines, all were long-sleeved and fronted with pointed flapped pockets. Also, there were a matching number of undershirts, long sleeved and long waisted, with a pair of buttons poking through their mated buttonholes for a distance of about four inches down from the center of the neck.

Dent had received the package that was similar to mine, but his contained a stack of pants, three were a blue denim, originally dark, but relatively faded and obviously pre-owned, the fourth a dungaree appearing to be made of light-weight cotton canvas dyed the color of a camel, with cuffs that were slightly frayed and dingy. Packaged with the authentic pants of the era, were white pieces of midriff-to-ankle length underwear, with thick folds of the soft cotton secured in the frontal crotch area with a set of five buttons that appeared to be made of polished bone.

"What the hell?" Dent scoffed, displaying the relatively odd and unusual garment.

Blaine's lumpy package was more of a bag, secured with a drawstring of heavy twine. He undid the tie and pulled out a leather boot dyed the shade of raw umber, then a second one that matched the first. Each was well-scuffed and fitted with a Cuban heel, a pointed toe, and a high shaft.

"Just what I've been dreaming of," Blaine said with a big, genuine smile as he admired the traditional cowboy boot. He then took from the bag a shorter black boot, more buffed and polished and with a rounded toe. "Somebody else can have this pair," he added, dropping it back inside the bag.

I looked to Kival and saw that he held a stack of headgear, the tops fitted into each other and inside the cavity of the bottom-most hat was a handful of colorful scarves and bandanas. It appeared that Morgan had thought of everything we would need to costume ourselves in the clothing of the 1870s. The idea made sense for a number of reasons. Practicality being one, especially where Blaine and Kival were concerned. But the underwear? I completely shared my brother's sentiment.

"Now," Morgan spoke, again as though he were our commanding officer, "go inside and change out of what you are wearing," Then, as though he anticipated the obvious question, he added, "all of it."

Dent and I exchanged glances.

"Keep the extra items. I would suggest storing them in your individual saddlebags I have provided for you," Morgan added with a nod toward the horses. "Return to me with the clothes you are now wearing. Each and every article."

Obediently, we left him and entered the dugout, leaving the door open so that we could literally see what we would be getting ourselves into. Across the table, Dent and I laid out the gently used pants and shirts and undergarments.

"JT, that dude is serious," Dent quipped. "Wearing somebody else's duds, though, seems a little over the top, doesn't it?"

"Yes. But this," I answered, gesturing to the clothing, "will eliminate people gawking at us because of the way we're dressed. You saw how Abelard and Karl looked us over."

"So that we blend in. Makes sense," Blaine said, nodding as though it was an ingenious idea.

"Right," I agreed, watching as he emptied the cloth sack of the remaining three pairs of boots. "And also save us from a boatload of questions. I don't think any of us want to get tripped up into telling folks we're from the future."

"They would think we are nut jobs," Kival suggested, laying out the hats and the twenty-four-inch square cuts of colored gingham.

"You're right, Kival, they would. So, let's just do what Morgan suggests."

"Suggests, hell!" Dent countered. "The dude is telling us what to do!"

"Yes, he is. But I trust him."

"Good thing Sedgwick's not here. He'd argue with him for sure," Blaine offered, and no one disagreed with him.

"Speaking of," Dent began, "he say anything about how Olly's doing?"

"Recovering," I reported.

"Anything else?"

"What do you mean?"

"Anything else," Dent repeated, "that he told you before we interrupted you?"

I thought for a moment of the cryptic conversation.

"Just … stuff. But he didn't deny being the guy you saw at the Pyramids."

"I knew it."

"So, let's get to it boys," I said as I peeled off my shirt. "Apparently, even this Western shirt from 1979 would still be a give-away."

"Probably the snaps on it, partner," Blaine said, holding a pale red shirt with grey stripes. "These all have buttons."

"No way!" Dent suddenly spieled, holding a pair of long, high-waist underwear in front of him. "I'm not wearing these."

"Suit yourself, brother," I said, "but, I have a feeling it's gonna be that guy's way, or no way."

"Shit!" Dent growled and began to strip.

The items Morgan had collected were relatively uniform in size, just as the four of us were similar in height and build, though Kival was the slightly taller and skinnier among us. I set aside a pair of underwear and two of the undershirts, not really caring about which, just hoping that they had at least been laundered. Then I chose a solid light blue shirt with brown buttons and slipped it on. The fit was reasonably good.

Being partial to green, I picked as my secondary shirt one similar in color to the meat of an avocado, which upon closer inspection had a subtle pattern of black plaid woven through it. I set it aside, not feeling as concerned about whether it fit as well as the blue one, then I began to change, removing every article of old clothing and replacing the lot with the new.

Or new enough.

The others did the same, and when I glanced at my brother standing in his nineteenth century long johns, it was all I could do to keep from busting out laughing. I turned away before he could see me smiling and picked up the last pair of pants left on the table.

The camel-colored canvas dungaree.

Great, I thought, noticing that the other guys had, without hesitation, staked claim to the genuine 1870s Levis, brass rivets and all. Then I noticed that a dusty beige round-top cowboy hat rested between a pair of moderately-brimmed, sombrero-esque options, and quickly I snagged the one flanked between the other two. I looked around for the fourth hat and found the Western chapeau of faded black sitting atop Dent's head of dark brown locks. Our eyes met and he smiled at me, and with the manner of a smart ass, he lifted and tipped the hat toward me, acknowledging that he had judiciously made his choice.

I dropped my eyes to the hat in my hands, and though it was strikingly opposite in color, it was nearly identical to the one Dent had claimed, including the chin strap ties which gave both hats a juvenile quality, but imparted a degree of practicality in a working hat. I turned it over and inside its cavity on the face of the sweatband I discovered the name Stetson.

"Good enough for me," I said aloud, and sat it on my head, only to have the hat swallow my ears and eyes.

"Litte big for ya, huh little brother?"

"What's new," I said, and Dent chuckled. He was keenly aware that I was the owner of a cranium with a below-average circumference, despite having an above-average brain. I plucked one of the gingham bandanas from the tabletop determined to rectify the ill-fit of the cowboy hat. Folding the square cut of cotton material in half, then half again, I continued repeating the action until I had created a thick band of cloth. Carefully, I tucked the elongated pad behind the sweatband of the hat, then refitted the Stetson to my head. It fit snug this time, held in an ideal position just above my brow and ears.

Without another word, I redirected my attention to the remaining items, and discovered that two pairs of the boots had already been claimed. The brown, pointed-toe pair that had put a twinkle in Blaine's eye were already on his feet. He had understandably been wishful for something to wear besides his thinly vamped athletic shoes.

Kival was seated on the bench tugging on the pull-straps of the round-toed pair of black boots, then stood and tested them for fit. He looked at me and shrugged.

"These are more my size," nodding at the remaining pairs, as if to inform me that he had already tried those on, and they were either too small, or too large, or at any rate, just not as right as were the ones now on his feet.

The two unclaimed pair of boots were of the pointed-toe variety, one a sand color, the other pair black. I chose those that were black, though they were neither as spiffy as my Noconas, nor as deeply pitched. Inside I discovered two pairs of socks, one with the feel of soft cotton, the other pair grey and itchy, likely made of spun wool.

Once dressed, I stepped out the door just on the heels of Blaine who had donned one of the straw quasi-sombreros, both of us carrying our old clothes that had labels or logos of manufacturers that had not yet been established, or like our blue jeans, displayed features that were too modern to go unnoticed. Kival had already returned to Morgan and was feeding his clothes into the flames of a fire that licked upward from a freshly dug hole in the ground. But still, I noticed that the bullet-holed derby remained perched on his head.

"Wow," I said. "You don't take any chances, do you Morgan?"

"I do not, Mr. Tescott."

"And yet," I said, tapping my head and pointing to Kival.

"I have learned from Kival, that his hat is genuine. Historical, one could say."

Knowing where the derby had come from, I couldn't argue. So, without protest, I waited while Blaine dropped his clothes into the fire, and noticed that Morgan watched with intense interest, as though he were itemizing or counting. After Blaine had fed his shoes into the inferno, I dropped in my socks and underwear, then my jeans, followed by my favorite Western shirt.

"Boots, too?" I asked, clutching my beloved shark skin boots I had bought and paid for with my own money.

"Yes, Mr. Tescott."

"Damn," I said, not relishing the idea of subjecting them to the fiery destruction of the evidence of our own time. Suddenly Dent was beside me, giving me an extra moment to say a materialistic good-bye.

"Shit," he sputtered at the sight of flames. "There's not a local Good-Will or something around here we could donate to?"

"No, Denton, there is not."

"Now hold on just a sec, Mr. Morgan."

"Not mister, just Morgan."

"God Bless America," Dent sighed, shaking his head. "Fine. But for the record, my name is Dent."

"Dent," Morgan responded, seeming to taste the name as he spoke it. "I will think about it."

I threw my brother a quick glance, barely able to swallow a laugh, especially upon seeing his lips purse into a clownish scowl.

"Now, if you please," Morgan continued, nodding to the fire. More annoyed now than he had been ten seconds earlier, Dent dropped into the smoking fire his BVDs and older, but ironically newer, pair of

Levis, though he held onto his keepsake shirt that our mother had made for him.

"You know," Dent said, casting Morgan a thoughtful look, "I was thinking I could get Karl to maybe just hide this somewhere. I mean, it's hand-sewn, not store-bought. My momma made it for me. It has a sentimental value that makes it priceless!"

I knew of the sentimentality of the shirt, and it had nothing to do with our mother. I looked at Morgan and read with ease that he was not persuaded. Then he showed Dent a curt nod of his head, aiming it at the fire.

"Ah, for chrissakes!" Dent whined. Lifting the shirt to his face he kissed it on the place where Mom had embroidered roses, then looked at me. "When we see her, you tell her I tried to save it." Then he tossed the gauzy shirt into the hole of incineration. He stared into the devouring flames for several moments, until Morgan recaptured Dent's attention.

"Continue," Morgan said, eyes wide and suggestive.

"What?" Dent stuttered. "Oh, yeah, almost forgot," he added before pulling his pair of red-striped tube socks from the blonde pair of boots he held in his hands. He tossed the socks into the flames, then innocently presented the boots to Morgan. "I don't need these. Got my own," he added with a comical click of his heels.

"No," Morgan countered with a sharp tone. "YOUR boots as well."

Dent looked at me, his eyes disbelieving.

"Is he serious?"

"Afraid so," I said, setting my prized dress boots into the fire.

"That's bullshit!" Dent blurted, followed by a few more colorful expletives as he kicked off his boots and pitched them into the blaze next to mine. Then he just gawked at the footwear he held in his hands and shook his head. My brother did not like to wear light colored leather, be they boots, belts or hats.

"Here," I said as I sat down on the ground, removing the black cowboy boots from my feet. "I'll trade you." Dent accepted the swap without so much as a thank you. As I refitted my feet with the blondish leather boots, it occurred to me that now that I was dressed in light pants, light shirt, light colored hat and boots, I had unintentionally attired myself with a color palette that was typical of the good guy of television's Westerns, an image I seemed destined to embrace even in the 1870s.

Dent stepped into the new boots, stomping and pacing in them for a few yards as he angrily tested them for comfort, then shot Morgan a peeved glare.

"Satisfied?"

"Almost," Morgan replied. "There is one item unaccounted for. It, too, will need to be destroyed," he added before shifting his gaze to Kival, who returned an equally impervious stare.

For a second, I thought that Morgan had changed his mind regarding the derby.

"Don't wear any," Kival said with a shrug. "Haven't for a long time."

Morgan then looked at me, his eyebrows lifted, his forehead furrowed. I realized then that Morgan was referring to underwear. And he needed my confirmation of the fact.

"He doesn't wear them," I said, with a shake of my head, Blaine and Dent joining me with the same cranial motion. Apparently all three of us had noticed.

"Okay," Morgan said, indicating his satisfaction was complete. "It is time we ride. We have a long journey ahead of us today."

CHAPTER 16

ecked out in our replacement duds and mounted upon the saddled backs of our new rides, the four of us began another journey eastward, though this time we had a leader who was not one of us, but who genuinely seemed determined to provide for our welfare. Though I didn't understand why, Morgan was clearly going out of his way to save us, assuming we needed saving. And by all accounts we did. Oleander, inarguably, being an example of that need. And considering our circumstances, it was comforting to have an ally here in a time that was foreign to us, though geographically familiar. And I said as much to him.

"I'm glad you're with us Morgan," I told him, strongly emphasizing glad. We were now riding side by side, and though he looked at me and smiled, he said nothing. I counted one hundred of my horse's hoof steps before expressing another personal thought. "Also, and I should have said this before, but—but with everything—I got distracted. Anyway, if you hadn't been there to free us, to untie us, we'd be dead. Or worse. So, thank you, for rescuing us."

"Rescue?" Morgan said glancing at me with a dubious smirk. "I apologize. I should not have made such a dramatic implication. Perhaps I assisted in saving your impetuous friend, Oleander, but perhaps not. His survival is optimistic, although not guaranteed."

"But, the Indians," I argued, "I think there was, maybe still is, a good chance they would have come back for us. To finish what they started."

"No. You were not going to die," Morgan stated with confidence. "Neither were the four of you likely to be victims of the Cheyenne Dog Soldiers' torture."

"Dog Soldiers?" I asked, trying to recall what I had read about them. Swifter than I had expected, I retrieved the desired file from the cabinet of my grey matter. "A society of militaristic resistance to the westward European expansion," I spoke, remembering a little.

"That is correct, Mr. Tescott. The Dog Soldiers first evolved in the 1830s. But, in the decades since, they have effectively become a separate band of the Cheyenne, rejecting the policies of their chieftains who want peace for their people."

"Like Black Kettle?"

"You do know your American Indian history, Mr. Tescott."

"It's practically a requirement at my school. Especially since our hometown is named for George Armstrong Custer."

At once it dawned on me that I had probably just revealed more to this stranger than I should have done. In this year 1870-something, it was doubtful that any towns or cities would have been named after a man who may not have yet achieved the fullness of his acclaim, or notoriety, depending on which side of the coin was one's favored viewpoint. But in any regard, Morgan had made it clear that he knew we were not merely lost teenage boys, but were, instead, inconveniently relocated into the present year that headlined his calendar. Yet neither had he pointedly expressed an opinion that he knew, with certainty, we were from the future.

"I detect from your tone that you do not hold this celebrated Lieutenant Colonel in high regard?"

"You detect right."

"A villain to some, a hero to others. However, I share your sentiments," Morgan declared with a hint of satisfaction. I smiled at him, glad that we were building a footbridge of shared ideology, but I wanted to know more of what he knew.

"So, Morgan, the Dog Soldiers. You said they wouldn't have killed us. Why not?"

"Their leader, Fire Wolf, known by his people as Ho'neeho'esta, is as much a businessman as he is a warrior. Having escaped from the reservations of the Oklahoma Territory, he has earned a reputation for capturing soldiers and settlers and an occasional stray cowboy, so that he might negotiate a ransom with the U.S. Cavalry."

"So, you're saying we were hostages, worth more to this Fire Wolf alive than dead?"

"Correct."

"Wow," I softly sighed, stunned yet completely buying into Morgan's explanation. I was also thinking that had Oleander kept his finger to himself, he probably wouldn't be in the condition he was in now, and likely would never have been subjected to the Dog Soldier's abuse. "So, why hasn't Fire Wolf been caught? You know, like tricked during an exchange?"

"Rumors exist that such an endeavor has been plotted, several times, but without success. And the cost for such attempts was high."

"How high?" I asked, though I was certain I knew the answer.

"Trust me, Mr. Tescott, "You do not want to know."

And I chose not to press him for details.

Instead, I thanked Morgan again, for his part in our rescue, though I still wondered why he had yet to mention anything about Sam and his disappearance. Neither had he offered an explanation as to why he was there at the Pyramids in the first place. When the time felt right, I would ask him those questions. Hopefully before the end of this day, since the gnawing of my curiosity was leveraging my patience. In the meantime, I focused on the gratitude I held for this man of mystery who claimed to have only a singular name.

Morgan.

Just Morgan, like Cher, I supposed. But without the figure or the voice.

But as much as I appreciated that Morgan was with us, I was almost more thankful for the horse that carried me. After the two solid days of traveling by foot, I had decided I was not particularly cutout for touring my home state of Kansas by walking it.

It felt good, and natural, to be on horseback again, though the steed beneath me was the second one I had ridden, so far, this morning.

Before we had left, Morgan had allowed us to say our goodbyes to our new Germanic friends, and so the four of us had strode out across the section of the wheat field we had helped reduce to stubble the prior day and claimed a few more moments of time from the brothers who were hard at work harvesting the remainder of their plot of cultivation.

I had offered a handshake, but I was given a hug. They were just those kinds of people. Affectionate and caring. It had been easy to like Karl and Abelard, despite our language barrier, and apparently within the short time of our visit, they had also grown fond of us. But it might have just been the fact that I and my brother, and Blaine and Kival had saved the two of them from an enormous amount of labor.

I had been the first to trek back across the field, leaving Dent a few more minutes to captivate his four-man audience with his wit and charisma and theatrical expressions, attributes of which I had not been as nearly blessed as was my brother.

I had rejoined Morgan, who had apparently been satisfied that our former wardrobes had been sufficiently destroyed by the flames of the fire. He had been there where we had left him, next to the incineration hole he had dug, refilling the smoldering cavity with dirt scraped and scooped by the edge of his boot sole. I gave him a moment to complete the burial of our collective items; things which, from his perspective, could easily identify us as subjects worthy of scrutiny and suspicion.

"So, Mr. Tescott," he said, tamping the grave with his feet, "the brothers informed me of your assistance."

"It was a group effort," I had replied. And that was the truth. All of us, Blaine, Kival, my brother and myself, had worked equally hard in the harvest of the wheat field.

"Of course." Then he had looked me in the eye, a solemn expression on his face causing me to question if our assistance had been a poor decision, though I couldn't imagine why that would have been the case.

"What is it?"

"I am … impressed," Morgan added, one corner of his tight mouth twitching with the hint of a smile.

"Well, you can give my parents the credit. They would have whupped my brother and me if we hadn't helped."

"Good for them!" Morgan had concurred with a laugh. "I would like to one day meet those parents and congratulate them."

Sure, I had thought, why not? Mom and Dad were not that far from here. Morgan would just have to leap forward a hundred years, more or less. It was then when it had occurred to me that I still did not know the exact year in which I had been transported backwards in time. I only knew of the dates of the newspapers Dent had found at the abandoned Butterfield station, and those could have been years old. And because I had escaped unscathed by my potentially errant mention of Custer, I had decided to take an intentional chance of airing a question that would otherwise have been exceedingly dumb to ask.

"Morgan, this may sound like a strange question, but what year is this, anyway?"

"Eighteen seventy-eight," he replied without a blink of surprise, then turned and crossed to the horses.

Easy math. We had time-traveled backward 101 years.

I had then followed Morgan, though I had first paused beside the grullo-colored stallion that I had coveted since I had first laid my eyes upon him. I had reached out and stroked his nose and scratched his ears while Morgan had begun to untether the rear horse from the one in front of it. Then my attention had fell upon a rifle scabbarded vertically on the rear cinch of Morgan's saddle, its barrel safely pointed downward. I ran my hand along the exposed wooden stock of the firearm. It was scarred and scratched and had certainly seen better days. Not as well cared for as the one displayed above the fireplace mantle in my home.

"An 1874 Sharps, single shot," Morgan had volunteered. "Almost new," he added with a smile.

"It looks like someone used it to crack open walnuts or crack down doors."

"Crack something, no doubt."

"We have one like it. It was my Great-great-grandfather Jermyn Thomas's rifle. But his is a hundred years old and looks way better."

"It was the best I could find," Morgan had said nodding, "in short notice. And the owner no longer had need for it. Or, his boots, for that matter," he added with a nod to my feet.

"Are you saying I'm wearing a dead man's boots?"

"Again, you do not want to know."

I had wondered where Morgan had shopped for our replacement clothes, but more importantly I questioned how he had acquired the horses. I knew enough of the 1870s to know that the price of a horse and a saddle was equivalent to about two- or three-months wages for a ranch cowboy.

"Are these your horses?"

"No, they are now yours. Consider them a gift."

"That's a lot of money," I had suggested.

"I have resources," Morgan assured me. "So, Mr. Tescott, which horse would you like to have?"

"Yours," I had said, and he had immediately chuckled.

"Not today."

My choice of the available steeds had ultimately been made for me.

Dent had picked first, choosing a dark bay that was relatively nondescript, having no markings of white anywhere and even its dark brown coat barely distinguished itself from the black points of the gelding's legs. I would have guessed that he would have claimed the red chestnut, a color Dad had always referred to as sorrel, since it was almost identical in color to his own horse, Copper, even sharing a similar blaze of white down its face.

But the bay was clearly a better-quality horse, its musculature and conformation both exceeding that of the sorrel gelding. And the cherry on top had been the bay's well-defined head, having characteristics that suggested it had an Arabian as a grandparent. It was the horse I would have chosen, if I had not decided to let the others choose ahead of me.

Blaine had staked his claim next, taking up the reins that were attached to another gelding, a buckskin, his coat an exceptionally pleasing shade of pale fawn, with striking black legs and a flowing mane and tail of shimmering ebony, and absent of any white except for a snip of a star between its clear, dark eyes.

Kival had migrated to the sorrel horse that I had expected to be claimed by my brother, leaving me with the strawberry roan, its red coat paled by the intense mixture of white hair giving it the appearance of being frosted, or even falsely grayed as though victim of advanced age. But the horse, the only one of the five there that was of the female gender, was certainly not old. I would have guessed the mare to have been the age of four or five years, judging from a spot check of her teeth. And, for better or worse, she was gentle, with an easy-going gait. She had also been used by Morgan as the packhorse, probably because of her calm demeanor.

Mounted singularly upon our personal modes of transportation, we had trotted along for less than an hour before Blaine had worn tired and frustrated by the spirited buckskin. Given his lack of horseback experience, he had not chosen wisely. The most suitable mount for him was unquestionably the roan mare. So, we traded horses, and Blaine and I both were happier because of the swap.

Riding now upon the strong back of the feisty buckskin, I had sternly, yet comfortably, convinced the horse that I was the one in charge, and the gelding had finally settled down after a few miles of coaxing. Ironically, Buck, the name I had begun to call him as we had gotten acquainted, was a color-match to my new threads. A coincidence that my brother had noticed and had then shared with me, finding the observation far funnier than I did. Dent had even joked that I could probably pass as a stunt-double for the character of Heath Barkley of the old TV drama, *The Big Valley*, though, by his smart-aleck assessment, I was too ugly to be twinned with the actor Lee Majors.

Another hour into our ride, Morgan slowed his horse's pace allowing Dent and Kival and Blaine to pass by him, though he reined in to ride jointly next to me. I wondered if he had contrived a new puzzle of words for me to decipher, but he offered nothing. In silence, we rode as a pair, and I could not help but let my eyes roam over the beauty of the cowboy's horse. The stallion was simply postcard quality.

"What do you call him?" I asked, curious to know what name the man had chosen for the athletically handsome animal.

"Viento," Morgan answered. "Spanish for wind," he added.

"Groovy," I replied, though I hadn't probably used that colloquialism since I was in the sixth grade. I rolled my eyes at my backward slide into adolescence.

"The buckskin suits you," Morgan volunteered, saving me from an inexplicable feeling of embarrassment.

"Yeah, that's what Dent told me."

"Your brother knows horses. And he rides extremely well."

"Yeah, well, we were raised on a ranch."

"I remember," he replied. And here we go again, I thought, with more statements of ambiguity.

We treaded along for another few minutes, keeping to myself, for now, a slew of questions I had waiting for him. Finally, I broke the awkward silence between us.

"Anything else?"

"No," he replied, then spurred the stallion forward, returning to the lead.

Ahead of me I watched as Dent broke his horse from our processional and turned him in a perpendicular direction, nudging him into a lope for some twenty yards. The call of nature had been the catalyst for his sudden departure. I glanced toward him as Buck and I sauntered by, observing that my brother was about as non-descript as his horse in terms of color, having a shirt that was a light shade of grey that pleasantly contrasted with the darkness of his hat. And though his denim jeans were a faded blue, the only real color he sported was a bright red kerchief tied around his neck. Only a minute or two passed before I heard the clomping of Dent's horse as it trotted to catch up with me.

"Hey, little brother," Dent said as he reined in beside me. "I gotta question."

"Shoot," I replied, confirming he could ask, but withholding the commitment of an answer.

"Funny you should say that."

"Wasn't trying to be funny."

"Mr. Morgan, he has a rifle," Dent announced, though Morgan's possession of the gun had not been a secret.

"He has. And a pistol."

"I would have thought he might of fixed us up with guns."

"Funny, I said the same thing to him," I admitted, referring to an earlier conversation I had shared with Morgan.

"What did he say?"

"He said we didn't need them."

"Don't need a gun? What do we do about snakes?" Dent added, his question reminding me that the .22 caliber pistol he carried in his saddlebags when riding Copper was standard cowboy equipment as far as he was concerned.

"Dance on them," I said, pitching him a smile.

"We're in the Wild West for chrissakes!" Dent argued, ignoring my attempt at humor. "Everybody else will have a rifle or a pistol, or something that goes bang-bang!"

"Not according to Morgan. He said there are actually very few men who carry a gun."

"I'll have to see it to believe it. On those TV Westerns you watch all the time, every last soul and his dog are armed up to their assholes. Did you tell him that?"

I looked at Dent. "No. Television hasn't been invented yet."

"Oh. Right."

"Besides, I've read quite a few articles about how Hollywood has inaccurately portrayed this era of American History, especially when it comes to defining the average Joe Cowboy. So, we probably don't need a gun, for defense or otherwise. Besides, according to my sources, cowboys were more likely to die from a fall from a horse than in a gunfight. So be careful," I chided.

"Ha, ha," Dent smirked. "JT, is there anything you haven't read?"

"Well, don't tell Mom, but I've basically just skimmed the Bible."

"You and me both."

We rode together for a while, talking about a variety of other things Mom, and even Dad, were better off not knowing, though we both admitted that if a confession of our sins to the big man upstairs was what it would take to reunite us with our parents, we would gladly cough one up. That said, we both knew the debaucheries of my brother were far more interesting than any misdeed I might list.

The morning passed as we continued our migration eastward, and twice we had ridden near to where soddies had been built upon contractually free homesteads. One appeared to have already been abandoned, but the second featured a family posing before the simple sod-bricked home, standing as though frozen, and staring at us as we rode by, seeming to have adopted the survival attitude that if they didn't move, we wouldn't see them.

However, my shrewd eyes did not allow them to go unnoticed. And it didn't hurt that our route past them was a mere thirty or so paces. I saw that the man was tall and thin, and held the hand of a little girl of around three years of age, the wind blowing her dark hair and fluttering the blue skirt of her dress. Next to him, his wife and the girl's mother, I assumed, a young woman who could easily have been my age, was plump and shorter than her husband by the half-length of a yardstick, herself posing steadfast with a quiet toddler cradled in her arm. I waved at them as we passed, being friendly, but curious to know if they were actually real people and not statues made of native limestone.

The little girl waved back, and I smiled.

We rode for several more hours, making as straight a line as possible for our destination, a tiny community called Schoenchen, founded and populated by the same ethnic group of which Abelard and Karl were members.

Volga Germans.

"They are good people," Morgan explained as we again found ourselves riding side by side, he upon the stallion I coveted, and me upon a horse I was content to settle for. "They work hard. They mind their own business. And they pray. Even now, they are building in their community, a grand church out of stone carved from the soft yellow rock that lies mostly hidden beneath the ground."

"Limestone," I said.

"That is correct."

"There are many structures in this part of the state that are built of limestone," I added, not giving the slightest thought as to how prevalent they might be in 1878.

"There will be. Only a few now. But yes, many later."

"A community?" I said, refusing to be annoyed by Morgan's insinuation that he was somehow as knowledgeable of my time as he was of his own. "With businesses?"

"Small ones," Morgan confirmed, as my horse suddenly side-stepped, brushing my stirrup against the stirrup of Morgan's saddle. I reined the buckskin, readjusting the gelding to a proper spatial distance between him and the grullo-colored stallion. "But enterprises mostly operated by different families providing products and goods for trade among themselves," Morgan continued without missing a beat. "There is a smithy, and a mill. Some families have specialized in livestock, choosing only to raise pigs, others nurture chickens and harvest eggs. And one particular family provides milk and cheese and butter."

"A dairy," I responded with an expression of fact as I had done earlier with the limestone.

"In general, yes," Morgan replied. "It is also the place we will stay the night."

"Oh," I said, his announcement catching me off guard. "Is that where Oleander is being cared for?"

"No. He is at a different place. In the town of Hays City."

"So why aren't we going to Hays?"

"Because the Beilmans are in need of some help. The father, Helmut Beilman, has been accidentally injured by one of his milch cows. And a month ago his only son, Ernst, was murdered, leaving behind a young wife."

I swiveled my head to look at Morgan, again caught by an unanticipated revelation.

"Did you say, murdered?"

"Correct."

"Who killed him?"

"A very bad man."

"I kinda figured that one out on my own," I snarkily replied.

"A sly and deceitful man," Morgan continued, unaffected by the attitude of my words. "A man who may at first wear a mask of congeniality, but is like a viper hiding in tall grass, waiting for the perfect opportunity to strike. But he will eventually strike. And when he does, you will know that he is indeed, a bad man. But," Morgan paused for a moment and held my eyes with his, "it is my desire that you should avoid him at all cost."

"So, why did this guy kill the son, Ernst?"

"Because he could."

"That doesn't make sense."

"No, it does not."

"Who is this killer? Surely, he's in jail."

"His name is Culver Headville."

"Culver Headville," I repeated, the enunciation of his name seeming to trigger a nasty taste in my mouth. Not a good sign.

"And no, he is not imprisoned. He is free and will likely remain free."

"Free? How?"

"He is a powerful man, Mr. Tescott," Morgan emphasized. "He is why it was prudent to disguise you. He is why I have changed your appearance, given you suitable and logical transportation."

"I don't understand. Why would this Culver guy care three licks about us?"

"Because you have something he wants."

"But I don't have anything," I said, disagreeing with him.

"No, Mr. Tescott?" Morgan asked, glancing at me with speculation. "Well, then one of you does."

I waited for a few moments, collecting my thoughts, organizing my theories and assumptions.

"I don't know what you're talking about," I said, but truthfully, I suspected that I did know. Then upon the completion of a thorough ten-second contemplation, I felt positive I knew exactly what Morgan was referring to, though I had no idea how he could possibly be aware of it.

"Perhaps, you are, at this moment, truly ignorant, Mr. Tescott. But I assure you, there is one among you who has it. It is the only way you could have gotten here."

"Here? Where we are now?" I asked, toying for time and praying for words that could bail me out of the conversation. I trusted Morgan, but I was not ready to lay bare all that I knew.

Morgan laughed.

"Ah, Mr. Tescott, you do like to play your games. Please make vigilance and acumen your best friends. Culver Headville has been waiting many years for this day to come. If he suspects that any of you have—*crossed*, he will be relentless. Relentless, but also cautious. For this reason, it is important that all of you leave from here and go as far away from that man as you can get. And as soon as your companion, Oleander, is fit for travel, you will go. And wait."

"Wait for what?"

"For your opportunity to return home."

Suddenly I understood. The suggestive words, the pointedly cryptic comments, and the statements that were spoken with an arrogance of surety, all had been building to this.

Morgan knew exactly how we had gotten here.

And Kival's talisman was suggestively our way back.

But I hoped there was another means for our return, because the talisman was, unfortunately, at the bottom of a river.

"You never answered my question. About Sam."

"The sixth member of your party."

"Right. You didn't ask about him, because you already knew, didn't you?"

"Correct."

"Then you saw—what happened."

"I did and I did not."

Instantly, I was frustrated and on the verge of becoming fairly pissed off.

"Enough of the bullshit, Morgan! I think you saw it all. Hiding, and obviously armed, but you didn't do a damn thing to stop them!" I barked at him, each of my accusations gaining momentum and sending my frame of mind leaping beyond pissed to being interminably angry. "You could have shot those Indians and saved Sam!"

"Could I have?" Morgan responded calmly.

"They could have killed all of us. You don't know for sure that they wouldn't have."

"But they did not."

"Dude, you had a gun!"

"Dude?"

I ignored him. "I want to know why you didn't kill those bastards and stop them from doing those horrible things they did to Sam, and to Oleander?" At once I realized that my voice was quavering. I did not want this man to hear or see me become overly emotional, so abruptly I pulled the leather straps of the bridle and braked my horse.

Morgan reined Viento to a stop, denying me my privacy. "I understand your anger," he said firmly, staring me squarely in the eye. I gazed at him and discovered a compassion in his countenance that instantly abated my anguish. "But is it fair to end one life to save another? For me, that is a dilemma that is most unpleasant. However, know this: I am not here to take lives, or to change them. My purpose is only to perpetuate the history that is known to the one I serve."

I surveyed his face for a clue, but I had no success in finding one. Caught between bewilderment and ignorance, I asked him, "Who do you serve?"

"You, Mr. Tescott."

"That's bullshit. And your riddles and crap-speech are getting really old. And getting there fast." I watched as the corners of his eyes crinkled just as his lips parted and formed a warm smile of pearly teeth. "What?" I asked, tacking on the question.

"Mr. Tescott, I am so glad to have this opportunity to meet this younger version of you."

"Explain that to me," I tranquilly demanded, though I knew I was only seconds away from begging him to affirm what I suspected to be true.

He knows me from my future.

"I know that you were transported through the 101-year passageway. I know how in a swirling cloud of animated figures and vaporous mist, your friend vanished before your eyes. I know of the object that must be used to return you to your own time. And I know of the ones who are responsible for the phenomenon that brought you here to this year of 1878."

"You know?" I asked, as the image of the creature with large ice-blue eyes flashed across my mind. "You know what they are? What they look like?"

"I do, Mr. Tescott. Like you, I am also acquainted with them."

At once, my planets aligned, and Morgan's ambiguity disappeared. He was like me.

A time traveler.

Though my thoughts began to overflow with what would avalanche into a hundred questions, I could not, for the moment, escape asking about the most enigmatic aspect of this world of mine that had been flipped inside out. "Tell me, Morgan, please. Who or what are they?"

"They are the Burmano-Ku-Partika."

I paused for a long moment, staring at him, feeling a little boorish that I had expected him to simply say the word Martians. "Burmano-Ku-Partika?" I repeated with a distinct pronunciation, before Morgan offered an interpretive description.

"Dust men who fly the earth."

CHAPTER 17

Burmano-Ku-Partika.

The name did not exactly roll off the tongue. I turned to Morgan, preparing to launch the first of several questions, but before I could get a single word to cross my lips, he nudged his stallion and the two of them abandoned me once again for the lead rank of our eastward procession.

Moments later, my brother and the dark bay had taken up residence alongside me and my buckskin horse.

"You and Mr. Morgan are getting pretty chummy," Dent said with a smirk. "What ya been talkin' about this time?"

I gave it to him straight.

"Burmano-Ku-Partika?" Dent said, repeating the peculiar name as though his words had to fight their way through the stickiness of peanut butter. "Jeez, JT," Dent said, twisting his mouth, "that sounds like something a rich bitch would spread on a cracker." Then added, "or smoke."

I could always count on a cheeky perspective from my brother. Still, he made me smile. Then in the next five minutes I explained and elaborated upon my hypothesis that Morgan was also a time-traveler, though from what specific year I had not a clue.

I also told Dent about what I had learned from Morgan about the Indian who had terrorized us, Fire Wolf, the Dog Soldier, and I mentioned Morgan's warning about the man he had called Culver Headville.

"Isn't that the dude who was humping Cruella de Vil?"

Apparently, as children, my brother had watched a different version of 101 Dalmatians.

"So, do you think he's shooting straight with us?" Dent asked me. "Seems like he's gotta have an ulterior motive, right?"

"Ulterior? That's a pretty big word for you," I chided.

"Yeah, spending way too much time around you, little brother."

"To answer your question, yeah, I think he's being truthful with us." Which was more than I was being with Dent. Suddenly I felt guilty for keeping my knowledge of the talisman secret from him. "Something else, Dent," I began, but held on to a pregnant pause for too long to change my mind.

"What?"

"I believe Morgan knows how we can get back."

"JT, you're shitting me?! How?"

"Well, my hunch is it requires the possession of an object. A talisman, at least—," I hesitated, "that's what I've been calling it."

"You've been calling it? You're saying you've seen it?"

"Yes."

"When? How?"

"At the Pyramids. After our fight. After we woke up, I found it in my hand."

"And you didn't tell me?" Dent asked, the pitch of his voice getting hard.

"I didn't know what it was."

"Where is it? I want to see it."

"It's lost."

"Bullshit," Dent accused, his tone angry. "You don't trust me? Your own brother?"

"No! Not always! I didn't then, and at the time, I had a damn good reason not to trust you, didn't I?"

I watched as the anger in Dent's face melted into shame and remorse. He had caught my drift.

"Okay," he said calmly. "I get it."

In silence, we rode side by side, for a good two minutes, perhaps three.

"So, what the hell does this talisman thing look like?" Dent asked, and I described it to him.

"Ok, so what happened to this talisman thing?" he asked before making an immediate accusation. "The sumbitch Indians took it, didn't they?!" he said, then promptly added a most vulgar expletive. Quickly, he cast me a glance, knowing that I had been a better stickler with our mother's rule regarding the use of obscenities. She had often professed to the two of us that she considered there to be a direct correlation between one's intelligence and the vulgarity of one's speech. Cussing, in her opinion, was a man's foolish boasting of his ignorance by demonstrating a limited vocabulary. Ironically, Dad really dumbed down when she was not around. "Don't tell Mom," he said, with a twitch of a grin.

"No, the Indians didn't take it," I assured him, believing now was the time to come completely clean with my brother. "Kival lost it in the river, where Oleander had wrestled him in the water."

"Kival?! Why the fu—heck did he have it?!"

"It was his to begin with."

We rode beside each other, adding another minute absent of conversation.

"So, if this tally-whop thing is so magical or whatever, then why does that weirdo have it?"

"I don't know. He wouldn't tell me anything. And now, it doesn't matter."

"But Morgan, he says we need it to get back home?"

"Pretty much, I guess. He doesn't explain things with a load of detail. I've had to kind of make some assumptions to fill in the gaps of what he says or implies."

"What did he say when he found out the thing was sittin' on the bottom of the Smoky Hill River?"

"Haven't told him that, yet."

"Interesting," he said, glancing at me with a raised eyebrow.

"See, you're not the only one I've been withholding information from."

"So, basically, without Kival's do-hicky, we're stuck here."

"So, it seems. But regardless of how Kival happened to come into possession of it, someone here in this time apparently knows of its existence and wants to get his hands on it."

"Morgan, of course."

"Well, I wouldn't rule him out. But according to him, this Culver Headville guy also knows about the talisman and will want to take it from us, if we had it."

"Cruella's boyfriend? How does he know about it?"

"No idea. Yet."

"Well, shit, JT!" Dent exclaimed, then clammed up. For several minutes we trailed along, the two of us behind the others. At once, he pulled his horse to a stop and turned him toward me so that we could talk, full face-on. "Dammit! As bad as I hate to suggest it, we need to turn around and go back and look for that talisman thing."

"And just how are we gonna find it? Dent, you know that river. It's lost! The only way we could possibly locate it would be with a metal detector—maybe. And I didn't pack one, did you?"

"Dammit," Dent sighed as he cast his eyes westward. "I guess then, we're hosed," Dent speculated. "Kinda wish you hadn't told me anything about it, now," he said, restarting his horse and reining him in the same direction as traveled by the others in our party.

"Man, I can't win, can I?" And he looked back at me and grinned.

We rode together continuing to bring up the rear of our five-man 1878 tour group. We talked, sharing with each other the things we were going to miss the most living in a century that had just barely birthed the light bulb, an era that was without movies and television, a time void of NFL football games, and without 8-tract tapes playing the songs of Kenny Rogers and Glen Campbell, not to mention the difficulty of now having to live without pizza.

It was enough to make us cry like babies, but like it or not, it was time to act like men.

We vowed to make the best of our new reality, though it pained both of us to think of our parents. However, my brother did rationalize that if we managed to live long enough, we might, as old men, get to see them again, except that our parents would, bizarrely, be younger than the time-transplanted versions of ourselves.

"Hell," Dent exclaimed, "if we timed it right, we might even get to help them out by changing our own diapers!"

It was an interesting thought. And I wondered, could I actually exist in a moment of time, as two versions of myself? And if so, how the hell would that work?

The sun was low upon the horizon behind us when we arrived in sight of the settlement town of Schoenchen. And my butt ached from being in the saddle for upwards of ten or eleven hours. I knew Kival and Blaine had to feel the same way, especially since they were new to horseback riding. I imagined, though, they were like me, just glad not to be walking on sore feet.

We crossed the river and our horses stepped out upon the south bank of the shallow waterway and within a quarter of a mile, we were riding into the small village. I noted the familiar layout of dirt streets flanked by small houses, some made of sod, but many built of milled lumber. And central to the tight cluster of homes was the limestone church Morgan had mentioned, its four skeletal walls towering upward supporting a sharply angular roof with a lofty steeple mounted skyward, the framework advertising the beginning of construction. And as we passed, we greeted eight, maybe nine men, each dressed in the fashion similar to Abelard or Karl. The German men humbly nodded and greeted us, though three of them took time to specifically address Morgan. It was obvious he was well-known in the community, and they appeared to like him.

Soon we arrived at a home on the far southern edge of Schoenchen, a house built of wood, not sod, though I noticed a soddy standing not too far behind it.

An upgrade had been made, I assumed.

We dismounted, and a large woman met us at the door, drying her hands with a small towel. An apron was tied around her waist, shielding a simple, homespun skirt, though her blouse was of finer, softer looking fabric, likely cut from a manufactured bolt of cloth. Her face was handsome, but her eyes were beautiful, and she greeted us with a smile that reminded me of my Grandmother Viola Thomas, who was just Gramma Vi to me. The woman then clucked a few words in her Teutonic language, and Morgan joined her in a brief conversation speaking what I guessed to be his own version of Germanic tongue.

Behind the matronly lady, I caught a glimpse of a younger woman who had stopped behind her and briefly raised herself upon her tiptoes to peer out at us, before vanishing into the dim light of the room. At once, the stocky lady-of-the-house chirped with delight and gestured an invitation to enter her home.

Morgan politely removed his hat and kicked his boots against the wooden steps of the wide front porch, knocking the day's collection of dust from them before entering the residence. I nodded, thinking Mom would probably like Morgan. She would certainly appreciate his consideration. Dent and I followed him in, repeating Morgan's gesture, head to toe, then glancing behind me, I saw that Kival and Blaine had also respectfully copied us.

Inside, the house was relatively spacious, with a large front room having one end temporarily converted into a bedroom. Propped up by pillows, an injured man sat upon the bed with his back against the wall. The room was warm, but he was comfortably shirtless save for the strips of white cotton cloth that bandaged his torso front to back.

Morgan made our introductions, calling my three companions by their given names, including Denton, but still he referred to me as Mr. Tescott, as though I was of the age of my father. The man, as I had assumed, was Helmut Beilman, and Ruta, his wife and the misses of the household, beamed at us before hustling away into an adjacent room. Her voice chittered from beyond the doorway, and when she reentered, she carried a pair of wooden chairs. Over her shoulder she called out a friendly order that was preceded by what I presumed to be the young woman's name.

Anja.

In a moment, the girl I had glimpsed earlier appeared carrying a single chair that matched the two Ruta had brought. Ruta spoke again, and Anja went about the room, lighting a pair of oil lamps stationed on an exquisitely crafted sideboard constructed of dark walnut.

There were other pieces of quality furniture dotted purposefully about the gathering room of the house, but I hardly looked at them. Instead, I watched the girl. She appeared to be about my age, eighteen, more or less, her hair a mousy brown with velvety reflections of red, tied in a long braid that traveled half-way down her back. Neither tall, nor short, she was undoubtably attractive, with proportions that had easily caught my eye. And I was not alone.

Kival stood beside me, and without trying to disguise his interest, he was also watching her every movement. He turned to me, and a partial grin twisted his face. I grinned back at him and thought, *Dude, you don't have a chance.*

With the supplement of chairs, the five of us accepted Ruta's invitation to sit. Morgan and Dent managed to seat themselves on a pair of upholstered and padded front room chairs, appearing to be absent of any remorse for obligating the remaining three of us to the discomfort of placing our saddle-sore fannies upon the hard-surfaced seats.

For about five minutes, we were left alone with Helmut. I listened to the gutturally melodic conversation he shared with Morgan, and I noted that there was just a rare word or two that remotely sounded familiar. It was hard not to ask, *huh?* So, Dent, Blaine, and I sat politely, and listened like obedient school children. However, Kival's attention was elsewhere, as he had the best view of the kitchen and essentially a front row seat to observe the activity taking place inside the smaller room, though I had a suspicion his captivation had less to do with what was going on but more focused upon who was doing it.

Soon, the subject of his interest emerged with a tray of porcelain cups filled with fresh milk. As Anja offered us the beverage, I noticed that she now had a pale blue ribbon tied around the braid of her hair. I speculated that when unexpected guests come a-knocking, adding a pretty hair accessory was often a priority for a girl, regardless of ethnicity or what century in which she lived. I thought of the spontaneous appearances I had made at Laurie's front door. For more times than I could count, I had observed that she had gussied up her blonde locks with a hair clip or one of those short combs with plastic flowers or beads glued to its spine.

Ruta then entered the room carrying a similar tray but set with small plates crowned with a generous portion of golden cornbread and garnished with an enormous pad of homemade butter half the size of a deck of cards. The sight of food instantly turned my mouth moist.

Surprisingly, I had not thought much about being hungry during our journey here, but suddenly I was famished.

A set of forks had been placed on the tray, and so I took one, as did the others, proving to the ladies that we did, in fact, have manners. I thanked the two women, and both politely returned a smile, though I could not help but notice that Anja hardly looked at me. It was obvious that as far as she was concerned, Kival was the only young buck in the room. Who would have guessed he had the mojo to hook the attention of an attractive young woman?

Ruta muttered something to Helmut, and as it turned out, she was apparently scolding him because he had failed to include in the introductions the girl with the blue bow in her hair. Helmut rolled his eyes and smiled as he gestured to her, and speaking what might as well have been gibberish, he introduced her to Morgan, who in turn, translated.

"This is Anja, the Beilman's daughter-in-law."

I had assumed the girl was their daughter. Instead, she was the young widow of Helmut and Ruta's murdered son, Ernst.

We ate and drank enthusiastically. The cornbread, butter, and milk were all pleasantly delicious, though I had a feeling we had, by an hour or so, missed arriving in time for a more substantial meal. I noticed that Kival had cleared his plate first, and Anja was quick to offer him a second helping, which he accepted with a smile and a blush. It was the only time I could ever remember seeing such an expression on his face.

All of us, including Morgan, ate heartily of the second round of our modest dinner, and once we were finished, Morgan stood and offered his German words of thanks to Ruta and to Helmut, then herded us outside.

We gathered our horses from where we had tied them to a hitching rail, and following Morgan, we led them behind the house and into a massive barn. Three stalls stood empty, each large enough to comfortably bed down two to three horses. Following Morgan's lead, we stripped our mounts of their saddles and lead them into the stalls, Blaine's roan mare and my Buck, sharing one of the compartments, and Dent and Kival's geldings were paired inside the adjacent stall. Morgan's stallion, Viento, ranked a room of his own, a reasonable situation given he was the natural alpha male, the only horse of his gender still in possession of his testicles.

Morgan took a thickly bristled brush from inside one of the twinned leather satchels tied behind his saddle and informed us we would find the same in our own saddle bags, a discovery I had already made when I had packed my extra articles of clothing. Inside the buckled and strapped compartment were also a round, toothy curry comb and a trio of hoof-maintenance tools. He had thought of everything, and I was glad the proper care of our animals had not been forgotten.

I removed the bridle from Buck and with the brush, I curried his sweat-soaked fawn coat from head to tail, and the sighs of the horse's deep breaths told me he appreciated the attention. Our first moments of genuine bonding were now in the books.

Shortly, Morgan brought to each horse a scoop of oats, and pointed us to a stack of freshly cut clover from which we gathered an armful for each of them. With the horses taken care of for the night, we transitioned to a large corner of the barn where shocks of straw were stacked upon a thick bed of dry, loose hay. This would be our sleeping quarters for the night, and I welcomed the opportunity to lie down and rest.

But R and R was destined to be delayed. There was much to be discussed.

Morgan began by sharing with the four of us the Beilman family situation, the primary aspect of which he declared to be an inadequate workforce. To carry out a routine twice-a-day milking required not just strength and dedication, but also good old fashion grit. But despite their work ethic, their agricultural business was on the line given that their eleven milch cows were literally the German family's bread and butter.

The labor had been easily manageable before the loss of their son, Ernst. But after his murder, it had become necessary for Ruta and Anja to assist Helmut with the task of hand-milking the small herd of dairy cows. Then upon Helmut's accident and subsequent injury, they had been forced to seek help from others in the community, all of whom had their own livelihoods to attend, but sacrifices had been made and their friends and neighbors had assisted as much as they could. And because Helmut was still a full week away from a comprehensive mending of his broken ribs, and since we, Dent, Blaine, Kival and myself, had nothing else to do, Morgan had volunteered the four of us to help the family.

"In return, you have a place to sleep, and food to eat. I hope that you are agreeable?"

He did not need to ask, and I suspected he knew that, but the man had manners. Besides, we did not have any pressing engagements, aside from Morgan's plan to sequester us far away from this Culver Headville person. But that plan was on hold until Oleander's recovery deemed him fit to travel. Until then, we were young men with strong backs, though from the sound of it, strong hands were the highest of prerequisites.

"Of course, we'll help," I offered. "Right, guys?"

"Absolutely," Dent concurred, as Blaine and Kival nodded in agreement.

Morgan expressed his appreciation, though it would have been hard not to submit to his request given all that he had done for us. And since the Beilmans were his friends, they had automatically extended their friendship to us, just like Abelard and Karl.

We sat around upon the stacks of straw and listened as Morgan gave us a summary of the milking routine, noting the specific aspects of the barn that had been installed to facilitate the task of efficiently managing the small dairy operation. He assured us that though we were without the experience of milking cows, the process was simple to learn.

"I wouldn't say I'm completely without experience," Dent said with a cocky grin. "These hands have been on a lot of—"

"Dent!" I said, cutting him off. "We know all about your experience," I added shaking my head.

"Just saying," he said, innocently shrugging his shoulders, though we all knew he was working us for a laugh. Instead, we sat there, unamused, and watched the strength of his bravado wilt to a gusty sigh. After a moment, he shrewdly shifted the attention away from him.

"I have a question, Just Morgan," Dent began friendly enough, but evidently felt the need to get in a dig because Morgan had introduced him to the Beilmans as Denton. He should have counted his blessings that I had not made the introduction because I might easily have added his middle name of Dean, just to see him scowl.

"Yes, Just Denton?" Morgan replied with a nod and a smile.

I could not help myself. I laughed.

"I would like to know exactly why you were spying on us at the Pyramids?"

And just like that, things got awkward.

Morgan and Dent squared off, staring across at each other as though they were preparing themselves for a showdown at the OK Corral. I glanced at the others, and by their expressions it appeared they had sided with my brother.

"Spying is your word. I would prefer observing," Morgan countered.

"Fine," Dent conceded, his tone a bit too sarcastic for the situation. "Why were you observing us at the Pyramids?"

"To learn," Morgan said simply.

"You talk like you knew we'd be there," Blaine suggested.

"Yeah, that's right," Dent agreed. "The Pyramids, they're on our ranch, out in the middle of nowhere. Why would you be there? You couldn't possibly have known that we were gonna show up. Hell, we didn't even know we were going to be taking this freaky-ass road trip!"

"You are incorrect," Morgan replied.

"Am I?" Dent asked. "Well, then, *es'plain* it to me, Lucy."

I rolled my eyes. Dent's imitation of Ricky Ricardo was a sure sign that he was quickly becoming impatient. Morgan raised his brow with admonishment and shot Dent a frigid look that captured my brother's condescending eyes, sending a message to all of us that he was not amused by such expressions of disrespect. For a moment, I expected Morgan to shrug and walk away, leaving us without answers, and I still had a ton of questions.

"Dent," I said, speaking his name in a tone similar to that which my mother had often used with him just before asking him if he'd like a time out.

He glanced at me, appearing as though he had no intention of giving in, but then turned to Morgan and apologized. Sometimes, my brother could surprise the hell out of me.

"Accepted," Morgan replied, then continued. "To answer your question, I had what you might call inside information." He paused for a moment before continuing. "Though I was expecting only one of you."

"JT," Dent suggested.

"Yes. And I was relatively certain of the day that he, and as it turned out, the rest of you, would cross over. On or near the third day of July. So, I was there, on purpose, in your middle of nowhere, as you put it, and I waited, curious to learn if I had calculated correctly.

"Morgan," I cut in, anxious to get in a few of my own previously contrived questions, but suddenly motivated to ask a new one. "What was significant about July 3rd?"

"It was the date of the aphelion, give or take a half day or so."

"What the hell is an aphelion?" Dent asked.

"I know," I said.

"Of course, you do, JT," he replied with a scoff, but his tone did not mask a hint of admiration.

"It is the point in the orbit of the earth that places it at its furthest distance from the sun."

"So?"

"Sorry, that's all I got. But I'm right, aren't I, Morgan?"

"Correct, Mr. Tescott. However, to satisfy your brother's second, more succinct question, the day of the aphelion, Denton, is to my knowledge the only date the passageway to a time past can be opened."

"But we didn't do the time travel thing on the third," Blaine said. "It happened to us on JT's birthday, the fourth."

"There is a margin of error that can be as much as eleven hours, forty-eight minutes, and twenty-three seconds, either side of the daylight hours of July 3rd. I have yet to understand or explain that discrepancy.

"Twenty-three seconds?" Kival asked, suddenly deciding to actively participate in the conversation. "That's being, you know, pretty—"

"Precise?"

"Yeah, that's what I was, you know, thinking."

"Seconds, Kival," Morgan replied, "can make the difference between going or staying."

"So, this time travel business, it's like a science," Blaine observed.

"Most certainly," Morgan replied. "The galactical phenomenon is the first of several aspects necessary for this method of time travel. There are other prerequisites that must be met. Place, is the second requirement."

"The Pyramids," I proposed.

"Not just any of those landforms, but specifically the one where you had gathered.

"The arch. That's what we call it."

"Aptly named, Mr. Tescott. And in this case, proximity is everything. You must physically be within a precise radius of the archway's center if you are to complete the third condition."

"Which is?"

"Signaling for your transport."

"The Burmano-Ku-Partika," I surmised.

"The what?" Blaine asked, perplexed.

"That's the weird-ass name for the alien dudes," Dent explained.

"Says who?"

"Him," Dent replied to Blaine, his finger pointing at Morgan.

"Okay, so this third thing. The signal," Blaine began, "I was there. But there was just the fight between these two, then boom. Blinding light. Nobody signaled anything."

"I did," I said plainly, understanding what I had used to make the celestial call to the Burmano-Ku-Partika.

"So, Mr. Tescott," Morgan cooed, his eyes piercing me with accusation, "you are not so ignorant after all."

"Not—not exactly," I replied, and I could sense his disappointment.

"And I thought we were friends."

"Are we?"

"Wait, I don't understand," Blaine interrupted. "What are you guys talking about?"

"A magic thingy-ma-jig," Dent replied.

"A talisman," I said, clarifying my brother's juvenile description.

"JT says it's like a thick metal lifesaver candy, only instead of a hole there's a different kind of hole—a black hole."

"I still don't get it," Blaine said, his face puzzled. "I mean, JT, you couldn't have just found it in a box of Cracker Jacks. Where did you get this thing?"

"From me," Kival announced. "He took it from me."

All eyes were on Kival, at least for a few moments. Then Blaine, aided by Dent began to question him like a witness in a prosecution. Morgan remained silent, and I looked at him as he quietly studied Kival.

"Then let's see it," Blaine demanded after firing off two questions that went unanswered.

"And there's the kicker," Dent exclaimed. "He doesn't have it. Lost the damn thing."

Morgan turned to stare at me, his eyes searching my face, looking for a confirmation, but likely preferring to find a denial.

"Mr. Tescott, is this true? Is the talisman lost?"

"Yes," I answered. And then I explained to him what had happened at the river.

"And I guess it's a safe bet that this magic metal Life Saver thing is, or was, our ticket home," Dent said. "Is that right, Morgan? Without it, we're stuck here, aren't we?"

"The talisman is absolutely essential. It is the only way to be transported by the Burmano-Ku-Partika. Except ..."

Suddenly, I was aware of the alternative. And I had already witnessed it. Sam was part of the exception. "Except," I said, echoing Morgan, though I completed his statement for him, "the Burmano-Ku-

Partika, they will take us back without the talisman. But we have to die first."

Dent, Blaine, and Kival all stared at me, their minds collectively pondering my words. Then my brother spoke, revealing the results of his contemplation.

"Like Sam."

Morgan did not offer a dissenting opinion, so I was certain I had to be right. For several long moments we hid within the silence of our thoughts. Then an unexpected shudder passed over Blaine. Seconds later, I watched as he raked his fingers through his hair and gripped his head in his hands as though he were experiencing an unbearable migraine. He exhaled, sharply, then again, and then a third time, as though he were suffering a panic attack. He turned away from us, his hands pushing down on the back of his head. Our reality had gut-punched him, and I suspected he had been wrestling with a well-concealed sense of hopelessness for the past several days.

Suddenly, he turned on Kival, his hands shoving him in the chest. Blaine's action had steam and it knocked Kival backward, stealing his balance and sending the derby hat to the floor of the barn. Then in the next second, Blaine advanced and pushed Kival again, forcing him against the wall of the barn.

"How could you?!" Blaine cried, seizing Kival by the front of his shirt. "How could you be so stupid to lose the one thing that could get us back home alive?!"

"Hey, hey, hey!" Dent exclaimed as he promptly intervened, roughly pulling Blaine away from Kival. Then Dent stepped between them and faced Blaine, gripping his shoulders. "Dude, it's not his fault. If you gotta blame somebody, blame Olly! He's the one who attacked him! You were there, you saw him bulldoze Kival right into the water!"

I crossed to Kival, first picking up his hat from the straw-covered floor, then I politely handed it to him.

"You alright?" I asked, and Kival nodded, and I noticed he seemed neither bothered nor surprised by Blaine's assault. When I turned around, I found that Blaine had distanced himself from Dent and stood ten feet away, his eyes lost as he stared hopelessly into the heap of tangled straw. I crossed to him and laid a hand upon the back of his shoulder. He turned and looked at me.

"I don't understand, JT," Blaine began, his head twitching back and forth as though he were nearing another break-down. "I don't. I don't understand it. I just don't understand it," his eyes welling with tears.

"What, Blaine? What don't you understand."

"This," he said, jerking his head, his gaze raking the rafters of the barn. "This place. I don't understand how we got here. I don't understand this time-travel shit. I don't wanna be here. I want to go back. I want to be back. Back with the things I know."

"Blaine, it's alright to be scared," I told him earnestly. "We all are, aren't we Dent?"

"Hell, yes," Dent replied, striding toward us. "And I'm in your boat, too. I don't understand any of this either. And I wish I could say it'll all be okay, that JT will figure it out and get us back home, but I don't know that. What I do know, is that you ain't alone. Just remember that. You got me and JT. Don't matter if it's 1878 or 1979 or any other damn year in between, or before or after. You understand that?"

The maturity of Dent's words resonated with me, and I was unexpectedly awed by my brother. Then I watched as Blaine's chin began to quiver, and saw a tear slip down his cheek, but a resolute smile found a place in his expression as his eyes darted from Dent to me then back again. He nodded to Dent, affirming his comprehension of my brother's question. Then Blaine glanced behind me and spoke to Kival.

"I'm sorry, man" Blaine apologized, his voice sincere and remorseful. "I freaked out, that's all."

At once, Morgan, who had remained a spectator throughout the scuffle, rose from the tableau of straw bundles he had been perched upon, and with a purposeful stride, he walked through the alleyway of the barn and entered Viento's stall. I followed him and saw that he was fitting his horse with his saddle.

"What are you doing? It's dark. I thought we were staying here."

"You are staying, Mr. Tescott. But I am leaving."

"Why?"

"The lost talisman. It changes everything."

"It does?" I asked, but at once, Morgan was in my face.

"Do you honestly not have it?" He questioned me, his eyes blazing with disbelief.

I shook my head.

"I don't. Search me, if you want," I offered, lifting my hands outward as if I were being held up and robbed. Then to my surprise, Morgan began to frisk me, checking my pockets, patting down my chest and back, his hands probing the length of each of my legs. He then seized my hat and began to search the folds and crevices of its interior. "Should I take off my boots, remove my socks and spread my toes for you?" I asked, annoyed that he did not believe me, though admittedly I had not been completely honest with him.

"Yes," he replied, and reading that he was sincere, I obliged, prying the boots from my feet. He thoroughly examined both their cavities and felt my socked feet. He was meticulous, so much so that his touch along my arches nearly tickled.

"Morgan, I don't have it."

"Open your mouth," he ordered.

I looked at him, gauging whether he was fully tripping out. Reluctantly, I did as he demanded, and with the gentleness of a dentist, he inserted his fingers, spread my lips wide and probed inside my cheeks and along my gums. He released me and stepped backward, his eyes astute.

"That's the only cavity I'll let you search," I said to him, an undeniable challenge defining my words. At once he turned and looked to where we had been. I followed his eyes and saw that my three companions had emerged from the storage area of straw and hay.

"All of you, come here. Now."

I had expected Dent to respond to Morgan's command with a crudely colorful phrase, but he did not. Instead, he silently complied, and surprisingly, Blaine and Kival imitated him. Morgan directed the three of them to line up against a wall of slatted lumber which Morgan had earlier described as a head-locking apparatus intricate to the design of the milking stations, and then demanded that they remove their boots and hats, and face away with their hands on the upper horizontal ledge of the wooden stanchion.

Unsurprisingly, Dent finally abandoned his foray of posing as a mute and protested.

"Do not challenge me!" Morgan spoke with authority as he drew a small revolver from inside his jacket. "I do not do this frivolously. It is a matter of life and death to know if the talisman is truly not in the possession of any of you. Perhaps, Denton Tescott, your own life could either be saved or lost with my confirmation of this detail."

"So, just shoot me then."

"Dent. Do as he says. Please."

Reluctantly Dent acquiesced, though Morgan went first to Kival, frisking him as he had done me, except when searching his legs, Morgan discovered a knife, the same one Kival had threatened me with, secreted in a thin sheath tied inside his pantleg and secured just above his ankle. After an examination of his derby and his boots,

Morgan likewise explored Kival's mouth. Then he moved on to Dent, then Blaine, repeating the identical procedure with them.

Then Morgan shifted his attention to our horse's tack, emptying our saddle bags, exploring every fold of our bedrolls, every pocket and crease of the extra clothes he had given us.

"Satisfied?" Dent asked.

For a long moment, quiet filled the air around us.

"I am. And I thank you, sincerely, for your cooperation. And I apologize to each of you for such a rude intrusion. But I had to know for certain."

"You said that this changes everything," I reminded him, "but you didn't explain why."

"The threat to your immediate safety, and more importantly the endangerment and devastation of countless innocent lives, is significantly reduced because of the unknown whereabouts of the talisman."

"Then there's no hurry to run off and hide out as you suggested before?"

"There is, perhaps, less urgency. But it would be prudent to keep a low profile. We will discuss this in depth once I return," Morgan added, then crossed to the stall where Viento waited.

"So, where are you going? Tonight?"

"To Nicodemus."

"Who's he?" Dent asked with a snarl.

"Not who. It is a place. And I must get there quickly. I have much to prepare before I begin my journey."

"Your journey? Where are you going?" I asked, not caring whether it was or was not my business.

"Gibraltar, Mr. Tescott. I must leave for The Rock."

CHAPTER 18

I awoke to a puff of sweet breath across my face, and when I opened my eyes, I was looking into a pair of soft, doe-brown eyes, lined with long, curled lashes, peering at me with a sense of curiosity. A female.

Apparently the first in line to be milked.

I quickly sat up from my simple bed of straw and stared at the dark face of the caramel-haired cow then blinked my eyes as I surveyed the corner of the barn looking for others who were of my species.

I found none.

Then my ears picked up the sound of multiple footsteps made by feet that were cloven as well as soled. From the shadowy light of the barn, Dent appeared, and my bovine alarm clock turned and lumbered away.

"Bout time, ya lazy bum," he jovially scolded.

"And what time would that be?" I yawned, feeling like I had gotten zero rest.

"Let me check. Oh, sorry, I forgot I left my watch at home, you know, a hundred years into the future, give or take."

"Score one for Denton Dean."

"Jackass. Now come on," Dent said, weaving the fingers of his hands together, then stretching them toward me, cracking his knuckles. "Time to play with some boobs."

Dent vanished as I shifted my legs beneath me, and I stood and stepped to the spot where my brother had just occupied. Blaine suddenly walked past and glanced at me.

"Morning," he said, appearing as though his understandable melt-down of the previous evening had never happened. I nodded to him and scratched the back of my head.

Then a soft voice rose from the far end of the barn, and I looked and saw Ruta entering with a lantern in her hand. She clucked a few words of her native tongue as she hung the light upon a peg, then turned and patted the head of the doe-eyed brunette that had awakened me. Then a voice I recognized sounded behind me, and I swiveled my head to find Kival entering the barn through the opposite end with a short lead rope connecting him to a big, boney spotted Holstein. And beside him strolled Anja.

He wasn't wasting any time.

Ruta motioned for the four of us to gather around and we watched as she lifted the lid of a large wooden keg. Using a metal scoop about the size of a two-liter bottle of pop, she loaded it with a measure of what appeared to be cracked corn. Then she crossed to the nearest V-shaped space constructed within the slatted-wood stanchion and poured the grain into the trough behind. The little brown cow eagerly stepped past Ruta and stuck her head through the purposely designed gap, upon which the matronly woman pivoted an angularly vertical board and braced it against the animal's neck then dropped a hinged locking block into place, securing her into the milking stanchion.

At least Morgan had not likewise used the head-locking feature when he had arranged Dent and the others for a game of peek-and-seek as he searched their persons for the talisman. And good thing, too, as Dent had been peeved enough as it was.

"Ich zeige ihnen," Ruta spoke, apparently ready to teach us our first lesson in Cow-Milking One-O-One. Anja then brought her a shiny silver pail, and after moving a short, squatty, three-legged stool into place beside the cow's flank, Ruta sat down and placed the container in front of her feet. With her plump hands she promptly seized two of the large teats of the milk-filled udder and squeezed powerful streams of the white fluid into the bucket. She clucked a few more words of German as she demonstrated the correct technique, but my fatigue had distracted me from giving her my full attention.

I was so very tired.

Last night, Morgan had departed from us as he said he would, and promptly Dent wasted no time authoring a few choice words that preceded his complaint of being practically violated. And Blaine had been just as unhappy. But the hour had become late, and I had been in no mood to talk, so I pointedly urged my irritated companions to man-up and get over it. They could bitch tomorrow. My tone must have convinced them, even though Dent was still grumbling when the four of us had settled upon the crumpled straw. Within a couple of minutes, Kival was snoring, and I was likewise eager to get some rest. But for me, sleep did not come easy.

My mind had been switched to full-throttle power, pedal-to-the-floor acceleration, all systems go. Without rest, I thought of nothing but questions. How had a small piece of alien-like jewelry been the catalyst to suck me into a convoluted time-shift of 101 years? How had Kival gotten possession of the talisman in the first place? And who had made it? Was it the Burmano-Ku-Partika? Or crafted by God himself? Or had Morgan manufactured it, and if so, was he its rightful owner?

Then there was the aphelion. That day. That specific day, the day of my eighteenth birthday, which had set the stage for this drama that had unfolded for the six of us, now a party of five, assuming Morgan's assurance of Oleander's fate could be believed. Without question, Sam was no longer a part of our story. And what of Sam? Dead, for certain. But to where, exactly, had his body been taken?

And why the Pyramids?

How had a cluster of relatively insignificant landforms in the west central part of the Sunflower State become a launching point for traveling through time? Had the arch been chosen for a specific reason? And if so, chosen by whom? Or by what? Or had we simply been in the wrong place at the wrong time when the veil between presumed parallel universes had suddenly split? Or even better, or worse, depending on the perspective, had I been an unwilling participant in an extra-terrestrial game played by other-worldly beings far more intelligent and imaginative than those of us that were merely human?

And there was the enigmatic Morgan. My thoughts of him had been the most sleep-robbing of all. Just who was that guy? He had been so determined to whisk us away from the danger and abuse of the Dog Soldier Indians, only to lead us into the neighborhood of a man who Morgan clearly considered a ruthless villain, and who, for all we knew, might also mercilessly ply us with cactus to get from us the talisman he so reputedly desired.

Morgan was also a time-traveler. He as much as said so, admitting that he had also been acquainted with the Burmano-Ku-Partika. And yet, he hadn't fully confessed to being a member of our seemingly elite little club of aphelion hop-scotchers. But I could think of no other reason to explain the things he knew, especially regarding his implied familiarity with yours truly.

Morgan had said he had met me before. So, our initial acquaintance had to have occurred sometime in the future. But where? Or more importantly, what had been the year? And had he used the arch as the gateway to get to my future? But if I were here, in his time, how could that be possible?

Perhaps the big question was one of practicality. What were we, my fellow time-trespassers and I, to do next?

It was no wonder I had barely slept.

After Ruta's demonstration, she moved away and gestured for us to give it a hand. Literally.

Dent stepped right up to the plate.

"Age before beauty," he told us, though I doubted he truly implied a compliment regarding our physical attributes. I watched as he struggled, noting that several of the squirts he had managed to get squeezed from the teat entirely missed the pail, one of which streamed upon my right boot. He looked up at me, grinning. "Oops!"

A few moments later, I was in the driver's seat and discovered the hand-action necessary for the process wasn't nearly as difficult as my brother made it appear. I stood and let Blaine take my place for his hands-on exercise.

I glanced across to where the big black and white cow had been stanchioned in the same manner as our patient little brown bovine and discovered that Kival was also being taught the art of milking a cow. His lessons, however, were privately one-on-one. His teacher, the young shapely Anja, was apparently more determined than was Ruta in providing specific instruction, evidenced by the fact that I was observing her leaning into Kival and reaching her arms around him, and not so innocently pressing her breasts against his back.

Already Kival was a teacher's pet.

I shook my head at the two of them. They had clearly made some sort of connection, and I was sure it had to have been the result of divine intervention. Admittedly, I was jealous. But curiously, Dent had not seemed to notice. Or at least he hadn't said anything. And that itself was unlike him.

An hour and a half later, our task was complete. The four of us had graduated from being inexperienced dairymen, to a few yahoos who, at a minimum, were novice milkers. Three of us, however, were obviously better than the fourth. Despite his optimism and his unabashed arrogance, Dent had underperformed. At least based on numbers. Of the eleven milch cows, Blaine, Kival and I had each drained the udders of three of them, while Dent barely finished milking his second cow ahead of the completion of my third.

It had been hard work, my hands ached, and my fingers were cramped. But between the four of us, we had kept the German ladies busy straining the fresh milk through a cheese cloth as they poured the warm liquid from the buckets into a larger can affixed with the white material that had been stretched across the mouth of the metal container.

We had just rinsed our hands and stretched the cricks from our backs, when the first customers of the Beilman dairy began to line up with empty pails and gallon glass jars. Mostly, they were women dressed much like Ruta and Anja, with funny-looking handkerchiefs tied around their heads and utilitarian aprons worn loose in front covering them from neck to hem.

One woman, in particular, caught my eye. She had an infant slung across her bosom and coddled in a pouch held by a strap behind her head, leaving her hands free to balance a yoke across her shoulders with a bucket attached at each end. Pulling at her skirt was a trio of youngsters, a toddler and two others barely older and just stair-steps apart in age. I had not often been around little kids, but I surmised that she and her husband had their hands full.

After returning the cows to their pasture, Ruta showed us a second fenced-in area that she indicated as a place where we could release our horses so that they could feed upon the lush grass, though we were advised to first take them to the river to drink. Then, she gestured to the house and motioned that we were to come inside and eat, but only after the animals were cared for first.

With the horses watered and enthusiastically munching away at their morning groceries, we went to the house and gathered around the bed where Helmut rested. He was beaming. And gibbering. Apparently, he had been given a favorable report from his wife regarding our efforts as milkers. He reached out to each of us and took us by our hands and squeezed and shook us with a strength that was a witness to the longevity of his experience at milking cows. I smiled at him, speaking words of English between his words of German, and I acknowledged his gratitude. I felt pleased with myself, and glad that Morgan had volunteered us to help. Despite being a foursome of outsiders, we were undoubtedly appreciated.

Soon, the four of us were seated at a table in the kitchen. Another meal of cornbread and butter had been set before us, but additional items had been added to the breakfast feast; a plate piled with thick slices of ham, and a giant bowl of red beans with a large ladle dipped into its center. We ate well, and I stuffed myself without a shred of discipline.

Yawning, Blaine reported that he was ready for a siesta. So, we thanked Ruta and Anja for the meal, and after a wave to Helmut as we crossed through the living room, we left the house and headed to the barn.

Blaine dove right into the straw, and as much as I wanted to do the same, I did not dare take a nap. I wanted complete and thorough exhaustion for the upcoming night. If I could help it, I would prefer not to suffer through a second sleepless bedtime. Kival, though, gathered up his derby and fixed it upon his head, then mumbled something about kicking around and looking for something to do, and disappeared from the barn. I, too, had my own plans.

"So," Dent said. "What now?"

"I'm going to town."

"There's nothing there, to speak of," he said, looking at me quizzically.

"Not Schoenchen. Hays."

"Hays? But what about Morgan?"

"I didn't hear him specifically tell us to stay put. Did you? So, why not explore a little?"

"I'm in."

"I thought you might be," I said with a grin.

We gathered our horses and brought them into the barn and saddled them, then told a sleepy Blaine we would be back before evening chore time. He grunted and I took it that he understood but was more interested in counting sheep than road-tripping. Apparently, the previous night had also been rough for him.

As we began to ride north through the little village, a chorus of male voices reached my ears. The sound was surprisingly pleasant, though the words were a mystery to me. As we neared the church that was under construction, we found the source of the harmonious choir. A half dozen German stone masons and carpenters were busy singing as they worked. If I had known the words, I might have joined in. Instead, I found myself humming along, at least until we had ridden far enough away to where I could no longer hear the men. I stopped the melodic vibration in my throat and glanced at Dent, finding that he was looking at me with his typical raised right brow and pursed lips.

"If we'd been in my truck, I would have turned the radio way up just to drown out that pitiful whining."

"Didn't know my vocal skills bothered you so much."

"What skills?" he replied, with a grin and I could not argue with him.

The ride to Hays City was about an eleven-mile journey and we arrived easily by mid-morning. The town, its skyline dominated by a three-story stone courthouse, was bigger than I expected it to be for the year of 1878, and more spread-out. We crossed a meandering tree-lined creek and entered the modest nineteenth century metropolis and found ourselves pulled into the traffic flow of wagons and buggies, equestrians and pedestrians. The dirt street was hard-packed, though powdered with a heavy film of dust, and flanked by a smattering of buildings, from simple board shacks to stone structures, several of which had second stories. Ahead I could see the density of people had more than doubled, with most appearing to merge left onto what I guessed might be the main commercial street.

Dent and I reined our horses into the flow and sure enough we found ourselves in the heart of a Western town that did not measure up to the neat and tidy representations built on movie lots in twentieth century Hollywood, California. Though relatively new, the wooden structures were rough, a few having never worn a coat of paint, with boardwalks that were barely nailed down, some sections with covers and some with just open sky for a roof.

Though there was barely any wind, dust billowed from every footfall and wheel tread.

Despite the earthy pall, I noticed many menfolk dressed in three-piece suits and derby hats, earnestly chatting with lesser-dressed ranch hands and jacketless storekeepers, their bright white shirts cut by dark suspenders that held up their high-waisted pants. Conversations were taking place on chairs within the shade of the wooden awnings of storefronts, while others chatted as they congregated at hitching posts where ponies stood at rest waiting patiently for their talkative owners. Several times cowboys leisurely angled across the street in front of us, and once a pair of cavalry soldiers crossed our path. Rarely did any of them look at us twice, and only once did I notice anyone even give us more than a three-second appraisal. It was enough to make one feel insignificant.

Which was Morgan's intent.

On the other side of the gender isle, I observed that most women were frocked in bonnets and fancy patterned dresses that draped to their ankles from high collars fastened with buttons that migrated up their necks not ending until reaching the line of their smooth jaw. Conversely, members of the gentler sex were not as socially integrated as were their male counterparts, being less inclined to linger and gossip, but instead moving readily as if on a mission constrained by an impending deadline.

In pairs of two or three, the well-coifed ladies scurried along boardwalks and disappeared into stores, while the simple-attired clusters of immigrant German women gathered at street corners, jabbering among themselves and pointing first one way and then another as they apparently debated the next direction of their morning outing.

We ambled along the streets and circled the blocks that comprised the main commercial area, twice crossing the railroad track that dissected the town. Flanking the tracks were two parallel streets I knew as Nineth and Tenth: Modern avenues I remembered from my trips to Hays in the company of my mother, though nothing else, a hundred years later, looked at all familiar.

Many of the establishments were clearly saloons or gambling houses, and one place even advertised "Faro Here", whatever that might be, but there were dozens of men bustling in and out of the sketchy-looking place. There were also several hotels, or at least hotel-looking structures. The Gibson House, Pennsylvania House, and the Union Pacific House to name a few that had, at face-value, the appearance of being reputable.

However, one especially noticeable building had large block letters aligned above its row of second story windows that spelled SPORTING PALACE, though there was nothing palatial about it. A woman, not especially attractive, swayed in a rocking chair on an outdoor balcony a floor above us. Her feet and her calves were bare, and she sat with one leg crossed over the other, and her dress, more of an evening gown than an otherwise acceptable daytime frock, was gathered up to her knees. She looked down at Dent and I as we passed and lifted the hem of her skirt a little higher and smiled. I looked away before she had a chance to turn me into stone.

Or worse.

Dent, always ready to make a new friend, waved at her, though I wasn't sure if he realized she was a representative of the world's oldest profession.

"I'm pretty sure she's a prostitute," I told him.

"Damn," he said. "And I left my wallet in my truck."

I laughed at him, but I was not entirely convinced he was joking.

We sauntered around on horseback, crisscrossing our way through the central part of town, exploring not just the busy avenues, but the narrower side streets that connected them. Returning to an intersecting corner of the central hub, we paused to observe the throngs of people seemingly busy doing nothing but keeping themselves and their horses and buggies and wagons constantly in flux.

Discussing where to go next, we sat there in the heat of a sun that was approaching its noon-time place in the sky, and I slipped my cowboy hat from my head and wiped the sweat from my brow. Suddenly, from behind us, I heard a shout, and instinctively I cringed.

"Hey, pussies!"

As one, Dent and I turned to the source and discovered a shirtless dude with exceedingly pale skin leaning out of an open window at the back of a narrow building that sat on the corner of the block, and his red hair was a match to whom I knew owned that voice.

Oleander Sedgwick.

We remained steadfast in our saddles, and I silently stared at him, mostly because I was in disbelief that we had unintentionally found our wounded comrade.

"Double D!" Oleander shouted. "Get your ass over here!"

"Damn," Dent said. "And I thought the hooker was ugly." He turned his horse, and I reined Buck in beside him and we crossed to where Oleander waited.

"Holy shit, just look at you guys," he exclaimed, with a broad smile. He seemed genuinely glad to see us. "All dressed up like you're back home on the range, you know, where the frickin' deer and antelope roam!"

"Olly," Dent said once he arrived at the window, "can you tone it down? We don't want to draw any unnecessary attention." I glanced around, and luckily, no one seemed interested in us.

"Oh, right. I forgot. That dude who brought me here, he told me to stay low and keep it cool, or something like that. Guess you've met him? Looks like Lamont Sanford, you know from that TV show, but without the moustache."

"His name is Morgan," I said, acknowledging our acquaintance with the man who had probably saved Oleander's life.

"Yeah, that's him," Oleander concurred. At once, a woman appeared beside him, her dark hands pulling him from the window.

"Please, Mr. Sedgwick," she said, "you need to rest."

"Jeez, woman," he said, though his protest was weak. "These guys are my buddies I've been telling you about," he added as he disappeared from the window. Dent and I sat there on our horses for a minute, then the woman appeared at the window, her face barely visible. She was a Black woman, petite, almost frail, but her eyes were bright, warm, and friendly.

"Please, come to the back," she said, then disappeared.

We tied our horses to the rail that stood next to the simple, one-story structure, and following her directions we crossed to the rear of the building to find her waiting at the door. She looked about, then motioned us to move quickly and join her. I likewise glanced up and down the road and seeing that no one was watching us, I followed Dent inside. The small woman closed the door behind us and within in the confines of a narrow hallway she introduced herself.

"I am Mrs. John White," she said. "I have been caring for your friend."

"I'm JT," I replied, "and this is my brother, Dent."

"Ah, yes, the brothers. Mr. Tescott and Mr. Tescott. Mr. Morgan said you would come to get him. But it is too early, I think."

"Well, we haven't actually come for Olly," Dent said. "We just sort of found him, by accident."

"That is good. That is good," she nodded then turned away after directing us with a hand gesture. "Come," she invited us, though it felt mandatory that we oblige her.

We followed her for only a few feet before she opened a door and entered the room where I expected to find Oleander. And there he was, sitting upon a low bed, a thick pillow behind his back, and a white cotton sheet covering him from his hips to his toes. Then my attention was drawn to his wounded hand that was wrapped in strips of cloth.

"Man," Oleander said grinning at Dent, "it's good to see a familiar face!" He then glanced at me. "Yours too, Worm." I pasted an insincere grin upon my cheeks and gave him a nod, just to be nice. Behind me I heard the door click shut and glanced to find that Oleander's caregiver had left us alone.

"Olly, you're looking ten times better than you did the last time we saw you," Dent informed him. Silently, I agreed with him, though I was equally impressed by Oleander's new haircut: A coiffure of half-inch length sheared hair that had replaced Oleander's beloved mullet he had been fostering in the nine months since he had been expelled from the football team. Apparently, Oleander had not been exempted from a Morgan make-over.

"No shit. And dude, I feel a hundred times better. But my feet are still sore as hell. Can hardly walk on 'em. But that lady, she's quite a doctor," he said, lifting his bare arms to show us that the swelling and wounds of his underarms had nearly disappeared. Then at once, he flung the sheet from him, exposing his groin area. "And look, my frank and beans are pretty much back to normal, but my balls still hurt something fierce, that bastard Indian."

I couldn't help but glance at his man-parts, noticing that all items were still accounted for, though I would not have been surprised to find something missing or misshapen, recalling how inflamed and swollen his punctured scrotum had been. He owed Kival a huge debt of gratitude, though I doubted he would say as much if he had known. And I could think of no good reason to tell him.

"We don't need to see your junk," Dent said, replacing the bed covering across his lap.

"Well, I've had to get way past being shy around here. That woman, she's been up in my business every day since I got here, and I've lost count how many times she's smeared me up with some weird-smelling shit. So, I don't even give a rat's ass anymore when that woman's dinking around with my goods."

"Her name is Mrs. White," I reminded him bluntly.

"Yeah, I know. And her old man is a barber or somethin'. Runs a lot of customers through his shop out front. I hear 'em yakking it up with him a lot. They sound like white dudes, but they seem to like ole John alright. He's nice. They both are," Oleander conceded, and I was glad he seemed to genuinely appreciate them.

"But still he probably doesn't like it that his ole lady gives me boners when she's doctoring me up," he added, as though that was her objective, and healing him was her secondary purpose.

"Still a class act," I said, my tone of sarcasm blaring. "I thought maybe you'd be a little more humble considering what you've been through. What we've all been through."

"I am what I am, you know," he countered, not in the least apologetic. "Hey, so where are the other guys? Sambo and Hollywood?"

Dent and I glanced at each other, and I sensed that he was checking with me for permission. I nodded, preferring him to be the one to tell Oleander.

"Wallace is nearby," Dent replied, reporting of Blaine. "And Sam is dead, Olly."

Oleander jerked his head.

"What?"

"He died."

"How?"

Dent glanced at me, but this time I subtly shook my head, and I hoped that Dent understood that I preferred not to tell Oleander the details of Sam's disappearance. But before he could say anything, Oleander supplied an answer.

"It was those goddamned Indians, wasn't it?"

"Yeah, it was them," Dent said.

"I swear, I'll kill the scalping sumbitches if I ever get the chance," he growled, shaking his bandaged fist at us. "Did you see they took my hair?!"

His accusation was misplaced, though I realized the trimming of his locks must have taken place during a state of unconsciousness. Morgan was obviously no dummy. "We should go," I spoke to Dent, and he nodded in agreement.

"You guys aren't stayin'?" Oleander asked, clearly disappointed that we would leave him.

"We're not far away. Staying with some folks south of town," Dent explained.

"And Morgan has left for a few days," I added. "But when he gets back, we'll come get you. Provided you're able to walk by then."

"I'll be able, trust me. Sooner I can fly this coop, the better."

We left the room, closing the door behind us. Mrs. White appeared through a doorway up the hall and crossed to us.

"Thank you," I said to her, feeling certain that Oleander had probably not expressed any appreciation for her care. "He can't have been an easy patient."

"I am happy to help him. As a favor to Mr. Morgan."

We promised her we would return for Oleander in a few days, though I wasn't at all excited about keeping the promise, though I knew that I would.

Dent and I left the building, exiting as we had entered, and remounted our horses.

"Where to next, Wild Bill?" Dent asked.

"We passed a newspaper office a block or so away. I want to go there and see if I can nab a paper. I'm curious to find out what's happening around here, without having to ask a lot of questions."

"Go ahead without me," Dent said, "I'm gonna just swing by the Sportin' Palace and you know, check things out."

"Tell me you're kidding?"

"I'm just curious, like you. Except your interest is current events and, well, mine is not. Besides, I'm just going to look. I've never seen an actual whore house before." He reined his horse away, then called to me over his shoulder. "I'll meet you in front of the newspaper office. I won't be long."

I watched as he disappeared around the corner. I shook my head. Another thing not to tell Mom if I ever got the chance to see her again.

I reined Buck around and headed him up the street looking for the office I had seen with the *Hays City Sentinel* painted in white letters upon a plate glass window. Arriving at the block where the office building was located, I was not too surprised to find the hitching rails in front choked with horses, but it didn't help that a two-horse wagon rig occupied a place that would otherwise accommodate at least a half-dozen one-man conveyances. I nodded politely at a fellow who was leisurely loading goods he had apparently just purchased from the adjacent building labeled C.F. Burnside Mercantile, and I guessed that his use of the space as a loading zone was not a violation of a city ordinance, if any such code existed.

I parked my horse a half block up, tying the rein around the end of a well-populated rail where several other horses were hitched.

"I'm telling you, Headville's got ole Moody on his payroll," I overheard a man say as I walked past him and a shopkeeper gossiping in the doorway of a shoe repair store. I walked a few more paces then paused to pretend to be window shopping.

"Horse nuggets," I heard the second man squawk. "Texas Jack Moody, he's too hot-headed to work for Headville. 'Sides that high roller is way too savvy to get hisself tied up with that no-good deputy! Hell, Moody used to be an outlaw! Mebbe still is one!"

"I dunno. Headville's done got the county judge in his pocket. Newspaper said about as much."

"Didn't know you could read?"

"I hear'd it was in the newspaper, that's what I meant."

"Hey, boy! Can I help you?" I turned to see the shopkeeper looking at me.

"Nope," I said with a shrug. "Just looking." Then I walked away, hoping my eavesdropping had not been obvious. I reached the newspaper office and began to study a sheet of newsprint taped to the window next to the door. I leaned forward so that I could get a better view of the small-sized format, vaguely aware of bootsteps clicking through the opened doorway.

"I hope you aren't one of those gullible citizens who believes everything he reads. The printed word can be as destructive to the reader as it is to the one who is the subject of slander."

I looked up and my eyes met a well-tailored man wearing a black, impeccable Stetson, and appearing every inch a cattleman as well as a gentleman. I straightened my posture and peered at him, my gaze pointing upward in an effort to address the tall man eye-to-eye. He was handsome, reminding me of the Hollywood actors of the silver screen, and appeared to be slightly older than my dad, late forties, with striking black hair and confident cerulean blue eyes and a friendly smile.

"I have made it a habit not to be gullible, sir," I said, respectfully.

"Good. A wise man recognizes the challenge to separate fact from fiction. Take this, for example," he added with a deep baritone voice, and tapping a headline printed on the newspaper he held in his hands. "A rather unflattering article about a local man. A reputable man. It could be true. Then again, perhaps not." I glanced at the caption.

DOES CULVER HEADVILLE OWN THE LAW?

"This Culver Headville person," I began, trying my best not to appear startled by the headline, "do you know him?"

"I do."

"And what do you think of him?" I asked, foolishly unable to suppress my curiosity. I knew Morgan's sentiments, and a few moments earlier a shopkeeper had voiced his point of view regarding the notorious Culver Headville. A third concurring opinion might ultimately sway me to keep my distance from him.

"Is this an interview?" he asked with a grin that quickly broke into a smile and then was accompanied by a soft laugh.

"No, sir," I said feeling very much at ease with the taller man. "I'm just an inquisitive sort of guy. I didn't mean to pry."

"Not to worry. I take no offense with your question. But neither will I answer it. I believe that a man should form his own opinions."

"Good advice, sir," I said, offering him a reciprocating grin.

"But I will say the opinions of others can be entertaining. Buy a paper and see for yourself."

"Well, I would, but I'm a little short of funds at the moment."

"Not even two bits?"

"Well, not two bits to spare," I said, avoiding the truth that I was flat broke and nearly destitute.

"Unemployed?"

"You could say that." Then at once I felt compelled to tell a fib. "That's another reason I'm here, wondering if there are any help wanted ads."

"Help wanted ads. Interesting," he said, studying my eyes. "Well, here, you may have my paper. And good luck," he said as he stepped away. Then he stopped and turned back to me. "Given your circumstances, I am quite positive that Mister Headville there," he said referencing the headline, "is looking for hired hands. He owns a ranch north of town. If you're any good with livestock, he might offer you a job."

"Thanks, but for now I think I'll keep my options open." I did not want to explain why and who had warned me about Culver Headville, so I quickly added, "But thank you, for this," I said, lifting the newspaper.

"My pleasure," the tall man replied, then he turned and sauntered across the street. I watched as he stepped up into a sleek, black-painted buggy with huge, spoked wheels and hitched behind a pair of beautifully matched palomino ponies, noting that his transportation suited him. But what captured my attention the most was the girl he had sat beside. Curls of honey blonde hair cascaded from beneath a blue hat held in place with a wide, white bow. Even from where I stood some twenty yards away, I could see that disguised within the shade of her bonnet was the face of a beautiful young lady.

The fatherly man then spoke to his driver, a stocky sort with a muscular barrel-chest wrapped up in a form-fitting grey button shirt. But my eyes lingered on him for just a fleeting second. When I returned my gaze to the girl, I discovered that she was looking at me. I smiled at her, and in my natural and awkward way of doing things, I lifted my hand and waved. She turned quickly away as the benefactor of my newspaper tipped his hat to me. I watched as the fancy buckboard rolled away behind the clicking hooves of the yellow horses.

If there was such a thing as love at first sight, I felt sure I had just experienced it. And to be clear, I was not thinking of the Palominos.

I returned to my horse just as Dent rode up.

"You got a paper? They givin' those away?"

"No. Call it a free sample," I said. "You weren't gone long. No free samples at the Sporting Palace, I assume."

"Dunno. Didn't ask for one. The place was like a livestock market. A pair of hefty cows, an ugly old mare and a tall bird with a beak as long my—my thumb. Those gals don't look like the ones in the movies. I couldn't get out of there fast enough."

And I couldn't help but laugh.

CHAPTER 19

At the Beilman farm, it had taken me a couple of days to really get the hang of milking a cow with my bare hands. For certain, just that task alone was strenuous work, especially fatiguing the small muscles of my palms and the tendons of my fingers, though already I could tell my grip was getting stronger. If I were to ever be a contender for the title of World's Strongest Handshaker, milking a cow would be an ideal part of the training program. But also, I had quickly developed a far greater appreciation for a simple glass of milk and the ice cream cone I had regularly indulged in every Friday afternoon when me and Sam and other friends would gather at Custer's local Dairy Delight.

It had also become distinctly evident that the level of daily commitment to dairy livestock was more of an investment in time and resources than was required with the raising of beef cattle, which had been my life-long experience. Other than the winter, when it became necessary to feed hay to the Tescott herd of Herefords, or the occasional need to break ice when temperatures dropped below freezing, our cattle would mostly fend for themselves.

The dairy cow, though, was a different story. On top of ensuring she had plenty to eat and drink, she also had to be milked twice a day, morning and evening. A dairyman was unquestionably married to a different lifestyle. But the rewards were atypical, as well. For one thing, it was easy for these milk cows to become like pets as one discovered that often each was inclined to possess her own unique personality. It was no wonder the Beilman's had names for each of their eleven milch cows.

One of my two favorites was called Birgit, a big cow, at least a thousand pounds, with a red coat splashed with spots of white over her back and shoulders, and a face displaying a white spot shaped like a valentine in the center of her forehead and eyes that seemed to beg me to scratch behind her big, floppy ears. And so, I found myself frequently obliging her, particularly upon the moment she stepped foot in the barn, and again before she left. The second of my new cloven-hooved pets was addressed by Ruta Beilman as Greta, the little brown cow that had awakened me on the first morning. Greta liked to lick the back of my head as though my noggin was her own personal salt block. With a tongue the size of a house slipper and as rough as sandpaper, Greta's affection was not quite as appreciated as was the face-licking

Zoey, a sweet Border Collie that had been a treasured family dog when Dent and I were little boys.

In the two days that followed, I had also managed to pick up a few phrases spoken by our Volga German hosts. The first was *guten morgen*, an easy interpretation of good morning. The second, *zeit fur das abendessen*, was not as straightforward but I liked what it meant: Dinner Time.

The morning following the fifth night we had spent camped inside the Beilman's barn, Helmut sauntered into the musky structure accompanied by Ruta and Anja. I had seen him up and about the day before, apparently testing the recuperation of his injured ribs.

"Guten Morgen, Helmut," I greeted him, and his jolly grin I had come to know flashed across his face.

"Guten Morgen, Jay—Tee," Helmut replied, then shared a nod and a smile with Dent and the others.

I had begun to repeat my greeting to Ruta but seeing that she was wearing a scowl in place of her usual cheery smile, I decided it was perhaps best not to poke the bear. She was clearly unhappy that her husband had apparently decided he was ready for his re-entry into the workforce, although I imagined she preferred that he convalesce for a while longer. Also, I had a feeling she was enjoying the company of the four of us chittery young Englishmen and was probably not quite ready to be rid of us. And to some degree, my feelings regarding the Beilmans were the same. They were, as Morgan had promised us, good people.

Helmut watched as the four of us easily managed to get the first set of cows locked into their respective milking stations. With affection, he commenced the routine business we had just learned a few days earlier, walking behind each cow, patting them on their rumps and calling them by their names. It was obvious that he had missed them.

When he circled back, he stopped at my cow, Birgit, and gestured that I should stand and give him the seat of the three-legged stool, and so I did. He eased down upon the squatty chair and within seconds the spewing of robust streams of milk mixed quickly with the gurgling of the liquid as it pooled into the pail.

Those sounds combined with his motions were as rhythmic and precise as a tempo set to a metronome, and within a short span of under ten minutes, Helmut had completed what I had begun and had accomplished the task in half the time it would have taken me. He stood and handed the filled pail to Ruta, who had waited nearby watching with her arms crossed, and grunted something to her with a pitch of satisfaction that might have been some version of "I told you so."

I told my eyes not to look at her.

With the early morning chores close to being wrapped up, Kival and Anja had led the last pair of cows from the barn, as they had for each of the previous four mornings, while Dent and Blaine and I tidied up the facility, particularly the milking stanchion, raking and replacing any soiled straw. At once, Anja appeared inside the large doorway, her breathing heavy.

"*Ein kalb wird geboren!*" She exclaimed, and I looked to see that Ruta and Helmut were beaming with excitement. Then from behind her, Kival entered leading a barrel-bellied Holstein that since our arrival, had been separated from the milking herd. The nearly all-white bovine waddled her way behind Kival, her tail pointing outward and the balloon of a liquid-filled placenta dangling from her birth canal. Dent and I had seen this before. And often.

A baby calf was soon to be born.

Helmut opened the gate to the empty stall where Morgan's stallion had earlier been sequestered, while Ruta met Kival and gave the cow a cursory inspection before taking the lead rope from him. She led the expectant new mother into the stall and the seven of us humans gathered around to watch and wait. However, the Beilmans had only a few minutes to spare before being called to the duty of the usual business of supplying fresh milk to their morning customers, but the laboring cow remained the focus of four attentive teenagers. Dent and I stood back and allowed Blaine and Kival front row seats, since this would be a first for the two of them.

An hour would pass, though, before the arrival of the newborn, and neither of them moved from their place outside the stall. And I could not blame them. The birth of a baby calf was simply a cool thing.

"It's here!" Blaine exclaimed, and Dent and I joined him to see the cute little guy, wet and gangly, and spotted with black patches across a coat of snow white. Then I sensed the presence of someone else joining us, confirmed by the sound of movement closing in behind me, but I was too enthralled with watching the miracle of new life and kept my eyes forward. Within moments, the momma cow was on her feet and instinctively she began to lick and clean her newborn, stimulating and encouraging him to test his ability to stand on his own four wobbly legs.

"Who is the lucky father?" the voice spoke from over my shoulder. A voice I had heard before but had not known its owner to possess a sense of humor. I pivoted upon my feet and smiled at Morgan.

He had returned from Nicodemus.

I knew little about Nicodemus, Kansas, other than it had been founded as a community for Black Americans, a destination upon the plains of Kansas that offered opportunity for slaves who had been freed because of the Civil War.

I had actually traveled through Nicodemus, once, by bus enroute to a high school sub-state tournament held in Osborne. My view of it, speeding by on US 24, had been little more than a blur of a handful of old buildings, most of which were in dire need of a fresh coat of paint. On the bus, I had heard someone mention it was a "Black town" and, of course, my curiosity had been piqued. Later, I had researched the history of Nicodemus, finding minimal information in my school library. What the community was like now, before I had glimpsed it a hundred years later, I had no idea, but something or someone was there that had necessitated Morgan's visit.

"We need to talk, Mr. Tescott."

Morgan's sudden appearance had not gone unnoticed by the others. Blaine was first to turn his back on the event inside the birthing stall, and he looked as though he might like to give Morgan an oral examination similar to the one he had received but using a pitchfork instead of his fingers. And that was not my imagination at work. Blaine had expressed that desire that night after Morgan had left.

Kival acknowledged Morgan's presence with a subtle bend of his head that allowed him a glance lasting all of two seemingly disinterested seconds before returning his eyes to the wonder of the newborn calf. Dent, on the other hand, leveled his full attention upon the dark cowboy, and of no surprise he was quick to begin a conversation with Morgan, albeit an unfriendly one.

"Well, well, well," my brother began as he stepped toward him, "looky who's back. The asshole with the big probing fingers."

"Dent," I said, stopping him with my hand firmly planted against his chest. "We talked about this. Let it go." My brother had been thoroughly pissed when he had literally "hit the hay" the night of Morgan's overly-personalized search, and he had awoken in the same mood, although he had tried to hide that fact. At least, at first. We had, however, discussed Morgan's words and actions the following day during our ride to Hays. I had not liked the oral examination Morgan had given me either, and I had said as much to Dent. But I had also reminded him that the man had saved our lives. There was no one else present in this time-past who had done as much for us. As far as I was concerned, we had no choice but to trust him. At least, up to a point.

"Where do you want to talk? Here?" I replied to Morgan's invitation, indicating the barn.

"No. Anja has given me permission to use her home. The soddy. It will provide the privacy that is needed."

"Okay," I said. "Come on, guys."

"No," Morgan commanded. "Just you," he said to me.

"Fine by me," Dent snarled. Blaine said nothing.

"And him," Morgan added, pointing at the back of Kival's head.

"Kival?" I asked, surprised.

Kival turned at the sound of his name and he found us all staring at him.

"What?" he asked.

"You and Mr. Tescott. Please come with me," Morgan instructed, then turned and left the barn and I saw that he carried his saddlebag with him.

"Come on," I said to Kival, and with a nod he affirmed his willingness to comply with my request, and together, we followed Morgan.

The earthen-walled home was in decent shape, well-constructed and more accommodating than Karl and Abelard's dug out had been. And cleaner. The inside floor had been fitted with an assortment of odd lengths of wood plank, most two feet long and shorter, obvious scrap pieces that were probably remnants from the construction of the Beilman's second and permanent home. The sod house, the first home built upon the Kansas prairie by Helmut and Ruta, I deduced had been given to their son and daughter-in-law as a starter home for the newly wedded couple. Now, because of a heinous crime, it was solely occupied by Anja.

A tiny wood-burning cook stove occupied the center of the one-room house, and a grey curtain of homespun wool partially divided the living area from a sleeping space located at one end. A simple eating table, intimately sized for two stood before a small window, and two chairs were positioned at each end. In the center of the table was a slender yellow vase inhabited by a fresh wildflower. And beside the vase was a hat.

A derby, with a bullet hole in it.

I had wondered why Kival had not been wearing it this morning. I looked at him and I thought I saw a momentary blush.

Morgan told us to sit, and we did as we were instructed, parking ourselves across from each other at the small table, but turning our chairs toward him where he remained standing.

"First, a bankroll for each of you," he said, unfolding the straps from the buckles of the saddlebag, before removing five identical leather pouches, each the size of a baseball, their opening drawn tight and tied.

"You're giving us money?" I asked, not particularly pleased with receiving a cash payment without having earned it. Even as kids, Dent and I had never been given an allowance. Instead, we did extra chores beyond what was expected of us, and those voluntary efforts earned us some extra cash to buy the newest Hot Wheels race cars or add to our collection of Spiderman and Top Cat comic books.

"Correct. You will need funds to function and survive as a contributing member of your new world of 1878."

I took one of the bags. It was heavier than I expected. I opened it and poured its jangling contents upon the table. It was a modest mix of silver nickels and seated liberty dimes minted in the early eighteen seventies, but there were also a variety of gold coins, most with denominations of $1, $2.50, $3, and $5, but there were a half dozen Liberty Heads stamped with a value of $20. I recognized most of the coins from photographs in a book I had on my shelf in my bedroom. All of them were highly sought after by twentieth century collectors.

"What I wouldn't give to take these back with me to 1979," I said. "I could almost finance my first semester of college."

"Perhaps, Mr. Tescott," Morgan responded. "But more importantly, their current face values have far greater worth to you here, and now."

"I get it, but—"

"Two hundred dollars for each of you, Mr. Tescott," Morgan said, cutting me off. "Enough to last you one year if you do not spend foolishly."

Across from me, Kival claimed a bag and emptied it onto the table replicating my actions. By all appearances, his cache was the same distribution of coinage.

"Thank you," I said, knowing how utterly broke were the five of us time-lost boys. "I'll pay you back," I promised him. "Somehow."

"You already have, Mr. Tescott," and I saw from his eyes that he was reminding me of our previous acquaintance, one of which he had exclusive knowledge, but was yet unknown to me. "If you are weakly disciplined and squander these monies, I have entrusted John White to supply you with additional funds, within reason. In fact, I would advise you to have Mr. White safeguard at least eighty percent of these assets until you are in actual need of them. This amount of money carried upon your person might make you vulnerable to thieves, or worse. Mr. White and his wife are the most honorable people I know. You can trust them as I do." After a suspiciously extended pause, Morgan looked at me and added, "I understand that you, Mr. Tescott, have already met them."

Busted.

"Yes," I admitted, feeling like I had just been caught with my hand in the proverbial cookie jar.

"The Jermyn Thomas Tescott I knew before, would not have been so foolish."

I had nothing to say in my defense, so I sat and played dumb.

"What is done, is done," he added somberly, though I expected him to thoroughly scold me for a full ten minutes.

"However, now, I have a question for you, Kival Freeman."

I looked at Morgan curiously, my mind alerting me that his knowledge of Kival's surname raised yet another question. I was certain I had not mentioned to him the last names of any of my friends, other than I had probably referred to Oleander as Sedgwick in casual conversation, but then technically, Oleander was not a genuine friend.

"K," Kival replied, leveling his eyes at his inquisitor. "Shoot."

"Where did you get the talisman?"

"From my mother."

"When?"

"A few months ago. Before she died."

"And how did your mother come to be in possession of it?"

"It was given to her."

"Not taken by her?"

"Given."

"By whom?"

"It was a gift from her grandfather."

"When?"

"I don't know."

"Morgan," I interrupted. "What's with the third degree?" But he spared giving me a courteous reply and continued with his questions.

"How old were you, Kival Freeman, when you first saw the talisman?"

"I was—I was very young."

"And did your mother tell you of its abilities?"

Kival glanced at me, his blue eyes seemed darker, and in them, I sensed fear, or at least apprehension. But there was also something else.

"You can trust me, Kival," I said, feeling compelled to reassure him. "I promise. Nothing you say here will be repeated by me to anyone. Ever."

He turned to Morgan. "Yes," Kival answered.

"Where is the talisman?"

"In the river."

At once, Morgan slapped his right hand upon the table, palm side down, the action appearing as if he had just trapped a rogue cockroach crossing the table but sounding as though he had just crushed a loose coin. He turned his hand over and the talisman lay there on the table before us.

I drew a sharp breath, shocked at what I was seeing. Kival had been equally startled, though his reaction had been an instant lunge for the missing metallic amulet. But he was not fast enough. With a flash of his dark hand, Morgan drew it away.

"Give it to me!" Kival demanded. "It's mine!"

I had heard those same words before.

"Calm down, Kival Freeman," Morgan spoke sharply. "This is not yours. It is mine." Then he offered it to Kival, and he took it without hesitation. "Look at it! There is a difference! And it is most obvious!"

Kival opened his fist and looked at the talisman lying in his palm. I watched as he touched it, then flipped it over, then back again. With a sigh, he laid it upon the table, relinquishing his mistaken right of ownership. As though it had called to me, I plucked the surrendered object and began my own examination. By all appearances this talisman was identical to the one I had pulled from Kival's neck, the same size and thickness, the same shape and weight, and with an abyss of fluid darkness in its center. Then I realized that this one was different from the one claimed by Kival. Instead of three holes spaced equidistant around its perimeter, this talisman had only one piercing.

"Morgan, where did you get this?" I asked.

"From someone with whom I share much love and respect," Morgan answered, offering no additional aspect of identity or relationship. Kival sunk back into the chair and Morgan studied him for a moment.

"What is your real name?"

The question struck me as though I had been hit on the chin. Of all the questions he had asked Kival, that had been the oddest.

"David," Kival said, barely above a whisper.

His answer punched me harder than Morgan's question. I looked across at Kival, stupidly gawking, I supposed.

"As I had suspected," Morgan spoke, his volume matching Kival's, or David's, or whatever the hell his name was.

"I don't get it," I said. "I've known who you were since the first grade. You've always been Kival."

Kival stared at me, silently nodding, his eyes seeming to illustrate the presence of a debate taking place in his head. Moments passed, then he sighed and spoke willingly.

"In the privacy of our home, my mother always called me David," he said, his eyes growing misty. "One day I asked her why she called me one name, but the teachers at school called me by another. In turn, she asked me if I remembered what she often said to me as a young boy before I was old enough to attend the school. 'You are Kiowa' was my answer. And I remembered being asked who I was by the teacher on my first day at the school, and I proudly told her I was Kiowa, but she had misunderstood my childish speech. My mother chose not to correct her."

I sat there, stunned by his explanation, then at once it dawned on me that he did not at all sound like the Kival I knew. The pattern of his speech and the relative eloquence of the words he strung together were in complete and un-stuttered sentences. And not just singular sentences, but a paragraph of them. I suddenly felt duped.

"I—I have never heard you talk like that," I said to him, obviously perplexed.

"I'm not so dumb, after all?"

"I never thought of you as dumb, Kival," I said earnestly, then shaking my head I added, "I mean David."

"No. I was David only to my mother. I am Kival to you, my friend."

Suddenly my eyes watered, and I blinked back the stinging of tears. Becoming instantly emotional was an unexpected reaction. But Kival had suddenly reminded me of Sam, and I knew then, in that moment, I had found a brotherly place for him in my heart.

"Who was your mother?" Morgan asked him.

"She was an Indian princess," Kival replied, his voice proud. "The granddaughter of a great Kiowa Chief."

"And what about your surname, the one you were born with as David?"

Kival shrugged. "Just David."

What was it with these guys? Just Morgan and Just David?

"And Freeman?"

"An invention by my mother. And precisely descriptive. She had told me that we had escaped from a place where we had been considered someone's property, owned, like dogs. That we were from a place where I could not grow up to be a free man."

"Do you know what year you were born?"

Kival looked at Morgan and shrugged and shook his head. "No, I do not."

"I believe I do," Morgan replied. And in my mind, I was sure that I knew, as well, since Kival and I were essentially the same age.

"Nineteen sixty-one, maybe sixty," I said, though I had not been asked.

"No, Mr. Tescott," Morgan said. "Earlier."

"How would you know that?" I asked.

"Because I knew his mother."

"What year was I born?" Kival asked and I saw the wonder rise in his eyes.

"Eighteen—fifty—nine."

My eyes widened, staring at Morgan in disbelief. I quickly looked back at Kival and found a face smiling though his chin was quivering, and tears were streaking down his cheeks. Wow! I thought. But more than wow.

Holy shit!

     Gary Stapp

CHAPTER 20

I sat reeling from the revelation that Kival was a time traveler. After all, I had been classmates with him since we were in kindergarten. But despite being essentially the same age, his birth year had actually been a full century ahead of my own. And here, in 1878, he was back where he belonged. Or more accurately, he was back to whence he belonged.

And his talisman had brought him home.

Given to him by his mother, the object had returned him to the history from which he had been taken, although he had expected to attempt the journey back through time as a solo traveler. At least, according to Kival, that had been his intention. But my birthday party at the Pyramids had become a monkey wrench in his plan, a rude coincidence that had inadvertently been poised to obstruct his chance to experiment with the talisman and learn if it could accomplish what his mother had promised him it could.

Despite the unwanted presence of others, fate chose to align with Kival's original plot. Ultimately, it was the tempestuous action of two dumbass brothers that brought Kival's plot to fruition.

My fight with Dent.

Just another disagreement that had manifested itself into a physical altercation. Mom often warned us that one day we would regret our behaviors outside whatever punishment she determined appropriate for our misconduct. And as always, she had been right. That day had been July 4th, and a mere eleven earthly rotations later I had experienced adventure beyond my imagination, but the price to ping around through time had been costly. Already, I had one friend less than I had in the beginning, and now I find out my newest friend is Buck Roger's prodigal brother. Or something like that.

"No offense, JT," Kival politely interjected, "But I wish you weren't here. I never wanted company."

I nodded in understanding. Though entirely by accident, I had been the one to signal for the Burmano-Ku-Partika, and they had come for Kival as he had hoped. But I and four others had unintentionally been swept into a galactic taxi ride with him, courtesy of the unworldly beings with ice-blue eyes. They had been our personal escorts, moving us from Point A in 1979 to the same point A, ten decades earlier and they did so in minutes, or perhaps hours, I was not entirely certain but either way it was an incredible feat.

"Unlike JT, I had nothing and no one to leave behind," Kival said to Morgan and to me. "My mother was gone, I had no one else. For months I had dwelled upon it, growing more and more eager to test the talisman. But I didn't know for sure it would even work."

But it had worked. And the transport of the six of us had been exercised in the way in which it was designed. Morgan's words, not mine, but the basis for his statement rested upon his own experience.

Morgan confessed to the two of us that the description of our ethereal escorts was a match to those who had transported him. And likewise, he acknowledged the same subjection to a blinding eruption of light, the abyss of heavy darkness, the suffering of unfathomable cold and searing pain.

Though one thing had been different.

His instrument to summon the Burmano-Ku-Partika was formed with a single perforation occupying the metallic space between the talisman's rounded edge and its central light-sucking black hole. Kival's talisman had three such apertures.

As intrigued as I was with Morgan's personal admissions, in the next moment I would learn he had an even greater surprise up his sleeve.

Without the etiquette of giving us some degree of advance notice, he reached into his mouth, and with a precise movement of his fingertips, he removed a complete lower plate of false teeth. If I had not often observed my Grampa Jake remove his set of dentures, I might have been reasonably grossed out. But the display of false teeth was not this show's headliner performance. Their removal was merely the opening act.

Morgan laid his denture plate upon the tabletop, and immediately I could see that these were not like my grandfather's. They were, for lack of a better word, sophisticated, almost artsy, as though it could as easily have been on display in an avant-garde galleria of abstract sculpture. But the oddest aspects of the device were the abnormally long, but otherwise normal-looking molars, one at each end of the horseshoe shaped apparatus. But beneath those relatively over-sized replicated teeth, the gum portion of the appliance extended downward at least a half inch and was semi-circular like a half-waning moon. And because of the extension, the plate of teeth sat upon the table tilted forward, instead of level as a normal denture would have been.

But like everything regarding Morgan, nothing had been normal.

I glanced at Morgan's cheek and wondered about the size of hole that had to have been cut from the bone of his jaw to accommodate the bulk of this denture anomaly. But I quickly found out that this display of his was only the beginning of the show-and-tell demonstration.

With the front edge of a fingernail, Morgan released some sort of miniscule lever along the simulated gumline next to the fake molar embedded on the right side. I heard a faint click, and I watched as the pearly white masticator popped up from its artificial gum. Morgan touched one end of it, and I observed that it tilted backward as though it were hinged. The deceptive tooth was merely a deep-sided lid concealing a cavity, though not the type that required an urgent visit to the dentist, but instead was a miniature storage compartment, the upper section of a cavernous space set inside the fake gum.

I was literally gobsmacked.

Then Kival and I watched as he installed his talisman inside the cavity of the false tooth where it fit with engineered precision, without so much as a hair's width of space to jiggle around. Then with a measure of gentle pressure, Morgan snapped the enameled lid back in place. I was awed by what I had just witnessed. It was simply genius.

He reached for his multi-purpose denture plate and prepared to reinsert it, but I suspected there was more he could share with us. "Wait," I said. Morgan paused and looked at me. "The other side. It looks the same. Is it also a hiding place?"

For a moment Morgan hesitated, then he moved his fingers to where I had questioned and a fingernail also found a secret lever there, and he sprung it open revealing a twin compartment. But what was inside made my head snap.

Hidden there was another talisman.

If Dent had been here, he would have dropped an F-bomb, probably a religious one. Again, Kival was startled, but managed to contain his impulsiveness to steal it away. Instead, he waited and watched as Morgan removed it and laid it upon the table so that we could more clearly examine its details. It was a match to the size, shape, and color of Kival's missing talisman, and the one Morgan claimed and had just secreted away.

Except for the holes.

Though otherwise identical, this talisman was designed with two holes equidistant from one another, both flanking the central black abyss. Kival's had three, the one Morgan had revealed to us earlier bore a solitary hole.

"Where—?" I began to ask, but Morgan stopped me with his hand, the gesture demanding I wait. Silently, Morgan replaced this third metallic disc into the space from which he had removed it and then returned the plate to its place upon the natural ridgeline of his lower jaw. Though I was experiencing the impatience of a child eager to unwrap the first gift on Christmas morning, I waited expectantly while he studiously endeavored to reset the apparatus within the cavity of his cheeks.

"There," Morgan said. "Now I will talk."

And he did.

He shared with us the story of his acquisition of the talisman with the set of two holes. He and his employer, as he dubiously referred to him, had discovered a lead in an Argentinian newspaper and the two of them had traveled to a remote village called Gan Gan, located in the central region of Northern Patagonia. There, they found an elderly man who had been the subject of their inquiries, and despite the assistance of an interpreter, there had been a long and labored attempt at communication. Having become exasperated with the language barrier, Morgan said he had impulsively decided to resort to a game of '*I'll show you mine, if you show me yours*,' and subsequently revealed to the Argentine his own talisman.

And the effort had paid off.

And a deal had been negotiated. But there had been one problem. The old man had no idea what it was and could not remember where he had found it, only that he had been a boy, walking with his father along a mountainous trail, supposedly having spied it lying within the loose rocks of the pathway.

"So, you don't know the exact geographic place this talisman is linked to?" I asked.

"Correct. Without that knowledge it is virtually useless in terms of its design and purpose to signal the Burmano-Ku-Partika. But it has helped in piecing together a premise that had been theorized by my great uncle."

"Your great uncle? How does he fit into this picture?"

"It is because of him that I have my talisman. He was born in Ethiopia, but his parents fled to Spain taking with them their two young sons, my great uncle, and his brother, who was my grandfather. My great uncle was a scientist and possessed a mind that would today be measured with an IQ most high. And he was an explorer, an unmarried man of adventure. In the year of his thirtieth birthday, he embarked upon an excursion to Gibraltar, and by accident discovered a unique and mysterious object," he said, tapping his left jaw, "this thing you call a talisman."

"This great uncle of yours," I began, "you don't mention his name. Why not?"

"I cannot. His safety resides in his anonymity. He had knowledge and abilities that were, and are still, dangerous in the wrong hands."

"You're mixing tenses. Resides, but had. He's passed away, then?"

"Yes, he has died in my time. He still lives in yours."

For a moment, I reflected upon the significance of his answer.

"And your uncle—"

"Great uncle."

"Great uncle—so, he found this talisman and eventually gave it to you, and I assumed, showed you how it worked."

"Correct."

"Why you? If you don't mind my asking?"

"Because I was the last in the lineage shared with my great uncle. My family all perished in a train bombing in Madrid in the year 2004, a cowardly act orchestrated by a terrorist organization called the Al-Qaeda. I survived, and my great uncle took me to live with him in Gibraltar, where I became his apprentice, if you will."

The loss of Morgan's family was tragic, and I realized that he had probably been nearly my age, perhaps younger, when his mom and dad had been horrifically taken from him. And then he was uprooted from a place that had been his home and transplanted to a foreign land. To some degree, I could relate to Morgan. I, too, had experienced an event that had separated me from my mom and dad, and though I was geographically still home, I was now living in a time 101 years in the past. A time long before my own mom and dad would be born. Or even my grandparents, or their parents, for that matter.

Though I was curious about this Al-Qaeda organization Morgan had spoken of, I still had unanswered questions about this mysterious relative of his.

"So, your great uncle was a scientist, but still, how did he figure out that these talismans were part of a convoluted method of moving through time?"

"When he found it, Mr. Tescott, he was simply in the right place at the right time. Purely coincidence. Or fate. Perhaps even divine intervention."

"So, obviously, he time traveled as well?"

"Of course. And ultimately quite often. But not for the sake of the destination. He was intrigued by the journey and the beings that carried him through the passageway between times. Secretly, my great uncle devoted his life to a study of the Burmano-Ku-Partika, whom he had initially met quite accidentally, much like you, Mr. Tescott."

"Yeah, only I'm not a scientist. I'm just an eighteen-year-old with a high school diploma. Though I might eventually write a book about all of this."

"Not yet. So far, I have managed to dissuade you from penning your memoirs," Morgan said smiling.

I ignored the bait and continued with my interview, "So, back to the Burmano-Ku-Partika. This great uncle of yours had obviously become well acquainted with them. Did they communicate their name to him?"

"No. During each of his encounters with them, there was never vocalized speech. He had theorized that the Burmano-Ku-Partika communicated with one another telepathically. Through his research, my great uncle believed he discovered multiple references to them in various ancient texts defined by three distinct languages. Ultimately, he deciphered the translation from his subsequent studies of associative linguistic documents. He also firmly believed these beings have existed for untold millennia."

I closed my eyes and summoned from my memory my own encounter with the Burmano-Ku-Partika, seeing the image of the one that had appeared before me, distinct, but dream-like, its face capped by a prominent cranial dome, its eyes large, and energetically ice blue.

"They must be alien, then?" I asked, opening my eyes.

"Non-human, certainly. Alien would imply they are not of this world. Even with the many encounters my great uncle shared with the Burmano-Ku-Partika, he told me he was not convinced they were from another planet or alternate galaxy."

"Then they could be ghosts, or angels, or maybe evil demons of the underworld," I said somewhat jokingly causing Kival to abandon his silence with the release of a soft chuckle. It was then I wondered what Kival's perception of the Burmano-Ku-Partika might be, especially since his experience with them was apparently double that of mine.

"Evil? No, I do not believe so. Not in the least," Morgan said. "My great uncle described them as gentle and intelligent and with skills beyond human comprehension. Once he told me how they reminded him of worker bees allegiantly performing the tasks assigned to them by an omnipotent designer."

"God?"

Morgan shrugged. "Who knows, for sure?"

I pondered the idea for a moment.

"So, back to the talisman," I said, then remembered that now there was more than one. "Or talismans," I added, pluralizing my subject. "You mentioned that your great uncle had pieced together a theory about them, I assume he developed an idea that explained their differences?"

"Correct."

"And what was his theory, this Great Uncle Einstein?"

Kival chortled in amusement, and even Morgan laughed at my stab at humor before answering my question.

In a nutshell, his great uncle had theorized that there were seven talismans, one for each continent, as designated by the different number of piercings, or holes, around the perimeter of each metallic disc. He had formed that conclusion after discovering a photograph of an image carved in a slab of rock that was among a cache of stone tablets excavated near the Chebika Oasis in the central part of the African country of Tunisia. The image depicted was a perfect match to the talisman possessed by the great uncle. Except it had six holes surrounding its black prodigious center.

"My great uncle also postulated that each of the potent discs were assigned unique time intervals measured by years, and that conclusion is valid with what we know today. Mr. Freeman's talisman separates dates that are 101 years apart. Mine takes me 145 years in either direction of the calendar. This one," he added, tapping the right side of his jaw, "is obviously unknown."

Then he paused and with his dark eyes, he captured my attention. "Additionally, my great uncle was convinced that these talismans are made of elements not found on our own galactical globe."

"Intriguing," I said, briefly contemplating that tidbit of news.

Then I decided to let my subconscious process and mull the information Morgan had shared, while I consciously and intentionally returned the conversation to the device sitting discreetly upon his jaw. "So that," I said pointing to his mouth, "is why you did what you did to the four of us, the other night in the barn. You thought maybe we had been accessorized in the same way?"

"It was a possibility."

At least, now, that explained his intrusive exploration of my mouth and the likewise examinations of my companions. But I wondered how and who had conceived such an idea, one that could easily have been an invention of Houdini or that of Leonardo da Vinci.

"Who came up with this hiding place in your mouth?" I asked.

"You did, Mr. Tescott. That is why I looked."

CHAPTER 21

I did not know whether to believe Morgan, or not. As he had frequently suggested, he and I were acquainted with one another in some future year. I could buy into that. How could I not, given that I, myself, was breathing the air of 1878, so certainly Morgan was, theoretically, as capable as I of being separated from the future. But to state that I was the engineering craftsman of a dental apparatus designed specifically to smuggle magical talismans was a freaky concept.

I was simply not that clever or industrious. At least, not yet. All modesty aside, I considered myself a pretty smart cookie, and I carried lofty expectations of what I wanted to accomplish with my life. So, why not accept Morgan's words as truth? Perhaps I would become an inventor of sorts. One thing was certain, I hungered to learn. And currently at the forefront of that gnawing desire of my mind were the Burmano-Ku-Partika and the talismans.

And Morgan's anonymous Great Uncle Whoever.

"So, Morgan, your great uncle theorized the existence of seven talisman, one for each continent. So, apparently his talisman with the single hole represents Europe, the one from Argentia with the set of two holes suggests that it's the South American talisman, and the three-holed one responsible for bringing Kival and me here confirms a North American association."

"Correct. And?"

"I'm seeing a correlation with the number count of the holes. From east to west, the number increases by one, excluding Antarctica. I'm thinking that's not a coincidence?"

"Great Uncle assumed the same. Especially since the African talisman from Tunisia bore six such piercings. However, he could only speculate that if a talisman existed with a correlation to Antarctica, he presumed it would either have seven symbolic holes, or none."

"If seven, then that would make Europe was the starting point."

"Gibraltar specifically. Do you have an idea of why that might be?" Morgan asked me.

I shrugged. In my mind, I would have thought the Burmano-Ku-Partika might have chosen a starting point in some location within the Fertile Crescent of West Asia's cradle of civilization, the bulk of which lies within the nations of Iraq and Iran.

"The Prime Meridian," Kival said aloud, as much a suggestion as a question.

I looked his way and imitated a churlish snarl. "Damn! Why didn't I think of that?" I turned my eyes to Morgan. "Is he right?"

"Perhaps. The concept of applying a grid of lines over the surface of the Earth was first suggested by a Greek astronomer and mathematician over two thousand years ago. However, I believe, as did my great uncle, that the creators of the talismans are significantly more ancient, and that their selection of the geographic locations of the portals were not random."

"That's hardly a concrete answer."

"No, it is not. Man can only know what is revealed to him."

"That doesn't help either."

Morgan laughed. "Nothing satisfies you, does it? But I can tell you this with the utmost confidence," Morgan began as he segued to a more relevant topic, "Culver Headville will come after you, Kival Freeman, if he learns of your true identity. And if that truth is made known to him, he will know your talisman brought you here."

At once my mind processed the implication of Morgan's comments. "Wait. Are you saying that Culver Headville is a time traveler—as well?"

"Of course," he replied bluntly. "I thought I had already made that clear to you during our journey here to Schoenchen?"

I felt my face flush, both with embarrassment and annoyance. After all, most of this man's comments had been fraught with riddles. "Sure, if you say so," I replied, then regrouped my thoughts. "Then Headville has been a visitor to my time?" I asked, "or did you already tell me that as well?"

"I did not," Morgan said, answering my second question. "Though it was implied," he added, signaling an answer to my first question.

For a moment, I thought about stretching the truth and telling Morgan my question had merely been rhetorical, but I was not eager to engage in a debate. Instead, I offered a third question. "Has Headville poked around in my time very often?"

"Often enough."

A fourth item of inquiry was on the tip of my tongue, but Kival interrupted me.

"Morgan, how did you know my mother?" Kival asked, and I was as keen to hear the answer, even more so than getting a reply to what I had wondered about.

Morgan studied Kival for a few silent moments. "I met her only once. She was not expecting me, but I proved to her that I was an advantage, an opportunity, and she took it. I spent two days traveling with her, and with you. But it was a journey wrought with anxiety and hardship."

"You were escorting us to JT's pyramid."

"Yes, to the portal of the archway. You see, with the help of a man named Isaiah, I had orchestrated a plan to procure the talisman in Culver Headville's possession and then convinced Kitty to use it to escape from him."

"Procured?" I asked doubtfully, then realized what was likely more truthful. "Wait—did you steal the talisman?" I asked, my voice pitching an octave higher than normal.

"I did."

"So, even fifteen years ago, you knew this Headville guy had it."

"I did not. But my employer knew it, and I trusted him completely. Unfortunately, I failed his faith in me."

"I don't get it. Obviously, you succeeded. Kival and his mom escaped into the future. How was that a failure?"

"There was an unexpected casualty."

"T'on P'ee."

"Wait—what?" I sputtered, my eyes pivoting to Kival.

"I'm right, aren't I, Morgan?" Kival asked, he and Morgan, both ignoring me.

"Yes. And no."

"You'll have to do better than that," Kival advised with a subtle shake of his head. "My memory of her is faint, but genuine. My mother called her T'on P'ee. Water sister."

I gawked at Kival. "Sister?"

"She was supposed to go through the arch with me and with my mother," Kival continued, his eyes lingering on Morgan.

"That was the plan."

"What happened?" Kivel asked.

"Culver Headville intervened."

"And?"

"That is all I will say of the matter."

"I deserve to know," Kival responded.

"Perhaps. But you will not hear it from me."

"But—"

"NO!" Morgan spouted, his voice firm. "Kival Freeman, I will not give you details. That is for someone else to decide."

My eyes shifted from one man to the other. The tension in the air between them was thick enough to cut with a knife. And Kival had just such a weapon. It was time to refocus the conversation upon Culver Headville before something regrettable occurred.

"So, Morgan, can you tell us why Headville is apparently willing to kill to get the talisman back?"

"Culver Headville," Morgan replied, seemingly willing to take the bait, "has often used that talisman to access times into which he should never have trespassed. He is an immoral man whose wealth has been predominantly compiled through his unscrupulous exploitation of a power of which the consequences of using it are unimportant to him. He feeds upon the ability to manipulate people, politics, and history. Without the talisman, he is rendered impotent to exercise further discord among this trilogy of subjects."

"Then what is there to worry about? Kival doesn't have the talisman. Nobody does," I argued.

"Lost or not, Culver Headville will never abandon his desire to repossess the talisman. With my assistance, Kival and Kitty used it to escape into the refuge of the future. There, in your time, the talisman was 101 years beyond his reach and Culver Headville was forced to resign to patience. I imagine he could only hope that the talisman would eventually be used to return to his time, and that anticipation birthed a tolerance in him to wait. And after fifteen years, his assumed faith has proved fruitful. The talisman is back within his reach."

"But he doesn't know that."

"And it is prudent, Mr. Tescott, that we maintain that secret."

"He'll never hear it from me," I assured Morgan.

"Or me," Kival echoed.

"The sincerity of your pledges are noted," Morgan replied. "Culver Headville must never be told about that place in the river. Keeping that secret from him will be the only way you will get back to your time. Unfortunately, far too many know of the talisman and its fate. Because of this, I cannot help but fear the worst."

"If you're implying that Dent or Blaine might let the cat out of the bag, I promise you, they won't. Not when they learn the importance of keeping their mouths shut."

"And what about your other companion? Oleander? Are you as equally confident of his discretion?"

Oleander.

I had forgotten about him.

"No," I confided with a sigh.

"Then, do not be overly optimistic. Remember, I have witnessed Oleander's behavior. I have overheard his words and I have observed his rebellious behavior."

"Then saving him was a major risk. Why did you do it?"

"Because it was the right thing to do."

Instantly, I was ashamed of myself. "It was the right thing," I admitted, but my gut was telling me that Oleander Sedgwick could easily be our downfall. "Luckily for us, Oleander knows nothing about the talisman."

"But he knows enough to be dangerous," Kival suggested.

"That's an accurate assessment. I'm not sure Oleander is smart enough to understand how critical it is that we blend in with this 1878 citizenry. That, frankly, is a challenge to all of us."

"Agreed," said Morgan. "That is why the intelligent thing to do would be to go elsewhere from here, to eliminate the possibility of crossing paths with Culver Headville."

"I'm not going anywhere," Kival interrupted, his tone adamant.

"Mr. Freeman, among your friends, you are in the most peril. If Culver Headville suspects that any of you are time travelers, you will not escape his determination to identify you specifically. There is a chance he might recognize you. For certain, if he learns that you have returned to your time, he will use any means necessary to extract from you the one thing he desires most."

"Doesn't matter. I'm staying here."

I looked at Kival, surprised by his conviction. Then my eyes fell upon the derby hat sitting on the table in front of me, in the home of Anja Beilman. Of course. Now I understood why he was eager to stay.

A moment later, I was struck by an idea. "Morgan, Headville can't take something we don't have."

"Exactly. But if you don't have it, you, or any one of your other companions might be expendable from Culver Headville's point of view."

"Are you saying, you think he might kill us?"

"What I am saying, Mr. Tescott, is do not tempt him. Neither do I believe he would be so foolish to harm any of you. Your knowledge of the talisman's location is far too valuable to him to risk being taken to the grave."

"Then if Kival stays, I say we all stay. I don't like the idea of splitting up."

Morgan shrugged. "You're the boss, Mr. Tescott. But may I offer two suggestions?"

"Of course," I replied, ignoring the implication that I was actually in charge."

"First, hide this man," Morgan said, staring at Kival.

"Where?" I asked.

"In the best place possible."

"And just where is that?" Kival asked him doubtfully.

"In plain sight. Here, among the Volga German community."

I caught the hint of a smile lift at the corners of Kival's lips. "I am good with that plan," Kival promptly agreed. I glanced again at the derby hat.

"Then what?" I asked.

"Distance yourself from him," Morgan said, nodding at Kival. "You and your brother, and the other two. All of you must empty Kival from your mind. Remove him from your conversations. Do not let your knowledge of his existence spill from your lips."

"I can keep a secret," I said. "And I'm pretty sure I can get Dent and Blaine on board."

"You promised!" Kival sputtered urgently.

"I won't tell them specifics. Only that you need protecting. That you're in danger because of the talisman. That's something they already know about. The real problem will be Oleander Sedgwick. He's a wildcard. I've never known him to keep his mouth shut. Even when it's to his advantage. He's missing a finger to prove his stupidity." I looked at Morgan. "You should take Oleander with you," I suggested.

"No, I will not," he said with a stern shake of his head. "Not under any circumstance."

"Then take Kival with you. Wouldn't that make the most sense to keep him safe?"

"No!"

This time it was Kival who objected.

"I won't go. I'm staying here. HERE," he emphasized, "where I belong."

Discussion closed.

"Then we'll just deal with Oleander. Somehow." I paused for a moment then added, "I could kill him, I suppose. I've often dreamed of choking him with my bare hands."

Kival chuckled softly, and I looked across at him, both of us pushing a grin into the corners of our mouths. "Get in line," he said, and my face bloomed into a smile.

Then suddenly I remembered the conversation Dent and I had exchanged with Oleander a few days earlier, and I was instantly optimistic.

"You know, I think that conceited, self-centered asshole may not be a problem after all."

"I advise you, Mr. Tescott, not to commit murder."

"No, no, no. I was just kidding, of course," I replied with relative sincerity. "The thing is, when Dent and I were in town the other day, Oleander asked about Blaine and Sam. But he didn't ask about you, Kival."

"I'm crushed," he smirked, but I ignored his sarcasm.

"Oleander's world revolves solely around things and people that benefit him. Truth be told, my brother is the only one of us here who means anything to him. Not me, not Blaine, and luckily, Kival, you are less than nothing. So low on the Oleander social ladder that he's apparently not given you a second thought. And since Oleander didn't ask about you, neither Dent nor I mentioned you at all."

"His indifference regarding Kival is promising," Morgan offered.

"Yeah, I think so," I agreed. "For the record, he did ask about Sam, and when we told him that Sam had died, he assumed it was because of the Indians and we didn't correct him. If the dumbass ever thinks to ask about Kival, I will just tell him he was a victim of the Indians as well. And he would believe me. And probably wouldn't even dwell on it again."

"Thanks, JT," Kival chided. "If I had an ego, you would have just flattened it."

"Sorry."

"So, Morgan, if I'm hiding here with the Beilman family, what is JT supposed to do in the meantime?"

"Right," I agreed. "Elaborate on the distancing suggestion."

"My advice for you, Mr. Tescott, is to adapt yourself into the society of this time. Hence the money I have staked for you. Though I would prefer that you integrate elsewhere, perhaps the risk is worth it to keep all of you close. When we recover the talisman, it will be imperative that you are nearby. The window for your return could possibly be just a few hours. Perhaps less. Time spent looking for you or for the others will be time lost. If you miss the window, your next opportunity will not come for twelve more months. I doubt you will want such a lengthy delay."

"Damn right."

"You speak pretty confidently about the talisman," Kival stated, though doubtful. "How do you know we'll ever find it again."

"I am confident because of him," Morgan replied, his eyes moving to stare at me with a glint of mischievous accusation.

"Because of me?" I asked. "And why, exactly, is that?" I added, though I suspected his reply would be enigmatic and evasive, as usual.

"Simply because I know you."

"So, you say."

Morgan laughed. "Ah, Mr. Tescott, you are truly an engaging young man."

"And you, Morgan, are incapable of giving a straight answer."

"I am obligated by a promise."

"To me, I suppose? Or more accurately, the future me."

Morgan laughed. "You are finally catching the drift, as those of your generation have coined." At once, he crossed to the door and opened it. "And now, I have a train to catch."

Waving off an anticipated litany of questions from me, Morgan emphatically suggested that I assemble Dent and Blaine for an immediate departure from the Beilman farm.

"And then what?" I asked.

"Then I will escort the three of you to Hays City."

"And after that?"

"You assimilate, Mr. Tescott. For the time being, 1878 is your home."

CHAPTER 22

With our meeting adjourned, we left the sod house, me going one way while Kival and Morgan crossed as a pair to the newer house and knocked at the backdoor. Ruta appeared and invited them inside. In that moment I noticed that Kival had remembered his hat.

I headed for the barn and found Dent squatting against the shoulder of his bay horse, an elevated front foot resting across my brother's bent knee. In his hand was a metal pick he was using to loosen and remove the jam of dirt, mud, and manure that had become packed around the frog of the horse's interior hoof. He dropped the animal's foot and straightened to look at me.

"Well?" he asked, and I knew he wanted details.

"Here," I said handing him one of the four bags of coins Morgan had unpacked from his saddlebag.

"What's this?" Dent asked, feeling the bumpy exterior of the soft leather sack, and weighing it in the palm of his hand.

"An apology from the man with the big intrusive fingers."

"Damn," he said, "suddenly I feel like a whore. So, what gives?"

"Morgan is supplying us with a bankroll. We're going to be on our own for a while."

"Good! That's music to my ears," he said, fingering a handful of coins from the bag. "How long is this petty change supposed to last us?"

"In this economy, a year."

"No shit?!"

"Saddle up. We're moving out."

"Where to now?"

"Hays City."

"Hot jiggety!"

"Where's Blaine?"

"Wondered into town. On foot, no less. About ten minutes ago."

"Hopefully he'll be back soon."

Without waiting for Blaine, Dent brushed and then saddled his bay, cinching the riding tack tight around the gelding's belly. I stepped into the stall where my own horse waited, though I first took a glimpse of the baby calf that lay at the feet of his momma, apparently content with his first feeding of his mother's milk. A cutie, I thought, and without intending to, I sighed. A part of me was going to miss this place. But only a small part.

I slipped the bridle over Buck's head and led him out into the wide-open space of the barn and copied Dent from brush to cinch. Inside my saddlebag, I packed the purse of coins I had been given by Morgan, as well as the two others I had yet to distribute.

Saddled and ready to go, we lead the horses outside just as Morgan and Kival and the three Beilmans exited the house.

"Where is Mr. Wallace?" Morgan asked, glancing around.

"He's not here," I told him. "He didn't go far, just a walk into the village."

"I cannot wait for him."

"You heard the man, Kival," Dent said, then tipped his head toward the barn. "Giddy-up."

"I'm not … not going with you," Kival stammered. "I'm staying … here."

I saw Dent give him the once-over, then raised his eyes to Anja, standing upon the porch, her hands wrapped around an awning post. "Of course, you're staying," Dent grinned then turned and winked at me, before returning his attention to Kival. "Now, come on, dude, go saddle your horse. Just Morgan here is anxious to hit the road."

"Dent, really, he's not going with us."

"Why the hell not?"

"I'll explain later."

Morgan crossed to the hitching rail where he had tied the grullo stallion he called Viento and mounted. "Come, Mr. Tescott. Your brother will wait for Mr. Wallace, then the two of them can meet you at John White's home."

"Fine by me," Dent assured Morgan. "I'd prefer Blaine's company, anyway."

I stepped close to my brother. "Dent, like he said, I'll meet you guys there. But listen, don't say anything to Oleander about Kival. Not a word. And tell Blaine the same."

"Why all the mystery?"

"I'm serious. Not a word. If he asks, which I doubt he will, just say Kival died with Sam," I added, then slid my foot into the stirrup and seated myself in the saddle, just has Morgan nudged Viento into a trot and entered the narrow roadway that connected the Beilman farm to the village of Schoenchen. "I promise, I'll explain everything to you later." And with a wave to Helmut and Ruta, I spurred Buck into a canter and followed Morgan.

Together, we trotted through the small community, and like a few days earlier, the singing masons were back on the job, and I noticed that considerable progress had been made with the construction of the church. It would not be long before the men would be harmonizing as a choir within the walls of their new place of worship.

We crossed the shallow ford of the river and headed north. I looked forward to spending more time with Morgan, especially since he was leaving. I still had a question or two for him. But truthfully, I anticipated asking him about multiple things.

"Morgan, what year in the future are you from?" I queried, hoping he was in the mood to talk.

"When I departed last, it was 2020."

"Wow, even from my own 1979, that's a lot of years in between."

"Indeed."

"So, anything fascinating going on in the world when you left?"

"A viral pandemic was spreading across the globe. It was devastatingly contagious. And deadly."

"Oh! Jeez!" I exclaimed, not expecting such a dire answer. "Wait— wasn't that risky? I mean, what if you had carried the virus back with you?"

"I assure you, Mr. Tescott, I was not oblivious to the risk. But Gibraltar was in a general lockdown, and I had been self-isolating for three months prior to the day of the aphelion. And I had under-taken multiple tests to ensure that I neither had the virus, nor was I an asymptomatic carrier of the contagion. But your concern is valid. If someone were to bring such a virus into this time, it would be as catastrophic as the predestined Spanish Flu will be when unleashed in four decades hence."

"I'm sorry, I did not mean to suggest you were careless. Sometimes I just speak my mind without thinking first. I need to work on fixing that."

"Do not worry, Mr. Tescott. You did fix it."

I looked across at him as we rode along. If I had not personally experienced the construct of time travel, it would be an incredible idea that Morgan was from my future.

"What, then, is the year of your current time?"

"It would be 2023. A decade earlier was the era of time in which I had first become acquainted with you, Mr. Tescott. Though in that time, you are of course a much older man. An esteemed elder," Morgan added with a bow of his head. I did the math. I would be age sixty-two. Damn, that was old.

"Wait," I said, suddenly doing simpler arithmetic. "If you left in 2020, then you've been here, in this time, for three years?"

"Correct."

"But you said you were expecting me at the Pyramids just a few days ago."

"Also correct."

"Then why did you come back to this time so dang early?"

"I have a—a fondness for this time and place."

His hesitation made me wonder. Was there a certain someone of whom he was also fond? Perhaps his abrupt visit to Nicodemus was more than just business. I decided not to ask, instead, I blinked at the thought of my own romantic notions of the Old West. "Yeah, well, I used to fantasize about living it up here in the time of Louis L'Amour's Western novels. But not so much now."

"It is a challenging era in which to live one's life. But all times have their unique difficulties and rewards."

"Tell me more about your time, Morgan. What was 2020 like? And 2023, when you get back, do you think the pandemic will still be raging?"

"I predict the Covid-19 virus will have largely been eradicated, but still active within the web of the human race. Perhaps even usurped by a new variant. There will always be some threat to humanity, whether natural or man-made. Sadly, I suspect that poverty and world hunger has continued to grow exponentially. I expect the income gap between those with means and those without has become wider than ever. And no doubt families are still being ripped apart by world-wide wars and domestic violence and by political differences fueled by immoral and corrupt men and women of power."

"You don't make my future sound very appealing. I mean, I don't have my head stuck in the sand in 1979, but I never considered it to be bad to be there, you know?"

"As coined by the English poet, Thomas Gray, ignorance is bliss," Morgan replied, implying that I did have my head buried somewhere. "But not to worry, Mr. Tescott, the future that awaits you in the twenty-first century is full of many miraculous things. You would not believe the technology."

"Such as?"

"Before I departed, I installed an audio-video doorbell on my home in Gibraltar. It is wirelessly connected to a variety of surveillance apparati that is affordable for the everyday man. I am able to monitor when my friend down the street, Mr. Saeed, comes knocking at my door, or when a delivery arrives from my favorite store, Amazon, whether I am home or not. There are automobiles that are capable of driving and parking themselves without human assistance. We have the ability to electronically talk to our homes, to tell them to adjust the air-conditioning or when to turn on the oven. And our houses, they listen and do as they are instructed!"

"There are monsters that have been created for the movie screen that with the proper eyewear they appear so real that you can be made to believe that you could be eaten alive while sitting in your theatre seat. There are computers capable of lightning speed calculations of the most complicated and complex formulas and are available in a size as small as a thin paper notebook and named as such. And despite forty years of inflation, this personal computer can be purchased for half the cost that you, Mr. Tescott, would have had to pay for an Apple II PC."

I glanced at him, preparing to lift an eyebrow of doubt to notify him that I was not going to be easily convinced to buy such a boast. But, I listened, and was awed by the prospect of his claims.

"The best, though, is the smart phone. With it, you can make telephone calls and send text messages to and from almost anywhere in the civilized world, but not such a big deal, right? What is most amazing is that you can also use this portable wireless device to watch movies and live broadcasts of sporting events, and access unlimited global data on an informational network called the World Wide Web. And this phone, it has proven to be an excellent camera as well."

Okay, now I was dumbfounded. For a moment I wondered if Morgan was also acquainted with a real-life George Jetson.

"What I wouldn't give to have one of those," I said, my mind reeling of the possibilities.

"You do have one, Mr. Tescott. You and millions of others possess them, including hundreds of thousands of children, if you can believe such an indulgence."

Suddenly, I felt impatient. If these things, and probably much more, were true, I did not want to wait to become an old man before experiencing them.

"Take me with you, Morgan. You can, can't you?"

"I can. But I will not."

"Why not?"

"Because you are already there, Mr. Tescott. At least you were when I left."

"But Morgan, I want to be able to see my parents again," I said, shifting to a more personal reason to be allowed to go with him. "I want to hug my mom, and to tell my dad that I'm sorry."

"That is not possible. They are gone."

"Gone?"

"They have passed."

At once, the weight of his words crushed my soul and I wept. I could not stop myself. It did not matter that the news of their deaths was related to a future I had yet to live. Those words, 'they have passed' cut deep, and I knew it was because I fearfully doubted that I would ever see them again. It took a few minutes, but the rational side of my brain finally got my shit together and reminded me that Mom and Dad still lived in my time. The time I had been a part of little more than a week ago.

"I'm sorry. I just—"

"Do not be apologetic for loving or grieving someone."

"Right," I said, then I exhaled deeply and brushed the wetness from my cheeks. I felt about as foolish as I had ever been. "This time travel business … it's confusing."

"Most certainly."

"So, I've been thinking about it, you know, the basic concept of time. To me, it's irrational to believe that the clock of the universe can just be rewound or spun forward then back again. Yet here I am breathing the air of absurdity. I suppose I could just buy into the existence of parallel worlds that are offset by a few years here and there and that the talisman is just a means to slide from one dimension to another."

"A reasonable hypothesis," Morgan said, adding "for a layman."

"Ok, sir," I began, more sarcastic than I intended, "please share with me a professional opinion."

"You will not like this perspective."

"Try me."

Morgan glanced at me and smiled.

"What?"

"We have already indulged in this conversation. Before, in the future."

"Indulge me again."

He waited for a count of ten, then spoke. "It has been suggested that time travel is all in the mind."

I looked at him, waiting for more enlightenment. "That's it? You're saying I'm just imagining all this?"

"No. I believe your existence here, in this time, is completely authentic. But, what if, all of this," Morgan said with a gesture of his hand, "is only a magnificently designed hallucination? A place populated by tangible, living things set within the scope of adaptive human experience, totally created and sustained in *their* minds."

"Whose minds?"

"The Burmano-Ku-Partika."

"Shit," I said, believing that Morgan was proposing that time travel was nothing more than a data file residing inside the head of an alien being. "That's—that's just too freaky to think about."

"I agree with you completely, now, as well as I did later, when we had this discussion before," he added, grinning at me again. "And for the record, this hypothesis was spawned by my great uncle, though I responded to his idea with a dissenting opinion. I prefer believing in the concept of parallel worlds, as you put it. That way, I can sleep easier," he added, and I noted that he did not offer a smile.

We rode in silence, a mile passing beneath the hooves of our horses, and I contemplated the infinite complexities of time and the improbability of understanding its shifting nuances, allowing a few seconds to anxiously wonder if I was truly inside the cranium of one of the Burmano-Ku-Partika. However, one thing I was certain about was that Morgan and I have history. So, to speak.

"Wait," I suddenly blurted, a thought flashing like a yellow traffic light, telling me to slow up and stop for a minute. "In my future where I know you, I assume Dent is there? I mean, he must be! Obviously, I get back, right? And what about Sam? Is he there?"

"Your friend Sam, died, Mr. Tescott."

"Did he? Do I know that? I keep thinking about the Burmano-Ku-Partika—they healed me when they brought me here. I had cuts and scrapes on my face, thanks to my brother. But I didn't have them when I woke up!" I looked at Morgan, expectant, but he said nothing. "Why couldn't they fix Sam, too? I mean, I know it was different when he died. We weren't at the arch, Sam didn't have the talisman, but still maybe they returned him, alive," I continued, my emotions again becoming raw, "to our time. It's possible, right?" I looked at Morgan, my eyes begging to know.

"Perhaps."

"That's it? That's all I get? Perhaps?! Bullshit! You have to tell me!"

"No. I do not."

"But I need to know!"

"No, you do not, Mr. Tescott."

"But you know, don't you, Morgan? You know!"

"A man whom I have recently come to love like a father, and of whom I greatly respect, once told me that I know nothing, and that I know too much. Knowledge of such matters can rob you of hope instead of giving it to you. It can diminish the importance of acting with caution and accepting responsibility. You have only one life, my young friend. If you knew you had the proverbial nine lives of cat, one day you would still become a dead cat. If I have learned one thing from my experience with time travel, it is better not to know what or who is in your future. That knowledge cannot necessarily comfort you. It only holds you back from living in the present. It keeps you from appreciating each and every day God has given to you. Trust me, you do not want to know."

I relented. There was wisdom in his words. I even understood the thing about the cat.

"So, I guess I'll just stick to Plan A and hang around here and wait."

"That is the best plan. But there is something else you should be wary of, Mr. Tescott. You are a trespasser. You have crossed into a time that does not belong to you, and neither do you belong to it. A time where even the smallest of your actions could change the lives of thousands of people, perhaps millions. You may find yourself drawn to interfere with a dynamic or to engage in a relationship with someone outside the parameters of your time, but you must not allow yourself to do so. You must not purposely attempt to rewrite history, as Culver Headville has done."

"What do you mean?"

"He did not subscribe to the logic of my great uncle, to act solely as a spectator when trespassing into other times. Instead, he has selfishly and contemptuously toyed with history and gambled with the lives of others. He has tangled and knotted and unraveled various threads of the fabric of the past while trespassing into the future. He has even attempted, with some degree of success, to change the course of American Politics."

"What did he do?"

"The year you were born, Mr. Tescott, who was the President of the United States?"

I thought for a moment. "John F. Kennedy. He was our thirty-fifth president."

"And who succeeded him?"

"Lyndon B. Johnson. He became president the day Kennedy was assassinated. I was only two years old at the time."

"And what was his number, this President Johnson?"

"Thirty-six, of course."

"Specific to the history of my time, Richard Nixon was elected as the thirty-sixth president of the United States. Succeeding the two-term presidency of John Fitzgerald Kennedy."

I stared at Morgan as though he had just confessed to me that he was an extra-terrestrial cross-dresser from the planet Neptune. "How is that possible?"

"Because I corrected an injustice, a blatant interference instigated as a mere amusement for a narcissistic and maniacal man."

"What are saying?"

"Culver Headville employed the use of the talisman and with the knowledge and ability to travel into the future, he assassinated Kennedy and framed the Lee Harvey Oswald of your history books, before fleeing back to the safety and obscurity of his own time."

With a countenance of disbelief, I just stared at him. Had I heard Morgan correctly? Had he just pointed the finger at Culver Headville as the true assassin of JFK? And what did he mean by *my history books?*

"Morgan, are you telling me that in my past, the one where you and I will ultimately share a future, John F. Kennedy was never assassinated?"

"That is correct. For now."

"What do you mean for now?"

"History is a fallacy, Mr. Tescott. There is not one single past, concrete and unchangeable."

"That sounds weirder to me than your great uncle's all-in-the-mind-of-an-alien theory."

"Perhaps. But know and remember this: There are others, dozens, or perhaps hundreds, like you and me who have crossed over into what is commonly described as parallel worlds of existence. For some of them, the crossing was accidental, as it was for you. For others, the crossing of time is purely for scientific purposes, to conduct research and exploration with a minimum degree of disturbance.

"Like your great uncle," I said.

He nodded. "But there have been others who have, or who will, exploit the ability to time travel for the benefit of their own wealth and power and entertainment. And they care not of what the cost might be to the lives of the innocent and unsuspecting. Culver Headville is one of those people. And he and others with like temperaments, have played games with what you have been taught to believe about history.

That is why Culver Headville should never regain possession of the talisman. It is also why he hungers to get it back."

"Not to sound like I'm in the same brotherhood as this Culver Headville guy, but why don't you just take him out? Kill Culver Headville and stop him from his madness."

"That, Mr. Tescott, is an immoral action I am not willing to take. Remember, the slightest event can profoundly change the course of a history, whatever version that might be. I do not want to bear such direct responsibility. And neither should you."

At once, I thought of the deaths of Morgan's family. "What about going back in time and making changes for the good. Like saving your parents. With your talisman, you could do that, couldn't you?"

"Perhaps. But, what of the others who died in the train bombings. I could not possibly save all of them. What if by chance or design I managed to deflect the death of one other person, and in the resultant future he or she becomes responsible for the death of another, or the demise of many innocent lives? No, Mr. Tescott, I could not live with that. I will not play God."

"But you're helping me, and Kival, and the rest of us."

"This is different. You do not belong here."

"Okay, okay. It was just a thought." And then I had another. "The talisman. This Culver Headville, he stole it from Kival's mother, didn't he?"

"Indirectly. If it had been a perfect world, his mother would have inherited the talisman. She certainly would not have abused it. But that is only my opinion."

"And with your help she got back what should have been hers in the first place and escaped with it by way of the arch and the aphelion," I suggested.

"Not exactly. The arch of your Pyramids, yes. But the aphelion is a day of the year allowing only travel *backward* into time."

I looked at him, suddenly confused. It was my understanding that he had already thoroughly and completely explained the prerequisites of this mode of time travel. "When then?" I asked, not having a clue.

"The perihelion, Mr. Tescott."

"Ah," I said, as I extracted the information from my brain. "The point in the orbit of the earth that places it closest to the sun."

"Correct. Again."

"And when is that, typically?"

"By the astrological calculations made by experts from my time, it is expected to occur in six months, on the third day of January."

"So, let me get this straight. You're telling me the perihelion works the opposite of the aphelion?"

"Yes. By means of its calendric arrival, it opens a passageway allowing one to travel forward into time."

I was thinking, my brain accelerating in over-drive. "The same number of years?"

"For the portal of your Pyramid arch, yes."

"Then that is my way back, isn't it? Back to the time that I belong to."

"Correct. So now, Mr. Tescott. You know the place and the date to be there. But you still need one thing."

"The lost talisman." I said, sighing with defeat.

"That is why I must leave for Gibraltar. It is there, in a place teetering near the sheer edge of the towering rock where lies the portal of 145 years that is interconnected with my talisman. It is my passageway forward to the new year of 2024. I must be there this January 1879. To be ready and in place for my transport. Obviously, it will take some amount of time to travel by train, then by way of a ship across the Atlantic. For your sake, and that of your friends, I must leave at once so that I can overcome any contingencies that could delay my arrival. And I will need as much time as possible to prepare for my return."

Suddenly the light bulb in my brain flickered to life and I realized what Morgan was going to do. And not only that, but days ago I had thought of it myself. "You're going into the future to get a metal detector and bring it back to here, to this time, aren't you?"

Morgan laughed. "Technically, yes. But it will be a more advanced machine than a simple metal detector known by you in your time of technology. What I plan to smuggle back here will be far more sophisticated and with capabilities that should ensure the location and retrieval of your lost talisman."

"What's it called?"

"I don't know yet. I will have six months to develop and test it," he said, more as a statement of confidence than one of arrogance.

"So, the best-case scenario is you travel back to Gibraltar in January, then return here a year from now by way of the aphelion, then we find the talisman, then I and Dent and the others get back home six months later passing through the portal of January 1880. Right?"

"Yes. At best."

"Jeez, Morgan," I sighed, "that's a year and a half away. At best." I thought of Mom and Dad. Eighteen months spent wondering and worrying and likely fearing the worst. Those months would probably feel like a decade or longer to them.

"If the talisman had not been lost, your way back could have been just a few months away. If more time is needed to develop my device, another year will pass. If, by some miraculous misfortune, Culver Headville finds the talisman before we do, the return to your time could be indefinite."

"That's a lot of ifs," I said, shaking my head. And despite Morgan knowing me from the future, his revelation of multiple versions of history had to also be applicable to versions of the future. Getting back home from this time could not be guaranteed. "I gotta be honest. Eighteen months is going to be tough enough. I don't want to even think about it taking another year, or two, or never."

"I understand your trepidation. I will endeavor to do my best to get you back home sooner, than later."

"Thank you," I replied with genuine gratitude, my eyes reading the sincerity reflected in the depths of his own dark pupils. Then, my gaze was drawn to Morgan's horse and suddenly I had a new question.

"What about Viento?" I asked Morgan. "Does he get to launch into the future with you?"

"He does not. He could if I chose to take him with me. Instead, I plan to leave him in the care of a good friend of mine."

"Oh," I said, doubting that I had masked my disappointment. "Who? Helmut?"

"You, Mr. Tescott. I am leaving Viento with you."

CHAPTER 23

Morgan and I crossed Big Creek and rode into the southern perimeter of Hays City pointing our horses toward the grand three-floor Ellis County courthouse peeking over the cluster of buildings in the commercial part of town where Dent and I had explored a few days earlier. Avoiding a ride down either side of Main Street, Morgan guided us along the side street that took us past the newspaper office where I had encountered the congenial man who had shared a ride with the pretty girl with blonde curls. A daughter escorted by her father, I had assumed. I could not help but wish for another glimpse of her. I furtively glanced around looking for three blondes, the girl or the pair of Palominos that pulled her carriage. I got what I expected, though not what I hoped for.

No sign of the lovely young lady. Or the horses.

A block and a half later, Morgan and I arrived at the law office of Nathaneil J. Penny.

We entered the quaint establishment and found it occupied by a tall man with a potbelly that strained against the buttons of his vest. He appeared to be around the age of fifty and had a crop of short gray hair surrounding the naked crown of his head, an example of the male pattern baldness of which I feared I was genetically destined. Briefly, it occurred to me to ask Morgan if the me that he knows in the future of his time has hair, but I figured he wouldn't tell me. Likely, he would suggest that my knowledge of that detail would also fall under the category of 'information best not to know about' in my future, and though I could debate otherwise, I was not going to argue the point, especially since Morgan was gifting me his horse.

Following introductions, Morgan asked the attorney to draw up a bill of sale, in triplicate, from him to me for Viento. Since Morgan was leaving his stallion with me, he wanted to ensure that no one could challenge my possession of the Thoroughbred, but at the very least guard against the possibility of a false accusation from someone declaring that I had stolen the horse, which, in this day and age was a hanging offense.

I was completely on board with the idea. I was, after all, rather fond of my neck.

Our next stop was a boarding stable for horses. There, Morgan introduced me to the livery's proprietor, Dub O'Brien, a stout little Irishman who looked as though he could beat a man to a pulp if he were so inclined. And considering his prominently broken nose and the long, jagged scar that traced its way downward from his left eye before disappearing into the thick kinks of his red beard, I could easily imagine the pummeling he could deliver to an opponent who would likely end up looking worse than, well, than the face of himself.

A regular customer, Morgan negotiated a boarding fee with the man, agreeing to fifty dollars for a year's stay. And informing Dub that he could expect me to frequently come and take the horse out for a weekly exercise, if not more often. I didn't say anything. I was just in my own little world, imagining myself getting acquainted with the grullo stallion as both his rider and his owner, and not just a two-bit cowboy who only gawked at his beauty and said things to him like 'nice horsey'.

Concluding our business with the Irishman, we circled back two blocks to a less-busy stretch of the main street, then crossed the railroad tracks and turned west on the next street, riding the length of that block. We passed two buildings that were in the early stages of construction, indicating that Hays City was a growing community.

Upon arriving at the Pennsylvania House hotel, we tied the horses out front and walked inside where Morgan was greeted by a tall, wiry man with a handlebar moustache stretching above a pair of thin lips.

"No mail for ya, today either, Mr. Morgan," the hotelman said as he slid a room key across the counter.

"Good. I was not expecting any, Mr. Keeler," Morgan replied, and I thought if he had perhaps received any letters or correspondence, they would have likely been sent from across the pond and stamped with a date one-hundred and forty-five years in the future. Keeping my thought to myself, I listened as Morgan asked Mr. Keeler if I, and three of my companions, could be allowed to use his room for the remainder of the month, since he had already paid for a full thirty days in advance.

"Well, Mr. Morgan, I don't know," the mustachioed innkeeper said with hesitation. "Four you say? I'd have to get another bed put in up there."

"I understand, Mr. Keeler. What would you charge for the inconvenience?"

"Well," the man replied, sending his eyes upward as he did a bit of mental math. "Two bits."

Morgan laid a dollar coin on the counter. "More than reasonable," he said.

"Each."

From his pocket he withdrew two identical gold coins and laid them next to the first. "Payment for the three extra guests. Mr. Tescott is temporarily taking my place, therefore his stay has already been paid, agreed?

"Of course," he said, sweeping up the money.

"And, please, Mr. Keeler, have the room ready for this evening, and make sure each of my young friends has his own pillow."

"Consider it done, Mr. Morgan."

We left the hotel lobby and took the stairs to the second floor and walked to the far end of the hallway and entered a surprisingly spacious room furnished with a full-sized bed, a large bureau of five drawers, and a small table set with a silver-backed mirror and a wash bowl, and paired with a chair. An oil lamp sat upon a tiny round table next to the bed, and a second lamp was perched upon the bureau. Though I had no idea, I assumed the place was par for a basic hotel room in the 1870s. For certain, it was not the Cosmopolitan Hotel in which I had stayed while in Denver on our last family vacation. For one thing, there was no sign of an ensuite bathroom.

I sat on the edge of the bed while Morgan emptied the top drawer of an assortment of extra clothing and shaped them into a roll and then packed the articles into one side of the saddlebag he had brought in with him.

"Nice place," I said.

"An adequate accommodation."

"After four nights of sleeping in a barn, it'll feel like I'm staying at a five-star hotel. Can you get a hot bath here?"

"Mr. Keeler can arrange it. Four bits. Soap is extra."

"I'll pay it. I'm starting to itch in places I'd rather not scratch."

"Speaking of assets," Morgan began, then bent and pulled open the bottom drawer of the clothes chest. He removed it completely from its cavity and laid it aside. "I managed a modification," he said, moving to his knees and reaching deep toward the back of the narrow space.

"Big surprise," I said, thinking there could be no end to what he might use to secret away things. When he sat back upon the heels of his boots, he held a relatively thin wooden box and inside were two small leather bags identical to the ones Morgan had given Kival and I. And they looked pretty darn full.

"You don't trust banks," I commented.

"Not trust," he replied. "This I have done more out of convenience for me. This way I am not restricted to access my funds based upon the hours of bankers."

"So, another one of your hidey-holes," I said with a grin and a tap to the side of my jaw.

He smiled. "That is one way to put it." Then he removed the money sacks from the box and handed the rectangular wooden sleeve to me. "I would recommend that you use this 'hidey-hole' to safeguard the money I gave to you and to your companions. It is not wise to leave so much wealth in an unsupervised saddlebag."

Shit.

Did I feel like an idiot?

"Good advice," I said, bolting up from the bed and leaving the hotel room. A few moments later, I returned with my saddlebag, but only after a quick check to confirm that I had not been embarrassingly robbed. I looked at Morgan apologetically, but he said nothing. His lesson had been successfully taught. His student not above learning things the hard way.

I loaded the secret box with two of the three bags still in my possession, then from one, I took a handful of coins and stuffed them into the front pocket of my tan pants. Having made the withdrawal, I placed my sack of wealth at the far-left side of the container, opposite the other two.

"Only three?" Morgan asked as he opened the flap of the brown envelope given to him by the lawyer.

"I gave Dent his already, back at the Beilmans. He—he meant to thank you, I'm sure."

"His gratitude was not expected. But do impress upon him, Mr. Tescott, that he and the others should spend frugally. You do not want to give anyone the appearance that you are men of means, if you will." I nodded with understanding. "Now," Morgan continued, taking one of the two documents from the envelope and handing it to me. "Keep this original bill of sale safe. I will keep the copy, and as you know, Mr. Penny has a copy for his records."

I refolded the piece of heavy paper and tucked it into the pocket of my pants. Then, prompted by a second thought, I replanted the ownership transfer letter into the box beside my cache. I then dropped to my knees and refitted the box into the low space of the bureau and replaced the drawer and stood. I turned and found Morgan gazing at me, his face sullen, seemingly apologetic.

"Mr. Tescott, I'm afraid I almost failed you, again. I had not realized my error until after I had left for Nicodemus."

"What then?" I asked, but his silence was heavy, and I realized whatever it was, it must be important. "There's a saying, you know," I said to him, 'Better late than never'."

"Indeed," he said sitting in the chair at the small table. "Earlier, I shared with you and your friends the prerequisites necessary to travel through the Burmano-Ku-Partika's passageway of time."

"I remember. There are three. The date of the aphelion, the archway of the pyramid, and the talisman."

"There is a fourth."

"Oh," I said, my surprise not well-hidden. Morgan did not strike me as one to forget anything of significance, especially as important as this.

"I recall mentioning to you the aspect of the daylight hours of the aphelion. What I failed to tell you was why the daylight is important. More than important. Absolutely necessary."

"Go on."

"Once you are in the archway with the talisman, on the day of the aphelion, or perihelion as may be the case, a specific source of energy is required to ignite the power of the talisman and summon the Burmano-Ku-Partika."

"Solar power," I said, realizing the significance of the daylight hours.

"Correct," Morgan said, nodding his head and smiling. "In the many years I have known you, you never cease to amaze me."

"To be honest, you gave me a pretty big hint."

"Perhaps. But, yes, sunlight MUST strike the dark core of the talisman."

"Which caused the explosion of bright light around us."

"If sunlight does not strike, nothing will happen."

"Nothing?"

"Nothing. So, remember, if all other requirements are in place, darkness can still rob you of the opportunity. As could also a veil of clouds."

"Okay," I said, thinking I'll have to remember to check the weather before I make my travel plans. "But nothing for me to worry about now, right? Until we get the talisman back, anyway. And then, well, you'll be back by then, so … "

"That is the plan."

"You are coming back, aren't you Morgan?"

"Neither heaven nor earth will stop me, Mr. Tescott."

I smiled at Morgan. Without realizing it, he had become my friend. Again, I thought, since he alleged that our friendship had already been formed previously in a future that was years ahead for this current teenage version of me. And provided nobody screwed up that future he was from, he and I were still together. As a team, of sorts. And I looked forward to knowing him there.

"One last question, before you leave."

"Only one?" he asked, with a raised brow of doubt.

"For now," I smiled. "You said earlier when you told Kival and me about your trip to Argentina, you said you went with your employer. Who was that? Who went with you?

"You did, Mr. Tescott."

I had surmised as much. "Which is why, I suppose, you call me Mr. Tescott."

"Perhaps," he replied with a shrug.

"But—"

"But?"

"When you get back to 2024, and you see me there, well I want you to demand that I make you a partner. I don't like the idea of being your boss."

Morgan looked at me and I watched as his eyes crinkled, just seconds before a most radiant smile broke across his face.

"That partnership, Mr. Tescott, you have already created."

I had then asked him about the significance of his trip to Nicodemus, but I learned little from him other than it was there where he had entrusted the cache of money he had given to me and to my castaway companions, the five of us accounting for the newest adult citizenry of 1878.

In Nicodemus, he had associates, a few of whom he considered incomparable friends. And though it was necessary that he leave for Gibraltar, he admitted regret with the timing. He elaborated with fewer words than a mute with laryngitis, but I sensed that something was amiss there in that unique community of former slaves. I offered to check in on them for him, but Morgan was adamant that I stay away. "It is far too risky for you to be associated with the people of Nicodemus," Morgan asserted. "At least, for now," he added, but refused to elaborate further.

An hour later, I watched Morgan step from the platform of the depot and board the eastbound train for Kansas City. Suddenly, I felt a sense of loss, and admittedly a wave of insecurity swept over me as I realized that I and the other guys were now on our own, without big brother

Morgan to look out for us. But then, we were all eighteen. Legally adults. Grown men.

It was time to pull on those big boy britches.

I crossed to the horses, untied them and climbed into the saddle on the horse I had named Buck. I would have preferred to have mounted the Thoroughbred stallion that I had coveted since the first time I saw him, but that could wait. For all I knew, Viento would not even like me, and would promptly dump me in the middle of the street if I took such a premature liberty with him. So, with pride and vanity twisting my arm, I decided it was best to wait, and hopefully bond with Viento first. Besides, we had plenty of time between now and Morgan's return via the next earthly aphelion.

Leading Viento, Buck and I rode through the center of town to the livery. Once there, I turned the grullo stallion over to Dub O'Brien, promising the fighting Irishman that I would be back shortly with Buck and two other horses, and then arranged with him to care for all three animals while Dent and I, along with Blaine and Oleander, figured out just what we were going to do for the next eleven and half months while waiting for Morgan to return. It was odd, I thought, realizing how easy it seemed for my mind to replace Kival with Oleander in such a subconscious and casual way. But then, that was the idea.

Forget Kival Freeman.

For his sake and for ours.

CHAPTER 24

Ideparted from the boarding stable and nudged Buck into a trot and headed for the rendezvous point where I expected the others to be waiting for me.

When I arrived at the place where Oleander had been convalescing, I found, as I had hoped, a dark brown gelding and a strawberry roan mare standing hitched to the rail. And beside them stood Dent and Blaine.

Nonchalantly, I aimed Buck across the dusty avenue and dismounted, then tied him to the hitching rail opposite of the building occupied by the barber John White and his wife, the salubrious healer endowed with golden patience and therapeutic skill. I glanced across the street and nodded at two of my unscathed time-traveling brethren.

"Howdy partner," greeted my brother.

"We thought we'd just wait outside here for you," Blaine added, and I looked to see that the window of Oleander's room was sealed with a closed curtain.

"Basically," Dent said, "Wallace and I decided we were in no hurry to hear—"

"Hey, pussies!"

"That," Dent snapped.

We looked to see the curtain drawn aside, and Oleander poking his head through the opening in the clapboard wall.

"What took you so long?!" Oleander bellowed. "I'll be out in sec," he added, then disappeared.

We waited, and in a few moments, the big oaf with a missing digit on his left hand appeared from the back corner of the building with a set of saddlebags draped over his shoulder, and, luckily, he had clothes on this time. And boots. And a black Stetson. Admittedly, Morgan had attired Oleander as though he belonged to our gang, which I suppose, for now, it was necessary to include him as a member of our new foursome.

"Check this out," he said, cocking his head and readjusting the cowboy hat with both hands, and striking a pose that was as fitting for him as it would be for a city slicker on a dude ranch. In the few days since I had last seen him, the flesh of Oleander's face had regained more of its natural pinky-beige complexion, and his stride spoke volumes proving that healing and strength had returned to his lower limbs. "So, dudes, which way to the party?"

Instead, Dent talked Oleander into a meal, and though I hesitated to leave the horses, we headed on foot to an eating establishment Morgan had recommended to me earlier called Tommy Drum's Saloon. Nestled between two similar places of business, our restaurant of choice was just down the block and across from the depot from which Morgan had voluntarily abandoned us. Though the distance was short, Oleander chattered the entire time, and not once, I was sure, did he take a breath. I could not wait to get some food in his mouth and shut him up long enough to allow the rest of us to impress upon him the importance of keeping a low, and quiet, profile.

"Score," Oleander said with a smile, noting the name of the establishment.

The first thing I noticed was the absence of a set of double-swinging café doors, typical of the Western saloons featured on Hollywood's silver screen. Instead, there was a relatively solid and substantial door, and as I squeezed the latch of the ornate handle, I noticed what appeared to be a few bullet holes that had at one time splintered the heavy oak.

We entered the place, which according to an account by Morgan, had been the scene of a controversial shootout several years ago between Hays City Marshall James Butler Hickok, and a pair of 7th U.S. Cavalry troops who had been stationed at nearby Fort Hays. The two soldiers, who were under the command of the infamous general who would become the namesake of my hometown of Custer, attacked the Marshall with one of the two pinning Hickok to the ground and putting a gun to his ear and pulling the trigger. Luckily for Wild Bill, the weapon misfired, and Hickok had survived.

Morgan had told me how Tommy Drum, the proprietor, had rallied from the misfortune of having his normally congenial place of business labeled as a dangerous location for law abiding citizens, and was now, as Morgan had observed, a highly admired man known for his generosity of feeding and clothing those in need, not to mention playing a Santa Claus of sorts to kids whose parents had found themselves short of means at Christmas time. His compassion had made him a popular man, and his saloon a popular haven for the milder citizens of Hays City.

In addition, Tommy's place of business also appealed to lesser-confrontational men from the nearby fort, especially the Buffalo Soldiers who were often rejected at other like establishments simply because of the color of their skin. Consequently, Morgan had been welcomed by Drum, and he had reciprocal respect for the saloon keeper.

Inside Tommy Drum's Saloon was an elegant and elaborately paneled bar built of what I guessed was top-grade mahogany, the behemoth piece polished to a splendid shine. Fastened at the base of the long, L-shaped bar was a gleaming brass foot rail with a row of spittoons spaced evenly along the floor next to the golden-colored boot rest. And behind the drinking counter was a large rectangular mirror edged with a frame five to six inches wide and carved with vines of primrose that shined from their covering of what I assumed to be gold-leaf.

Opposite the bar was a row of eight square tables grouped with four chairs each, and draped with clean white linens, half of them occupied by a variety of customers. A young man, who was probably only a hair older than we were, met us at an empty table where the four of us had seated ourselves. Wearing an apron and carrying a friendly smile, he bid us a good day, introduced himself as Gordy, then asked what he could get for us.

"I want a beer," Oleander promptly stated. "Cold with a big head." Silently, I noted that his words could also be a description of the mannerless school yard bully I had always known him to be.

"And just how do you plan to pay for that beer?" I asked him, just loud enough for him to hear me.

"Oh," he said, swallowing his disappointment. Then perked up and smiled at me. "You said you were treating us to lunch!"

"I am, but I'm not buying you a beer. Or any other alcohol."

"Fine," Oleander snipped, then turned to Gordy, "I'll have Coke, or a Pepsi, I don't care which."

The young man gave him a curious look. Jeez, I thought, regretting that I had not schooled Oleander before taking him out in public. I glanced and saw a middle-aged couple seated at a nearby table and looking our way.

"And a cheeseburger," Oleander added with a nod of his head.

"A cheese…what?" Gordy asked.

"You know, a hamburger patty, inside a bun," Oleander chided with sarcasm. "With a slice of cheese on it. It ain't that hard to make here in the good ole U-S of A!"

"Four waters," Dent broke in. "And a plate each of whatever you would recommend for four hungry morons, us, I mean."

"We've gotta good side roast served with red beans and a mean-tastin' gravy. Got some tomatoes, too, fresh from the garden of some of the German-folk."

"Gordy, that would be perfect, thank you," I said. And I watched as the smooth-shaven dining attendant left our table, making a stop to speak to an older gentleman behind the bar.

"Olly! For chrissakes!" Dent exclaimed. "This isn't 1979 for cryin' out loud."

"I know it. It's like a hundred years earlier. Least that's what that woman told me."

"Right. So, you gotta think," Dent said, leaning in toward Sedgwick, his voice low. "Think before you open that big cake-hole of yours. If people around here get the idea that we're from the future, they'll lock us up and throw away the key. Or worse, they might just shoot us. Hell, I could shoot you right now."

"Sorry, Double D, I didn't think about that. I get it now. I'll fix it."

"Don't try to fix anything," I pleaded. "Just let it go." Then I looked past him and saw the barman approaching us, and I fought against a sudden urge to run. "And let us do the talking, okay?"

"Who do you think you are, my daddy?"

"Olly!" Dent snapped, his tone stabbing.

"Alright, alright."

"Afternoon, boys," the man said, sporting a big grin beneath the shock of a thick grey moustache that matched the hair on his head.

"Hello," I said. I watched as he darted his eyes around, appraising each of us, his gaze pausing on Oleander. Shit, I thought.

"That's a nasty looking stub you got there," he said, nodding to Oleander's left hand.

Sedgwick looked at me smugly, indicating to me his intent to follow my orders and say nothing.

"He had an accident," I said, looking at the half inch that remained of his middle finger, its end covered by a thick scab.

"There are men around here with a lot worse," he replied, his words unjudgmental and his voice absent of any expectation for additional information. "You all are friends of Morgan's, aren't you?"

"We are," I said, just slightly surprised. "He recommended this place to us."

"I'm Tommy Drum. This here is my place. Morgan has been in a lot lately. He's a good man. Told me to keep an eye out for the four of you. Welcome."

"Thank you," I said.

"Thanks," Dent offered as well.

"My pleasure. Friends of Morgan's are friends of mine. Sorry I can't fix you up with the, uh, things you wanted to drink. Out here on the plains, we're a little behind the offerings you can get back East, 'cept for what might come in on the train."

"No problem, Mr. Drum," I said.

"Call me Tommy. We don't use a man's last name around here too much. And you fellas?"

"JT," I said, then allowed the others to introduce themselves.

"Dent."

"I'm Blaine."

Oleander smirked at me for a second time, and I reluctantly gave him a fraction of a nod.

"Oleander Sedgwick, at your service," he said to Tommy Drum, then looked at me, and added, "sir."

"Good to meet all of you," he said, as he began to turn away, but stopped and fixed his eyes upon us again. "I've got a barrel of reasonably tame sarsparilly, if you'd rather have it instead of water."

I glanced at the others, or at least the other two who mattered, and gauged their preference.

"I think we're fine with just the water. Thanks, Tommy."

He left us alone, returning to the bar just as a trio of men dressed in grey-striped trousers, and black jackets and bowties, entered and stepped up to the counter. Immediately, they slipped from their heads, nearly identical black derbies that sported sharply rolled rims though were each minus any tell-tale signs of bullet holes or other misfortune. "The usual?" I heard Tommy ask them and a mix of positive replies responded in unison.

A short time later, we sat eating the meal that had been recommended, and it tasted good. And I had been hungry, having missed my usual breakfast prepared by Ruta. All four of us put the food away, sopping up the gravy with a piece of hard-crust bread that had been added to each of our plates. After we had finished, Gordy came to our table to take away the dinnerware.

"How much do I owe you," I asked, as I began to dig in my pocket for the gold coins.

"On the house," he said, and I glanced up at him, unsure that I had understood him correctly.

"Excuse me?"

"There's no charge today. So long as you promise to come back another time. Straight from the boss," he clarified. I glanced over and saw that Tommy Drum was in a spirited conversation with the three men who had moved from the bar to a table.

"Thank him for us," I said. Then we left the saloon, our bellies full, but so far empty of a sip of beer or whiskey or sarsaparilla for that matter. We walked back along the boardwalk that fronted the strip of businesses, and I felt the pinch of anxiety building with each step. But when we rounded the corner of the barber shop, I let out a soft sigh of relief. I had worried about nothing.

The horses were still there.

It was going to take some getting used to when it came to parking a horse in this day and age. It was like leaving my pickup parked on Custer's Main Street with the keys hanging in the ignition, which, come to think of it, was exactly how and where I had left it. I was sure to get an earful from Dad for that oversight, and given my current situation, I looked forward to the opportunity to be reprimanded by him.

Oleander began whining about the heat and complaining about his thirst, but I crossed the street to retrieve Buck, leaving Blaine and Dent to babysit. I gathered the reins of the bridle, then led the horse to where the others waited.

"Now what?" Dent asked.

"We have a hotel room just on the far side of the depot," I said, as I stepped foot in the saddle. Dent and Blaine likewise mounted their horses and the three of us turned them toward the street that ran parallel to the railroad track.

"Hey, pussies!"

I turned to look over my shoulder at Oleander.

"What about me?" he inquired.

"Yeah, what about him?" Dent asked. "I sure as hell don't want to ride double with him."

"Me either," Blaine said adamantly.

"Don't worry. Morgan has indirectly taken care of that," I said, saving the details for later. "Oleander, the hotel is just at the other end of this block. You can walk that far. Then once we're in the room we'll figure out how to get some transportation under your ass."

"I don't know how to ride horse," he volunteered and spoke without shame.

"Neither did I, a week ago," Blaine said to him. "It's not that hard."

Surprisingly, the three of us on horseback arrived at the Pennsylvania House hotel just steps ahead of an irritated Oleander who had kept pace with us making sure we knew he did not like being subjugated as a lower class of traveler than that of Blaine and Dent and me. Ignoring his ranting, I led the three of them inside and got our room key from Mr. Keeler, who informed me that the room had been prepared for four occupants.

We climbed the wooden staircase, Dent and Blaine toting their individual 1870s model of overnight luggage. Treading single file, our foursome of accidental time-travelers moved down the hallway to the room that was to be our home away from home. At least, I assumed, for as long as we could afford it. I slid the key into the lock and opened the door and stepped inside, the others on my heels. It was, as Mr. Keeler had said, prepared for the four of us, two to a bed. But at least there were four feather pillows, as Morgan had requested.

Dent looked at the two small beds, then at me. "Dibs on the bed by the window. You three can share the other one."

"Funny," I said. "Two to a bunk, that's the deal."

"Then I get dibs on you, brother. I am not sleeping with them."

I then noticed that an additional wooden chair had been placed beside the small table, raising the seating count of the room to two. It would have to do. I glanced down the hall before closing the door and when I turned, I found that Oleander had already set up house on the bed my brother had first claimed, and Dent and Blaine had parked their butts in the chairs, having dropped their saddlebags on the floor beside them.

"Make yourselves at home," I said with a bit of jovial sarcasm as I crossed to the bureau and knelt to pull open the bottom drawer, sliding it fully out from the space it had been designed for.

"What the hell ya doing?" Dent asked.

"Preparing to play Santa Claus," I replied, then leaned low and reached deeply into the drawer space and retrieved the secret box.

"That's got Just Morgan written all over it," my brother added, as I placed the wooden container on top of the empty bed.

I handed a bag of coins to my friend, Paul Blaine Wallace, Jr. wondering if the two-hundred dollars in his hands was perhaps the most he had ever been given at one time, knowing how his alcoholic father had kept the Wallace family on the brink of poverty. Blaine opened the sack and peered inside.

"Money?"

"Gold and silver coins. Enough to hopefully get you by for the next year."

As though a carrot had been resplendently dangled in front of him, Oleander sat up and threw his legs over the bed. "I better be getting my share of that," he said boldly, his sense of entitlement irritating me.

I tossed him the second bag. "Here," I said. "Two hundred dollars for you, too, Sedgwick."

He caught the bag and scoffed. "That'll last me about a week. Or weekend, depending on what there is to do around here," he added before dumping the contents of the leather sack.

"Again, dude, this is not 1979. Morgan said this should be enough money for each of us to get through to next summer."

"Next summer?" Dent asked, looking at me with a head beginning to explode with questions. But Oleander stopped him.

"Well, pussies, I'm outta here," he said, scooping up the coins and pocketing them.

"Oleander, for once, don't be so dumb," I told him. "That's too much money to be carrying around. You need to leave most of it here. That's what we'll be doing."

"Screw that," he said crossing to the door.

"Where the hell are you going?" Dent said, jumping to his feet and blocking Oleander's path.

"Out."

"You're staying here. JT has things to discuss with us. Important shit, you catch my drift?"

"No. But you can catch mine, Double D," Oleander spat, jabbing a pair of hard index fingers into both sides of my brother's shoulders. "I'm not your bitch. I'm a Sedgwick. And like my dad, I don't take orders from Tescotts. I give them," he added pushing Dent aside.

Oh boy, I thought. The situation, I was sure, was about to get ugly. I didn't know if Morgan had paid a damage deposit, but if he had, it looked as though he might not get it back after Dent was through with Oleander. "Dent," I said, my tone begging him to stand down. But I had not been persuasive enough.

As expected, Dent was pissed. He grabbed the bigger man-boy by his shoulder and spun him around and backed him up against the wall beside one of the two windows that offered views of the limestone courthouse and a variety of other buildings built on the north side of downtown.

"No, you listen to me you stuck-up piece of shit," he growled, his face so close to Oleander that it wouldn't have taken much to think my brother was moving in for a kiss. "If you go out there and screw around and talk stupid and get the rest of us in trouble, I'll do far worse to you than those Indians did."

They stood, the anger between the two of them thick and palatable.

"Do you understand me, Olly?"

A full fifteen seconds passed, then a grin arose on Oleander's face. "Dude, you worry too much. And that could get you killed. You know, a heart attack … or something."

The threat was poorly veiled, and I was suddenly concerned. I didn't doubt that Dent could handle himself against Oleander in a fair fight. But would Sedgwick fight fair? I doubted it.

"Let him go, Dent," I said. "Both of you need to cool down."

Dent stepped away, but I held my breath expecting him to launch a wicked right hook or a solid left jab or something akin to a hard slap across the mouth. But he didn't. Oleander brushed past him, knocking against him shoulder-to-shoulder and left the room leaving the door open behind him.

I crossed and closed the door and turned to Dent and Blaine. "If I had it to do over again," I said, thinking of the help we had given an unconscious Oleander as he knelt splayed at the base of the tree, "I don't know if I—"

"We should of left him there, that's what we should of done," Dent said, reading my mind.

"No," Blaine spoke. "We're better than that." His sentiment essentially duplicating that of Morgan.

And like Morgan, Blaine was right.

"Honestly, it's probably better he's not here," I said. "There's no trusting him with too much information."

"Can't argue with that," Dent said, blowing out a heavy breath of frustration. "So, what's the deal with next summer? Sounds like you and Morgan have made a plan."

"We have," I replied. And then the three of us sat down and I shared Morgan's admission as a time traveler and his plan to retrieve the lost talisman, and thus help the five of us get back home to our time to which we belonged.

"And what about Kival?" Blaine asked. "What's the deal with him?"

I hesitated for a moment, remembering my promise regarding his true identity, and the concealment of his real story as a kid born a hundred years before any of the three of us.

"It's the talisman," I said, deciding to keep my promise. "Because it was Kival's it makes him vulnerable to the man who would probably kill him to get it back, if you are so inclined to believe that warning from Morgan."

"Which you do," Dent said.

"One hundred percent."

"How did Kival get it, the talisman?" Blaine asked, "I mean, it sounds like this Headville guy Dent told me about must have known something about the thing, right? So how?"

"I don't know, for sure," I said truthfully, as the only things I could be certain about were those I had personally seen or heard or experienced. "Kival said he found it one time when he was hanging around the Pyramids," I added, rationalizing that the creation of a little white lie was acceptable given the circumstances.

"He found that magical do-whopper at the Pyramids?" Dent asked seeking confirmation.

"The talisman, yeah, I guess."

"Then really, it's ours. He found it on our land, so it should belong to us."

"I suppose, but it doesn't really matter right now, does it? The thing is, if we let it slip to someone that Kival possessed the talisman that got us here and this Culver Headville guy hears about it, Kival could get in deep shit. It's doubtful this Culver person would believe the talisman is lost, so, no telling what he might do to Kival to get him to tell him where the talisman is at. That's why Kival has to stay hidden, and we've got to make sure he stays that way."

"I don't see how any of us could avoid being suspect if that Headville turkey gets the idea we all got here through the arch," Blaine suggested.

"That's true," I said, though I knew another piece of the puzzle that I had promised not to share with any of them: Kival had returned home to the time where he belonged. And therefore, there was a strong probability that Culver Headville could discern who Kival is and who had been his mother.

"So, what do you think happened?" Blaine asked, his curiosity aroused. "Did this guy travel into our future and just accidentally drop the talisman on his way back?" It was as good of a theory as any, I thought, given he lacked what I knew. It was becoming quite obvious to me that simply feeding Dent and Blaine a half-baked story regarding Kival and his background wasn't going to go unquestioned as I had hoped. The two of them were not dummies.

"Could be," I said.

"One thing for sure," Dent offered, "our asshole buddy, Olly, is going to be a problem."

I could not have said it better myself.

CHAPTER 25

Wᵉ had spent another hour in the hotel room, Dent, Blaine, and I, talking about several things, but the subject of employment had been the most significant topic of our conversation, and I was relieved that attention had been directed away from Kival.

"I gotta do something," Dent professed. "There's just no way I can hang around here with nothing to do but twiddle my thumbs." And I knew he was serious. Dent had never been one to laze around watching endless hours of television or entertaining himself by reading a book, whereas I had been content to immerse myself in the pages of an adventurous novel or even a volume of the Britannica encyclopedia. He preferred to do and to go and to get his feet wet and his hands dirty.

"Well, we are here in cattle country," I said. "And we have ranch skills."

"I don't," Blaine countered.

"Yeah, but you're catching on," Dent said. "You handle that mare like you were born to it."

"Ha," Blaine retorted, and Dent grinned.

"I suppose we could ask a few of these cowboys we've seen floating around town and find out if their boss could use a few more employees," I suggested. "Or we could take a ride out in the country and knock on a few doors."

"I'm in," Dent said. "But, hey, what about Olly Asshole? You said Morgan has set him up with a horse?"

"Yeah," I replied, then turned to Blaine. "So, Blaine, how comfortable would you be taking on Buck again?"

"Well, I think okay. I've learned a lot from riding the lady horse."

"Mare," Dent corrected.

"Mare, right. And you guys ride geldings which are—"

"Nut-less," Dent interjected.

"Right. But, yeah, I'd give Buck another try."

"It's just the mare would be a good trainer for Sedgwick, just like she was for you. Though I have a feeling he'll still struggle."

"Big time," Dent affirmed. "But then that would leave you without a horse." Then immediately the clouds parted for him, and he knew the answer. "You're shitting me?"

"What?" Blaine asked.

"JT's gettin' the stallion! You are, aren't you?"

I smiled. I was apparently not the only one who had coveted the beautiful bald-faced grullo.

"Aren't you a lucky sumbitch? If I'd of known that horse was up for grabs, I would have kissed Morgan's ass, too!"

"Hey, brother, it's only fair. At Abelard and Karl's place, you got the first pick, and the best pick."

"Of course. That chocolate brown bay is a top-notch cow pony. Dad would have jumped right on him, too."

I agreed.

"But—"

"You know what they say, good things come to those who wait."

"Kiss my ass," Dent replied cordially, and I snickered wickedly.

With the horse and rider situation settled, and after Blaine and Dent deposited the majority of their funds into the box where I had secreted my own bag of money, the three of us left our room and stopped at the front desk to turn in the room key and to ask about how to arrange for a bath. From Mr. Keeler, we confirmed the cost was fifty cents for a hot bath, but soap was an extra nickel, just as Morgan had said. But Keeler also shared with us that cold baths were half-price, but the water would not only be cool, but also probably pre-used.

"Hot," the three of us said in unison.

"For all of you, then?" Keeler asked.

"Yeah," Dent replied. "But not in the same tub at the same time."

Mr. Keeler gave my brother a cross look. "Of course not, sir," he said, though I had the feeling he would have liked to have substituted the expression of respect with 'you idiot.' But I was just guessing.

"Thing is, we only have two tubs in our bathing room, so one of y'all will have to wait for another hour or so later."

Continuing to campaign as the aforementioned idiot, Dent sniffed under his arms, just to be funny, though neither Keeler nor I were amused. "I can wait," he said.

"That'll be two bits for the two of you, then," Keeler stated, adding "in advance, if you want the guarantee of hot water." Blaine and I paid him and arranged for our bath appointments later in the evening.

We left the lobby and stepped outside and retrieved our horses, though I turned Buck's reins over to Blaine, encouraging him to seat himself upon the upgrade of the buckskin gelding. Having swapped for the gentle strawberry roan mare, I stepped into her saddle and then led the others through the dirt-covered streets heading for Dub O'Brien's livery. As we rode along, I was constantly casting my eyes about, not wanting to miss catching a glimpse of Oleander if he happened to be out in the open somewhere. But I saw no sign of him.

Oleander Sedgwick, what the hell were you doing?

Blaine had gotten along fine with Buck, even though the ride to the enormous stable was only a short four-block test run. At the horse hotel, I made introductions and then Dub showed us to a large interior stall that was suitably sized as a bedding place for the brown bay, the buckskin, and the red roan that would either make or break Oleander in terms of a horseman.

On the opposite side of the building was Viento, standing proud, though he pawed into the straw bed with a couple of heavy thumps of his hoof, seeming to say hello to the other horses he had grown accustomed to being around. Either that, or Viento was just flirting with the roan mare and letting her know there was more than enough room for her in his little bachelor pad.

We unsaddled our horses, storing our riding tack on wide wooden perches, cleverly attached to the nearby wall. I brushed the mare down with a curry comb I found conveniently hanging on the post of the stall gate, since our usual grooming tools were in our saddlebags at the hotel. After a quick scratch behind her ears, I handed the comb to Blaine, giving him an opportunity to score some points with his new ride. Dent stood at Viento's stall, one foot on the lower board rail, his hand caressing the white face of the grey horse. I crossed to them.

"He's a beauty," Dent said. "I'm glad for you, JT. Really I am."

And I knew he meant it. He had been equally happy for me the day he and Dad had brought Jericho home to me as a birthday gift four years ago.

"I hope I can handle him," I said, genuinely concerned by the fact that I had zero experience with a stallion, and they had reputations for being fiery and high-strung. But I was optimistic since I had not noticed Morgan having any problems with him.

"You'll be fine," Dent assured me. "But if not, I'll be glad to take him off your hands."

The three of us left the stable and began to meander our way back to the hotel, choosing a route that took us by the prominent limestone courthouse and past the office of Nathaneil J. Penny, sharing with my companions that he was the attorney who Morgan had solicited to draw up a bill of sale for Viento.

"Smart move," Dent commented.

Just as we drew near the exit door, a young woman stepped from inside the law office, a clutch of loose, folded papers in her left hand, the sheath pressed against her bosom. We paused politely, being the young gentlemen that we were, and waited as she passionately closed the door behind her, its windows rattling. I smiled at her, my curiosity piqued by the manner of her brusque exit and because I enjoyed looking at pretty things. She glanced at each of us, her emerald eyes fiery and determined.

"Excuse me!" she sputtered, then abruptly moved ahead of us, whisps of her red, curly hair fluttering from beneath a green, floral-print bonnet that matched her ankle-length dress. She strutted to the edge of the boardwalk, then stepped down onto the dusty side street.

"Have a nice day," Dent called out to her sarcastically before adding, "ma'am."

I swiveled my eyes to look at my brother and found him with his hat in his hand and a grin pinned to his face. Then after a half dozen pointed steps, the young lady abruptly stopped then spun around to confront us. Or more aptly, to challenge Dent.

"Oh, boy," Blaine whispered apprehensively.

At once, the redhead charged forward.

"He stepped in it this time," I assured Blaine, seconds before the young woman met Dent as he moved down onto the street to intercept her.

"That sounded rude," she spoke to my brother, her words expressing disapproval more than anger. "I don't believe you meant it."

"Meant what?"

"Have a nice day. You didn't mean it, did you?"

Dent was silent for a moment, the two of them in a showdown. "Sorry," Dent said, genuinely apologetic. "Hungry?"

"Pardon me?"

"You're right, I was rude. So, how about I treat ya to a nice dinner? You know, so I can show ya I'm sorry in the way a woman like you deserves."

"A woman like me?"

"Dent, you better quit before you get any further behind," I chided him.

"Fine," she cut in. "A restaurant, not a saloon."

"Of course," Dent agreed, then shot me a look that said, 'don't worry, I got this.'

"On one condition," she began, "my husband must join us."

I laughed out loud.

"Husband?"

"Yes. Him," she said, nodding toward the office. "Nathaneil."

"Well—"

"That's what I thought," she replied smugly. "Here," she added, handing Dent a pamphlet.

"What's this?"

"A continuation of my grandfather's work. Perhaps you've heard of him? John Beeson?"

Dent glanced at me. I shrugged. That name did not ring any bells with me. "Can't say that I have," Dent replied to her for both of us.

"I'm not surprised. But you can read, can't you?"

Dent smiled, "I've been known to crack a book on occasion."

I laughed again.

"My grandfather was, and still is, an advocate for the rights of Indians. His crusade began in Oregon Territory, and he carried his campaign to Washington D.C. Twenty years ago he wrote and published a pamphlet much like this one," she said tapping her finger on the front of the brochure in Dent's hand. "I've modified the original and have made it current and applicable to the Plains Indian whom as an Indigenous nation is suffering at the hands of unscrupulous white men just as the Takelma peoples did in grandfather's beloved Oregon."

"You're a long way from home," I said to her. "Oregon, I mean."

"Everywhere there is the need to elevate the whole human family. Here is no exception."

"I quite agree."

"Which is why I must press on with my work. Only, my husband thinks I'm wasting my time. And his money. He refuses to print more than ten of these a week. So," she said, snatching the brochure from Dent, "if you're not going to read it, I'll give to someone who will."

"I'll take it," I told her, holding out my hand. She looked at me for a moment, then crossed to me and offered the pamphlet. "Thank you," I said. "I'll read it, I promise."

With a firm nod of her head, she stepped in front of my brother. "Have a nice day," she said bluntly, then turned around and crossed the street.

"Dodged a bullet there, didn't I?" Dent asked with a grin.

I shook my head at him, then pointed my eyes at the document in my hand and read from its front cover. "A Plea for the Indians. Authored by John Beeson and Abigail Beeson Penny."

"Man, oh, man," Blaine said with a sigh, "sure hope she doesn't try to give Oleander one of those."

"Yeah," I agreed. "That would not go well."

"Abigail. Now it makes since. I dated Abigail Hanniford for a while when we were Sophomores."

"She dumped you, too, didn't she?" I said with a snicker.

"What you mean, too?!" Dent exclaimed, then without waiting for an answer he took off ahead of Blaine and me. I folded the brochure and tucked it inside the front right pocket of my tan dungarees where I had previously stowed Viento's bill of sale. I would read it later when I wasn't trying to keep up with my brother.

Shortly we were walking past the front of John White's barber shop, and I glanced in and saw a short, slender Black man sweeping the floor. And he was alone.

"Guys," I said, nodding at the shop. "I don't know about you two, but since I didn't pack a razor from '79, I wouldn't mind losing these whiskers of mine."

"Don't be foolin' yourself, JT," Dent said, adding "that's peach fuzz, not whiskers."

We entered and the man looked up from his task and shot us a gleaming smile.

"Welcome, gentlemen" he said, sitting his broom aside.

"John White?" I asked.

"Yes, sir."

"I'm JT Tescott. This is my brother, Dent, and our good friend Blaine Wallace."

"Ah!" he smiled, and clasped his slender, bony hands, "The young friends of Mr. Morgan!"

I smiled back. "Yes, that's us," I said. "Earlier, we came by and picked up—"

"The ass—", Dent began.

"Associate," I interrupted before he could complete his intended expletive or begin an itemized list of other colorful adjectives he might use to describe Oleander. "Didn't know if you knew that or not. Oleander met us outside and I didn't get the chance to thank your wife, again."

"Yes, sir, I knew. Mrs. White came into my shop here and did a dance!"

I looked doubtfully at him, certain that he was kidding us.

"No, sir, it's the Lord's truth," John said, reading my skepticism. "Mrs. White, she danced," he repeated, then he, himself, kicked his feet around in a humorous little jig.

We all laughed, and he smiled at us.

"The Good Lord will bless you for your suffering," he added with a raised brow that told us he was sincere.

"So, Mr. White—"

"No, sir," he interrupted. "All you boys can just call me John."

"You bet," I said smiling at him. It was impossible not to immediately like the man. "So, John, do you have time to give us a shave, you know, help us clean up a little?"

"Always have the time for you, Mr. Tescott," John replied, and I was about to reciprocate his request to be less formal with me, as well, but he turned his back and scurried. "Come," he said motioning me to a big chair.

I sat down and Blaine and Dent sat opposite me on small chairs that lined the windowed side of the wall, preparing to watch me as though my shave might be entertaining. The only thing that was missing was a bag of popcorn.

John tilted me backward and peered over my head, examining my bristled cheeks.

"It's been ten or so days since I've shaved," I said.

"No matter," said John, patting my cheeks. "Soft whiskers."

"Told you so," said Dent with a smirk.

John tucked a thin cotton napkin around my neck and covered my front and shoulders with a towel, then went about wetting my face and applying a shaving cream he had whipped up in a little bowl taken from a wood ledge mounted beneath a cheap mirror. Then he was hovering over my lathered face, armed with a slender straight-edge razor. I rolled my eyes to look at its menacing appearance, though I was not naive. I knew how shaves were accomplished in the years before there were cartridge razors. But still, I felt submissively vulnerable as I tipped my head backward exposing my jugular to the mercy of this man who was a stranger to me.

I closed my eyes and prayed.

With gentleness and caution, barber John White returned my face to the smoothness of a baby's bottom. And with attention to detail, he cleaned me of all remnants of the shaving crème. Then I heard him fiddling behind me with a bottle of some kind, and immediately a strong whiff of alcohol touched my nostrils. Oh, boy, I thought and when John's wet, sterilized hands met my cheeks, I could not help but cry out.

Blaine and my brother sat there giggling like little girls.

John sat me up and I stood from the chair, my face stinging, and my eyes watering.

"Who, please, will be next?" he asked. Without a blink, Blaine bravely took to the barber's throne.

Blaine's shave was as uneventful as mine, neither of us experiencing a serious cut, fatal or otherwise. Though to my angst, my friend managed the application of the aftershave potion far better than I did and Dent was happy to point that out to me. Blaine relinquished the chair and John White wiped a speck of cream from the arm and looked at Dent with an invitation on his face.

"No thanks," Dent said, rubbing his whiskered chin between the fingers of his right hand. "I'm kinda diggin' this badge of virility."

"Virility?" I asked, giving him a suspicious look. "Didn't know that was in your vocabulary? Have you been reading—you know, books?"

"Nope," he replied, "but I do read a certain kind of magazine, but mostly I look at the pictures," he added with a wink.

I ignored him and looked for a sign or posting of the barber's rates. On a small square of white paper were the words HAIRCUT, 35 Cents and beneath was lettered Shave, 15 Cents. The cost of both adding up to four bits. Also advertised was a hot-water bath with soap for fifty cents. With soap inclusive, John White's rates were a better deal than what Blaine and I had gotten at the hotel. Regardless, the cost of appearing civilized and smelling nice might be more than I could afford on a regular basis, given the fact that the allowance bestowed to me by Morgan was just over sixteen dollars a month. And as soon as I had the chance to enjoy a hot bath, the one-dollar expense for hygiene and hair taming seemed certain to be worth every penny. I reached into my pocket and pulled out several denominations of change.

"No, no, Mr. Tescott," John said to me. "No charge."

I thanked him for the generosity of his gesture, but I insisted on paying him, leaving him a trio of nickels on the wood ledge. Blaine likewise paid for the service, thanking John with a handshake.

"Hey, Dent," I said, pointing to the sign. "Maybe Mr. White can fix you up with a bath here, so you don't have to wait on us."

"Now that I'll go for," he said. "How long to heat the water, John?"

"Twenty minutes, Mr. Tescott, sir."

"Let's gitter done, then," Dent said, then added, "John, Mr. Tescott is my daddy. My friends call me Dent."

A broad, bright smile spread across the barber's face. "Yes, sir, Mr. Dent. Glad to call you my friend."

"And, same for me, John," I said, wishing I had spoken up before my brother. "Please, call be JT."

He nodded and smiled at me as Dent stood and primped in the mirror.

"I'll meet you at the hotel," my brother informed me.

"Remember, we're at the Pennsylvania House" I said to him with a smile, adding, "not The Sporting Palace."

"Don't worry, I'd have to be three sheets to the wind to confuse the two, and twice that to be fool enough to sample that menu."

I chuckled at his sense of humor, and after Blaine and I were outside, I explained to him that the palace I had referred to was by name a grandiose exaggeration. Sporting, possibly. A brothel, for certain. Then I summed things up for my friend with a recitation of Dent's description of the women he had seen there. Blaine was not impressed.

From the barber shop, we strolled up the boardwalk toward our hotel and by happenstance, I glanced across the railroad tracks to the other side of the street and saw Oleander exit from a one-story shop with a false front that advertised Johnson Bros. Outfitters.

I stopped in my tracks, gawking at him. From that vantage point, I could clearly see he was brandishing a set of holstered pistols upon his hips.

Oleander Sedgwick was now armed and dangerous.

CHAPTER 26

I watched as Oleander glanced around, his right thumb hooked into the gun belt, his fingers tapping one after another, appearing to imitate the legendary Wyatt Earp or Billy the Kid, or someone in between. Then he caught me staring at him. He returned my glower, then lifted his left hand and folded his three unsevered fingers into his palm, evidently forgetting that he was missing his flipping-bird digit. Regardless, I got the message. Then he smiled like he had just been named gunslinger-of-the-year and sauntered toward us. I watched him as he crossed the wide street and the railroad track that dissected it, moving confidently as though he embodied the essence of the cock-of-the-walk. Or an arrogant prick. Six one way, or half a dozen the other, as my Granny Evelie would say.

"Look out," I said to Blaine.

"I see him. Hard to miss him, actually."

"Hey, hey, hey ... Pilgrims," Oleander said, emphasizing an alternative P-word as his choice of greeting. Given the fact that he was accessorized with weapons, I was not sure I liked the new salutation any better.

"John Wayne, huh?" I suggested, being as friendly and un-antagonistic as I could be."

"Caught that, did ya?" he said with a grin. "Check these babies out," he added, slipping one of the pistols from the holster and laying it across the palm of his hand.

Surprisingly, he had the good sense to point the barrel toward the ground.

"Nice," I said. And it was. It had a shiny nickel-plated finish fitted with Ivory grips and a barrel about six inches long.

"Colt Peacemaker, forty-four caliber, six-shot, single action, brand spanking new."

"Impressive," I said aloud. My mind, however, was screaming *get this idiot off the streets!* But I kept calm, not wanting to poke the bear. Especially since the bear was armed with an Army revolver loaded with bullets twice the size of a pencil eraser.

"How much did these guns cost you?" Blaine asked.

"Cheap," Oleander declared. "Stoled 'em for thirty-five bucks."

"For both?"

"Don't be stupid, Hollywood, thirty-five each. Only paid eighty bucks for the two of them."

"That's forty dollars each."

"Well, I got the holsters and some ammo, too, durr," he countered with a lift of his shoulders, a gesture that would also have been my reaction to anyone who asked me if Oleander had any brains.

"So, you've already spent almost half of the money you got from Morgan?"

"Told you it wouldn't last me long. But look at me, you can't say I don't fit into the scene now."

"Oleander," I said as even keeled as I could manage. "In case you haven't noticed, hardly anyone actually wears a revolver or carries a rifle. This place isn't *Gunsmoke*, or some movie set. It's real. Not make believe." But admittedly, neither had this town been as I had expected, thanks to the mythologized representation of the Old West I had grown up watching on television.

Oleander stared at me before displaying his maimed hand inches from my face.

"No shit."

"JT," Blaine said, tapping me on the elbow, "we've got things to do."

I nodded. "Why don't you come with us," I suggested to the embryonic gunslinger, though I was certain he would decline.

And I was right.

"I don't think so. And I sure as hell don't need you pussies babysitting me."

Pilgrims. I did like that better.

Blaine and I left Oleander to the devise of whatever his little mind was up to, and as we walked along the wooden decks that fronted the stores of the busy avenue, I decided that Sedgwick was right. We were not his babysitters. And I knew if Sam were here, he would remind me of that. *Play it cool, JT,* I could imagine him saying. *Ignore him and do your own thing,* would probably have been another piece of sapient advice delivered to me by my deceased friend.

When Blaine and I reached the entry to the Pennsylvania House hotel, I stopped and checked behind us. Oleander was gone.

"He's going to blow it for us, isn't he?" Blaine asked, also looking in the same direction.

"Probably."

"That would be a shame," Blaine added. "I mean, just look at us. Here we are way, way out of our natural environment, and yet, there's nobody pointing at us, or looking at us like we're space cadets or something."

Blaine was right. Morgan's costuming of us had been spot on. We had, so far, ostensibly blended in as though we were chameleons. Well, three out of four of us, anyway. Four out of five, if you counted Kival. Oddly, I felt reasonably confident the high school outcast would assimilate well with the Volga German immigrants. They were good folks who would help him. Earlier when Morgan and I had departed the Beilman farm, I had thought then that Kival had already begun to mimic their appearance and postures, as though he were born one of them. Maybe that's what we needed; someone to take the rest of us underwing, but without knowing the truth of our origin.

Something to wish for, though probably best not to get.

Blaine pushed open the glass-windowed door of the hotel and walked inside, and I was on his heels. From a doorway at the far end of the narrow hallway that was partly obstructed by the lobby counter, Mr. Keeler appeared and strode toward us.

"Five minutes, boys," he said, "and I'll be ready for ya. Down there," he added with a backward nod of his head.

We thanked him, then climbed to the second floor. In our room, we unpacked our personal saddlebags which we had earlier stowed under the bed, sitting aside a clean set of underclothes that Morgan had provided for us. A few minutes later, we entered the back-room Keeler had indicated and found a relatively large space furnished with four sets of tables and chairs, and positioned against the rear exterior wall was a huge black cast iron stove with thick pails lined upon its wide flat surface. Keeler was there at the stove, evaluating the temperature of the bucketed water with the tip of his finger.

I did not know about the water, but the room was hot.

"Over there," he said, gesturing toward a corner that had been partitioned by a tea-colored piece of drapery that looked to have been made by sewing together several old sheets. I walked to the wall of fabric and parted a space wide enough to accommodate my modest frame and stepped through it. Then Blaine appeared through the same split and joined me.

Two round galvanized tubs sat on the floor; their size barely large enough for a grown man to sit in cross-legged. Between them was a long, narrow wooden bench, the height of a footstool, and exhibiting a set of folded towels and two thin bars of soap that appeared to have been used frequently by someone else.

"Wow," Blaine huffed, his singular word saying it all.

The setup hidden behind the questionable curtain of modesty was not the arrangement I had expected. I had imagined a deep copper tub with a lofty backrest and of a length long enough to stretch my legs, just like those appearing in my favorite Western movie, *The Good, The Bad, and the Ugly.* In that film, there had been an unexpected surprise unfold in a scene where Tuco Rameriz, the Ugly, shot another bad guy with a gun hidden beneath the soapsuds of the bathwater. Apparently, I was as guilty as Oleander when it came to preconceived perceptions of the Old West. His being the fanatical brandishing of a pair of loaded pistols, mine a less dangerous bathtub.

On the wall were pegs where upon one I hung my hat before kicking off my boots. Keeler entered through the curtain carrying two pails of steaming water and emptied one into each of the tiny metallic tubs.

"A nickel for the soap, if you use it," he said. "And if you want me to pour water over you after you're in, that will be an extra fifteen cents."

"I'll pass on the pour," Blaine said. And I shook my head at the man as well, though I was not sure I wanted the soap either.

About a half hour later, we had redressed after a surprisingly pleasant bath and a primitive shampoo, having decided to use the soap after all. In addition, Blaine and I rinsed out the underclothes we were wearing when we had entered, and we wrung them of as much excess water as possible. Upstairs in our room we reasoned we could spread our laundry over the metal framed headboards of the beds where they could dry. We had thought ahead, both of us having been judicious Boy Scouts in our youth.

Heading back to our room, we treaded along the hallway when suddenly Dent entered the front door, himself freshly bathed. Following a quick appraisal of each other, we then shared mutual nods of approval, then together we took the stairs to our room, but not before Blaine and I placed a nickel each on the counter in front of Mr. Keeler.

"What was that about?" Dent asked as we reached the top of our climb. "The coins?"

"Soap costs more, remember," I said.

"Suckers," Dent said playfully hooking his arm around my neck and feigning a wonky punch toward my jaw. In that ordinary moment, I silently recognized how genuinely glad I felt having him here, and that the two of us were coping, as brothers, with an unexpected adventure into a dangerous past. In spite of our differences and disagreements, and polar opposite personalities, I loved my brother. I should break my silence, I thought, and tell him that.

Later. I would wait and tell him later.

Once in the privacy of our room, Blaine and I reported on our encounter with Oleander, leaving nothing out. Dent shook his head, agreeing that there wasn't much we could do about him, short of putting him on a train bound for California, or the Yukon, either of which would be fine and plausible as we figured it wouldn't take much to point him in the direction of the fabled locations where gold and silver lie in wait for the lucky or the skilled.

The evening wore on, and not one of the three of us was eager to venture out for dinner or entertainment. Even Dent, surprisingly, did not seem motivated to visit a saloon for a taste of 1870's beer. Instead, in the darkness of the room, we shucked down to our nineteenth century skivvies as we prepared ourselves for a comfortable night's sleep on a mattress, something I vowed to never again take for granted.

Tucked beneath the thin sheets of the two beds, the three of us talked about a variety of things, but mostly though, we reminisced of our glory days in high school, and recounted stories from our childhoods. I was glad to see Blaine and Dent laughing and talking again, being the friends they had been before whatever had happened between them this past spring. We also pondered upon our future, both the one we hoped to experience once Morgan returned, but also the future we might have here if, alternatively, Morgan failed his quest to find the lost talisman.

Dent and I both had plans for college, and presently we both intended to first enroll in the nearby Junior College located in Colby. There I planned to whiz through my general college requirements before transferring to one of the state universities where I would major in history.

Dent's goal was vastly different from mine. Though he had reported to our parents that he aimed to achieve a degree in business, he had secretly confessed to me that what he really wanted was to lead a multitude of fraternity parties, each one of which he intended to make legendary in their own right. I had no doubt my brother would succeed in his non-educational ambitions. But, as it now stood, both of us would miss our enrollments next month. Perhaps we would miss them altogether.

Blaine was scheduled to enlist in the Army. He would need that experience and income in order to afford the cost of earning a teaching degree in physical education and enjoy a career as an educator and coach. And I knew from experience that he would be an inspiration and an example for his students, especially those who would relate to Blaine's background.

Finally, we called it a night, with Dent and me basking in one bed and Blaine in the other. For now, he had the second bed all to himself. I was quick to close my eyes, but my mind did not surrender to sleep right away. In a long, unexpected moment of reflection, I lay awake, not thinking about any of my roommates, but instead my thoughts lingered upon a girl. A girl wearing a blue hat with a white bow and curls of honey blonde hair framing a face as lovely as that of a porcelain doll. I wondered if I might also dream about her at some point during my nighttime slumber. With a yawn, I shut my eyes and prepared myself for the possibility of a subconscious encounter with a girl whose name was unknown to me.

When I awoke the next morning, I had no recollection of any dream. Not of a blonde, a brunette, or even a nightmare starring a certain male redhead of questionable intelligence. Though when I opened my eyes, I saw Blaine lying on the adjacent bed, curled up under a white linen, and he was still the only occupant upon that mattress.

Oleander had not returned.

After a surprisingly robust breakfast composed of a thick sausage patty, fried eggs, and biscuits and gravy that had been cordially offered by Mr. Keeler in the room next to where Blaine and I had bathed, the three of us amigos left the hotel. A waft of smoke met my lungs, courtesy of a man loitering near the entry door puffing away on a cigarette. He was impeccably dressed in a dark grey pinstriped suit, his jacket fitted over a white shirt, and sporting polished black boots and a thin black bowtie. I also noticed his accessories; a top hat that coordinated with a black holster that peeked out from the bottom edge of his suitcoat. He appeared to be a lodger of the hotel, though I had not seen him before. He gave me a nod and a smile as he took another drag of his cigarette.

I nodded back to him, then picked up my pace so that I could catch up with Blaine and Dent who had gotten ahead of me as they walked in the direction of the livery stable. We had decided to go for an explore of the countryside, and perhaps see if we might land ourselves jobs as ranch hands. We greeted Dub O'Brien telling him we were here to take the horses out for a while and wondered if they had been fed and watered. He looked at us, then glanced outside to where the sun had already been shining for a couple of hours.

"Aye," he said, "took care of 'em first ting dis mornin'."

I thanked him, though I was a little embarrassed by his insinuation that we had slept in till nearly noon. We groomed and saddled our respective mounts, and I was excited and nervous to get Viento beneath me. He stamped a foot and snorted as I stepped into the saddle, but he stayed calm, attentive, ready to bow to my commands. Or so I hoped. One thing I did was pray that he would not dump me to the ground, especially in front of my brother.

We exited the wide door of the spacious barn, and I allowed Dent and Blaine to lead the way. We first did a little sashay through town, and I imagined that the choice of that very public route had been intentional. Knowing my brother, he was anticipating a show from the stallion. No doubt he hoped for a spectacle that would feature the white-faced horse theatrically depositing my backside upon the dusty street, and if that were to happen, he would prefer I have an audience. At least, that is what I suspected, though it could easily have been for some other reason.

And as it turned out, I was blessed with a second sighting of the girl I had hoped to see in my dreams. It was a brief glance, one that caught the sway of a yellow skirt as she disappeared into a mercantile shop following upon the heels of the man who had given me the newspaper. For a second, I thought that she had also glimpsed me riding proudly upon my picturesque stallion, but that was only wishful thinking.

Then it occurred to me that Dent was probably doing a casual, though detailed, reconnaissance of the town, seeking to locate our classmate who had never, according to Oleander's crowing, obeyed curfews. After a sweep through the central streets of Hays City, we pointed our horses eastward with Dent and Blaine still in the lead, crossing in front of the three-story limestone courthouse. But we did not get far.

"Hey thar, boy!" I heard someone call from behind me. Then I heard the cocking of a rifle.

I reined Viento to a stop and turned him at an angle just enough to look behind me to see who happened to be the subject of the firearm's attention. As it turned out, it was me. Standing in the street not more than twenty yards away posed a man with his weapon leveled in my direction. And the man wore a badge.

"Hans in the ahr," he scowled, one eye peering through the sight of the gun barrel. I raised my hands, keeping the reins in my clutch and praying that Viento would not use this opportunity to show me that he was boss and take off running, with or without me in the saddle.

"Is there a problem, sir?" I asked, swallowing my tonsils.

"Thet depends," the law officer spoke as he crossed toward me. "I knows thet horse. It belongs to thet edgycated Negro. Why ahre you on it?"

"He sold it to me," I said, realizing I had just inadvertently lied to the man since no money had actually exchanged hands.

"I don't believe ya," he said, his eyes narrow and doubtful.

I heard the nearby sound of hooves beating the dirt street and at once Dent was beside me.

"What's going on?"

"The sheriff, here—"

"Depudy, ackshully," he corrected through a mouth of stained and crooked teeth.

"Deputy, right," I said. "He thinks I stole Viento."

"That's bullshit!" Dent spoke to the deputy. "My brother's got a bill of sale."

"Shit," I whispered just loud enough for my brother to hear me.

"Show him," urged Dent.

I exhaled a deep, regretful sigh. "I don't have it. Not on me." In an inexplicable moment of second-guessing myself, I had transferred the document from my pocket and stashed it where I thought it would be kept safer. In the hotel room, inside the secret box behind the bureau drawer.

"Why the hell not?"

"I decided to keep it with—you know," I paused, then lowered my voice, "with the stuff Morgan gave us."

"Look, Officer Fife—Barney, is it?"

"Jeez, Dent, put a lid on that sense of humor, will ya? Now's not a good time to be funny."

"Moody. Texas Jack—Not Fife." He said, keeping his gun aimed at me.

"Right," Dent confirmed, but I did not know if he were speaking to me or to the man that could, with a squeeze of his finger, shoot my head off. "So, Deputy, sir, my little brother's bill of sale is at the hotel where we're staying. We can go get it and show it to you, sir."

The change in the tone of Dent's speech relieved me. Perhaps I would get to keep my ears and the lump of grey matter between them.

"I don't tank so," Deputy Moody snarled. "Both a yous, down offa dem horses."

I stared at him in disbelief. After all, we had done absolutely nothing wrong.

"I says—git—down."

I dismounted first, though it was not easy because I was still holding my hands in the air as the man had instructed. And I was not about to ask him if he expected me to follow the game rules of Simon Says. The law officer then motioned with his rifle for the two of us to step away from the horses, and we did as he indicated. I noticed that a fair number of bystanders had gathered around us, onlookers seeking a little entertainment for the day. I hoped that the girl with the golden curls was not watching.

Deputy Moody then crossed to our horses and took their reins. It was then that I saw Blaine, still mounted upon Buck and close enough to us that I knew he had to have heard the conversation. I looked at him and nodded toward the direction of our hotel. He nodded back and I could tell in his eyes he knew what I needed him to do. Then casually, without drawing attention to himself, he eased Buck away and headed slowly toward the Pennsylvania House hotel.

"Eenside," the officer said, pointing his gun at the stout square building next to him that advertised Sheriff lettered on a window sheltered beneath a wide wooden awning. Dent and I moved past him, our fingertips still pointing skyward. "Tie 'em up," I heard Moody tell someone, and I assumed he meant the horses. At least that is what I hoped. However, we entered the small office unrestrained.

"Weapons on da table, dehre," he ordered.

"Does it look like we have guns?" Dent asked, the cutting edge of his characteristic sarcasm causing me to wish he would, for once, just keep it to himself.

"Knifes, too, smahrty mouth," the man spat.

I knew Dent always carried the little pocketknife, and I hoped he would relinquish it. And he did, removing it from his jeans and laying it upon the top of the wide oak table that served as the office desk. "Thet way," he said, nodding toward a doorway that led to the back half of the building, the space that would undoubtedly be partitioned by walls of vertical bars. I crossed through, with Dent behind me, but suddenly I drew to a stop. Behind the locked gate of the nearest cell was an athletically beefy young man reclining upon a narrow canvas cot, his red hair disheveled.

"Well, ain't this a hell of a reunion."

Oleander Sedgwick was now present and accounted for.

CHAPTER 27

Deputy Texas Jack Moody, who seemed long on distrust and short on patience, pushed me forward into the cell where Dent had already entered ahead of me, then shoved the iron-bar gate closed and it clanked hard in its lock. I was nervous. No, more than nervous, I was worried. And not just about me and Dent, but for Viento. I had promised Morgan I would look after him. A difficult thing to do from inside the Hays City hoosegow.

"Now, yous two titty-bit horse theifs kin jest sit yous asses tight! Ah'll be back," Moody sneered before he hurried outside, slamming the front door behind him.

"Olly, what the hell are you doing in here?!" Dent exclaimed peering at our rogue castaway through the iron bars that separated our dank cell from his, though I was certain the stench of urine and the olfactory assault of stale alcohol were complimentary to both accommodations.

"Funny thing," Oleander began, "I don't exactly remember how I got here."

I stood at the front of the cell facing toward the office area. I did not want to look at Sedgwick, much less hear him, but short of busting into a rendition of Elvis Presley's "Jailhouse Rock", it would be impossible to ignore his senseless blabbing.

"You look like shit," Dent told him, and I peeked over my shoulder to give Oleander a second glance. He did look rough. His hair was mussed and caked with some substance that had once been liquid, or mostly so, appearing as though he had slept with his head in a spill of vomit. And his eyes were almost as red as his hair.

"Gotta hell of a headache, I know that much," he said, then touched the back of his skull and winced. "Umm! I think some jackass clobbered me from behind, too."

"You've got a hangover, you dumb shit," Dent told him. "Where the hell were you?"

"At a party, dude," Oleander replied. "Drank some mean stuff, too," he added as he began to drag his fingers through his matted hair. "Started with something called coffin varnish—nasty, nasty stuff. Smelled like that chewin' tobacco crap we were into for a while, you know, before we had hair on our balls. Then I had a couple of shots of what that pickle-faced bartender said was tarantula piss, or spider piss, some kinda piss. And tasted like it, too. Then next thing I know, I'm highrollin' in a card game."

"You were playing poker?"

"Sure the hell wasn't bingo."

"You're a shitty poker player, Olly."

"That's what I thought! But, man oh man, was I drawin' the cards. Got a big house once. Sixes and eights. Or was it sevens and eights? Anyway, I had those guys by their nuts."

"Guys?"

"Three, I think. But I run one of 'em from the table with my big house."

"Full, not big."

"Right," Oleander said, then his chin dropped. "Bastards," he whispered.

"They cleaned you out, didn't they Olly?" Dent asked, though we both knew the answer.

"The cheaters stoled it all."

"Moron," I whispered, turning away from him. I shook my head. Oleander had foolishly burned two-hundred dollars in less than twenty-four hours. Money that was meant to last him close to a year. But no, not for Oleander Sedgwick, the idiot boy born with a silver spoon in his mouth.

"Are you sayin' you don't have single dime of your money left?" Dent asked.

"Nope. Don't even have my damn guns, neither," I heard him snarl, his breathing suddenly deep and rapid. "They stoled my brand-new guns."

"Good!" I spat out loud, not giving a crap whether he heard me or not. At least one problem had been solved by his night of idiocy and depravation.

"What did you say, Worm?" Oleander hissed.

"I said good. And I called you a moron, which deserves repeating."

Then I heard him push himself up from the cot, the bottoms of its wooden legs scraping backwards across the floor.

"Bitch, you're lucky there's a wall between us, or I'd bust you across that nerdy face of yours."

"Yeah, I'm feeling lucky," I said, but I imagined my sarcasm was lost on him.

"So, what the hell did you do, Olly, try to fight them, too? The guys who tricked you out of your money?"

"Crooks, that's what they were," Oleander growled, then piled on a string of vulgarities. "Stoled my pretty new guns," he said as though he were on the verge of whimpering. He sighed as he dropped his two-hundred pounds down onto the cot, the primitive bed itself squeaking woefully. "I told that dude I'd buy 'em back."

"And how would you do that, Olly? If you pissed away all your money, you don't even have two nickels to rub together. You're broke!"

"Told him I could get the money. If he'd just give me the time to get back to the room."

"The room? You mean our hotel room? You don't have any money there, Olly. You took it all, remember?"

"Was gonna ask you for a loan, Double D."

"You shithead. What did you do then? Punch him?"

"Nope. Just lowered my head and tackled him like he was a skinny-ass third-stringer like that pussy brother of yours."

Dent crossed to me and stuck his arms through the bars and clasped his hands together. "He's a prick."

"Yep."

Quietly, we stood next to one another, and I pondered our predicament. The only upside was that Morgan was not around to see any of this. Or Dad, either, for that matter. Our father had periodically warned us that if we ever got ourselves into trouble for doing something asinine, neither Dent nor I should expect him to bail us out. So far, I had yet to do anything I would call stupid. My brother, on the other hand, had begun building a resumé, though I doubted Dad knew half of the things Dent had done.

"What are we gonna do, JT?"

"Wait for Blaine. He went to get the bill of sale. Hopefully, that will get us out of here."

"Right. Good for him. He knows where it's at?"

"Yeah, its, you know, in the bottom drawer."

Dent and I stood waiting, our backs to Oleander, who continued to bemoan his victimization in a swindle instigated by a sophisticated gang of plausible gambling sharks, and he cursed the little weasel who had kept him locked up like a monkey in a cage. I could not argue with the monkey part, and wanted to say as much, but I kept quiet, preferring to interact with him as little as possible. Another half hour passed, though it was probably closer to ten minutes or less, when I heard the front door open and close.

"JT? Dent?"

"Back here, Wallace!" Dent called. Blaine stepped through the doorway and his face told me something was terribly wrong.

"What's the matter?"

"Our money."

"What about it?"

"It's gone."

"What do you mean, it's gone?" Dent asked incredulously.

"It's just gone. I got there and found Keeler tied and gagged in our room. The place was all tore up, our saddle bags emptied, and the drawers pulled out." Then added emphatically, "clear out."

Suddenly, I remembered the man smoking the cigarette. He was dressed like a gambler. Odds were good that he was there waiting for us to vacate the premises.

"Oleander," I said, his name seething across my lips. Dent looked at me, and we both knew.

"Oleander?" Blaine asked, and I jerked my head indicating where the idiot could be found, and Blaine peeked around Dent, his eyes spotting our prison mate. "What's he in here for?"

"Drunk and disorderly, but mostly for being insanely stupid," I replied.

"He just had to go and shoot off his big ass mouth!" Dent exclaimed, then turned on Oleander. "You sumbitch, our money's gone because of you!"

"What about the bill of sale?" I asked as a wave of nausea cramped my stomach. "Blaine, was that gone, too?"

He shook his head and pulled the folded document from his shirt pocket. "No," Blaine said, shoving the paper through the bars. I unfolded it and with a glance of confirmation, I blew a sigh of relief. Before I could thank Blaine, the sound of the front door being flung open and the anxious stomping of a pair of boots upon the wood floor silenced me. Quickly I tucked the bill of sale into the front pocket of my pants, deciding I was not at all comfortable letting the officer know, without other witnesses, that I possessed evidence that would exonerate me as the horse thief he accused me to be.

"Got 'em locked up back here," I heard Deputy Moody declare just before he appeared in the doorway. "Horse theifs. One ub 'em, enyways." Then he spied Blaine, and after a brief gawk, he spat and spewed, "Who da hell ahr you?!"

"I'm a friend—of theirs," Blaine replied with a nod.

"Git yer scrawny ass back up thar agin thet wahl," Moody ordered, pointing his rifle at Blaine. As a precaution, Blaine held his hands out in front of him and followed the lawman's instructions. Then a movement behind the deputy drew my attention. Filling the doorway of the cellblock, was a tall, striking gentleman.

I had met him before.

He glanced at me, his face hinting of sympathy, then looked at Dent and Blaine, before returning his commanding blue eyes to stare at me.

"We meet again," said the handsome, middle-aged benefactor of a certain copy of a newspaper that had been gifted to me a few days earlier.

"Hez the wun dat was ariddin' that smart-talkin' Negro's bald-faced pony," Moody snarled, and if I had not been behind the bars of his jail cell, I might have congratulated him on the details of his description. But I kept my mouth shut.

"Jack," the expensively suited man said to Moody, "they don't look like horse thieves to me," he spoke, his voice a soothing, pleasant baritone. Then he turned to me and smiled. "You aren't, are you? A horse thief?"

"No, sir," I said, then feeling reasonably confident that I could trust this man, I took the paper from my pocket and passed the evidence to him through the bars, not realizing I had instead handed him Abagail Penny's pamphlet. I watched his eyes flinch curiously before I noticed my mistake. "Sorry! Wrong pocket," I exclaimed, then I fumbled into the correct pouch of my pants.

"I see you've met Mrs. Penny," he said nonchalantly. "I admire her advocacy. I, too, am sympathetic of the dying race of the Native Indian."

"Here," I said, barely acknowledging his commentary, and anxiously presented him with Viento's bill of sale.

We traded papers, and I watched as he carefully passed his eyes over the transfer document.

Twice.

"Well, Jack," he spoke congenially, his tone a stark contrast to that of the prickly lawman. "This young man has a legally binding bill of sale."

"Whut?" Moody coughed.

"You've arrested the legitimate owner of that stallion," he explained showing Moody the document. "This bill of sale, drawn and witnessed by our own esteemed Nathaneil Penny, unquestionably makes young Mr. Tescott the horse's legal owner."

"Tescott? Is thet hez name?

"That's what it says, right here," the man gently replied, tapping the paper, and offering the deputy an opportunity to look at it. "JT Tescott."

Moody pushed the paper away, "You knows I cain't read."

"Probably best to let Mr. Tescott go, Jack. And his friends, too."

"Pro'ly," Moody replied. "But only cuz yous say so, Mister Headville."

I froze.

Oh shit, I thought. Then thought it again. And then a third time. And I imagined Dent was thinking the same thing. But probably with a more colorful choice of expression. Culver Headville turned his eyes back to me and I quickly fashioned as genuine a smile as I could pretend.

"Thank you, Mr. Headville, sir," I said taking the bill of sale from his outstretched hand.

"My pleasure," he said then turned to leave. He stopped and faced me again. "By the way, how is the job hunting going? Any luck?"

"No. Not yet," I replied.

"As I alluded to the other day, I could use a few more ranch hands. Assuming, of course, that you have experience working with horses and cattle."

Dent and I exchanged glances, but I got nothing conclusive from him one way or another. So, when my brother spoke, he startled me, though I hoped I had hidden my astonishment well enough.

"We've got skills," Dent replied. "Solid skills, scouts honor."

"We'll think about," I quickly intervened.

"Of course. Talk it over. I have an appointment at the U.S. Land Office. If you decide to take me up on my offer, catch me there in an hour," Headville added with a smile that would turn a politician green with envy.

"Hey—dude, sir!" Oleander called as he appeared at the front of his personal cell looking Culver Headville over, head to toe. "I'll work for you."

Instantly, I cringed.

"And who would you be?"

"Oleander Sedgwick, at your service, sir. I'm a friend of the Tescott brothers," he added with a gesture of his head, falsely supplanting an exaggerated friendship, at least as far as I was concerned. But in that moment, it did not seem wise to argue with Oleander given we were squarely in the company of the one man whom we wished to avoid.

The notorious Culver Headville turned upon Oleander a more scrupulous study, then grinned. "A friend of JT Tescott is a friend of mine," said the man Morgan had referred to as a viper. "Come by the land office, after you've cleaned up, and I'll visit with you for a few minutes about your possible employment."

"How much?"

"Salary?" Headville asked, noticeably annoyed.

"Yeah, how much dough are you talking about paying me?"

"More than you could earn working for anyone else," Headville replied, though when he spoke, his eyes were directly on me. "And of course, it depends on your—abilities." With a nod, he left the room and exited the building.

Deputy Texas Jack Moody pulled a ring of keys he had hitched to his belt and unlocked the gate of the Tescott brother's short-term place of residence. We stepped out and I was glad to once again be a free man. Thankfully, Mom had not been here to see her boys wrongfully incarcerated. Knowing her, she would have a few words for the deputy, if not a scalding speech.

Moody then released Oleander without giving him so much as a warning to keep out of trouble. We spilled from the front door of the city jail, and I immediately crossed to Viento and stroked his neck. Dent came and stood next to me, tucking his pocketknife into its rightful place.

"We're in a hell of a mess, little brother. A hell of a mess."

"That we are," I agreed, my anxiety pushing my stomach into my throat.

"I hate to say it, but I don't see how we have much of a choice."

I knew what he meant. We were flat-ass broke, except for some change in our pockets. Thanks to Oleander's drunken stupidity, we were without any means of financially supporting ourselves, much less afford to buy our next meal. And neither would my pride allow me to seek additional proceeds from the coffer Morgan had left in the hands of the executor, John White. I wanted neither man to know that we had, indeed, stupidly squandered our funds in just one day. Somehow, we would have to find a way to earn a living now that our collective bankrolls were likely long gone and destined to be wagered in another gambling joint far away from Hays City. Getting our money back was undoubtedly a lost cause. Especially considering the caliber of the law enforcement officer who had arrested us.

"He's Culver Headville," I said, shaking my head. "Morgan warned us to stay away from him."

Then Blaine joined us. "He wasn't as bad as I expected him to be."

"No, he wasn't," I agreed. Then I remembered Morgan's words.

Who may at first wear a mask of congeniality.

"But, like a viper hiding in tall grass," I added, verbally quoting the man who was rambling eastward by rail, his mind set on returning to his home in Europe.

"Waiting for the chance to bite you in the ass," Dent cautioned.

"Exactly."

"Do you think he'll really hire Oleander?" Blaine asked.

"If he did, he'd be a fool," Dent replied.

But I was thinking differently. "Or a fool not to."

The three of us studied each other for a long moment, I, myself waiting for a lightning bolt of an idea that was better than the alternative we were contemplating.

"Well, what's that saying?" Dent asked, rhetorically. "Keep your friends close and your enemies closer." It was hardly the inspiration I was hoping for, but there was wisdom in those words.

Quietly, the three of us continued to ponder our situation, while the fourth of our group stood in the middle of the dirt street, looking first in one direction, then another.

"Hey, Double D," Oleander called to my brother. "Which way to that land office?"

"You're right, Dent. We really don't have a choice."

Then in my mind I thought of something else that suddenly made the risk seem foolishly worthwhile.

The girl with the honey gold curls.

CHAPTER 28

Dent and Blaine and I mounted up, instructing Oleander to follow us to the livery stable where we had a horse waiting for him. He cussed at us, reiterating his inexperience as a horseman, and expressing his displeasure with being forced to travel about on horseback, and he also muttered a few choice expletives regarding the inconvenience of having to walk to get to the place that housed his ride. There was no pleasing the imbecile.

After first insisting Oleander dunk his head in the horse trough to clean up his face and hair, Dent took Oleander to the stall where the roan mare waited. Once there, my brother began to school the fledgling Westerner on how to saddle a horse, making it explicitly clear to Oleander that the job would be his going forward, so he had better pay attention. I listened to him grumble and cuss as I shared with the livery owner our plans to work for Culver Headville.

He laughed, though he didn't sound amused. "Watch yer back, Laddie. And keep a sharp eye on that fella who rides with him. Mean one, he is."

I politely thanked Dub O'Brien for his advice, then asked him for directions to the U.S. Land Office, only to learn that the place of government business was just caddy-corner from our hotel. I felt foolish as I realized my powers of observation were apparently beginning to tank. But at least the office location was convenient to the hotel since we needed to return and gather our gear from the scene of the crime that had rendered us desperate and destitute.

During the following ten minutes, Oleander hesitantly committed to joining the ranks of the cowboy, albeit a novice one. Neither his arrogance nor his family wealth offered much assistance with the task of learning to ride a horse. Dent bestowed upon him far more patience than I would have, still it was pitiful to watch him flounder about in the saddle like a catfish out of water. Somehow, Oleander managed to stay on top of the roan mare. But that was more to the credit of the horse than it was to her rider.

After a five-block round-about maiden ride to literally give Oleander the reins of sole control, the four of us eventually arrived at the Pennsylvania House hotel. With poorly disguised hesitation, Oleander announced he would stay outside and wait on us and watch out for the other horses. I assumed the reason for the offer had more to do with his preference to remain in the saddle in lieu of an awkward dismount and an unsure remount. Though he was athletically gifted, Oleander had demonstrated an embarrassing clumsiness when it came to getting himself onto the back of a horse. I guessed that his mounting ineptitude was mostly due to an undeclared fear of the equine species, however the roan mare was as gentle as they come. But it had not helped alleviate Oleander's anxiety when Dent had earlier warned him that the horse liked to bite.

I had looked at the smirk on my brother's face and then had given him the sincerest eye of admonishment that I could fake. "That ole mare doesn't bite," I had reminded him.

"Sure, she does," Dent had replied, still smiling. "She bites grass and hay. I've seen her do it tons of times!"

Blaine, my brother, and I entered the hotel, but there was no sign of the manager.

"Mr. Keeler?" I called out, but coincidentally there was no reply. Dent was first up the stairs, and Blaine was only two steps behind him when he stopped and looked down at me.

"JT, you know what?" Blaine asked, though the guilty expression on his face told me that he had something else to say. "I was in a hurry. Didn't think—"

"You left Keeler tied up, didn't you?"

"Yeah, I did."

When we reached the room, the door was open and Dent was standing inside, staring into the corner behind the door.

"I'll be damned!" he chortled. Once Blaine cleared the threshold behind me, I swung the door aside and found Keeler, tied and gagged, and glaring. Dent knelt and untied a rolled bandana that muffled the hotel manager. At once, Keeler spat out a second saliva-soaked kerchief from the cavity of his mouth, and with dismay I recognized that it belonged to me. And I had already done my laundry for the week.

"You ungrateful little shithead!" Keeler spat, his eyes shooting daggers at Blaine.

"Sorry," Blaine offered with sincerity.

"Sorry?! Sorry?! You left me here like I was a stinkin' chamber pot!"

"He said he was sorry," Dent politely reminded him.

Keeler spun his eyes toward Dent and gawked at him as if he had just stepped out of a spaceship, which if he had been at the Pyramids two weeks ago, he might have witnessed that very thing.

"Nobody treats Fergus Keeler like that!"

I squatted near the prostrate man and reached for the bindings around his feet, but Dent raised his arm and placed a hand against my chest.

"First, Mr. Fergus Keeler, sir, I'd like to know how a thief managed to get into our room? I mean, you keep the keys, right?"

"I let them in."

"Them?"

"Two of 'em," he said with a nod.

"Well, that was nice of you. Did you know them?"

"Never saw 'em before."

"So, you let two strangers into our room and watched them rob us blind."

"They had guns," Keeler reported dispassionately.

"Did they? Had them pointed at you?"

"Not exactly. But they meant business!"

Dent paused his interrogation and glanced at me. "Wild Bill, do you have any questions for the witness?" Clearly, Dent was suspicious, but I did not know exactly why. Though I had to admit that sometimes he had a sixth sense when it came to reading people.

"I ain't answerin' no more questions!" Keeler screeched, bestowing upon me his full attention. "Now get on with it, you dumb little asshole, and untie me."

"Oh, now Mr. Keeler, that, well that was entirely uncalled for," Dent reprimanded. "My brother, JT, he's twenty times nicer than I am, and twice as smart. You're going to need to apologize to him, and while you're at it, you should tell my friend Blaine you're sorry for calling him a bad name as well. You know, if my momma was here, she'd wash out your mouth with a bar of soap. For free, no extra charge."

"You smart mouth sumbitch, I ain't—"

"No, no, no, no," Dent cut him off. "You've crossed the line now, Mr. Fergus Keeler," and in the next instant Dent was stuffing the kerchief back into his mouth. Then my brother looked at me. "I take it very personal when somebody insults my mother."

"Me too," I admitted, then we stepped away from Keeler, leaving him to thrash and bemoan in protest of our lack of assistance. Quickly, but thoroughly, the three of us gathered and sorted the disarray of our gear, including that of Oleander's, and repacked our saddlebags. As we headed out the door, I caught Dent by the elbow and nodded over my shoulder.

"Shouldn't we ..."

"Should we?"

"I didn't the first time," Blaine said without sounding the least bit apologetic. "Don't see a point in starting now."

I couldn't disagree. Besides, I had decided to let Fergus Keeler keep my kerchief. A little something to remember us by.

We left the hotel and found Oleander still waiting for us as he had promised. Seemingly brooding, he sat quietly focused on the animal beneath him, and said nothing as the three of us attached our gear onto the back end of our horses' saddles. In the next minute we were mounted and pointing our rides down the street, where just a half-block away, a potentially unpleasant destiny awaited us.

Culver Headville exited the two-story limestone structure and found the four of us prospective cowhands punctually waiting for him. He smiled at us, though this time I believed I could see the sly expression of deceit Morgan had warned me about. But maybe not. This man would not be an easy read, nor would he be as openly uncouth as Oleander Sedgwick. He was polished, suave, and borderline charismatic. And so far, damn too easy to like.

Gathered there in front of the U.S. Land Office, Culver Headville offered each of us a generous thirty dollars a month plus room and board, and it was clear to me he would neither indulge us with a counter proposal, nor entertain the idea of a negotiation.

"We accept," I said, having earlier been elected our spokesperson with a vote of three to one. And though I had explained to the dissenter what the current wage would likely be for a ranch hand in 1878, I was not remotely convinced Oleander understood the concept of inflation.

Still Sedgwick scoffed and informed our new boss that he himself was worth far more than any of the other three of us. And by virtue of his words, he included Dent as his subordinate. Not a smart move, considering my dear brother was the closest thing Oleander had to a friend, and even that relationship had been perilously deteriorating at an accelerated rate.

"There," Headville responded to Oleander, pointing his finger down the street in the general direction of the place where Sedgwick had spent the night, "is the road. If my offer does not suit you, then, by all means, look elsewhere."

The symbolism of Headville throwing down the gauntlet did not go unnoticed. Additionally, it was impossible for me not to appreciate the fact that he exuded confidence and authority, especially since he was clearly unimpressed with the cockiness of Oleander Sedgwick. Without doubt, Culver Headville was the man in charge. It was plain to see that working for him would be a choice between his way, or the highway. I hoped all of us would be up to the challenge, though a voice inside my head argued that Blaine, Dent, and I would be far better off if Oleander would flip Headville the bird of his intact right hand and then just ride off into the sunset. But that did not happen.

"Naw, no need for me to do that, Mr. Headville, sir," Oleander said, glueing a grin on his face that looked surprisingly sincere. "You suit me just fine."

Before we left town our new boss informed his entourage of four that he had a detour to make, so we followed him after he had mounted an exquisite example of what I knew a premier Quarter Horse should look like.

Stocky and well-muscled, with a sleek and elegant head and fox ears, and with a snip and a star marking his face, the chestnut stallion could easily have landed the coveted cover of any of the horseman magazines subscribed to by my father. But the horse was small, by most standards, and I guessed him to be short of fifteen hands at his withers, a good six inches less than Viento. But the lengthy size of the man who rode upon him unfairly diminished the appearance of the ranch animal's height.

On horseback, the four of us followed Headville as he traversed along a low-traffic street that ultimately intersected with the road I had decided was a direct southerly route to nearby Fort Hays, the same street that lay adjacent to the length of John White's home and barber shop structure and was only a few addresses away from The Sporting Palace and a spattering of other houses of ill repute. Given the logistical convenience, I imagined the soldiers were the preeminent customers who kept those lucrative businesses safely out of the red, so to speak.

Surely, I thought to myself, Headville was not making a personal pitstop at a brothel prior to leaving town. Or worse, he was taking the four of us boys there to exercise a right-of-passage necessary to make men out of us before putting us on his payroll. If that were the case, I was minutes away from resigning from my new job.

Two changes in direction put the five of us squarely in the throng of the busy main street, where we were practically rubbing elbows and stirrups with a deluge of afternoon shoppers. But within a few clips, Headville stopped his horse at a hitching rail that fronted Krueger's Dry Goods, an impressively large stone building two stories high and fronted with large plate-glass windows. At once, the senseless worry concerning a certain den of iniquity evaporated. Instead, the focus of my attention fell upon the occupants of a fancy, black-lacquered buggy parked in the space along the boardwalk and harnessed to a pair of flashy palomino ponies.

The driver was the same thick, stout man I had observed from a distance a few days earlier, but up close he appeared thoroughly menacing, and from an appearance perspective, he was the polar opposite of Culver Headville. A scraggle of salt and pepper whiskers sprouted from beneath a broad, flat nose, and poorly veiled a heavy scowl that anchored the corners of his mouth. He wore a gray cowboy hat, and had it comfortably fitted down against his ears, one of which was missing a lobe. And in the shadow of the hat's wide brim, I detected eyes that were dark and cold. Without question, he was the man Dub O'Brien had cautioned me about, but the warning was unnecessary. The buggy driver was plainly someone worthy of vigilance and concern.

I looked away, but not before my gaze wandered over the man's Stetson. Apparently, it was a favored hat, but one that had clearly seen better days. A greasy set of smudges graced the crown, where obviously a dirty hand had frequently been used to put it on and take it off. But most noticeable was a sprinkling of dark speckles across the front dip of the rim. The dots appeared to be in the pattern of blood splatter, but whether they were his or the coagulate of someone else, I could not tell, but I also knew I would not be asking him which.

Besides, I was more curious about the young lady who sat upon the rear seat of the carriage, her eyes and chin dipped toward a small leather-bound book in her hands that appeared to be a bible. Telepathically, I implored her to lift her head and bless me with a smile I imagined to be as radiant as the dew on the petals of a white rose, but she remained static and focused. Perhaps, she was praying. If that were the case, I could hardly compete with God.

Headville introduced the four of us new hires as the Tescott brothers, JT and Dent, Blaine Wallace, and Oleander Sedgwick, and then presented the man parked in the driver's seat as Willard Sherlee, who grunted an acknowledgement that seemed to say he had heard and had recorded our names into the dark recesses of his mind. I hoped that this man who was without any semblance of a personality, would not be our foreman or supervisor.

Then, and only because I suspected etiquette demanded it of him, Headville introduced us to the shapely young woman who sat in the buggy behind her driver, Mr. Sherlee. Having been thinking of her off and on for the past several days, I was now mere seconds away from learning her name.

"And this young lady is my ward, Kate," Headville said smiling at her, as her guardian, and not as the father I thought him to be.

Kate, I repeated in my mind. A nice name, and it fit her well, much like her dress. Then she glanced up, looking first at Headville, before casting a disinterested gaze in the direction of me and the other guys. Despite her lack of enthusiasm, she was a natural beauty, even if she chose not to smile, and I guessed her age to be fairly close to mine. For certain, she was not a girl, but practically an adult.

Subconsciously, I straightened my back and repositioned my butt inside the confines of the saddle, hoping to improve my posture to match the manly pose I pictured of myself. Unexpectedly, she directed her attention toward me, her green eyes nearly the same shade as my own. Then Kate creased her brow and appeared to gaze at me with disdain. At once, I wondered if she thought she had caught me squirming, perhaps speculating that my underwear had irritatingly ridden its way upward and inward. Or maybe my movement was the excuse she needed to give me a second look. Either way, there was nothing I could do but smile at her. But unfortunately, I did more than that.

Like a fool, I tagged on a wink, and for a long embarrassing moment she just stared at me. Instantly, I felt like a pubescent idiot, but still, I could not help but hope for a similar reciprocation. But I did not get my wish. With a sudden purse of her cherry red lips, Kate looked away as though to inform me that she was definitely not interested.

"I am Kate's guardian," Headville added, rescuing me from my failed attempt at flirting. "And I take that responsibility very seriously," he added, giving each of us who were steeped and brimming with testosterone, an unspoken warning.

I looked at Dent, hoping he had not seen my misguided eye twitch, but also trusting that he had clearly caught the man's drift and understood that if there was ever a time to keep it in his pants, it was now. Preferably, my brother would not be interested in Kate in the first place, but I doubted that possibility. Still, I wondered if I should tell him I had my own designs for the young beauty, as improbable as they might be at the moment. After all, he did owe me.

I shook my head, silently cursing the doom of my fantasy. I had to put such ideas from my mind. This girl, Kate, was essentially the daughter of a man who might just kill me for my knowledge of the location of a certain talisman. And the fact that I had plans to return to my own time in a future that was not meant to be hers made Kate an impractical choice for a potential love interest.

But I could dream.

With introductions completed, we left Hays City, traveling northeast along the path of a narrow-tracked road, its edges sprinkled with sunflowers, its breadth a perfect fit to the axel width of the Western carriage. The four of us underlings rode a respectful distance behind the transport of our new boss who had tied his handsome, white-footed horse to the back of the buggy and was now seated next to the golden-haired girl named Kate. I watched as the long curls of her hair bounced from beneath the back edge of her bonnet and at once it occurred to me that her locks were nearly the same color as those of Laurie, and I wondered if I had, without realizing it, a certain type I was attracted to? Dent, though, interrupted my self-analysis.

"That horse," he said, and I looked to see his gaze was fixed on Headville's chestnut stallion. "I could swear I've seen him before."

I returned my eyes to my brother. "You probably saw him the other day when we explored Hays," I suggested.

"No," Dent said, shaking his head. "I would have remembered seeing him then. No, what I'm thinking is, I've seen a picture of that horse."

"A picture? Where?"

"In one of Dad's horse magazines."

"That's impossible," I said to him.

"I know," Dent agreed. Then he turned to me and added, "Or is it?"

I knew what he meant, but still, it did not make sense. But before we could discuss the idea further, the noise of trotting hoofbeats sounded behind us as Blaine and Oleander rode up and bookended Dent and I, one on each side.

"Guys," Blaine was quick to speak. "Sedgwick just asked me about, well, about Kival."

Shit, I thought. But then I knew it would only be a matter of time before a rogue pair of Oleander's brain neurons accidentally collided sparking an unfortunate memory. I glanced warily at Blaine.

"I told him Kival had died with Sam," Blaine added assuring me he had stuck to the plan.

From the other side of Dent, Oleander spoke. "I don't remember any of that," he said, seeming to be genuinely confused.

"So," Blaine added, "I told him to ask Dent about it."

I looked at Blaine and nodded. He knew, as did I, that Dent would be the only one Oleander would believe.

Without missing a beat, Dent turned to the inquisitor. "Listen, you dumb shit, of course you don't remember what happened. And be glad you don't. While you were passed out under that tree with cactus practically shoved up your ass, those sumbitchin' Indians just whacked 'em up right there in front of us! I wish I didn't remember it. JT and Blaine, they don't want to be reminded of it either. So, just—just drop it, okay, Olly? Just forget that either one of those poor bastards ever got sucked into this godforsaken time capsule we're trying to bullshit our way through. Okay?!"

"Okay," Oleander said with the most amiable tone of submission I had ever heard come from his normally obnoxious mouth. "I guess I should count myself lucky, huh?" he added apologetically.

"Yeah," Dent said. "You were straight up lucky."

I rode along in silence, staring at the ears of my horse, literally stunned by what my brother had just improvised. Then I glanced at Blaine whose brow was raised to full mast and could offer me nothing more than a shrug. Apparently, he was equally impressed. Then I gambled a peek at Dent and coincidentally found him turning to look at me, his face grim and serious.

And then he grinned and bobbed his eyebrows, securing my vote for him to win the Oscar for best actor in either a comedy or a drama, depending on one's point of view.

"Damn, I could sure go for a pizza right now," Dent announced, returning his attention to the carriage ahead of us.

"Ah, me too, Double D," Oleander agreed. "And a beer."

"Damn straight."

Three hours later, and roughly twelve miles overland, the primitive road brought us to a grand entrance with a meticulously lettered sign that immodestly proclaimed in a font of shiny metal letters CH QUARTER HORSE RANCH. The signage hung from an expansive frame of gnarled and twisted timber stretched between lofty posts of thick red cedar set in bases of limestone masonry that were every inch as tall as I stood with my boots on. To describe it as impressive would be an understatement.

I glanced left and right, consciously acknowledging the presence of formidable post rock fencing that infinitively disappeared in both directions from the ranch's access point, and I surmised that the network of fence had been built upon the perimeter of the entire ranch. A property of an uncommonly grand size, or so I felt drawn to believe.

We followed the buggy through the massive gateway, noting that the only way I could have reached the bottom edge of one of the letters would have required me to be fully standing on the back of Viento. And the extravagant width of the entrance was also noteworthy, though I was surprised it had not been designed to accommodate the full name of the ranch's baron, and not merely the abbreviated use of the man's initials.

Dent and I exchanged glances. Our own ranch, the Sweetwater, had a similar entrance, but was far less pretentious.

The private roadway we were now traveling upon was noticeably well-maintained and situated within a wide gap bordered on each side by secondary fences sternly dominated by the square-cut limestone posts, that were, in my own time, common fixtures along pastures and roadsides of Central and Western Kansas. Symbolic of innovative homesteaders, and evidence of backbreaking labor, the cream-colored rock posts had been set into the ground and spaced ten feet apart. Five tight strands of twisted barbed wire linked the posts, and together the twinned fences disappeared over a rise ahead of us that seemed to swallow the road.

Just after crossing the boundary that defined the ranch, there was one characteristic of the landscape that immediately captured my attention. The pasture was like a field of virgin grassland, unflawed by any vestiges of prickly pear cactus, or prairie yucca, or even so much as a visible sprig of sagebrush. It was as though the pasture had been picked clean, cleared of anything other than the fluttering of native buffalo grass.

How Culver Headville had accomplished such a task was mind-boggling. The hours of labor, particularly in this era of Mid-Western settlement, would certainly have been daunting. Yet somehow this man, whom I was to heed as much as I would a rattlesnake, had somehow managed it. And it was difficult not to be impressed. But suddenly I wondered exactly what I and my companions had been hired to do. I had assumed the work Headville had planned for us involved horses and cattle, not shovels and rakes.

As I gazed around, I discovered that Dent was equally awed by the pristine pasture. Without a word to each other, we studied the terrain as we continued eastward, riding along the wide pathway that had dropped abruptly before beginning to skirt a knoll that rose from what appeared to be a basin within the rolling plain of the ranch. Then, as we rounded the low hill, we found ourselves looking across a wide shallow valley, the little road needling along the edge of a wood that feathered southward and sprinkled its trees into the natural hideaways nestled between ridges and rills.

Flanking the northern side of our roadway were coves and draws hollowed from hillsides, the vegetation thick and green. The aesthetic panorama that had unfolded before us was so abruptly different than just a mile back west from which we had come. The only explanation I could think of for the abundance of trees and the lushness of the grass was that this was an oasis born of natural springs. But as impressed as I was with the landscape, the scenery that was even more spectacular was that of a living portrait of horses.

Hundreds of them.

Broodmares with nursing foals. Yearlings and young fillies frolicking about in the early evening air. And among them was a kaleidoscope of coat colors, from white and dapple-grey, to dun and buckskin, and sorrels and blood red bays and blacks. At once, Viento whinnied causing dozens of his species to lift their heads and gaze in our direction. Apparently, Viento was also impressed.

And in the distance, I could see bands of cattle grazing along the slopes and valleys beyond the central site of a cluster of buildings that commanded an equal nod of admiration.

And admire, I did. Even from where the structures stood a good half mile away, the homestead of the CH Quarter Horse Ranch was stunning.

There were three long barns, seemingly identical, with doorways and paddocks flanking the length of their limestone walls. And a fourth barn that was easily the largest of its type that I had ever seen, boasted a lofty profile that would have otherwise dwarfed its neighboring windmill had the water pumping structure not been of an unusually enormous scale in and of itself. Then a fifth barn, or something else, veneered in matching limestone rock sat strategically near the livestock housing, and as my mind connected the dots, I realized it was probably the bunkhouse, the place that I expected to be my living quarters for the next several months.

And opposite the bunkhouse, towering across from the collection of outbuildings, was a sprawling two story house, slightly elevated upon a bank of ground and cuddled by a treescape that pushed into the home's backyard. And like the other homestead structures, the exterior of the extravagant domicile was likewise clad in walls of pale limestone that caught and reflected the sun giving the dwelling and its counterparts an appearance of being almost golden.

It was a palace. At least in comparison to what was the norm here on the plains of Western Kansas, regardless of the century. Inarguably, it was a home built for a king.

And his Highness was Culver Headville.

PART THREE

A Matter of Time

CHAPTER 29

s we entered the spacious ranch yard, dotted here and there with cottonwood trees thick with leaves and hinting of namesake specks of willowy fluff, a black and white Border Collie dashed from the shadowy space of the giant barn and raced for the buggy. I watched as the little herding dog pranced about, wagging its feathery tail as it impatiently waited for Sherlee to help Kate down from the carriage.

"Such as good girl," Kate cooed, kneeling before the devoted animal, and playfully ruffling the top of the dog's sleek head. "Did my little Poppy miss me?" I heard Kate ask as she pat the thick fur of its back.

A dog person, I thought to myself and smiled. Another gold star for the golden-haired beauty. I wondered if I would ever be as lucky to get a similar greeting from Kate. And with that thought I realized I had gone there again, to that place that was not meant to be.

"JT, check out this cottonwood," I heard Dent call to me.

Reluctantly, I let my eyes trail away from the girl and her canine companion and found my brother staring upward into the branches of the largest tree I had probably ever seen on the high plains of Western Kansas. How I had not noticed its impressive size from afar had to have been because of the hypnotic effect of the grandeur of structures comprising the heart of Culver Headville's ranch. Without question, everything around me was disproportionately large in comparison to my family's Sweetwater ranch.

"Ain't she a beauty?" Dent added, twisting his neck to look over his shoulder at me. Instantly, I began to gesture to him to cut out his brazen joshing, thinking his comment was directed at Kate. Then at once a flash of déjà vu blinded me as I looked across at my brother sitting there upon the horse, seemingly mesmerized by the sprawling limbs above him, and I was momentarily overcome by an ominous feeling of grief. I shook my head. "What? You don't think so?" Dent added, looking at me like I was an idiot.

"Uh—yeah," I replied, shaking the illusion of the phenomenon. "That tree is—impressive," I added, not feeling at all comfortable with the trick my mind had played on me.

"Can you imagine the hell of a fort we could of had when we were kids if this thing had been standing in our yard?"

"For sure," I agreed, knowing Dent was referencing the scant square footage of a treehouse we had nailed together in our own backyard when we were ten years old. Then as if we were both controlled by the same set of marionette strings, we scanned the structural landscape around us, until Dent made a gesture with a flex of his head that I, Blaine, and Oleander, should follow him.

The four of us freshly employed ranch hands, or cowpokes, or cactus pickers, or whatever we were to be labeled, reined our horses toward the nearby corral, an enclosure superbly constructed of milled wooden planks painted bright white and flanking the easterly wall of the massive barn. We paused at the nearest side of the animal pen, though I sensed Viento would have preferred to trek to the opposite side and partake of filling drink of water from a large trough set at the base of the towering windmill, a typical necessity of cattle ranching in the semi-arid climate of much of the Great Plains.

"In a minute," I said to Viento, giving him a pat on the neck, preferring not to be presumptive that it was okay with Culver Headville to allow the horse to drink before being given the green light to do so. As if choreographed, Dent and I dismounted in unison, the two of us easing from our saddles that bespoke of years of experience. I glanced in time to see Blaine manage a respectable slide down from Buck, especially given he had only had a week or so of practice. Oleander, though, climbed out of the saddle hanging onto its horn and cantle like a third grader dropping from a playground monkey bar.

"Holy shit!" Oleander exclaimed feeling for the ground with the toes of his boots as the patient red roan mare rolled her eye toward him as though she was considering a quick little side-step to send the greenhorn tumbling to the ground. At least that is what I would have done had I been in her horseshoes. Once replanted on terra firma, Oleander reached both hands behind him and began to massage his gluteus maximus. "Chrissakes, my ass—"

"Yeah, its fat," Dent piped up. "But I won't tell anyone."

Blaine laughed, and I could not help but snicker. Oleander did not find Dent's joke funny at all and said as much with a two-word phrase of profanity having F and Y for acronymic initials.

We tied the reins of our horses to the top rail of the corral fence, and I turned to see King Culver standing before his castle, his hands on his hips and his elbows splayed, and the black Stetson royally crowning his head as he surveyed the distant lands of the ranch he had assumably built with blood and sweat and tears. I was just not sure of whose bodily fluids it had taken to accomplish it all, but I doubted if much of it had been his own. Though by reputation he had figuratively gotten his hands dirty, he did not, however, seem the type to do so literally.

Then for a moment he focused his attention on Kate, saying something to her before she turned toward a walkway of fifteen or more steps that led upward to the limestone home, the little dog obediently at her heels. From the corner of my eye, I watched as she effortlessly climbed the outdoor stairs and crossed to a sweeping veranda where she was met by a slightly taller young woman with skin the color of rich fudge and attired in a long red velvet dress that was decidedly both prim and provocative. As the two of them entered the house, a short, slender, feisty Black man dressed in dark pants and an equally dark jacket skimmed passed them and spoke to Headville, though his words were inaudible.

As Headville and the man who matched the stature of a professional jockey engaged in conversation, I shifted my attention to watch as the man called Sherlee led the chestnut stallion toward the nearest of the three identical structures that were clearly designed as horse stables. For a moment, I wondered about the familiarity Dent had perceived regarding the horse, though I felt sure that we would eventually chalk it up to coincidence that the animal resembled the photograph of another horse that would live in the next century. Besides, in the natural order of things, there were not as many differences among ranch horses as one might think, despite the variations in color and markings. However, the opposite was true when describing a ranch hand where the spectrum of that sub-species of human being could range from someone like my brother to someone like Oleander.

"I'm serious, Hollywood," Oleander said with persuasion, his voice distracting my thoughts. "I'll give you fifty bucks to massage my ass."

Enough said.

As we waited for instructions from our new boss, a pair of cowboys, each riding a specimen of horseflesh that reflected a similar gene pool of that of Headville's stallion, trotted into the ranch yard arriving from behind the massive limestone barn. Living examples of authentic 1870s cowboys, the two men stopped in front of the building I assumed to be the bunkhouse, then dropped from their respective saddles and promptly tied their mounts to a long hitching rail anchored upon the edge of the covered porch of the masonry building. They glanced in our direction, then spoke to each other, before heading our way. I had guessed they were planning to speak to us, but a voice rose behind me,

and I realized the two cowboys were striding toward us purely because
of the presence of the land baron himself.

"Mick, Boyd," Headville said, greeting them with a simple nod.

"Evenin' Mr. Headville," they replied in near unison.

"You solved the issue," Headville stated, though his words could
have easily been meant as a question.

"Shore-for, Mr. Headville," said the older cowboy, pushing sixty,
with grey shaggy hair spilling from beneath the bent rim of his sweat-
stained cowboy hat. He had a red checkered bandana tied around his
neck, and a dusty blue work shirt tucked loosely over a potbelly, and
brown work pants, with the legs pushed down into his pointed mud-
colored boots.

"And the bulls?"

"Put 'em down, just like you said, Mr. Headville."

"Good," Headville said approvingly. "How many, Boyd?"

"Four of 'em. Big, onery rascals they was."

"Two bull buffalo for each of you then," he said, turning his eyes to
the younger cowboy who looked to be a few years older than me.

"Not 'zackly," Boyd said. "My Mick, here, had hisself a bit of
trouble with his rifle."

"Is that a fact, Mick?" Culver asked, obviously expecting an
explanation.

"Uh, my gun jammed, Mr. Headville, sir," Mick stammered.

"Again," Headville spoke, and as before his tone was not a
question.

"I'll—I'll get it fixed, sir. I promise."

"It's a good thing, Mick, you are not depending on that rifle to save
your life."

"Yes, sir, Mr. Headville. It's a good thing."

Without so much as a blink, Culver Headville switched his attention
to the four of us who had accompanied him from Hays City, now
having found ourselves gathered like lost sheep in the heart of his
swanky ranch. "Rogue buffalo," he offered succinctly. "Tearing
through my fences."

Now I understood why the animals had been shot, but as far as I
was concerned a death sentence for simply damaging a few strands of
barb wire was offensively inhumane.

In my time of the second half of the twentieth century, the regal
male bison had been hailed as unlucky admirals of the grassy sea of
the Western Plains. By the thousands they had been nearly slaughtered
to extinction as recorded in annals of the history of the late 1800s,

which I reminded myself was in the midst of my present calendar year. I admired the beasts, respected them, and was glad that their numbers had been growing, albeit slowly, in the era of my rightful time, both in the wilds of national parks and within the confines of many private reserves.

Granted, I had a soft spot for the American Bison, so if it had been up to me, I would have instead herded them back through to their side of the pasture fence. Assuming, of course, that they could be herded.

"Why shoot them?" I asked as casually as I could, unable to ignore a jab from my conscience to speak up for the wild bovine.

"Why not," my boss responded.

Again, not a question.

"Boyd, Mick," Headville said, smiling as genuinely as he had the first day I met him, "Meet your inquisitive new bunkmate, JT, and his brother Dent, and friends Blaine and Oleander. I hired them today to fill in while the others are away. Boyd, see to it that they are productive."

"Yes, sir, Mr. Headville."

"Howdy," Dent greeted the two ranch hands, his smile as charming as always.

Fearing that I had crossed the line by questioning the shooting of the buffalo, I merely nodded at them, choosing to refrain from saying anything else that Culver Headville might consider insubordinate. My self-imposed silence was my way of wordlessly promulgating the wisdom of the adage, 'better to be quiet and thought of as a—'

"Hey, I gotta question," Oleander said, interrupting my thought.

'Fool,' I added, completing my unspoken recitation of the first part of the lauded proverb. And likewise, I mentally shook my head wondering what stupid thing Oleander thought he needed answered.

Culver Headville shifted his gaze to my illustrious companion. "And to whom, Oleander, are you speaking?"

"You. I was just—"

"No."

"But I haven't asked—"

"No," Headville repeated, his voice firm, but calm, his eyes determined. "Oleander, as a youngster, I was raised by a man whom I considered to be boorishly old-fashioned. However, he did teach me the value of possessing proper manners. As your employer, your commander-in-chief, your—superior, I demand to be addressed with respect. Here, on my ranch, I am Mister Headville. I am not *hey*,"

Headville added gently, though only an idiot would mistake his placidity for weakness. "Understood?"

It was going to be fifty-fifty if Oleander comprehended Headville's expectation. A generously long moment passed and from the expression on his face, Oleander appeared to be thoughtful, but then he often looked that way seconds before busting a fart.

"Yes, sir, Mr. Headville. I hear you loud and clear."

Oleander's response was better than I had expected. A high B plus if I were grading him.

"And?"

"So, I was wondering, Mr. Headville, if I could shoot one of them buffalos for ya?"

And just like that, I lowered the grade to a C minus.

Headville bestowed upon Oleander five full seconds of consideration, then without comment, he turned and crossed toward his home, treading the stone steps before disappearing through the wide nine-foot-high doorway of his grand house. Unquestionably, the man exuded arrogance, but also intelligence.

And danger.

Upon instructions from Boyd, we gathered our horses and led them through the gate of the corral, then across the pen to the watering trough. One after the other, they dipped their muzzles, breaking the surface of the clear water and sucked the liquid into their thirsty mouths.

"Looky," Dent said to me, nodding at the waterworks next to him. Like the windmills of our ranch, this one was likewise fitted with a pipe that fed water to the trough. One difference though was that at the dispensing end of the pipe was a T-joint with a valve that was apparently used to redirect water into an alternative location, one that was seemingly subsurface. "What do you make of that?" Dent asked.

For a prolonged moment, I studied the convergence of the pipe with the ground, then lifted my eyes and looked about. "There," I said my gaze pointing him toward the house. "Modern plumbing, or so it appears."

"What the hell? Is that a water tank up there behind the house?"

"That's my guess," I replied, studying the squatty round structure sitting upon a wooden platform built onto the steep face of a hill that rose beyond the backyard of the home.

"So, this valve switches the water pumped from this windmill and sends it up there," suggested my brother.

"And gravity does the rest," I added. "Despite the isolation, Culver Headville is clearly a man who prefers the conveniences we've taken for granted."

"And no doubt the money to pay for it," Dent agreed, scanning our surroundings.

After satiating our own thirst from a trickle of water from the dispensing pipe of the windmill, the four of us acolytes exited the corral with our respective horses in tow and joined the man called Boyd who waited for us inside the great masonry barn that was as spacious as its exterior promised. There were two tack rooms, one at each end, and a granary built in the southwest corner. Two exterior rows of individual horse stalls lined both sides of the cathedralesque alleyway, their number more than enough to accommodate our four horses and would certainly be an upgrade for them compared to both the Beilman's milk barn and Dub O'Brien's livery in Hays City.

After Boyd's assignment of stalls, I walked Viento inside his new compartment and slipped the saddle from his back and began to prepare him for his first night on the CH Quarter Horse Ranch. A moment later, Mick entered the barn leading the mounts that he and Boyd had been riding. He was quiet, much like Blaine, and similar in height, though his face was landscaped with a short growth of beard identical to the style of facial hair Dent had decided to embrace.

"Say, dude," Oleander blurted as Mick passed by the stall that Boyd had appointed for the roan mare. "Any chance you could show me how to un-do this thingy?"

Mick shifted his eyes to look at him as though Oleander had just performed a ballerina's pirouette while wearing his tutu around his ankles, an imaginary sight that was as ridiculous as the question. Mick neither paused nor replied to Oleander, though I wondered if the admonishment he had been given by Headville was the cause of his bashfulness, or perhaps he just did not care to engage with Oleander. Or maybe the young cowboy was simply a quiet type, in contrast to the older man, Boyd, who had hardly taken a breath between sentences.

"Nothin' against 'em personally, but Mr. Headville he don't like squat 'bout those ole buffs," Boyd went on, having begun the wagging of his tongue the moment we had entered the barn. During the first five minutes of his introductory monologue, I must have heard the man say shore-for a dozen times and a few of his words and phrases were initially a little tricky to comprehend, but not nearly as challenging as the dialect of the lawman Texas Jack Moody. "Luck'ly not been many of 'em round here for a while, what with the railroad terminatin' at Hays City. Been lots and lots a them ole Injun meat wagons shot dead on the spot right from the windas of them train cars. I hear tell that shore-for there's a handful of 'em still roamin' round west of here and into the Colorady."

I had seen one such herd. And it had been an inspiring sight.

"So, Boyd, is that you're first name or last?" I asked, cutting in.

"Boyd be my given name. Last names don't matter none round here, 'cept for Mr. Headville. You boys surely be from back East. Otherwise, you would'na asked such a meddlin' question."

"Yeah, we're in from the East" I replied, thinking our arrival in Hays City might at some point be questioned, so why not point folks in the opposite direction of the truth. "Followed the railroad," I added.

"Didn't ask. Shore-for don't care," Boyd replied, busying himself with the chore of putting his horse in an empty stall. "Most boys out here usually got somethin' they wanna be keepin' in the past, and by gum that be nobody's bidness but their own. So ain't no call to ask nobody what their whole name is, and we don't 'zackly tell other folks ours neither. Hard to trust nobody with too much knowledge 'bout yourself. Could cause a man a big sight of trouble. So be warned, mind ya."

"Well, just so you know, you can trust us. We aren't running from anything." Which was basically the truth.

"Then you be the 'ception, not the rule."

"What the man is saying, JT, is that we should just mind our own business," Dent said, as he parked the bay into a vacant stall next to Boyd's horse. "And him and Mick will mind theirs."

"That be 'zackly right. You catch on a sight faster than your brother," Boyd said, poking me with his eyes.

"Happens all the time," Dent said, tossing me a smirk.

"So, Boyd," Dent continued, capitalizing on the old man's distraction, "Can I ask you this—just how many hands does Headville have working for him here on the ranch?"

"*Mister* Headville. Best you 'member that, boy."

"That's what I meant—Mr. Headville."

"Be how many of us here, Mick? Ten, lebben?"

"There abouts," Mick replied.

"Lessee, there's Little Pete, he's out sweepin' the Saline bottoms. I sent him out there so's he could check 'n see if any of the CH cattle got themselves on the outside of the ranch by sneakin' through that hole in the fence them ole buffs tored through. And there be Sonny,

Roy, and Evrett and Hershel, they be out in Nevady roundin' up some Mustang mares for Mr. Headville."

"You forgot Big Pete," Mick reminded him.

"Oh, hell, how'd I forget 'bout Big Pete?! He's out on that wild horse roundup with the rest of 'em. So that be how many?"

"Six," Dent and Mick said simultaneously.

"Right," Boyd said, "plus Mick and me makes us eight, I figger."

"What about Willard Sherlee?" I asked, making a point to use the man's full name.

"Well, 'course, but he ain't one of us reg'lar hands. Sherlee's the horse wrangler."

"Sherlee? Not just Willard?"

Boyd shrugged. "I guess I should clar'fy the rule a smidge. A man on this ranch wears whatever name Mr. Headville calls him. Jest hope Mr. Headville don't decide to call you Buttercup, cuz if he does, Jay-Tee, that's what we'll all be callin' you."

From behind me, Dent laughed.

"Got it," I said. "So, Sherlee, is he also the foreman?"

"Hells bells, boy! What do you think I be? A butler man?!"

A soft chortle sounded from the stall where Mick curried his horse. And then Boyd joined him with a snort and chuckle. Then from down the length of the barn I heard a scuffle and a thump, followed by a pair of select curse words.

"He's practically worthless," Dent said of Oleander, then strode away in his direction.

"That brawny peckerhead friend of yours, he don't know nothin' much 'bout horses, does he?"

I could not deny his observation. "No," I admitted. "He's … well, he's only had an afternoon to practice, if I'm honest."

Boyd shook his head. "Mr. Headville is 'spectin miracles from me if I'm s'posed to figger somethin' for that greenhorn to do. And him missin' a finger too. You know, out here in this open country, ain't ever-body fit for it! And if I knowd any better, I'd say you boys didn't get here followin' that railroad neither. What you really done was rode in on the damn train, ain't it?"

"Well, no," I said, feeling the squeeze of my little white lie. "Actually, we—"

"Don't matter. Don't care. You gotta past. Who don't?"

Suddenly I had great respect for the "don't ask and don't tell" philosophy of the 1870s semi-modern man of the West. Given that the four of us, five counting Kival, were a hundred years out of our element and striving to keep that fact a secret, it appeared we might get lucky enough to dodge unwanted questions. At least where Boyd was concerned. Hopefully we would be as fortunate with Mick and Willard Sherlee and Little Pete, though I knew better than to be as optimistic when it came to Culver Headville. But as much as I liked the acceptance of anonymity, I still had a problem. I was too damn curious for my own good. And nosey, to quote my mom.

"Who's the other guy?" I asked.

"Boy, you gotta be more specified," Boyd replied.

"The Black man at the house. I'm not sure what his proper job description might be, but he looked like a butler or maybe a manservant?"

"Cain't tell ya."

"You don't know?"

"Course, I know. Been here workin' for Mr. Headville long enough to learn a few things. Most impotanly, around here you don't ask questions 'bout who people are. Sides, if Mr. Headville wants you to know somethin' 'bout the folks up in the big house, he'll tell ya. If he don't want ya to know, then you don't need to know!"

There had to have been something profound about that statement, I just wasn't entirely sure what it was. One thing that was certain, the man liked to talk.

A short time later, Boyd and Mick grained their horses after showing us where the feed sacks of oats and corn were kept in the room designed as a granary, then the two of them headed for the bunkhouse where the old chatterbox mentioned supper would be served just before sundown. Dent was continuing a hands-on demonstration on the proper way to unsaddle a horse, while Blaine and I grabbed our saddlebags and bedrolls informing the teacher and his pupil that we would be waiting outside.

"So far so good, wouldn't you say, JT?" Blaine asked, as we occupied ourselves by playing fetch with the Border Collie.

"I suppose," I replied pensively, tossing a stick across the ranch yard, and watching the little dog speed eagerly after it. "If it were just you and me and Dent, I wouldn't be so worried."

"But Oleander, he's a wild card."

"He's a joker in our deck for sure. Wanting to shoot a buffalo, Jeez Louise."

"We're not telling him we suspect our new boss is a time traveler like us, are we?" Blaine asked as our furry little playmate returned to him the prize of the game.

"Hell, no," I replied, pausing to wonder if I should share with Blaine what Morgan had revealed to me regarding Culver Headville's escapades into the time that belonged to us. If Morgan was to be believed, Headville was John F. Kennedy's true assassin. What other atrocities he may have instigated, I could only imagine, but it would not take much to convince me there were more than just a singular incident, though killing a U.S. President was itself, bad enough.

For a second, I thought I would tell Blaine that wildly incomprehensible testament Morgan had divulged to me, but I changed my mind. The revelation of that construct could easily avalanche into other questions I would rather not be asked, so I rationalized that, for now, it was in all our best interests to keep that bit of information to myself. Besides, what was one more secret?

"As far as Oleander is concerned," I continued, "there is no talisman, no Kival, no Burmano-Ku-Partika, and certainly no one but the four of us shuffling between centuries. If Oleander were to find out that Headville has crossed into our time, I don't know what he would do, but it wouldn't be anything good."

"What wouldn't be good?" Dent asked, striding from the barn with Oleander three steps behind him, both laden with their personal gear.

"Missing supper," I replied extemporaneously, pitching a stick as far as I could and watching the little dog chase after it. "I'm starved."

The bunkhouse was an easy sixty feet long and half that wide, with windows evenly spaced three on each side of the entry door that stood dead center in the limestone wall. The four of us stepped inside and found the room spacious, looking much like the sleeping quarters of my youth's boy scout camp, only the beds were single story, not stacked. In front of the door was a long table made of thick planks of hewn timber, and flanking its length were a foursome of benches that collectively could accommodate eight grown men giving each plenty of elbow room but could manage the seating of as many as sixteen ranch hands crowded beside one another. This gathering spot for our impending dinner divided the room into equal halves, six beds on each side, twelve total.

Impulsively, I did the math. Eight beds belonged to the old hands, the two who were present and the six others out on assignment, and one bed I assumed would be claimed by Willard Sherlee, leaving three beds for the four of us. Somebody would be getting the short straw.

"Take off your boots," Boyd abruptly instructed. "We keep us a clean floor in here. Pract'ly civilized we be."

We set our saddlebags and bedrolls down onto the smooth surface of floorboards that, by all accounts, were immaculate. "Where do we put them?" I asked, as I removed my boots.

"Pick ya a bed, and stick 'em under it," Boyd said from where he sat at the table, tapping what had to have been smoking tobacco from a tin can and aligning the ground fragments along a slip of a paper lying on the surface in front of him.

The four of us spread out, peeking under beds as though we were checking them for the presence of the monsters that had haunted us as kids. Oleander was the first to stake a claim, choosing the bed on the east end nearest the door and next to where Mick sat upon the top of his bunk reading a thin paperback book.

"Cept there, greenhorn," Boyd told him. "That be Little Pete's bunk."

"But he ain't here now, is he?" Oleander challenged.

"Suit yourself," Boyd replied. "He'll be movin' ya tomorra when he gets back."

Oleander puffed up and enlightened the man who was our supervisor that he was not worried about anybody with Little for a name.

"Three spare ones over here," Mick offered to the rest of us pointing across the aisle.

"Thanks," Dent said to him, then my brother and Blaine and I chucked our boots under the beds Mick had indicated. It was then I noticed the corner bed had a pair of worn boots tucked beneath its edge and on the wall next to the bunk was a photo of a showgirl hung up by a rusty nail. Boyd's domain, I surmised.

"Good choice," Boyd called to us. "That end down yonder is where the mustangers been sleepin.' But they ain't likely to be back for a while yet, but s'posedly one of them boys has hisself a head of lice."

"Lice?" I asked, suddenly feeling itchy.

"Nothin' to worry 'bout. Lizanny she's done gathered all the bed covers and cleaned 'em good with lye soap and bit a kerosene I 'spect."

"Lizanny," I said, pouncing on Boyd's slip of the tongue as I moved to sit across from him. "She dresses nicely for housekeeping," I added, recalling the long, flowing red dress, with embroidered cuffs and a neckline that wasn't shy about dipping southward.

"No, boy" Boyd grumbled, as he rolled his cigarette. "You didn't see Lizanny. She only comes on a Saturday now and then. Gets here early, stays the whole day, then gets picked up by her folks and rides back home to Nicodemus after they been into Hays City for supplies. Who you seen was Beverly Carniero."

As I had observed earlier, Boyd liked to talk.

"Who is she?"

"Reckon she be Miss Kate's readin' and writin' teacher," Boyd said striking a match and lighting up. "I don't ask. That be why I keep my job," he added, giving me a cautionary eye.

"Mr. Headville calls her Dove," Mick casually remarked, looking up from his book.

"Says who, Mick?" Boyd challenged.

"Heard him call her that once, that's all."

"And the butler?" I asked, circling around to my earlier question that Boyd had squashed.

"Isaiah," Boyd said through a puff of smoke. "I'll tell ya, he shore-for knows his way round a kitchen I can tell you that! He's—hold up!" Boyd spat, glaring at me. "You be tryin' to trick me, ain't ya boy?"

"No," I said, giving him my most sincere smile. "I was just listening to you. I like conversation."

Boyd squinted an eye at me and took another puff on his cigarette. But before he had a chance to make another accusation, which I would be compelled to deny, we were interrupted.

Willard Sherlee entered the bunkhouse. And behind him was the Black man whose name I had just learned was Isaiah, and within his grasp he carried a square basket covered with twin lids that folded down from the center. With a subtle grunt, he hefted the woven container onto the table. It was not until that moment that I made the connection. Morgan had shared with Kival and me that he had recruited an accomplice on the night he had thieved away the talisman from Culver Headville.

A man named Isaiah.

When Morgan had divulged the identity of the wiry little man, I doubted he thought I would ever actually meet him, much less be on the receiving end of his culinary abilities. More intrigued than I might otherwise have been, I watched Isaiah as he opened the basket and took from it a stack of plates and began to position them upon the perimeter of the tabletop. Immediately the aroma of broiled beef wafted through the air. At once, my mouth turned moist with anticipation.

Seven employees of Culver Headville gathered around the bunkhouse dining table and though I could not speak for everyone, I considered the food exceptionally delicious. But then again, I was hungry.

Crowding my plate were firm slices of sweet potato smothered with a ladle of red beans seasoned with onions and diced bell pepper, and a set of dinner rolls the size of baseballs, each slathered in honey and butter. But the main attraction was an inch thick steak, flash grilled with just the right amount of charring and perfectly cooked with a warm red center and plenty of melt-in-your mouth fat trimming the edge. Without knowing, Isaiah had prepared the steak just as Dad would have done when flexing his cooking skills on the barbeque grill at home.

With Headville's right hand man, Sherlee, sharing the table, I had nixed any further inquiries regarding, well, pretty much anything or anyone. Instead, I ate and listened, determined not to give the horse wrangler any pertinent information which he might feel compelled to report to his boss. That said, there was not a lot of talking. Even Oleander had been unusually quiet having made only a pair of off-handed comments, luckily neither of which had caused me to shit my pants.

But one thing I learned, thanks to Dent's turn at casual interrogation, was that Sherlee did not sleep in the bunkhouse, so the bed count stood at twelve and guaranteed that none of us would have to sleep double. But neither did Sherlee reside in the house, though judging from its size it had to have a minimum of three or four unoccupied bedrooms. Instead, he had his own personal quarters in one of the horse paddocks, which given the fact that he was the ranch's horse guru, made perfect sense.

I also learned that there was what Boyd called the range hut, a place near the north end of the Headville spread where Little Pete was spending the night. Boyd explained that it was a little sod house originally built on a 160-acre homestead that Headville had acquired in a trade with an exasperated farmer swapping the land for two cows bearing Headville's brand. The place was small, and according to Boyd was hardly a house at all and was a 'sight far away,' but convenient for the cowboy called Little Pete to 'hole-up' for the night.

From that and other comments by Boyd, I was left with the impression that the ranch was far grander in size than I had first imagined. But I did not ask for specifics, having already been informed that Headville would tell me if he wanted me to know. However, I had learned in just a short couple of hours that Boyd would probably spill the acreage dimensions if given the time and the opportunity.

After dinner, Sherlee, whose age I finally concluded was right at the big five-o, give or take a decade in either direction, left us and shortly afterward Isaiah returned for the dirty dishes. When he had gone, I grabbed my boots and stepped outside, and was soon strolling into the barn. I crossed to Viento and through the rails of his paddock, I patted him on the smooth plane of his cheek and caressed the end of his velvety nose. I was about to tread into the feed room and sneak a handful of extra grain for Viento before tucking him in for the night, when suddenly at my feet was the little Border Collie. She sat down in front of me, her paws nearly resting on the toes of my boots, apparently determined not to be excluded from any distribution of my affection. I gave her a good scratch-and-rub on the top of her furry head.

Though night had fallen, there was a fair amount of moonlight, so I decided to walk around for a while before returning to the bunkhouse for the night. With the dog as my companion, I began casually exploring the premises. As I passed the most northern of the three identical horse barns, a figure suddenly appeared through a doorway, causing both of us to halt in our tracks. A subtle gasp of surprise escaped through her lips, and at once the little dog expelled a soft bark before quickly trotting toward her.

"Hello," I said. "Kate, right?"

"Who are you?" Kate asked. "And how do you know it's me?"

"Well," I paused to ponder the details of my reply, thinking it might be best not to reveal that my identification was based upon her shape. "I recognized you because of the reflection of moonlight upon the golden color of your hair," I blathered, realizing the words I had strung together were poorly Shakespearean, and sounded more like a half-ass stab at coining a nerdy pickup line. But luckily, she saved me from the embarrassment.

"I'll ask again, who are you?"

"I'm JT," I told her, realizing that the moon was to my back, shadowing my face, and I was also without my hat, which can easily change a man's appearance. "I'm one of the new guys Mr. Headville hired today."

"I remember," Kate said, her voice as soft as a kitten's purr. "You're the one with the handsome—"

She let it hang, suspiciously intentional, but I took the bait hoping she would complete her sentence with the word face, but prayed the word would not be brother. It was neither.

"—grey stallion."

"That would be me," I confirmed, thinking that Viento was giving me some unwanted competition. "And yes, he is a handsome horse," I added, as the Border Collie trotted back to me.

"Poppy likes you," she said, gesturing to the little dog.

"She's a cute little thing," I said, and I thought the same thing of Kate. "We played fetch with a stick earlier," I said offering a reason for the dog's attention.

"Poppy likes anyone who will play with her. So, you're not special, just so you know."

"Got it," I said, then we stared at one another for several uncomfortably quiet moments. "You're out kind of late, aren't you Kate?"

"That's none of your business!"

"Don't worry, I'm not making it my business. It's just that its dark out you know."

"I'm seventeen, for your information. I'm not a little girl and I'm not afraid of the dark."

"Okay, no need to get defensive. I'll leave you to your … business," I said, and turned away.

"I was just checking on a new baby foal. It was born this morning just before we left for town. I wanted to see it before I went to bed."

"Understandable," I said, then spoke over my shoulder. "Goodnight, Kate."

"And just because I like your horse, doesn't mean I like you."

"Not a problem," I told her, as I kept walking, but judging by her attitude, I couldn't help but think this seventeen-year-old young woman might actually like me. She was, I deduced, just playing hard to get.

But I could be wrong.

Either way, I strutted back to the bunkhouse with a smile on my face.

CHAPTER 30

oyd wasted no time putting us to work. After a hearty breakfast of biscuits and ham and red-eye gravy delivered again by Isaiah, and escorted, again, by Sherlee, Boyd clapped on his hat and informed the four of us to get our butts moving, or else he'd *build a boot factory in our ass.*

With Mick already ahead of him by three strides, the two of them were the first to step out into the fresh air of a morning just beginning to show a skim of light on the eastern horizon. Excited to be doing something he both liked and was patently familiar, despite the breadth of a century of time, Dent left the bunkhouse right on the heels of the two tenured ranch hands. Some thirty seconds later, Blaine followed him, though with less enthusiasm than that of my brother.

Like Dent, I was eager for the day to get rolling, but I had decided to delay my departure just long enough to gather and stack the plates and cups before wiping the crumbs off the table and catching them in my hand.

"What ya playin' housewife for, Worm?" Oleander asked me from where he had returned to recline on the top of his bunk.

"Just helping out, that's all," I replied with indifference.

During breakfast Boyd had rattled on about a dozen different things, including what he had in store for us for our first day on the job, but he had also talked about Isaiah, saying more than he had probably intended.

Apparently, Isaiah wore several hats and various aprons as a member of a household staff that was basically just him, except for the periodic Saturdays when the girl called Lizzyann stopped by to do the laundry. Not only did the little Black man cook and keep the house, but he was also responsible for the milking of two cows, the feeding of a pen full of hogs, and caring for a flock of laying hens. From Boyd we learned that these species of traditional farm animals were housed behind a bump-out of a tiny hill that reached from a glen of trees that sprouted just beyond the back end of the huge central barn. And according to Boyd, there was a half-acre garden, fenced on four sides to keep stray livestock out, nestled between the hog pen and the chicken coop, and it, too, was the dominion of Isaiah.

The inconvenient location of the pigs, and milk cows, and egg producers was evident, though I imagined it was purposely chosen as a means to render those perceivably unsightly aspects of the homestead far from the palatial home of Culver Headville. And if the slopping and the milking and the planting and gathering were being done by someone else, it wouldn't matter to Headville if those chores required extra time and effort. But admittedly, I was just speculating on the why. There could have been a good reason for the isolation. The smell, for one, given there was swine involved.

All the same, I knew I could not let myself give Headville the benefit of any doubt. And despite his initial charm, I had my mind made up about him, in a large part because of what Morgan had told me about the man. Evil, Morgan had said, and a viper hiding in the grass. But worse, he was responsible for the murder of Ernst Beilman. At any rate, I had decided to err on the side of caution, and trust and believe in the opinions of the man who had gifted me Viento.

"Cleaning up our mess," Oleander spouted, "is that little monkey man's job."

In two seconds, I had crossed the five steps to where Oleander relaxed prostrate on the bed, and I grabbed his shirtfront with both my fists. My temper lost, I jerked him upward, putting us within an inch of being nose to nose, and glared angrily at him. "If I ever hear you call Isaiah that again, I'll bust you right in the face, I swear I will!"

Oleander stared back at me, his eyes twinkling with amusement. "Careful there, sweetheart, you're gonna wrinkle my shirt."

I let him drop. "I'm not kidding, Sedgwick. I'm not the same kid I was two weeks ago. So just try me if you want."

"That time of the month, is it?" he said, goading me. "Lucky for you, Mr. Headville probably wouldn't like it if I gave you the bitch-whippin' you deserve. Would he, Sherlee?" he added looking past me.

I had been impulsive, forgetting that Willard Sherlee had been sitting at the end of the table, nursing the last sips of his coffee. He grunted in response to Oleander, and I turned to see him peering over the rim of his cup, gazing nonchalantly at the two of us. I cursed to myself. I had just given the man something of which to tattle. Then I noticed Isaiah standing outside beyond the door that had been left open by the four cowboys who had departed moments earlier. I glanced at him apologetically, but he looked at me as though he didn't have a care in the world, and I hoped that he had not heard Oleander's offensive remark.

"Excellent breakfast," I said to Isaiah. "Thank you," I added, and then without a word to either Oleander or Sherlee, I grabbed my hat and boots and exited the bunkhouse. I would finish my dressing outside on the porch.

I headed for the barn with the intention of getting Viento ready for the tasks planned for the day, but Oleander had me so overly irritated, I needed to let off a little steam before I joined the others. Cutting around the corner of the massive building, I strode to the horse paddock I had seen Kate exit from the previous night.

I stepped inside the limestone barn and found myself gazing down the generous alleyway of a structure that had been perfectly designed for the comfort and care of animals that were obviously of paramount importance to the man whom I now worked for. Though I didn't want to be, I was impressed. I had never personally seen a facility quite like it, though I had seen photos in numerous horseman magazines of similar horse paddocks that were, albeit, more modern, but then that was a hundred years into the future.

I walked down the alleyway, noting that the stalls of the barn seemed to be virtually empty, but then I heard a stamp of a hoof and a healthy exhale of breath. I walked softly in the direction of the sounds and near the far end I found what I was looking for. A mare, and a new baby foal.

The mother horse was a dun color, with a mane and tail a few shades darker than the beige of her smooth shiny coat. She had a blaze of alabaster down the front of her face and a white sock on her left rear foot. The mare looked at me and nickered softly as though to say, *come see what I made.* So, I did.

Stepping to the wood-planked wall, I peered through the metal piping of the stall gate and saw the fuzzy shape of sorrel-colored foal lying curled upon the fresh straw that covered the floor, its nose resting against its flank. It was no wonder Kate had wanted a peek at the little guy.

"Why are you in here?" asked a voice, low and husky, its source reaching me from the end of the stable where I had just entered moments earlier.

Startled, I turned to the man called Sherlee. "Uh, I'm just admiring the little colt," I said, which was the truth. I quickly crossed toward the horse wrangler, who was naturally stoic and seemingly unperturbed, but with him it was genuinely hard to be certain of his frame of mind. "I apologize, if I'm not supposed to come in here."

"It's fine," he said. "So long as you keep the gates shut."

"Of course."

"How did you know there was a newborn in here?" he asked, eyeing me curiously.

I shrugged. "Heard a noise. Sounded like a youthful whinny," I said, lying this time. I didn't want to risk getting Kate into trouble. "I grew up on a ranch," I continued, "back east," I added, finding it surprisingly easy to fudge the truth.

He grunted, the same as he had done earlier in the bunkhouse. I hoped I wasn't about to get a beating after all.

"Well," I said, feeling nervous around the stocky, muscular man. "The others—I don't, well … I better go." I said, stepping past him. I had gotten almost to the door when he called out to me.

"JT."

I turned back toward Sherlee, slightly astonished that he had called me by name. "Yeah?"

"I don't care much for that Oleander, either," he told me. "Takes guts to stand up to someone bigger and more powerful than yourself."

"Well, he's not easy to like, sir," I replied, choosing to bypass the compliment.

"Sherlee," he corrected me. "Mister Headville is the only *sir* around here."

"Right. Sorry. Sherlee," I stammered. "Thanks," I added, then left with my feet pointed toward the barn where I was expected to be and feeling relieved that I still had all my teeth.

Twenty minutes later, Boyd led our train of men and horses through the expansive doorway of the north end of the central barn and across a wide, grassy lot nestled between a modest embankment on the west, and by a thicket of trees on the opposite side.

We followed him for the distance of a city block, passing within yards of Isaiah's garden, and the secreted and stenchy hog pens. I counted at least thirteen pigs of various sizes, lounging in a muddied area just outside their squatty shelter of scrap planks and tin. I noted that if I had not been detoured by Kate the night before, I might have passed by the place on my moonlight walk, though my nose convinced me that I would not have needed any kind of light to know what was nearby.

In front of us, a wooden gate set within a stout fence of post rock and barbed wire temporarily blocked our advance. Without dismounting, Mick expertly maneuvered his horse against the latch-end of the gate, tripped a metal bar and pushed the gate open, guiding it along a ninety-degree arc while the cowpony tiptoed in tandem, its hooves high-stepping as though he had been trained by a Scottish folk dancer. I glanced at Dent.

"Piece of cake," I said to him, smiling. My brother had been trying for months to train his horse, Copper, to do the same thing with the corral gates at our own ranch. Dent glanced at me, looking as though he was ready to launch a snide remark, but instead, he returned his attention to Mick.

"Impressive," Dent commented.

"That be why I brung my Mick along," Boyd concurred. "He ain't worth a shite otherwise," he added, grinning. I saw him and Mick trade smiles, and it was obvious the two of them were fond of one another. A team, I assumed, even though three or four decades separated them in age.

Boyd cut his horse through the gateway, and Dent and I, a team in our own right, reined in behind him.

"Go!"

I looked over my shoulder at the sound of Oleander's voice. He and Blaine sat upon the bench of a buckboard wagon loaded with scraps of lumber and cuts of firewood and conveying a set of branding irons, all necessary items for the task Boyd had planned for us. Oleander had taken charge of the reins of the two horses pulling the wagon, and he had openly expressed his appreciation to Boyd for assigning him transportation that didn't require his ass to be in a saddle. But he was as inept with harnessed horses as he was with saddled ones. And as equally impatient.

"What the hell? Move your fat asses!" Sedgwick whined.

Boyd shook his head and glanced at me. "That boy gotta be the dummest peckerhead that ever shit behind a pair of boots."

I nodded in agreement, but Dent laughed. "I'm gonna have to remember to tell that one to Dad!"

"You gotta talk to 'em, boy!" Boyd growled, returning his attention to the driver of the stalled wagon.

"Are you deaf, old man? What do you think I'm doing?"

"Cluck to 'em like this," Boyd scowled then made a 'chk-chk' sound that echoed across his tongue and out the side of his cheek. "And snap them reins at the same time! That's how ya talk to 'em!"

Oleander uttered his favorite four-letter word suffixed with "that".

"Here!" Blaine scoffed, grabbing the reins and flicking them along the backs of the animals as he simultaneously voiced the universal sound horses are taught to respond to. "Chk-chk!"

At once, the pair of part-time draft horses stepped forward, pulling the wagon through the gateway of the fence, its wheels fitting perfectly in a set of tracks that were worn into the surface of the pasture, a roadway that bent downward through an expansive, but shallow basin.

We traveled northeasterly for a mile across the pristine grassland, passing by dozens of horses, mostly mares with young foals, though many were the size and character of yearlings and two and three-year-old adults, the males of which had been gelded. All of them, I noticed, were quality animals. Suddenly, I felt motivated to engage in conversation with the man who was my supervisor. I nudged Viento and he trotted forward, and within a few seconds the horse had positioned me where I wanted to be. Riding next to Boyd.

"Mr. Headville has an impressive herd of horses," I said to my foreman.

"Shore-for," Boyd replied. "He be what them educated folks might call a visionary."

"Visionary?" I asked, surprised that the word was in Boyd's linguistic wheelhouse. I guessed that Culver Headville had planted that seed.

"Yep. He shore-for has a passion for these horses of his. Quarter Horses," Body added unnecessarily.

"I noticed the sign," I said, referencing the grand entryway into the ranch.

"Ever cowboy's fa-vor-rite horse," he said, leaning over and running his fingers through the flaxen mane of his sorrel gelding. "Yes, sirree, Mr. Headville has been buildin' hisself a legacy, goin' back twenty years and more. He be just a young man, too, 'bout twenty-five I 'spect when he got him a job workin' for a fella called Mid Perry down Texas way. That be how I first met up with him."

"You knew Mr. Headville as a young man in Texas?"

"You got that right. Course then, I knowd him as Culver. We spent a heap a time together back in them days, cowpunchin' for some of them big-wig Texas cattlemans. An afore I knowd it, Culver, I mean Mr. Headville, he done saved him up a bag full of money, pro'ly cuz he stuck his wages in a sock instead of doin' what I done—spendin' most of the fruits of my labors on whiskey and, well, uh, on companionship. Anyways, he goes and buys a half dozen young mares that be bred to a stud owned by Ole Perry, a famous racehorse of a name a Steel Dust."

Steel Dust.

I knew of the legacy of the blood bay horse and suddenly I was more interested in Culver Headville's quarter horse ranch than I had planned to be.

"I've heard of Steel Dust," I said, keeping to myself my specific knowledge of the stallion that had been credited by many as championing the most dominant bloodline in the development of the Quarter Horse breed.

"I betcha have at that!"

I recalled a few vague details from an article I had read about the history of the American Quarter Horse Association, an organization which was, in my present time, decades away from being founded in the era of the forthcoming World War II.

I also remembered from my reading that Steel Dust had been a preeminent racehorse and was the most sought-after sire of his time. And now I find out that Culver Headville's horses apparently had pedigrees listing the famous horse as a sire somewhere in the linage of their family trees. Again, against my better judgement, I was impressed. But I was also growing suspicious.

"And then a few months later," I casually suggested, "Mr. Headville has a crop of valuable Steel Dust foals to look after there in Texas."

"No, no, not in Texas. He took them six mares back to his family's farm somewhares in Illinois. I didn't go with him. But boy, I be as jealous as a cactus is sharp. A cowboy couldn't go anywhares in Texas without you'd hear of some high dollar horse trades claimin' Steel Dust blood in the winner of 'bout any a horse race that mattered squat. And Culver, he was smart and got his hand in the pie right off, too."

Smart, without question. But likewise, opportunistic.

"Then 'bout six years ago, I guess now, he buys his first twelve hundred acres of this here ranch, right back there where the house and barns be. The best two full sections of land for miles and miles around. Paid the U.S. guberment a dollar and two bits for each acre, too."

"That's a lot of money," I said, doing the arithmetic and knowing that $1500 to $1600 hundred dollars would take an ordinary man a dozen years or more to accumulate in this era in which I now resided.

"Oh, that be shore-for," Boyd agreed. "But worth ever penny, I tell ya, what with that land straddling the springs and headwaters of the Sweetwater Crik. Ain't been dried up not even a day in all the years I been here."

"Sweetwater?" I asked, instantly intrigued by the parallel with my own family's ranch.

"That be what Mr. Headville calls it. Don't rightly know if it be 'ficial or not."

"That would have been a good name for the ranch," I suggested. "More of a romantic tribute to the landscape, instead of—well—"

"I hear what you be sayin'," Boyd responded. "Mr. Headville is nothin' if he ain't proud of hisself. But I gotta hand it to him, he's smart. And tough, too, he is. Don't let them fancy duds of his fool ya. Before he homesteaded the place, he was out in these parts soldierin' for the army, fightin' Injuns, 'specially the Cheyenne. Big battle up northwest of here ten, lebben years ago on the Solomon Fork. That's how he found this place, scouting around for that Colonel Sumner. Anyways, according to what Mr. Headville told me, he brung thirty some horses with him, ever one be havin' Steel Dust blood running through their veins," Boyd added, returning our conversation to the subject of the famous equine.

We ambled northward, following the faint pasture road, Boyd and I in the lead, Mick and my brother paired up behind us and riding just a few yards ahead of the wagon. Earlier, Oleander had reclaimed control of the transport, and was frequently, and annoyingly, practicing the clucking Boyd had managed to teach him. At any rate, the wagon rolled steadily along, having less to do with Oleander's guidance and more to do with the natural instinct of the horses to herd with those they followed that were under saddle.

A first-rate conversationalist, Boyd had jabbered along most of the distance we needed to travel to get to our destination, but I didn't mind. I appreciated the fount of information that flowed freely from the talkative man. I learned that even though Boyd had first met Headville down in Texas when they were both much younger men, Boyd had later, by accident, crossed paths with Headville in the stock yards of Hays City where Culver had been negotiating the purchase of heifers and young cows, specifically chosen from among a herd of longhorns Boyd had driven from his native state, following the relatively new, but thoroughly challenging Western Trail.

Ultimately Headville purchased a hundred head of cattle from Boyd, the trail boss, and had then offered him the opportunity to work on his fledgling ranch. Boyd accepted the job offer from his young friend, but quickly learned that with Headville positioned as his boss, calling him Culver, as he had in the earlier years of their relationship, was no longer acceptable.

Though he tried to mask his feelings, it was obvious that Boyd harbored at least a small degree of resentment. But promptly, he changed the subject, purposely avoiding any further incrimination of his umbrage, and began to ramble on about the price of tea in China, and other nonsense, until I had finally excused myself, falling back to ride next to my brother.

The six of us arrived at our destination after a journey of nearly three miles from the ranch's homestead. Fundamentally, the facility had characteristics that were familiar and expected. But someone with imagination and forethought had artfully designed a unique layout that appeared to be exceptionally functional. I had neither before seen nor heard of anything similar.

At its core, was a large corral, circular in shape and a hundred feet in diameter. Its fencing was comprised of five rows of solid wood planks, two inches thick and nearly a foot wide and spaced horizontally with gaps of about six inches between the long edges of the boards and mounted on hefty, square posts that looked to have been cut for railroad ties. Accessing the pen was a singular gate that blended with the wall of the enclosure. A full six paces out from the inner corral was another circle of fence identically built, though with a half dozen gates that opened inward and were of the appropriate width to completely block, trap, or direct livestock within its donut-shaped perimeter.

I had noticed as we neared the facility, that the same barbed wire fencing that had streamed from the grand entrance gate of the ranch also radiated from this working hub in five separate lines, and if I were a bird flying overhead, I imagined the cross fences would remind me of spokes of a wagon wheel, though curiously none radiated in the south and southeast directions.

Boyd had informed me that the design of the corral had been Headville's idea, one that worked *neater than a skeeter's peter*, though I wasn't at all sure what that phraseology meant. Regardless, the foreman also explained to me the rationale for the divisions of the vast pastureland, and I could see that this centralized livestock holding and processing compound could be easily accessed from any of the three northern triangular pastures occupied by cow and calf pairs, and the southeasterly one that was reserved for yearling age heifers. Conveniently, the pristine grassland dedicated exclusively to Headville's horses also had a connection to the circular corral system. Undeniably, the facility was impressively practical.

I also learned from Boyd that Headville's ranch was just over twenty-five thousand acres in size, a substantial spread six times larger than my family's Sweetwater Ranch. Rectangularly shaped by a boundary of five miles on the north and south sides and bordered with eight miles of post rock fence along each of the eastern and western sides, subdividing the massive CH ranch was not only practical but allowed for better management practices.

"So, here be what you boys are gonna do," Boyd said, speaking to Oleander and Blaine, "whilst the four of us goes out and gathers in the cattle, you two get a good hot fire goin' over there in that pit," he explained, pointing to a large divot in the very center of the inner circle of the corral.

"Huh?" Oleander uttered, gawking at the foreman.

"Now who be deef?" Boyd asked, affirming that Oleander's earlier snide remark had not gone unnoticed, though I doubted that Sedgwick picked up the connection.

"It's gonna be like a hundred degrees of ball-scalding hot out here in just a little while," Oleander said as he issued his version of the weather forecast. "Why the hell would we want a goddamned fire?"

Obviously, Oleander had not reasoned that having been informed at breakfast that we would be spending the day branding the crop of calves born in April, that the task would require a fire to accomplish the permanent identification of the young animals.

"Olly, you dumb shit," Dent interrupted, "we have to have a fire to heat the branding irons. What did you think we were going to do, finger paint?"

"So, what you're saying is we're gonna burn 'em?"

"Right."

"Groovy," Oleander nodded, and I would have expected nothing less from him.

Promptly Oleander crawled over the bench of the wagon and began to pitch the cache of wood onto the ground, now clearly eager to participate in our assignment for the day.

The four of us mounted ranch hands crossed into the outer circle of the corral and exited through the northeastern gate that would be the receiving point for the cows and their calves that were born in April. However, the ranch foreman had mentioned that *a handful of stragglers that didn't hatch until the early parts of May*, would be among the calves born in the prior month. Boyd and Dent and I filed past Mick as he secured the gate into an open position, and then we all headed for the far reaches of the wedge-shaped pasture.

"What do you know," Dent said to me after we had passed fifty or more full-grown cows. "I wasn't expecting there to be so many Angus-cross cattle."

I agreed with him. "Yeah, me neither." Then I noted, "Hardly a Longhorn mamma out here so far." Based on Boyd's comment that the herd had begun as transplants from Texas, I had expected to find a relatively pure herd of lanky cattle with the signature massive horns. "A visionary," I said, recalling Boyd's earlier description of his boss, though I said it with an edge of sarcasm. Still, it hadn't occurred to me that Culver Headville would have so quickly engaged in a program of crossbreeding.

"Mick was telling me that Headville got his hands on a set of half-Angus bulls a few years ago," Dent began.

"Hands on? Are you implying they were rustled?" I asked frivolously, resorting to the vernacular of the present time.

Dent looked at me. "You have a pretty low opinion of our new boss, don't you?"

"Well, you know the rumors," I replied.

"Right. Anyway, like I was saying, it looks like those Angus boys have been busy spreading their chromosomes around."

"Looks that way," I agreed, taking note of the predominance of not only black coated animals, but half of the cows and all the calves had the characteristics of the thick, muscular breed that had been imported from Scotland. And what was also noticeable was that most of the crossbreeds we observed were without the horns typical of their Longhorn parentage. Having been a member of the Future Farmers of America club in high school, I knew enough about the dominance of the polled gene of the Angus and how it didn't take too many cycles of selective breeding to genetically eliminate the nuisance of bovine antlers from subsequent generations of the horned breeds of cattle.

Upon reaching the furthest and most isolated area of Headville's ranch, I split away from Dent, as Boyd and Mick broke from one another, and the four of us began to individually scout for cattle. Before long, Viento and I had flushed a dozen rogue mommas and their respective calves from the heat-relieving canopy of the elms and cottonwoods that banked the river that knitted its way across the northern tier of the vast ranch. We pushed the twelve pairs southward, convincing them to ford the shallows of the Saline River. Suddenly, the waterway triggered recent memories of the Smoky Hill River that dissected my family's land, and I realized that my personal ranching experience, though the breadth of a hundred years into the future, was relatively unchanged from that of this nineteenth century I currently called home.

Nostalgia unexpectedly clouded my mind like a cool blanket of fog. I closed my eyes and began to recall images of Dent and Dad and I, riding the range of our beloved Sweetwater, the three of us Tescotts cowboying just as it had been done for decades past. I couldn't help but smile, though if I wasn't careful, I'd be risking a potential tear of regret. Admittedly, I was missing my dad. And my mom. And to be honest, I missed my horse, Jericho. But at least I had my brother to help get me through this time that would otherwise be solidly in the past, if it had not been for a talisman and a contingent of Burmano-Ku-Partika.

CHAPTER 31

An hour later, after I had tripled the count of four-legged beasts in the group that plodded unhappily ahead of me, Dent and I melded our small herds of cattle and another thirty minutes later, we merged them into one greater herd with the livestock rounded up by Boyd and Mick.

Heading southward, and taking less time than I had expected, the four of us horseback riders were within sight of our destination. Eagerly we pushed and drove the cattle onward, though I realized that from a practical perspective, the natural funneling effect of the wheel-spoke cross-fencing was contributing greatly to the pooling of the livestock toward the central corral, essentially replacing the typical impact of an extra cowboy or two. Not that the job was easy. Still, I was actually having fun, smiling often, even occasionally laughing a few notes as Viento and I became more accustomed to our partnership as cowboy and horse.

So far, my first day as an employee of Culver Headville had been a satisfactory one. Then suddenly, as if to say *not so fast, bozo*, Viento sidestepped, quickly cutting in front of a wild-eyed, brindle-marked Longhorn cow, convincing her to twist into an about-face and resume her original direction of movement. I had barely managed to keep my ass in the saddle but was nonetheless impressed with the reactionary ability of the horse beneath me.

"Good boy," I cooed as I leaned forward and patted Viento's neck. Though Morgan had shared next to nothing with me regarding the horse's background and training, he seemed eagerly adaptable to function as a cowpony, though I had no idea whether he had any previous experience interacting with cattle. But if not, I was prepared to argue that the grullo stallion was a natural.

As we pushed toward the hub of the ranch, I tried to count the number of adult cows, coming up with tallies that ranged between ninety-seven to one-hundred-four. Boyd had advised us that today's task would be a full day job and given an average of one-hundred cows and thus a corresponding number of calves that needed to be branded, it would likely take at least eight to ten hours of grueling work, even with two teams, to catch and process the little critters.

We packed the herd of cattle into the outer ring of the corral and the four of us on horseback wasted no time in separating the mammas from their babies by isolating the calves into the working center of the circular enclosure. Earlier, Boyd had outfitted Dent and I with a cowboy's toolkit that primarily included a rawhide lariat, different from the engineered nylon ropes we were used to, but clearly top-quality, no expense spared. And since my brother had assured Culver Headville that we Tescott boys had cowboy skills, it was time to put up or shut up.

Dent and I volunteered to catch the first batch of the three-to-four-hundred-pound bovine youngsters, and since he and I had for several years worked as a team on our own ranch, we fell into our respective roles with Dent roping as the header, and me as the heeler.

The first catch took us both longer than normal since we each had an unfamiliar animal beneath us and the real-world experience of our horses modeling as cowponies was essentially unknown to us. Luckily, Dent's adopted brown bay acclimated quickly, likely because the gelding had previously been exposed to some nuance of ranching. The opposite was true of Viento. As I propelled my lariat above his head, he shied and dodged in what seemed like fifteen different directions all in the matter of five seconds. But I calmly exercised patience and reassurance, leading him to settle down surprisingly quick.

Our first calf was a chunky fellow with dark red hair, and once we had him roped and stretched out on the ground between us, Boyd, carrying a hot iron, hurriedly led Blaine and Oleander to the animal. Quickly and expertly, he began his demonstration of the proper technique for permanently marking the ownership of the calf as property belonging to Culver Headville. Because the marking end of the branding iron had been taken from the coals of the fire pit, it's red glowing tip had barely darkened by the time Boyd had laid the hot iron against the calf's skin. At once, the calf bawled with pain, and I winced with sympathy as I telepathically messaged the animal that his suffering would be over quickly.

In that moment, we were players in a typical Western motif, where the day's branding took center stage in the embodiment of ranching, including the scene of a wooden corral, with ropers on horseback and cowboys kneeling next to a calf and wielding a hot iron, all performed before a big, open sky spread above the background of an arid Kansas prairie. It was, in my opinion, a scene worthy to be immortalized by the talent of the American artist, Frederic Remington. Except that I would give the painter permission to leave Oleander out of the picture, seeing that he stood next to Boyd grinning like a perversive twelve-year-old ogling his first *Playboy* magazine.

For the duration of two full seconds, Boyd held the hot branding iron in place, its blistering heat burning into the calf's thick hide as the acrid aroma of singed hair blatantly wafted into the late morning air. Stepping back, Boyd handed the iron tool to Mick, then sent a nod to Blaine informing him to open the exit gate that would offer the calf an escape and a reunion with whichever momma cow decided to claim it. Boyd shifted his eyes to my brother and gave him nod. Dent responded by gently urging his horse forward. I watched the rope slacken around the calf's neck, and quickly the temporarily muted foreman slipped the lasso over the animal's head.

In the next moment, and without waiting for a nod, I nudged Viento toward the calf, loosening the taunt hold of my own counter lariat. By the time I had counted to five, the calf was up on his feet, free from our capture, and sporting upon his right hip the sear of a stylized letter H, its crossbar a double headed arrow whereas one end pointed left and the other right.

For a moment I pondered the meaning of the brand. H was logically representative of the name Headville. But the horizontal line truncated with a pair of arrow points caused me to wonder if it meant something more than opposing directions. Perhaps the left arrow symbolized Headville's past, the right arrow his future. Then at once I had an epiphany.

Time travel.

Was the brand symbolic of Culver Headville moving freely forward and backward in time? Or was the left side of my brain looking for something that was simply not there?

"Say Boyd," I spoke aloud, my curiosity aroused. "What do you call the brand? Left-Arrow-H-Right-Arrow?"

"Ha! That be a dead on 'scription of it, but by gum that be one heap of a mouthful! Anyways Mr. Headville, he calls it somethin' else," he replied, pausing for a moment. "In—fin—ity," he continued. "I think is the word, if I be sayin' it right."

Infinity. A geometric line, never ending in either direction. And with Headville in the center of it all.

The brand: It fit the visionary rancher like a glove.

"Okie dokie, boys, that be one down," Boyd said, his mathematical tally perfect so far. "Now go on and fetch me another little doggy."

From catch to release, the complete process took less than five minutes. But Dent and I both hoped to shave some time with our second go. With our ropes recoiled and readied, we peeled away, pointing our horses at the milling cluster of calves from which Dent quickly chose the next unsuspecting young bovine.

Our second attempt was perfect, neither of us missing with our first throw. And no sooner had we positioned the roped calf flat upon the dusty ground, Mick was there with a fresh iron. After a burn and a bawl, the white-footed black heifer was on her feet and scurrying through the gate held open by Blaine, eager to find her mother among those milling at the far side of the corral.

With a third calf caught and waiting, Boyd offered the branding iron to Blaine who hesitated just long enough to give Oleander the opportunity to step in and take the primitive instrument from the older man. With an excess of enthusiasm, Oleander pressed the hot iron onto the calf, smiling with unnecessary glee as the bovine youngster cried out.

"That be long enough, boy! We ain't needin' to brand 'em clear through their hide!"

Oleander stepped away then gazed at the results of his work. Just a single day earlier, I had doubted that there would be any ranch task that would align with his limited aptitude. But I was wrong. And forty some calves later, Oleander was still going strong.

Like the cogs of a well-oiled machine, the six of us worked as an efficient unit. Blaine kept the fire stoked and the irons hot and ready, Oleander performed the ritual of branding, while Boyd and Mick joined Dent and me, roping and heeling. Rarely was there a moment when there was not a calf tethered upon the ground.

At mid-day, we took a break and quickly ate a thick slice of salted pork sandwiched between a cold biscuit and washed it down with fresh water skimmed from the cattle tank that had been filled by water pumped from a subterranean aquifer by a symbolic windmill that was not quite as enormous as the one next to the great limestone barn.

The sun was fairly low in the sky when we finished with the last calf, and after reuniting with its impatient mother, I watched as the pair trotted away into the direction where the others had retreated, seeking refuge as far from us as their legs could get them. When I turned around, I saw a lone horseman approaching, his mount clipping along in a gentle lope. There was no question as to his identity.

Culver Headville.

"Look who's here," I said to Dent, though I directed my eyes askew in Headville's direction as he rode in on his exquisite chestnut stallion.

"That horse!" Dent exclaimed. "I don't know why he seems so damn familiar."

"Well," I said, "if you play nice, Headville might let you ride him."

"Yeah. And I'm the King of England."

Dent and I carefully recoiled our ropes and tied them to our saddles, then when I glanced back toward Headville, I saw that he had dismounted and Boyd was talking to him, though the foreman was looking in our direction.

"Hmm," I coughed. "We should go see what Boyd is saying about us. We may need to defend ourselves."

We led our horses in the direction of the two older men, and as we drew near, I could plainly hear Boyd's words.

"Top notch cowboys they is," Boyd said, looking at us with a grin and a nod.

"I expected as much," Headville replied, watching us intently as we strode up. "Dent, JT," he nodded, "you boys have impressed Boyd. Not an easy feat."

"Thanks," Dent said to Boyd.

"Hate like fire to say it, but you two boys be a better team than me and my Mick."

"We've had a crap load of practice," Dent replied, then glanced at the taller man. "That's one fine looking horse you got there, Mr. Headville, sir. I meant to tell you that yesterday."

"This fellow," Culver said, reaching up to stroke the horse's nose, "is my pride and joy. My greatest trophy, you might say. But he's more than that. Doc, here, he's family." he added patting the stallion's neck affectionately. The chestnut nuzzled the man's shoulder, as though to say *ditto Dad*.

The stallion was unquestionably an older horse, at least the age of twenty I would guess, with a light frosting of greyish hair filtering through the brown fur of his muzzle and around the arches of his eyes. But still, the animal with a senior age had the tone and bulk equal to that of much younger peers.

As if Headville had been reading my mind, he added, "He's getting some age on him, but he still has the eye of an eagle and the step of an antelope and the prowess of a mountain lion." Unquestionably, Headville was proud of his horse. Then with a broad gesture of his hands, he added, "Every single Quarter Horse on my ranch carries his blood in them. A Grand-Sire many times over. He's as biblical a father as was Abraham of the Old Testament."

An interesting comparison, I thought.

"He's a stud, that's for sure," Dent commented, pushing the envelope of a joke. But both of us noticed his humor went unappreciated.

"One of my three stables houses the best dozen of his stud offspring. A favorite of mine is a rare black stallion that boasts an ancestry dominated with Steel Dust lineage."

"Steel Dust?" Dent asked, surprised. Like me, he also knew of the legendary equine thanks to a passion for horses passed on to us by our father.

I glanced at Boyd, who met me with an expression that said, *I told you so*, but also a look that implied, *but don't tell Headville I told you so*. I gave the older man a subtle nod, assuring the chatty cowboy that I would say nothing that would get him into trouble with the boss.

"Boyd, what about the other two boys?" Headville asked cocking his head around. Blaine was behind me, standing near the pit, talking with Mick, the two of them having just smothered the fire with a thick covering of dirt and dust.

"That one over there with Mick—"

"Blaine," Headville said, acknowledging my friend's name.

"Yeah, Blaine, he be a worker, that boy. Kept the fire stoked and hot. Learned quick 'bout gettin' the gates opened and closed the right way and helped keep the calves all sorted and such. But I don't think he be havin' no stomach for the brandin'. Still shore-for he be worth his salt."

I glanced at Headville, ready to defend Blaine if needed.

"No one can be perfect," the boss man replied, then he glanced at me and grinned, just before his eyes shifted to the left, peering at what I assumed to be Viento. "Isn't that right, JT?"

I was unsure how to accurately interpret his statement or to read what was behind his eyes, but I sensed Headville meant something very specific, yet he spoke as if the question was rhetorical, so I kept silent.

"What about Oleander?" Headville asked, giving me no time to respond, even if I had been so inclined.

"Oh, that boy, he be a hard worker," Boyd began, and I looked at him wondering why he was inventing such a story. "for 'bout as long as two twitches of a horse's tail," he added. "I had to keep on him to hurry his butt over with the irons. But that big ole peckerhead shore-for liked to lay on the brand. Liked it too much if you ask me. Had to bop him on the noggin a couple times for keepin' the iron on too long."

That sounded more like it, I thought, and I scanned about for the presence of Oleander. It took a second glance past the buckboard wagon, before I noticed a pair of boots sticking out from underneath the bed. I shook my head. Sedgwick was apparently taking a nap. And as much as I wanted to point that out, I didn't, but instead I excused myself and led Viento toward to the wagon and gave Oleander the favor of a kick to his feet.

"What the hell!" Oleander exclaimed.

"Mr. Headville is here. I doubt you want him to find you sleeping on the job."

Oleander rolled out from under the wagon. "Who said I was sleeping? For your information, Worm, I was doing an inspection, making sure there wasn't any damage. My ass lost count of the number of holes we hit on that shitty road we drove in on."

I stared at him, oddly impressed. He had given me a plausible answer, though I still knew that he was bullshitting. I started to call him on it, but realized the hypocrisy I would be committing. In the infancy of my legal adulthood, I had resorted to stretching the truth on numerous occasions, and at least twice today, albeit for one particular reason.

Survival.

At least that was how I rationalized it. As Morgan had implied, I had an enemy of whom I was to be extraordinarily wary. And fool or not, I had practically placed myself into the palm of his hand.

A few moments later, my presumed nemesis, Culver Headville, and his beloved stallion, Doc, departed from our company, leaving the rest of us to eventually follow him back to the heart of the ranch.

Leisurely, the six of us branding crew cowpokes made our way south over the same trail we had followed earlier in the morning. It was late when we arrived at ranch headquarters, the sun was already lost beyond the rise of the western ridge.

Once inside the interior of the massive barn, we stripped the horses of their saddles, then groomed and fed them. To my surprise, Oleander had been reasonably conscientious to give the roan mare a little attention, though she had enjoyed the day off.

Dog-tired, we left the barn in single file, with Boyd leading the way. I followed the pack in the caboose position, with Oleander just two strides ahead of me. As I stepped onto the porch of the bunkhouse, I caught a glimpse of Sherlee exiting the nearest horse stable in which the wrangler had led the chestnut stallion the evening before after we had arrived from Hays City. Without doubt, it was the building exclusively used to house those Headville deemed to be worthy members of a selective equine fraternity, a reverent place reserved for the most genetically elite.

I would have to explore that place, I decided, taking the time to lay an eye upon its occupants and judge them for myself. Mostly, though, I was curious how Headville's stallions matched up with Viento. And then I wondered what Headville thought of my grullo horse, an animal I considered on par with Doc, though for all I knew their bloodline had nothing in common. Suddenly, I was intuitively uneasy.

With the bunkhouse doorway looming before me, I shook the cloud of concern from my mind and stepped across the threshold, bumping squarely into the back of Oleander Sedgwick.

"What the hell?!" he exclaimed, but his words were not for me, they were directed at someone or something in front of him.

I stepped around him and discovered his bedroll and collection of extra socks and shirts and underclothes scattered across the floor as though they had been mindlessly, but purposefully pitched there to get them out of the way. As one, we both turned our heads to the bunk that sat behind the opened door and discovered a stranger reclining upon it.

One extra-large cowboy.

Little Pete had returned. And he had reclaimed his territory.

CHAPTER 32

"That's my shit you've thrown on the floor, you little bastard!" Oleander scolded, though plainly he had used an inapplicable adjective. Even horizontal, the man was clearly huge, and if I were inclined, I would wager that Oleander would be the tiniest of the two.

Nonplussed, the thickly bearded cowboy continued to lounge atop the bunk as Oleander barked at the man with a fit of profanities, while the rest of us piled behind him and listened to his explosive tantrum. I held my breath, hoping the mouthy baboon would not say or do anything that would lead him to losing another finger.

"Didn't 'spect a welcome party like this, did ya, Little Pete?!" Boyd mused as he stepped to one of the table benches and sat and began to remove his boots.

"I did not," replied Little Pete, as he swung his socked feet over the edge of the bed and stood up, towering an arms-length away from Oleander. "Who are you—squirt?" he asked, peering down at the teen who was unexpectedly displaying a minimal amount of intelligence, while my puerile first thought was if Sedgwick was a squirt, then I was hardly more than a dribble. Either way, the dude towered at least six inches above me, and though he was not perceptually fat, I imagined he still outweighed Oleander by forty or fifty pounds. Then at once I wondered just how colossal the absentee mustang wrangler called Big Pete might be, if this guy owned the prefix of little?

"I'm Olly Sedgwick," was the reply, spoken with noticeably less hostility than had been in his tone three seconds earlier. Without a doubt, the looming bulk of Little Pete had influenced the shift in Oleander's attitude.

A big hand suddenly thrust toward Oleander, but stopped short of making contact, and instead its fingers formed into an offer of greeting. "Name's Pete," said the man whose head was not too far from the ceiling above him. It was then I realized Little Pete had the same shade of reddish hair as Oleander. Though facially, neither looked like the other, especially since the bigger man had a relatively long, kinky beard as opposed to Oleander's cheeks sporting a couple weeks' worth of bristle. But because of their hair color and their above-normal size, they could reasonably be mistaken as brothers.

As if I really needed another Oleander Sedgwick.

Resentment still painted his eyes, but Oleander grasped the young man's hand anyway, and I could tell from the expressions of both men that the grip of each was exceedingly firm. "Friends," Little Pete declared as though he was offering a truce.

"Well, we'll see—," Oleander began, and I saw his face crinkle as his arm collapsed inward. "Yeah, yeah, right!" he cringed, his hand obviously at the mercy of the giant. "Friends!"

Little Pete nodded, then stepped past Oleander and began to gather the items of clothing that lay on the floor. Oleander watched him, then glanced at me and snarled. I had no idea what I had done to deserve the look, but I was not at all pleased that the playground bully had made an ally of someone the size of Paul Bunyan, or perhaps as big as the character's blue ox, Babe.

Oleander stooped next to his new friend and assisted with the scattered laundry. "So, Pete," Oleander said to him, "you okay with me calling you Ox?"

I had just begun to sit on the bench next to Boyd when the request caused me to flinch. Though I knew it was coincidence, the idea that Oleander might be able to telepathically intercept my thoughts was a sure sign that my nervous circuitry was getting trounced by an overload of science fiction. Except now, time travel and aliens were no longer as fictional as they had been fourteen days earlier.

Throughout the next hour, all of us newcomers got better acquainted with Little Pete, specifically being informed that he was only seventeen, but going on thirty if judging him by his thick crop of whiskers. And we learned that as a twelve-year-old, he had hid himself in the back of a buckboard wagon that by chance was headed for the CH Quarter Horse Ranch. Orphaned and desperate for a place to call home, his gamble paid off. Boyd had discovered the stowaway, and after learning of the kid's circumstances, the foreman had persuaded Culver Headville to let the boy stay and learn the ropes of a ranch hand.

"Kid, my ass!" Boyd coughed. "That boy there be pract'ly full-growed when he got here! Shore-for ass and elbows taller than anybody else, 'cept for Big Pete who'd done been cowboyin' for me for a year or more. So's to make it easy on me, I gots to callin' this dern boy Little Pete and nat'rly the other Pete I went to callin' Big Pete on account he was a good two inches taller."

"Didn't last that way for long, though," Little Pete chimed in.

"That be damn shore-for! Time he turned a year older, Little Pete was four fat fingers taller than Big Pete!"

"So, by then, the names just stuck," Blaine suggested with a knowing smile.

"Zackly," Boyd confirmed, and I chuckled realizing that there was the answer to my earlier pondering that had now diminished the immense size I had imagined the other Pete to be. Additionally, the conversation we shared with Little Pete established him as a credibly nice guy. I hoped that perhaps he might be a positive influence on Oleander Sedgwick. Especially since the two of them had seemed to bond over their physical similarities.

Dinner came and went as usual, as did breakfast the following morning. With the sun barely up, Foreman Boyd gave the four of us recent graduates of Custer High School's class of 1979 a tour of all the ranch buildings. Whether the sightseeing was his own idea, or was the result of instructions from the top executive, Boyd led us around the campus of ranch structures, explaining the specific details of each building he thought to be pertinent. But as far as Dent and I were concerned, he was preaching to the choir though Boyd probably knew it. Which gave me cause to believe the tour had been delegated by upper management. Then again, the exercise could have been essentially for the benefit of Oleander, whom the foreman had already identified as a greenhorn. And a peckerhead.

We skipped the big barn where our horses were lodged, for the obvious reason, so our first stop was the nearest of the trio of identical stables, the one where Headville's beloved stallion Doc was housed. Its floorplan was the same as the paddock two doors down where I had laid eyes on the newborn foal, equally spacious and luxurious from the feed bunks down to the straw. But what I found most interesting was that each stall was equipped with a bucket-size watering container that sat beneath a spicket that Boyd explained was fed by the windmill that had been erected adjacent to the main barn.

"So, what you're saying is, these horses and the folks in the big house get to enjoy the convenience of indoor plumbing," Dent suggested sardonically, knowing the horses were at least a rung higher on Headville's corporate ladder than were the men who worked for him.

"Yep, that be one way of puttin' it," Boyd agreed.

"So, what about us?" Oleander said, asking a reasonable question. "I didn't see no faucet in the bunkhouse. And the shitter out behind didn't have running water either!"

"Hells bells, boy! Least you gots a bed to sleep in. If'n we had water piped in and porsee'line tow-lets and sissy-ass bathin' tubs, we wouldna be cowboys!"

"So where do I take a bath?"

"Anywhares you want!" Boyd said, seemingly bringing his stump speech to a conclusion. 'Cept in the big house," he continued, unable to resist feeding us more information. "Mr. Headville's place be off limits to the hands. Even for me," the foreman added, and I believed I detected a hint of resentment. "If you be a feelin' like you wanna wash up, there be a nice cold pond rite-char behind the bunkhouse. But it ain't Saturday yet, so no need to be gettin' your britches in a twitch!" Boyd scolded, clearly getting a burr under his saddle where Oleander was concerned.

I looked at Oleander, expecting to find him fuming. Instead, he appeared thoughtful. I wondered if he was trying to determine a way to get an invitation to lodge inside Headville's palatial residence, a place that would be more like home to him than the bunkhouse. My speculation aside, based on what I had observed of Culver Headville thus far, there was no way Oleander would receive that upgrade.

The horses, though, were a different story. Not only were they pampered with running water, the stalls that were their individualized domains were also equipped with Dutch doors, split horizontally for the management of air circulation, which opened outside to fenced-in exercise runs partitioned with thick milled and white-washed lumber. Recipients of royale and red-carpet benefits, Culver Headville's Quarter Horse studs were undeniable VIPs, or in this case, VIHs.

After our group of new recruits progressed halfway through the barn, I caught Sherlee emerging from within a room, and before he closed its heavy door, I glimpsed a bed and a washstand inside, realizing the corner location contained the horse wrangler's apartment of which Boyd had spoken. Without necessarily being rude, Sherlee ignored us, and I watched as he stepped into the nearest stall where the prolific chestnut sire had the honor of being nearest to the barn's main entry door, not to mention being stationed next to the man who was his trusted caretaker.

Pushing open the lower half of the solid Dutch door positioned on the exterior side of the stallion's abode, Sherlee coaxed the old horse outside then closed the door behind him. It was then that I noticed my brother was also watching, but his focus had been entirely on the fetching white-footed horse marked with a snip and a star upon the handsome plane of his reddish elongated face.

As he escorted us down the broad alleyway, Boyd gestured to three specific occupants, sharing with us a colorful summation of each horse, concluding with an anecdote he considered important or amusing. I noticed then that Sherlee had followed us, though he stopped at each stall, and repetitiously escorted each horse outside.

We exited the barn through the broad doorway that overlooked the open pastureland that unfolded westward, and then we skirted the far side of the trio of buildings. By-passing the middle stable, which was currently unoccupied, Boyd explained that it was primarily a facility used to care for horses that had become injured or ill. We did, however, enter the last one, its sole purpose being a maternity ward for expectant mares, as well as it being the stable of which I had caught Kate leaving two nights earlier, though I assumed Boyd had no knowledge of the encounter.

The foreman paused just long enough to cluck at the little two-day-old colt as he stood pressed against his mother's flank and enthusiastically nursed from her full udder. Dent made some comment about the resemblance of the foal's white markings to those of the grand sire that was Headville's favorite horse, but I hardly heard him as my mind was seemingly stuck on a loop of my memory recall involving my moonlight chat with the lovely and somewhat sassy Kate.

We followed Boyd from the barn where he paused and pointed at a shed that garaged the buckboard wagon and the fancy black-lacquered carriage, that if still standing in my time it would likely have been converted into a garage housing modern automobiles. It was a modest structure situated behind the big barn, a mere molehill to the mountainous size of its neighbor, and even though we had seen it the day before enroute to the centralized circular corral three miles deep into the ranch, Boyd was apparently compelled to mention it.

Likewise, he gestured to the other three out-buildings we had also noticed yesterday, all comparatively lesser structures, but still significant as far as I was concerned, since ultimately, they contributed to one aspect of Isaiah's responsibilities of which we all benefited: His preparation of meals, whether it be in a bunkhouse or in the dining room of a mansion.

For a second or two, I tried to think of a better word to describe Headville's stately abode, but lair was the first thing that popped into my mind, and before I could mentally regurgitate an alternative, Boyd shared a new and unexpected piece of information with us.

"And back yonder in them trees behind the hogs and the milkin' shed, there be an old house built into the side of a hill, widda front wall made of them limestone rocks. It be the first house ever built here on the ranch, but not by Mr. Headville. An old place, it is. That be where the Injuns was kept afore they was took to the reservations."

I looked at Boyd. "Indians?" I asked as I glanced at Oleander, whose face immediately flushed red, though not from embarrassment, but because he was spontaneously angry. He had talked very little, at least to me, about his near-death experience with the wolfskin-hooded savage, but the absence of his finger had to have been a daily reminder of what had happened to him, and knowing Oleander, he harbored intense hate for the abusive Indian.

"Yep," Boyd went on, "a few years ago before the guberment first went to roundin' up the Injuns and scootin' 'em down to them Oklahoma reservations, Mr. Headville give quite a handful of 'em a place to stay and put some food in their bellies, too."

Culver Headville, a humanitarian? It was possible, I supposed. He would not be the first bad guy to conscientiously man up with compassion and mercy. The idea was nice, but I would not bet my life on it.

"Why the hell would he do that?" Oleander asked, his tone sardonic.

"Well, them Cheyennes worked for Mr. Headville, that be why!" Boyd replied, moderately annoyed by Sedgwick's question. "No need to get your feathers all ruffled up."

"Worked?" Dent asked. "Doing what?"

"Digged up that dadgum cactus and soapweed and brushy sage, that be what. Not much else they could do to earn their keep. Injuns they be hunters and nomads, shore-for not ranchers." Though he may not have planned it, Boyd's penchant for talking had supplied the answer that explained the pristine condition of the horse's pastureland.

"And Mr. Headville paid them for their labor, right?" Dent questioned, his tone ringing of doubt.

"Yeah, 'course! Room and keep. And lucky for it, too."

And there it was, the proverbial writing on the wall.

"But no wages?" Dent asked, his tone caustically elevated. "What— Headville just considered them sub-human labor? Nothing but property?"

I knew what was going through my brother's mind. Despite growing up in a rural Western Kansas community where the latest federal census had tallied a grand total of one inhabitant belonging to the race of Black, he and I both had developed an instantaneous empathy for those who had historically been owned as slaves. The catalyst for our compassion had been the television miniseries *Roots* that had aired in January of our sophomore year and was one of the few TV programs that had ever fully captured Dent's interest.

But we had both been mesmerized by Alex Haley's story. And appalled. And ashamed. But ultimately, the show had anchored our entire Tescott family in believing that it was wrong to own people, to strip them of their dignity, and humanity, and freedom, regardless of their ethnicity. Most importantly, however, the show had offered a platform to engage in meaningful conversation between generations, and after each episode, Dent and I, along with our parents, had heartfelt, emotional, and mature discussions regarding Blacks and Indians and other minorities and how the uninhibited actions and narcissistic motivations of those who considered themselves superior brought consequences that had severely damaged the integrity and principles of our young nation.

So, I could not blame Dent for challenging the obvious subjugation of these people who had become easy prey for men like Culver Headville. But not everyone in our little circle of 1870s cowboys shared my pardon.

In Boyd's eyes I could see resentment building, and I waited as he stared at my brother for an uncomfortably long, intense moment, seeming to contemplate the gravity of Dent's suggestive words. "You be steppin' out of line, boy, askin' questions like that," he growled, his voice low and defensive, yet surprisingly calm. "Ain't no bidness of mine or yours neither how Mr. Headville manages his affairs."

"Them Indians were slaves!" Oleander said with a laugh. "Genius!" he added, beaming. I glared at him, sickened by his imperialistic attitude. In that moment, I was the most disgusted I had ever been with Oleander Sedgwick. Suddenly, the moment was ripe with emotion, and not just mine.

"You listen up here, you mouthy shithouse toad!" Boyd spat, breaking his composure. In the next instant, he was storming toward Oleander and shaking an angry finger in his face. "Mr. Headville be a God-fearin' man! Respected! Not just here on the ranch, but in town, too! And you, callin' him a slaver! That shore-for will get your good-for-nothin' ass tossed outta here quicker than you can say scat!"

"Easy old man," Oleander said raising his palms in surrender, his smug expression disclosing his contempt for the elder cowboy.

"You're not hearing me right. I ain't got nothin' but respect for Mr. Headville."

"You best mind them lippy words you let fly outta that big yam of yours," Boyd sneered.

Clearly, the man who probably knew Culver Headville better than anyone else on the ranch was stanchly loyal to his employer, and quick to defend him against any dishonorable accusation, intentional or otherwise. But despite his reaction, I did not believe Boyd to be a man who would knowingly condone the ignoble treatment of others. But I also knew that often people could get caught up in the illusion of honorable principles at the expense of losing their personal kindness and compassion.

"I 'spect maybe a swollar or two of humble pie might do you some good," Boyd added, and I could not have agreed with him more. "And that goes for all ya'all."

Oleander scoffed, but I quickly butted in. "Sure, Boyd," I said, eager to defuse the situation, even though I knew Blaine and I would be paying for part of the cost of my brother's insinuation and Oleander's unbridled tongue. "Whatever you want us to do, we'll do it."

He looked at me, his dander settling back down. "In the barn, there be some pitchforks and shovels. Git 'em."

"And then what?" Oleander asked, truly without a clue.

"You gonna shovel some shit," Boyd answered.

The four of us spent the early part of the morning mucking out the horse stalls, but there was really very little to clean up. Sherlee, I assumed, kept the horse barns exceedingly tidy. But still, we went through them, one by one, finding the stud paddock having the highest density of droppings due to its full occupancy. As directed by Boyd, we worked in pairs and loaded wooden wheelbarrows with the manure, then emptied and spread the fruits of our labors in an area next to Isaiah's garden where, according to our loquacious superintendent, horticultural expansion was planned. When we had finally reached the last of the littered stalls, Boyd came and told Oleander and Dent to follow him, informing me with a cackle of delight that he had another job for them that was "shore-for gonna put some fur on their balls."

That did not at all sound like fun.

After Blaine and I completed the less-manly job, in terms of inducing the growth of scrotal hair, we rolled the last ladened wheelbarrow from the stud barn, and passed by our comrades who were laboring with the transfer of six-foot-long cuts of limestone bedrock from a reserve stacked next to the buckboard and buggy shed. With dramatically loud and breathy grunts and groans they heaved a hefty fence post onto the bed of a low wagon custom fitted with wide, solidly spoked wheels on a heavy axel crafted from what I assumed to be steel. Boyd stood near them, supervising, but as one of the two remaining muckers, I kept my eyes down and my face free of the smile that would not belie my relief at dodging that toilsome bullet. I did not know about Blaine, but I would rather be working with horse nuggets than rock posts.

Though I had purposely minded my own business, I was also being consciously poked and prodded by my curiosity. More precisely, I was overwhelmed with a desire to snoop. So, after we had completed the task of pre-fertilizing the garden annex, I was simply too inquisitive to leave alone what I had been thinking about. I told Blaine what I wanted to see, and he did not discourage me.

Together, we slipped into the perimeter of the trees beyond the garden and after wading through the narrow strip of scrub willow and elm we arrived at a clearing that was twenty yards square and standing at its edge was an old limestone building. I paused for a moment, noting that the decades-old structure was half the size of our bunkhouse, its sidewalls merging into the sharp slope of a hill rising behind it.

I pursed my lips and furrowed my brow as I thoughtfully digested Boyd's impromptu information that this was the place where Indian workers had slept.

Or had been contained.

The construction of the building was far better than I expected it to be, and the door swung easily and quietly on its hinges. I stepped inside and was even more surprised. I had anticipated an empty room, with an earthen floor and perhaps disheveled remnants of blankets and pallets lying scattered on a packed surface of earth. Instead, there was a wood stove and a table with benches, similar to the furnishings outfitted in the bunkhouse where I had taken residence. And there were a few make-shift cots, and in one corner, a bed topped with a generous layer of wool blankets, every bit as big as my bunk, in fact, it looked large enough to sleep two. And what was more, nothing about the room left me with the impression that Indian slaves had been living here.

"Looks like our bunkhouse," Blaine spoke, stepping through the doorway and into the room of a dug-out that was notably more sophisticated than the home of our friends, Abelard and Karl. Lured by his own curiosity, Blaine crossed to the stove and peeked inside a wooden box sitting on its top. "Huh," he said, and I saw his hand disappear inside, then pull away with an object grasped in his fingers. It was a smoke-charred book, a dime novel, like the one Mick had been reading. Then Blaine took another book from the box, its edges also seared. "A box full of fire-damaged stuff."

Then from behind me I heard a noise accompanied by a voice I recognized, but still, I could not help but flinch.

"They're mine," said Mick. "Boyd won't let me keep them with me."

I glanced at him, hoping that he had not noticed that I had been startled. "Your books, they've been in a fire." I said, stating the obvious.

"Yeah, last winter. In the bunkhouse," Mick explained. "A spark or something from the woodstove, Boyd guessed." I heard the doubt in his words. I wondered if one Boyd's cigarettes could have been the cause. "Anyway, my books, they kinda stink because of the smoke, but I can still read them. So, I keep them here."

"So, you guys moved in here for a while?" Blaine asked.

"Yeah, several of us did. Boyd and Little Pete and a couple of the others set up beds in the barn. Half our bunks were ruined, these we salvaged for temporary use here."

"And the bigger bed?"

"Mr. Headville brought it from his house for us to use." And I read between the lines that Headville apparently did not want it back. "He took care of us. Hired a few of those German men to come out and fix the bunkhouse. Got it done pretty quick, too. We were back in there in a couple of Sundays, and with new bunks and new bedding for all of us."

"Nice," I said, genuinely glad to hear that Headville had rose to the responsibility of taking care of his men.

"Anyways, Boyd sent me to get you. Looks like you guys are going to be building a fence today," Mick added with an apologetic smile.

I was not surprised. I knew the purpose of those rock posts Dent and Oleander were loading. "Fun," I said, though I did not mean it.

Two hours later, I and my fellow low-ranking laborers who yesterday had been up to our elbows in livestock, were back at the same corral where we had been roping and branding, and essentially having fun. Unfortunately, digging holes in the ground and setting heavy ball-busting rock posts into the freshly excavated cavities would not be nearly as entertaining.

Boyd had led the way astride his flaxen-maned sorrel gelding, with the remaining four of us having piled into two separate horse-drawn wagons to follow him. With Oleander at his side, Dent had guided the low-bedded wagon laden with the rock posts, while I, partnered with Blaine, had sat at the helm of the general-duty buckboard we had used yesterday, the two of us taking turns between driving and riding shotgun. Behind us, in our wagon were spools of barbed wire and the tools necessary for the construction of pasture fencing.

Once at the centralized corral, Boyd explained the trajectory of the new fence line, an angular direction toward the southeast, splitting the pasture currently occupied with last year's crop of yearling heifers. With an arthritically crooked finger, he pointed out a previously set single post rising about a hundred yards out. Across the indicated distance, I could discern that next to that vertical marker was a stack of posts that had presumably been brought here at an earlier time and were ready for placement by a degenerate and naïve club of time-traveling teenagers. Or something like that. Thoughtfully, I doubted that there had been a shortage of volunteers raising their hands to go west and wrangle mustangs, if this project had been the alternative summer job for those select cowboys.

But as my Grampa Jake would say, a man's gotta play the cards he's dealt. But knowing what was ahead of me, I wouldn't have argued against a reshuffle.

Our objective for the day, and likely for weeks or months ahead, was to partition off another section of prairie from the remaining south half of the ranch that had yet to be completely subdivided.

It was no wonder Culver Headville had offered us employment. There was a lot of work to be done on his twenty-five-thousand-acre ranch. It was apparent that our above average wage of thirty dollars a month was going to be earned not just from the preferred back of a horse, but by our sweat of fence building. At least we were not toiling with cactus. Though there had been others who had not been so lucky.

After being convinced by Dent that the Tescott brothers were well acquainted with the fencing process, Boyd left us with instructions not to leave until the last of the posts from the wagon had been set. What my brother failed to mention was that our fencing experience was with steel posts, not rock ones. At least our quota was relatively small.

I had counted sixteen.

But the natural stone posts were likely fifty times heavier than the metal ones I was familiar with. Not to mention our backs and our fingers would be subject to risk, and we were decades away from a chiropractor and an emergency room.

Studying the space between us and the distant limestone marker, I estimated that the fence posts we were expected to set today would be roughly equivalent to the modest measurement separating the out-of-bounds line of a football field endzone and mid-field. Still, even with the four of us, it would likely take us most of the day to accomplish the work. And from experience, I knew that the amount of time and effort would be dependent on the ground. If the topsoil was deep, the dig would be relatively easy. If shallow then we would be hitting the underlying bedrock from which the limestone posts had been quarried, and that would be a much bigger problem.

Dent assumed leadership of our workgroup but considering Boyd's absence and the inexperience of Blaine and Oleander, someone needed to be in charge, and I did not need it to be me. Fitted with leather gloves, we wrestled a spool of the wire from the wagon and after tying the end of the barbed strand to the appropriate corral post which Boyd had pointed out to us, we took turns pushing the heavy spool in the direction of the marker, the wire unrolling along the ground.

Immediately Oleander had questioned the logic of stringing the wire before setting the posts, and Dent, with more patience than I was willing muster, explained to him that the wire would establish a straight line between the point of the corral post and the marker that was our second point.

"Hands-on geometry," I said aloud to no one in particular. Surprisingly, Oleander seemed to grasp the mathematical concept and said nothing smart-assed as I had expected of him. I had a feeling the ride out here with my brother had been a butt-chewing for Oleander, and if anyone could reprimand him and get away with it, it would be Dent.

Having established our line, adjusting it here and there as we walked back to our starting point, Dent immediately paced off five long strides from the corral post and marked a spot next to the wire guide with the heel of his boot.

I took the post-hole diggers and went to work on the place where Dent had scuffed into the surface of the prairie. Though not as hard as rock, the ground was still solid, the natural result of lying undisturbed for God knows how many millennia. It was no wonder the bricks of the sod houses bolstered walls that were nearly as sound as those made of stone. Gripping the twin-handled digging tool, I hammered the sharp metal blades into the earth, lifting scrimps of loose soil, sometimes chunks, and piling the fruits of my labor a half-yard away from the place where I dug.

After a few minutes, I had formed a hole, a foot or so wide, though it was barely six inches deep. Already my face dripped with perspiration, and I felt the trickle of sweat down the core of my back. I paused for a moment, leaning upon the oaken handles of the digging tool, and wiped my brow with the cuff of my sleeve.

"Here," Blaine said, gently tugging the post hole diggers away from me. "My turn." Having watched my example, he copied me, digging another six inches into the ground. I relieved him for my second shift and found that the soil had gotten firmer, and after several minutes of huffing and puffing and stabbing and lifting, I had managed to add a few more inches to the depth of the hole. Then Blaine volunteered a second turn, and it was then I noticed Dent and Oleander watching us from a few yards away where they waited beside the wagon of rock posts.

"You know, Wild Bill," Dent said with his usual smirk, "I would have already had that hole dug out and the fence post set into it."

"Right," I replied, knowing that his postulation would prove to be false. And I had an idea he was only trying to goad me into trading him hole-digging for rock-wrestling. But I did not take the bait. Besides, those limestone posts were damn heavy, and because he was a patron of the school's weight room far more often than me, Dent had more strength in his muscles than I had, so he was innately better suited at setting the posts, especially with a brute like Oleander helping him. And then I had a thought. Well, it was more like a poke, and in more ways than one.

"Tell you what, big brother," I said, looking at him as seriously as I could, "I'll trade jobs with you, providing, when we get back home, you do the needle work with the pinkeye problems."

"Jackass," he growled, his mouth turned down. But in his eyes, I saw a smile.

After Blaine and I had carved out a cavity in the ground to the width and depth that was necessary to accommodate the size of the rock post, we stepped away and embraced our turn to rest and assume the roles of spectators. With as much accuracy as they could manage, Dent and Oleander carefully maneuvered the three-hundred-pound rock post off the end of the wagon and into the hole we had prepared for it. Then between the two of them they balanced the post upright and plumb, and following my brother's instructions, Oleander used the edge of his boot to scrape dirt into the hole, while Dent tamped and packed the loose soil with a smooth oaken rod that looked to have once been the handle of a shovel or a pitchfork.

One down. Fifteen to go.

All said, it had probably taken us a good twenty-five minutes, start to finish, to set a single post. We were undoubtably going to be here for a big part of the day.

In our self-assigned teams of two, we worked steadily throughout the afternoon, our shirts and the waists of our pants soaked from the sweat of our toils. And though it was hard work, I enjoyed being partnered with Blaine. He had certainly proven himself a competent fence builder, enduring the summer sun while putting his arms and shoulders and back to the strain of manning the labor-intensive instrument of a post-hole digger. It was something he had not done before, and probably never expected to try. But then, neither had he planned to take a trip back into the 1870s either.

With the wagon empty and the last post in place, the four of us led the two teams of horses to the corral. Soon, all eight of us, men and beasts, drank from the tank that had been filled with water pumped from beneath the surface by the mechanics of the windmill that towered at the edge of the corral. Then, without any of the three of us paying much attention to him, I looked up and found that Oleander had stripped down to his underclothes and was crawling into the tank.

"What the hell, Olly!" Dent cried. "That's our drinking water you're dipping your sweaty ass into!"

"Don't care!" Oleander replied sliding his body beneath the surface, "Come on in, pussies, the water's fine!" And in an instant, he had surrendered his head underwater.

I looked at Dent and he looked at me, and then we both shifted our eyes to Blaine who shrugged as though to say he had read our minds. Seconds later we were kicking off our boots and our outer layer of shirts and pants. As if we were ducklings wading into a pond, we crawled into the refreshment of the water tank. But truth be told, we entered the trough like sea lions flopping into a teacup.

We laughed and splashed at each other as though we were all playing in the backyard as five-year-olds in a plastic kiddie pool. It was nice, honestly, to be sharing with each other a few moments absent of worry or apprehension, and even Oleander had been pleasant company for a change. After a bit of teenage frolic, I sat there in the water, my back to the wall of the tank, and smiled at my companions.

Clothed in nothing but soppy underwear and cowboy hats, I thought to myself what a sight we would be if someone saw us. And in the next instance I was made aware that we had, in fact, been under observation.

"Hello, boys."

I looked up and peered around Oleander, and there behind the wagons and horses was a man perched upon a chestnut stallion.

We had been busted by our boss.

"Mr. Headville, sir!" Dent said, abruptly rising to his feet to face Headville, the top of the water hitting him just above his knees. From my angle, Dent's wet underpants and undershirt clung to his rear-end and back like a saggy sausage casing, and though I knew he was over-playing the respectful employee bit, I wished he would sit down and spare Headville the saturated and sculpted view of his cotton-covered bits and pieces. "We were just cooling off after, you know, working our butts off for you."

I winced at his choice of words, but like Mom, I had long ago given up on his sense of decorum.

Headville smiled, and then walked his horse to the tank and allowed him to drink at the place where Dent had been sitting. "And well deserved," he said, then gestured toward the fence line we had been constructing. "I have just inspected it. Good work."

"Thank you, sir," Dent replied. And the rest of us likewise paid him a tribute of our appreciation for his appreciation. But, still, the entire moment was weird.

After his horse drank his fill, Headville reined Doc aside and then glanced at each of us. "Enjoy your evening," he said, then clipped his horse with his heels and trotted away.

Dent then turned to face me and said, "Well, I'm gonna call that a win."

I laughed.

"What's so funny?"

"I didn't realize the water was so cold," I said, and Dent was quick to realize my meaning.

"Shut up," he said, shielding his hands in front of him, as Blaine and Oleander joined me in a snicker.

And despite the sudden appearance of Culver Headville, and the grueling work of our day, I was thoroughly enjoying the sense of peace and contentment offered by this moment I was sharing with these young men, Oleander included. As a group we had become accidental trespassers, having crossed together into an unnatural time that had too often been cruel and unsympathetic. Yet, so far, we had adjusted and endured. But I had no doubt that in the months that lay ahead of us, there would continue to be tests of our fortitude and resolve.

It would be almost a full year before Morgan would return. And after that, there would be another six months of our lives spent displaced in this time of the Old West before the arrival of the perihelion in early January 1880. That repeated date in time would be our first opportunity to return home. It was then that I realized I would be completely absent from the year 1980. But that was only if things went according to plan. And if our recovery of the talisman was a success. Admittedly, those were pretty big ifs.

Suddenly, the realist in me reared its ugly head and mocked me with a consequence I had once pondered before but had willfully buried in my subconsciousness.

Prepare for Plan B.

CHAPTER 33

Dinner in the bunkhouse had been pleasant. The food prepared by Isaiah was hearty and delicious as usual, and Boyd, who had been cantankerously ill-tempered earlier in the day, was back to being his affable, chatty self. And Little Pete proved to be more than just a giant of a young man, he also exhibited a sense of humor to match his stature.

"While passin' a house on the road, two Kansas City salesmans spotted a very—funny-looking—chimney—and it made 'em stop and to ponder about it," Pete began his drollery, and the excitement of his voice and the animation of his gestures easily captured our attention as we sat around the dining table listening to him. "And standin' there beside the house was a flaxen-haired lass, so the salesmans—"

"Why she gotta be a lass?" Boyd interrupted. "We ain't no bloody Irishmans!"

"I'm just tellin' you like I heard it down to Tommy's Drum's place."

"And just 'zackly who be the flibbertigibbet doin' the tellin'?"

"Dub O'Brien."

"Eh, 'course it be!"

Dub and Tommy. Two men with whom I had become acquainted, both of whom I liked, which was more than I could say for the ordinarily sullen man currently sitting at his usual spot at the end of the table.

"Let him finish the joke, please," Oleander said with a politeness I had rarely witnessed.

"So, the two salesmans asked her," Pete continued, "if the chimney—drawed—well? But the lass she just snips at the men and looked at 'em like they was looney birds and told 'em course it does!" Then with a switch to a feminine inflection in his voice, Little Pete delivered the punch line. "It draws the eyes of all you damn fools that pass on this road!"

Pete slapped the top of the table and let out a guffaw that in and of itself made me laugh, and Boyd was quick to join him with a robust chuckle, and I saw that even the normally joyless Sherlee let a flicker of a grin sneak past him. I then realized that blonde jokes had been around for a while.

"I don't get it, Ox," Oleander said. "What's the joke?"

"Well, Olly," Pete replied, "a chimney draws smoke, right?"

"Yeah, I guess so."

"The lass thought they was askin' her if folks were *noticin'* the funny chimney."

Oleander remained confused.

"It's a blonde joke," I said, "Don't strain yourself."

"Hell, I know better jokes than that," Oleander spouted. And I and Dent and probably Blaine knew of the blatant perversion that would define his attempt at humor.

"We don't need to hear them tonight, Olly," Dent said and the look in his eye told Oleander to just keep his mouth shut. "What I want to hear is another joke from Little Pete."

And Pete shared with us another, and then another.

Finally, the party broke up and Sherlee left for his sleeping room in the stud stable, and Mick and Boyd and Blaine and my brother retreated for the quiet comfort of their bunks.

I, too, was exhausted, but not necessarily tired, so I padded outside in my sock feet and sat on the step of the bunkhouse porch. The little dog Kate had named Poppy trotted over to me from her lookout post on the veranda that fronted the grand House of Headville and sat at my feet waiting for a pat on the head or the toss of a stick. I opted for just the pat, and she appreciatively licked my hand.

I glanced toward the house and saw several windows of the two-story stone home glowing with light from lanterns and candles, and I wondered if Kate was still awake and perhaps planning another late evening visit to the foaling barn. I had not once seen her in the daylight of my first two days here. I would have to make sure the streak did not extend to three. And perhaps with a little help from Poppy, I could make that happen.

But in spite of my plans, an additional day had been added to the stretch. The four of us who had been whisked away from our rightful time had been assigned a second day of fence building, and because we had hit an area of hard, rocky ground, the digging of holes had taken much longer than I had anticipated. Ultimately, our workday ended with barely enough daylight left to get us back to the bunkhouse before dinner was served.

And that was the good news. Unfortunately, the bad news came with Boyd's announcement that a third day of setting limestone posts was on our agenda, so again, we would be absent of the activities of the ranch headquarters for a fourth straight day. Unless, somehow, I managed to get back from fencing duties early. But that would require that I bust my ass, and somehow likewise motivate the other members of my construction team.

In the early light of the next day, and after only one wagon had been hitched with the team that bore the duty of being the draft animals of the ranch, we loaded another set of sixteen rock posts onto its low bed. The buckboard wagon would not be needed today, since Boyd had determined that two loads of wire would suffice for now, especially since we were not even ready to string it upon the posts. So, having gotten the approval from Boyd, Dent and I saddled up our own horses and followed Oleander and Blaine as they rode in the wagon leading us toward "corral central" as Dent had begun to call it.

"What do you think of Headville?" Dent asked me out of the blue.

I glanced across at him, "As a boss, so far so good."

"As a nemesis?"

"Well, listen to you," I said with surprise.

"Yeah, well, I picked that fancy word up from talking with Mick. He's about as smart as you are," Dent said with a grin. "Anyway, I thought I'd try it out and see how it fit."

"Like a glove," I said.

"Still think he's as bad as Morgan says?"

"One hundred percent."

"Wow, that doesn't leave any room for doubt, does it?"

"And you doubt Morgan?"

"Well, I didn't get a present from him like you did," Dent said, nodding at Viento. "But, no I don't trust Headville, not even as far as I could throw him."

"Which wouldn't be far," I said, curtailing my sibling's machoism as any respectable brother would do.

Dent ignored my jab. "There's just something about him, isn't there? And that horse!?"

"Again, with the horse," I said, knowing he was referring to a certain old stallion that was prized by our employer. "Dent, your obsession with Doc is borderline annoying."

"I can't help it. And even though I can't explain why, my gut tells me I've seen him before," Dent replied. "Somewhere. I just know it."

"Well, you know, he's marked a lot like Samson," I said referring to our father's horse, "the face and the white feet, a red coat, just not as dark. I think you're just homesick, brother. Seeing things you wish were there. Like Dad."

"Okay, I'll say it. I am a little homesick. The weird thing is, I'm starting to feel like I'm just away on some vacation, you know what I mean? It's like one side of my mind is telling me that I could just hop on this horse and ride west seventy miles or so and see Mom and Dad again, anytime I wanted to. But then there's another part of my head that says to me, *dipshit, you're a hundred years away from them, so miles don't matter,*" Dent said with a sigh. "I miss them both. Lots." he added and there was a catch in his voice, and from the corner of my eye, I saw him look away.

"Me, too, brother. Me, too."

We rode silently for a while, my thoughts sending me into a melancholy state of mind where I wondered about our parents. It was the twentieth of July. We had been gone for sixteen nights now. All they could possibly know was that their two sons had vanished. Literally into thin air. They had to be in a living hell, especially Mom. Instantly, my eyes welled with tears.

"Olly's coming along some, don't you think?" Dent said suddenly, and I was glad for the interruption. I wiped the tears from my eyes before they had a chance to streak my face, and I knew that Dent saw me, but reciprocating the silence of my observation, he pardoned me without a color commentary. Then again, I knew him well enough to know that when we got back home, he would undoubtedly embellish to anyone who might listen to him that he had caught me crying like a baby.

"If you say so," I replied. "Still, every time he opens his mouth, I worry he's going to cause me to piss myself."

"With him, you never know," Dent agreed. "But me and Olly, we had a serious heart-to-heart the other day."

"I thought you might of," I said with a smile.

"I painted the picture for him. It was a masterpiece!"

Suddenly, I was wary. I looked at Dent. "You didn't tell him everything, did you?!"

"Hell, no. I'm not that stupid. But I did my best to persuade him that under no circumstances was he to tell anyone, especially Headville, that we're from the future. Olly wants to get back home, too. This kind of life is way, way too rough for him."

"Well, that's good to hear."

"He's really not as bad as you think."

"That's your opinion."

"Anyway, this place, it'll do him some good. And when we get back home, I think he'll be a changed man."

"I hope you're right." But I doubted that he would be.

About nine hours later, and after the placement of another stretch of posts, I stepped into the saddle and headed back toward the ranch homestead, getting a head start on a little plan I had contrived. I left

Dent and Blaine and Oleander at the water tank where they talked of another dunk in the pool, but I was not interested and did not wait to see whether they did, or they did not.

I returned to the heart of the ranch and as I led Viento through the gate behind the mammoth barn, the little Border Collie met me, her tail wagging, and her eyes gleaming. The dog seemed genuinely excited to see me. And coincidentally, in that moment, I felt the same way.

The three of us, man, horse, and dog, entered through the north doorway of the imposing limestone structure, and I quickly unsaddled Viento, and noted that as expected, the horses of the three tenured cowboys were gone. And with them their riders, who had all planned to conduct an inspection of the perimeter fencing of the vast ranch. However, there was an unfamiliar horse occupying the stall next to the one shared by Buck and the roan mare.

I crossed to the pen and peered inside. Like the roan, it was also a mare, though its coat was the color of sand, and her ebony mane and tail were frosted with creamy strands of the characteristically coarse hair. She was a pretty thing, her finely shaped ears tipped in black, and with dark eyes that exuded intelligence, and a body that matched the composition of a hundred other horses that were at home on the Headville ranch. I was curious why she had been stationed in the barn, and who might lay claim to the horse. I wondered if perhaps one of the mustangers had returned from Colorado.

Then a yip sounded from the Border Collie demanding my attention, so I knelt and gave the little dog a pat and rub. "Okay, Poppy, you're going to have to work with me here, okay?" Then I untied my bandana from around my neck and after folding it into a particular shape, I wrapped it around the left front leg of the dog and tied it into place. She looked at me as though she sensed that I was up to something, and she was right.

I picked Poppy up, and carrying her in my arms, I left the barn. Following a quick glance around at the empty ranch yard, I crossed over to the stone steps that rose to meet the great house that was the home of Culver Headville and plodded upward. With an edge of apprehension, I stepped between the center pair of colonnades and crossed the grand porch and firmly tapped my knuckles on the pretentiously large door.

I held my breath.

This was only going to work, so long as Headville didn't answer the call of my knock. When the door opened, Isaiah stood there. I exhaled. And then smiled.

"JT?" Isaiah said looking from me to the dog, his face a portrait of surprise.

"Hello, Isaiah. Is Kate home?"

"Uh-huh, but you're not allowed to be in the house, no sir."

"No, no," I said, "I just wanted to speak to her about the dog," I explained. "I just got back and found her limping. I thought Kate would want to know."

Wow, I thought to myself. I was getting pretty good at fabricating lies. My mother would be so disappointed in me.

"Wait here," Isaiah said, buying my story. He closed the door, and I stepped off the porch and started counting seconds. When I had ticked off the number eighty-three, the door opened, and standing in my presence was a very attractive representative of the female gender of the human species.

But it was not Kate.

It was the older and darker beauty, Beverly Carneiro. She looked at me, her brow raised in suspicion. Instantly, I felt a wave of guilt wash over me, and though she hadn't said anything, I was almost compelled to tell her that my intentions were honorable and that I had no plans to sully the reputation or the virtue of the one I had hoped to see in her place. But then, I had lied to Isaiah, so maybe I was not completely honorable.

"Miss Kate is busy with her studies," Beverly informed me, her voice soft and silky, but stern.

"Right," I said. "I'll just come back later, then."

"Perhaps you should first check with Mr. Headville."

"Right, again," I said feeling a little flabbergasted.

"He is there, I believe," she said with a nod toward the nearest stable. "With his horse."

"Perfect," I replied, but even that singular word was an un-truth. "I'll go see him." And I turned away, Poppy still in my arms, and strode toward the place where Headville was believed to be, though I had no intention of finding out. When I had crossed half the distance, I glanced behind me to confirm that the coast was clear, but it was not. Beverly Carniero stood in the doorway watching me.

"Shit," I whispered to the dog. Outwitted, I reluctantly strode the rest of the way but stopped just inside the doorway of the VIH barn.

Headville and Sherlee were there in the alleyway with the progenitive sire called Doc. Sherlee, his back hunched forward, held one of the stallion's front feet across his thigh as he examined the underside of the horse's hoof.

"Just a bruise, then, you think?" I heard Headville ask.

"That's my opinion," Sherlee responded, easing the foot to the floor of the building. "I wouldn't ride him for a while. Wait at least a week, or so," he added, then his eyes fell upon me. "You need something?"

Headville turned and stared at me, and I felt as though I had just been caught trespassing into the lair of my enemy. "JT," he said to me, then smiled. "Come on in." His invitation had been friendly enough, but his words reminded me of a childhood story where a spider had essentially said the same thing to an unsuspecting fly.

"Is there something wrong with the dog?" Culver asked.

"Uh, well, I just got back from fence building and I found her limping—a little, so I thought I'd, you know, bandage her leg."

"Must be something in the water," he said, patting his favorite horse on the neck. "I found Ole Doc here favoring a sore foot this morning."

"Weird," I said, then immediately wondered if the expression was not itself weird for the time, but Headville seemed not to question it.

"I'm glad you're here, JT. There's something I've been wanting to ask you."

I stared at him for a long moment, wondering and fearing where this might be going. I shrugged, and set Poppy down on the ground, my heart racing. "Sure," I said with as much courage as I could muster. I straightened my knees and looked evenly at him across the space that separated us. "What do you want to know?"

I prayed that he would not ask me something so bold as what century I was from, or did I enjoy my transportation through the arch of the pyramid rock?

"Your horse," Headville began, and my heart caught in my throat. Though he knew from my bill of sale that I had obtained Viento from Morgan, I had hoped I would never need to explain how or why that transaction had occurred. "He's a fine animal."

"Viento?" I replied with circumspect naivety. "Yes, he is," I concurred. "But I doubt he has the pedigree of your Doc."

"Doubtful," Headville agreed.

We stared at each other, as fifteen seconds of excruciating silence ticked away. If his intent was to unnerve me, it was working. I did not like the quiet scrutiny, but neither did I want to propel the conversation that had begun as his idea. Suddenly, a smile spread across his face, and I perceived it to be genuine.

"You are waiting for my question," he stated.

"Yes, sir."

He nodded. "I appreciate the respect." Then he turned his attention to Doc, and stroked the stallion's neck with the affection one would give to a child, then whispered into the horse's ear. "Time for a rest, ole boy." Then Headville turned to the wrangler. "Sherlee, when you are finished with him, take Ulysses out and knock the burrs from beneath his saddle."

"Yes, sir, Mr. Headville," Sherlee replied with a perceptive emphasis on his employer's name.

"Walk with me, JT," Headville said, extending his hand toward the opposite end of the stable.

"Yes, sir," I began, then added, "Mister Headville." I had not missed Sherlee's subtle reminder. I stepped forward, and the two of us walked side by side, with Poppy padding along behind me. I hoped Headville would not notice that the little dog moved without the slightest sign of injury.

"How did you meet him?"

I gulped as discreetly as I could. It did not take a genius to know of whom Headville referred, and I could think of no logical reason to pretend ignorance by asking to whom he was referencing. Or maybe it was the little voice inside me who sounded, at the moment, like Mom, reminding me of the virtue of honesty. Perhaps now was the time to come clean with the truth.

"I met Mr. Morgan by pure luck. He stopped me outside of Tommy Drum's saloon and asked me if I would do him a favor. He was needing to leave by train and said he couldn't take his horse with him and offered him to me."

Not bad, I thought to myself. There was some truth to my story. Under the circumstances, I think my mother would have approved.

"And you had the funds to buy him?"

"Well, no, not really. The truth is, I had nine dollars and six bits in my pocket. He sold the horse to me for half of what I had," I said, my story sounding as though I were writing a fictional best-seller. "I would have given him my last dime for that horse," I added as a statement of fact that I could legitimately swear to with my hand on a Bible.

"And you didn't know him before?"

"No, sir. First time I met the guy," I said, once again lying through my teeth. "But it was like fate, Mr. Headville, sir. Kind of like you offering the four of us jobs when we needed them. Mr. Morgan offered me a horse when I needed one. And, well, I couldn't say no, I mean I'd never owned a horse like Viento before." Then I decided to flip the script and ask Headville a question. "Do you know who he is, this Morgan person?"

Headville pinned me with cold eyes that unmistakably informed me that he would be the one asking the questions. Then with a blink, his mask of congeniality reappeared.

"What do you think of my horses?"

I looked at him and read from his expression that his question was sincere.

"Well, they are finely bred animals," I replied, stating the obvious, and feeling cautiously optimistic that I had successfully sold my employer a plausible bill of goods. "And all beginning with your shrewd investment in those first six mares," I added, then at once I regretted the slip.

Headville smiled. "Boyd has been—talkative."

"Well, it's not his fault. I ask a lot of questions," I said, attempting to keep the old cowboy out of trouble. "That said, he duplicates your pride in your horses, Mr. Headville, sir."

"He does, at that. He and I, we go back a long way."

I said nothing, refraining from taking what I assumed to be bait.

"But what Boyd has shared with you is true. Steel Dust was the sire of my first crop of foals."

"There's no denying your good luck to have begun your breeding program with his bloodline."

"Luck had nothing to do with it," Headville countered, then he raised his hands and spread his fingers widely, pointing the digits of one hand near his face, the other toward his heart. "Within me," he began, his hands shifting and rotating as if he were conjuring the essence of his mind and soul, "indwells sheer determination to achieve my desires." Abandoning the theatrics, the posture of his hands and arms returned to normal. "When I was a young man, JT, just barely older than you are now, destiny chose me to forge the finest specimens of the breed of horse born of this new, untamed country of ours." He then stepped ahead of me and walked along the edge of the right row of stalls where there stood examples of his selective breeding expertise. I followed him, as though he were a doyen and I, his protégé.

"Here, in the American West, there were those who wisely accepted a complete dependence on the horse for every economic and social function. With grit, and imagination, and innovation, I seized that wisdom, adopted it as my own and because of that judicious perspective I have an invaluable appreciation for the nature of the equine species and their inarguable nobility. And none are more befittingly noble or more deserving of such esteem than the Quarter Horse, a beast that proved to be most ideally suited in physique and temperament for the challenge and hardship of settling this Western continent."

I listened to the particulars of each of his sentences and could not help but feel as though I was an audience for a well-rehearsed speech.

"A hundred years from now," Headville continued, "nay, a thousand years, these animals will be regaled for their contribution to the history of our young nation. Some of them have been used to power the breaking of virgin sod so that the industry of farming could be born here on the prairie. Others have been heroic and trusted mounts that have carried cavalry soldiers and buffalo hunters across miles of unexplored plains. The Quarter Horse will be revered for generations to come as the key breed of horse in the remudas of ranching enterprises from the Rio Grande and north to the open ranges of Canada."

I smiled at Culver Headville, pretending to be awed by his oration.

"And as you can see, I have succeeded in my ambition," he added, and I could almost perceive the band of his black Stetson bulging from the expansion of his cranium.

"Certainly," I agreed. Headville's pride in his horses was undisputedly evident and begrudgingly deserved. Another thing that was certain, was that Culver Headville was an educated man, though I doubted there would be a university diploma displayed on his wall.

"It was a serendipitous day, my young friend," Culver continued, "when the horse of the Cavalier in Virginia was crossed with the wild Spanish pony lost by the Conquistador, a result that would gift to the world what was to ultimately become this Quarter Horse," he said, looking now at a young, black stallion, the horse's forehead bearing a large star with five points. "A naturally engineered hybrid with speed and compactness inherited from English sires and born with the endurance and cow-sense of the dams of its Spanish ancestry."

I stood and admired the horse's intelligent eyes and small alert ears, and noted the ideal sloping of his shoulder, and the short but deep barrel chest, and thighs and upper forelegs thick with heavy muscle, and appendages that were firmly jointed with the knee and pasterns sharing a close spatial relationship. All these features being desirable characteristics of the American Quarter Horse.

"He's a beautiful animal," I said, and I meant it.

"Yes, he is," Culver replied. "I named him Ulysses, in honor of the president."

"Good choice," I said, though I was surprised. Ulysses S. Grant had been an advocate for the Fifteenth Amendment, openly supporting the citizenship and associative rights for Blacks and Native Indians, neither of which I believed Headville genuinely championed.

"It was either that or JFK."

For an instant, it felt as though my heart stopped beating. But luckily my mind kept working, and it told me to act as though those initials meant nothing to me. But still, Culver Headville was obviously testing me. Was it because of my story of Morgan and Viento? Or was I simply being paranoid?

Diligently, I masked my fear and concern then turned to him with a bold determination to change the subject quickly and to do so without causing any undue suspicion.

"I imagine the quality of your Quarter Horses, Mr. Headville, are leagues ahead of what anyone else has developed," I said, hoping that the stroking of his ego would steer him from another attempt at catching me off guard.

"Indeed, they are, and my reputation as a breeder of first-class Quarter Horses continues to grow. In fact, I host several lucrative auctions each year. Advertisements are placed in all major city newspapers. Attendees come from all corners of the country to bid for the ownership of one of my own. Future generations of horsemen will hail me as a father of the modern Quarter Horse," Headville added, his blue eyes glinting with egotistical confidence. He looked at me, "Do you think I am arrogant to make so bold a claim?"

"No," I said without hesitation, though a reply of 'yes' would have been more truthful. I had researched and read much about the breed to know that in the annals documenting the history of the American Quarter Horse, there is no mention of Culver Headville, a father or otherwise. But I was not foolish enough to tell him that. "Doc and his progeny are undeniable evidence that such a goal is achievable."

"Not a goal," Headville corrected me. "An inevitability."

I smiled at him. His confidence would have been admirable if I had not been suspicious of his integrity. "Is Doc one of your first Steel Dust foals?"

"No. He was—" Headville hesitated. "He was a serendipitous acquisition from a later time."

Serendipitous. Twice now Headville had used the ostentatious adjective.

My Grampa Jake had introduced me to that word when I was barely nine years old. He had often called me his little professor, encouraging me to explore the English language, but I had always struggled with the pronunciation of serendipitous, and found it preferable to instead use its rambling definition of accidentally being in the right place at the right time. But Headville had spat it out with ease.

I waited for several moments, expecting him to elaborate. Instead, he waited, his eyes capturing mine as if to analyze my reaction to his choice of words, or perhaps to challenge me to ponder the existence of an obscure meaning behind the composition of his statement.

Either way, I was overwhelmingly uncomfortable with the silence between us. "Well," I said, "all of your horses are superior animals— even the ones we've been using to haul the fence posts. They're tough, but not your typical draft horse."

Headville grunted thoughtfully, then obliged my attempt to re-establish conversation. "I decided years ago that I would utilize the sturdiest of my horses to adapt to the tasks typically performed by the ordinary or genetically disadvantaged. Why look at something ugly, when one has options?" he asked, though I refrained from offering an alternative opinion. "And so, I went a step further and decided that my horses would exclusively be used for every aspect of the ranch. Boyd and the others all ride horses that were bred by me and are animals that are accountably my property."

Immediately, I felt the pit of my stomach leap upward. I did not like where this was going.

"Which brings me to issue I am compelled to rectify."

I looked at him, and I could see a hint of glee dancing in the blue sea of his eyes.

"That nag belonging to Oleander."

It was a harsh word to describe the gentle strawberry roan mare. Granted, she would easily land at the bottom of a beauty contest if compared to any of Headville's horses. But still, she had qualities that were worth defending.

"Yeah, she's not much to look at. But she puts up with Oleander's lack of horsemanship."

"Agreed. But I have similarly dispositioned horses within my remuda. Therefore, I have chosen to upgrade his ride."

"I see," I said, vying to sound objective.

"And the buckskin, too," Headville informed me. "Neither does it have the physical refinements that are characteristic of my horses. Sherlee will also be choosing a replacement horse for your friend Blaine," the ranch commander stated with a casual smile and a discriminating gaze. "Any objections?"

I knew better than to try to persuade him differently. All signs I had observed so far pointed to Culver Headville as a man who did as he chose regardless of the preference of another.

"I think it's a great idea," I said, again practicing my newly acquired penchant for lying. But I could not shake the dread that throbbed in my heart. "And Viento?"

He studied me as though I required a thorough appraisal, and I wondered if he could detect in my eyes the obstinance I felt straining against the buttons of my shirt. If Headville thought for a second that I would let Viento be taken from me, I had news for him.

"Well, I'm not unreasonable, JT. Obviously, your horse is a specimen in his own right. So, for the time being, you may keep him."

"Thank you, sir," I replied, releasing some of the pressure in my lungs.

"I admit, your grullo stallion could have instilled in me a moderate degree of envy if it were not for Doc, or for that matter, any among the hundreds of his progeny that reside on my ranch. However, come next spring I am confident you will have determined that one among my herd will suit you far better than your Viento."

Headville's arrogance was nauseating.

"You could be right," I agreed, though my thoughts sternly proclaimed that the man was dead wrong. "And what about Dent's horse?" I asked quickly, in the event Headville possessed the power of ESP.

"Your brother's bay is safely above my threshold. So, for now, I will also let him keep the gelding. Unless you think he would prefer to switch to one of my horses sooner than later?"

"I'll let my brother know of his options. And Blaine and Oleander—when do get their new horses?"

"Tonight, for Oleander. Sherlee has a flawless dun mare waiting for him in the barn."

"I saw her," I said. "A fine-looking horse. And for Blaine?"

"Sherlee will choose one for him on Sunday."

"Not tomorrow?" I asked, glad that Blaine would have a day or so to process. When it came to horses, he did not particularly like change.

"Tomorrow is Saturday," Headville stated pragmatically, though I didn't understand why.

"Right."

"It's your day off, JT."

"Oh! I didn't realize."

"You boys are not my slaves. You're free to enjoy the day as you wish. Boyd and the others typically spend their holiday in town. I'm considering riding into Hays City with them tomorrow. Make it a family day," he said as though to imply a degree of sentimental affection for his employees. "Kate would enjoy that, I'm certain."

"As would we," I said. "I'll let the guys know, Mr. Headville, sir."

Headville nodded as though sanctioning my intent to dispense the information, then turned away from me. Twelve steps into the promenade of his exit, he stopped, then turned and faced me. At once, the gunfight at the O.K. corral blazed across the silver screen in my mind, and I had neither a pistol nor Wyatt Earp for defense.

"One other thing, JT," he said with an intimidating lift of his brow.

"Yes, sir?"

"Your stallion," he began with a foreboding tone, "my hospitality toward him will be forfeited if he doesn't behave like a gentleman around my mares. One slip and I'll have him castrated."

"Understood," I said, nodding.

"And that applies to any Casanova, be he four-legged, or two," he added, then turned and left the paddock.

The message had been received loud and clear. My intended ruse, aided and abetted by Kate's little dog, had been discerned by Headville after all. Laurie's protective dad, Chief Edwards, and my boss Culver Headville were apparently members of the same school of patriarchal thought. And I believed in the sincerity of both of them.

At some point, little Poppy had abandoned the barn, perhaps discouraged by the company of the older man who had not once shown the dog any sign of interest or affection. So, I left the building short of the furry accomplice I had brought in with me, but grateful that my flirtatious plan had failed. With all my bits still accounted for, I focused on a safer female subject with which to get better acquainted and crossed to the main barn. Though I was not by any means a fan of Oleander Sedgwick, I did not want him to get hurt by an animal more highly-strung than he was himself. I hoped that Sherlee had, indeed, wisely chosen a suitable replacement for the inept rookie horseman.

When I stepped into the grand doorway of the barn, Poppy ran to me, apparently having retreated to a cool place she had found somewhere inside. I bent and ruffled her head, and she licked my hand, then lifted a paw to me. Immediately, I noticed the bandana I had wrapped around her leg was gone.

"Looking for this?" A voice summoned me from inside.

I glanced down the wide corridor and in the shadowy light I could distinguish the shape of a young woman with flaxen hair, though I doubted she was as clueless as the lass from Pete's funny story. Unlike me, I was, in an instant, a blonde completely dumbed down by the effect of testosterone.

"Maybe," I said, smiling. "Looks like mine." I told her as she crossed toward me. It appeared that my plan had worked after all. And with that thought I proved that I was one-hundred percent stupid.

"I found it."

"Did you?"

"On Poppy's leg. Someone tied it there."

"Wonder who?"

She smiled, and her eyes told me she was not as annoyed with me as her voice wished me to believe. "A little bird told me that it was you … what's your name again?" she asked with a grin that denied a genuine loss of memory.

"JT."

"Oh, yes, the boy with just two letters for a name. They must stand for something, J and T."

"They must."

"You're not going to tell me?"

"I don't know you well enough."

"Well," Kate began, as she stepped near me and slipped the bandana behind my neck, "thank you anyway, JT, for curing my dog. She seems completely healed of any lameness in her leg."

"You're welcome," I replied, looking into her eyes as she tugged the ends of the scarf under my chin.

"You should become a veterinarian," Kate cooed as she tied a knot around my neck.

"You sound just like my mother."

We stared into one another's eyes, our faces near enough to initiate a kiss. And I definitely wanted to kiss her. And then she smiled, and I was certain she shared my desire. So, I leaned my face toward hers, but she ducked aside and turned to the little dog.

"Come on, Poppy," she called, and then without a glimpse in my direction she left the barn with the little black and white Border Collie trotting behind her.

Without a doubt, the two of us had just flirted. She with me, and I with danger.

CHAPTER 34

Early Saturday morning we left the ranch, heading south for Hays City, but there was no buggy or team of palomino ponies traveling with us. Therefore, no Kate.

Mick had also stayed behind, volunteering at the last minute to be the home watchdog since Kate was not, for some unexplained reason, joining the entourage into town.

Eight riders and nine horses filed through the gateway of the Culver Headville Quarter Horse Ranch. Headville, mounted today on the black stallion he had introduced to me as Ulysses, led the way, though the unassuming second in command, Willard Sherlee, rode beside him and was leading the only horse that did not have a rider.

Oleander's strawberry roan mare.

Headville had followed through with his edict, thus the gentle horse was being ceremoniously banished from the ranch with the apparent objective of finding her a new owner in Hays. And without asking Oleander whether or not he preferred the status quo, Sherlee had simply informed him that he would be changing mounts. To his credit, Oleander had enough respect for the menacing wrangler to refrain from debating the issue with him.

However, Oleander had later balked at the reality of changing to a horse he knew nothing about, but our esteemed commander-in-chief had stepped in and explained to him that the roan mare was essentially a Chevy and the dun mare that Sherlee had chosen for him was a Cadillac, though the automobile analogy was very much my own private interpretation. At any rate, Oleander, having zero amount of horse judging expertise but plenty of hands-on experience with owning the finer things in life, promptly got on board with the switch. And just as quickly, he had lumbered his way into the saddle of the replacement horse.

I had watched Oleander and his new ride plod ahead of me as the duo followed behind Boyd and Pete, and I had to concede that Willard Sherlee had, in fact, found a comparably dispositioned horse for Oleander, just as Headville had indirectly promised.

As hard as it was to admit, I was apparently going to have to be somewhat more trusting of the man who Morgan had advised me not to trust. Still, I hated that Buck was going to likewise be taken from Blaine, though I had not yet found the heart to tell my friend what was forthcoming from the top brass.

Riding side by side, Dent and I brought up the rear of our convoy, and as we passed beneath the ostentatious sign spanning above the entrance of Headville's property, I looked over my shoulder, thinking again of Kate. For a moment, I considered turning back.

If I had foreseen her absence, I would have done two things differently. One, I would not have bothered to check out of bed a half hour earlier than I needed to, just to take a bath in the cool water of the secluded swimming pond that lay nestled in the trees behind the bunkhouse. After the previous impromptu exchange with Kate, I had decided that if she should find herself compelled to tie another bandana around my neck, I would prefer to smell as fresh as a daisy, but I had no such ambition if my company for the day were a band of similarly fragrant-less cowboys.

Secondly, I would have volunteered ahead of Mick to remain behind and act as the sentry and guard the welfare of Kate, but then if I had successfully procured that assignment, I would have needed the bath anyway.

Either way, it was likely I would not see her today, and that disappointed me despite the effort of my short-term memory reminding me that the anatomical items that defined me as male had been threatened by the captivating young woman's dutiful custodian.

Culver Headville.

Also known as a distinguished breeder of Quarter Horses and presumed castrator of misbehaving males.

Then I wondered about Mick. I was not naïve. I knew I could not be the only one smitten by the charms of the girl who was the ward of the boss. But I imagined that Mick, and probably Little Pete and any other red-blooded ranch hand, had undoubtedly received from Headville a warning similar to the one he had given the four of us freshmen employees.

I am her guardian and I take that responsibility seriously.

That was what Culver Headville had said to the four of us before we had departed from Hays City a mere five days ago. But there had been another word. Very.

Very seriously.

Headville had been arguably subtle with the meaning of his words, at least from my intrepid, albeit foolish, perspective. Although last evening his warning had been clearly more specific.

Castration was routine for livestock males. But a whole different story for adolescent young men. Not that I really believed Headville would be so barbaric as to go that far, but then maybe I was more naïve than I was willing to admit.

Besides, I was not scheming to get into bed with Kate, so my testicles were currently not as threatening as perhaps were the pair that belonged to Viento. I just wanted to talk with her again, to be near her. To engage with her on a purely platonic level.

Right.

But there was a problem with my rationale. I had tried to kiss her.

Hells Bells, to quote both my dad and my current supervisor. What had I been thinking? Again, I reminded myself that I was not on a romantic holiday. I was a hundred years away from being where I should be, and if tomorrow I was given the opportunity to return home, I would take it without hesitation. And in that moment of lucidity, I knew a relationship with Kate was absurd. Certainly, unfair to her, in the event she was to develop an interest in me. But that was a longshot in the first place.

Or was it?

"Damn it!" I said aloud, cursing myself for caving again to a romantic daydream.

"Forget something?" Dent asked me.

I looked across at him and found that he had a knowing grin pasted upon his face that was by all accounts the goofiest smirk I had ever seen him wear.

"That's not a good look for you, brother," I said, dodging the question.

"She's a pretty gal."

I wanted to say, 'she who,' but what would be the point? Dent could always read me.

"Yep."

We rode for a full sixty seconds without another word between us. But that was longer than Dent could stand.

"So, that's it? Just yep?"

"Yep."

"Look, JT, if you're worried about me trying to move in on her, I'm not. I've learned my lesson. No girl is worth getting between the two of us, right?"

"Right," I said, and started counting to myself.

"Besides," Dent began as I hit number thirteen, "I, for one, have no intention of getting my neck stretched for a pretty girl with pretty green eyes and pretty blonde hair, and who is obviously already spoken for."

"What?"

"Headville. Clearly, he's got his own plans for her, and when she says yes to him, I'll let you cry on my shoulder."

"You don't know what you're talking about."

"Maybe not. But when you step back and look at the big picture, you know, with an open mind, it looks about as plain as the nose on your face, to borrow a phrase from Dad."

"That's a fairly abstract picture, in my opinion," I said, then I clicked my tongue against the roof of my mouth and simultaneously nudged Viento with my bootheels urging him into a trot, leaving Dent and his hypothesis behind. I was uninterested in continuing that conversation. Not because I thought he was totally wrong, but because I knew he could be right.

Moments later, Viento and I were neck and neck with Blaine and the buckskin.

"What's up with that?" Blaine asked me right away, nodding forward.

Ahead of us, Sherlee had suddenly separated from the group and had taken a path that was at a right angle westward. I watched curiously as he trotted away on the back of his muscular sorrel mare and with Oleander's former transportation, the roan mare, in tow via a halter and a lead rope.

"Dunno," I said quietly, keeping in pace and in position with our caravan. I watched until the wrangler and the two horses disappeared beyond a knoll. I wondered if an urgent call of nature had prompted Sherlee to seek some privacy.

"JT," Blaine said to me, and I switched my eyes to look at him.

"Yeah?"

"I've been thinking."

"About what?"

"Well, we're about a year and a half away from getting back home, right?"

"Right," I agreed, realizing there was no need to qualify his statement with a list of ifs of which he was already aware.

"I don't really want to do this."

"This?" I asked, waiting for further explanation that did not come as quickly as I had expected. So, after a lengthy pause, I added, "I'm not following you, Blaine."

"The ranch," he said, finally spitting it out.

"You don't want to do the ranch?"

"That's right, JT. I don't mind the work, but, well, it's just not for me. Not like it is for you and Dent."

"Okay. That's fair," I said, not totally taken by surprise. "But honestly, you've done great with everything you've been asked to do. I've been impressed. Dent, too."

"Thanks," Blaine replied. "I appreciate that, I do. But, well, I just feel really out of place there. Like I know I don't belong."

"We are all out place here by a hundred years," I reminded him.

"Yeah, I know, but it's different for you guys, and you know what I mean. It's just that I don't want to be a cowboy or a ranch hand or whatever, even if it's just temporary. I gotta do something else, something that's more worthwhile to me, you know, just in case."

"Just in case, what?"

"We don't get back home."

I understood where he was coming from. And though I was usually a glass-half-full kind of guy, I knew there was a significant chance that we would be here in the era of the 1800s for a long time to come. He and Dent and I had already talked about the real possibility of never getting back to our own time.

"So, what are you going to do?"

"Well, first, I won't do anything that would risk you guys, I want you to know that."

"That goes without saying. You're not Oleander," I said with a grin.

"Lucky you, right?"

"Right. I couldn't take two of you."

"Well, to answer your question, I thought I might go out to the fort."

"Fort Hays?" I asked, surprised.

"Yeah. I want to talk to someone about enlisting."

I did not see that coming. "Wow," I said, then whispered, "shit."

"Do you think that would be stupid?"

I thought for a long moment, processing not only what Blaine was suggesting, but how, if at all, his decision would impact the rest of us.

"No, I don't think it's stupid. I mean, after all it's exactly what you were planning to do in a few weeks anyway, if we had not gotten ourselves sucked into this century."

"Yeah, that's why I've been thinking about it. I mean, it's not exactly the army I was planning to join. And it won't get me scholarship money for college. But at least it would be keeping with my plan, you know? Giving me a sense of purpose. And I need that, more than most I suppose."

I knew of what he referred. His father was a bona fide alcoholic who spent eighty percent of his time in The Wigwam, Custer's local beer joint, and could keep neither a wife nor a steady job. Blaine

Wallace, Sr., had often told his namesake son that he would never amount to anything. But that detestably cruel prophecy made by the elder Wallace carried no weight, especially with anyone who knew of the courage and determination that were the pillars of Blaine's personality. But still, Blaine embraced his father's negativity as a challenge to succeed.

BANG!

I heard the gunshot but was not immediately sure from where it had come. Blaine and I both pulled our horses to an immediate stop, and we looked around. Then there was a second shot, and I realized it had reached my ears from the west. From the direction where Sherlee had gone.

Dent trotted up next to us, his eyes also looking westward. "What the hell?"

I glanced up ahead and saw that Oleander had stopped and was looking at us, but Headville and the two tenured cowboys continued to trek onward, neither appearing to give any notice of the gunshots, though there was no way they could not have heard them. And then I knew.

"That's bullshit," Dent whispered, and I saw that his eyes were upon a horse cantering toward us. Without so much as a glance our way, Sherlee passed by the three of us and I saw attached to the pommel of his saddle the lead rope and the halter.

Presumably, Sherlee had just slain the gentle roan mare.

I heard Oleander say something to Sherlee, though his words were indistinct. The wrangler slowed just enough to mumble a reply to him, then loped onward, catching up with Headville and retaking his place at the boss's right hand. The deed, if proven true, had been a cold execution, an act of shameless loyalty for the appeasement of the Culver Headville ego.

My naivety had just gotten a reality check.

I stared ahead, determined to keep at bay any sympathetic tear that might try to slip from my eyes. Then I saw Oleander shift in the saddle and turn and glance back at the three of us who sat stoically upon horses gifted to us by Morgan, all still appreciatively underneath us. For a moment he seemed as though he were about to rein his new horse around and join us, but instead he kicked his heels into the dun's ribs and trotted onward, taking him to a position next to his new best friend, a cowboy he had nicknamed Ox.

I wondered, then, if Oleander had just symbolically chosen which side his allegiance would lean toward, not just in this moment, but in whatever future that was destined to unfold for us. A sense of foreboding overwhelmed me, and I felt an unexpected loss, as though we had been abandoned by a brother musketeer who had just shunned his pledge of one for all.

Sometimes, I admit, my thoughts can be overly dramatic.

The three of us kept our distance from the group of five that led us toward Hays City, but we still maintained a course in the same direction. Dent had fired off a mouthful of cusswords, each one something our mom would have wanted to clean up with a bar of soap and a warm glass of water, but I could not blame him. The horse did not deserve a bullet. And there had been two. I only hoped Sherlee had been merciful. Then I told them of my conversation with Headville, and that I feared Buck was next in line for the same fate.

"I'm not letting him do that to Buck," Blaine declared.

"He won't," Dent said. "I guarantee that."

I hoped that it would be a promise my brother could keep. But not at the cost of him getting hurt.

When we arrived in town, we found it bustling with far more folks than we had seen thus far. Saturdays, as they were in the 1970s, were apparently the preferential days for citizens of the surrounding smaller communities and individual homesteaders to seek opportunities to trade and to fraternize with one another. What caught my attention most was the number of Volga German folks; men, women, and children, all clamoring around the town, choking the covered walkways of storefronts and crowding the hitching posts where their wagon teams lined the streets.

Promising that he had no specific agenda, Dent informed me that he had earlier agreed to join Boyd and Pete at a saloon they had called The Bull, and he had supposed that Oleander would be with them since he did not have a dime to spend on himself. Not that the three of us had a lot of money for that matter. Our current liquid assets amounted to only what we had in our pockets at the time our hotel room was being plundered.

With genuine brotherly love, I asked Dent to be careful and I hoped that he wasn't planning a drinking binge just because he could. But he assured me his pockets were just barely deep enough to pay for a few beers and with the first of the month payday still ten days away, I knew he was pragmatic enough to keep his spending to a minimum. I just hoped he would not charm his way into getting wasted because of the drunken generosity of the others.

Blaine squandered no time expressing his intent to go his separate way. Per his plan, he had a fort to investigate, but I suggested we make a stop at Tommy Drum's place first and see if he would happen to know if there was a specific man Blaine should ask for at the barracks.

Tommy's saloon was busy, not even elbow room was available at the bar. But, when he saw us, he waved us over.

"Morgan's friends!" He greeted us with a smile.

"Hi Tommy," I said.

"JT, right? And you are, hmmm, let me think. Ah, Blaine?"

"Right, on both counts," I told him.

"Let me find you a spot here somewhere, and get you something to drink," Tommy suggested, but I held up a palm to stop him.

"Actually, neither of us drink, so…"

"Well, some food, then."

"Not right now, sorry," I said to him.

"It's going to be hard for me to make a living with customers like you!" he said with a big grin.

"I know, but later though, I promise. Blaine here is wanting to talk to someone at the fort."

"About what?"

"Joining their ranks," Blaine volunteered.

"I see," Tommy said with a grimace. "There are worse places I suppose. Don't get me wrong, most soldiers that come in here are good men. But not all of them." Then he looked at me. "I heard you boys went to work for Culver Headville." Apparently, the Hays City grapevine was adequately fruited with wagging tongues.

"We did," I said, not planning to elaborate much.

"But I take it, not a good fit for you, Blaine?"

"Not really."

"Headville can be a hard man to work for. But pays well, I hear."

"It's not him," Blaine said, "I'm just, well, I'm just not a cowboy."

"Really?" Tommy eyed him, "well, you look like one."

Neither of us said anything.

"Tell you what, if you hang around here for a while, there's a Corporal Jenkins that usually comes into my place most every Saturday. I expect he might get here any minute. I'll introduce you. I just wouldn't recommend that you ride out there unexpected."

"Thank you, that would be great," Blaine replied.

"And, if it's only a change of employment you want, I heard that the smithy off west of the courthouse is looking for some help. Name of Billings, Ross Billings. Anyway, there's a chair at the end of the bar.

Wait there and I'll bring you a Sarsparilla and bowl of peanuts to chew on while you wait."

"Thank you," Blaine repeated.

"And what about you, JT?" offered the kind proprietor.

"Nothing for me, Tommy. I've got some things I need to do."

"Next time, then," Tommy said, and stepped away from us to tend to his customers.

I looked at Blaine. "Sounds like you've got a lead," I said to him. "I'm going to go explore the town a little more, I think. How about I meet you back here in a few hours?"

"It's a plan," Blaine said. And I left him to advance the plot that was of his own design, though secretly I did not care for the idea.

Mounting Viento, the two of us ambled down the street. I opted for a few different turns at intersections I had crossed the previous week, looking about for nothing in particular, but with a purpose to eventually visit John White again. I needed another shave even though my stubble was not nearly as thick or dark as my brother's. Nevertheless, there was a girl I felt irrationally compelled to impress.

When I eventually entered the barber shop of John White, I discovered four men in line ahead of me, though one of them was already seated in the chair of honor. John glanced at me and flashed a warm and welcoming smile.

"My friend, JT, come in, come in."

I couldn't help but return my best smile to him. John White was an especially easy man to like. I sat down in the only empty chair and watched as John completed the finishing touches of a haircut for a heavy-set youngish cowboy who I guessed to be around thirty years old, with chubby cheeks and eyes that laughed as loud as his voice. After a peek in the old mirror, the jovial young man thanked John and paid him, then taking his cowboy hat from a row of hooks next to the door beside me, he nodded in my direction.

"Howdy," he said grinning, and up close I saw a nick or two on the jowl of his throat.

"Howdy," I replied.

"Name's Fred," he said, offering me his thick, meaty hand. I took it.

"JT."

"Nice to meet you, JT. Spiffin' up for a night on the town, are ya?"

"Probably not. But, we'll see," I said, giving Fred what I imagined to be my second-best smile.

"I work for the Shank outfit, east of here. Harfon Shank."

I held on to my smile, wondering if the name of his employer was supposed to be someone I should know. I finally caved. "I'm sorry, I don't know him. I'm new around here."

"Didn't think I'd seen you before. So, you lookin' for a job?"

"Nope."

"Oh, so who do you punch cows for?" Apparently, like Blaine, I also had that look, which was exactly what Morgan had desired. "If you don't mind me asking?" Fred added congenially.

There was no jumping ship now. "Mr. Headville," I replied, including mister as a precaution.

"Ah!" Fred said, and I saw that I could see more of the whites of his eyes than was visible before. "Culver Headville."

"You know who he is then?"

"Who don't?! He's … well, he's an important man around here. Course, I don't need to tell you that." Then he shoved his cowboy hat down over his freshly sheared head. "Well, good luck, JT. If ya see me around town, be sure and let me know and I'll buy ya a drink."

"Thank you, Fred. Good to meet you," I said, deciding I could be a little more sociable.

"Same," he replied then left. I turned back and found the three men ahead of me in line looking at me with a mixture of expressions. Great, I thought. So much for keeping a low profile. As the executive decision maker for a company of which I was the sole member, I decided a polite grin would be good enough for them, and so that is what I locked in place, noticing though how differently the men were attired in comparison to one another.

Nearest to me was an older gentleman, with a thin grey moustache and decked out in a charcoal suit arrayed with pinstripes the color of Western Kansas dust. The second man was also a sharp dresser and I had to look twice to make sure he was not the gambler I had seen outside our hotel who I was sure had to have been the man who had robbed me and the others of our cache of funds. The third guy looked to be slightly older than Fred but dressed for the same profession. Clearly, John White's clientele came from all walks of life.

I leaned my head back against the wall, and tipped my cowboy hat down to my eyebrows and pretended to nap while I waited my turn. I was not interested in another beauty shop chat, and I hoped my ruse would work for me. And it did. But I did not sleep. I listened. And though nothing was said that was especially interesting, what was evident was that John White's customers were clearly fond of the little ebony-skinned proprietor.

When it became my turn, I took my place in the chair and gave John the instructions for what I wanted. We easily fell into a friendly conversation, and neither of us brought up the subject of Culver Headville. After completing the business of a shave and then letting him talk me into a haircut, I left the chair and took my hat from the wall and was about to bid him a good day when I remembered that I had also planned to ask him a question before I left.

"John," I began, "do you know Beverly Carniero?"

For a moment, John paused the movement of the broom he was using to sweep up the hair on the floor. "Yessir, I know Miss Beverly. She lives out there where you works," he added plaintively.

"Yeah, I've talked to her once. Briefly. She's Miss Kate's teacher, I guess."

"That's what we heared, me and Mrs. White. Miss Beverly, she make a fine teacher."

"She seems—well, is she from the east coast?"

"No, no, she from Nicodemus, most lately. I knows her folks. They was slaves down to South Carolina, freed by President Lincoln. They more educated than most of us Black people out here. Their master was a good man they tell me. Made sure they all could read and write. Not many like that, Mister JT, I can tells ya that."

"I imagine that's true," I said.

"Miss Beverly's daddy told me that the master 'bout lost everything though, cuz of the war. But he had a son come out here with the Carnieros and five, six other Negro families and helped 'em get settled in Nicodemus. I heared he bought some land for hisself out somewhere, but we's hadn't seen him for a long while now. A good friend he is."

"Can't have too many friends."

"Lord knows that be right."

"So, I'm curious, Morgan told me he went to Nicodemus before he left. Was he, by chance, friends of the Carnieros?"

"Oh, yessir, Mister JT. That's how I gots to know Mr. Morgan. A good man, he is, too."

"For sure," I said, "So—

The door opened and a pair of cowboys, twice my age, lumbered in, laughing at something the two of them had found overtly funny.

"Hey, Johnny!" One of them exclaimed. I glanced at John White to gauge his reaction. I was prepared to stay if I needed to, though I was hardly a suitable candidate for a bouncer.

"Mister Benny and my friend Joseph! Come in, come in," John welcomed them. He was, without a doubt, a popular barber.

"See ya, John," I said, fixing my hat back in place. He wished me a safe week before I closed the door behind me.

I stepped into the saddle and reined Viento away from the barber shop and began to meander through the stream of folks crisscrossing the main street. Shortly, I was passing by the saloon with a sign that featured an impressively artistic image of a buffalo and lettered with the words THE BULL. I was tempted to take a peek inside and check on my brother, but like it or not, he was an adult, and I was not his keeper. Besides, I had my plate full of my own crap, specifically the torment of infatuation.

Without pause, I kept Viento moving along, though after a while, we found ourselves near the grand courthouse and within view of the jailhouse of which I had recently been a temporary guest. And tied in front of the small, square building were two horses that might as well have been neon billboards beckoning me to look their way. One was a splendid sorrel mare with one white sock, the favored ride of Willard Sherlee. The other, the black stallion that had been the day's substitute transportation for Culver Headville.

Interesting, I thought. Though it had been obvious that Deputy Texas Jack Moody and my boss had some sort of relationship, an oddly suspicious one if I were to be asked for an opinion.

I swung wide of that place of incarceration, not at all feeling an urge to spy through the windows with the hope of learning the grisly details of some imagined evil plot that might be hatching between the three men. Instead, I continued to ride around, exploring some of the residential streets. After Viento and I had wasted a good half hour looking around, we rounded a corner and found what was certainly the town's schoolhouse, modestly sized and situated in the middle of a city block. And parked in front of the limestone structure was another horse I was as familiar with as the one beneath me.

Buck.

I reined Viento toward the place and just as we edged in next to the buckskin, the door of the building opened and Blaine and two men, both old enough to be his dad, stepped outside talking and shaking hands. By all appearances, some sort of agreement had been consummated. And here I was imagining similar alliances were developing in the jailhouse. I sat there watching them, then Viento tossed his head and nickered at Blaine as though he had given up on me to say, *hello, what are you doing here?'*

CHAPTER 35

Blaine looked up and saw me, and after a quick word with the pair of older gentlemen, he hurried in my direction.

"JT, perfect timing!"

"Is it?"

"I've got a job!"

"No shit?" I asked, glancing back at the school. "Doing what?"

"I'm going to be a schoolteacher!" Blaine said excitedly. "That's Orville Bascom and Theodore Schmidt over there. They're on the school board. They've been testing me with all sorts of math questions and asking me to spell like a hundred different words. It seems like I've impressed them with what I know, at least they seem confident enough to trust me to teach the local kids math and reading and such."

"How'd you find out about the job?"

"At Tommy Drum's place. I had been waiting for the guy Tommy told us about, when those two came in and happened to sit at a table behind me. I heard them talking and decided to let them know that I had plans to teach someday, which is true."

"Right."

"So, anyway, we ended up here, with me standing in front of a chalkboard and taking an easy pop quiz."

"Wow!" I said with a laugh.

"What do you think, JT? This will be better than the Fort Hays army, right?"

"Oh, yeah, Blaine. For sure," I agreed wholeheartedly. "I didn't want to discourage you earlier, but honestly I was worried that you might not be stationed nearby, you know, when the time came for our trip back home."

"I know, I thought of that, too. But this is perfect." I smiled at the excitement in my friend's voice and the genuine happiness that painted his face. "There's a catch, though," Blaine added, and instantly his face darkened with worry. "There are three men on the school board."

"Okay. Looks like you've got a majority in your pocket."

"You'd think. But they won't commit to hiring me until they get the approval of the third."

"A unanimous thing, then?"

"Apparently so. And guess who number three is?"

I looked at him, and I could read the answer in his eyes.

"Culver Headville," I said.

"Yep."

"I should be surprised, but I'm not. Headville seems to have his fingers in a variety of pies: Law enforcement, now public education, and who knows what else. Well, I happen to know where we might find him. Let's go see what he says."

Blaine returned to the committee of two while I stayed with the horses, and after a brief explanation, he departed with handshakes and smiles all around. Blaine mounted Buck and together we rode into the midst of the bustling Western village but as we neared the jail, I discovered that neither the sorrel horse nor the exquisite black one was there.

"Damn," I said. Then looked around.

"There!" Blaine said, pointing to a pair of riders moving patiently along a lesser populated side street. We urged our horses into a light trot and headed their way.

"Mr. Headville, sir," I called as we neared him and Sherlee. He turned and saw me, and as though it was second nature to him, he broadcast a congenial smile that reminded me of a TV evangelist.

"JT, Blaine," he addressed us. "Sherlee and I were just heading back to the ranch. The two of you are not also calling it a day, are you?"

"No, sir. Not exactly. But could we have a minute? Blaine wants to talk to you about something important."

"I'm intrigued."

The four of us reined our horses over to a space that fronted a vacant lot nestled between the side street and the rear walls of two stores with long, peaked rooflines extending from their square false-fronted facades that overlooked the street on the opposite side. Without dismounting, we gathered in a circle and Blaine boldly and unapologetically told Headville of his meeting with his fellow school board members.

"So, Blaine," Headville began with an expression that seemed to be leaning in a negative position, "you would prefer a job educating children over the employment I've provided for you at the ranch?"

"Yes sir, I would."

Headville nodded. "I appreciate your honesty, Blaine." Then he glanced at Sherlee before returning his flickering blue eyes to Blaine. "It has been obvious to Boyd and Sherlee that ranch work is new for you. And that is not to say that I don't think you've done a respectable job for me. If I did not believe you were worth it, I would have already sent you packing." He shifted his eyes to me. "What about you, JT? Are you also looking for alternative employment?"

"No, sir. I'm right where I want to be," I said to him, and it was relatively liberating to speak truthfully, although my desire to be at the ranch had little to do with him. "And as far as I know my brother feels the same way."

"Good. Well, Blaine, it looks like luck is on your side today. If our young schoolmarm had not decided to get married, we would not have had a position available for you to fill."

"Yes, sir, that's what Mr. Bascom and Mr. Schmidt told me. Right place and the right time, I guess."

"I'll speak to them before I leave town. And well done, Blaine."

"Sir?"

"You're making your own way here. I admire that."

"Thank you, Mr. Headville."

Headville and Sherlee reined their horses around and headed in the direction of the school. I waited for a count of ten, then exhaled a deep breath.

"For a minute, I thought that was going the other way."

"Me, too," Blaine admitted.

"So, when do you start?"

"Monday."

"Well, let's go find my brother and tell him your news."

We headed for The Bull, and as we entered its neighborhood, sounds of laughter and sporadic versions of drunken "yee-haws" echoed through the streets. But not just from the one saloon that was our destination, but from many like establishments that lined the main street of Hays City. Without expending much time and effort, we found a place to tie the horses, but as I expected, Blaine preferred to wait outside. But not just because of his father but also because I had just learned that Theodore Schmidt and Orville Bascom had openly postulated that they expected their teacher to abstain from patronizing places of depravity, saloons being one such place, but listed second were the popular businesses where the proprietors were women of questionable reputation.

I walked inside, and the acrid smell of cigarette smoke, stale beer, and man sweat permeated the air, and I could not help but frown at the assault on my olfactory senses. I glanced around the crowded room, but my eyes were immediately drawn to the massive head of a taxidermized buffalo bull mounted to the wall behind the bar. Then I heard a familiar voice yell, "*Hey, Worm,*" and I begrudgingly looked to find Oleander and the not-so-little Little Pete seated at a table with Boyd and some other man of similar age.

I crossed to them, anticipating that an intoxicated Oleander would flip me his trade-mark gesture by the time I arrived at their table. Surprisingly, none of my three co-workers seemed worse for the wear after spending an afternoon in a saloon, though the elderly stranger was unquestionably inebriated. I shifted my eyes to Boyd and nodded at him, surmising that perhaps he had exercised some degree of influence on them, especially Oleander. But then there was no sign of my brother.

"Where's Dent?" I asked.

"He done skedaddled," Boyd said.

"Where to?"

"Back to the ranch, so he told us."

"I see."

"Pull up a chair, JT," Pete said. "Olly here has been teaching us some jokes!"

"Jokes?"

"Funny, too!"

"No doubt," I said without much confidence.

"They shore-for be different kinds of jokes, too. Tap-taps, ain't that be what ya called 'em?" Boyd asked Oleander.

"Knock-knocks," corrected my red-haired quasi-comrade.

Boyd laughed. "That be 'zackly what I said!"

Great, I thought, wondering if Oleander had just pushed the introduction of the knock-knock formula of humor up by a good seventy or eighty years. Hopefully, Oleander's potential impact on the history of comedy would be a thing quickly forgotten until it had a chance to come into the time in which it was meant to arrive. I stood for a moment and listened to Little Pete try his hand at repeating an Oleander goody, but he was not quite up to task just yet, but still, I laughed a little, before I turned and left them alone.

Blaine and I rode the twelve miles back to the ranch, with Blaine doing most of the talking, at least for the first mile or two. According to him, the pair of elected school administrators had not only evaluated Blaine's knowledge but had also advised him of various expectations outside of the classroom.

To avoid any future question of his integrity, tobacco use, whether smoked or tucked in the cheek, was prohibited. But the easy pass for Blaine was that the consumption of any kind of alcoholic spirits was strictly forbidden, although he was, however, allowed to occasionally patronize a saloon but only one of the reputable ones that provided a full restaurant service. The men had verbally given him a short and select list of those approved businesses, noting that Tommy Drum's saloon had just recently made their cut.

Courtship had also been addressed. Blaine would be allowed one evening each week for courting purposes, but two evenings in any given week were permissible so long as he attended church on the prior Sunday.

I laughed. "Well, you know where I'll be if you need a groomsman."

"Maybe, but only after plan A is completed."

"And what about your salary?" I asked him.

"Sixty dollars a month!"

"Ah, you'll be banking double what you are now," I said.

"Right, but I'm not bragging, you know."

I laughed again. "Of course not!"

"Sad thing is, though, they were only paying the previous teacher forty dollars, and didn't act at all like they were ashamed to have paid her a lot less for doing the same job."

"Sucks to be female," I said. "There's no escaping wage disparity between genders. My mom frequently rants about it."

"Good thing she's not here."

"Good thing."

"Oh, and get this, there's a room in the back end of the school building that is set up for living quarters. Not a big space, but it will be nice to have my own place."

"Be honest, you're going to miss bunking with a bunch of farting men." We both laughed, knowing that would not be the case.

There was hardly a quiet moment on our ride back to the ranch, and I was genuinely glad to see Blaine happy. Unlike me, he had grown up as a kid without a mom, and instead had lived a hard life with an alcoholic father who had never shown him the slightest degree of affection. And not only that, but my friend also had an older half-brother who had, at his first opportunity, bolted for a better life, one presumably far from the man who had been made his stepfather. But Blaine did not condemn his brother for his escape, but neither had he seen nor heard from him in the six years he had been gone.

I could not imagine that degree of estrangement from Dent. Despite our occasional disagreements, or even the rare physical confrontation that can get a guy transported back in time, I would miss him. A lot. And given what we had been through in the last eighteen days, I knew I should communicate to Dent that endearing feeling sooner, than later.

By the time we had ridden to within a mile of the ranch entrance, the late afternoon sun was edging into the first part of evening. And though my conversation with Blaine had been a welcome distraction, I was compelled to glance toward the hill that shielded the secreted spot where Sherlee had allegedly slain the roan mare. A part of me wanted to confirm her fate, but I had little doubt that what I would find would be evidence of what I already knew to be true. I was positive that Sherlee had not alternatively set her free and then deceptively fired a pair of shots into the air as the means to frighten her into running off. But it was a nice thought. And not impossible. But maybe I was better off not knowing for certain. At least now that Blaine was leaving, the threat of a similar fate for Buck was squelched.

When we entered the ranch yard, Isaiah was rounding the barn, a bucket of milk in one hand and a basket of garden vegetables in the other. We both called out to him and said hello, and he smiled and hurried along toward the house. No one else was in sight, not that I expected them to be, but I was surprised that little Poppy had not run out to greet us. We dismounted, then walked the horses into the barn and sure enough, Dent's brown bay was there.

Thank you, Jesus, I thought to myself, relieved that he was here and not so drunk that he might have found himself waking up in bed with one of the soiled doves of the Sporting Palace bordello he had intentionally stumbled into on our first visit to the 1878 version of Hays.

We unsaddled Viento and Buck and brushed and grained them, then led them outside toward the smaller pasture nestled behind the bunkhouse where the work horses had a forty-acre pasture designated just for them. As we passed by, Dent stepped from inside the place that was our sleeping quarters, his white-socked feet matching the markings of many of Headville's horses. I called for him to come with us, and with a nod he ducked back inside to grab his boots. As quick as a New York minute, he had caught up to Blaine and me just as we released our horses.

"What's up?" Dent asked.

"Well, Blaine has some news," I said, closing the gate and watching as Viento proceeded with his routine rolling on the ground, his hooves thrashing skyward. As always, this amusing antic would cause me to smile, despite knowing that it was just his horse-way of relieving the skin discomfort created by the saddle, even though I had just brushed loose hair and road grime from the velvety side of his hide.

Excited by his turn of fortune, Blaine shared with Dent his unexpected opportunity. And then Dent surprised me, as he does on occasion. I had guessed he would voice a paragraph of reasons why Blaine becoming separated from us was not exactly a clever idea. Afterall, Kival had already been split from our group. But, instead, my brother was believably pleased for Blaine. Perhaps Dent was beginning to become more discriminating when it came to picking his battles. Especially since he and I both shared the blame for getting all of us into the pickle we were in.

We headed back toward the bunkhouse, Blaine leading the way, my brother and I walking side by side.

"You came back early," I stated conversationally.

"Yep."

"I think I know why."

Dent turned to me as we walked, looking at me doubtfully. "Let's hear it," he said.

"I think you wanted to check on the roan mare," I said. "Without anyone seeing you." He had not said much to me since the presumed execution of the horse earlier that morning, but I knew it would have been bothering him. When it came to animals, Dent had the softest of hearts.

"Busted," he said returning his eyes forward.

"So, it wasn't just for show, was it?"

"Nope. The bastard shot her. Twice in the head."

"It wasn't Sherlee's decision."

"Hell, no. That was all Mr. Culver A. Headville's doing."

"I didn't know he had a middle name," I said, knowing what the A meant from Dent's witty perspective.

Dent had been, for a year or so now, adding the snarky initial when referring to people he did not like. The first time I remembered him using the singular acronym was after Mr. Clarkson, our high school English teacher, returned to Dent an essay he had written as an assignment to pen a brief one-page summary of the first two chapters of the book, *The Lord of the Flies*. Dent of course had not read it, but he did fill a page of a notebook describing men's underwear and their associative and functional flies. The grade had been an F, and Dent had argued that he had given the teacher exactly what he had asked for: A brief summary, which from Dent's humoristic perspective was a short essay on tighty-whities.

A soft laugh got away from me as I remembered my brother's annoyance with Mr. Stephen A. Clarkson.

"What?" Dent asked.

"Nothing."

"I see you've been to see John White again."

"Maybe."

"Too bad. I hear she likes whiskers."

"Bullshit," I said as we stepped inside the bunkhouse. We found Blaine was already at his bunk pulling his saddlebags from under his bed. "You're not leaving this afternoon, are you?" I asked as I customarily removed my boots.

"Thinking I might."

Reclining on his bunk, Mick looked up from a dime novel he was reading. "Leaving? What's going on?"

"I'm taking on a new job," Blaine told him. "I'm going to teach … at the school."

"Really?" Mick said, sitting up. "I didn't know they were needing a teacher."

"Opening just came up. Believe it or not, they basically fired the previous teacher because she was getting married."

"Oh, yeah, I believe it. Folks out here are pretty darn conservative," Mick said. "Married women aren't allowed to be teachers of children. It doesn't make much sense, does it?"

Times had changed. And for the better.

"New book?" I asked Mick, noticing the dime novel he was reading had an unfamiliar cover.

"Yeah," he said, offering it to me. His appreciation for literature glamorizing the Old West was something we had in common, and after I had been on the ranch just two days, he had loaned me one of his paperback books.

"Kit Carson, Jr. the Crack Shot of the West," I read from the cover of the Beadle's Dime Library's volume one, issue number three, that featured an artist's portrait rendering what was itself an impressive depiction a handsome young version of the fabled frontiersman.

"Dent picked it up for me."

"He did?" I asked, glancing at my brother.

"He asked me to, you know, since he wasn't going into town," Dent explained. "It's not like I haven't bought a book before."

"You haven't, to my knowledge," I said, with a grin.

And at once, the four of us heard the scream.

Quickly I scrambled back into my boots, but Dent had dashed outside ahead of me, again sock-footed.

I looked toward the house but saw no one.

"Somebody! ... Help me!"

It was Kate, I was sure of it. Then suddenly she appeared from around the side of the grandiose home, and in her arms, she carried the limp form of an animal with black and white fur fluttering in the heat of the summer breeze.

There was no doubt of the critter's identity: Poppy.

Dent and I both rushed to Kate, just as the front door opened and Isaiah scurried onto the veranda. Dent took the lifeless dog from her and after crossing to the grand porch, he laid it gently onto the wooden platform. I followed him as Blaine and Mick gathered beside us. The little dog's face, though covered with a glossy coat of hair, was swollen to an enormously grotesque size, the pooling of the fluid beneath her skin nearly engulfing her dark sightless eyes. I knew at once what had happened. Dent and I had seen these characteristics before. More times than either of us cared to remember.

The deadly bite of a rattlesnake.

Beverly appeared on the porch, and Kate rushed to her and the slightly older woman enveloped Kate in her arms as she buried her head against the woman's breast, her sobs gently muffled.

"Damn," Dent whispered, stroking his hand along the animal's quieted chest. I sighed, realizing I was going to miss having the playful little dog around.

It had not been a good day for the innocent of God's creatures.

CHAPTER 36

A half hour later, the seven of us had assembled in the yard behind the two-story limestone home where we quietly loitered beside a little ten-foot square structure that I learned was Kate's childhood playhouse. Her guardian, Culver Headville, had it built for her as a gift for her eighth birthday. Its walls were wood-framed instead of limestone but painted a sand color to match the shade of the masonry of the Headville mansion, and it had a natural pine six-paneled door and two false windows, each framed with brown faux shutters.

A simple building but compared to the dugout abode occupied by my new German friends, Abelard and Karl, it was arguably an extravagance for a child to play pretend.

The playhouse even had its own miniature yard that was fenced with a rectangle of short, white pickets. In its center was a circular area defined by small fragments of limestone and within the boundary were horticultural remnants of perennial flowers that had struggled to flourish. But what held my attention and steered my thoughts was a wood plank marker with the name of SAM carved into the wood. Kate had shared with us that it was this place where her first dog had been buried just five years before. I could not help but think of my childhood friend who shared the same name. Only he did not have a marker. Or even a grave for that matter.

Earlier, Kate had asked that everyone, the four of us young ranch hands, as well as Isaiah and Beverly, help make immediate arrangements for the burial of her beloved Poppy. She was bereaved and was unable to bear the thought of her little dog lying about without being properly laid to rest. And none of us, save for Isaiah, had attempted to change her mind. Though sympathetic, he had suggested she wait for Mister Headville.

"I don't want to wait for him. He won't care anyway," she had said to Isaiah, her tone conveying a hint of resentment. But maybe that discernment was just wishful thinking on my part. Especially if Dent was right about Headville's matrimonial intentions for his ward.

As a sister might console a younger sibling, Beverly had cradled Kate within the crook of her arm and had eventually persuaded her to wait and relax inside the house while the men made the necessary preparations. Though before they left, Kate had given Mick a brief instruction.

"Out back, Mick. You know where," she had added somberly.

Minutes later, Mick had returned from the barn with a shovel and a rake, as my brother hurried back from the bunkhouse where he had gone to retrieve his boots. Immediately, Dent volunteered to do the digging and politely took the spade from Mick then the two of them, followed by Blaine, strode toward the back yard of the lofty ranch home. With the lifeless dog cradled in my arms, I joined them and watched as a spot was cleared and a shallow excavation completed.

Isaiah had found a piece of burlap and together he and I shrouded the dog's body in the coarse fabric and then had tied it with ribbons that looked like they could have been from the same spool as those I had seen adorning Kate's hair.

Shortly, the women had appeared, entering the area from the backdoor of the house, and in Kate's hand she carried a Bible. With the help of Beverly, they settled upon a verse they agreed would be perfect. Though I was not as familiar with the book as my mother would have liked, I could not recall any mention of scripture that had been penned for the funeral of a beloved pet.

With the preparatory tasks completed, Kate glanced around at our solemn group, then made requests for specific favors from among us younger men, choosing Blaine to place the deceased canine into the empty hole of the grave, and asking Mick to read from the Bible. It had been a sweet and earnest gesture for the little dog for which I, myself, had developed a fondness. Then it occurred to me that I had essentially been excluded as an active participant in the reverent occasion, and as I looked around at the others, I caught Beverly Carniero staring at me as though she thought I might somehow be responsible for the little dog's demise. I prayed that Kate had not entertained any such possibility.

Despite my imagination of Beverly's suspicions and the conceived oversight of being denied a role in the event, I stood quietly while the little dog was buried. Kate had been somber but seemed more at peace with her grief.

If only she had not gone to my brother for solace.

After Dent had smoothed the loose soil over the grave, Kate crossed to him and wrapped her arms around his shoulders. I reasoned that since Dent had been the one to dig the grave, it was natural for her to express to my brother her appreciation for his kindness. But then he returned the affectionate of her gesture, and had done so with more intimacy than I expected of him. I should not have been surprised.

Instantly, I was seething. And yet in the next second I was cursing myself for being ridiculously jealous. But my mind found it impossible not to feel that way. When it came to my brother and the recent revelation of his alleged indiscretion with my former girlfriend, Laurie, I was painfully insecure, and I hated the feeling. But still, I could not bear the sight of the two of them embracing, so I turned and marched away though I hoped I did not look too much like a drama queen.

Moderately irritated, I passed from the backyard of the house and ambled down the slope of the front yard and hastily stepped into the space that managed the horse and wagon traffic only to look up and discover Culver Headville and Willard Sherlee intercepting my advance. I had not noticed that they had entered the ranch yard, my mind resentfully elsewhere. Headville pulled Ulysses to an abrupt stop and looked down at me with a cold eye of suspicion, then Sherlee grunted a couple of words that took Headville's attention from me and directed it toward the gathering in the backyard of his palatial home.

"What is going on?" he demanded, his voice calm, yet hard.

"We … well, Mr. Headville, sir, the little Border Collie, she got a snake bite. The guys—well, we just helped Kate bury the dog, sir."

"I see," he said returning his eyes to the group. "Silly girl. I hope she didn't carry on too much. It was, after all, just a dog."

I offered neither an affirmation nor a rebuttal.

Then he looked down at me again. "A word of advice, JT. Keep your eyes open and your head out of your ass." I stared at him, surprised by his condescending attitude. The sympathetic gathering had seemingly put Headville in a sour mood. "I wouldn't want you to get trampled," he added, nudging his black stallion toward me. I stepped out of his way, and without another glance to where his ward was loitering among the staff of the Headville ranch, he and Sherlee reined their horses toward the nearest of the three stables and disappeared inside.

Kate had been right. He did not care.

Passing beneath the age-old cottonwood that anchored the center of the ranch yard, I strode to the pasture where I had released Viento and picking up the halter and lead rope I left hanging on the gate, I whistled for the horse, just as Morgan had taught me. Within seconds, my grullo stallion was trotting toward me. Obediently, he allowed me to fix the halter onto his head, and I led him out through the gate. But instead of taking him to the barn, I knotted the end of the rope to the halter forming a makeshift rein, and sacrificing the convenience of a saddle,

I pulled myself up onto the back of the horse hoping that Viento would be agreeable to my riding him bareback. Viento did not so much as flinch, and so I patted his neck expressing my gratitude. Then I reined him toward the exit of the ranch.

I wanted space. And I needed time. I had something of an anger issue to deal with, and it was solely mine, not Dent's. He had done nothing, this time, to cause these feelings, yet there they were. And the last thing I wanted was to let the heat of the moment trigger me to say or do something that would cause an unnecessary rift between us.

When I returned to the ranch yard with Viento, our shadows were long, flat shapes crawling across the ground, foretelling that less than an hour of daylight remained. I dropped from the horse's back and untied the temporary knot I had made, then opened the corral gate and led Viento to the water trough at the far side of the pen. Behind me, I heard a door close, then the sound of bootsteps shuffling along the ground toward me.

"Kinda late for a ride," Dent spoke as he stepped next to me. "You know, considering you've been in the saddle for half the day already."

"Well, it was kind of an impromptu thing," I said, congenially. The ride had calmed me, and it had given me the time to erase the temporary feelings of ill-will that had spontaneously developed toward my brother.

"Bareback?"

"Yep. Viento didn't seem to mind."

"Just like Jericho, huh?" Dent said, speaking of my horse back home. "I don't get how you like riding without a saddle."

"Just being lazy."

Quiet closed in upon us, as I waited for the stallion to drink his fill from the tank.

"Are we okay?" Dent asked suddenly.

"Sure," I said, looking at him. "Why wouldn't we be?"

"Well," Dent said with a hint of hesitation, "that hug. It was all her doing."

"Hug?" I asked as though I had not a clue what he was talking about, but my face had told him otherwise.

"Nice try."

"Okay, I didn't like it, I admit. But I'm good with it. It's not like she's my girlfriend," I replied, and as soon as the words spilled across my lips, I knew what they would sound like to Dent, and that was not at all my intention.

"I deserve that."

"No," I said. "I didn't mean it like that. I'm just saying Kate's not my girlfriend, that's all."

"But you like her."

"Yes! And, yes, I know, I'm being stupid."

"Probably."

I looked at him. "You're lots of help."

"Doubtful. But let me make something very clear to you, JT. Honestly, I have no interest in Kate Headville or whatever her last name is, I swear."

We locked eyes in the typical fashion of a stare-down between the two of us brothers who were incidentally cut from different bolts of cloth, and instantly I read the sincerity in his expression. "I believe you," I said. "Straight up, we're good."

"Straight up?"

"Straight up."

Then a distant voice suddenly hailed us.

"Hey you—you proossies!"

"Damn," Dent spat. "I was half hoping he wouldn't find his way back."

"More than half for me."

We looked to see Oleander riding toward us, sandwiched between Boyd and Little Pete. They entered through the open gate of the corral and stopped their horses next to us at the trough, then Oleander peered down at us with glazed and groggy eyes and a ridiculously cocky grin.

"Knock, knock," he said, and there was a distinct slur attached to his two words.

"Not now Olly, we don't wanna hear it."

"F—-fine!" he replied, as he slid from the saddle, his knees buckling as his feet touched the ground. Dent stepped in next to him and held him up.

"Somebody's been drinking."

"Little bit," Oleander admitted, then a prolonged giggle stuttered from him as he shook his head idiotically.

"It's my fault," Pete spoke up.

"That be damn shore-for," Boyd tacked on as he swung down from his horse. "Why don't you boys take him inside and Little Pete and me we'll take care of his horse."

Since it was more or less an order issued from the man who was my superior, I complied, though I was not in the least interested in dealing with an inebriated baboon.

"Dude!" Dent exclaimed turning Oleander so that he could get an arm around the taller man's waist, "your breath smells like horse piss!"

"And that bothers you, why?" I asked my brother, who would normally have been in a similar condition.

"Shhhssss," Oleander gushed, "I think that's what I've been … been … been drinking."

I positioned myself opposite Dent and we escorted Oleander toward the bunkhouse. Blaine stood there with the door opened wide for the three of us to squeeze through. We led him to the south half of the building where he had been sleeping alone, and we dumped him on his bunk. He landed facedown, and I suspected that he had passed out before he even hit the bed. Dent pulled his hat from his head and tossed it on the empty bed next to him, and I likewise removed his boots before shoving them out of the way.

"Man does this bring back memories," Dent said with a shake of his head.

"Doesn't it though?" I asked, looking at him with annoyance. He grimaced, realizing that I was referring to my frequent experiences of putting his drunken ass to bed.

"Brother, my sincerest apologies."

The following morning was Sunday, which meant it was a workday, just like any other on the CH Quarter Horse Ranch, and it started early before the crowing of the rooster. As usual, we gathered at the table for breakfast though Oleander was an exception since he was still lying on top of his bunk, fully clothed and passed out, or sleeping, or playing possum, I didn't care which. Then after breakfast, Dent and I went with Blaine and helped him with the saddling of Buck, not that he needed our assistance, but we did it as a gesture of friendship. I was happy for Blaine, but it was not going to be the same without him around. Just as he was tying his saddlebags and bedroll in place, Sherlee walked in and handed the resigned cowboy a handful of coins.

"Four days wages," Sherlee told him, then turned and left.

I looked at Blaine. "I think you'll miss him most of all."

"Where have I heard that before?"

"Well, basically that's what Dorothy said to the Scarecrow," I replied to Blaine.

"Oh, right," he said, stepping into the saddle. "Well, guys, you know, when you get into town, look me up, okay?"

"Will do," Dent told him.

"See ya. And, good luck," I said to him, then patted Buck on the rump as Blaine reined him away. Dent and I stood for a moment and watched as our friend left us behind.

"Just you and me, now," Dent said.

"I'm not complaining," I told him.

"And Oleander."

"Okay, now I'm gonna cry."

Suddenly Boyd came storming out of the bunkhouse and tromped toward the water trough. "Damn hon-yock!" he cussed, then we watched as he dipped a bucket into the water. "Shore-for I be gettin' that peckerhead woked up!" he sputtered heading back with Oleander's final wake up call.

"This is gonna be good!" Dent said.

And it was.

Then quickly, almost without realizing it, the week had passed, and on that first Saturday after the burial of little Poppy, a pair of buckboard wagons rolled into the ranch yard, both empty except for the passengers. Four men, all of whom were likely former slaves now free because of Abraham Lincoln, and with them was a young woman of their kin who I assumed to be the laundress of whom Boyd had spoken.

Lizzyann.

Lord Headville himself stepped from the privacy of his lavish house and greeted Lizzyann in the flash of a conspicuous moment that left me with the impression that she was either excessively bashful or modestly afraid. Though because of the distance that separated us, she could have smiled at Headville and giggled before disappearing through the front door, hurried by the fact that she had too much work to do to and could not afford to forfeit a single second spent idly chatting away with her imposing employer. But considering what I knew about the man, I doubted that she was genuinely happy to see him.

Sitting on the edge of the bunkhouse porch and acting as though I was completely disinterested, I pretended to be fully focused upon a personal project I hoped would prove to be worth its weight in gold. But with my eyes masked in the shadow of my hat, I covertly observed the assembly of the men and cocked an ear in their direction hoping to hear them better. But all of them had kept their voices low, but I could read their body language. None of the Black men appeared to be comfortable, one driver seeming to be especially anxious. But given what I knew about Headville and his penchant for slave labor, I was not surprised by their discomposure.

However, the men who were surely citizens of Nicodemus did not stay long. And when they left, Lizzyann remained behind. As Boyd had informed me, she had the frame of most of the remaining day to complete her work for the Headville household, and as it turned out, I had my own task to finish. A gift for Kate.

A few days earlier, while nosing around in the giant barn, I had happened upon a thick plank cut from an oak tree, a likely leftover from the construction phase of the great Headville home. It was a board two inches thick and two feet tall and half as wide. At once I knew it was the perfect size for something I hoped would be considered special enough to earn me some much-needed brownie points.

This morning, on my day off, I had built a small temporary fire, and with the aid of its flames I heated the end of a discarded horseshoe, and I began to neatly sear and center a precise set of letters into the smooth surface of the board and spelled a name, capitalizing it from beginning to end.

POPPY

An hour later, I had completed my project, and was loitering on the porch of the bunkhouse, waiting inconspicuously for the chance to catch Kate leaving her home. Luckily, I did not have to linger for very long.

CHAPTER 37

I trotted toward Kate, with the bulky marker hidden behind my back, but as soon as she noticed my approach, she hurried her pace, striding with determination toward the trio of horse stables.

"Kate! Wait!"

At once, she stopped and turned to glare at me. "What do you want?" she asked me. "I'm too busy. Especially for you."

What I had done to offend her was a complete mystery to me, though my conscience suggested that my failed attempt to kiss her was a good candidate for the offense. "I have something for you," I said to her.

"It had better not be a frog, or a horned toad, or something stupid like that."

"No," I replied. "Nothing like that." Then from behind my back I revealed to her my gift. Instantly, her eyes filled with tears, and I cursed myself for not giving her more time to grieve for her dog. "Sorry, I didn't mean to make you cry."

Then she smiled and looked at me in a way she had not done before. "I love it," she whispered. And then together, we walked side by side to the place in the back yard and meticulously planted the marker at the head of the fresh grave.

Afterwards, we sat on the stoop of the little playhouse, and she told me about her first dog, Sam, and I shared with her the loss of the canine companions I had known during my childhood. And then we talked about stories from the Bible, which were familiar to me from the days of my Sunday School attendance, but Kate was clearly better educated from an adult perspective, particularly regarding the Book of Ester. Though she dominated the biblical discussion, I hung onto every word, enjoying the sound of her voice, and basking in her company.

Then our conversation shifted to horses. She asked me the name of my grullo stallion, and I obliged her, adding that Viento meant wind in Spanish, or so that was what Morgan had informed me. Then without intending to, I told her about my first horse and how he had been a special gift from my dad but omitting several relevant details including Jericho's delivery by pickup and horse trailer, not to mention he was waiting for me on my family's ranch 101 years into the future.

Soon, we were chatting about the cities of New York and Boston and San Francisco, all places she had seen in pictures and hoped to one day visit, while I concurred with her that I also looked forward to one day exploring those grand metropolises. Kate had even talked of clothes and dresses and millinery shopping, none of which I found particularly interesting, but I loved the excitement in her voice, so I smiled and paid close attention. An hour later, we parted. And although I had no idea how she had perceived our time together, I had confidently elevated myself to cloud nine.

Over the course of the next two weeks, I orchestrated three other encounters with Kate that ultimately resulted in similar conversations, each seeming to last longer than the previous one, but all ending sooner than I would have liked. And I felt something happening to me that I had not experienced with Laurie.

I believed I was falling in love.

At least that was what I presumed to be the explanation affecting my heart. Unfortunately, this tumble of my head over my heels was for a girl who lived in a place and in an era that was abundantly filled with uncertainties. Worse yet, my brain had lost its influence over my feelings, and neither did I have any ability to control the ambiguities of a century past that was now my present state of time.

Of one thing I was certain: The complexities of time travel could give a give a guy a headache.

Between the rare moments of my romantic socializing were long days that were often a duplicate of those before and after. I, along with three of the other hired hands, had predominately spent our time working on the new fence that was now stretching into a fairly long line toward the eastern boundary of the ranch, though we still had a long way to go.

Thankfully, Little Pete, who was always ready to entertain us with a joke, had been assigned to take Blaine's place and he and Oleander proved to be a matched set of redheaded muscle men in charge of moving and lifting the ball-busting limestone posts. And weirdly, Oleander had seemed eager to work, despite his natural tendency to avoid mundane and burdensome activities. But I surmised it was probably because of his newfound friendship with a co-worker he called Ox, who genuinely seemed to enjoy being around him. Though Pete, I noticed, was like Dent, often demonstrating that he would not put up with Oleander's bullshit.

A lot of my worktime, though, was spent on horseback, doing ranch hand tasks with my brother, and laboring alongside Boyd and Mick. But it was in those hours where I had felt most at home, although not quite there. Typically, it was just the four of us riding range and checking on cattle and the Quarter Horse breeding stock, while Little

Pete and Oleander occupied themselves with other odd and end type jobs. But for me, the cowboy work was satisfying, and I was growing comfortable with it, at least for now. But I was also beginning to ease my guard in terms of keeping an eye out for Headville, though inherently I knew better.

But still, I could count on seeing Headville at least once a day, though usually from a distance. On two separate occasions he had entertained horse buyers who had arrived in packs of four riders one time and five the next, and when they had left the ranch the tally of their steeds had at least doubled the number they had come riding in on. According to Boyd, this would be a common occurrence as the brood of horses having the bloodlines of Steel Dust and coupled with the genetics of a show-quality stud by the name of Doc, made a desirable and enviable reputation for Culver Headville.

On a Wednesday that I had mentally checked off as the beginning of my seventh week living in the year 1878, Dent and I, and Mick and Boyd had been cowboying for the afternoon. Our task for the day put us on horseback, riding through the three northern sub-pastures of the ranch and splitting apart from the cows and calves, the herd bulls that had been contributing their half of the genetic creation of a new generation of Culver Headville cattle. After separating the bulls and collectively penning them inside the circular corral where the previous month's branding had taken place, I studied the twelve regal males from my place on the back of Viento and I noticed that four of the black hornless bulls were noticeably different, despite their color and their general beefy characteristics.

"Boyd," I began, getting the foreman's attention, "four of these guys are stockier. Are they just older?" I asked, thinking of the Hereford Bulls used on our own ranch, where the elder ones tended to carry more muscle and weight.

"Not 'zackly. They carry more meat on their bones mostly cuz they be pureblood Angus. The younger eight of 'em be their get."

"Oh," I said surprised. "I thought all of them were Angus-cross bulls."

"Was just them younger ones at first. Mr. Headville bought 'em from a feller south of here at that Victoria settlement. Grant be his name, I think. Some big shot who come over from that Scot-land. First Angus brung into the country, too, and ri'chere on the plains of Kansas. Made a big ta-do at the Kansas City fair the year he brung 'em over. Cattlemen from all around talkin' about 'em. Some liked the look of them black bulls, but not all. Some thought they be hard on the eyes, like me. But I be a Longhorn man, and 'spect I always will."

"But Mr. Headville was obviously impressed," I said.

"Shore-for! Course he's one of them, whatta ya call 'em, men who plans and speculates about the future?"

"Visionary?" I offered, remembering that Boyd had previously used that word to describe his reverent employer, Culver Headville.

"Yeah, that's it. That's what he calls hisself. So, a few years ago, Mr. Headville goes and rides down to Victoria, takin' me with him, and he brung a saddlebag full of money, too. Guess cuz he done set his mind that he be a buyin' those ugly, round-noggin' purebloods. But didn't do him no good. That yahoo Grant, he wouldn't part with a one of 'em. Headville had to settle for those youngins' thet was born outta them la-tee-da pures."

"But, he has them now," I said, more as a statement than a question of the obvious.

"Yeah, afor we left, Headville told that cattleman if he goes to change his mind, he'd take the lot of 'em and pay a pretty penny for 'em too."

"So, obviously, Grant changed his mind."

"Dunno 'bout that, but the man's widda sent word to Mr. Headville that she be glad to sell them four bulls to him."

"Widow? So, Grant died?"

"Shore-for. This past spring, facta-matter. Just after the grass started turnin' green."

"What happened to him, this yahoo fellow?"

"We heared it was some kinda accident."

Suddenly, I was, again, suspect. Had Culver Headville been just a lucky beneficiary of a fatal misfortune, or had he orchestrated it?

"Now this next year, they gonna be a bunch of calves outta those ole boys. And that shore-for will hurry up Mr. Headville's breedin' plans. Won't be but a few years and Culver Headville pro'ly be the star of that Kansas City fair."

I had no doubt. The man exhibited vanity when it came to livestock. But was he willing to kill for it? I decided that it was probably in my best interests not to ask Boyd if he harbored a similar suspicion.

The four of us cowboys departed corral central, herding a dozen bulls south and eventually sequestering them in an isolated pasture east of the homestead.

For management purposes, the breeding season had ended. Per Boyd, Headville wanted next spring's calving to be completed by mid-

May, since the year's calf crop would be sold as weanlings in the fall, except for the heifers that were judged to be top tier. Those chosen few would be kept and later introduced as replacement breeding stock. My father had also subscribed to the same autumn-time livestock marketing concept, so this aspect of a cow-calf operation was nothing new to either Dent or to me.

Leaving the bulls to begin their nine-month hiatus of reproductive rest and recuperation, we began to return to the heart of the ranch just as the sound of six quick repetitious gunshots popped through the stillness of the mid-August air. Dent and I immediately exchanged glances of concern, but Boyd seemed to be as alarmed as a slug on a cow turd, so we finished the last half mile of our homeward trip walking our horses as though we had not a care in the world. But I did not share Boyd's apathy. I was as apprehensive as a street cat in an animal shelter. And as it turned out, I had a good reason to feel that way.

Dent and I broke from Boyd and Mick, and after dismounting and tying our horses to the corral fence, we sauntered over to where target practice was apparently taking place. Near the little barn that housed the dairy cow, Oleander and Pete had set up a target range comprised of old cans and bottles and had the display positioned immediately in front of the steep slope of a knoll. At least care had been considered with the choice of the shooting location, although immediately my brother and I confirmed our suspicion that Oleander was in possession of a firearm.

Again.

"Olly," Dent piped up. "What the hell are you doing with a gun?"

"Mr. Headville gave it to me."

"Loaned it to you," Little Pete corrected him.

Either way, I had no words, other than *what was the boss-man thinking*? But I kept those shut deeply behind my gums.

"It's a Colt Navy, that's what Mr. Headville called it. Had it converted to something or other, but can't remember exactly what he said."

"Had it modified to take thirty-eight caliber cartridges," Pete clarified.

"Shoots good, too," Oleander said, and I glanced at the line of targets, noting that none were broken or even nicked by a bullet. "A manly pistola, from the big man himself," he added, and I saw that the weapon was a more practical looking firearm, unlike the fancy show pistols that Oleander had bought and ultimately lost in a poker game after having owned them for only a few hours. What I did not like was the careless way he had displayed the revolver. "Ain't it nice?" he asked, callously pointing it toward us.

"Damn it, Olly!" Dent cussed at him.

"Uh-uh, Olly," Pete scolded. "You don't point a gun at folks like that, especially when they're your friends!"

"Sorry, Ox," Oleander said. "Sorry Double-D, but no big deal, it's not loaded anymore," he added, completely oblivious of his irresponsibility.

As for me, I had been instantly distressed because of this unexpected development. The last thing any of us needed was an armed Oleander Sedgwick. Yet, Headville had given him a lethal weapon. And what would unfold as being more disturbing was that this particular afternoon had been the beginning of what would become a daily practice for Oleander. The only respite I could hang my hat on was that he was always supervised by Little Pete.

But at some point, that would undoubtably change.

When the third Saturday of August arrived, another caravan of human residents left the Headville ranch for a day of distraction in Hays City. Unlike the previous procession that occurred four weeks earlier, this time there were notable differences.

One: The twinned palominos were pulling the buggy that was Kate's transportation and was being driven by the dependably sullen Sherlee. And within the Western coach's black-lacquered shell sat the girl who I knew was looking forward to getting away from the isolation of the ranch, not to mention the fact that she also happened to be a young lady with whom I had become completely enamored.

Two: There was no sacrificial horse being led away this time, so Dent was able to make the trip without that precursor of angst and agitation.

Three: Headville was instead mounted on his beloved chestnut stallion, Doc, the horse having apparently recovered from a bruised hoof and given the green light for long, distant travel.

Four: My friend Blaine was not among us, though I looked forward to seeing him and checking out his new digs.

Five: Boyd, the consummate ole cowboy who preferred being in a saddle was unhappily driving a buckboard wagon that was apparently needed to haul supplies back to the ranch.

Six: Oleander was staying behind with Little Pete, the two of them deciding to spend the day exercising their pistols with more target practice, so we had Mick replacing the company of Oleander, a difference I personally appreciated.

Then I smiled.

And seven: Kate was going with us. Admittedly, she had already been named in the first entry of my list, but what the hell, I was in a good mood.

But as it turned out, the most interesting thing about the day had nothing to do with any of the people named on my mental manifest, even though the noteworthy episode had not begun until after my visit with Blaine.

When I left the schoolhouse, I crossed to the hitching post where I had tied Viento and as I approached, I saw a familiar object that had been placed over the horn of my saddle. It was a black derby hat with a distinct bullet hole piercing its crown.

Kival was in town.

I glanced around but saw no one, although I happily expected to see a movement in the shadow of a nearby tree, or a wave of his hand from some other place of concealment. I picked up the hat and examined it. Tucked within the interior hatband I discovered a small slip of paper. I slid it out and found that a word had been scrawled upon it.

Stockyards.

I mounted Viento, and we went to that place on the east side of town, where plank-railed pens were often tightly crammed with milling and noisy beasts, though not so much today. A dozen or so men were gathered here and there in sets of two or three, likely dickering over the price of an animal between spits of tobacco juice. I stepped down from Viento and tied him to a rail of fence and walked a short distance away, staring through the rows of pens, seeking a glimpse of the man I was in search of.

"Nice day," Kival said from behind me, and I nearly jumped from my skin. Though I had not seen him in over a month, and despite the fact that we had not particularly been the greatest of friends, I was happy enough to want to give him a hug. But I didn't.

"It is at that," I said to him, keeping my eyes forward and appearing as though I was not especially interested in having a conversation. Kival then stepped up to the fence, arranging an inconspicuous distance of ten feet between us. From the perspective of a casual observer, we would not appear to be anything more than two strangers appraising a handful of cows and sharing with one another an opinion of their worth. I glanced around finding that the only eyes that were fixed upon me and Kival were those that belonged to the cows that stood staring back at us.

"It's good to see you, JT."

"And I am glad to see you, my friend," I said to Kival as I shifted my eyes momentarily toward him. But at once, my cursory observance of his physical appearance forced me to honor him with a second look, only this time I gave him a more thorough study. His clothes were far different from the duds Morgan had secured for him, but the biggest change had taken place above his neck.

Gone were the long strands of black hair that had easily covered the back of his neck and beyond. Instead, he had wisps of short-cut bangs hanging over his forehead, and his ears were now visible courtesy of a pair of scissors that had been used to trim away his dangly side-locks. I was not at all sure I would have given him a glance of recognition if I had met him on the sidewalk. And I said as much.

"That's funny," Kival replied. "Because we did meet."

"You're kidding?"

"About an hour ago, in front of the Burnside store."

"Well, no wonder," I said, remembering the large gathering of Volga German folk that I had seen gathered there. "You've got new duds," I said, gesturing to his attire that was one-hundred percent authentic immigrant dairy farmer.

"From Anja. She gave me all the clothes that had belonged to her husband, Ernst. They're a little big, but I'm growing into them."

"I bet," I said, smiling. "Ruta is a good cook."

"That she is. And a good person too. And Helmut, also. They have been gracious, and … and, uh…" I heard the emotion leap into his voice. I looked at him and saw him quickly blinking his eyes. "And loving," Kival added, with a grin that looked profoundly good on him.

"Lucky you," I said, putting a less serious grin on my own face. "I still have Oleander hanging around my neck."

He laughed.

"Nice haircut, too, by the way."

"It was Anja's idea."

"And how is Anja?"

"Pregnant."

I turned to him and gawked. "That, that was fast work," I said to him as though I were a parent who had failed to give his son a timely speech about the birds and the bees.

"The baby is not mine. It's Ernst's. Anja is five months along now."

"Wow," I said. "She hid it well."

"Not anymore," Kival said with a grin.

I smiled at him, noticing a twinkle of excitement in his eyes as though he possessed a secret too juicy to keep to himself. "I have a feeling you're about to tell me something."

"We're getting married."

"But Kival, we hardly know each other," I said without missing a beat. We both chuckled, then I added, "Because of the baby?"

"No. Because I'm in love with her."

I heard not just the declaration of his words, but also the sincerity in which they were spoken. His statement not only sounded genuine, but also rang of a maturity that seemed far beyond his age.

"Congratulations, my friend. Jokes aside, I'm happy for you, really, I am."

"I want you to come."

"To the wedding?" I asked, wanting to make sure I understood him correctly.

"Yes. I need a best man. And I want that man to be you."

In an instant, my eyes grew moist, and the muscles of my neck squeezed my throat. Kival's words had immediately taken me back to a conversation I had shared with Sam a few months earlier when we had both wondered if our girlfriends would one day become our wives. I remembered Sam being quick to point out to me that I could do better than Laurie, and I reciprocated a similar sentiment since neither was I much of an Alex fan. But we had agreed to be one another's best man if, or when, we ever managed to talk some girl into marrying us. Only now, Sam was gone, and so was the life he had planned to have.

"I would be honored, Kival. Deeply, deeply honored."

And in that moment, I realized that it did not matter if it were 1979 or 1878. Life would go on.

With or without a talisman.

CHAPTER 38

"Next Saturday," I said, telling Dent about my unexpected meeting with Kival and the news of his impending nuptials.

"Wow," my brother replied as we distantly followed the entourage northward. Even though it was Saturday, Headville had firmly suggested that we all return together and assist with the unloading of supplies that were currently in transit via the wagon Boyd was driving ahead of us. To be off the clock the next morning had been our promised compensation in lieu of our voluntary forfeiture of the latter half of what was supposed to be our scheduled full day off, although unofficially there was nothing voluntary about it. Anyway, I knew what I was going to do with the liberty of my gifted time.

Sleep.

It had been weeks since I had last enjoyed the opportunity to languish in bed for as long as I wished, and so far, not once had I overslept in this, the nineteenth century.

"He knocked her up in hurry," Dent mused.

"The baby's not his," I said glancing crossly at him.

"Don't look at me, I didn't touch her, I swear."

"The father is Ernst, dipshit," I explained. "She was already pregnant when he was killed."

"Murdered, you mean."

"Yes."

"By Headville, no less. According to your buddy, Just Morgan."

"Well, about that," I said, recalling the details of a second-hand version of the story as retold by a certain groom-to-be. "According to Kival, that's not technically true."

I then shared with Dent the details Kival had relayed to me by way of Anja, who had been an eyewitness. From the farm in Schoechen, Ernst and Anja had made a mid-week trip into Hays City, a day that had been extremely windy. As the two of them crossed a street, her scarf had been whipped from her head and had unfortunately blanketed the face of a horse, frightening the animal. Rearing back, the horse had snapped its tie and was blindly bolting toward them, nearly knocking Anja to the ground. Ernst had managed to capture the reins of the horse and was trying to calm it down. But then a gun had been fired.

"Let me guess, the horse was Headville's Doc, right?" Dent asked.

"The description fits."

"I see where this going," Dent conjectured. "Headville claimed Ernst was stealing the horse."

"Yeah, that's what Anja told Kival."

"So, he shot him?"

"No," I replied. "Willard Sherlee did."

Dent stared at me for a moment, processing the identity of the actual shooter. "Of course," Dent spat. "Headville wouldn't get his hands dirty. Sherlee does his bidding, and we know of a dead mare that proves that."

"Yeah. And I think that's why Morgan stated that Headville killed Ernst. Sherlee was simply used as Culver Headville's weapon of choice."

"I get it," Dent conceded. "But killing Ernst was bullshit. And no one did anything about it?"

"The City Marshall was there and had arrested Sherlee. But that's all Anja knew. I'm guessing Headville put the screws to somebody. The Marshall, maybe—but probably the County Judge. I've already overheard some boardwalk gossip about him, so that fits."

"You know, if we were smart," Dent said seriously, "we'd haul ass and get as far away from that man as possible."

"I can't argue with that."

"But we're not that smart, are we," Dent asked rhetorically, and I knew he was implicating my feelings for Kate. I just hoped she would not be my Achilles Heel.

"I can't argue with that either," I said.

"Makes two of us," Dent replied with an edge of hesitation. "So, this wedding, it kinda complicates things."

After the newly indoctrinated Volga German had departed from the stockyards, I had thought the same thing, after first having a half hour to digest Kival's intentions.

"So, what's Kival going to do? Leave the little wife and baby behind after we get the talisman back? Or does he plan to pile them into the arch with the rest of us and the Burmano-Hoochie-Doochies for the ride back home?"

"Neither," I said. Then I told Dent what I knew. But only part of it. Kival had been adamant. He had no intention of returning to the future, 1979, 1980, or nineteen any year for that matter. But if we didn't retrieve the talisman from the depths of the Smoky Hill River, all of us would be in the same boat with Kival: Sailing through the remaining years of the 1800s.

My heart apprehensively leapt within my chest as that uncomfortable possibility crossed my mind. Then I thought of Morgan and crossed my fingers.

A week later, I was preparing for a secret trip to Schoenchen, my departure only minutes away. Dent was with me in the quiet of the majestic barn, standing at Viento's head, politely holding the strap of the bald-faced stallion's bridle as I pushed my foot into the stirrup and seated myself into the saddle I had cinched onto the horse's back.

"Sure you don't want to go with me?" I asked him with a grin.

"That would be a solid pass."

"I'd be happy to wait for you while you saddle up Mister Brown," I said, calling the horse by the name Dent had finally settled on after going weeks without calling his dark bay anything but the informal and generic 'Good Boy.'

"Hey," Dent growled, glancing quickly left, then right. "Watch the Mister Brown shit. He might hear you."

"You gave him the name, not me." I then grinned a second time enjoying the thought of my brother's onery rationale for giving his horse the prefix of Mister, and thus privately elevating the animal to the same level of respect demanded by Culver Headville.

"Are you trying to get me axed by Sherlee?"

"Chicken shit."

"Cluck, you," Dent said with a smirk, and I snickered at his humor. "Be careful, little brother," he added, then I nudged Viento into a gentle canter leaving the ranch yard as a lone rider.

Even though it was a Saturday, it was still a week away from our first-of-the-month payday, so none of my bunkhouse mates were motivated to make the trip without their pockets being properly funded for whatever proclivities they might choose to enjoy. I had half expected Boyd to argue against my leaving alone, but he was indifferent when I told him I was going into Hays City to see Blaine. He might have had more to say if I had told him the truth about where I was going, and who I was seeing, and why.

Kival and Anja's wedding was a simple service, and it took place in the newly completed stone church that occupied a central place in the little town. As expected, Ruta and Helmut were there, along with twenty or so others, some of whom I remembered coming to their farm for milk and butter. A Catholic priest had presided over the event, confirming to me that Kival had, as he had confided in me a week earlier, declared his faith in the Holy Church.

I stood next to him as his friend and witness, grinning from ear to ear. It was undeniably evident from the way he and Anja looked at each other, that they were genuinely in love. For a moment, I imagined that it was I, instead, standing centerstage, although in my vision Anja was replaced by a certain blonde who had completely cast me under her spell.

At the conclusion of the vows of matrimony, Kival kissed his new bride, and immediately I was moved to applaud. But I had been the only one to clap. I glanced around and saw at least fifteen sets of eyes looking at me like I had just sky-dived from the moon wearing my cowboy hat and my boots, but nothing in between. Obviously, I was ahead of their time.

An hour later, I left Schoenchen and rode into Hays City, deciding a quick stop to see Blaine would legitimize my fabricated story. I found him outside the school, stepping off a measurement in the play-yard where a sand lot displayed signs of tracks and depressions where America's favorite pastime had apparently been a regular activity enjoyed by Blaine's students.

After swapping handshakes and pats on the back, I told Blaine about where I had been, and he expressed more merriment than I had expected.

"That's pretty, well, pretty groovy!"

"Speaking of groovy, what ya got going on here?" I asked him.

"Well, the kids have been playing softball, but the field is laid out all wrong. I thought I'd plot it out a little better, get the bases at least equidistant apart like they should be. Oh, and I got some old feedbags from one of the parents. I'm going to fill them with sand and set the kids up with real bases."

"Sounds like you've got recess figured out. What about reading and writing?" I asked jovially.

"Ha-ha!" Blaine laughed. "That kind of sass will get you detention."

I then spent a half hour listening attentively to a synopsis of Blaine's experiences since I had last visited with him, and it was more than groovy to see him so happy and content. He and Kival had both embraced a new way of life, and their assimilation gave me something to think about. I wondered if Dent and I should be more like them and just let go of our yearning to get back home and make the best of what was here in 1878. But there was a difference between us. My brother and I had a family waiting for us in 1979, parents who were no doubt worried sick. The same was not true for Blaine or Kival.

The following week, on Thursday, Mother Nature unleashed a powerful thunderstorm across the ranch bringing not only the saturation of needed rain, but also a reprieve from the usual work of building that damn never-ending post-rock fence. The cloudburst's lightning and thunder arrived first, just after breakfast, and so Boyd kept us inside the central barn where we occupied ourselves with busy work which amounted mostly to spending the morning up in the barn's massive second-story loft, shifting and repacking the loose hay that had been shipped in by the wagon loads from suppliers located in the Flint Hills area of the state.

According to Pete, we had luckily missed the hay party by only a few days prior to our arrival at the ranch, and he and Mick and the five other hired hands had suffered in the heat of the stuffy barn, packing the Bluestem hay into the loft of the massive structure.

"Sucks that we missed out on that," Dent told him sarcastically.

"Don't worry, there's another wagon train pulling in here in a few weeks."

"Thanks for the warning," Dent replied, then looked at me. "Wonder if John White needs any help sweeping up hair?"

Then Little Pete pointed upward at a platform-type structure with heavy jute rope attached on four corners and knotted together as a single rope that was fitted through a set of pullies high in the center of the building.

"Up there, Olly, that's how we get the hay up into the loft," Pete added, "Mister Headville's idea."

"That's genius," Oleander replied, though I doubted he had the foggiest idea how it worked. But admittedly the mechanics of the lift were clever, though my admiration for the man was otherwise overwhelmingly faulty.

By noon, the rain had subsided to a heavy sprinkle, and as we climbed down the ladder from the loft, Isaiah was waiting for us with a bowl of ripe tomatoes, each nearly the size of my fist. The five of us, Dent, Oleander, Mick, Pete, and myself ate the red tangy fruit, enjoying a rare midday snack. I stood leaning against the edge of the broad doorway, looking toward the house, daydreaming, when Kate suddenly appeared wearing pants and boots. I had to look at her twice to make sure it was her and not Annie Oakley or some other quasi-masculine figment of my imagination.

She strode across the muddy ground in the direction of the horse stables but then I saw her glance my way. She paused just long enough to nod her head as a gesture of invitation, or so that was my interpretation. Then she shifted into a dainty little trot and disappeared past the side of the barn and from out of my view. I turned and through the barn I scampered, as manly as one can scamper while wearing cowboy boots and an anxious grin, and quickly I reached the opposite wide entryway.

"Where ya going?" Dent asked me as I passed him.

"Nowhere," I said as I exited the barn and took a sharp left. Behind me I heard my brother explain to the others that when you gotta go, you gotta go, but I had no intention of countering his humorous snipe with the truth. They could think what they wanted. I stepped between the barn and the wagon shed just in time to see Kate enter the third and nearest of the three horse barns.

I entered to find Kate standing five stall spaces inside, petting the dark nose of a dapple-grey horse as it poked its head through the space above the feed trough. She turned and looked at me, her lips twisted and pursed as though she had just bitten into a sour apple. But darn, she was still pretty cute.

"What are you doing here?"

"I thought I had been invited," I told her.

She shrugged coyly, then flashed me a Farrah Fawcett smile, and I came within a half second of telling Kate who she had reminded me of.

"So, who's this?" I asked as I walked up to her.

"Belle," she replied. "That's what I call her. Culver has a paper that has her official name as something else, Steel Bar Belle, I think. But just plain Belle suits her better."

"Culver?" I asked, but not before I glanced behind me. I had not heard her call him by his first name before.

She sighed. "You know who I'm talking about. He's being nice today, so I'm calling him Culver."

"He's not usually nice?" I asked. In all our conversations, none had so far centered around Headville.

"Well, he's strict with me. Not mean or anything."

"Glad to hear it."

"Culver promised to take me riding today," she said informatively, though hearing her speak his given name a second time with such causal familiarity was cringe-worthy. "Anyway, Willard brought Belle in from the pasture last evening. But now with all this rain, I have to wait until tomorrow to ride her."

"I didn't know you knew how to ride. Or even liked to."

"That's because you don't know very much about me, do you JT?"

"Not yet, I don't."

"You're being presumptuous."

"That's a big word."

"That's because I'm a good student. You can ask Miss Carneiro."

I laughed.

"What's so funny? Don't you think a girl should know how to read and speak properly?"

"Yes! Of course," I said lifting my hands to gesture my surrender. "I just laughed, I guess, because I love—"

"What?" she said, cutting me off, yet looking at me expectantly.

"To hear you talk," I finished.

"Hmph," Kate sounded, then returned her attention to the horse. "So, what do you think of her? Belle, she's so pretty, isn't she?"

"Certainly is," I said, my answer being identical to the one I would have given her if the subject of the question had been Kate herself. "Not too many dapple greys on the ranch," I told her.

"No. But I think that's one reason why I like her so much. She's different. Like me."

"Didn't know you were so different."

"Beverly, I mean, Miss Carniero says I am. But only because of my imagination. Sometimes during our lessons, I tell her things I think of, things that just pop up inside my mind."

"Such as?"

"Flying, like a bird. Sometimes I get these pictures in my head where I'm like looking down and I can see what all this land looks like from way up high. Trees that look like clumps of broccoli, and rivers and streams that glisten like threads of blue and silver, and houses that look like little toys."

"That is imaginative," I said, and I thought about my first ride in an airplane as a fifth-grader when my family had made a sudden trip to Pennsylvania for the funeral of a great aunt I had never met, but who had faithfully sent birthday cards and Christmas presents to Dent and I. Houses and cars and people did in fact look like toys from thousands of feet up in the air.

"Miss Kate."

At the sound of her name, she turned and looked past me as I bent my neck around to look at the man who had called to her.

"Hi Willard!" she said with a big smile. "Thank you for bringing Belle in," Kate added, then crossed to him. I could not help but notice the attractive fit of her lady dungarees.

"I'll take her out this afternoon and knock the rust from her," Sherlee spoke, his tone expressing a fondness for Kate, as though she were a favored niece. "It's been a while since she's been ridden."

"Not since late June, I think," Kate replied, then she turned to me as though I expected an explanation for the two-month interval since her last ride. "I don't like to ride when it gets hot. Neither Belle nor I like to get … well, we don't like to perspire."

I nodded and said nothing because from behind her there was a fierce set of masculine eyes staring like an evil serpent and making me feel as though I had been caught plucking the forbidden apple from the infamous tree in the Garden of Eden.

"Miss Carneiro is looking for you," Sherlee said plaintively.

"Back to my studies," she said with a sigh, then looked again at me. "We're reading Shakespeare."

"All the world is a stage," I told her, but she just looked at me funny, then quickly scampered outside, scampering in a far more appealing manner than I had done earlier. I glanced at Sherlee, but I did not wait for him to exercise his authority by telling me to get back to work. Instead, I moved to walk past him, managing to give him my most innocent of smiles, and hoping that he was not there to shoot me per orders of Culver Headville. Suddenly his hand reached out and grasped my arm. I stopped and passively looked at him.

"Mind your manners, young man."

"Yes, sir," I said. Then he let go of me and I did not wait around for anymore advice.

The next day, those of us who were the entirety of the cowboy crew saddled our horses and had just mounted up when Culver Headville and Kate appeared in the frame of the barn's expansive doorway, each of them astride the backs of their favored horses. Kate wore a Western hat, with a tie strapped under her chin, and her golden hair pulled back into a ponytail. She looked exceedingly attractive, especially on a horse. Suddenly, I wished that my mom could meet her.

Then Sherlee appeared into view behind them, and all three of them peered inside where the six of us had been preparing to leave through the opposite doorway.

"Good morning, men," Headville greeted us, much like a cavalry general addressing his minions.

"Morning, Mr. Headville, sir!" Oleander chirped in quick reply.

"Morning, sir," I said, as the rest of the guys simultaneously added to the group response.

"Headin' out to check on the cows, make shore-for none of 'em got spooked by the storm and tord through any fences," Boyd informed him. "Got us split up in pairs, two boys for each of the north pastures."

Headville stared for a moment as though he was mulling a thought. And I was right, unfortunately.

"Oleander?"

"Yessir, Mr. Headville?"

"Who's your partner?"

"Ox, uh, I mean Pete, sir."

Then Headville turned and spoke to Sherlee. "Swap places with Oleander." I watched as Sherlee gave Headville a compliant nod before obediently reining his horse toward us and entered the barn. "Oleander, you are riding with me today. And with Kate."

Seriously?!

That had been my impassioned thought, though I was not entirely sure I had not spoken it aloud. But after a quick glance at my brother, who seemed unmoved by the rearrangement, I felt some degree of relief. Still, I was annoyed that I had not been chosen instead of Oleander. Then I wondered if Headville had shrewdly caught on to me, and not because of a talisman.

"Oleander, do you have the Colt with you?" Headville then asked. Instantly, I thought what a dumb question, of course he did. Oleander practically slept with the revolver under his pillow.

"Right here," Oleander said, patting his saddlebag.

"Good," Headville smiled. "Let's go," he said, then he nudged his chestnut stallion into low gear and headed across the ranch yard with Kate and Belle behind him. Within seconds, Oleander was trotting out from the barn astride the sandy dun mare that had been the replacement for the roan mare whose carcass lay rotting a few miles outside the kingdom ruled by Culver Headville.

I watched them leave, following a pathway that cut eastward through the trees that skirted past the spring-fed pond that had been frequently used by us ranch hands for recreational swimming as well as bathing. Apparently, the Headville trio would be scouting the area where the Sweetwater creek meandered through several six-hundred-forty-acre sections of pasture that were reserved exclusively for the wintering of livestock.

I shook my head, feeling both annoyed and jealous of Oleander. Headville had, by all appearances, taken him under his wing, often joining him and Pete in shooting practice, and once, just a few days earlier, he had invited Oleander to join him for the dinner meal inside the grand residence. Oleander had puffed up like a rooster on steroids, which was pretty much what he looked like anyway, but with an arrogance more cocky than normal.

"Birds of a feather," Dent had reasoned, giving me the only explanation he could fathom for the inexplicable bond that seemed to have suddenly developed between Oleander and Headville. But I had thought of a different motive. I wondered if Headville was cunningly ingratiating himself with Oleander as a means to pump him for information or insnare him with a trick of words, like he had tried with me when he had mentioned JFK. I hoped Dent was right, but my money was squarely upon my suspicion. And yet, I could do nothing about it. I had to trust Oleander.

But that was like letting a dopey coyote babysit your chickens.

The six of us crossed through the wooden gate behind the great barn and trod along the narrow road toward the corral hub that was more than two miles away. Our horses left prints in the damp earth, scrapes where the ground was hardest, but deeper gouges where the dirt was soft and still slightly muddy.

At corral central, we split up, Dent and Mick going through the northwesterly gate that was the mouth of the triangular pasture Boyd had called 'Febry', while Pete and Sherlee filed through the opposite gate that opened into the pasture of which I had already been introduced to on branding day as April. I wondered if Pete had prepared a few jokes to loosen up Sherlee's grim personality, otherwise it was likely to be a far less entertaining day than he had probably planned with Oleander.

And since Boyd had chosen me to partner with him, we passed through the centermost gate where there lay faint signs of an old road that the foreman casually mentioned as the trek to the range hut. My memory flickered as I recalled the hut as being the place where Little Pete had stayed on the first night Blaine, Dent, and Oleander and I had spent in the bunkhouse.

Boyd and I rode together, zig-zagging our way across the pasture, connecting the dots of livestock with a close inspection of any cows or calves that might show signs of illnesses or ailments, and also appraising fences for damage. As was par, Boyd jabbered most of the time, which was fine by me. Better to be the student in a new environment, especially one where the critter at the top of the food chain was Culver Headville. And then Boyd sputtered something about Big Pete and those other *peckerheads* and so I looked at him.

"The mustangers?" I asked, speaking of the five ranch hands who had been away somewhere out west, rounding up a new set of wild mares to breed with the Headville stallions.

"Good a word for 'em as any, I reckon, but peckerheads fit 'em best, least for now. Shore-for Headville he got another name for 'em."

There had been only one or two times I had heard Boyd refer to Headville without the prefix of Mister. "So, when are those guys supposed to be back?" I asked.

"Um-um-um," Boyd mumbled. "That be a sixty-four dollar question, and a sore sub-jeck."

"And why is that?" I asked, gently prodding him into the 'sub-jeck.'

"Well, for one, they shore-for shoulda done been back here two weeks ago!"

"Do you think something bad happened to them?"

"If it didn't, then by gum it gonna be bad! I have me a feelin' them ole boys ain't comin' back. Big Pete pract'ly said as much, but I didn't believe him. But lawdy, those yahoos be plum stupid if they don't come back. They left outta here on Headville horses. Be they don't come back, they same as stole 'em far as Mr. Headville be concerned. And out here, you don't steal another man's horse."

Immediately I wondered if the same principal applied to shooting another man's horse, but I saved my breath. Boyd was talking and nothing would be gained if I pointed out the obvious double standard.

"Don't matter if it be the only horse a man gots or if he owns a hunnerd of 'em like Mr. Headville. Shore-for wish them peckerheads would come back. Be for their own good, and ours too."

"Why for our good?"

"Well, boy, without 'em, we be damn short-handed goin' into witner."

"I see. So, what does that mean for the rest of us?"

"Shore-for we be stayin' on the payroll."

"Okay, I get the job security thing, but what I meant was, can just six of us manage a ranch this size?"

"Pro'ly. Done it before. Likely be workin' sunup to sundown, but least the days be short. But hoo-wee livestock shore-for be lots more work in the code of witner."

I knew what he meant, even if some of his words were a little whacky. A green and growing pasture was a self-serve buffet for horses and cattle, but the cold months of winter required a lot of man-hours devoted to the routine feeding of hay, and sometimes the breaking of ice to allow access to water.

"Tell you one thing though, I be damn glad you boys are here to hep us out. You two brothers anyways. Both of ya work harder than any two of them hon-yockers put together. And I 'bout hate to say it, but with them other boys up 'n leavin' us high and dry, makes me be some bit a happy to have that Oleander teamin' with us, though he don't know shite from shinola, he least gotta strong back that be shore-for. And I 'spect he's a doin' better now with Little Pete teachin' him like." Then he turned to me, his face energized with an idea.

"Think maybe we could get Blaine back here to hep?"

"I doubt it," I replied with confidence. Then up ahead I saw something that I recognized as bad news. "Uh-oh," I said, gesturing with a nod of my head. A cow lay on her side, her feet extended outward, parallel to the ground, and a brownish colored calf, four months old or so, milling nervously nearby.

"By gum that don't look good, do it?"

We rode up to the prostrate mama cow with a horn pointing upward toward the sun of the last day of August. With just a glance, my suspicion was confirmed. She was dead.

Though I knew that bloat could kill a cow within a few hours if she were unable to sit herself upright, but I could see that the cow was neither lying in a depression nor caught between thickets of sage brush or any other things that might have prevented her from rising up and expelling the natural buildup of ruminal digestive gases.

"What do you think happened to her?" I asked.

"Lightnin' strike, I 'spect."

"What about the calf? What do we do with him?"

"Nothin.' He be plenty big enough to make it on his own without his mamma's milk. Figgered you woulda knowd that. Sides, even if he be a baby, we'd hafta leave him here."

"Really? You wouldn't try to take care of a newborn calf and bottle feed him?"

"Bottle feed?" Boyd looked at me funny and I wondered if I had, again, spoken out of century. "Hell, no. Culver shore-for don't believe in none of that soft-heart shite. Survive on his own or he don't survives atal, that's Headville's way."

And it was either Headville's way, or the right way. But, again, I saved my breath.

CHAPTER 39

The thirty days of September came and went quietly as the month ushered in an autumn that was relatively peaceful and pleasant. The only aberration from the normal routine of my ranch-hand responsibilities happened when the first week brought to us a wagon train of hay from the east, just as Little Pete had promised, and though he had referred to the first shipment of hay in July as a party, there had been nothing fun about it. It had simply been hard, sweaty, and sticky work that made the fence-building seem like a vacation.

It was no wonder the mustangers had not returned in time for the subsequent hay delivery. In my book, this hay-unloading task was a totally acceptable reason for the postponement of their return, though I would have preferred their help. As my Granny Evelie would say, *many hands make light work.* But Culver Headville operated between the covers of his own book. And Dent and I had gotten an illuminating glimpse of it within a few days north of mid-October.

"WHERE THE GODDAMNED HELL ARE THEY?!"

The voice had echoed from inside the main barn, easily amplifying across the two hundred feet to the pasture gate through which Dent and I had just entered. We immediately exchanged looks of concern having recognized the voice, though we had, so far, been luckily unfamiliar with the livid passion of his anger. Then an explicit F-this and F-that shaped the context of another outburst, as the man who was our boss vented and bellowed.

"I sure as hell hope he's not looking for you and me," Dent said as he closed the gate behind us. We had been conducting a routine equestrian inspection of the horses inhabiting the uniquely pristine pasture that occupied the southwest quadrant of the ranch, and because those elite residents were many and the acreage an enormously large ten-square mile subdivision, we had spent the entire day there. The only downside had been the discovery of a gimpy mare.

"We could go back," I suggested, but with no serious intention to do so since my stomach had been running on empty for half the day and dinner was fast approaching. Additionally, we were close enough to the barn to have already been noticed, and besides, we had a horse in tow that needed medical attention.

"You first," Dent challenged me.

"Then here," I said handing him the lead rope that tethered the injured blood bay mare, as I pretended to return to the pasture. Instead, though, I turned Viento around and reached for the rein of Dent's ground-tied horse.

"What the heck are you doing?"

"Assuming the front line," I told him. "I'll take care of the horses and let you bring in the casualty. Might be a reward in it for you!"

"I'll get the short end of the stick on this one, you just watch."

I laughed at him, then took the lead with Viento and Mister Brown and entered the barn a solid ninety seconds later and just in time to hear a more subdued complaint from the ranch CEO.

"They have been gone for over three months. As far as I'm concerned, they are now horse thieves. And you told me they could be trusted." Headville said to Boyd, his words sharp and biting.

I held my breath and watched as Headville disappeared through the opposite doorway without even looking in our direction. After a pause, I heard Boyd whistle a breath of exasperation.

"Hey, Boyd," I called out softly, and he immediately turned to me looking as though he had just been paddled by the school principal. "Mr. Headville's not looking for us, is he?" I asked, though I knew that the three-months remark I had heard Headville speak moments before had already exonerated us. Then Dent stepped up beside me with the mare limping behind him.

"What be goin' on here?" Boyd croaked.

"She's got a shitload of cactus needles covering her back left foot," Dent volunteered. "I'm pretty sure she's broken some of them off below the surface of her skin," Dent added.

Boyd crossed to the mare and examined her. "Looks infected. Best get her to Sherlee and let him take a gander." Then he glanced at my brother as though to accuse him of lying. "I ain't seen a lick a that durn cactus in the horse pasture for three, four years, now."

"Guess one of those *somebodies* who could not be forced to give a shit, missed getting it all," Dent said, glancing at me, his irritation over Headville's exploitation of the Cheyenne still at a boil beneath a poorly disguised façade of indifference. Both of us had been appalled when we had learned from Boyd that the Indians had been fed and housed, yet confined, under the guise of a wolfish humanitarian. But Headville's provision of those basic needs did not justify the indentured servitude, so as far I was concerned Culver Asshole Headville and George Armstrong Custer were cut from the same despicable cloth.

"Well, it be either missed, or it growed back," Boyd speculated, oblivious of my brother's bitter sarcasm. "Mr. Headville ain't gonna like that none, either way. And shore-for he be already up for a fist fight with the devil."

"Clearing a pasture of native cactus," I said as I began to strip the saddle from Viento, "was a spectacular concept. And I get why Mr. Headville would have such as idea, but it wasn't really practical."

"Boy! You best not let him hear you yak like that!" Boyd warned me. "Ain't our place to judge. You be just a two-bit cowboy like me. Mr. Headville, he's way smarter than you two boys and me put all together."

"Right," I agreed, then added flippantly, "he's a visionary."

"And if you wanna keep your hide in one piece, best you 'member that," Boyd concurred, my sarcasm clearly going over his head.

"I got it," I said with subtle surrender. "But what I meant was the man-hours it took to clear that area of prickly pear cactus had to have been in the thousands."

"Don't know nothin' 'bout that, but gettin' the job done would'na be no problem when the Cheyennes was here. Mister Headville still ain't happy they got took from him and what with just a part of the work done, too."

"You mean, Mr. Headville had plans to remove the cactus from the whole ranch?" Dent asked incredulously.

"Not just had, but by gum still does. He got the idea in his head with the first acre of this here ground he bought and I 'spect come hell or high water he be gonna make sure he gets it done, too. Just like this Angus cattle bidness. He set his mind to raise up the finest black cows either side of the Mississippi, and you watch him, he'll do it, too! Specially now that he gots the four most prized black bulls in the whole damn country."

"He has unwavering determination," I agreed. "Or just damn good luck," I added, thinking of the opportune demise of the Scottish cattleman.

"It ain't always been sunshine and roses for him, I can tell ya that. Fact is, some l'il Injun gal got the best of him long time back and right from under his nose she gone and stole some kinda somethin' that was real impotant to him, too."

Instantly, Boyd had my full attention. I was certain he was referring to Kival's mother, but I kept that thought to myself, remembering that Dent did not know about her. Neither had I told him the truth about Kival. And as much as I wanted to get more details from Boyd, I could not risk asking him and inadvertently waving a red flag at my brother.

I had promised to keep Kival's secret. And though I wrestled with the guilt, that promise extended to Dent.

Without saying a word, I switched my attention to Mr. Brown and began to remove the gear from his back.

"Hell, one day I 'spect whatever it be that was took from Mr. Headville, he be gettin' it back. If he don't find the luck, he shore-for will just make it. Or buys it. The man be like that for as long as I know'd him. Back when he worked down Texas way, he got a notion he be gonna have him a herd of Steel Dusts and make a name for hisself as an impotant Quarter Horse breeder, and by gum he done it, too. Just look 'round ya."

"You're kind of proud of him, aren't you, Boyd?" Dent asked, cautiously goading him.

"Proud?" Boyd said, twisting his lips in three different directions before settling on a frown. "Some proud, I 'spect. Mostly I be jealous of the man. Always have been. Shore-for I never had the money or the balls to do what he's done. And there be plenty of doubters, too, folks tellin' him he didn't have the where-fors or the what-fors to do it, and I hear'd 'em say it with my own ears. But that didn't matter squat, cuz he shore-for showed 'em. Thanks 'specially to that fancy stallion of his."

"Doc," Dent said, "he be one first-rate horse, shore-for," my brother added snarkily. "Did Mr. Headville buy Doc, or did he raise him?"

"Hell, if I knows!" Boyd spat. "I asked him one time if ole Doc Bar come from one of them first Steel Dust mares, but he tells me maybe, maybe not, and that some things be just his own biddness, not none of mine. Shore-for never asked him again."

I heard the full name Boyd had just used for the grand sire of the ranch, and I recalled Kate telling me that her dapple grey mare had the official name of Steel Bar Belle, something that had then sounded as though her horse had been named for an item of standard weight-lifting equipment, but now it flickered in my mind as a potentially enlightening piece of information. I glanced at Dent and saw him looking somewhat catatonic, staring into the eye of the injured mare that stood at his side.

"Doc … Bar," I heard my brother faintly repeat.

"Say, boy," Boyd said suddenly to Dent. "Best you git that horse to Sherlee."

"Right," said Dent, and he glanced at me with a glassy look in his eyes. Then he shook his head and slowly he led the limping mare through the barn, and out the expansive doorway, before the two of them disappeared behind the wall of the building.

I retrieved a bristle brush from a hook beside the stall gate and began to comb it through Mister Brown's dark coat. "So, Boyd, the Indian gal you mentioned. Was she one of the Cheyenne who worked here?" I asked looking at him from across the horse's back.

"Nooo," Boyd drawled, shaking his head from left to right. "That squaw be long gone afore then. She was a Kiowa, seems like."

That checked a box relative to Morgan's narrative. "I wonder what exactly she took from Mr. Headville?"

"Shore-for, I ain't got no idey. Just called it his ticket, seems like. And I only knows about it cuz he got to drinkin' with me one time just after I started workin' for him. Didn't make no sense to me, but then that whiskey be mighty mean, so's I might not be memberin' it all right. But far as I know, he ain't never got it back neither," Boyd said with a slight grin before his countenance returned to a more serious state. "For some reason, he don't drink with me no more."

I ignored Boyd's moment of melancholy and thought of this ticket he had mentioned. Had Headville's remark been a reference to the talisman? Reasonably the talisman could be described as a ticket; a necessary item required to board a mode of transportation, like a train or an airplane, or perhaps an interplanetary ride provided by the BKP.

Though talisman had been what I had labeled the magical object, it was unlikely Headville would coincidentally use the same descriptive name as I had chosen. It was reasonable to assume he might refer to it by another word, such as amulet or charm, so calling it a ticket was equally valid.

I finished brushing the brown horse and had begun grooming Viento when Dent stormed into the barn. "He's out of his mind!" Dent growled, kicking at a scruff of lose straw.

"Whoa, whoa, there boy," Boyd said, trying to hush him. "Keep your lid down and your yap shut afore your alligator mouth overloads your hummin' bird ass!"

"What?" Dent glared at him as though Boyd had badly misquoted a phrase from a Dr. Suess storybook. I, however, was startled to hear him recite the same phrase my dad had often used. Apparently profound statements of such nature transcended the centuries in which both men lived.

"What I be sayin' is you shore-for don't be wantin' Mr. Headville to hear you spoutin' like that. Not if you wanna be keepin' your hide."

"What's the matter?" I asked.

"Headville just laid into me like it's my fault. Told me to go out there in that big-ass pasture and find that little spiky-ass piece of shitty-ass cactus that that fat-ass mare stepped into. He's crazy!"

"Calm yer self down, boy!" Boyd said, quickly stepping in front of Dent and laying a thick-knuckled finger into my brother's sternum. "You ain't gonna be doin' no cactus pickin.' He be just a spoutin' cuz of Big Pete and Hershel, and them, that be all."

"Oh, yeah, he's mad all right," Dent agreed. "If he was a fire-breathing dragon, I'd be a little shitty pile of smoking ashes right now."

I laughed.

"Shut up!" Dent spat at me over Boyd's shoulder. "Headville says you gotta help me."

I looked at him and analytically searched his eyes for any signs of bullshit. I found none.

"Ain't neither of you boys gonna be diggin' up cactus, I'm tellin' ya," Boyd reiterated as he turned to face me. "He done told me and most of the others, too, the same dadgum thing when he gets all puffed up 'bout somethin,' but he shore-for don't mean it. Trust me."

"Why are you so sure?" I asked.

"Cuz your skin ain't the right color, that be why."

I stared at Boyd for a moment, then shifted my eyes to Dent.

"Mr. Headville he gots his own way a lookin' at things. He's told me more times than I can count on two hands that the job of clearin' out that damn cactus ain't gonna be done by no white man."

"Headville's a racist. Big surprise." Dent scowled.

"I dunno what that is, boy, but you better 'member one thing, it be Mister Headville, no matter what your color!" Boyd spat at Dent's absence of respect.

"So, Boyd," I interrupted as if I were an ardent supporter of Switzerland's philosophy of neutrality, "Lizzyann's people," I began, remembering the posture of the men from Nicodemus. "Mr. Headville has been trying to recruit them, hasn't he?"

"That ain't none a your bidness, or mine neither," he growled at me, then as if he couldn't help himself, he added, "but they keep turnin' him down. Even with him offerin' to pay 'em a wage 'long with food to eat and a place to sleep."

Boyd was an endless fountain of information.

"Shore-for don't make no sense to me why them folks keep turnin' down a sweet deal like that," the foreman added.

"Well, gosh, Boyd," Dent began, his tone sarcastic. "Maybe they've got better things to do with their lives than to add cactus to a resume of cotton, and peanuts, and tobacco."

"That's enough, Dent," I said urging him to exercise some restraint.

"Yeah, I 'spect they do pro'ly wanna try to make a go of it with they own farms," Boyd replied, oblivious of my brother's facetious cynicism. "Ain't been free slaves for very long, you know," he added, gently plying the two of us with a Cliff Notes education of the Civil War.

Eventually, Dent settled down, and by the time dinner time rolled around, we had both avoided any additional call of duty to scour the immense horse pasture for the rogue prickly plant. But then, there was an impending task of major importance planned for the entire ranch crew.

A roundup.

And because there would be a pot of money at the end of the rainbow, this event was undoubtably a priority for Headville. And since he had hired us white boys to work as bona fide cowboys, the roundup required all of us to be accessorized with a rope and horse, not a spade and a wagon. And that included Oleander, though reluctantly I had to admit that my irritating comrade had bungled his way into becoming comfortable in the saddle more quickly than I had expected of him.

The following morning, the six of us bunkhouse boys awoke before the chickens, and were fed an early breakfast by Isaiah, a rare meal that was not shared by Sherlee. The promised sun had just barely put a haze of violet into the sky when we set out on our horses for the far north central corral. Once there, we split up into three pairs, just as we had done six weeks or so earlier, only this time Boyd had announced that he would ride with Pete, and that Mick would be my partner, leaving Dent with the short straw thereby getting teamed with Oleander. But typical of my brother, he did not seem to mind the arrangement, but if I had been paired with Oleander, it would have required an Oscar-worthy performance from me to have hidden my displeasure.

Boyd and Pete headed northwest, and Dent and Oleander embarked into the northeastern pasture, leaving Mick and I the central one that was home to the range hut situated about three miles due north.

With Viento under me and Mick riding his sorrel gelding that had almost identical white markings to that of Headville's propagative stallion, we headed northward, not getting very far when we began to come across the first cattle of our assigned pasture. They were a motley trio of cows but each was nursing a black calf that if grouped together, the Angus-cross calves would look like triplets in the eyes of a city-slicker. But I had learned that despite solid coats of ebony hair, there were differences that made each one unique.

The three cow-calf pairs eyed us with a modest amount of concern, but none moved, apparently determined to allow the morning meal to be delivered and consumed without interruption. But Mick and I rode past them, giving the cows and their respective offspring no reason to suspect that in a matter of a few hours ninety percent of the happy couples would be permanently separated by the end of the day.

We took our time ambling across the acres of short-grass prairie, both knowing that once we arrived at the furthest reaches of the pasture, there would be an intense amount of work involved to get the herd of scattered cattle moving southward toward the destination of the central corral.

Between rare moments of observatory conversation, Mick and I traveled in prolonged intervals of uninterrupted silence, each of us wrapped in whatever thoughts were preoccupying the two of us moderately social introverts. Mostly, I thought of Kate. But then Headville would rudely creep into my subconsciousness.

But I also thought about the young man who rode with me. Despite knowing him for a couple of months already, I had not spent a great amount of one-on-one time with Mick. Most often Boyd had partnered with him, though lately I had observed that the young cowboy could frequently be found in the company of my brother, but understandably so. Dent was a full-fledged extrovert and had far more charismatic personality than anyone I knew, so it was easy for others to migrate to him.

As a kid, I had often felt like a square-shaped third wheel when Dent's friends came to our house to hang out, and I grudgingly admired my brother's ability to be completely at ease within the presence of other people, whether they were relative strangers or long-time friends. And during these two months at the Culver Headville ranch, I had admittedly felt a twinge of jealously as I watched his and Mick's friendship develop.

But there was a reason for my envy.

I was missing Sam. We had been practically joined at the hip since our first meeting as five-year-olds in kindergarten class and I supposed that oftentimes genuinely close friends were few and far between. But in Sam's absence, I had been drawn to develop an alternative relationship, one that I secretly imagined would develop into something more intimate and mutually desired.

"So, you like her a lot, don't you?" Mick said suddenly, as though he had been reading my mind.

"Who?"

He laughed. "You know who."

"Dent told you, didn't he?"

"Your brother didn't have to say anything. I've got my own eyes."

We continued to ride without words for another fifty yards. "Yeah," I said, breaking the silence, "I do like Kate. A lot."

"She's a pretty girl. And pretty flirty, too."

"Not with me," I said. "Well, not at first, anyway."

He laughed again. "I noticed that, too."

"So, I bet Kate didn't ignore you, when you first came to the ranch."

"Why do you think that?"

"Well, you just said she was flirty, and you're a handsome guy, so one plus one is an easy two."

"Don't know about that, but you got part of it right."

"And?"

"And what?"

"Did you flirt back?"

"No," he said pragmatically. "She's, well …"

"She's the boss's daughter."

"Exactly."

"Which probably makes you a hell of a lot smarter than me."

"I'm not as smart as you might think," he replied. "But, JT, be careful. Culver Headville is not a man you want mad at you. Especially when it comes to Kate."

I thought for a moment, holding a question on the tip of my tongue, debating whether to ask it. Yes or no, it was a tie, so what the hell. "Mick, do you think Headville has plans for her himself?"

"You mean, like do I think he wants to marry her or something?"

"Yes. Do you think he does?"

"I think he might. Most of us have thought as much, even Boyd, but while sober he'd never admit it. But you have to remember, Kate is Headville's ward, not his daughter."

"You mean, Mr. Headville?" I said, scolding him with my eyes.

"Sure," Mick replied with a grin, but the rocking of his head defied the affirmative.

Within minutes we were at the range hut, the small homestead soddy still used for an occasional overnight stay. Adjacent was a little corral, large enough to comfortably hold three horses, but would be overcrowded with five.

"So, Mick, have you stayed there before?" I asked, gesturing toward the tiny house.

"Yeah," he replied. "Springtime, mostly. We take turns staying up here so calving can be monitored."

"Ah," I said, "gotta keep a close watch on the first-time heifers, right?"

"Right," he said, confirming the necessary birthing assistance that is sometimes required to help a new mother bear her first calf. "It's nice inside, though," Mick added. "You wouldn't guess to look at it, but its got a wooden floor, and the interior walls are covered with wood planks, too. And a heavy cast-iron wood stove keeps it cozy for those early spring nights."

"Nice," I said, thinking Abelard and Karl should make similar improvements to their dug out. But then, they probably had plans to build themselves a free-standing home someday, so why waste the lumber?

"Want to see inside?"

"No," I replied. "I'd rather get these doggies gathered up. You know, sooner the better."

Mick agreed, and we picked up our pace, nudging our horses into a trot. We crossed the shallow river I had previously learned was the Saline, and together we began pushing livestock out of the two square miles of that portion of bottom land pasture that formed the northernmost tier of the ranch. Initially, the cows and their weanling-aged calves that were born in the month of March, were reluctant to submit to our guidance, but once we started yelling at them with sounds and voices unique to motivating cattle, their moods elevated to a modest level of excitement, and they began migrating southward.

The first two hours were filled with repetitive maneuvers of riding from one side of the pasture to the opposite, comprehensively shifting cattle from being stoically comfortable homebodies into a begrudging herd of head-to-tail travelers. East to west and back again, we guided our assigned group of livestock within the channel of the two quasi-longitudinal fences that eventually connected to the central corral. As our herd neared the holding pen, a veil of dust rose up around them, stirred by the cloven hooves of their legs that quadrupled the total of the head counts. And to our right, in the adjacent pasture, Boyd and Pete were neck and neck with us as they closed in on the collection point. I looked left and to my surprise, Dent and Oleander's cattle were not that far behind.

All told, when the last gate was shut on the outer circle of the corral, we had penned just shy of one-thousand cattle. Despite Boyd's assurance that the corral would physically accommodate that number, I had sincere doubts. But Boyd was ultimately proven right.

But the enclosure was also abundantly crowded. Luckily, very few of the cattle had the horns of their Texas ancestors.

The four of us residing on the lowest rung of the ladder of tenure dismounted and tied our horses to the outside of the corral while Boyd and Pete pushed their way through the milling and mooing livestock and opened one of the gates that would allow the filing of a portion of the ranch animals into the perimeter of the second concentric circle of corral space. Immediately, dozens of cows and calves poured through the opening until Boyd was content with a number he considered manageable for the next task. After Pete had closed the gate behind him and the foreman, Boyd called for the four of us to join them, though we were obliged to traverse the space carefully and cautiously on foot.

Mick, Dent, and I took quick advantage of reasonably safe opportunities, but Oleander had been overly cautious, which given his lack of experience around cattle was understandable and likewise forgivable. But he was funny.

"Okay, okay," Oleander pleaded as he practically tip-toed between the animals. "Nice cow," he said. "Nice cow," he repeated with nearly each step.

Putting into operation the gating system that we had used on branding day, we worked and separated the cows from the calves and finally had about fifty of the young isolated in the inner most pen. Unhappy with the separation, they constantly bawled in distress, seeking the attention of their mothers. Like most aspects of ranch life, the young were destined to grow up fast.

Three hours later, we had well over four-hundred crying calves gathered and divided from the cows. But there was more work to be done before we could call it a day.

After reopening the gates that lead to the pastures, very few of the cows took advantage of the opportunity to escape any further than a hundred yards away. Most stayed close by, raising a chorus of bovine voices, assuring their young that mama was nearby and not planning to go anywhere without them. At least not until their maternal instincts were suppressed by those of self-preservation. Hunger and thirst were often enough to modify one's intentions whether you walked on two legs or upon four.

Taking just enough time to rinse our heads in the cattle tank and drink the cool water that had been pumped from the subterranean aquifer, we looked to Boyd to give us our next instructions.

He stood peering through the fence, appraising the young animals, getting a fix on the forty-odd heifers that he would ultimately judge to be the best prospective herd replacements, those adolescent females that would not go to market, but would instead be kept as breeding stock for future calf crops. The first dozen had been quick decisions, and it had been easy to agree with him. Boyd, like my dad, was a keen judge of quality livestock.

After identifying a worthy specimen, the five of us underlings cut the calf from the group and with the precise timing of the gates, we released the young animal back into the throng of anxious cows. Another two hours later we had this important task completed. And I was overwhelmed by exhaustion.

After another drink and a head-dunk, the six of us piled back onto our horses and began our fifty-minute ride back to ranch headquarters. Tomorrow, we would be back. Then somehow, with just the six of us, we would leave corral central and begin a fifteen-mile drive of nearly five-hundred weanling-age calves and herd them across the south half of the ranch, then out into the wide-open Kansas prairie that was without fences or pens.

If my mom were here, I know what she would call this impending experience.

A herding of cats.

I did not see how six of us ranch hands would be enough, even if Headville and Sherlee participated. In previous years, there would have been the addition of the five absentee mustangers, bringing the total number of cowboys nearer to a more practical and efficient number. And knowing calves as I did, I was not particularly confident that our mission could be accomplished without an excessive amount of aggravation. I wished for all our sakes, calves and cowboys alike, that help might come from somewhere.

And then when we got back to the Taj-Mahal of barns, we found four strange horses penned together in one of the larger stalls. And when we entered the bunkhouse, we discovered that those of us with only two legs also had new roommates.

Four Hispanic men, appearing to be in their late twenties or early thirties, were gathered at the table. And from their attire, it was obvious my wish had come true.

Vaqueros.

"*Buenos tardes*!" said one of the two men who faced the door, his dark eyes glistening with congeniality, his smile a welcoming beacon of iridescent white teeth set against the deep bronze of a whiskered face.

And with what was as quick as a snap of my fingers, there was a promise that tomorrow would be easier than I had expected.

CHAPTER 40

From horseback, we pushed the herd of spring calves southward from corral central, the six of us who had gathered and penned them the day before plus the four vaqueros, all of us collectively working as a team of ten. The sun had barely cleared the eastern horizon when we arrived at the ranch yard guiding the anxious young weanlings through the gate behind the great barn, then across the grassy lot and into the space flanked on the west by the remuda pen, and finally threading them between the bunkhouse and the Headville mansion and onto the roadway that led toward the main entrance of the ranch just over a mile away.

Entering the core of the congregated set of buildings, Boyd, Dent, and I brought up the rear trailing behind the last of the calves, and straightaway I saw an audience standing on the veranda of the grand limestone home. Kate and Isaiah and Beverly Carneiro were watching the parade of cattle as attentively as if there were instead firetrucks displaying locally prominent politicians, and civic floats decorated with paper streamers, and a marching band complete with acrobatic majorettes.

Keeping my face pointed forward and the rim of my cowboy hat parallel with the ground, I shifted my eyes discreetly toward the house and found Kate smiling and watching me with noticeably less discretion. I considered signaling to her with a covert wave of my hand, but I stymied the foolish action. Propriety was, at the moment, a priority, especially with Beverly standing guard. I was ninety-five percent positive she did not like me, though in my opinion, I had given her no valid reason to feel that way.

Then in the distance, perched upon the knoll that gave the road an elbow, sat Culver Headville upon a black steed. He had apparently given Doc the day off again and was back in the saddle of the younger stallion, Ulysses. Although he was more than a thousand feet away, his presence there within sight of me was another reason not to greet Kate so openly. And from that quarter-mile distance, I believed I could feel his eyes upon me, though I had no evidence to support that sentiment.

As I rode past Headville, I let my eyes casually glance in his direction as he lorded over the herd of calves whose sale would provide significant proceeds for the coffers of his ranch budget. With the light of the Autumn morning illuminating his features, he formed a striking image as he posed upon the stunning black horse; his broad shoulders fitted with a white shirt and a red bandana knotted around his neck, and a cowboy hat that was fittingly the color typical of a villain in a melodrama.

For a moment his appearance caused me to think of Johnny Cash, sans the white shirt and the villainous reputation. And of course, Headville didn't have a guitar, or a hit song as far as I knew.

Once all the calves and cowboys had funneled through the signature gate of the CH Quarter Horse Ranch and were pointed southwesterly toward Hays City, the big kahuna himself galloped by on the back of his black stallion, passing the herd and assuming the prominent frontal post as the honored point man. And within the distance of a mile, myself, and the remaining cowboys, plus Sherlee, had likewise assumed our assigned positions for what was basically a modest version of the illustrious cattle drives I had often imagined and yearned to experience.

But still, the real-life event was promising to compete with the fictional pages from a favorite Western novel or from a scene of a 1950s Hollywood film. I relished the creaking of my saddle, the sway of my body moving as one with the horse beneath me, and the astringent smell of Viento's sweat mingling with the tart scent of my own perspiration. And the sight of the herd of young cattle that stretched ahead of me, their hooves shrouded in billows of powdery soil, was the cherry on top. And, despite being assigned to one of the least pleasant rider positions, I was not inclined to complain. I was living the dream.

To my left, Oleander twinned me as a co-drag rider, and the vaquero named Carlos, who had last evening enthusiastically greeted us in his native language, rode nearby on my right side. From behind the throng of young cattle, the three of us were tasked with moving the herd forward, a responsibility that required a near constant push against the dragging pace of the slower animals. And, as an unwelcome bonus, we were automatic beneficiaries of an insufferable amount of dust.

My part in the drive was not the most glamorous role, and my brother had been quick to laugh at me when Boyd had barked our respective assignments.

"And that's what you get for courting the boss's daughter," Dent said, before blasting me with his manly giggle.

"She's his ward," I corrected with a hard edge to my voice as I simultaneously shot him my best impression of a stink eye.

"Not much difference," he called out to me as he and Mick loped forward to assume the coveted roles as swing riders for the right side of the herd. Opposite of them, on the left side rode Boyd and Sherlee, and behind them, two on each side nearest to the back of the herd were the remaining three vaqueros and not-so-little Little Pete, the four mounted riders responsible for preventing the calves from fanning outward.

A compact and uniformly moving herd was the preferred intermediate objective. Getting the calves securely and safely delivered to the Hays City stockyards being the eventual goal. At that point, our little soiree of a morning-long cattle drive would be completed as far as the herd drivers were concerned. Then ultimately, the exchange of money for beef on the hoof would be Culver Headville's bailiwick.

We had gotten about three miles from the ranch when I caught a glimpse of Oleander waving at me in a gesture that indicated he wanted me to come to him. I didn't know what he wanted, but I doubted it was very important. He waved at me again, and with a sigh of annoyance I acquiesced, turning Viento toward him and pointing to a spot roughly fifty or so yards mid-way between us. He understood my side of the signing conversation and kicked his horse into a trot and met me halfway.

"What?" I asked him, with less benevolence than I probably would have bestowed upon any of the other riders.

"I think Ox lied to me," Oleander scowled, the planes of his face already coated in a layer of grime.

"About what?"

"He told me I got the choice job riding here at the back. But this is crap," he declared, his resentment obvious. "I can't hardly breathe!"

"Yes, Pete lied," I said.

"That sonofabitch," Oleander cursed, but he didn't seem exactly angry.

"Actually, the positions we're riding in are typically handed to the less experienced cowboys. So don't take it personal."

"Well, that would be me, obviously." Then he looked my way, and I saw his brow furrow. "So, why are you back here eating dust and shit?"

"I've wondered the same thing myself. But I'm not complaining."

"Seems to me those other three wetbacks should have been riding here with their other guy, instead of us."

"Mexicans," I said, correcting his offensive slang. "Vaqueros, professionally," I added.

"Big whoop," he countered without apology. "So, what about Double-D up there? He's in a way better spot, isn't he?"

"Yep. Way better," I said, then I spent the next two minutes explaining the positions of the riders, including Headville, and their respective roles in the cattle drive.

"So, you've done this before?"

"Nope. Just read about it."

"Figures."

"Anything else?"

"Yeah, so where do these little cows go to after we get them to town?"

"East, I suppose is the most likely place. A train ride to denser population centers. They'll likely be confined and corn-fed for about a year or so until they are fattened and ready."

"Ready for what?"

"Slaughter."

Oleander stared at me for a long moment, digesting the information. "So, you're telling me these little guys are gonna be butchered?"

"Yeah, but not before they get bigger."

"That's a shitty thing to do to 'em."

"Oleander, it's just a reality of the livestock industry. Where do you think your steaks and your hamburgers come from?" He was silent, his eyes glued forward, his profile contemplative. I could relate to him, recalling my first lesson when I had learned that the cattle my family raised were at the bottom of the ranch food-chain. As an eight-year-old, I had vehemently sworn to my parents I would never eat beef again, or would I make a pet of another orphan calf. Eventually, I broke the first promise. Keeping the second one though, spared me of an unknown number of resentful tears.

"Are you okay?" I asked Oleander, realizing that perhaps he held some small measure of compassion in him after all.

"Yeah," he replied.

"Anything else?"

"Nope."

"Then I've got a question for you, Oleander." He looked at me, waiting. "Why did you bring the pistol with you?" I asked, nodding to the gun holstered and strapped around his hips. "There won't be any target practicing in town, you know?"

"No shit," he snarled, and then just like that the Oleander Sedgwick I knew, but could not quite love, was back from a sentimental state of mind. "Who knows, I might need to shoot something. Or someone." His voice resonated with an ominous tone.

"That's a dangerous mindset, Oleander," I warned. "There will be no reason for you to shoot anyone."

"Never know, Worm. There is such a thing as self-defense," he said with an arrogant smile, then he reined his horse and trotted away from me.

"Great," I said out loud, then seeing a straggler calf trailing from the place I had left a few minutes earlier, I nudged Viento into a lope and positioning the two of us behind the black speckled youngster, we encouraged him to catch up with his four-legged comrades.

Three hours and some change later, the calves were penned at the stockyards and done so without mishap and free of any serious angst and frustration. And as far as I was concerned, the smoothness of the drive was fully due to the assistance of the vaqueros. Where and how Headville had recruited them, I didn't have a clue. And being wholly aware of the binding regulation of if-you-need-to-know-he'll-tell-you, I did not bother to ask. Not that Headville's rules totally stopped me from an occasional crafty extraction of information from Boyd.

I glanced to the nearby place where my Mexican colleagues congregated, the four of them laughing and grinning and yammering with one another in their cultural language that would occasionally impart a word I could interpret to English, but that wasn't often. Then as if he sensed I was observing them, Carlos pivoted his head and looked at me and smiled with his illuminating set of pearly whites and waved. I reciprocated his friendly set of gestures, but to be honest, the man was a little weird. Not because of the way he looked or acted, but because of the creepy thing he carried in his shirt pocket that, at present, was sitting on his shoulder.

A Horned Toad.

Last evening, after the initial round of informal introductions, I had noticed a heavy twist of twine tied around a button of the shirt worn by the vaquero who had been the first to greet us with his exuberant expression of hello, followed by, *Mi llamo Carlos*. The string sagged from the second button south of the man's Adams apple, but looped upward, disappearing into the Mexican's shirt pocket. That accoutrement had been peculiar enough, but something had been moving around in the shirtfront's pouch.

Oleander had noticed it, too, and had made an inquiry that was more colorful and less diplomatic than the configuration of my un-voiced question, but he had gotten a result. Carlos had responded by tugging on the string. A moment later, a squatty and hideous wide-bellied lizard with a crown of short spikes crawled out of the pocket, leashed by the opposite end of the twine tether. Oleander had promptly shuffled backwards, each step paired with an expletive. The four vaqueros had laughed, as had Boyd, Little Pete, Mick, and my brother. But like my red-haired antagonist, I didn't find anything about it funny. Perhaps the only thing Oleander and I had in common was that those native little reptilian devils gave us both the heebie-jeebies.

Deciding to cowboy-up, I sauntered over to the Spanish-speaking buckaroos, determined not to let Carlos's unconventional pet keep me from expressing my admiration for their collective droving skills. But neither was I planning to get within leaping distance of that creature tethered to a certain piece of string.

Unscathed, I returned to Viento and mounted up.

I had planned to stop by the school and see if I could catch Blaine functioning in his new environment, but the boss-man had nixed that idea, ordering those of us under the age of forty to return immediately to the ranch. But the management team of Headville, Sherlee and Boyd would be staying behind.

So, the nine of us, including the vaqueros, left Hays City riding as a group. Though I had not been informed otherwise, I had assumed that the Hispanic cowboys were also recruited to be long-term replacements for the mustangers who had punched a one-way ticket when they had left the Headville ranch in the early part of summer. If so, the bunkhouse would be full again, tonight, and perhaps for months to come.

But knowing Headville's obsession for pristine pastures, I wondered if our head honcho had other plans for them. I genuinely hoped that he did not have the ulterior motive of turning them into the cactus crew. The vaqueros didn't strike me as bending to any task that would not keep them on the back of a horse, and as they had proven today, that was where their skills matched those of the Tescott brothers.

The ranch was quiet and seemingly deserted when we arrived, and we wasted no time in unsaddling and grooming the horses before watering them and leading them to the small pasture behind the bunkhouse. We were one dusty and dirty group of young men, and already the five of us with tenures exceeding twenty-four hours were eager for a dip in the spring-fed pond that lay neatly sequestered in the trees behind our sleeping quarters.

Pete was the first to head for the water, and though he couldn't speak but five words of Spanish, three of those being questionably profane, he invited the Mexicans to join us using a mixed communication of his own native language and a signaling of his hands and arms that clearly demonstrated that we were going swimming.

Gathering on the wooden pier that protruded a dozen feet across the dark, clear water, Pete, and Mick, and the three of us who were born in a different century striped from our jeans and shirts and socks, having already carefully secured our beloved hats and boots on the grassy, hard-pack bank of the pond. And because I, and Dent and Oleander had already been taught by Mick and Pete of the advantages of simultaneously bathing and doing our laundry, we kept our underpants and undershirts on, jumping partially clothed into the cold water.

The vaqueros, however, didn't see the point of multi-tasking, and without hesitation they had joined us as skinny-dippers. I was half-surprised Dent hadn't impulsively decided to abandon his remaining clothes since he was the most immodest person known to the Custer, Kansas community, famous for a streak down Main Street on a cold November night after he had over-indulged in the celebration of his birthday. I smiled, remembering that in the dawn of the next day, after having spent all of the dark hours past midnight as an involuntary guest at the Custer City Police Station, he had been released into the custody of our dad. Outside, Dent had been the recipient of a round of applause from his friends who had been waiting out the night for the pardon of their brazen hero. Mom, however, had grounded him for a month.

I was the first to climb from the chill of the autumn water. I didn't particularly like cold baths, no matter what time of year, and Pete was just seconds behind me. With a quick rinse and wring of my socks, I gathered up my dry clothes and picked up my hat and boots and turned for the path that led to the bunkhouse only to find that we had unexpected company.

Kate.

"Hi JT," she said with a sly grin.

"Kate!" I exclaimed, shocked to see her here in an environment that was much like the boy's locker room at school, a place that should have been off limits to anyone of her gender. Quickly, I began to pull on my pants, not immediately concerned that they would easily become saturated from my sopping wet long underwear.

"Hello, Pete," she added, looking past me, and waving her fingers.

I glanced back to see Pete standing head to toe in his dripping wet underclothes with both hands sharing the responsibility of concealing his crotch, and his face turning a bright shade of pink that was quickly heading toward the color of his hair.

"*Ayi, yi, yi!*" I heard one of the Mexicans call out.

I glanced toward the water and saw Carlos, sans the horned lizard, wearing nothing but a big grin and standing knee-deep in the shallows of the pond. Then he spread out his arms and gyrated his hips. "You like, *Senorita*?" He said with a laugh, and his comrades joined him in a cackle of Spanish commentary that was clearly inappropriate for the ears of a young lady. In that split second, my opinion of Carlos tanked from what I had thought about him three hours earlier.

"Kate!" I said again, taking her by the elbow and turning her away from the naked man who had just assaulted her presumed innocence.

Then from behind us I heard Dent.

"Asshole!" he scowled, as I heard him splashing quickly through the water targeting, I assumed, Carlos. I turned in time to see him punch the exhibitionist in the face. "She happens to be my brother's girlfriend," I heard him add, and instantly I was even more embarrassed.

"Come with me," I told Kate, and I promptly led her through the trees, not stopping until we were at the porch of the bunkhouse. Behind us, I could hear a melee of commotion. From the sounds of it, a free-for-all fight had swiftly developed.

"What do you think you're doing?" I asked rhetorically. "Back there is no place for a girl."

"I'm not a little girl, I'm a young lady. I thought you had noticed that."

"Doesn't matter. That pond is no place for you. Not when—when boys are there!"

"It's not like I haven't seen one before," Kate said with an air of nonchalance.

I caught her gist, but I was not about to question her about it. And frankly, I did not want to know any details, though I suspected she was stretching the truth anyway. Culver Headville was nothing if he was not protective.

"Did your brother hit that new guy?"

"Yes! Dent is like that. He'll jump on any excuse to punch somebody."

"And what about you, JT? Would you punch someone like that, too?"

"I don't know, probably not," I replied seriously. "I'm not a naturally violent guy. Besides, the last time I lost my temper it cost me this trip back into time."

Instantly, I realized what I had said.

Kate looked at me quizzically.

"A trip where?" She asked.

"Never mind."

"Miss Kate!" I heard a womanly voice screech from across the yard and I glanced and saw Beverly Carniero striding toward us, the front of her dress gathered high enough to allow for a seriously paced march of determination. It was the first time I was genuinely glad to see her. Beverly stopped within four or five steps of infiltrating our personal midst, and then assaulted me with a glare that promised to whup my ass if I so much as touched Kate. Then at once I realized I still held her arm in the clutch of my hand. As if Kate's flesh had instantly turned to molten lava, I let go of her. "Young lady, you need to return to the house this minute!"

"Of course," Kate conceded. "We'll talk later," she informed me, then crossed to the finely attired private educator who hastily escorted Kate to the grand house before both disappeared inside. I watched until the door closed.

"Oh, boy," I said aloud, wondering how I was going to explain my words to Kate. My first thought was that I had better start rehearsing another pack of lies. Then I thought surely, I could come up with a spin that would be relatively truthful and still be a plausible explanation for my slip of tongue. Still, the last thing I wanted to do was purposely lie to her.

I sighed, realizing I had also done exactly what I had worried Oleander would do.

Two hours later, the nine of us had gathered around the dining table of the bunkhouse having been served our evening meal. As Isaiah went about setting food and plates and utensils upon the table, I saw that his eyes roamed from one of us to the next, lingering on the four cowboys who bore the facial evidence of a brawl. But he said nothing, though before he left the building, he turned at the door and looked collectively at us with a raised brow of which I interpreted to be a warning to eat in peace and leave any further fighting for outside.

In silence, we lifted healthy spoonfuls of beans and thick bites of ham into the quiet cavities of our faces. But our eyes were as busy as our mouths, checking each other for signs of truce or signals of what might lead to a second scuffle.

Then the door opened, and Sherlee stepped inside. He paused long enough to immediately ascertain that Oleander had a busted lip, and Mick sported an inflamed and inflated nose that still hinted of the presence of blood in one nostril. Then Sherlee saw that the vaquero who exhibited a crooked row of bottom teeth had one eye nearly swollen shut, and Carlos was similarly injured having an eye radiantly red and encompassed by a deep bruising of its lower lid that was entirely a gift from Dent, who just so happened to appear unscathed. Not only could he hit well, but my brother also knew how to duck.

"Two to two," Sherlee said in the direction of my group. Then he looked at those at the opposite end of the table and said, "*Dos a dos.*" Then he did something I had not seen him do before.

He smiled.

"*Bueno,*" he added, and all of us broke into laughter.

And in that moment, unexpected friendships were born among the nine of us young ranch hands, and for the next four weeks we not only shared in the work required of the Headville hacienda, but we also shared in a lot of laughs as we struggled to bridge the communication barriers that separated us. All said and done, the vaqueros were fun, jovial guys, and I had even decided that Carlos wasn't too bad of a guy, so long as he kept his pants on when Kate was in the vicinity.

But then on a brisk, cloudy Friday afternoon that launched the second half of the month of November, a rider appeared as we were gathering hay into a wagon inside the great barn. Boyd saw him first.

"Oh, hells bells!" Boyd cursed, then with a whisper of dread so thick it barely left his lips he added, "Ignoramus." I looked at him and saw deep concern fill every corner of his face.

Then I looked at Little Pete, seeking in him an explanation only to follow his eyes to the hitching post next to the giant cottonwood in the center of the ranch yard. When the visiting cowboy turned toward us, I watched as Pete turned as pale as a ghost.

"Shit," he said, shaking his head.

"Who is it?" Dent asked as we stopped what we were doing and peered out from the barn.

"It's Pete," Mick said. "Big Pete."

One of the five prodigal cowboys had returned. And having heard the criminal description Headville had denounced them to be, I feared this guy had just made his second big mistake.

At once Boyd threw down his pitchfork and quickly left the barn in an assumed attempt to intercept the man. "Pete!" he cried out. "Where the hell ya been, you dumb sumbitch?!"

"I can explain," I heard Big Pete tell him as I edged toward the door in order to improve my ability to eavesdrop. Behind me, the others on the ground floor followed me.

"Don't 'splain it to me! Shore-for Mr. Headville be gonna have your hide! He done got in his head that you ain't nothin' but a dadgum horse thief!"

"But I ain't, really. I mean, I brung the horse back," Big Pete countered.

"You be a fool, too! You knows what he be like," Boyd spat at him.

And then Headville and Sherlee appeared from inside the stud barn, and I watched as Headville crossed toward him. Even from where I stood, I could see the rage flickering in the rancher's eyes.

"Mr. Headville … sir," the man said nervously as he took a few steps forward in Headville's direction. At once, both men stopped dead in their tracks, their eyes locked on each other. I imaged that Big Pete had to be scared shitless. I know that was how I felt, and I was only a bystander.

With my eyes glued to Culver Headville, I watched as he raised his hand toward the convicted man, and pointed at him with such intensity that I could see the outstretched finger shaking. Boyd stepped aside as though he knew better than to be within striking distance of whatever supernatural force might inexplicably fire from Headville's fingertip. Then the man known by his former colleagues as Big Pete, began to utter another word, but before he could manage to spill a second syllable across his lips, Headville jerked his hand with a fierce repointing of his finger that appeared powerful enough to pierce through body and bone. I held my breath. The scene was like nothing I had ever witnessed, and the quiet was eerie.

"Boyd," Headville hissed, breaking the silence like a bullet shattering a glass window.

"Yes, sir, Mr. Headville?"

"Is there a rope tied to that saddle?"

I saw Boyd's head hesitantly swivel to look at the blue roan horse that was tied several feet away from him. He gulped, reluctant to answer.

"Well?" Headville asked, his eyes never leaving Big Pete.

"Yes, sir, they be a rope there."

Surely, I thought to myself, I was not about to witness a hanging. Not without a judge or a jury. But in context of the 1870s, I knew this was a different place and time, one where too often justice was imparted at the whim of the one who had been wronged.

And horse thievery was after all, a hanging offense.

Then Headville called for Sherlee and the wrangler obediently went to his side. A few private, inaudible words were spoken to Sherlee, then he sauntered toward the horse the mustanger had supposedly been returning, and I watched as Big Pete's eyes grew wide with fear.

"I'm sorry, Mr. Headville!" he cried, shaking his head in disbelief.

"Get. Off. My. Land."

Without another word, the doomed cowboy turned and raced from the yard and onto the roadway that led to the ranch's exit. Then Sherlee had the horse's reins in his hands and stepped into the saddle. Steering the animal around, I watched as the wrangler shook out a lasso from the rope and kicked the horse into a lunge as he set out in pursuit of the fleeing pedestrian.

Suddenly, Dent was beside me, and we looked at each other knowing that we were about to abandon the sensibility of doing nothing, despite an outcome that would certainly land us in big trouble. But still, we took a step forward, but immediately I was grounded by the clasp of strong hands upon my arms. I turned to discover my brother was likewise being held at bay, the two of us under the restraint of Mick and Little Pete. Both quietly shook their heads, silently and sternly warning us to stay out of a business that was not ours to interrupt.

I looked westward just in time to see the loop of Sherlee's rope drop over the man's head and shoulders, knocking his hat to the ground. With a snap that sounded the demise of any remaining slack in the rope, I watched as the snare cinched itself tightly around the man's arms and chest. Then with a quick trot past his captured prey, Sherlee wrapped the rope around the saddle horn and jerked the man with such ferocity that his body dove forward, temporarily causing him to be airborne.

Big Pete fell to the ground, but Sherlee did not give him even a second of opportunity to clammer upright to his feet. Instead, he dug his heels into the horse's ribs launching the animal into a lunging run, and mercilessly dragging the man behind him. Faint masculine cries of torment melded with the horse's pounding hooves as the man who Boyd had correctly called a fool was brutally escorted from the kingdom of Culver Headville.

If I had entertained any doubt before, it had now completely vanished. There was an evil in my presence, and I should have, at that very moment, saddled Viento and rode away from this lair of wickedness with as much haste as I and my horse could manage. And though I knew Dent would agree with the decision and join me, I knew with certainty that I could not abandon Kate and leave her future in the malicious hands of a madman.

Then Headville turned to those of us in the barn, and it was then that I noticed that the vaqueros had gathered beside us.

"Anyone else want to take something of mine away from me?"

I looked at him, and his eyes bore into me a truth I could no longer dismiss as impossible. He knew of my knowledge of the talisman.

But then I thought perhaps he was referring to Kate.

Or maybe both.

Both. Somehow, in my heart, I knew it was both.

CHAPTER 41

Boyd had ushered us back into the barn to resume our task of gathering hay for the livestock, but soon we heard the telling sounds of a trotting horse as Sherlee returned to the ranch yard after being absent for less than ten minutes. I guessed that he had only dragged the elder Pete just beyond the entrance of the ranch, thereby banishing the accused horse thief from Culver Headville's land. I was relieved when the henchman had returned, mostly because there had not been a gunshot, which would not have come as a complete surprise. I assumed, then, that his life had been spared, but not the proverbial rod. My fear was also allayed by the fact that there had not been a hanging, which had been my initial concern.

Culver Headville's act of mercy, though to call it that was a charitable exaggeration, did not at all elevate him to be anything other than what he was. A despicably evil man.

By early evening we had completed the day's feeding of hay and during those hours it had been a subdued and somber atmosphere. Even Little Pete had refrained from sharing his usual daily joke. The vaqueros had also been reserved, having postponed their retirement to the bunkhouse long enough to discuss something in private. And I had a good guess as to what that conversation was about. I fully expected them to waltz into the bunkhouse, gather up their things, and bid to the five of us *adios amigos* just before riding off into the sunset. But surely, they would eat supper first. Culver Headville's temperament aside, it would be difficult to pass up Isaiah's home cooking.

But the sunset came and went, and the vaqueros had sat down at the table without packing their bags. However, the nine of us ate without much conversation. And then at Boyd's discretion, he doused the lanterns and sunk us into an early bedtime. But I was fine with that. I had a lot of thinking to do. Tomorrow was Saturday, our day off. And I wasn't entirely sure whether I would spend the day in Hays City, or just stay put on the ranch and wallow in my feelings of sorrow and dread.

Before I fell asleep, I had ensconced my thoughts in self-pity. In just over six weeks, Morgan would be hailing his ride via the January third perihelion. Then upon his return to the future, he would begin the necessary preparations to return in July with the instruments designed to locate the lost talisman. Therefore, my next window of opportunity to return home would be the perihelion of 1880, a date with the Burmano-Ku-Partika that was still more than a year away.

And that was only if Morgan made it back in time.

And only if the talisman could be located.

And only if I could survive until then.

Culver Headville epitomized the dog-eat-dog world in which I currently sojourned. But there were others just like him living in my day and time. The difference though, was that I was not personally acquainted with any of them.

Hours later, when I awoke, dawn had crept into the room. I lay still for a few moments, listening to the gentle breathing of others who were still sleeping. Then, I realized the rhythmic breaths were not noisy enough for eight men. Curiosity sat me upright, and I glanced around. Nearby was Dent and Mick and Little Pete, all sighing with the soft labors of sleep, the lingering effects of the Sand Man.

Then, I heard a snore and turned toward the other half of the bunkhouse and could make out the bulky shape of Oleander lying flat on his back, but he was the only one there. In the pale light I could see well enough to confirm that the vaqueros were not present in the cluster of bunks that had been theirs for the past month. Boyd was also unaccounted for, but that was not unusual. He was often the first one up and out.

I sat for a moment, wondering about the Mexicans. Had they actually vamoosed during the night just as I had speculated they might? Then suddenly I heard a guttural noise that sounded like someone was retching. I waited a moment, then heard it again as the sound pierced through the exterior walls of the bunkhouse.

Someone was definitely sick.

I got up and pulled on my boots, then shivered against the presence of a chill that had managed a nightly visit during the past few weeks. From a peg next to the one that held my hat, I took my sheep-wool jacket that I had purchased upon my last visit to town, and wrapped myself within it, glad that I had saved enough money to buy the coat. The Burmano-Ku-Partika had not thought to pack one for me.

Pulling my hat down to my ears, I stepped outside and quietly closed the door behind me. Then I heard the retching again, and it was clearly coming from the barn. I crossed to the massive building and when I entered, Boyd was there, bent over in a corner nearest the door.

"You okay, Boyd?" I asked.

"I shore-for the hell ain't," he moaned. "Been up half the night. Sicker than a snake-bit dog," he added, turning toward me. Even in the darkness of the barn, there was just enough light splitting the shadows of the early morning to give me a clear enough view to see that Boyd did, in fact, look sicker than a dog.

"You look like hell," I told him.

"Spect so. Feels like it, too. Least I ain't got no pro'lems in my south forty. Couple months back I had the squirts so bad I coulda shit through a screen door and not hit a wire."

That was more than I needed to know. "Why don't you go crawl back in bed," I suggested to him.

"Don't wanna be keepin' you boys up."

"It's nearly breakfast, so I wouldn't worry about it," I said before glancing toward the stall where the horses of the vaqueros had been quartered. It was empty. "The Mexicans, did they leave in the middle of the night?"

"Nooo—ohhooo," Boyd said, then quickly he turned and without the product of a regurgitation, he dry-heaved into the straw of the barn floor. For better or worse, he seemed to have emptied his stomach. "Them boys rode outta here, maybe—" he whispered, bending his face to look at me, his eyes pitifully moist and red. "Maybe an hour ago," he concluded.

"They quit?"

"Don't reckon. From what I could figger of that Spanish, they just be goin' to town. I 'spect they prol'ly just horny."

I grimaced. I did not need to know that, either. Then I thought of who they might visit, and I grimaced again. I spent the next five minutes talking Boyd into returning to the bunkhouse. Afterward, I got Viento and Mister Brown from their stalls and led them to the little pasture. As I was walking back, I heard the rattle of a buckboard wagon and the rolling of wheels on wooden axels and the clopping of the hooves of work horses.

After I had passed through the trees, I saw not one wagon, but two. The same ones that regularly came with their delivery of the housemaid, Lizzyann. The driver of the first wagon circled around the tree passing by me. I gave him a wave and he hesitantly lifted his hand, though without enthusiasm. Their arrival was earlier than normal, at least as far as the sun was concerned. But then I realized the days were growing shorter and the journey from their isolated community of Nicodemus to the bustling cowtown of Hays City was a lengthy one. And though they probably preferred not to, they would have to ride in the dark for at least one portion of their round-trip.

The second wagon stopped at the Culver Headville mansion, and Lizzyann eased down from the old buckboard, then climbed the stone steps that led to the sweeping veranda. In a blink, she had crossed beneath the portico, and she was knocking on the door. As I watched her, it occurred to me that she and the men who were her escorts were likely friends of Morgan, or at least acquaintances, and I wondered just how much they knew about him. Had he confided in them that he was a time-traveler? Would they have believed him if he had?

I was struggling with a similar predicament of honesty with Kate. Several times already, she had asked me what I had meant about *my trip back into time*. I had given her answers that had barely dodged insulting her intelligence, and it was obvious I would not be able to avoid the subject indefinitely. If they had been her words, instead of mine, I would be equally relentless in my pursuit of a believable explanation.

I saw Isaiah open the door and allow Lizzyann inside, and I, in turn, ambled toward the barn. I busied myself mucking out the stall that was shared by the horses temporarily belonging to me and my brother, when Dent walked in, bundled up in his own new wool-lined jacket that was among the winter clothing upgrades both of us had made, including long underwear and insulated gloves.

"Mornin'," he said to me with a yawn.

"Morning," I replied.

"Boyd's damn sick," Dent informed me.

"I know."

"Hope I don't catch whatever it is he's got."

"Ditto," I said.

"The Nicodemus folks," he said glancing over his shoulder, "they been here long?"

"Just a few minutes."

"Guess they can't leave until Culver A. Headville has made them kiss his ass first."

"Seems like."

I continued to run the pitchfork through the straw, not feeling particularly social. And Dent noticed.

"You're all sunshine and cupcakes this morning."

"Sorry, got stuff on my mind, I guess."

"I get it," he said stepping over to the pen to watch me. "Looks like our friends from south of the border have lit a shuck, to quote one of Boyd's little ditties. Think Carlos and his amigos will come back?"

"Boyd thinks they will."

"I'm surprised Headville hasn't tried to get them to glean and clean a few acres of land by now," Dent said, without stating the obvious that they were eligible cactus diggers due to their darker-than-white skin pigmentation. "I don't think they'd do it. And I wouldn't blame them any."

At once a murmur of voices filtered into the barn, and one of them was the smooth baritone of our boss. Dent walked away and stood within the shadows near the doorway and peered toward the main house.

"They don't like him," Dent said softly.

"Neither do we," I replied.

Dent sauntered back. "they're scared of him, I think."

"And they should be."

Moments later, the sound of the horses and wagons pulling away scratched through the brisk air. Then I heard bootsteps and looked up to see Headville entering the barn. He stopped and studied us for a moment.

"Where's Boyd?"

"Sick," Dent told him succinctly, omitting sir, though I was not sure if it that was intentional or purely accidental.

"He's gone back to bed, sir," I promptly chimed in.

Headville looked at us as though we were fabricating a fairytale.

"Really, Mr. Headville," I added, "He's been vomiting half the night."

Headville scowled, then barked an order in a tone that warned us not to disobey. "You two, get the buckboard. We're going into town," he added, then he turned to leave without offering a please or a thank you.

So much for our day off. But I was not inclined to remind our boss of that fact, and I was relieved that Dent had also kept his mouth shut.

Then as he stepped through the wide doorway, Headville said to us over his shoulder, "the team is already in the middle paddock. Be quick about it." Then we watched as he made a right-hand turn and marched in the direction of the barn that was Sherlee's domain.

Paraphrasing Shakespeare, *something was afoot.*

"Something's up," Dent said.

"That's what I was thinking."

We went and found the two horses, one a mare, the other a gelding, that bore the regular duty of pulling the supply wagon to and from town. Dent and I quickly led the pair across to the carriage shed, and from the corner of my eye I saw Headville and Sherlee enter the northern most paddock nearest us. This barn, where foals were born, had been a busy place for the last few days.

Without dawdling, we harnessed and hitched the horses to the wagon then led them around the corral side of the colossal barn. As we passed by the bunkhouse, Oleander stepped outside, stretching his arms, and scratching himself in places where those itches would have been more politely dealt with while still privately secluded inside.

"What's goin' on?" he asked.

"Going to town, Olly," Dent told him without either of us missing a step.

"Hang on, I'll go with you."

"You weren't invited," I said more bluntly than I should have. Why I let Oleander get under my skin so quickly was a personal issue I had yet to resolve.

"Kiss my ass," Oleander snarled.

I ignored the invitation, though admittedly, I had deserved the remark, but I was not going to do any kissing in penance either. Suddenly, Headville appeared from around the corner of the great barn and headed for us. We stopped and waited for him.

"You," he said, his black Stetson nodding toward Oleander. "Saddle up. You're coming with us."

"Yes, sir!" Oleander said and I glanced at him expecting to see a subservient salute accompanying the enthusiastic affirmation. Instead, my obnoxious schoolmate smirked at me, then stuck out his tongue as though he were still the age of seven. I pivoted my eyes back to Headville, hoping he had not seen the juvenile gesture. Apparently, he had not. Instead, Headville was examining the horses, and he did not look happy.

"You didn't brush them," he said, clearly annoyed.

"We … I thought you were in a hurry, sir," Dent explained.

He glared at my brother. "My horses do not leave this ranch unless they have been properly groomed, do you understand?"

"Yes, sir," Dent said. "I'm on it," he added, hustling into the barn.

Headville returned his attention to me. His eyes were penetrating and sharp as knives. It felt as though his gaze was surgically peeling away the layers of deceit I had built as a mask to hide from him the truth of who I was and how I felt about him. Or maybe he didn't know anything, and instead he just didn't like me. And if he had in some way discerned just how fond I had become of Kate, I could understand his disdain. Especially if she reciprocated my feelings. At any rate, I stood my ground and matched his stare with as brave of a façade as I could pretend, given I was once again the subject of a mental dismantling similar to the one I had experienced yesterday. Then I watched as a sinister smile grew across the plane of his face. Shit, I thought to myself. He was on to me.

No question about it.

And in that moment, I was one-hundred percent afraid of the man.

"Uh, sir," Oleander said, unknowingly rescuing me from Headville's intangible assault on my psyche. "Today's Saturday."

"Clever boy," Headville said to him with a biting flair of mockery. "Get dressed and get on your horse. Or it will be your last Saturday," he added with unmistaken sincerity. He repointed his eyes at me just long enough to send another quiver through my bladder, then he returned to the place from whence he came.

Not Hell. But the horse barn.

Luckily, I had so far managed to keep my satirically subconscious thoughts to myself. And after a quick check, I was also pleased to find that I had not peed myself.

"Who the hell pissed in his Cheerios?" Oleander mumbled, then retreated inside the bunkhouse. He had, I hoped, wisely deduced one or both of Headville's implications.

From the barn, Dent returned with a bristle brush in one hand and a curry comb in the other. Handing me the comb, we began to thoroughly, yet expediently ply the grooming tools to the coats of the two horses that were currently harnessed from shoulder to flank and spent extra attention on their flowing manes and tails, being sure not to miss a burr or tangle. Within five minutes, I believed we had the animals looking adequately presentable. But what I thought would matter little to the man in charge, and he certainly would not be asking me my opinion.

Ten minutes later, the four of us left the ranch yard. Dent had automatically sat down in the driver's seat of the horse-drawn wagon, an unspoken reminder that between the two of us, he was a notch above me in the pecking order of our brotherhood. Seated beside him, I stared forward and watched Oleander and his horse plodding ahead of us but trailing twenty yards behind the governor of the Infinity-H branded ranch, who again had chosen Ulysses, the young black stallion, as his transportation.

And again, Oleander had belted around his waist that damn pistol. Apparently, he could not leave home without it.

CHAPTER 42

Within two miles of our exit from the Culver Headville spread, Oleander had maneuvered his horse up to ride beside our nefarious boss, and I fully expected he would be immediately reprimanded to return to his place following behind the man in black. But that did not happen. Instead, Oleander seemed to be a fitting replacement for Sherlee, who we learned was staying behind to monitor one of the most prized of Headville' mares, one that had just begun to show the early stage of labor. That announcement came as a rare bone of information Headville had decided to toss our way.

"I wish Morgan was here," I said suddenly to my brother. "I wish right now it was a year later already and we had the talisman back, and I wish we were only weeks away from getting back home, not months and months from now."

"Okay," Dent said to me, "if we're going to be rubbing the genie's bottle, why not just wish we never got sucked into this time in the first place."

I let his words soak in for several long moments. "I can't wish for that," I replied quietly.

"Of course, you can't," Dent said, and we both knew the reason why.

Kate.

"So, JT, what happens a year from now? Are you going to ditch this place without regrets, or with them?"

I waited for another long moment then told him what I had been secretly thinking of for weeks. "I'm taking her with us," I said frankly, and I meant it.

"That's nuts," Dent responded. "But I like it," he added with a mischievous grin.

Dent said nothing more. He knew me well enough to realize I had already weighed the absurdity of such a notion and had probably compiled a solid list of a dozen reasons why taking Kate with me into my time was a bad idea.

"He's on to us, Dent," I said, breaking the silence while slightly altering the subject. "He knows we're from the future."

"Why do think that?"

I thought of the JFK taunt, but that was less persuasive than my gut instinct. "I can feel it. I know how that sounds, but I do. I just know it."

"Then it must be on Olly," Dent declared, "He's said something that's let the cat out of the bag and the dumbass probably didn't even realize it."

"Maybe," I said, thinking of my own trip-up with Kate a month earlier. Several times since, she had asked me what I had meant when I told her I had been party to *a trip back into time*. I had so far avoided an out-and-out lie, but I had certainly danced around the truth. But, if I were going to take her forward into my time, I would have to tell her eventually. And when I did, would she agree to go with me, or would she just think I was crazy?

"Or maybe not," I debated my brother. "Headville is evil. Who knows, his knowledge might have gotten to him as a whisper from Satan himself."

"Olly's big mouth or a dude in long red underwear waving a pitchfork," Dent mused. "I'd say it's fifty-fifty." A minute passed. "But, so what, JT? What if Headville thinks he knows we're from the future?"

"Then he will know how we got here. He'll know we used the talisman."

"Be we don't have the talisman."

"He doesn't know that."

"Does it matter? The damn thing is laying somewhere in the bottom of the river back on our ranch. And even if he knew that, it wouldn't do him any good."

"We don't know that for sure. So, we can't tell him where it's at. Ever," I said definitively. "Under no circumstance can Headville know where to look for it. If he finds that talisman, or takes it from us, we'll never get back home."

"Then we better hope he doesn't try to drag it out of us."

"That's what I'm worried about," I said, thinking of the spectacle we had witnessed the day before. "What if he does to us what he did to that Big Pete guy? Could we be tough enough to keep our secret from him?"

"Yeah, I could," Dent said candidly. "I've still got my balls, don't you?"

"What if he tortured us, like say what those Indians did to Oleander. Would you still be able to keep your mouth shut?"

"Mmmm," Dent shuddered. "Headville wouldn't be that sadistic."

"You're naïve."

"You know me, I'd rather party today and worry about the consequences tomorrow."

"And that, big brother, is why you scare me."

Dent glanced at me preparing to laugh, but he saw that I was deeply serious. "Got it, little brother. You don't need to worry about me."

But I did.

A couple of hours later, with the railroad settlement of Hays City within our sight, we had nearly caught up with the pair of wagons that had left the ranch a good thirty minutes ahead of us. The men from Nicodemus had decent horses, but not as powerful or agile enough to outpace the horses born and breed by Culver Headville.

Hays City was as busy as usual for a Saturday, but the day had developed into an Indian Summer, warm enough that neither Dent nor I needed to wear our jackets. As the density of people began to notch swiftly upward, Headville held our group for a few moments just inside the edge of town.

"Here," he said to me, handing me a small, folded paper. "You two go to Krueger's Dry Goods and get these things. Purchase them on my account and be sure to get an itemized receipt. Is that clear?"

"Yes, sir," I said, forcing myself to exercise the level of esteem that was expected of me, though it was as false as were my grandfather's teeth.

"And then?" Dent asked, finally tagging on "Sir."

"Leave the wagon and get lost." I looked at him curiously, but he did not seem to notice. "I don't care what you do or where you go, just stay away from the mercantile."

"What about Oleander?" Dent asked.

"You let me worry about Oleander," Headville growled, and I glanced to see that our time-travel companion had looked away, ignoring eye contact with either me or my brother. "I'll meet you sometime later."

"And where will that be, sir?"

"Again, JT, the two of you do not need to worry. I will find you."

Then Headville reined the fancy black stallion around and with Oleander at his side, they melted into the fray of other riders and wagons and pedestrians all moving like ants in a jar of dirt.

"I wonder what Headville is up to?"

"Something, that's for sure," Dent agreed. "And he's got Olly mixed up in the middle of it."

Dent pulled the wagon into the traffic and headed for our explicit destination. The general store was a handsome two-story stone building on the southside of the railroad tracks, and one of the few mercantiles in town willing to do business with Negro customers.

The place was busy, and Dent had to park the wagon on the nearby side-street. I unfolded the paper Headville had given me and scanned the detailed list. Most of the items were ordinary staples: A barrel of salt, three barrels each of sugar and flour, and five one-gallon jars of molasses, and a dozen five-pound bags of coffee beans, plus a crate each of dried apples and figs. But also listed were three cases of .38 caliber bullet cartridges, and a count of twenty gallons of kerosene. That was a copious amount of fuel, but I supposed that between the main house, the barns, and the bunkhouse, there were a fair number of lanterns required to light up the evenings that were progressively growing darker.

But there were things on the list that were not so normal. And I read them to Dent.

"An enamel coffee boiler, box of cigars, premium stove polish, a castor set, whatever that is," I said feeling a little exasperated at the thought of shopping for things of which I had little knowledge. "And this, Woodworth's Ursina Bear Grease," I said turning to Dent. "What the hell is bear grease?"

"Probably that shit he puts in his hair, would be my guess."

An hour later, we had Custer Headville's personal shopping complete, including an expensive silver-plated dining table caddy with four fancy bottles we learned were typically used as containers for vinegars and oils and mustards and ground pepper and other spices, and a similarly elegant coffee pot of grey-mottled enamel that was the cream of the crop of the coffee boilers offered by Mr. Krueger. I had expressed my angst over having to choose from among several options of the household items that ranged from simple to exceedingly fancy, but Dent didn't even blink.

"Nothing but the best for Culver A. Headville."

With the goods loaded and stowed in the wagon and covered with a heavy cotton tarp, Dent and I left the rig at the mercantile as instructed and sauntered across the railroad track and into the heart of town.

We assumed we had several hours to kill, so Dent and I decided to pay John White a visit, but not until we first patronized Tommy Drum's place, taking time to indulge in a slice of deep-dish apple pie, though we were disappointed that Tommy was off-site on some errand, according to Gordy. With food in our bellies, we headed for the barbershop and found this proprietor where we expected him to be, chattering and scissor-clipping above the head of a man seated as John's current guest of honor. And as usual he had other customers lining the wall. And as was predictable, he greeted us with the brightest smile.

After exchanging pleasantries, we waited for our turn to be groomed. I procured my usual trim and shave, for which I was weeks overdue on both counts. But I didn't look nearly as unkept as Dent who had opted months ago to forfeit a haircut and at the same time see how long and scruffy- looking he could get his beard to grow. So, when he sat down in John's barber chair and asked for the works, I didn't believe he meant it, until I heard him give the barber very specific instructions.

When John White had finished with him, Dent looked completely different. Five months of unfettered hair lay on the floor, his head now trim and neat. But his face still boasted of those enviable thick walnut brown whiskers, but instead of a scraggly beard, he had a trimmed moustache and a corresponding goatee, and James Dean sideburns shaped like the profile of a boot gracing the upper portion of each cheek. If there had been a cigarette clamped in his lips, he could pass as a model for a Marlboro Man.

"Damn," Dent said, looking into the wall mirror and admiring his appearance. "I forgot how good-looking I was."

I rolled my eyes, and two seconds later, the door opened, and a towering figure of a man stepped inside. He was in his late thirties, which was twice my age, but younger than Dad, and ordinary looking, neither Dent-handsome nor mud-fence homely, just somewhere in between. But he was tall, six-six, maybe even six-seven, with broad, square shoulders and a posture that emanated with confidence and strength. And adding a flair of gusto to the man's persona was a gun holstered at his hip. If it had not been for his smile and the gentleness in his eyes that reminded me of my mom, I might have been intimidated.

"My friend, Mister Tall John!" the barber exclaimed.

The stranger glanced at me and nodded then removed his cowboy hat revealing a shock of unruly hair nearly the same sandy color as mine. Then I noticed a scar in the shape of a crescent above his left eye though barely below his hairline.

"John White!" he said, with a voice low, but brassy.

Dent stepped aside, and since we were the only four in the shop, it was easy to give the big man space. And in the customary way of the discretionary Old West, introductions without surnames were made by our jubilant barber. I shook hands with the man, noticing not just a powerful grip, but likewise a palm with a span that easily swallowed my slender digits. That said, the coincidence that the two friends shared the same first name also did not go unnoticed.

"But not John Black," the Caucasian said with a grin, and instantly John White laughed at the humor sparked by the charm of the stranger.

Then quickly, the frail Negro scuttled to the door, locked it, and flipped a sign to indicate that business hours were temporarily on hold. "Mrs. White will be so pleased to see you!" Then he merrily exited through the door that led to the living quarters behind the shop, the place where Oleander had convalesced as a patient of John White's dear wife. Within moments, she poured into the room and greeted Tall John with an enthusiastic embrace. Then seeing us, she crossed and patted our cheeks in a grandmotherly way, before taking a step backward in order to give Dent a second appraisal.

"Mr. White!" she said with a smile, "Lord have mercy, what have you gone and done?!" She said to her husband before laying her eyes on my brother for a third time. "Sure to the world this handsome man gonna get married-up with a shave like that!"

Four of us laughed, including Tall John, though unexpectedly, Dent blushed with embarrassment, something I had rarely witnessed. Then in the next moment Mrs. White backed away a few steps and paused looking at the three of us white men who stood clustered together in her husband's popular shop.

"Lordy!" she said, raising her hands to her own cheeks as her eyes darted between us. "The feelins I's gets sometimes!" And it appeared as though she were about to cry, though her dark eyes were nothing less than orbs of joy. Then she dropped her hands and turned to the man who towered an easy half-ruler above both Dent and I.

"Where you be stayin' at, Mr. John?" she asked him.

"I've got a room at the Pennsylvania," he replied. Naturally, I recognized the name of the hotel, the place where we had been robbed of a substantial amount of money that had ultimately forced us to accept employment with Culver Headville.

"Shame on you, Mr. John. You should be stayin' here with me and Mr. White! You know you are always welcome."

"I know."

"Then, you come back for dinner tonight, okay?"

As they made their plans, I was beginning to feel a pinch awkward and moderately intrusive, so I turned to Dent and suggested we leave and visit Blaine at the school. Immediately, Mrs. White invited us to join them at their table, reminding us that as friends of Morgan, we were always welcome. Then in a flicker, she left the room.

"Morgan?" asked the John who was neither White nor colored. "The grullo stallion Morgan?" he added, glancing between the two of us.

"Yes," I said. "You know him?" I asked, my curiosity heightened.

"I certainly do. We have common friends northwest of here. A little settlement called Nicodemus."

"JT, this is the friend I tell you about, who helped to settle the folks there to Nicodemus."

Ah, I thought to myself, this man then was the son of the Southern plantation owner who had once been a slave master. The Emancipation Proclamation had changed this man's and his family's livelihood, though according to John White, they had embraced the act of freedom, though it had come at great personal cost. They were undoubtedly among a fractional Southern minority who favored that outcome of the Civil War. I glanced at the man who I now felt privileged to meet. I had nothing but admiration for his respect for the new law that had been the subject of a paper I had written for history class in my junior year of high school.

"So, you know of Nicodemus, then?" the man asked.

"We've not been there," Dent replied. "Well, we've driven by—," then instantly he severed his sentence and glanced at me realizing he was about to put his foot in his mouth with a reference to a year far, far into the future. I glared at him.

"What Dent means, is there have been men from Nicodemus who have driven their wagons by the ranch where we work."

"Yep, that's what I meant," Dent said with a nod and smile.

"And who, exactly, do you work for?" Tall John asked, but his eyes told me he had already guessed.

"Culver A. Headville," Dent promptly informed him, emphasizing the initial. I glared at Dent a second time. "You've probably met the man," Dent continued, "tall dude, dark hair slick with bear grease, with blue eyes and a black heart." I just stared at my brother, my eyes blinking. He had not been drinking, but he was in rare form.

"No, I've never met him. But his reputation is … noteworthy."

"Quarter Horses. Best ones around," Dent suggested.

"Right. That's—that's what I've heard."

"In fact," I said, steering away from the uncomfortable subject of my boss, "we actually followed some of your friends from Nicodemus into town today. They're here for supplies."

"Great! I'll have to catch them!" he said, acting genuinely pleased of the convenient opportunity. "Thank you for sharing that with me."

"So," I said, taking two hats from the wall, and handing Dent the one that was his, "we have a friend to see."

"Nice to meet you," Dent said, shaking the man's hand. Then with a nod to John White, I said goodbye and stepped through the door with my brother behind me.

As we began to saunter along the boardwalk, I turned and admonished Dent with what was a third glare in the timespan of less than two minutes.

"What?" he asked innocently.

But he knew what.

As Dent and I headed for the schoolhouse, the most direct path led us to a street just one dirt road over from the mercantile where we had left the wagon. And after a two-block walk, I happened to glance in that direction just as we entered the intersection of streets and observed that an unusually large crowd had gathered outside the nineteenth-century Five and Dime. I stopped and tapped Dent on the arm. He looked in the direction I had pointed my eyes.

"That can't be good," I said.

"Any time a crowd gathers like that, there's either gonna be a fight or a naked woman just popped out of a cake."

"I'll cross my fingers for the cake," I added, concluding that the alternative could have Oleander at center stage. "You don't think—?" I asked Dent, reluctant to finish my suggestion.

"Yeah, I think," Dent replied. "Him and his damn gun."

We made an immediate left turn and headed to where we feared something was happening that was worthy of drawing a crowd of spectators. We just hoped that we were wrong, and that Oleander was not involved. As we drew near, I noticed the group was comprised of folks from all walks of life, though mostly they were men, whose masculine voices lifted in a mumble of noise as the on-lookers chattered and pointed. Then an all too familiar voice rose above the din, his cadence and tone similar to that of a suave attorney.

"Now, Bishop, the evidence is against you. It's there, in your wagon," said the voice that belonged to Culver Headville.

"No, sir, we's didn't have nuthin' to do wit it. We swears on the word of God."

"Then how do you explain why the supplies I bought and paid for are not in my wagon, but are in yours?"

Dent turned to me, and whispered, "That asshole has set them up."

"Smells that way," I said, then we cut slightly deeper through the crowd until I had a buffer of five men between me and the back of my cunning boss.

"Cain't says to you why, Mr. Headville," the Black man spoke, bewilderment filling both is voice and his eyes. "There's no sense to it."

"So, you admit, these items aren't yours?"

"No, sir, we's didn't buy any of those things," he said, pointing to the back of a wagon. I followed the direction of his finger and saw a display of items sitting at the rear of the supply transport. There was an enamel coffee pot, a silver and glass condiment caddy, a wooden box of Havana cigars, a red paper-wrapped rectangle of Rising Sun Stove Polish and a small, wide-necked jar with a label that boasted an image of a bear. Immediately I recognized the so-called exhibits of evidence as the unique items that Dent and I had purchased earlier for Culver Headville.

"Thet be alls I needs to hehr! Boy, hans in the ahr!" said another familiar voice that had once cracked a similar command for which I had been the beneficiary. I craned my neck around and there he was, standing on the far side of Headville.

Texas Jack Moody.

And then I watched as he aimed his rifle at the man from Nicodemus. Instantly, a rumble of alarm sounded throughout the crowd.

"Deputy Moody," Headville said, calmly. "There is no need for a gun. Folks could get hurt."

The twitchy little man reluctantly lowered the barrel of his weapon, but not quite low enough to eliminate the possibility of an injury should there occur an accidental squeeze of the trigger.

"Wull, theys thiefs, I needs to lock 'em up, don't ya thank?"

"Well, Deputy Moody," Culver purred. "I'm not the law, but, sadly, they should probably be arrested, for their own safety, until we can get this sorted out."

"But, Mister Headvilles, sir," the spokesman for the four men pleaded, "we's ain't done nuthin' wrong! We's didn't take nuthin' that was yours. You knows we wuddna do that, no, sir!"

"I want to believe you, Bishop, I really do," Culver said, his declaration a total sham of sincerity. "Let's just take a walk to the marshal's office and see if we can determine how such an unfortunate mistake has occurred. You trust me, don't you, Bishop?"

"Yes, sir," Bishop replied, but I could see in his dark eyes the unmistakable fear of suspicion.

"Now folks," Headville began, as he swiveled his head to address the crowd. Intuitively, I shrank back into the folds of bystanders, and Dent likewise moved with me. Quickly we ducked our heads and hurried away, hiding ourselves among the growing number of curious onlookers. Within moments, we had secreted ourselves around the corner of a building and stopped to consider our next move.

"What should we do?" I asked my brother.

"We find tall, white John, that's what we do," Dent said definitively.

Of course.

And I wondered if the crossing of our path with his had been the result of a divine coincidence.

CHAPTER 43

With haste, Dent and I covertly made our way back to John White's barbershop, and when we got there, the proprietor had reopened for business and even had a customer in his chair. But the John we were looking for, the tall one with a fair complexion, was not there.

"I am sorry, he is already gone, JT. Back to his hotel room, so he said to me," the barber answered, replying to my inquiry as to where his friend might be located.

"Thanks!" I told him.

"You have a worried face, my friend. Did something bad happen?"

I looked at the customer whose eyes studied me curiously. "No," I told him. "Nothing for you to worry about. I just have a question for him." Then I ducked back outside where Dent had waited.

"So?"

"The Pennsylvania House hotel."

We made our way to the hotel walking as quickly as we could without drawing suspicion. When we stepped inside the lobby, the man in charge didn't immediately identify who we were.

"How can I help you?" Fergus Keeler asked congenially, then in a flicker, he recognized us. "Oh, it's you. Get the hell out."

"We're looking for a man who's staying here," I said, giving the hotelman a thirteen-word description.

"His name is John," Dent added.

"John who?" Keeler asked, without seeming to really care.

"We don't know his last name," I said. "But it's important that we talk to him. Can you give us his room number?"

He scoffed. "You of all people should know better than to ask me that. How do I know you aren't gonna rob the man?"

"Didn't stop you from letting someone rob us," Dent countered.

"I didn't have a choice; he had a gun."

"I can get a gun," Dent informed him bluntly.

"Dent, that doesn't help."

Then from behind us, the entry door of the hotel opened, and I turned fearing that I would find Headville poised with a rope and sneer. But instead, it was John Whatever-His-Name.

"Hey, boys," he said upon seeing us.

"John," I said, "we need to talk to you in private. It's urgent."

John got his room key from Keeler, who fired a peevish glare at me before the three of us made our way up the stairs and entered a room. John closed the door behind us.

"What's wrong?" he asked.

Dent and I took turns filling him in with the details of what we had witnessed. We further explained to him why we thought the situation with the men from Nicodemus was a planned manipulation by our employer, Culver Headville.

"I don't think Headville intends to jail your friends permanently," I said.

"We think the asshole wants to blackmail them into working on his ranch."

"Seems to me there are better ways to recruit workers."

"Not when you want them to basically be slaves to clear away cactus and shit," Dent retorted. Then I stepped in and explained the most radical of Culver Headville's obsessions.

"I've ridden by there," John said, "I've seen the pasture, at least from the outside. It's impressive."

"So, what are we going do?" Dent asked him.

"And don't forget about Texas Jack Moody," I added. "He can't be trusted to do the right thing."

"I know Moody," the tall man reflected. "I met him a couple of years ago just after Sheriff George Bardsley appointed him to work as a deputy. I never understood that. Anyway, let me think for minute," John said, then turned and stood at the window, contemplating the situation. A few minutes passed without a word. Then at once he looked at us.

"This list of things you bought that Bishop is accused of stealing; do you still have it?"

From my pocket, I produced the list and the receipt from Krueger's Dry Goods and handed them over to him. He studied them both for a full minute.

"I have an idea. I don't know if it will work, but if nothing else, it will be unexpected."

"Sounds good so far," Dent responded. "If Headville can't see it coming, then that gives us an advantage," he added with a crisp nod. "Let's hear the rest."

Tall John smiled. "You're a feisty lad, aren't you?"

"Oh, that's an understatement," I offered. If our towering cohort only knew of the snips and snails and puppy dog tails that defined

Dent's machismo personality, he might have instead called him a gladiator.

"So," Tall John began as his eyes measured our resolve. "Here's what we're going to do."

Within just a couple of minutes, he had laid out his plan to derail Headville. And very little of it included our involvement.

"You guys need to just lay low. I've heard some interesting rumors. Culver Headville isn't liked much, or trusted. And based on what you've told me first-hand about him, it would not be in your best interests to be seen with me." Logically, Tall John made a good point. Dent and I could not risk further association with a man who was likely to become an adversary of Headville. Already, Fergus Keeler was a loose end that could one day unravel and fully bite us on the butt.

Dent immediately protested, but ultimately, we did as John suggested, and the two of us headed for the schoolhouse to wait just long enough to avoid the possibility of being found guilty by association. We arrived at the school and knocked at the back door of the living quarters. When Blaine answered our call, the expression on his face clearly conveyed that he was not happy to see us.

I looked at him quizzically.

"I've got company," he said, and then the door was promptly pulled wider, and Oleander pushed his way outside.

"Shit," I heard Dent whisper.

"Hey pussies," Oleander exclaimed. "Where the hell have you been? The boss-man wants to see you, Worm."

"What for?" I asked innocently.

"He wants that receipt."

"What receipt?" I asked, trying to buy precious seconds of time.

"I don't know. But you better have it. Mr. Headville is waiting for you to bring it to him."

"Well, he can wait five minutes," Dent interjected. "We just got here. Olly, why don't the four of us sit around and shoot the bull for little while, you know, like old times."

Oleander stared at him for a good ten seconds, then started shaking his head. "Do you think I'm stupid? You're stallin' for time, Double-D."

"Now, why would I do that?"

"Because you can't be trusted, that's why."

"That's bullshit, Olly, you know that. We're friends, remember?"

"Naw, we're not really friends, are we? Mr. Headville's showed me that. And now I see it plain as day. Let's go, Worm."

But I stood, unmoving, daring him to lay a hand on me, but expecting an assault that would lead to some pain and suffering on my part, but at least a scuffle would buy us some time.

"Now!" Oleander snarled, then casually drew his pistol in acceptance of my challenge.

"What the hell, Olly?!" Dent admonished. "Put the damn gun away!"

"Then tell your little pussy-assed brother to get the move on."

"Where to?" I asked as I turned and started walking away.

"Good girl," Oleander smirked. "The jailhouse."

"What about me?" I heard Dent ask.

"Come if you want. Mr. Headville didn't say to bring you. So, I don't give a shit one way or the other."

By the time the three of us had arrived at the business address of Texas Jack Moody, Oleander had holstered his weapon, having been persuaded to do so by Dent. Oleander was first to the door, and he opened it with a grand gesture and led the way inside. I purposely closed the door behind me, with the intent to quarantine Dent outside. I hoped that he would have worked out in his head that I needed his babysitting less than Tall John needed a heads-up upon his arrival at the headquarters of the community's questionable administrator of law and order.

I glanced around the small office area, reacquainting myself with its details and remembering that I had previously been compelled to enter the building courtesy of the threat of a rifle. Moody leaned against the edge of the desk, its wooden surface currently displaying the items that Dent and I had procured at the behest of our boss. Culver Headville sat in what should have been the deputy's seat, appearing as though he was the legal trinity of judge, jury, and prosecutor. And slumped in a chair next to the doorway that led into the room of cells, sat Bishop, worried and nervous. I assumed the others in his group were confined just beyond my field of sight, unfairly locked behind bars. Something with which I was all too familiar.

"It's about time, Oleander," Headville said coolly.

"Sorry, Mr. Headville, I had to wait a while. But you were right, they came to the school."

"Oleander said you needed the receipt?" I asked Headville casually, beating him to the reason for my summons.

"Ha!" Oleander blurted. "So, you do know what he wanted after all, you slimy little jackass."

Headville glanced between me and Sedgwick, but I evaded eye contact while I dug the hand-written form from my pocket and offered it to him.

"Is there a problem?" I asked. "We got everything you wanted, I'm sure," I added, pretending not to know the subterfuge of the cooly composed man in black.

Headville took the paper from me and carefully studied it, then handed it to the deputy.

I watched as Moody's eyes roamed aimlessly over the paper.

"The castor set, the coffee boiler, stove polish, the jar of Woodworths', and my box of cigars," Headville said to Moody, as though he were instructionally reciting the items. Oddly, I thought of the cigars and realized I had never once seen the man smoke. But then, who knew what went on in the privacy of his home?

"Uh, yeah, yeah, thet's right," Moody said, hesitantly, "Uh, kester set, an a, uh—coffee pot—

"Boiler," Headville corrected, before the deputy continued his recitation.

"Ceegars—"

Then suddenly the front door opened, and Tall John stepped inside. I glanced at Headville and saw his eyes flash with irritation. Across from me, I watched as Bishop lifted his posterior two inches from the chair, his eyes instantly glimmering with hope.

"This is a private conference," Headville informed John. "Deputy Moody and I are in the middle of resolving an issue. You'll need to wait outside," he added, delivering the same smile he had first introduced to me some four months earlier. "Please," Headville added for good measure, and I could only imagine how difficult that had been for him.

Without being too obvious, I eased back and stood near the wall next to Oleander, worrying that he might rationalize the need to rise up and answer an ill-conceived call of duty and brazenly produce his revolver again. After all, he was pinch-hitting for Willard Sherlee.

"The middle, you say?" John asked rhetorically, then smiled. "Good, then I'm in time to clear up the matter without any further erroneous accusation."

My employer stared at the stranger who had boldly invited himself to what was effectively Headville's private party. With bated breath, I studied his face and vaguely perceived a slight movement of his mouth and lips, and I wondered if he was gently biting his tongue. "Perhaps I didn't make myself clear, this is a confidential—"

"Deputy Moody," John interrupted as he handed to Texas Jack a paper form that twinned the size and shape of the one already in his possession, "these things you have here on your desk, they're mine. That's my receipt from Krueger's Dry Goods. The coffee boiler, the cigars, all of it, itemized right there. I bought them earlier and stowed them in my friend Bishop's wagon. He wasn't around at the time, but I knew he wouldn't mind. Naturally, when I heard of this ridiculous arrest, I rushed over to set the record straight," he added, fixing his eyes on Headville. "With evidence, of course," John said with a smile that was as genuine as Culver Headville's had been fake.

"That's not possible," Headville politely countered, but his eyes were seething.

"It's a receipt," John said with an edge of sarcasm, as he began to subtly lecture Headville. "It lists all these things on the deputy's desk that my friend Bishop has been accused of stealing. Go on, Deputy, tell this fine, upstanding citizen what's on—oh, wait," John paused then glanced at Moody, "I forgot, you can't read, can you, Jack?"

The ambushed deputy sputtered a couple of incoherent words, and I watched as his eyes pinged between Headville and John. Suddenly John turned to me, and I felt a flutter of nerves quiver against my bladder. I prayed that I would not dribble.

"You, kid," he said to me, "Can you read? Or are you with this gentleman?"

"I'm with him," I said nodding to Headville.

"I see. Well, that wouldn't make you impartial, would it?" Thankfully, he did not wait for me to answer, adding "Hold on, I've got an idea."

At once, John maneuvered his towering six and a half feet to the door and opened it and leaned his head out. "Hey, sir!" he called suddenly. "Yes, you, come here for a moment, will you? We need an impartial witness." Then as though he were practicing the dance of the Cotton-Eyed Joe, John took a quick step outside through the door, and then with an equally expedient move, he stepped back into the room bringing with him a man around the age of thirty. With awkward hesitation, the young man crossed the threshold, though I imagined the strength of John's powerful hand grasping his elbow had been persuasive.

"What's your name?" John asked the man who was dressed as though he were a bartender at one of the swankier gambling halls in town.

"Sid," he replied.

"So, Sid, would you read out loud, the items on this list please?"

"Okay," he agreed though he looked thoroughly confused. "Enamel Coffee Boiler, Rising Sun Stove Polish, Woodsworth's Bear Grease, Box of Havana Cigars, Eastlake Silver-Plated Castor Set."

"Thank you, Sid."

"Sure. But I gotta go. I need to get to my job."

"Of course," John said extending his hand toward the doorway. Without hesitation, Sid scooted outside, and John closed the door behind the young man. "So," John continued, turning to Moody, "like I said, those things are mine. And since I was the one who put them in my friend Bishop's wagon, he couldn't possibly be accused of stealing them, could he, Deputy Moody?"

"Wull … uh … uh … I—I s'pose not," he said glancing at Headville, who looked at no one but the man who had just foiled his plot.

"Good. Then, Jack, please release Bishop and the others. They have a long drive ahead of them. And it will now be a delayed journey, thanks to this unsubstantiated inconvenience."

At once, Moody clambered to his feet and taking a ring of keys from a desk drawer, he exited to the back.

"Sorry for the mix-up," John said to Headville, whose face was surprisingly subdued, though I knew he had to be boiling inside. "I hope you find your things," he added as he picked up the box of cigars. Then he paused for a moment and smiled at Headville. "You know, on second thought, just to show you there's no hard feelings, I'll let you keep these items for yourself," John added returning the cigars to the table.

I was in awe of the performance. If this place had been a theatre, John would have easily earned a standing ovation.

In the next moment, the three incarcerated men from Nicodemus entered the room and Tall John opened the door for them, and they, along with Bishop, quickly and quietly filed through it.

"What is your name, if I may ask?" Headville said calmly and distinctly, his voice sugared with false amicableness.

"Name's John."

"John—what?"

"Just John. Out here in the West, it's considered bad manners to ask a man his last name. Best to be courteous and wait and see if he wants to tell you himself."

"Then for your future reference, John," Headville cooed politely, "my name is Culver Headville."

John paused for an instant and shot Headville a glance. "I didn't ask," he said, then stepped outside, closing the door behind him. Suddenly, I wondered how things might have gone differently if Sherlee had been there.

Oleander and I stood against the wall, waiting. I for one, had no plans to speak unless spoken to, and I doubted that even Oleander would be dumb enough to say anything to our boss who had just had his ass handed to him. But with Sedgwick, you never knew. A minute ticked by, then Headville rose to his feet and crossed to Texas Jack Moody and leaned into his face.

"You have just lost your job," Headville told him icily, his tone solidly making the threat sound like a promise. Then he crossed by the desk, and without any warning Headville swiped his arm across the topside, scattering the items noisily onto the floor.

Yep, I thought. Culver Headville was royally pissed.

Then like a fool, Oleander jostled across the small room and stooped to begin picking up the remnants of Headville's fury.

"Leave it, you stupid boy," then he stepped outside, and Oleander and I followed him.

Twenty minutes later, we were leaving town. Dent and I leisurely navigating the horse-drawn wagon. Oleander and Headville galloping northward ahead of us.

By the time we arrived at the ranch, I had of course recounted to Dent every detail and every word spoken inside the jailhouse. Dent cussed with disappointment for having missed the spectacle, but he reveled in the knowledge that he and I and the man we knew only as Tall John had thwarted Headville's plan to subjugate the men from Nicodemus. At least, for now.

My fear, however, was what wrath would Headville subject us to in the hours or days, or even weeks to come. I doubted he would take defeat with a casual win-some-lose-some temperament.

Immediately upon our arrival at the ranch, we unloaded the food supplies at the back door of the house, Isaiah allowing us to step inside the palatial Headville domicile just far enough to place the barrels upon the floor and to set the crates and the sacks upon a bench that sat against the wall of the enclosed porch. Before I left, I noticed as an adjacent room, hardly larger than a closet, its door propped open revealing a small bed, neatly topped with a gray blanket and a thin pillow. Isaiah's bedroom, I wondered. Apparently, he was not favored with second floor sleeping quarters.

The kerosene, we stored in the barn along with the bullet cases. And by the time we had gotten the horses unhitched and brushed and returned to their place in the paddock, dusk was settling into the shallow valley. Other than Isaiah, we had seen no one, though when we had first returned to ranch headquarters, there was audible evidence that there were inhabitants in the bunkhouse. A warbling of voices peppered with a chorus of hoots and hollers met our ears and amalgamated pleasantly with the unbridled laughter of the vaqueros, whose horses we had discovered were once again at home in the barn.

Boyd had been right. They did come back, apparently getting what they wanted in town. I could easily imagine that the gaiety of the party was due to a crude game of charades as the Mexicans conveyed the details of their illicit conquests. Though a half-hour later, the revelry had ended. When we stepped inside the bunkhouse, we found Boyd sitting at the table nursing a cup of coffee, and not appearing a bit better than he had looked in the earlier hours of the morning. Mick lay on his bed, reading another dime novel, and he smiled and nodded at us, then did a double take with Dent.

"Look who got a haircut," he said approvingly. "Looks good."

"That's what folks keep telling me!" Dent said smiling as though he were fishing for another compliment. But instead, Mick returned his eyes to his book, apparently more interested in the written word as opposed to those spoken with shameless conceit.

On the far side of the room were the merry Mexicans, and Pete who seemed to be the only remaining member of their captive audience. However, one who belonged to our pack was suspiciously missing.

Oleander Sedgwick.

"Where's Olly?" Dent asked, and I could sense he was concerned.

"Ain't seen him," Boyd said weakly.

"I have," Mick volunteered. "Saw him ride in with Mr. Headville. They got here just after this tall fella left with Lizzyann."

"A Tall dude?" Dent asked, feigning his actual knowledge of whom Mick referred. Then Mick described him, and the horse he had ridden on.

Good, I thought. John had wasted no time trekking to the ranch in order to escort Lizzyann to her home in Nicodemus. And as planned, he had sent Bishop and the others directly to their settlement. That part of Tall John's strategy clearly proved he cared about the welfare of the isolated Black community.

Without question, Bishop and the others needed all the friends they could get, and with Tall John in their corner, they clearly had an alliance they could count on.

CHAPTER 44

Later in the evening, Isaiah brought dinner, accompanied by Sherlee and Headville's newest yes-man, Oleander. Pushed into a disappointing conclusion that Sedgwick had become a turncoat, I kept the accusation to myself and asked nothing about where he had been. And given that Headville's right-hand man was in our presence, neither did I expect Oleander to offer an explanation. Throughout dinner I furtively watched our wayward comrade and based upon his body language and the absence of his otherwise boisterous personality, I decided that it was unlikely he would tell us anything. Considering his words and actions, Oleander had gotten himself into Headville's pocket, for better or worse. But was the coalition voluntary on Oleander's part, or had he been coerced? Or bribed?

The meal ended without any mention of what had happened in Hays City, but neither had anyone asked. Dent and I were both glad to avoid the subject. Tall John had purposely and perfectly staged our alibis, so we hoped we could profit by being above suspicion. Still, it was going to be awkward enough to interact with Headville given I had witnessed what had to have been a humiliating defeat. But I would not have been surprised if Dent and I were to be summoned to an interrogation, though to assume that we had a hand in the foiling of Headville's plot would have required our boss to give us credit for being smarter than he, and that, I felt certain, was something the man would never admit.

I welcomed Saturday's bedtime, wholly ready to put the day's events behind me. And before I knew it, three days of the week had rolled by, and I had seen Headville on numerous occasions, but not once had he acted as though he was bothered or embarrassed by anything in the least. Good for him, I thought, but better for me. And for Dent.

However, when Thursday morning arrived, I discovered that not everything was as rosy as I had hoped. When I opened my eyes, Boyd had already lit the lantern on the table, and across the room I discovered that Oleander was up earlier than normal. I watched as he stepped into his boots, strapped on his beloved gun, and began to stuff his bedroll into one compartment of his saddlebag.

Oleander Sedgwick was moving out of the bunkhouse.

But going where?

I sat up, then saw that Boyd was at the wood stove, pouring a cup of coffee.

"Want some?" he asked me.

"Sure," I said, looking at him intently. I then nodded toward Oleander, subtly questioning the foreman. Boyd glanced at Sedgwick, then shifted his eyes back to me and shrugged with genuine ignorance.

"Where are you going?" I said, not worrying about waking any of the others.

Oleander looked my way and smiled, saying nothing.

Then across from me, Dent sat up from his cot and swung his feet over the edge of the bed, taking in the scene.

"Olly? What the hell are you doing?" Dent asked him.

"None of your damn business, Tescott." Rarely had Oleander referred to my brother as anything other than Double D.

"Why so pissy?"

"I said, it ain't none of your business."

"Then you can kiss my ass," Dent declared, standing up as though he was preparing to fight.

A wordless quiet filled the room, but around us, Little Pete and Mick had roused awake, and at Oleander's end, the vaqueros had become alert and one by one they rose to their feet. Then Oleander strode toward Dent and I, pausing to smirk at the two of us. Then he raised his right hand and flipped Dent the bird, inches from his face.

Dent's eyes flickered and his elbow cocked backward as he prepared to throw a spontaneous, and angry, right hook. Quickly, I pushed my hand against his chest, "Don't do it," I begged him, praying he would not allow himself to be suckered into a confrontation with Oleander. Dent jerked his arm but didn't manage to move his fist forward more than an inch. Then from the corner of my eye, I saw Mick standing close behind Dent, and I looked and found that the young cowboy had my brother restrained at his elbows.

"And that," Oleander said, pivoting his offensive finger toward me, "goes double for you, Worm," he added, as he paired the first hand with a similarly posed left hand, apparently forgetting the fact that he was missing the appropriate digit. Then in the next second, he poked into my chest one of the fingers the Indian had not taken from him. I held back. He wanted me to start something, but why now, I had no idea. Then Oleander grinned and laughed before crossing to the door. He lifted his hat from a wall peg and sat it down over his shock of red hair. "See ya 'round, pussies." And then he was gone.

Dent pulled away from Mick and stepped within the open doorway and filled its space, watching. Several moments ticked by. "You gotta be kidding me," Dent whispered.

"What is it?"

"That—that—"

"Peckerhead," Boyd said, offering to fill in the blank.

"Yeah, that peckerhead just waltzed right into the big house."

Oleander, then, had been expected.

A half hour later, with breakfast under our belts, Boyd and Dent and I stepped out onto the bunkhouse porch, just as Sherlee appeared from beyond the great barn mounted upon his horse but leading two others. Headville's black stallion and Oleander's sandy dun mare, both saddled and ready for riders.

The three of us watched as Sherlee crossed to the house, and as if on cue, Headville and Oleander exited the front door, paraded down from the stone steps and climbed into their respective saddles. None of the three men looked our way, purposely ignoring our speculative countenances, just as Oleander and Sherlee had similarly boycotted sharing breakfast with us. Obviously, our societal ranking at the ranch was not worth even a glance.

From the porch of the bunkhouse, Boyd, Dent, and I watched as the less scrupulous trio of men trotted their horses from the ranch yard, heading west along the road.

It was an ominous moment. I just didn't understand why.

The day came and went, and it was otherwise uneventful. I had, however, stolen the chance to knock at the backdoor of the limestone mansion where I engaged in a brief conversation with Isaiah. I had a favor to ask of him, and with a grin, he promised to oblige me. Then, after a little bit of begging, I convinced Isaiah to tell Kate I was there and that I needed to talk to her. Luckily, Isaiah liked me, as opposed to the ill-feelings of Beverly Carneiro.

"Kind of late, isn't JT?" she asked me with a smile that could melt away any gloom of discontent.

"Is it?"

"Unless you're here to court?" she asked, switching her expression to one that dared me to say either yes or no.

"I was just in the neighborhood."

"You're avoiding my question. Culver's not here, you know. I could invite you in. There would be supervision, of course."

"Not that I wouldn't love to spend time with you and Miss Carneiro, but I'd rather just live a few years longer, if I could."

Kate laughed. And then I told her why I was there.

The next day dawned and the eight of us remaining ranch hands, along with our foreman, began the arduous task of gathering hay from the barn loft and loading it onto the long flatbed wagons that were utilized daily for the feeding of the range horses and the cattle. It was a cold morning, our breath wafting from our mouths in moist coils of personalized fog.

Weeks earlier, we had brought in the cows and the few remaining heifer calves, and the yearlings born from the previous season, and had collected them into the southeasterly quadrant of pasture that had been purposely vacated during the growing season in order to naturally reserve the untouched grass for the lean winter ahead. Additionally, the location was not only a more convenient arrangement for caring for the livestock but was also a more efficient way to dispense the supplemental winter feed stored in the loft of the great barn. But still, it took us hours to care for the hundreds of animals on the Headville ranch. It was easy to pine for the months that shaped the seasons of spring and summer when grass grew plentifully and thus diminished our hands-on responsibilities in the occupation of animal husbandry.

As normal, Boyd and Pete and one pair of the vaqueros took one wagon full of hay to the horse pasture while Carlos and I and his crooked-toothed amigo named Ramon drove the second wagon into the pasture of cattle. Maneuvering a smaller wagon laden with a set of buckets containing a mixture of oats and ground corn, Mick and Dent headed for the smaller pasture where the twelve herd bulls were sequestered. So far, the beefy patriarchs had not needed hay since the grass there had also been off limits during the grazing season. However, the honored genetic donors were pampered with the supplement of grain.

Shortly, my brother and his partner joined me and my team of Hispanic cowboys, and the five of us doled out the cured grass and returned to the barn for a second load of hay.

Then the morning was gone, followed by an afternoon of piddling around and working hard to look busy. Finally, evening had arrived, and still there had been no sign of Oleander or Headville or the ranch wrangler, Mr. Sunshine Sherlee.

Something was keeping them in town, I just hoped it had nothing to do with my new friend, Tall John. Silently, I assuaged my worry with the knowledge that he had proven that he was more than capable of taking care of himself. Besides, as far as Dent and I knew, John could already be long gone.

The cold of the day pushed us into the bunkhouse a little earlier than normal, and Boyd was quick to stoke the woodstove and had managed to coax a roasting fire by the time Isaiah arrived with our supper meal. When he entered with the covered basket, I glanced at him, my eyes seeking confirmation and Isaiah indulged me with a covert nod and smile. A few moments later, with the food on the table and the nine of us hungry cowpokes gathered upon the set of long benches, I felt a nudge from Isaiah, and intuitively I opened my hand and felt the small, cloth-wrapped package secretly touch my palm. I wrapped my fingers around its softness, then casually stood and went and slipped the appreciated fulfillment of my humble requisition into the pocket of my coat.

I decided then, that I would have to think of something special I could do for Isaiah to express my gratitude.

Later, I went outside and sat on the porch, retreating as usual from the cigarette smoke that boiled like chimney stacks from Boyd and all four of the Mexicans. And as was also customary, Dent joined me.

For a few moments, I was quiet, gazing up at the stars.

"What ya thinkin' about little brother?"

"You."

"Me? Why?"

"I got you something," I said, pulling the soft gift from my pocket and handing it to him.

"What's this?" he asked, taking it.

"Birthday cake. I arranged for Isaiah to make it for you. It's just a small one, enough for two."

Dent was quiet for a moment. "Thanks, brother," he offered, his voice soft, but his appreciation legitimate. "Man, I feel stupid. I didn't even realize. I don't keep up with the days of the month like you do."

"The big one-nine," I said. And then quiet fell upon us again. He said nothing for a moment and finally I turned to look at his profile and I saw a faint glint of light flicker upon a tear that slid from his eye. Instantly, my own eyes welled.

"You're thinking of Mom, aren't you?" I asked him.

Dent nodded. We both knew this would have been a difficult day for her.

"We've been gone four months, JT."

"One-hundred and forty-two days to be exact," I informed him.

At once, my brother began to shudder. "She's probably cried her eyes out every single day," he sobbed, as tears trekked down his cheeks, racing against an anguished string of snot dripping from his nose. Through the misty veil of my own heartache, I dropped my blurry gaze toward the ground as I placed my arm around him. "And you know what the worst part is? She might be thinking we left her on purpose!"

"She won't think that, Dent," I assured him, my own voice beginning to crack. "Dad might, but not Mom."

Dent laughed, and I was glad my attempt to lighten the mood had succeeded. "Yeah," he agreed, though we both knew better. "But then, you did say some mean things to him that night, remember?"

I nodded. I remembered. I had said to him that I was damn glad I was nothing like him.

"You didn't mean it," Dent said to me.

"No, I didn't," I whispered.

"He knows that," Dent reassured me and in the next second I was the one leaking from my eyes and my nose, praying that my brother was right.

We sat quietly for a few moments while we pulled ourselves together and belted on our big-boy britches. And because nothing else needed to be said, I took the package from his hand and unwrapped it, and the two of us somberly shared a few minutes enjoying Isaiah's cake, as I silently slipped away into my memories of other birthdays and celebrations with our mom and our dad.

"Makes me crave Mom's chocolate chip cookies," Dent said with reminiscence.

"Nobody makes those better than her," I said, giving him my two cents.

Both of us picked at the dessert slowly, working to make it last more than what could have easily been two bites each. When it was gone, Dent turned and affectionately punched my shoulder.

"Thanks, again," he said. "Really, I appreciate it."

"I was going to throw you a party," I said suddenly, breaking away from the sentimental melancholy. "Like the one you did for me, you know, a few months back," I added, grinning.

"Sure, you were!" Dent laughed. "But that's okay. I'm starting to think that maybe I drank too much anyway."

I looked at him. "So, it took a ride with the Burmano-Ku-Partika to figure that out?"

"Kiss my ass," he said to me, as though I hadn't heard that before.

The next day was Friday, and there had still been no sign of our boss or Sherlee. On the other hand, Oleander's packing had implied that he would not be returning in the near future, so I had abandoned the expectation that he would show his face any time soon. However, I would have given my eye teeth to know what he was up to. Boyd, though, was glad he was gone, and understandably so. But he was also getting concerned. From him we learned that Headville often disappeared for days, sometimes weeks at a time, occasionally taking Sherlee, but more often than not leaving him behind. But Boyd had always been kept in the loop.

Except this time.

By noon, all three of us were fidgety, and so I suggested to Boyd that he send Dent and I into town on an errand, some ruse or excuse that would be believable in the event we were caught. He was reluctant at first, but then he warmed up to the idea.

"S'pose I got sick agin, and be shore-for in need of some sort a tonic to git me over it? Make some bit of sense if I was to send you boys into town for it."

"Sounds reasonable," I assured him.

"Think you could fake it?" Dent asked.

"Won't be no fakin' it. I be already sick to my stomach just thinkin' bout it." A few minutes later, Boyd put on a scowl of nausea and coughed and gagged a few times before giving Mick and Pete instructions pertaining to an errand of their own with the intention to occupy them without their knowledge of our secret mission.

"You two boys saddle up and check on the windmills and the water tanks. Make shore-for they ain't sprung no leaks. And while you be at it, go do a look-see 'cross the far ends of the pastures. Just in case."

"Case of what?" Little Pete asked.

"I dunno. Just look around!" Boyd grumbled impatiently. "Maybe Mr. Headville or Sherlee is up there somewhares hurt or somethin'. Ever think of that?"

"Why would they be up there?" Pete said, questioning the foreman for a second time.

"I dunno! Just do what I tell ya and by gum don't be askin' me no more dumb questions! Can't you tell I'm sick?" he added before faking another cough and gag.

As soon as our co-workers were mounted and heading north, Dent and I saddled up and began our journey to Hays City.

When we were less than a half-mile away from town, a rider appeared on the main road at the city's north edge, urgently heading in our direction. A quarter mile later, both horse and rider were near enough to be recognized.

It was Blaine and Buck.

"What are doing out here?"

"Coming to see you guys. I dismissed class a bit early."

"Something wrong?" I asked, naturally ignoring the obvious.

"You might say that. There's been a lot of chatter and gossip going on. Mostly, I only know what I've picked up from the kids. But one of the parents brought by a load of coal for our heating stove, and he confirmed a rumor I overhead one of my students yammering about."

"So, what is it?" Dent asked impatiently.

"It's Oleander."

"Big surprise," I said.

"What about Olly? What's he done?"

"Nothing he's done, specifically."

"Then what?"

"He's been appointed the new deputy sheriff."

We stared at Blaine, both Dent and I surely looking like a pair of deer caught in headlights.

Neither of us had seen that one coming.

CHAPTER 45

laine knew very few details about how Oleander had been chosen to be the replacement for Texas Jack Moody. But I would have bet my 1970 Ford F-150 pickup that Culver Headville was responsible for the appointment. Though how he had managed it was the sixty-four-dollar question, to quote Boyd. However, we were acquainted with a certain popular businessman who through his clientele was well-connected and would likely be knowledgeable of all news-worthy events occurring in town. But Dent and I both conceded that we should not get John White involved in our inquiries. Instead, there was one other who met the same criteria. And we decided we would go to him for answers.

Tommy Drum.

We sent Blaine back to his school, deciding that the two of us Tescott brothers could maneuver through town less conspicuously than three, besides, it was best for Blaine to keep his distance from us in the event things went south. Then Dent and I headed for our first stop, carefully making our way to the grocery operated by R.W. Evans. Surprisingly, his store provided an extensive selection of food choices, items that were shipped in by train, but also fresh milk and eggs and butter and when in season were offerings of perishable fruits and vegetables presumably raised locally by farmers and gardeners, most of whom I guessed to be Volga German immigrants.

The store had a reasonable selection of drinks and tonics suitable for the treatment of gastro-intestinal disorders, coughs, and sniffles, and for those consumers inclined to try anything, sanitized tapeworm pills: A treatment for women touted as *the most effective way to banish fat and still eat like a man.*

Our shopping eventually led us to discover that the structure was also home to the official post office, a small space carved out of a far corner of the long, narrow building. A countertop display advertising postal cards caught my attention, and I picked one of the three-by-five-inch cards from the stack and examined it.

Unlike the modern postcards from my time that typically featured a souvenir photo on one side and a place to write a message on the opposite face, these were uniformly beige in color, entirely plain on both sides except for a one-cent stamp impression in the upper right corner profiling the Goddess of Liberty and an ornately designed icon denoting US POSTAL CARD and the phrase *NOTHING BUT THE ADDRESS CAN BE PLACED ON THIS SIDE.*

Inexplicably, I felt inclined to buy one.

"Excuse me, how much is this?" I politely asked the clerk who stood with his back to me. He turned away from his task and glanced at the item in my hand, then gave me a look as if to say he was unamused.

"One penny," said the middle-aged man whose pinstriped vest matched the streaks of grey within his black hair that lay combed backward over his scalp and looked to be as brittle as candied sugar. For a second, just out of curiosity, I considered asking him if his hair gel happened to be Woodworth's Ursina Bear Grease.

"No charge for the card?" I asked, instead. Again, he looked at me as if he thought I was trying to pull his leg.

"Nope."

"Cool," I replied, deciding to give him a sample of the vernacular from 1979. "Are these pretty popular?" I asked him, laying a coin on the counter. I had not realized postcards had been around for as long as a hundred years, at least relative to my time zone.

"Too popular, if you ask me," the clerk said shaking his head and loosening his tongue. "And not at all private. Some folks will write anything on them. Once a lady wrote to her sister describing a quarrel she had with her husband."

"You're right, they aren't private at all," I concurred with a brassy edge of sarcasm.

"My wife's mother posts them to us from back east. Sends my Millie recipes. All the time. Like she don't already know how to cook?"

"Weird," I agreed, teasing him with another word from my era, though he didn't seem at all intrigued.

"Just a new thing the government come up with, but they won't last. I expect another year or two and folks will go back to letters with envelopes."

"You're probably right," I told him, though I knew he was completely wrong and felt mischievously inclined to enlighten him of that fact. "So, are you the proprietor?"

"Nope, that would be my dad," he said with a nod in the direction behind me. I turned and saw Dent engaged with an older gentleman who appeared to be three times more hospitable than the man in front of me. "Same initials, though," he added without much enthusiasm.

"Ah," I said, then smiled. "Well, RW, I'm JT. My folks couldn't give me my own name either."

He opened his mouth as if he might laugh, but he asked me a question instead. "Exactly, where are you from?"

"You'd be surprised," I told him before wishing him a good day.

I tucked the postcard into my pocket and rejoined Dent. When we finally left the establishment of R.W. Evans, we had purchased a couple of bottles of what the elder Mr. Evans promised to be the most suitable for the gut and the bowels, treatments that would be reasonable for Boyd to take to cure his ghostly illness, should we get caught in town by Headville or Sherlee. Or by Deputy Oleander Sedgwick.

Our second destination was the livery owned and managed by Dub O'Brien. If we were going to traipse about town as stealthily as possible, we needed to ditch our horses, especially Viento since he tended to catch a lot of notice with or without me. Even Dub seemed glad to see the grullo stallion, though he was hardly interested in giving neither Dent nor I the time of day. But still he agreed to board the horses short-term for a few hours, though something was obviously troubling him.

As we were leaving to head for destination number three, Tommy Drum's Saloon, a thought occurred to me.

"Say, Dub," I began, waiting for a moment to get his full attention. "Have you heard anything about the new deputy?"

"That blarney-ass friend of yours?" he asked me, his eyes narrowing. "Can't say that I like him." Apparently, Dub remembered Oleander from his embarrassing first encounter with the ill-fated roan mare.

"That's him," I said with a nod. "What's the story there, do you know?"

"Aye. Bardsley was a good friend of mine."

"Bardsley? What does the sheriff have to do with our jackass friend?" Dent asked.

"Nothin' far as I know." But Dub's previous use of a past tense raised a flag.

"Then what about your friend, Sheriff Bardsley?" I asked.

"Texas Jack killed him, that's what!" he replied, spitting nails.

"I thought that the sheriff was gone somewhere on business?"

"Aye, lad, that's what we all thought. Moody told anybody who would listen to him that Bardsley rode down to San Antone with a prisoner, some no-name a Texas Ranger wanted to lay his fists on. Seemed right. Bardsley had done that before."

"But you think Jack Moody murdered him?"

"Appears so! Bardsley's badge was found in his pocket. Wasn't any reason why Moody should have that unless the scallywag took it off him. And Bardsley would no'ave given it to him. He'd be dead before he'd hand over that bloody badge."

"Who found the badge in Moody's pocket?" I asked him.

"His high and mighty—Culver Headville."

And there it was.

"When was this, Dub?" Dent asked, casting me a glance that said he shared my suspicion that the date would be two days earlier.

"Wednesday."

Bingo.

"So, then what happened?"

"The County Judge was sent for, and he declared the evidence to be as plain as the nose on the deputy's face, so he jailed Moody there on the spot, least that's what I heard. And before you can bat an eye, that holier-than-thou judge appoints that mouthy friend of yours as temporary deputy." Dub added, shaking his head. "Far as I'm concerned, he's a'no different than Moody was. But what the judge says is what goes."

I again heard the use of the past tense, but I assumed Dub meant it in reference to being a former deputy.

"So, Moody's waiting for a trial then?" Dent asked.

"Not anymore, he's not."

"Then where is he?"

"Boot Hill. Hanged himself in the wee of the night. And good riddance," Dub added before walking away, leaving us to chew on the information.

"Convenient," Dent said glancing at me.

We left the livery and five minutes later we slipped into Tommy Drum's restaurant and bar. Since it was a weekday and, in the afternoon, the patronage of the saloon was thin, with only one table occupied by a pair of men who looked to be bankers, but no one was at the bar. Tommy looked up as we entered and gave us a nod. We met him at the counter.

"Haven't seen you boys for a while. What can I get you?"

"Information," I answered him hopefully.

"Nothing to drink or eat?"

"We're short on time," I told him.

"What's new?" he said smiling.

"Sorry. Next time, okay?"

"Right. I bet I know what you're here about. Moody and your hamburger friend."

"Exactly."

Tommy motioned for us to follow him, and he led us to a small room isolated just off the hall behind the bar. We told him what Dub O'Brien had shared with us and he confirmed that it was the same story he had heard. But he also had additional details, beginning with the fact that it was widely believed that the judge was deep in Headville's pocket, and would do whatever the influential rancher would ask of him. Including the appointment of Oleander as acting deputy. And, since I had personally heard Headville tell the deputy himself that he would have his job, it was evident that he had meant it. But would he really kill Texas Jack Moody just because the swashbuckling Tall John had convinced him to release the incarcerated men from Nicodemus?

No, Headville would not have gotten his hands dirty. But Sherlee would have done it. I just hoped Oleander had not been bullied into taking part in Moody's murder, if it was murder. It could have been suicide, but like Dent had said, that was convenient. Too convenient.

"So, Moody's death? Any speculation on that, or is it a cut and dried suicide?" I asked.

"Maybe. The judge has ordered an inquest. My feelings are the formal proceeding is only meant to be a dog and pony show. It's set for tonight at seven o'clock."

"Why so late?"

"The judge wants a specific panel of jurists. Frank Jessup is one but he's on a bereavement call over east of Victoria. He's a Presbyterian preacher, and most of the folks over there are Catholic, but some Protestant farmer died, and Reverend Jessup is conducting the funeral. Can't make it back until seven."

That situation was a Godsend. Frank Jessup had unknowingly bought me and Dent time to return to the ranch without being missed by Headville or Sherlee. Both of them, I was sure, would be giving testimony at the inquest, though I would not be surprised if Sherlee were also a co-member of the jury.

"Who else is on the inquest panel?" I asked.

"Orville Bascom. He's a school board trustee."

I was distantly acquainted with him. Another Culver Headville yes-man, I suspected.

"And, unfortunately, I'm the third member," Tommy informed us, and he was clearly unhappy about it.

"Ah," I said. "Why you?"

"I'm an upstanding, law-abiding businessman, haven't you heard?" he said smiling. "Mine and the opinions of my distinguished colleagues would satisfy the citizenry and close the case quickly and quietly, I suppose."

"So long as you bought the story that Moody had killed the sheriff for his job and then hung himself out of guilt," Dent suggested. "So do you?"

"I will not render my opinion until I've heard the testimony and have examined the evidence. That's the responsible thing to do, though I can't speak for the other two."

"Good to hear," Dent said. "JT and I might need your unbiased judgement one day soon."

He studied us with an expression of both concern and curiosity. "I hope the two of you aren't looking for trouble?"

"No," Dent replied. "But with Olly as the flippin' deputy, trouble will be coming for us."

We thanked Tommy for his time, and after a quick reconnaissance of the street, we stepped outside.

"JT, why the hell would Headville want Olly to be the acting deputy?"

"You're guess is as good as mine. But I'd bet money Oleander will be played like a puppet," I said glancing down the boardwalk, seeing that the coast was clear.

"Wild Bill, looky there!" Dent softly exclaimed.

I swept my eyes left and then right again, searching for one of the three men we were keen to avoid.

"Where?"

"Over there," Dent nodded, and I glanced at him to determine the direction I needed to focus my attention. Within seconds, I saw him, but it was not who I expected.

Tall John.

He was seated in a wagon, flicking the reins of a hitched pair of Mutt and Jeff horses, one an exceptionally tall, athletic looking dark chestnut and the other a shorter, but stoutly built animal sporting a dull white coat and a greyish mane. Trying not to appear interested, I watched as they rolled across the railroad tracks and passed within a hundred feet of where Dent and I stood shadowed beneath the canopy of the saloon's open porch. Then Dent casually eased himself two doors down before stopping at the corner, with me close behind.

For a moment we watched as the wagon moseyed along, its deep-sided bed teeming with lumber though a portion of the cargo was covered with a tarpaulin protecting what I assumed to be a large quantity of supplies. And tethered by a heavy rope and a halter, a white-faced springing adolescent heifer followed obediently after the wagon, her mousey coat bearing a dapple of snowy spots over her shoulders.

"Where do you suppose he's going?" Dent voiced, echoing my own thoughts.

"Dunno," I replied. "But it looks like he might be gone for a while."

"Let's ask him," Dent suggested, but before I could put in my two cents, my brother was already five steps away from me.

We followed along at a discrete distance primarily keeping to the outer boundary of the dirt street, walking on a boardwalk if one happened to be there, but mostly skirting the edges of buildings or the front yard of houses, and all the while keeping a watch for Headville, Sherlee and Oleander. Three blocks north he reined the horses to the left and plodded along a street predominantly flanked by residences. As Tall John neared the western perimeter of town, he pulled his team to a stop and stepped down from the wagon. With perfect aim, he looked our way.

"Busted," Dent said. "It's a good thing we don't tail people for a living."

Then the man whom we had been conspicuously following lifted a hand and fluttered his fingers in unison, inviting us to join him.

"I hoped you might catch up to me," he said smiling at us when we had gotten within a few feet of him.

"Saw us, did you?" Dent asked rhetorically.

"Eyes on the sides of my head."

"Bishop and the others get back home, okay?" I asked.

"Sure did. And Lizzyann, too."

"Good," I said, returning the smile.

"Thanks to you boys. That Culver Headville, he's something else, isn't he? Honestly, I'm surprised the two of you work for him."

"It's complicated," I told him. Then I quickly changed the subject. "Looks like you've got some plans," I added gesturing to the wagon.

"Sure do. Just left the land office. Filed a homestead claim. Found a place a few years back when I was out buffalo hunting with a friend of mine. Of course, that was before when the beasts were still as plentiful as the leaves of a summer tree. Lord, what a sight they were then!" Tall John said with an air of nostalgia. "A damn waste," he added, and I assumed he referred to the mass slaughter of the bison, their numbers substantially diminished for both sport and for their hides.

"Not much settlement in that direction," I said looking westward.

"Just the way I like it," John said flashing a grin. "Looking forward to the solitude if I'm honest. Hopefully come March, I'll have a little soddy built, and maybe a lean-to for these animals."

"Better hurry then," Dent said gesturing to the heifer tethered behind the wagon, "from the looks of her she's gonna drop a calf in a few weeks."

"Know your cattle, do you?"

"It's in our blood," Dent said, nodding his head.

Suddenly, I heard a whimper and the sound of claws scratching against wood. John turned to glance into the wagon bed behind him. Then he reached over the edge and lifted a puppy into his big hands.

"Little rascal," he said, gathering the young canine into his arms and rubbing his head. The dog had a streak of white between his eyes and white legs speckled with dots of grey and black, and a thick coat of brown fur. He licked John's hand. "This fella is all the company I'll be needing for a while."

Dent reached over and tousled the pup's head and ears.

"You like dogs, do you?"

"Oh, yeah," Dent replied.

"I've got an extra one, if you want it?" he said, handing Dent the pup before turning and retrieving a second puppy that was nearly a twin as far as markings and coloring were concerned, but obviously possessing a much quieter disposition. He cuddled the doe-eyed youngster in his arms. "This one is a little bitch, sweet as pie. Both of them, gifts from Bishop. I couldn't refuse, but I really don't need two of them."

"I do like dogs, John … but sorry, I gotta pass. Doubt if the boss would approve."

"I'll take her," I said suddenly. "I know someone who would love to have her."

"Great!" John said, handing the pup to me. I smiled and stroked her sleek head and her furry back, then glanced at my brother.

"You give her that," Dent said to me, "and she'll want to marry you."

John raised a brow as he looked at me.

"Ignore him," I said. "He's a bullshitter."

"Whatever," Dent said with a laugh.

"Well, boys, I gotta be going," John said, returning the feistier little dog to its place in the wagon bed. Then he faced us and offered his hand. "It was a pleasure to meet you both. I hope our paths cross again."

"Same here," Dent said, shaking the tall man's hand.

Then it was my turn, and we clasped hands with a firm gesture of friendship as my other hand cupped the quiet little pup safely against me. "I know it's not necessarily polite to ask a man his full name, but I was wondering—"

"We're friends," he interrupted. "Nothing impolite about it. Thomas," he said, "John Thomas. And you boys are?"

"We're Tescotts," my brother jumped in.

"Dent and JT Tescott," he said, confirming that he had remembered our first names. "JT," he repeated thoughtfully. "Funny, those are my initials," he said with a grin, and in that moment my breath caught in my chest, my hand still in the tall man's clutch. "You're not a John, too, are you?" he asked me.

"No," I replied in a volume barely above a whisper as I stared at him with bated wonder.

"To be honest, John's not my real name. I changed it. Didn't care much for my given name. Same initial, though. Jermyn."

In an instant, being the sentimental softy that had been my life-long bane, I was completely overwhelmed with emotion. I continued staring at him with disbelief, my fingers tensing around the palm of his hand, struggling mightily to muster the restraint I needed to fight back tears that would be impossible to explain.

Tall John, a.k.a. Jermyn Thomas, smiled at me. "Can I have my hand back?" he asked.

"Sorry," I said, and I could hear the crack in my voice. Then quickly I broke our handshake. I glanced sideways to look at my brother. Dent stood there, his jaw hanging open, gawking at the man who was our great-great-grandfather.

"The two of you look like you could use a drink," he said to us as he turned and stepped foot into the wagon and sat down upon its bench seat. Then I noticed the Sharps rifle positioned near him, and wondered if it could be the same gun honorably displayed above the fireplace mantel in my family's home. And though I practiced sobriety, in that moment I would have gladly tossed back a shot.

"You Tescott boys take care," said the man who had no idea he was saying good-bye to descendants of his who were decades and decades away from being born. "And if you ever find yourselves heading west, look me up. You'll find me near a wide bend of the Smoky Hill River."

Dent and I stood and watched as the wagon rolled away. For several minutes we said nothing, waiting until he had disappeared beyond a house and barn that stood at the fringe of the town.

"That dude, he's …" Dent whispered then paused, I guessed, to do the generational math.

"He's my namesake," I said. And never had I been more proud to call myself Jermyn Thomas Tescott.

CHAPTER 46

Gobsmacked, we turned and looked at each other, my brother's eyes a reflection of my own, filled with wonder and awe. Meeting our great-great grandfather was surreal, not that any aspect of our journey back in time wasn't equally fantastical, but never once had it occurred to me that I would encounter an ancestor, much less shake his hand as an accomplice in a plot to rescue four citizens of a remote Black community from the clutches of an evil time-traveler named Culver Headville.

Minutes passed as we stood our ground at the outskirts of town, then Dent confessed that he wanted to run to the man who was our living, breathing relative and tell Jermyn Thomas who we were, and I admitted to the same thought—at first. But we couldn't do that. And we both knew why. Besides, we had the timeframe of an entire year in front of us to see if fate would, indeed, merge our paths once more. But if not in Hays City, we knew exactly where to find him.

Still reeling with excitement from the familial revelation, Dent and I, and the little fur mop I had tucked under my arm, hiked to Dub O'Brien's livery and retrieved Viento and Mister Brown. Then cautiously, we bypassed the busiest parts of town and made our way toward the north side of Hays City to begin our three-hour trail ride to the ranch.

We were just a block shy of the soft boundary of the city limits, when ahead of us I saw a small, horse-drawn wagon loitering at the side of the road parked between a pair of naked trees. As we drew nearer, I discerned the twitch of the horse's ears framed between the cranial silhouettes of a couple who sat huddled upon the wagon bench, a grey blanket wrapped loosely around their backs and over their shoulders. The woman had a shawl draped over her head, and the man beside her would have had a hat shielding his head from the coolness of the late afternoon breeze if, instead, it had not been lying upon the back edge of the wagon.

And the funny thing was, I felt certain that once I had gotten near enough to see its details, I would discover a bullet hole in the crown of the black derby.

"Somebody's waiting for us," I said to Dent as we plodded forward. "Who is it?"

"Kival. And the misses."

We stopped next to them and Kival cocked his head and presented to us a visage that suggested impatience.

"About time," he said seriously. "It's getting cold out here."

"We didn't get the memo," I told him, smiling. "Hello, Anja," I said, and then I saw the bundle she held in her arms. It was a carefully wrapped package the size of a large loaf of bread.

"You're kidding me?!"

"What is it?" Dent asked.

"I thought you might want to meet my daughter," Kival said, his countenance shifting into an expression of joy that was led by the grin of a proud new papa.

"I'll be damn!" Dent said, pushing his horse closer for a better look.

Anja tilted the newborn up and a plump rosy face greeted us. The tiny infant was a doll, and I told her parents as much, then Anja shared with us that they had named the baby Elsa.

"A cutie, for sure," Dent agreed.

"Not an ideal place, though, to spend an afternoon," I said to Kival. "How did you know we were in town?"

"I saw you just a bit ago going into a stable. Figured you were grabbing your horses, so we swung around and waited here for you, expecting you'd soon be riding by. We've only been here a few minutes."

"Nothing gets by you, does it?"

"Nope. I even see that you now have a baby of your own," he said, gesturing to the little pup nestled in the crook of my arm.

"Hold on a sec," Dent said suddenly. "Dude, why are you talking so damn different?"

I glanced at Kival. I had said nothing to my brother about his altered, though natural, speech pattern.

"It's all Anja," Kival replied. "For months now, she's been giving me speech lessons."

"You're a damn good teacher, Anja," Dent said.

And Kival is a damn good liar, I thought to myself. Then I opened my mouth preparing to share with him that Dent and I had been enjoying the opportunity of hanging out with our Grampy Jermyn Thomas, but Kival interrupted my sensational announcement.

"JT, there is something—well—something important I need to tell you," Kival said suddenly, then glanced at Dent. "In private," he added then looked again at my brother. "No offense," Kival said to him.

I looked at Dent, who shrugged with disinterest, then turned his head to look toward the center of town.

"Shit!" Dent immediately spat, and I swiveled in the saddle to look back at what had alarmed him. A familiar rider was galloping his sandy dun mare toward us, the horse's frosted black mane fluttering and flowing in the brisk wind of the run.

Deputy Oleander A. Sedgwick.

Dent laid the reins of the bridle sharply against his horse's neck and spurred the dark bay gelding into a pivoting forward lung, then urged him into a swift interception of Oleander, the two horses and their riders looking like medieval knights in a jousting tournament.

"It's Oleander. We've told him your dead."

Both Kival and I instinctively surveyed the limited options of retreat, and when our eyes met, neither of us had a solid plan. It was impractical to hastily drive off, particularly in the opposite direction of Kival and Anja's home in Schoenchen, south of town. But neither was there a side road exiting left or right. The less suspicious choice was for Kival to just rein his horse around and pull them and the wagon back into the midst of town, but that would mean facing Oleander head on.

"Just—just sit tight," I told him, and he nodded in agreement. I refocused on the two riders, who had met each other, stopping less than fifty yards away, their voices within the distance of my hearing.

"If it ain't my ole pal, Dent Tescott," I heard Oleander spout with an edge of contempt.

"Olly," Dent, said, barely loud enough for me to hear him.

"What's going on over there?"

"Nothing. It's just JT."

"I know that. I saw that bald-faced horse of his from a mile away. Who's with him?"

Without waiting to hear Dent's reply to Oleander's question, I turned to Kival. "I don't know how this is going to play out, but you might as well turn your wagon around and get Anja and the baby home."

"He's not going to like finding out I'm not dead."

"No. And worse yet, he's the acting city deputy." Kival looked at me, his eyes clearly shocked. "Guess some things do get by you. But listen, don't try to hide your face from him or he'll probably come after you for sure."

"Okay," Kival said, and he took the reins of the horse and clucked to him. Then a moment later the wagon was rolling, its path arcing in a U-turn. I nudged Viento into a trot, holding the little dog tightly against me, and aimed my horse toward my brother and my childhood adversary.

"The weirdo?" Oleander asked Dent as I joined them. "Thought those shitty-ass Indians killed him. That's what you told me, right?" Oleander said, his eyes dark and angry.

"I did, but—"

"We didn't want you to know," I said bluntly, crashing their conversation. "We didn't want you to feel guilty because of what they did to him."

"Why would I give a rat's ass?"

"Olly, it was you, remember, who got those Indians all pissed off," Dent said, picking up my lead.

Oleander looked at him, his expression seemingly clueless. Then Dent casually demonstrated the fateful gesture of the bird and nodded at Oleander's maimed hand.

"Ok, I get it. Not one of my smartest moves," he said as the wagon with Kival at its helm rolled past. "You sure that's him?" Oleander asked, as he watched Kival gazing bashfully forward.

"Pretty sure," I said, pondering my next crafty white lie.

"He had long hair before, a regular hippy shithead," Oleander mused. "What did they do to him, scalp him?"

"Yeah, well, they tried."

"I gotta see for myself," he said, but before he could move, Dent reached out and clutched his shirt where the upper-most button was fastened.

"Olly!" Dent barked, "Leave him alone, okay? For once in your life stop shoving your nose where it don't belong."

Oleander looked down at the hand that held his shirt, then lifted his eyes to glare at my brother. "Who do you think you're talking to, Tescott?" Then he tapped the badge pinned to his shirt.

"I'll tell you who," Dent snapped, his grip noticeably tightening. "I'm talking to you, Olly. A guy who I thought was my best friend. A guy I went through school with, who I got drunk with, who I played football and basketball with. A guy who was always on my team and— and always had my back. And a guy who knew he could also count on me! That badge isn't who you are, Olly. You're one of us. One of the six of us who got our asses hauled away from our time and brought here to a goddamned place we don't belong. A place in time we never should have been thrown into. And we just wanna get back home, Olly," Dent fervently confided. "Don't you?" he added, releasing his hold on the replacement deputy.

"Yeah … course," Oleander said hesitantly.

"Well, to get back home, we gotta do it together. We gotta help each other. That guy," Dent continued, pointing toward Kival, "that weirdo you call him—he got down on his knees next to you after those Indians tied your smartass up to that tree, and he helped you. He pulled shitloads and shitloads of cactus needles out of you, from your legs and from your dick and your balls, and he did that for you, even after you had thrown him in the water and dragged him back onto the riverbank and pinned him down to the ground like he was nothing to you but a piece of shit! Hell, Olly, all of us helped you out there. For chrissakes, it's your turn to help us. To help him. Leave him alone, please," Dent pleaded, then brilliantly added, "Do you think he wants to yak with you after handling your junk?"

Oleander turned and watched as the wagon faded into the fray of traffic, dozens of seconds ticking by as he appeared to genuinely process the words of my brother's heartfelt speech. "Fine," he said, then returned his attention to Dent. "I just wish you hadn't lied to me—friend." Then he reined his horse around and trotted away.

Still holding my breath, I watched Oleander melt into the distance of the long street, until he turned his horse at a corner and disappeared around the far side of a building.

I looked at Dent, who appeared to be exhausted by the passion of his impromptu address. "Good speech," I said. "If I were a debate coach, I'd give it a solid B plus."

"Kiss my lily-white ass," he said, unamused by my attempt to sugar-coat the moment with a little humor.

We pointed our horses north and headed out of town. But we didn't get far. Gunshots rang out.

Two of them.

I looked at Dent. Fear clutched my throat. "God, no," I rasped.

With the power and speed of our horses, we galloped back into the heart of town and turned west onto the main street.

People hurried helter-skelter across the roadway in front of us, forcing us to slow our horses to the pace of a fast walk. Up ahead, I could see folks merging south onto the street that connected Hays City to its namesake fort. I leapt from Viento's back and threw a rein around a hitching post in front of Goddard's Saloon, then I handed the pup up to Dent before worming my way through the fracas of the brave and the foolish, passing as quickly as possible by Tommy Drum's place, and Paddy Walsh's gambling house, until finally I turned at the corner where John White's barber shop stood. I paused for a moment, my eyes falling upon a crowd of spectators gathered around what I deduced to be a wagon, though I could hardly be certain because of the camouflage of the milling crowd of bystanders.

I hurried through the people, pushing and squeezing past them, not giving a damn what they thought of my rudeness. Before I managed to worm my way to the front of the circular line of people, I found myself close enough to see Oleander standing at the back of the wagon, his pistol still pointing at a body splayed across the wooden bed. I exhaled a heart-pounding sigh of relief. The victim was not Kival, as I had feared it might be. But it was someone with whom I was acquainted, though I held no sympathy for the man.

"Why the hell did you do that, you jackass?!" shouted a man standing next the wagon, his voice angry and frustrated. "We was takin' him to the fort to get us our reward!"

The dead man's eyes stared sightlessly into the sky, his hands tied behind his back, and his wolf-skin headdress still clinging to his skull. Morgan had said his name was Fire Wolf, but all I knew for certain was that he was the dog soldier who had viciously severed Oleander's finger with a hatchet; a savage who had unleashed a brutal regime of unnecessary torture upon a red-haired boy who had barely transitioned into an adult. Only this time, the bloodletting had been violently performed on the Indian, the unconscionable evidence oozing from two lethal bullet wounds that had pierced his bare chest. Oleander had administered payback.

I hoped he had not also forfeited his soul for the dark privilege of vengeance.

CHAPTER 47

The sun had already hidden itself for a full hour before we had made our way back to the ranch, but there was just enough residual light in the evening sky to guide us along the road.

Dent and I had spent the early leg of our clandestine journey discussing Oleander and postulating how Headville intended to exploit him, but we both hoped some part of Dent's soliloquy would resonate with our time-travel cohort. But mostly we talked about our twice-great grandfather, Jermyn Thomas. And though we both wished to be returned to our time and place as soon as possible, we were also grateful, and admittedly exhilarated, to have been gifted the extraordinary opportunity to personally meet our ancestor who had been the one that anchored the roots of the legacy of our family's beloved Sweetwater Ranch.

That chance encounter with the clever, bold, and compassionate man had given our accidental journey back to 1878 a uniquely different perspective; an unforeseen reason to erase all regret of trespassing into this era of the Old West. Jermyn Thomas had now become more than just a name written on the page of our family tree. Mom had never met him, and even her dad, my Grampa Jake, had probably just been a little boy when Jermyn had died at the age of an old man.

And as Dent and I talked about him, I knew in the back of my mind, that when we eventually returned to our home year, Jermyn would have long since passed on. And the thought saddened me more than I expected. But worse yet, I realized the same thing defined Kate's potential longevity, a life that would be lived and finished decades before I would be born. That reality was emotionally suffocating.

If Kate chose not to go back with me when my chance finally arrived to abscond from this time, could I leave her behind? I wasn't sure that I could. But I had thirteen months to figure that out.

Later, after arriving at the ranch, Dent and I dutifully began the routine tasks of caring for our horses. Several feet away, the little dog that had been gifted to me by my doubly great granddad sat patiently beneath the lofty roof of the barn and watched us, her chocolate brown eyes bright and curious.

"What are you gonna to do with her?"

I had also been wondering the same thing.

"Tonight, I'll keep her with me, if Boyd will let me. Tomorrow, I guess she'll just have to be found, I suppose."

"Like a stray?"

"Why not?"

"Out here, in nowhere? A solid dozen miles away from town, and a puppy, small enough to fit inside my boot, suddenly appears on Kate's doorstep," Dent proposed, answering my question.

"Do you have a better idea?"

"Yeah. Just give the pup to her and tell her you found it in town. Knowing Olly, Headville's eventually going to know we were in Hays City anyway."

Dent had a point.

"Guess I'll just play it by ear," I said, not sure of the best way to spin the situation. But I was confident about one thing: Culver Headville would not appreciate the gesture of my gift. Not when the recipient was his ward. But to be there when Kate first laid eyes on the little pup might make any degree of retribution worthwhile.

Saturday morning arrived after a night spent cuddling with the little pup. Boyd had given the thumbs up so long as my bunkmates had no objections, and none did. In fact, everyone, the vaqueros included, joyfully spent a few minutes getting acquainted with the fluffy young canine, and she, in turn, enjoyed the attention. I would not have been surprised to discover she had wagged her tail completely loose from her body.

Though Saturday was generally a weekly holiday for us ranch hands, during the months of winter all species of livestock expected their appetites to be satiated whether we preferred to spend our free time doing something else of our own choosing. But at least Boyd let the guys sleep in, giving us until noon to begin the chore of loading and distributing hay.

By mid-morning, neither Headville nor Sherlee had returned. They had now been absent from the ranch for three consecutive nights. Their reappearance was surely imminent.

As I waited for an opportunity to connect with Kate, I happened to have the little pup with me in the great barn when I thought I heard a heavy door closing loudly nearby. And since the bunkhouse door was little more than thin planks and rusty hinges, I took a quick peek outside and caught Kate, bundled in a coat and long pants and boots, pausing for a moment on the wide veranda of her home, her head owlishly rotating as she scanned the ranch yard.

I wondered.

Had Kate's loud exit from the house been a ploy to get my attention? If so, it had worked. If not, well, I could pretend otherwise.

Without seeing me shrouded within the shadows of my hiding place, she buttoned her coat, then strode toward the horse barns. I was sure I knew where she was going. A week-old black foal was still enjoying the accommodations of the third paddock. And Kate seemed to like nothing more than a baby horse. But I was anxious to find out if I could melt her heart with a different sort of youngster.

I ducked into the tack room where I had been playing with the pup and gathered the dog in my hands and headed for the far end of the barn, past where Dent and Mick were yakking about things I had not been particularly interested in, and after scuttling between the building and the carriage shed, I saw her. However, instead of entering the third horse barn that I had anticipated was her most probable destination, she entered the middle of the trio of buildings. I wondered if Boyd had moved the newborn horse and his mother into there, but that seemed unlikely, since the management of the horses was Sherlee's responsibility.

Clutching the little pup, I crossed the ground and hurried into the third building as planned, feeling confident that Kate would eventually find her way to me, which was a better plan. I began walking through the center of the building and within moments I came upon the stall that had been home for the young colt and saw that he and his mother had ventured outside into the adjacent private paddock and were enjoying the morning sunshine.

The foal was feeling frisky, and I watched as he frolicked about. At once the pup whimpered and I discerned that she was also enthralled with the leggy colt, feeling her own stubby little legs squirming against me as though she wanted down to play.

"He's too big for you to romp around with," I said to the pup. "You could get stepped on."

"Who are you talking to?"

Before I turned around, I smiled.

Perfect, I thought, then I faced her. Immediately, Kate saw the furry little canine in my arms and her face lit up like that of a child at a circus.

"Ooh," she cooed, and quickly crossed to me, and I offered her the dog. "How cute!" Kate exclaimed, her emerald eyes sparkling with pure joy as she gathered the pup and placed its fuzzy little body against one of her lovely cheeks. At once the little dog began to lick Kate's chin, causing her to laugh.

Score.

"Where did you find it?"

"In town. I was there, yesterday," I said, deciding I could tell Kate only the truth. "My—a man I met, gave her to me."

Most of the truth.

"She's adorable!" Kate grinned, turning the dog so they could look at each other face to face. Then I watched as the two of them swapped kisses, and I couldn't help but feel jealous of the dog. "What have you named her?" Kate asked.

"I haven't."

"You must give her a name! I can't just call her dog."

"I thought maybe you should name her," I said. "Since I, well, actually I got her for you."

Kate looked up at me with an expression of genuine surprise. Then, I saw her eyes growing moist as a quivering grin was formed by her lips. In one long stride, she was in my face and before I knew it, she was kissing me. And I didn't care that the tongue of a dog had just been on her lips.

Then she pulled away, far too soon. But our eyes stayed locked in an intangible embrace, the depths of our pupils reflecting mutual confessions of genuine affection, now confirmed by the seal of a spontaneous kiss. In that moment, I felt as though I were hovering, almost floating out of my boots. And then I couldn't wait a second longer. I reached for her, cupping her face in the palms of my hands, and leaned my chin over the pup cradled against her breast. We kissed again, only this time it was my prerogative. Her soft lips melted against mine, and I savored the intimacy.

"Well—well—well."

I froze for a dreadful instant, then looked up, knowing my eyes would find Culver Headville. I gently eased Kate away from me, and I glanced into her eyes and saw that she was likewise concerned.

"Mr. Headville, sir," I said, gulping. Then I wondered if Sherlee had entered through the doorway behind me, preparing to disembowel me, or worse, castrate me with a dull knife.

"Culver!" Kate said, turning to face him. "I was just thanking JT. Look what he got for me!" she exclaimed, attempting to disguise our moment as nothing more than an expression of gratitude. "Isn't she just the prettiest thing?"

Headville said nothing, though his eyes roved from me to the dog, then back again.

"I thought she might like another, you know, since Poppy—," I began, but before I could conclude my pitifully weak explanation, Headville turned and left, as though he could care less, or more likely, he was too incensed to speak. "Sir," I added just before he disappeared through the doorway.

Kate cleared her throat. "I should go," she said, and crossed the length of the barn, following Headville's retreat. But before she left, she turned to me, smiling. In spite of my overwhelming concern for my man parts, I could not help but smile back at her.

"Toto," she said.

I looked at her curiously, thinking she had meant to say bye-bye, or some other double worded phrase. "What?" I asked.

"I'm going to call her Toto."

Instantly my mind flashed to a favorite childhood movie, *The Wizard of Oz*. Interesting, I thought. And the irony of Dorothy's magical sojourn into a world of munchkins and witches was almost in parallel with my own unexpected adventure. But Toto, that had to be a coincidence.

"It just came to me," Kate said smiling. "From a book I've read."

"It's perfect," I told her.

We held onto the moment for a few seconds longer, then she opened her mouth as though to tell me something, but she only managed to say "I—," before changing her mind and leaving.

Then I thought of what Dent had said concerning my idea of giving Kate the dog. Perhaps he was right. Maybe now, she did want to marry me.

A week crawled by and not once did Kate and I cross paths, neither by accident nor by design. I did catch a glimpse of her from afar on a mid-week, mid-afternoon while helping Boyd and Pete feed the pastured horses. From the distance, I could see that she was amusing herself with little Toto near the extravagant playhouse in the backyard of the formidable limestone home. It appeared the little dog had been allowed to stay in the house, at least for a while.

And then a second week passed, ushering in the month of December that brought several days of bitter cold, followed by a weekend that was slightly warmer, but ominously quiet. My penchant for worrying, a trait my dad said I inherited from Granny Evelie, fed me with a profound sense of foreboding. But no matter what I did to distract myself, I could not shake the feeling that something unpleasant was about to happen at any time.

Naturally, I believed Headville was at the heart of my dread.

In the two weeks since he had caught Kate and I kissing, he had said nothing to me about it, even though we had encountered one another several times. Instead, he had surprised me, greeting me congenially as though my interest in his ward was acceptable, though it was difficult for me to imagine that it was sincerely okay with him. Yet, I didn't have the guts to seek his clarification of the issue. And there had been opportunities to ask.

On one occasion, Headville had engaged me in a conversation about his horses, particularly his prized stallion, Doc. In fact, he had shared with me that he had secured the services of an artist who resided in France, a woman with a prominent reputation for painting spectacular equine portraiture. According to him, he had, months earlier, convinced her to travel to America for an all-expense paid adventure into the heart of the Wild West. And by his comments, I reasoned that he had also promised her a lucrative commission for her talent, and as a cover for her trouble and her travel. Culver had wealth. I did not require his personal confirmation of that fact.

But though he had money, he didn't always get what he wanted. And the incident with the men from Nicodemus, a plan thwarted by my great-great grandfather, was proof that Headville could occasionally be denied his ambitions, however grand or otherwise mundane they might be. But the question that constantly pricked my anxiety was what would Headville do if he learned that Dent and I had been involved with Jermyn Thomas?

So justifiably, I was wary of every subsequent encounter with Culver Headville, expecting at some point, the hammer would fall. An ambush, perhaps, by means of a statement about Kate, or Oleander, or even another crafty suggestion that would again articulate to me that he knew of what century I truly belonged.

Without realizing it at first, I had succumbed to living in a constant flux of paranoia, which was probably what Headville had deviously planned and had devilishly hoped. He was obviously not a man who acted irrationally, but he was a cunning individual who might avert one's expectation of a confrontation, at least until it suited him. He was, I believed, methodical in his preparation for action. I just worried about what he might currently be scheming, and when it would unfold?

More and more often, my brain reminded me of Morgan's description of Headville: *A viper patiently waiting for the very best moment to strike.*

Then with the onset of the following week, the cold and gray that had defined the first days of December was whisked away by an unseasonably warm southerly wind that arrived on the shirttails of a gloriously sunny morning. And the veil of despair that had been my dull shadow, lifted and I felt less worried, and appreciatively unshackled by those uncomfortable feelings of trepidation.

That date of liberation came on Monday, December the 10th, the day after Headville had met the *la femme étrangére* at the train depot in Hays City and had brought her to the ranch to stay as his guest. It was a day that would ultimately be a reminder to me of a guarded promise that was destined to split apart a relationship.

It was late morning, and the painter, a rather masculine-looking woman coiffed in a chopped cut of jaw-length hair and wearing trousers and a loose blouse befitting of a male French peasant, had sat up an easel in the center of the ranch yard. Placed next to the spindly tripod was a table of dark mahogany, elegantly footed with three decoratively carved legs that curved outward from a thick pedestaled center, conceivably a European import with an origination matching that of the eccentric artist. Procured from the house, the oval piece of furniture was set with a palette, an ensemble of brushes, and containers of paint, and looked as out-of-place as did Rosa Bonheur.

But the chestnut stallion, Doc, stood nearby, very much at home. A handsome specimen, though his coat was not as lustrous as it would have been in summer, still he was picturesque having earlier been thoroughly groomed by Willard Sherlee. Courtesy of a warm-water shampoo and a meticulous brushing of his coat, mane, and tail, with special attention given to his white socks that were arrogantly flashy and pristine, the horse exuded breeding and style.

It was easy to admire Doc. Unquestionably the animal was a product of ideal equine genetics, especially for a quarter horse born in the infancy of the development of the breed. And standing next to Rosa was Headville, watching her brandish the magic of her brushstrokes, and being clearly pleased that he was immortalizing the horse through a painting being rendered by an artist of whom he openly revered.

Throughout the mid portion of the day, I and the other ranch hands had passed through the area as the fifty-some-year-old artist worked, and neither she, nor her show-stopping subject, seemed to be at all bothered by our activity. At one point, Dent and I stood at the corner of the great barn, watching as Sherlee would pose the horse at the direction of Madam Bonheur, then minutes later, walk the stallion in a circle around her, accommodating the artist's every whim.

Suddenly Dent grabbed my arm, his grip tight and painful.

"What the hell is wrong?" I asked him, as I tried to tug my arm from his clasp.

"Doc!" Dent exclaimed.

"What about him?"

"Now I know why he's always seemed so damn familiar to me!"

"We've discussed this already."

"I know. And I thought you were right, that the horse just reminded me of Dad's ole gelding. Same facial markings and the white feet and the color. But that's not it, JT," he added, continuing to stare at the stallion.

"Then what is it?"

"I've seen his photograph. Looking at him now, it's as plain as day. It was the June issue of *Western Horseman*. There was an article, most of it republished from an older issue, I don't know fifteen years or so earlier, I guess. But it had his picture, a photograph of him as a champion show horse. I actually read the article." I looked at him doubtfully, for more than one reason.

"I know, big surprise. But Dad and I—we talked about it. Dad had even remembered the original news story, one about a theft in California of a prized Quarter Horse that had been a disappointment on the racetrack but had made a name for himself in the show ring!"

"Okay," I said, not fully understanding where he was going with what was probably just a coincidence of color and markings.

"JT, the horse was never found!" Dent continued. "Never!" he repeated with emphasis. "And now, it makes sense! That's him, I'm sure of it! The time of the horse-napping, Doc's age—it all fits!"

"I don't know, Dent, that's—"

"Shit!"

"What?!"

"I just remembered the official registry name! Doc-Bar!"

I stared at Dent, remembering that Boyd had mentioned that name to us a few weeks earlier. Then instantly I recalled a conversation with Headville when he had referred to the exquisite horse as a serendipitous acquisition from a later time. Had that been Headville's second tease after having first mentioned JFK? If the dates of Dent's recollection were correct, then Headville would have thieved Doc Bar in 1962 or '63. He would have been in possession of the talisman at that time, so it was arguably possible. I also knew that when it came to horses, my brother had an exceptional eye and a keen memory.

"Do you believe me?" Dent asked, looking me in the eye.

"I do now," I said, and I meant it. Not only because Dent believed it, but also because I knew it was completely feasible. After all, Headville had, according to Morgan, made numerous trips into the future. He could have easily brought a horse or anything else back with him.

"How did he do it, then?"

"Obviously, Headville brought Doc back with him."

Dent looked at me. "Back with him? From where?"

"From, well, from our side of the arch," I said, then suddenly remembered that I had not told Dent everything I knew about Headville.

Dent stared at me for moment, his brow furrowing. "That's news to me. I didn't know he ever went forward into our time."

"A few times, yeah."

"Says who?"

"Morgan."

"Morgan told you that Headville time-traveled?"

I nodded.

"Seriously?!"

"Yes," I replied, hearing my brother's disappointment and perceiving his egotistical injury of being excluded from the informational loop.

"But you, little brother, didn't bother to tell me that, did you?"

"Dent, don't get mad. Why else would Headville want the talisman?"

"Exactly. Why else? I'm not stupid, JT! I may not be a genius like you, but I figured out months ago that Headville had jumped time like us, and that was why Morgan warned us about him. And all on my own, my brain came up with the idea that Headville would probably kill to get the talisman back," Dent added, shaking his head indignantly. "But I've been waiting for you to tell me yourself. Cuz I knew damn well you knew, but for some bullshit reason you hadn't bothered to tell me."

"I'm sorry, Dent, really, I am. It's just—"

"What? You've got other secrets?"

I stared at him, unable to lie to him with words, but my silence betrayed the truth.

"You're keeping something else from me, aren't you JT?" my brother asked, the accusation in his eyes far more stinging than the allegation in his words. "It's Kival, isn't it? Just what exactly was so damn important he wanted to talk to you about? Huh? You know, that thing that was private—not for my ignorant-ass ears."

"I honestly don't know what he wanted to tell me."

"Bullshit."

"Dent, I don't know!"

He stared at me, his eyes hard and hurting.

"Did he really lose the talisman?" he pointedly asked me, and the significance of the question hit me like a rock.

"Yes, as far as I know," I said truthfully. "That's what he told me." But suddenly I wondered. I had only Kival's word that the talisman had been lost during his struggle with Oleander in the river at our ranch.

"Maybe he lied," Dent hissed. "Seems like keeping secrets from each other is what we do. Why should you be excluded from being shit on?"

"He wouldn't," I replied softly, unknowing that in a few seconds I would be defending my evasiveness.

"Why not?"

"Because I know who Kival really is!" I barked at Dent, feeling hounded to oblige him with a whisper of information. "So, there's no reason he would lie to me." Instantly, I was grieved by my betrayal of Kival's trust. I shook my head, my eyes begging my brother not to pry any deeper.

Dent studied me for a long, painfully restrained moment, then he snubbed my silent plea. "Who Kival really is," he said, repeating my words. "What the hell are you talking about?"

I stared at him. Layered within the core of my being, and fostered by the blood that bonded us as brothers, I longed to tell Dent what I knew, but I had made an earnest promise to Kival. If I caved to his interrogation, I would be sacrificing my word of honor. And if Dad and Mom had taught me anything, it was that you do what you promise to do, no matter how big or how small.

"I can't tell you."

Dent glared at me, his eyes resentful and angry.

"I'm your goddamned brother, JT."

Instantly, my mind teemed with my own buried feelings of resentment. My own anger ruthlessly pounding against the brick wall I had built to separate and contain emotions that were regrettably still raw, though I had convinced myself otherwise. But I would not keep them suppressed. Not now.

The gauntlet had been thrown down.

"Brother? You call yourself my brother?" I snarled at him. "What about Laurie, Dent? You didn't bother to tell me about the two of you! I had to find that out on my own. On my birthday no less! And in front of my friends. In front of Sam and Blaine. And what about Blaine?" I said, crossing to him and jabbing my finger into his chest. "What about what happened between the two of you last spring? I asked you. I asked you time and time again, what had happened—what terrible thing caused the two of you to suddenly throw your friendship out the window? But you wouldn't tell me. So don't get all high and mighty with me! Not when you have your own damn secrets!"

Dent stared at me, enduring the assault of my words, his eyes burning as though he hated me because I had ultimately forced him to take a good look at himself in the mirror.

Then I watched as he began to nod, his eyes defensive, yet insecure. "Go to hell," Dent whispered, and then I saw tears begin to pool. He turned from me, taking a step away, then without warning he spun around wielding a fist I was not prepared to meet.

I took the brunt of the blow to my chin, my teeth cracking from the impact. I felt my head explode, and my knees buckle, and I sensed that I was falling. But before I hit the floor of the barn, Dent pummeled his body into me, knocking me backward. I heard him grunt and groan as the two of us fell heavily upon the unrelenting ground. Then a hard punch of a right hook landed against my ribs, and Dent growled as he planted another blow on the opposite side. Dazed, I instinctively lowered my arms to defend myself, but then the assault returned to my head, and I reeled from the impact of another jab to my face. And then I heard voices and shouting.

And for a fleeting second, I believed I glimpsed a figure shadowed and grey, its ice blue eyes wide and wary. Appearing patient, but prepared, he who had been named a Burmano-Ku-Partika floated toward me.

I closed my eyes.

Then I felt as though my head was suddenly as heavy as a limestone post, and as the faint impression of light melted into darkness, I sensed my pain slipping away as my consciousness surrendered.

CHAPTER 48

As my consciousness returned, I could hear a strange voice filtering into my ears, but I lost interest in it the moment I moved and was informed by my network of neurons that my head was throbbing and my jaw ached like a sonofabitch.

Despite the pain, I tried to sit up, and then realized I could add ribs to the list of things that hurt. Although the vision of my left eye was oddly defined by a narrow gap curtained by the fringe of my lashes, I knew I was stretched out on the floor in the tack room of the barn, with itchy, woolen saddle blankets beneath me acting as both cushion and insulation against the cold ground. I touched the eye and felt its swollen condition and added a fourth thing to the list. This was now the second whupping I'd gotten in just over five months. I was not tough enough to make a habit out of fighting with my brother.

Then my thoughts began to focus on Dent.

I lay still, thinking, and wishing I had kept my mouth shut, and my emotionally charged insults to myself. Not only because of the beating from which I now suffered from head to toe, but also because I regretted that my scorching words had so passionately provoked my brother into inflicting these injuries upon me in the first place. Though my wounded pride tried its best to weigh me down with resentment, my thoughts kept returning to the truth I knew and fervently believed mattered most: I loved my brother.

No matter what.

"Hey," a voice spoke, causing me to open my good eye, if you could call it good, and found Mick standing in the doorway gazing down at me.

"Hey," I responded, with little enthusiasm.

"Glad you're alive," he said, curling a corner of his mouth. Mick had a quiet, yet confident way about him that made it easy to admire his level-headedness and his engaging ability to avoid drama, neither of which I had managed very well in the last hour, or however long I had been lying on the floor. "I think the Mexicans have been making bets between themselves on whether you live or not."

"Odds are fifty-fifty."

"From the looks of you, I'd say that's about right."

"Where's Dent?"

"Right now, he's milking the cows. And before that, he was busy slopping the pigs and feeding the chickens. But Boyd was so mad at your brother that when he gave him those orders, he actually told Dent to slop the chickens and milk the pigs. Pete laughed so hard Boyd sent him into the bunkhouse to sweep the floors."

"That's a pretty harsh punishment for both of them," I said, trying to smile, but failing. "I don't remember coming in here," I added, gesturing to the confines of the room, its walls lined with saddles and bridles and various straps, ropes, and gadgetry specifically used by a horseman.

"That's because you were knocked out cold. Pete and I carried you in after Boyd threw down that makeshift bed for you."

"Why not take me to the bunkhouse?" I asked, feeling a little put-out that I wasn't given the benefit of a more comfortable arrangement.

"Well, if we had done that, it might have distracted the painter lady, and Boyd said he wasn't going to risk that, but I think he mostly wanted to keep Headville from knowing that he didn't have the two of you under control."

"You mean, Mr. Headville," I said with a grin that sent a twinge of discomfort across my battered face.

Mick smiled with another curl at the corner of his lips. "Oops."

I began to sit up, and as I expected, the movement hurt like hell. Mick stepped in and offered me a hand to hold onto and I pushed through and finally managed to get my head positioned vertically above my spine. "I need to talk to Dent."

"That's not a good idea," Mick said more confidently than I would have expected. "He's pretty angry, but not at you so much as he's mad at himself. You know him better than I do, but I'm guessing he could probably use a few days to get his head put back on straight."

"That's a good guess," I said, relinquishing to his advice, for now.

Mick stayed with me for a few minutes longer, and I learned from him that Rosa Bonheur was still outside, painting the masterpiece she had begun hours earlier, and it was then that I realized the unfamiliar voice I had been hearing belonged to her. But it was long afterward, following the disbandment of the hubbub surrounding Madam Bonheur and the subject of her canvas, before I sensed that a calm had descended upon the ranch. Then like a thief, the first hour of evening stole any remaining warmth from the air, and soon I was beginning to feel chilled.

Rescued from the impending cold, Mick and Pete assisted in moving me through the cloaking haze of dusk to the bunkhouse where the promise of a more comfortable cot awaited me. Once inside, I sat at the table arriving just in time for the dinner that was delivered as usual, though without the company of Sherlee.

Isaiah looked at me and winced. "Mmm-mmm-mmm," he mumbled, shaking his head. "Mister Boyd, should I bring him some ointment of some kind from the house?" Isaiah asked. I noted the use of the prefix that was supposedly reserved only for Culver Headville. But perhaps with some relationships on the ranch, it was not a rule, but a guideline.

"Naw," Boyd replied. "We done doctored him up with a tincture we made ourselfs," he added, eyeing me with the assurance of a licensed physician. "What was in it, boys, some tabaccy spit, and horseshit, and sumpin' else?"

"Iodine," Little Pete volunteered, "to make him look purdy."

I looked at the assemblage of my coworkers, desperately seeking a sign that I was being made a fool.

To their credit, they kept straight faces longer than I imagined they could. Luckily for me, Pete busted out with a laugh, and it contagiously spread among all of them, including the vaqueros. I even noticed that Isaiah had smiled, something that was rarely expressed in our presence. For certain, my brother would have found Boyd's joke to be funny, but then he was not in the bunkhouse with us.

He had, by his own volition, chose to forego supper and had informed Boyd that he would be sleeping in the Indian's old soddy. I was glad, though, to see Mick slip out with a pair of biscuits he had wrapped up in neck-kerchief.

I did, however, see my brother several times throughout the following two days, but we didn't speak, and neither did we make eye contact. It was, I suppose, emotionally healing to give each other space and time, though my facial bruising had gotten worse before getting better. And a chance encounter with Kate a day later reminded me that I carried tell-tale signs of the physical injuries of which I preferred not to be reminded.

"Hey, stranger."

I flinched. I had been mucking the stalls of the great barn, shifting the horses between pens so that I could clean them without risk of injury to the animals or to myself, and was at that moment standing at the wide northern entrance watching the activity of my colleagues performing the duties of the daily chore of feeding hay. I had not heard the slightest indication that Kate had entered the barn. But I was smiling before I turned to face her.

"For Heaven's sake, JT! What happened to you?!" Kate exclaimed, staring at the persistent dark bruising that was around one eye but had faded to a yellowish shade of purple beneath the opposite one.

"I ran into a door."

"Did the door have fists?"

"If you make me laugh, it will only hurt me."

"Who—?" Kate asked, and I could see in her eyes she was suspecting Culver Headville.

"No, not him. Dent," I told her, then she crossed toward me, and I finally noticed a pair of eyes peeking at me from the top of Kate's coat. She had wrapped Toto inside the winter garment but given the fact that the little dog had her own thick coat of fur, I assumed the young canine was feeling well-baked.

"I see you've brought company," I said, reaching out to stroke the pup on the nose. Naturally, it licked at my hand.

"Of course," Kate said, touching my face with gentle fingertips. "Does it hurt?"

"Not now, it doesn't."

"What were you two fighting about?"

"Stuff."

"You know, JT, you tend to avoid answering a lot of my questions."

"Do I?" I asked, though I knew exactly what she meant. "This with Dent is no big deal. We're brothers. We've had other skirmishes."

"Oh? So, what was the last one about? And don't tell me stuff."

"Okay," I said, hesitating.

"Well?"

"Technically, it was over a girl."

"Really?" She asked, her hands landing upon her hips, her eyes a mix of humor and allegation. "Is there something you need to tell me?"

"Nope. I don't need another beating," I said with a smile. Then Toto started squirming and inadvertently saved me from further explanation.

Kate unbuttoned her coat and lifted the little dog into her arms.

"She's getting big," I said, but the furry babe was still a fairly tiny thing and would probably not get much larger than a native bobcat.

"Isaiah feeds her well," Kate agreed, then handed Toto to me. "So, two questions. One, does your brother look better or worse than you? And two, why aren't you out there working with the rest of them?"

"Dent doesn't have a scratch on him," I said, suddenly feeling as though my young manhood license had been stolen by the Cowardly Lion, though I preferred to defend my ego with the biblical adage that

I had turned the other cheek, but neither was true. I had simply had my ass handed to me.

"Good. I don't like a man who's violent."

Instantly, I smiled. Well, beamed would be a better description. The girl I had fallen in love with had just referred to me as a man. I relished the moment, then saw that she was waiting for an answer to her second question. "For some reason, Boyd thinks I'm hurt worse than I am, so he's given me a few days off from hard physical labor to recuperate. But honestly, I'm bored out of my skull."

"I see," she said looking at me as though I had forgotten her name.

"What?"

"Third question."

"I wasn't expecting a quiz."

"Why haven't you kissed me?"

I looked at Kate, pleased by the direction of her interrogation.

"You know Culver and Willard left to take that French lady to town to catch—"

I shut her up.

I kissed her gently, feeling the softness of her lips against mine, and then our passion began to blossom, probably more than it should have considering that we were standing in a musty barn with a little dog umpiring our embrace. Then Kate pulled away from me and looked into my eyes.

"I really like you, JT."

"I more than like you, Kate," I said, surprising myself at my willingness to share my deepest feelings with her.

"More? What does that mean, exactly?" she asked, and it was obvious she was teasing me.

"Do you want me to say it?"

"No. Not yet."

"When, then?" I said, giving her my best beguiling expression.

"Not until you tell me."

"Tell you what?"

"You know what, JT. I've asked you several times since."

I did, in fact, know what she meant. Nearly two months previous I had, by accident, alluded to time travel. And on multiple occasions since that moment, I had circumvented all discussion of the subject. But because I professed deep feelings for Kate, my heart had obligated me to eventually explain my words to her, sooner or later. Especially now that I planned to persuade her to return with me to the year to which I belonged. Perhaps it was time to bite the proverbial bullet.

Time to act. Time to own it. Time to be a man. Time to be completely honest with her.

"I'm from the future, Kate." I said, deciding to candidly lay the raw truth in front of her and prepare myself for the coming onslaught of laughter, or worse, a silent ogle with eyes that would clearly judge me as certifiably crazy.

"I believe you."

CHAPTER 49

I gawked at Kate, wondering if her belief in me was even crazier than my truth.

"You do? Just like that, you're buying it?"

"I probably wouldn't have believed you if you had said that to me when I asked you the first time. Or the second, or third, or the fourth, or—"

"I get it," I said, unable to deny she had questioned me repeatedly. "So, what changed?"

"Well, I have overheard Culver talking about you."

I gawked at her again. "What—what did he say?"

"He was saying he knew that you had used this thing, something that I imagined to be wonderfully magical, and it had brought you and your brother here from the future. He called it a talisman, and he offered a lot of money to get it back."

I stared at her, trying not to look shocked by her casual declaration that she was privy to information pointing her toward the origin of my existence, not to mention her reference to the talisman.

So, Headville had given the object the same term that I had settled upon. But talisman was what fit. It was a magical thing, and powerful, both because of its intrinsic ability, and through its effectual influence on the feelings and actions of those who possessed it. Or, likewise as influential upon those who were obsessed with getting it back. And Culver Headville topped that list.

"Who did he offer the money to?" I asked, though I knew who the recipient of the proposal had to have been.

Oleander Sedwick.

"Your brother."

I gawked a third time, but in this instance, I felt as though I had again been gut-punched. It wasn't possible. I knew Kate had to have misspoken. "You mean, Oleander?"

"No, Dent."

"When?"

"Three nights ago. He was drunk to put it bluntly. He came to our door demanding to see Culver. You didn't know?"

"No," I said, realizing the significance of the date. Three nights previous was the evening of the ass-whupping Dent had given me, the night he had moved out of the bunkhouse.

"I don't believe Culver would have let him inside the house, if Dent hadn't accused him of stealing Doc."

"Shit!" I whispered, my mind reeling. Damn Dent and his alcohol, and I knew where he had gotten it. The vaqueros had a cache of whiskey hidden in the barn, away from the eyes and lips of Boyd. It had been just a week earlier when my brother and I had caught Carlos concealing bottles of liquor upon their return from Hays City, where the Mexican cowboys had again enjoyed their free day by amusing themselves with the vices of a frontier fun-town.

"I heard the accusation, and so did Miss Bonheur," Kate continued. "We had just finished dinner when your brother started pounding on the front door. I don't think she understood what was said, but I was certainly curious to hear more details. And when I realized Culver had let your brother into the house, I was not surprised to hear the door of his sanctuary close. So, I excused myself and left the dining room and headed upstairs to my room, but I snuck down the backstairs and slipped into the hall closet."

"Okay," I said, not following the closet aspect of her story.

"It's a secret place where I can eavesdrop," Kate explained, sensing my confusion. "The walls are thin, as I found out years ago playing hide and seek with Isaiah."

"Then you heard what Dent told him?"

"Yes."

"Tell me, Kate. What did my brother say?"

"Naturally, I thought I was going to hear more about the horse, but by the time I was in place, Culver was in control of the conversation and was demanding that your brother return to him that talisman thing, but Dent said he didn't have it. That you had lost it. And did you?"

"Did I what?" I asked, distracted by my concern for other details my brother may have shared in his state of inebriation. Kival, for one. I prayed Dent had not mentioned him.

"Did you lose the magic thing? The talisman?"

I looked at her, alarm bells sounding in my head. *Why had she asked me that?*

"I don't know about any ... magic thing," I said, my survival instinct persuading me to lie to Kate. Immediately, I regretted it. Kate seized Toto from my hands, looking at me as though I had just slapped her in the face. She turned away and began to leave, but I reached out and caught her arm. "I'm sorry," I said, as I stepped around in front of her. "I don't want any more secrets between us."

Kate looked woefully into my eyes, and in a flash, tears began to slide down her cheeks.

"Oh, don't—don't cry, please," I whispered, as I wiped away a tear with the back of my fingers. "The truth is—"

"Stop!" Kate commanded, pushing the tips of her fingers against my mouth.

I took her hand away, just far enough to fold the fingers and then kiss them. "I want you to know—"

"JT! Please," she said, shaking her head, "don't tell me anything else. I don't trust myself to know!"

I looked at her, wondering if my hunch had been right.

"Culver … he sent me to ask you. He said if I didn't ask you about the talisman, he'd send me away. Six months ago, I wouldn't have cared! I would have been glad to get away from him. I hate that man!"

"Kate," I whispered, withered by the pain in her eyes.

"But now, I can't bear the thought of leaving. To not see you again, JT. You—you are my rescuer. In my heart, that's the truth I know. No matter where you've come from, I know that God sent you to save me … from him!"

I pulled her to me, embracing her as tightly as I could considering there was a little doe-eyed puppy between us. I stroked her hair. "It's okay, Kate. It's okay. We'll figure it out. I promise."

"But what will I tell him? What will I tell Culver?"

"Tell him," I began as my mind plotted, "the truth. At least, the truth that you almost had gotten something from me." Then I shifted my head and pressed my forehead against hers. "Tell him I denied knowing anything about a talisman. Can you do that?"

She pulled away from me and for a long moment I stared at my reflection in her eyes. Then she nodded. "Yes. I think so. I want to, I'm just not a good liar."

"I didn't used to be," I said, "at least not until I got here."

She gazed at me, her green eyes transforming into windows of her mind, and I could see her thoughts forming into questions before she could even ask them.

"Tell me, what year are you from, JT?"

"Nineteen-seventy-nine," I replied, feeling that I could tell her anything and wanting to tell her everything.

A soft gasp escaped her.

"That's a hundred years from now. One-hundred-one to be exact."

"Right," I agreed. "But nonetheless, 1979 is the year where I belong. Though here, in Kansas, is still my home place."

"Are you going to go back? Are you planning to return to your home?"

I nodded.

"Then take me with you. I don't want to be here with him, JT. Please!" Kate spoke, her voice pleading. "Take me with you!"

I looked into her eyes, loving her more than I thought possible. "Don't worry. When the time comes, I'm not leaving without you."

"JT, I don't want to wait! Let's leave! Now!"

I rocked my head, wishing I could grant her request. But there were contingencies and complications that were precursors of an unavoidable delay. And that was the best-case scenario.

Quickly, I glanced outside to confirm that no one was nearby, then I gestured to her to follow me.

"Best to leave Toto here," I said, pointing at a wooden crate tucked along the edge of the barn wall.

"Stay, Toto, stay," Kate commanded as she sat the puppy inside the box.

Then we ascended a ladder that was attached to the wall and climbed into the vast hayloft of the barn and found a quiet place where we could sit and talk. And then I told her why leaving right away was not possible, explaining to her that a passageway had to be opened in order to return to the future, the timeframe of my true existence. Then I informed her it would be just over a year before that passageway could be opened. Her disappointment was defeating, but at least there was hope. But that optimism required patience.

I explained the aphelion and perihelion to her and dressed those orbital phenomena with as much detail as I could retrieve from the files of my memory, though I intentionally omitted that most of what I knew I had learned from a man named Morgan. Kate seemed to accept the science unquestionably.

"JT, you sound so very smart."

"I read a lot. And I mean a lot."

"So do I," she replied with a smile. "So, the aphelion brought you here, but the perihelion takes you back," she recited, eagerly returning us to the subject of time travel.

Morgan is going to like her, I thought. Although, he was certainly going to be unhappy with me for taking Kate into my confidence. Not to mention, I could expect a reprimand for ignoring his warning to abstain from engaging in a relationship with someone outside the parameters of my rightful time.

"When did you learn all of this?" Kate asked.

"Truthfully, just a few months ago."

"How?"

"I suppose I was in the right place at the wrong time. But before, I would have argued I was in the wrong place at the right time."

"Before what?"

"Before meeting you," I said to her, knowing then that she was the one with whom I wanted to share my life. The one I would be taking home to meet my mother. Despite Morgan's advice.

Kate smiled. "You are even smarter than I thought," she cooed, her appreciation of my sentiment clearly pleasing her.

Smart? Well, intelligent enough, I suppose. My mom would be the first to tell her that I had been my senior class Valedictorian. That I had learned to read third-grade level books by the time I completed kindergarten and had recently scored remarkably well on my SAT exams. But there were other things I wanted her to know about me. Things that were far more personal and intimate. But I could save sharing those details with her at a later time.

Instead, I stayed on script and told her about the arch of the chalk rock pyramids, and how its geographic physicality made it the place that had launched me and my brother and Blaine and Oleander through decades and decades of the past, though currently those years now resided in the future beyond 1878. Intentionally, I left Sam and Kival out of my story. She did not know who they were, but when we had more time and greater privacy, I would tell her about them. But not yet.

"Tell me more," Kate begged. "What was it like, flying through time?"

I looked at her, wondering if she would still want to go with me once I told her about the creatures who escorted me through the gap that separated my time from hers.

"Well, I don't know if I'd call it flying," I said to her. "Not to terrify you, but I believe we underwent a transformation—that we were disassembled molecularly, then reassembled. I know that sounds crazy, and you may not even understand what I mean, but—"

"I know what molecules are, JT. I'm smart, too, just so you know. At least, Beverly says I am."

"And I don't at all doubt her evaluation of your intellect," I concurred, nodding, and smiling. And I did not say that just to placate her self-esteem. I meant it. But I could sense Kate was still hungry for more information and greater understanding.

And then I enlightened my beautiful and eager student about the Burmano-Ku-Partika, sharing with her Morgan's meaning of their name.

Dust men who fly the earth.

"That is so amazing!" Kate bleated with awe. I studied her face, looking for a sign of skepticism that would reveal to me she might have a doubt or two—or three, but within the depths of her wonderous eyes, there was no hint of suspicion or reservation.

"Kate, do you really believe everything I'm telling you?" I asked her, feeling somewhat incredulous, myself, that she was so willing to blindly buy the idea of the BKT, not to mention time travel and magical amulets.

"Yes. Why shouldn't I?" Kate replied. "I believe in God, even though I have never seen him. But in my heart, I know he is real. And also, in my heart, I believe you. I know now that you are probably the only person on earth who I completely trust. I can trust you, can't I, JT?"

"Completely," I assured her, feeling myself falling another thousand feet in love with her.

"Do you believe in God?" she asked, catching me off-guard. My mother had often professed her faith and had, like clockwork, escorted Dent and I to church for our weekly visit to Sunday School. Despite the Bible stories headlined by Moses and Noah and a giant-killing boy who would live to rein as a Hebrew King, I had not wholly reconciled within my mind and my soul that the triumphs of these biblical characters were the expressed will of an alleged Higher Being. But, as I had personally experienced on the recent eve of my eighteenth birthday, there were facets of this universe that I never dreamed to exist.

"I'm beginning to believe," I said to Kate, maintaining the integrity of my honesty toward her.

She smiled, and reached her hand to my face and touched my cheek. "I can see that," Kate said, staring into my eyes. "You have a genuine quality of goodness in you, JT. That is a God thing."

"If you say so," I smiled at her doubtfully.

"So," she began, removing her palm from my face and finding my hand to hold instead. "These dust men who fly about, these Burma-coo-particle things—"

"Burmano-Ku-Partika," I corrected, with a laugh at her expense.

"Yes, them," she agreed, squeezing my fingers in retaliation of my chuckle. "They sound like they could be angels," Kate said, her eyes glinting again with wonder and excitement.

"Maybe so," I agreed. "Or ghosts," I suggested. "But for certain they are some kind of supernatural being. Probably not of our world. At least not of the world as we know it."

"Then they could be Martians?" Kate asked, looking at me as though we were engaging in an ordinary conversation after having just watched a re-run of *Star Trek*.

"You've heard of Martians?"

"I've read about them."

"Really?"

"In a novel. *The War of the Worlds*."

"H.G. Wells," I said, looking at her, suddenly curious. I was almost positive the book had not been written until near the time the calendar had flipped into my century.

"So, you've read it, too?"

"Yes. A requirement of my Sophomore English teacher," I responded, still stunned.

Kate smiled. "I know what you're thinking."

"I doubt it."

"It hasn't been written yet. This book, *The War of the Worlds*. Its publication date isn't until 1898. Twenty years from now."

"I was wrong," I said, returning a smile that was accompanied by a raised eyebrow, and not the one that sat above my blackest of two eyes. "How—"

"I found it. In Culver's library."

"He has a library?"

"Yes. That's the room next to the front door, where I listened to him and Dent. Of course, Culver is cold and controlling, but he's a very educated man. All of the books I've read and those that Beverly has taught from are in his library. But, one time, I came across a section of books that Culver had made me promise to leave alone, which of course only made me more curious. Anyway, that's when I found it. And another written by Mr. Wells called *The Time Machine*, one he wrote a few years earlier, but still years from now," she added with a shrug.

I could do nothing but stare at her, amazed that she acted so indifferent regarding the books and their publication dates.

"At first, I thought the dates were misprints. And then I found other books with them, books that were older. Texts that talked of time travel, like *The Critique of Pure Reason* though it was written about one hundred years ago. And that was when it dawned on me that somehow Culver had experienced time travel himself. I mean, how else could he have those novels by H.G. Wells?"

"No wonder," I said looking at her with intensity, "you were not surprised when I told you I was from the future."

"Well, right away I knew you were different."

"Excuse me, but right away, you didn't like me."

"Not true. And don't ask me to explain!" Kate said, with a giggle. Gosh, how I loved her laugh. "So, JT, are there any—there—in your time?"

"Any what?"

"Martians? Are there Martians in 1979?"

"Well, only in the movies, as far as I know, but we call them aliens now, not Martians."

"Movies? What are movies?"

Oh, boy, I thought. I could see this conversation lasting for hours, one thing leading to another, and then another. Weeks, more likely. "That will take a while to explain," I said.

"Fine, but would you answer one more question for me?"

"I'd rather kiss you again."

She ignored me, but I saw a twinkle in her eyes that betrayed that she had heard me and was perceptibly agreeable to my suggestion, though my timing was off.

"This talisman thing that Culver wants. Don't tell me if you have it, I still don't want to know. But what does it do? How does it work?"

"Well," I began, my hormones rebuking the idea of more talking and less doing, "think of it as a key that you have to have to unlock a door. Without it, being in the right place at the right time will get you nowhere."

"I see," Kate replied. Then with a nod indicating my answer had been acceptable, she leaned into me, her lips finding mine. We laid ourselves backward, reclining into the hay, our kisses tenderly touching and tasting.

It was confirmed. She had liked my suggestion.

We had barely begun to make out when I heard voices. I scrambled to the edge of the large opening in the loft floor, the space where hay was pitched down into an empty wagon and saw Boyd and the swashbuckling Carlos cross below me. I turned to Kate and held a finger to my lips to shush her. She nodded, but she was smiling. I, however, was not amused.

"JT?!" Boyd suddenly called out. I rolled my eyes so far into the back of my head, I was almost able to get a good look at my brain.

"Yeah?" I said, peering down at my supervisor.

"Why the Sam Hill you be up there?"

"Thought I'd pitch some hay closer to the hole here," I said, silently congratulating myself on coming up with a feasible answer to his question. It was better than telling him I was locking lips with the boss's daughter, or his ward, to put it accurately. I turned to Kate and found her holding her hand over her mouth, apparently stifling a giggle. Then she waved her fingers at me. In response, I glared at her.

"Git down here," Boyd ordered. "I gots a project for you and Carlos."

"Yes, sir," I said, then scrambled to the ladder that rose through an opening of the loft platform and made my way down to the ground floor. I crossed and met him in the center of the barn, pausing to flick away a few strands of hay from my pants and shirt.

Boyd glared at me, his eyes looking just above my hairline. "You shore-for ain't been sleepin', has ya?"

"No. I have not been sleeping, I swear."

"You gots hay in your hair."

"Oh," I said, reaching up and dusting away at the top of my head, and watching as a few remnants of dried grass fluttered toward my feet.

"Where's your dadgum hat?" Boyd asked.

"Uh, must have left it up there," I said, pointing.

Suddenly my second-hand Stetson sailed down from the expansive opening in the loft and landed at my feet. I rolled my eyes upward, expecting to see Kate waving at me again. But she was not there. I shifted my eyes to the two men who stood in the barn with me, and both were looking into the shadows of the loft above them as though they were wondering what else might miraculously appear if they were to just ask for it.

"Pardon me, Boyd!" said a voice behind me, and I turned to see Beverly Carneiro standing in the doorway, a heavy cape wrapped around her head and shoulders. "Have you seen Miss Kate?"

"No, Ma'am," Boyd responded, "I shore-for ain't. Would you like me to look for her with ya?"

Beverly sneered at him for a moment, then she glanced at me. I regarded her with an innocence that was probably not as convincing as I had hoped for, but since she didn't ask me if I had seen Kate, I didn't volunteer an answer. If I had, it would have been an unapologetic lie.

"No, thank you," Beverly said answering Boyd's invitation, then turned away, heading, I presumed, for the horse barns. I waited until she disappeared around the corner beyond the doorway before reluctantly returning my attention to the others. I found Boyd and Carlos looking at me. My supervisor was shooting me a silent but an ironically loud glare, but the vaquero stood grinning at me, his eyebrows bouncing with humor.

"Miss Kate?!" I heard Beverly callout, her voice somewhat muffled by the barn, but bleeding through its exterior walls. Suddenly, the sound of feet scrambling overhead met my ears, and in the next second the young woman who was the subject of a determined search and rescue was descending the corner ladder that I had myself used moments ago.

Shit, I thought, and I could feel myself blushing even though I had nothing to genuinely be embarrassed about. Still, I was inclined to invent an explanation to Boyd assuring him that *I had no idea she was hiding up there.*

"Hi Boyd," Kate said once she had her feet planted on the same plane as the rest of us. "JT's been showing me his—," she paused, looking at me with a mischievous grin, knowing the hesitation would be intermediately construed as something ungentlemanly. "Pitch-forking skills," she said, finishing her sentence, however, I wasn't at all sure that sounded much better.

I glanced at Boyd, though I didn't really want to look. He was, as it turned out, redder than I was, but I couldn't tell if his facial coloring was from embarrassment or because he was pissed.

"Good girl!" Kate said as though talking to a child, and I glanced at her as she lifted the little puppy from the box and tucked her inside the space at the front of her coat. Then she turned to Boyd. "Nice hay, by the way," she added, then left the barn, skipping toward the house.

"You, *mi amigo*, are a scoundrel," Carlos said to me with a heavy Spanish accent that demonstrated some of the English he had been learning from us gringo caballeros. I glanced at him seeing that he was still smiling.

"It's not what you think," I began, speaking more to Boyd than to Carlos. The old cowboy stood peering at me with one eye nearly squinted shut. I had observed that look before and undoubtably knew one of his stump speeches was about to begin.

"Carlos, git on outta here," Boyd said, motioning for the vaquero to leave. "JT ain't gonna need no hep after all."

Thirty minutes later, I was chopping firewood.

With a dull axe, I might add.

I'm not sure what project Boyd had originally had in mind for me and Carlos, but clearly, it wasn't the punishment I was currently being dealt. But I didn't complain. The time I had spent with Kate was worth every swing of the axe.

But there was one big problem that had reared his ugly head.

Culver Headville.

Sending Kate to pump me for information proved he was no longer pussyfooting around.

PART FOUR

In No Time Flat

CHAPTER 50

A light blizzard blew into our midst two days later, and the cold that it brought was comparable to Dent's frosty attitude toward me. Five days had passed since our quarrel and my subsequent beating, and still he was avoiding me. But his appetite had returned, forcing him to gather at the bunkhouse table once again for communal breakfasts and dinners. And there among the others, he laughed and told stories and pretended everything was just hunky-dory, but it wasn't.

Not between us.

Not once during those mealtimes, even when circumstances positioned us at the table sitting face to face, did Dent look at me. As far as he was concerned, I appeared not to exist. In the evenings, after our supper, he would eventually leave. Per Mick, Dent had decided he would permanently bunk in the ranch's original limestone-faced dugout that had once housed the Indian laborers before they had been relocated away from the control of Culver Headville. The place was a definite downgrade from the modern bunkhouse but provided my brother with a degree of solitude which appeared to be his priority.

Fine.

I would give him time and space—if that was what he needed. But another week passed, and nothing had changed.

Nothing, except for me.

I'd had enough of his cold shoulder. And tonight, I had plans to tell him about it.

I glared at the back of Dent's head as he faced away from his dinner companions, sitting backwards on the long bench between Pete and Mick and pulling on his boots. As he stood and slipped on his heavy coat and topped his head with his cowboy hat, I kept my eyes pinned on him, noting his resolve to act as if I wasn't there. Then he bid goodnight to the young men beside him and to Boyd and Sherlee, calling each of them by name.

"Adios, Amigos," Dent said with a nod to the vaqueros, then he stepped outside and closed the door.

Instantly, I shoved my way from the end of the bench where I had sat quietly next to Boyd and in fifteen seconds, I had my boots on and was outside the bunkhouse, slamming the door behind me. I didn't bother with a coat or a hat.

I was already hot.

I stepped down from the porch and peered through the gloom of the late winter hour and looked to the right and saw that my brother was halfway past the barn's corral, hiking briskly toward the place where he had chosen to relocate and sleep. A place that was conveniently away from me.

I went after him.

Walking fast.

When he passed by the garden that had fallen into its winter rest and was almost to the gate of the pasture road, I called out to him.

"Dent!"

In the light of the three-quarter moon, I saw him hesitate for an instant, but he continued to lay tracks clearly choosing to ignore me.

"I'm talking to you!" I shouted, louder than I intended. "Denton A. Tescott!" I added, emphasizing the initial my brother often used when referring to someone acting like an asshole.

Dent braked, and I watched as he turned to face me. I closed the gap between us, my eyes staring into the dark lunar shadow beneath the rim of his hat. "I know I didn't hear you right," he said, his voice relatively unemotional.

"You heard right, asshole," I said, making sure he understood my temperament.

"Do you want another go?!" Dent asked, his voice now elevated.

"Is that what you want?"

"Maybe this time you'll fight back!" He snapped at me. "For chrissakes, JT!" he added, pitching his hat from his head, where it landed askew on the ground just feet away from where he stood. Then he splayed his arms outwardly, taunting me with his gesture of self-righteous vulnerability. "Hit me! Do it! Damn it, hit me in face! Kick me in the balls! I don't care! Punish me, damn you! I deserve it!" he cried.

I just stared at him, confused. Each of us studied the eyes of the other, then at once the anger that I had allowed to build within me crumbled away as I realized an unvarnished truth: My brother was genuinely hurting. I could count on one hand the number of times I had witnessed him being emotionally distraught and I would still have a thumb and three fingers folded into my palm. Without a second thought, I took advantage of his defenseless posture and stepped into his personal space and wrapped him in my arms. I felt him briefly try to pull away, but I locked my hands and squeezed him harder. I was not letting him go. Not until I had some answers.

"What's wrong, Dent? I'm your brother, for crying out loud." I did not always understand him, and often I wondered how we could be so different. Yet there was not another person in the world more like me, genetically speaking. Embracing him, I waited. Then I felt his body shudder.

"I'm—I'm—," he said, his voice squeaking.

"It's okay. You're sorry, I know."

"You don't get it," he whimpered, and I felt his head rocking against my ear. "I should have told you—"

"About what?" I asked, then it occurred to me. "About Headville?"

"You're not listening, JT."

"Kate told me what happened," I said, reassuring him. "So, big deal, you accused Headville of stealing Doc. We already know he's on to us."

"No, not that—this is different."

Suddenly the tone of his voice alarmed me. I shifted my hands to his shoulders and took a step away and looked into his eyes.

"You didn't tell him about Kival, did you?"

Dent looked back at me, his eyes moist, his face awash with uncertainty.

"What?"

"Dent, you didn't say anything about Kival, did you? About him or the talisman?"

He shook his head, clarity filling his eyes. "No," he said to me. "I didn't tell him anything."

"Then, what? What are you so angry about?" I looked at him, then at once he jerked free of the hold I had on him. "Dent, I don't understand."

He shook his head. "No, you don't."

"Then tell me! Help me understand."

"I can't," he said, his head rocking. "Not now." Then he stooped to retrieve his hat, before he turned away and walked to the gate and opened it.

"When then?" I asked, giving him a few moments of time.

I waited as he closed the gate. Then he began walking the footpath he had worn into the surface of the December ground over the course of the preceding ten days. Then he stopped and spoke over his shoulder. "Soon," he said. Then I watched as he disappeared into the tree line and onward toward the place where Indian slaves had been sheltered. My brother's guilt was palatable, and I was ninety percent sure I knew what he would tell me when *soon* arrived. But surely, he and Kate hadn't …

But he and Laurie had.

No. Surely, surely not.

Throughout the next few days, nothing about Dent's attitude toward me improved, as I had hoped it might.

We were estranged.

There wasn't a better word for it. And it was heart-wrenching. And worse, he had planted a suspicion in my head, though I couldn't imagine that it was true. No, I had imagined it, though I preferred not to believe it.

But Kate, she would tell me, if I asked.

But could I ask?

Or should I?

If my suspicion was wrong, then she would be the one hurt because I had not trusted her. And then what would she think of me?

Damn it!

"A penny for your thoughts."

I was standing in the stall with Viento, grooming him with a bristled hand-brush, absorbed in my thoughts and obviously paying zero attention to my surroundings. Either the intruder had an uncanny ability to quietly catwalk, or I just sucked at being naturally aware of my surroundings. Either way, Kate had startled me.

Again.

I gasped, sounding much like a spooked little girl than the man I hoped she was in love with, if I were, in fact, a man and not still an eighteen-year-old boy operating without a permit to manufacture excessive amounts of testosterone.

Suddenly, my mind retrieved a memory of a conversation shared between me and my Grampa Jake, although I acknowledged the fact that my recollection of our dialog had likely become embellished with the passing of years. However, the gist had clearly stayed with me.

"Grampa, when will I grow up and be a big-boy man like you and Daddy?"

"Squirt, I don't have that answer for you," he had said to me, as he sat me upon his knee. *"At some point, you and your buddies are going to go out and play together as boys for the last time, but not one of you will know that. Next thing you will know, is that your childhood has quietly and completely deserted you."*

I remembered thinking then that Grampa could have given me a better explanation, one that as a four-year-old I would have bought hook, line, and sinker, instead of feeding me that spiel of doo-doo that had then made no sense at all. But I understood it now. Playtime, for me, ended when Sam died.

"What was that?" I asked, turning toward Kate, being sure to check down the register of my voice a full notch lower than my normal baritone.

"A penny for your thoughts. That's what I said when I scared you."

"You didn't scare me," I refuted. Then I gave her my best smile.

"What's wrong with your voice?"

"My voice?"

"You sounded funny, that's all."

I cleared my throat pretending I had something in it, like a frog, or a toad, or given the level of adolescence I was sinking back into, I might as well have been trying to dislodge a Galapagos tortoise from the confines of my esophageal tube.

"Where is everyone?"

"Around about somewhere. I think most of the guys are just hanging out in the bunkhouse. The vaqueros play cards a lot, maybe they're doing that. Boyd gave us the rest of the day off. You know, since we don't really get a full free day when we have livestock to feed and such. But I don't mind, it helps make the time pass. And besides—"

"JT, *around about* was good enough."

"Right."

"Is something wrong?"

I studied her for a moment, finding nothing that I could discern as being a clue to anything other than true concern embedded within her expression. But admittedly, I was looking for a hint of guilt, and relieved that I had not found it. "Just Dent," I said, gazing at her with what I hoped was unperceived curiosity. "You haven't seen him lately, have you?"

"I've not seen anyone. Culver has been keeping me locked up in my room."

"He's locking you up?" I asked, stepping out of the stall and closing the gate behind me.

"Not literally, no. It just feels that way."

Because of the cold, the barn doors were nearly closed shut, save for a gap just wide enough for a man to slip through, or a girl. I glanced toward the narrow opening, confirming that no one was there, then I wrapped both hands around her waist. "So," I asked her "how did it go with him?"

"You mean about what he wanted me to find out from you?"

"No, I'm asking how well he took the news that you and I were going to run off together into another century and spend the rest of our lives holding hands while reading the novels of H.G. Wells."

She stared at me, one eye nearly closed, the other appearing slightly peeved. "JT, if you're trying to be funny, you're failing miserably."

"Guilty. Sorry. So?"

"I didn't tell him anything."

"Nothing?"

"He didn't ask. It was like we never had the conversation. I don't understand the man. And that's partly why I'm afraid of him."

"I've noticed that about him. He excels at playing word games."

Suddenly, Kate rose upon her toes and kissed me. The contact was brief, but the quality was first rate. "That was nice." I told her, tipping my forehead against hers.

We held each other for a few moments, then she dropped away and looked me squarely in my face.

"What?" I asked.

"I'm just going to say it."

"Say what?"

"What I started to tell you a month ago, after you had …"

"After I what?"

"Kissed me."

"Oh, that."

"Do you remember?"

What a silly question, I thought, but I wasn't so dumb to speak it out loud. "Of course," I said smiling. "I remember … every detail."

"Then did you hear me tell you that I love you?"

I looked into her eyes. Her words were unexpected, but I kept my girlish gasp contained this time. "I did not," I admitted.

"That's because I didn't say it, you goof!"

Okay, I thought to myself, I had apparently missed something, but I wasn't sure what it was. "Okay," I then verbalized, but I paired it with a facial expression that was meant to convey *huh?*

"So, I'm telling you now, JT. Besides, I'm weary of waiting for you to tell me how you feel about me."

"So, you're telling me you love me?" I said, teasingly seeking confirmation.

"I just told you! Weren't you listening?"

In that moment, she might as well have been the only human being within a million miles of the two of us. There was no barn, no horses, no ranch. Just two people, Kate and JT. I stood gazing at her, my heart swelling within my chest as though it had grown three times larger, just as the cartoonish Grinch had likewise experienced. Love was a powerful thing.

"Well?"

"Sorry?" I said, pulling myself back into the reality of the moment.

"Do you love me back, or not?"

"Don't you know?"

"Of course, I know. I just want to hear you say it!"

She was my dream come true. As surely as the sun would soon set in the west, I would, come hell or high water, make her my wife. And the mother of my children. Great aspirations for an eighteen-year-old, but I believed them. I smiled at her, my eyes feeling as though they were grinning as much as my mouth. "Kate, I have loved you from the moment I first saw you," I confessed, then I pulled her back into my arms, and we kissed.

Softy. At first.

Then with great fervor.

At once, she pulled away and shook her finger at me.

"You are going to get us both into trouble if you keep kissing me like that!"

"Ditto," I informed her.

"Ditto? What's that mean? It sounds Martian."

I laughed. "Probably—"

"Never mind, I don't have time. Culver could pop in here any minute."

"Talk about a buzz kill," I said, and Kate looked at me again like I was actually from that other unearthly place.

"I made you something," she said, and I watched as she slipped her hand inside the pocket of her coat. Then in a moment she was displaying in her open palm, a ribbon-like thing, braided and colorful, with a half dozen loose cuts of thin fabric extending out from each end. "I made it from several of my bows and hair ribbons. Just something I thought you might like to have to remind you of me," she added then placed the token of her affection into hand. "Like Toto. Every time I see her, I think of you."

"I like that," I said. "And, this, too," I added smiling at her.

"You don't know what it is, do you?"

"Well—"

"Here," she said, taking it from me, then she pushed the cuff of my coat toward my elbow. "You wear it like this," Kate informed me as she placed the braided band above the joint of my wrist and began tying pieces of loose ribbon into tight knots, forming the hand-crafted gift into a bracelet. "There," she said, completing the last hitch of a tie before looking at me. I could not help but grin at her. "What?" she asked, then quickly her face muddled into disappointment. "You think it's silly, don't you?" and she reached for my hand as though she intended to remove the token of her affection.

"Don't," I said, my voice and my free hand stopping her. "I love it," I told her, and I meant it.

"Isn't—that—sweet."

A surge of surprise coupled with instantaneous anxiety caused my throat to constrict, and simultaneously I felt my scrotum voluntarily contract as the jewels within its purse sought to better shelter themselves against the possibility of an assault that would violently separate them from my person.

"Culver!" Kate exclaimed, looking past me.

I turned to see him in the doorway, a silhouette at first, but then he crossed to us and within moments he was holding the sleeve of my coat and examining the keepsake Kate had just placed there. I could not find words, but I had feelings, and they were not optimistic ones.

"I had no idea the two of you were becoming so … friendly," Culver said with a smile, the same smile that I had seen before. An expression that was neither genuine nor comforting. "Kate, my little bird," Culver said, dropping my arm. "I think it's time young JT joined us at our table for supper. A friendly little dinner party would give us all a chance to get better acquainted."

"That's—" I began, politely intending to scuttle his suggestion.

"Tonight, then," Culver said, taking Kate by the arm and cutting off any effort from either of us to quell his invitation. "Eight o'clock," he added then strode toward the door, taking Kate with him. He stopped and turned toward me. "I'll inform Isaiah to permit you inside my home, JT. And please, bring with you a ravenous appetite. For both food and conversation. We will surely have a lot to talk about." Then he and Kate strode quietly from the barn.

I considered the dinner invitation. It was polite enough, but it came with connotations that gave me an instant and severe case of the proverbial butterflies. And even though my testicles were doing their best to send a message to my brain to launch, without delay, into survival mode, it was time to suck it up, I told myself. This day had been a long time coming.

But my gut told me that a discussion of my relationship with Kate would only be Act I of the drama that would unfold from the pages of Headville's script. Act II would no doubt place at center stage a certain metallic disc augmented with a supernatural power.

Time would tell.

CHAPTER 51

Irapped my knuckles against the face of the front door, hoping my knock would be somewhere comfortably between that of a timid Girl Scout selling cookies and a bold *I'll huff and puff and blow your house down* kind of attitude. To say I felt nervous was an enormous understatement. The delay between the dinner invitation and this moment of which I was determined not to flee, had not alleviated my concerns by a single butterfly. I stood there waiting, glancing back toward the bunkhouse, wondering if any of my co-cowboys would rise to my rescue. Then I heard another round of laughter and concluded that the vaqueros were continuing to have a good time at my expense.

Isaiah had brought dinner an hour earlier, setting the bunkhouse table with nine plates instead of the usual ten, despite the fact that my brother continued to be absent.

Dent had, during the past three days, returned to a reclusive status at mealtimes. But nevertheless, Isaiah set a plate on the table for him. And because of either friendship or pity, Mick repeated his role as the Good Samaritan, gathering upon the extra plate three servings of fresh bread and a thick cut of meat before ducking outside with the take-out meal for my temperamental brother. Boyd had on one occasion chastised Mick for *coddlin' that stubborn peckerhead,* though he himself had just yesterday taken the evening meal to Dent with the intent to persuade him to return to the bunkhouse. The determined negotiation had failed.

Dent was, and had always been, stubborn as a mule.

After Isaiah had left, the men noisily gathered around the table while I stood near my bunk shaking out the wrinkles of my clean green shirt of which I generally wore only for special occasions, like going into town. Or when attending a wedding. And perhaps on this night, as guest of honor at my personal funeral.

"Jay-Tee, *mi amigo!*" I heard Carlos call to me. "*Ap'urate!* Before theese *denar es devorado!*"

I had slipped on the shirt, then turned around and began to button the sleeves. "Not tonight, Carlos," I had said with a subtle shift of my head, but my eyes had stalled on Boyd as I caught him gawking at me with a spoonful of beans in pause mode just inches from his gaping mouth. Then his eyes went to the remaining singular empty plate that had been set for Dent, and his cowboy accounting seemed to have instantly summed things up for him.

Tonight, I would not be dining with the hired hands.

Then Boyd had glanced curiously at Sherlee, who sat in his usual spot at the far end of the table, and my eyes followed those of the foreman, and I saw that the wrangler was staring at me, chewing slowly, appearing to be almost grinning. A quiet had fallen upon the room, and I had glanced around and found six additional sets of eyes pinned upon me, as though I were the unlucky target of a firing squad.

Then as if I weren't already uncomfortable enough, Little Pete noticed the woven bracelet of ribbons tied around my wrist, and he had stated the obvious, though adding jovially that he was surprised it was not tied to my peepee. His words, not mine, but still I had been instantly embarrassed. Carlos had then said something in Spanish, followed by a series of lewd gestures that sent the other vaqueros into a frenzy of laughter.

Feeling my face blush, I had wanted more than anything to flee from the friendly ridicule of the Mexicans, but I still had clean trousers and socks to change into and it would be senseless to kick around inside a cold barn waiting for an hour in advance of my dinner reservation. And neither was a visit to my brother at his current address a favorable option.

"Shet up! All ya all!" Boyd cut in, not for my sake, but for the offensive insult that obscenely implicated Kate.

Ignoring my comrades, I stayed put, tinkering with the items I kept stored in my saddle bag. Then after Sherlee left, I asked Boyd the time and he pulled a round, tarnished pocket watch from his vest and looked at it.

"Seben minutes till the hour," he had said, and I then thanked him for the information. A few minutes later, I opened the door of the bunkhouse.

"Nice knowin' ya!" Little Pete had said as I gladly pulled the door closed behind me. We both knew his teasing was benign and playful, but what he didn't comprehend was the precarious situation I expected to find myself floundering in before the night was over.

But then, that was just speculation on my part. I didn't really know. Not for certain.

But my gut said otherwise.

I began to knock for a second time when the door opened, and Isaiah stood there looking at me, his eyes not in the least appearing pleased. In fact, he looked worried. And that expression did nothing to help settle my angst.

I politely removed my Stetson, realizing I should have left it at the bunkhouse, but habits are hard to break. I then stepped across the threshold of the front door and was met by a relatively grand foyer, complete with a broad set of stairs sweeping gently upward to the second floor. I lifted my eyes just long enough to notice that the balcony wall was laminated with what appeared to be a flocked wallpaper patterned with an ornate floral design similar to the covering I remembered being on the walls in the front room of my Gramma Vi Thomas's home.

Flowers and Headville.

That was as conceivably incompatible as fire and ice.

After relieving me of my hat, Isaiah then invited me to follow him, and we crossed through the intricately paneled foyer, passing by a room that was dark, but light enough to reveal shelves of books. Obviously, it was the room that was Headville's library. A place of knowledge. Both past and future.

Turning right, I followed Isaiah into a short hallway and at the end we arrived at a doorway, where he paused and gestured that I was to enter ahead of him. When I did, my eyes were immediately drawn to a large mahogany dining table, dark, long, wide, and ornamental. And seated on exquisitely upholstered chairs were those who would be my dinner companions for the evening.

Kate, Beverly Carneiro, and of course, the dishonorable and narcissistic Culver Headville.

Without question, the three of them had been waiting for me.

"Sorry, Mr. Headville, sir," I said, glancing quickly around for a clock and finding one sitting prominently upon a tall bureau positioned between two darkened windows framed in red velvet drapes.

It proclaimed a time of Eight-O-Six.

Shit.

"I thought I was right on time. I don't have a—a timepiece."

"That's quite alright, JT," Headville cooed, not so much like a gentle dove, but like a hungry tiger. At least that was my impression. "I would have been more surprised if you had been punctual."

Score one for Headville. He had been quick to exploit the opportunity to assail a less-than subtle strike against me.

"Please," he said, gesturing toward the complimentary place opposite from where he sat, and I noticed then that Isaiah had a captain's chair pulled and waiting for me to park my unpunctual ass. I had not expected such formality.

Immediately I moved, passing behind Kate, whose back had been toward me, and noticed that her head was tilted reverently forward. I sat down, and Isaiah helped me position the chair comfortably near the table edge, then he took a cloth napkin and laid it in my lap. Suddenly, I felt like a turd in a punch bowl.

I was way, way out of place.

I glanced at Kate and found her staring at an undefinable spot a few inches beyond the edge of the bone China dinner plate stationed in front of her, then noticed that Beverly was a near duplicate of Kate, both in poise and in proximity. Both were seated near Headville, Kate at his left, the esteemed educator and assumed sultry mistress at his right. From where I sat, there was easily enough space on each side of the table for three other people between the pair of them and myself.

"You must be feeling overwhelmed," Headville said to me, his face a mask of fatherly concern. "But don't fret. Dining with me is an event to be enjoyed and relished. Not something hastily consumed simply to satiate one's hunger."

"You have fine taste, Mr. Headville," I acknowledged. "I would have been more surprised if there had not been such extravagance." As soon as I said it, I wished I had simply answered him with a *Yes, sir*, or better yet a *Sir, yes, sir*.

I sat uncomfortably watching Headville stare at me, weighing my words and ostensibly measuring my attitude. I cursed myself for not being more contrite. Afterall, I had a lot at stake.

"I like you, JT," he said, suddenly smiling. "Really, I do. You speak your mind. That is something to be admired. However, a word of advice: Tread carefully. We wouldn't want these charming ladies to think we were preparing for a pissing contest, would we?"

He was frank, I could give him that. Though his advice had been two words, not just one. I did, however, manage to keep that observation to myself. "I meant no disrespect, sir," I replied apologetically, as I adopted his advice and began to carefully tread the uncertain waters of the evening that was set to unfold.

"None taken," Headville responded, flashing his magnetic smile at me, though for a second, I imagined I saw fangs shimmering like alabaster stalactites among the upper row of his even white teeth. "It's no wonder Kate is so taken by you."

I glanced at Kate and saw that she had not seemed to have moved as much as a hair, let alone did she reveal any sign that she had heard Headville speak. She was simply somber, and joyless.

"Well, let's eat. We have much to talk about!" Headville declared, then turned to Isaiah and nodded.

The meal was good. More than good, it was perfection, though at first, I was too nervous to enjoy it. However, the conversation directed by Headville had been surprisingly pleasant and unpretentious, and greatly helped to settle my nerves well enough to savor the dinner. Kate, too, had relaxed and when invited to share her opinion, she had done so with more enthusiasm than I would have expected. Despite my initial discomfort, her presence had so far made the evening worthwhile.

In the span of at least two hours, we talked about horses, and religion, and the implications of an invention recently patented by a man called Alexander Graham Bell, whom according to Headville, had reportedly named his communication device the telephone.   Then Headville moved the conversation to politics, focusing predominantly on the policies of the current U.S. President, Rutherford B. Hayes. Luckily, a section of my senior year government class had focused on post-civil war presidents, so I had some knowledge of the man who had been elected the nineteenth president the United States, even though the term election had been loosely re-defined by Hayes' ultimate win.

Rutherford Hayes had assumed the presidency following a contentious election where he had lost the popular vote to Democrat Samuel Tilden, though neither candidate had initially secured the requisite number of electoral votes. Ultimately, a House of Representative's congressional committee was appointed and subsequently awarded Hayes twenty contested electoral votes as a backroom deal whereby the Southern Democrats acquiesced to Hayes's election on the condition that he would bring to an end federal military occupation in the former Confederate States.

"I voted for him," Headville informed us, "though I didn't particularly care for the man. But, at least he withdrew federal support for Negro voting rights. Ridiculous to think that this country would allow slaves the right to vote and potentially direct the policies that affect those of us who are true and entitled American citizens."

I cringed at his utter disregard for the human rights of those who were employed by him, especially with Isaiah and Beverly being callously subjugated there in his presence, and in mine.

"Former slaves, you mean," I corrected him, unable to stop myself.

"For now," he said flippantly. "The order of the universe has been temporarily insulted by the political antics of Lincoln. One day, I believe, this country will realign itself upon the correct course of thinking. If only the Lecompton Constitution had not been rejected, this Kansas of ours would have tilted the scales of justice in favor of nationally successful pro-slavery politics. I helped draft the document and I signed it believing in my fellow white man," Headville added, pausing long enough to pierce my sympathies with his supremist eyes.

"Supporting the cause," my host continued, "I fought against the Free-Staters joining my comrades with the sacking of Lawrence. Alas, it was all for nothing … then. But things have a way of changing. I've been seriously considering a run for Kansas governor. And with my win, I would then secure a promising steppingstone to the Presidency. What do you think of that aspiration, JT?"

God help us, was my first thought. Followed by *not if I can help it*, even though I knew that neither the political history of Kansas, nor that of the United States, had identified Culver Headville to be among the elite roster of its elected leaders. But then I remembered that Morgan had confided in me his declaration that history is a fallacy. And unfortunately, Headville had the means and the motivation to change it. And if what Morgan had said was true, Culver had already attempted to change the course of this country with his alleged assignation of JFK, which was a fact in my history, but not a reality of Morgan's timeline. I still could not wrap my head around it. And probably never would.

"Well," I replied, choosing my words carefully, "If you win, I hope I am here to be the first to congratulate you." In the forefront of my mind, I was emphasizing *if*, but praying that I would not be *here* but instead living in my own time again. And hopefully the United States as I knew it, was continuing with the progress of equal rights and equality, regardless of race or gender.

And then, without realizing it was coming, my subconscious was insolently overruled by the sound of my voice. "But, if you don't mind my honesty, you won't get my vote," I added, glancing at Kate who was visibly shocked by my words.

"I appreciate honesty, JT," Headville replied without missing a beat. "In fact, I expect it from you," he added with that charmingly ingenuine smile. "So, tell us, why wouldn't you vote for me?"

If I were ever to be my own man, convicted to stand up for what I believed to be right and Godly, now was the time. "Mr. Headville, sir, I believe in the words of our country's Declaration of Independence which proclaims that all men are created equal, that they are endowed by their Creator with certain unalienable rights, that among these are life, liberty and the pursuit of happiness."

Headville nodded, then chuckled softly. "Your naivety is surprising, JT. Those words were written as propaganda to ignite a revolution against an imperialist King. No, our revered, and white founding fathers simply used poetry to imply equality, and they certainly would not have suggested that the Negro should engage in American policy, directly or indirectly."

"You talk as though you knew those historic representatives personally."

"Perhaps, I did. I do like to travel," Headville added, his implication obvious. "But to be clear, I live by a different slogan. *Quocunque Jeceris Stabit,*"

I studied him. "Latin, I'm guessing. Meaning what?"

"Wherever you throw it, it shall stand," Headville replied, obliging me with the translation. "And by that, I'm referring to power and influence, both of which I have learned to master. However, neither attribute should ever be wielded by common slaves, or other less-capable peoples. I for one, concur with the opinion of our Representative Sam Cox, that our government should always be a leadership of white men, and that the founders who made this government never intended to elevate the black race to be equal to the white."

"Sam Cox does not represent me."

"Obviously. But without an established and supported hierarchy of ethnicity, our country will ultimately be subjected to chaos."

"Chaos for whom?"

"For me. And for you."

"White men."

"Precisely. Because, JT, we are pre-ordained to rule, so we will rule. White over black. Manifest destiny takes many forms." Then Headville paused and peered across the table at me, his countenance stern and disapproving. "I suppose you also are a champion for the savage?"

"The American Indian, yes, I suppose I am."

"That surprises me," Headville mused. "Considering your alleged recent experience," he added, studying my eyes and daring me to deny the truth of his statement. "But then, you know Oleander better than I do, perhaps he embellishes his storytelling."

"He's been known to exaggerate things," I admitted.

"His maimed hand says otherwise."

"To be frank, Oleander's stupidity is why he lost his finger."

Headville laughed. "We could all learn from him. If only Custer had not been so foolish he might have experienced more success. And your friend, Sam Chambers, might still be alive."

My heart had leapt to my throat, though I held my gaze steady, refusing to express any reaction to the audacity of his declaration. If he presumed that I would attempt to avert the avenue of his subjective conversation, I intended to prove him wrong.

"If Custer had not been an arrogant asshole, hundreds of innocent lives, both Indian and White, could have been spared, then and now. Including my friend, Sam."

"You're not an admirer of the Colonel."

"No, I am not. A man with his ego should never have been given so much power. He habitually raided Indian camps knowing the men were out hunting, then with cowardice he slaughtered unarmed women and innocent children in an attempt to incite entire tribes to engage in a fight he believed they could not win. Ultimately, Custer underestimated his enemy and ended up with a very bad haircut."

"Bravo!" Headville laughed. "I am awed by your conviction! I wonder, would your speech have been different if you would have known that George was a close friend of mine?"

"Probably not."

Headville laughed again. "I don't doubt that! Kate, my little bird, your JT is a man to be admired, especially for one so young."

I glanced at Kate, but she didn't look as though she shared his counterfeit admiration. In fact, she looked nauseously ill.

"But, JT, you are as naïve as you are immature. It will surprise you to hear that I was once a champion for the Indian. However, I also fought against them. Once, though, I saved a young Kiowa maiden from her enemies, the Cheyenne. I rescued her, offered her a home, provided her safety and protection. She was my kitten," he added with a believable note of fondness. "And then, she betrayed me," his tone instantly dark and ominous.

Just that quick he was nakedly bitter.

"She took from me two things that were mine," Headville said, pausing and staring at me as though his loss was my fault.

I looked at him, struggling to maintain an appearance of ignorance. But I knew that the woman he referred to was Kival's mother. And the talisman was one of the things she had taken from him. But what would have been the other? Then it clicked. But the click had a big question mark.

Was Culver Headville Kival's father?

"Luckily though, you, JT, are in the position to return to me the talisman. The other, I could care less about."

I stared at him, genuinely surprised he had been so bold in front of witnesses. Obviously, he did not feel threatened by the two women. I hesitated, pondering the context of my reply. Affirmation? Ignorance? Or a ballsy kiss-my-ass?

"If you deny your knowledge of the thing I so dearly desire, then you would be even more fatuous than Oleander, though less careless than your brother. But you are not idiotic. You know it, and I know it. In fact, you are well-educated, are you not, JT?"

"I've read a few books."

"Come," he said, rising to his feet. "You will appreciate my library."

I glanced at Kate, her eyes firmly cast downward, staring blindly into the tabletop. She did not attempt to look at me, and she seemed to be holding her breath. She was frightened, I could read that much from her catatonic state.

"Thanks. But it's getting late," I replied.

"I wasn't asking you," Headville informed me, as he stood waiting for me to follow him.

I got his message. Loud and clear.

CHAPTER 52

I exited the grand dining room, following Headville but leaving Kate and Beverly behind. When we entered the foyer, light glowed from the doorway of the library. Apparently, Isaiah had prepared the room while the four of us had dined. Retiring to his realm of books following an evening meal was apparently customary for Culver Headville. Inviting an ordinary ranch hand into his home was undoubtedly not so routine. But neither was I ordinary.

I had information.

And information was power, at least for some people. But I didn't feel at all powerful. In fact, I felt utterly vulnerable.

But Headville was right about one thing. It would be stupid of me to argue against the truth. I did know about the talisman. In fact, I had for a time, been in possession of it, though during those few hours, I did not know what it was, nor did I have the vaguest idea of what it could do. Ultimately, though, I had been transported because of it. Regardless, I was certain that Headville presumed I knew of its exact location, though if I told him otherwise, he would justifiably call me a liar. For certain, I would sooner die than reveal to him any aspect concerning the talisman's whereabouts. At least I kept telling myself that my secrets, all of them, were worth dying for. I had, after all, made promises.

One could argue that the vow was essential considering Headville's escapades into the future. For all I knew, he might have already brought back with him a cache of inventions that might be used to locate an item as small as the talisman, that necessary piece of the time-travel equation that hailed the Burmano-Ku-Partika. It was reasonable to assume that he would not be so humbly and inadequately prepared, given the conceit of his personality.

Still, without twentieth or twenty-first century equipment, the talisman was surely lost.

Lost beneath the surface of a river a good seventy miles west. Probably buried in mud and silt, its minute size blending with hundreds of thousands of river stones and pebbles. So why not tell Headville the truth, if he forced my hand? If he looked for it, he would have a one in a billion chance of finding it. Or one in a gazillion. More or less a chance as remote as catching a hair from the leg of a gnat as it whirled within the dust of a Kansas tornado. I was not a statistician, but I understood the nature of the odds. There was still a chance.

No.

I could not risk it.

Headville was an evil dude. And if he did get his hands on the talisman, who is to say he wouldn't go forward into my time and wreak revenge upon those I love. My mom. And my dad.

Besides, I had fashioned a plot of my own to use it and return to the time and place where I belonged. And going with me on that journey home would be Kate, she and I, side by side.

But first things first. I had to survive the night. I had so far prevailed in the dining room. Next up was the library. Suddenly I felt as though I were playing a real-life board game, moving from room to room where at any time I might meet Miss Scarlet or Professor Plum.

Upon entering Headville's presumed sanctuary, I discovered a sturdy, ornate desk was central to the room, and it would have been an easy focal point had it not been for the wall of books behind it. From floor to ceiling, and across the entire twenty-some foot span of the library wall were shelves filled with an eclectic display of spines, their widths and heights fluctuating between publications a mere half inch thick to volumes as much as three inches wide. Most of the books appeared to have leather-bound covers and were colored in assorted shades of umber, sienna, and cocoa, and were positioned without regard to the variation of their heights. Consequently, that arbitrary arrangement denoted the likelihood that the majority of Headville's library was comprised of individual works, though there were exceptions, notably a minimum of three obvious clusters of books of identical proportion and color.

The overall collection of Headville's library was impressive, and if I had not been from the future where I had already browsed through entire buildings with multiple floors populated with miles of shelving filled with research publications, and non-fictional biographies and how-to books, and the endless imaginings of the authors of novels, I might have been awed.

But I wasn't.

Though what did impress me, for better or worse, was the gun.

The pistol was handsomely displayed upon the corner of the otherwise immaculate desktop, resting upright above a polished block of ebony-stained walnut affixed with gleaming metal U-shaped brackets propping the weapon into a position that mimicked being aimed by an invisible hand.

Peripherally, my eyes registered Headville crossing behind his desk and reaching toward the center shelving of books to a place that was comfortably elbow high, though my focus remained glued to the weapon.

"A gift," Headville said, and I switched my eyes to him. He pivoted in my direction and in his grasp, he held a timeworn leather-bound book, a full inch and a half thick, and sized similar to the dimensions of an eight by ten photograph.

"The book?" I suggested attempting to redefine the subject of my attraction.

"No, the gun," he countered, as though he had been observing me with eyes in the back of his head. "It's a Colt .45 caliber single action, army issue. A gift to me from my friend, George Custer."

Of course, I thought.

"It has personal sentimental value. It's also remarkably deadly," he added, smiling. He paused for a moment studying me, seemingly waiting for my comment. I did not pounce upon the opportunity. "Believe it or not, the Colonel and I often strategized here in this room, sitting across this desk from one another, planning and postulating all sorts of things. A brilliant man. We would have made quite the pair on a ticket for President and VP. Damn his impetuousness."

"The book," I said, nodding at the item in his hand, refusing to be drawn into a debate regarding the questionable intelligence and undisputable inhumanity of his historical friend.

"*The Works of Plato*, volume three," Headville said, displaying the book. I glanced behind him and saw that there was an empty space between two sets of identically twined volumes, obviously one, two, four, and five. "Translated by Thomas Taylor in 1804. Together, they include his Fifty-Five Dialogues and Twelve Epistles. These are my literary pride and joy. Fascinating reading. Have you had the privilege, JT?"

"No, not yet."

"Then let's make sure you get that chance, shall we?"

I looked at him, trying my best to appear unconcerned, even though my stomach was beginning to churn uncomfortably.

"Wait! I've got something I know will impress you," he said, and he stepped toward his desk. I felt myself flinch, convinced his objective was the pistol.

But I was wrong.

Headville paused long enough to fish for a key from the pocket of his dress trouser, and I watched as he unlocked a shallow center drawer and slid it open and reached into its rectangular cavity.

"Look at this," he said, tossing a newspaper onto the desktop, it's headline boldly visible from the ten feet of distance that separated me from a renowned copy of *The New York Times*.

KENNEDY IS KILLED BY SNIPER

That was the first line of three headlining the Saturday, November 23rd, 1963, edition of the famous newspaper giant.

"This happens to be the only copy in existence, anywhere in the world. For the time being, of course."

I lifted my eyes from the newspaper and looked at him with as minimal interest as I could plausibly perform.

"JT, you don't seem at all surprised. Old news, I suppose. But then you were just a toddler at the time," he added, his poise as steady as his stare. He exuded patience, though I imagined he was acting as much as I was. "You realize the two of us have significant commonalties. We're both time travelers, for one. And then, Kate, of course, we both plainly have feelings for her."

I had no desire to delve into either of the two directions he was mapping out for me, but one was slightly safer than the other, so I decided I would do the steering.

"Okay," I said, with a minor shrug of my shoulders. "I'm from the future, Mr. Headville. You figured it out. Or someone told you."

"Someone, yes."

"Oleander."

"Oh, no," Headville said shaking his head. "It was you, JT. You were my unwitting informant."

I studied his eyes, saw that they were twinkling with amusement, but his words sent my mind into rewind, flipping through the pages of each of my encounters with the man. No, I was positive he was toying with me.

"When, then, did I tell you?"

"The second time we met," he replied smugly.

At the jailhouse.

That place where I had been unfairly incarcerated by the late Deputy Texas Jack Moody. That day had marked my second encounter with the imposing man who towered before me. But what the hell had I supposedly said?

"You showed me your bill of sale for that horse, remember? And there you were, standing next to your brother and in my hands was a document with your name on it. J-T-Tescott. And it was then I realized

I had met you once before. Both you and Dent. And your father, Dean Tescott."

I could not help it. I sucked air.

"Sit down," Headville told me, his words clearly a demand, not an invitation. "I have a story I must tell you." And then he confidently lowered himself into the seat of an extravagantly crafted leather throne.

I glanced behind me looking for a chair of my own so that I might yield to his command, and it was then I realized the walls that flanked the doorway into the room were almost a mirror of the main wall, a vertical surface filled with shelves and shelves of books. Then my attention was drawn to an easel that easily matched my height and displayed upon it was the oil-painted canvass of Doc-Bar.

The rendition was beautifully done. Whatever price Headville had paid to Rosa Bonheur, she had earned her commission.

Beside the easel was a Queen Anne chair, its Cabriole legs and sleekly curved arms boasting of quality and craftsmanship. It was an expensive seat. I hoped that my britches were clean enough to sit upon its fine upholstery. Regardless, I moved toward the chair intending to park myself upon it.

"No, no, JT," Headville stopped me. "Bring the chair here," he added, gesturing to the space across from his desk.

Apparently, our conversation was meant to be a cozy one. I lifted the heavy chair and carried it to the desk, placing it gently where he had indicated, and then I sat to face him, determined to remain calm.

"You're going to love the irony of what I'm about to tell you," he said to me, leaning back and clasping his hands across the ivory buttons of his vest.

"If you say so."

"It happened at the end of my last adventure into the future, JT. It was July 1964, and I had been stealthily making my way north from Dallas, after having been responsible for the most startling assassination since Lincoln," he said, nodding to the newspaper. "That sniper was me, if you haven't guessed already," he grinned, as though he had just been named *Time Magazine's* Man of the Year.

"Luckily for me, the inept Dallas police and the fumbling Federal law enforcement got it wrong, and it made my return to Kansas rather uneventful. I simply retreated into relative obscurity, laying low for several months, spending the first part of the summer in a cabin in the Colorado mountains, before my planned overnight stay in a motel in that charming little town named in honor of my heroic friend, George.

Then and there, I was mere hours away from the arrival of the big day," he added, his eyes daring me to be man enough to admit I knew of that specific planetary phenomenon.

Little did he know, the magnitude of my relative knowledge had been fostered by the man who had robbed him of the talisman in the first place. A twenty-first century scientist named Morgan.

"The aphelion," I stated, deciding to play his game.

"Yes!" Headville exclaimed, sitting up and leaning toward me, his face a countenance of glee. "Finally, you and I are getting somewhere!"

Yippee-ki-yay, I thought sarcastically, knowing my expression did not reciprocate his joy.

"The aphelion!" He concurred, returning to a recumbent posture. "So, of course you know of my specific destination on that day?"

"The arch."

"Hmmm," he looked at me curiously, "I was informed it was called the keyhole."

"By some, yes."

"But it is a keyhole! IF you have the key? Correct?"

I shrugged.

"We'll come to that in good time," Headville said. "I promise," he added with the grin of a snake. "So, deciding there was no reason to delay the return to my time any more than was necessary, I decided to depart from the motel just before daylight, making the final leg of my journey in the belly of an automobile. A spectacular invention, but not my cup of tea as the expression goes."

"Your preferred mode of transportation, a horse, no doubt."

"Of course. Although that morning, the car was conveniently more expeditious, given I had with me an additional passenger."

"Car?" I asked, my curiosity heightened in the flash of a second. "You mean a pickup and a horse trailer?"

"I'm aware of the difference, JT. But why would you assume I would be brandishing about in such a cumbersome combination?"

"Doc-Bar."

Headville smiled. "It was clever of Dent to piece that together. But, no, I had acquired Doc during an earlier expedition."

Suddenly I knew, but I did not dare to say it aloud. Stunned, I just stared at the man and watched as he quickly recognized that I had solved the riddle.

"Yes, I had Kate with me," he coldly gloated. "But more about her later."

For the next few moments, I vaguely registered his words. My mind was swirling. How the hell did Kate truly fit into his story? Had she actually time-traveled with him? Then at once I began doing the math. In July 1964, I turned three years old. Kate was now 17, so she could have been two, maybe two and a half, more or less, realizing then that I didn't even know her birthdate. I would have to rectify that oversight.

But given my assumptions, it was possible Culver Headville had taken Kate with him into my time at the previous perihelion in January. But no, Headville had killed Kennedy and that was in November of 1963, so Headville would had to have taken the time-forward window of the January perihelion earlier that year, which would make Kate a one-year-old child, but less than two years of age.

Or, alternatively, he could have transported her with him into the past, into his time. I was betting on the latter. It made sense. And it fit his character one hundred percent. Culver Headville was not only a murderous brute, but kidnapper was also on his résumé.

"So, there he was, Dean Tescott, a rancher, much like me, up at the crack of dawn installing what he called a cattle guard across the very road I was traveling upon, an obstacle inconveniently between me and the rock that was my destination. But he was a pleasant man, your father, but then I had little choice than to engage in polite conversation with him. Especially after I learned that the landform that was my window back home, was located on his land. That in itself is ironic, is it not, JT?"

"If you say so," I quipped for the second time since I sat down across from him.

"Oh, I do. And it gets better. Dean Tescott had in his company, two little sons who looked to be twins, though one was a rambunctious boy with dark hair, while the quieter one had a mop lighter than corn silk. And so," Headville said, rising to his feet and crossing to peer through a curtained window, "there at the jailhouse when I saw your full name on that bill of sale, and knowing that the keyhole stood upon land that would one day be owned by a Tescott, that moment became ecclesiastically revealing. A vision, if you will. Of course, it helped that your brother was the spitting image of the man I remembered from fifteen years ago. That meeting was irrefutably a God-ordained gift of revelation. One I had been waiting for, for a long, long time."

"Ironic," I said, hating the fact that it had been me who had revealed to Headville the key to our identity. I had been quick to assess the blame on Oleander. I had worried that the guilty party might be my brother. But no, it was I, without thinking, who had openly and unintentionally provided evidence of mine and my brother's origination, both in terms of place and time.

"I knew you would appreciate that," my host added, after giving me an adequate amount of time for my guilt to soak in. Then enduring another uncomfortable moment, I watched as his expression transformed. "Now, enough of this bullshit. Tell me," Headville rasped, shifting his posture forward. "Where is my talisman?"

"I don't have it."

"I KNOW YOU DON'T HAVE IT!"

Spontaneously, I scrambled from the chair, fearing that he was prepared to strangle me with his bare hands or throttle me with the pistol displayed upon his desk. And though I hoped the weapon was unloaded, I assumed otherwise and lifted my hands and held them at my sides, palms toward him, determined to minimize any threat he might perceive in me. But Headville didn't even glance at the gun. Instead, he stepped around the desk, striding boldly toward me, and in his eyes, I could see profound anger. An almost liquid hate.

"You are a zealously incompetent and ignorant boy. Did it not occur to you that I would have had your belongings searched knowing that I knew who you were after our meeting in the jailhouse? Perhaps it will surprise you that I have personally combed through all pockets and scoured every fold and crease of each garment you and your friends possess. I have examined your saddles, searched your saddle bags, inspected your bedrolls, leaving no stone unturned as a potential hiding place of my talisman. That said, the only enclosure I have not explored would require me to slice open your gut and spill your entrails upon the ground, denying you the opportunity to confess its secret location. But, neither of us want to see me pushed into such desperate measures, do we, JT?"

"Honestly, I don't know where it is."

"Honestly, I don't believe you," Headville said, calmly dismissing my relatively truthful denial. "Sherlee owns an exceptionally sharp knife. Perhaps he should ask your brother the same question."

"Dent doesn't know, either. I swear."

Headville shook his head at me. "No, I doubt that he does. Certainly, Oleander doesn't. I offered that nine-fingered buffoon a roll of Benjamin Franklin $100 bills, fresh off the press in 1964, and the oaf took them without blinking an eye. He's too stupid to have noticed anything of such incriminating importance. And obviously too foolish to be trustworthy. But you—you're the smart one. Not Blaine. Not

Dent. You. We're a lot alike, JT. We understand and respect the value of keeping secrets."

Suddenly a knock sounded behind me, and I turned just enough to see the infamous Willard Sherlee standing there as though Headville had conjured him merely by saying his name.

"What is it?!" Headville growled, surprising me by the tone of annoyance he directed toward his number one man.

Sherlee crossed to Headville and whispered in his ear. For a moment, I considered running for it, but knew I wouldn't get far before a bullet found its way into the back of my skull.

"You don't say?" I heard Headville speak, his voice cold as ice. Then he turned and looked at me, and I could see an idea formulating in his eyes, and when a corner of his mouth twitched in a failed attempt to smile, I knew something dire was about to happen. But now, knowing the malevolence of which Headville was capable, knowing he had an unexpected connection with my family, I had to be fearless. I had to be the man I needed to be. No matter what Headville did to me.

"Bring him," Headville ordered Sherlee, then he took the Colt .45 from its honored place on the desk, and checked the rounds, then nodded. "This is going to get interesting," he said to me as Sherlee grabbed my arm, his hand clamping around my bicep as if it were the jaws of a steel trap. I winced at the pain but swallowed it without noise. Then Sherlee was forcefully pulling me with him.

The three of us stepped outside into the chill of an inky night, and Headville picked up a lantern that had apparently been left on the veranda by Sherlee. With purposeful strides, we headed into the space between the massive barn and the trio of horse stables. I glanced toward the bunkhouse but saw that there was no light. Bedtime for ranch hands came early in the winter, and it had to be near the midnight hour.

Shit, I thought to myself. Where the hell were they taking me?

We passed between the building that housed the transport wagons and the last of the trio of stables, and within the perimeter of the lantern's light, we circumvented the grand barn. In the distance, I heard the lonesome howl of a coyote prowling about in the dark, and moments later we, ourselves, were passing clandestinely through the gap between the milking shed and the garden. Then I knew.

Headville's destination was the old limestone fronted dug-out, the place where he had quartered his Indian slaves. The structure Dent had been using as his sleeping lodge.

My heart was pounding. My breath racing in short bursts. I was about to call out a warning to my brother, but Headville turned to me as though he had read my mind and pointed the gun at my head. In the glow of the lantern, I could easily read his eyes. One sound from me would bring mortal consequences. Twenty yards later, Sherlee let go of me, and stealthily eased to the entry door of the old dwelling and pushed it open.

The soft sound of Dent's snoring met my ears, and then Headville entered, raising the lantern shoulder high. Sherlee motioned for me to follow Headville, and I cooperatively went inside, hearing Sherlee's bootsteps behind me. Knowing Dent was a heavy sleeper, I doubted he was aware that he had unexpected visitors.

Light spilled across the room and found the bed close to where the old iron stove stood against the far wall, and I could sense a subtle amount of heat emanating from pulsing embers ensconced within its metal bowel. Atop the bed, lay a jumble of blankets heaped over the form of a man far too large to be that of my slumbering brother.

Then suddenly, a movement flashed across the bed, as a masculine cry of startled surprise pinged against my ears. In the next instant, Mick, shirtless, was sitting upright upon the mattress.

"Shit," I heard Mick whisper, as he stared across at us, his eyes fearfully focused on the man who held the source of light.

Then next to him, Dent arose, likewise appearing to be naked.

"JT!" Dent called out to me as the numbness of his sleeping mind awoke and fired on all cylinders. I stared back at him, profoundly speechless. For a moment, it felt as though he and I were the only two in the room. Stunned beyond words, I had forgotten about Headville and Sherlee, and though Mick was next to him, I could only look at my brother.

"Oh, God," Dent breathed, then his head began to rock from side to side, and in his woeful eyes I discerned how thoroughly mortified he felt in his moment of personal exposure. "I'm sorry," Dent whispered, as though he feared the shocking rawness of his secret had just inflicted an unforgivable wound.

Struck dumb, I stood there facing him, my feet weighing me in place, my heart and mind wondering how I could not have known. How I could not have picked up on some clue or at least a hint of some kind. But there he was, my brother sharing a bed with Mick, and the evidence of his words and the tears that swelled in his eyes was enough to convince me that the two of them had been sexually intimate. Maybe only tonight. But possibly for longer. But still, I could barely believe my eyes.

"What do we have here?!" Headville chortled, seemingly more amused than angry. "What do you call them in your time, JT? Queers, I think?"

"Mr. Headville," Mick stuttered, sliding out from under the covers, revealing that he was at least clothed from the waist down. "It's not…"

"Not what, Mick? And don't you dare lie to me," Headville warned him, and there was nothing but vicious contempt supporting his words.

Mick stared back at Headville, and I could see he was perhaps less concerned with Headville, than Dent was with me. But then, Mick's chin began to waver. "It's not easy to explain," he uttered apologetically as he stepped around the bed, positioning himself between the bossman and my brother sitting upright on the mattress.

"I get it," Headville said flashing his trademark smile of insincerity. "Two young, handsome, men nearly pissing pure testosterone. And the whores in town, well, let's be honest, they are worse than pigs. And it gets lonely out here, isolated on the ranch. That's why I have a dark little dove to take care of my fevered needs."

"It's more than that, Mr. Headville, sir," Mick said, his voice cracking. "I care about him," Mick whispered, "a hell of a lot," he added then turned and peered down at my brother, his eyes filled with affection. Without a hint of warning, I watched as Dent's face crumpled into an expression born of both anguish and joy.

"But I take full responsibility, Mr. Headville, sir," Mick conceded, returning his attention to the man who controlled his fate. "I'm older. I seduced him. So, fire me. Or drag me off from your place like Sherlee did to Big Pete. But, please, don't take your anger out on Dent."

Silently, I listened to Mick, moved by his brave declaration of the genuine feelings he held for my brother. But I knew Dent well enough to suspect that he was more likely to have been the one making the first overture. Boldness was his nature. But Mick's protectiveness and his open profession of his affection for my brother said something, and I sensed that Dent had not expected to hear either of those things.

"Mick, I'm not going to fire you, or have you dragged away like a lowly horse thief. Not when you've provided me with this golden opportunity that I, myself, had not thought to orchestrate. But," Headville said, pivoting upon the wobbling apex of his psyche, "I can't have … people … talking … I mean, I have a reputation, and I have aspirations, both of which would be damaged beyond repair if it were known that I employed … freaks."

BANG!

Within the close confines of the thick-walled building, the gunshot burst against my eardrums, but the sound was nothing compared to the assault on my eyes as I watched the impact of the bullet blast through Mick's chest. In linked seconds of heart-retching revolt, I leapt upward, my hands flailing defensively, my mind and my mouth cursing the horror as Mick fell backward across the bed, his life insolently snuffed out. But seeing his blood splattered across the face of my brother was far more than I could handle. Instinctively I turned toward Headville, intending to defiantly grapple with the monster and steal the weapon from his hand before he could fire a second lethal round into Dent.

But Headville was unarmed.

As though I were part of a slow-motion sequence of some B-grade slasher film, I retardedly swung around and discovered the Colt .45 in Sherlee's hand, it's barrel smoking.

"Mick!" Dent cried out and I turned to see him grasp the dead man by his shoulders and lift him into his arms. Then in an instant, Dent's characteristic temper flared violently, and he let go of Mick and flew from the bed, Sherlee the target of his rage.

I panicked, fearing for Dent's life. But before I could do anything to stop him, I watched as Headville reached for my brother's head, mercilessly grasping a fist full of Dent's thick hair, and with an unexpected but potent force of strength, Headville jerked him backwards upon the hard floor. The move had caught Dent by surprise, and the fall clearly knocked the wind out of him. But before he could recover, Headville leaned down and entwined his fist into a second grip of his hair and heaved his semi-clothed body upward and stood Dent upon his bare feet as though he was as light as a rag doll. In the next second, Headville shoved him toward the door.

I stepped toward them, intending to intervene in the brutality of Headville's assault on my brother, but a hard thick hand clinched the back of my own hair and jerked me away. And then I saw the gun and felt its warm barrel against my neck.

Ruthlessly, Headville and Sherlee led us away as though we were a pair of marionettes being manipulated with very short strings, a relatively easy task given they were both bigger and stronger, outweighing us by at least twenty and thirty pounds respectively. Not to mention, we had nothing with which to defend ourselves against a lethal Colt .45. By sheer happenstance, I saw Dent look at me, his eyes brimmed with tears of grief, though he seemed to clearly notice the weapon pointed at my head, convincing him, I hoped, not to attempt to wrestle himself free of Headville's grasp. Considering both of us had just witnessed a cold-blooded murder, it would be nothing less heinous of Headville to assign the same fate to either of us.

We were at the mercy of a madman.

Neither of our captors relinquished their brutal hold on us until after they had callously steered us along the dark path and delivered us into the center of the ranch yard. Together, they released their tangled grips from the natural harnesses of our heads as though they had obliged us with a mercy we did not deserve.

"BOYD!" Headville called out, as Sherlee corralled the two of us with just the mere threat of the gun.

Hostage to the whims of a lunatic, we stood obediently as the chill of the December air cruelly caressed us with its icy fingers. I glanced at Dent, his torso naked, his feet bare, and the dressing of just his long underwear peeled down over his waist was pitifully inadequate to protect him from the elements, though I was glad, at least, that he was still breathing. Sherlee could just as easily have fired two shots. Or three, for that matter. Luckily, my brother and I were worth more to Headville alive than dead.

For now.

Abruptly, Boyd appeared in the doorway, wearing barely more clothes than Dent.

"Culver?" Boyd said groggily, peering at our midnight gathering. "That you?"

"Get dressed and get the hell out here!" Headville replied with intense animosity.

"It shore-for gotta be way late. What be goin' on?"

"The Tescott boys," Headville replied. "One of them just murdered young Mick."

CHAPTER 53

Definantly, I shook my head, but my brother voiced his dissent. "He's lying!" Dent spat. "It was Sher—"

With a malicious arc of speed, Headville's arm swept outward stymieing my brother's speech with a vicious, fisted backhand across Dent's face. The blow was offensively harsh and characteristically vile, and it knocked him backward sending him brutally to the ground.

"You bastard," I cursed, preparing myself for the same strike from Headville but it didn't come. Instead, Sherlee pinned my arms behind me and lifted me up by my elbows, painfully pinching and binding my joints causing me to howl in anguish.

Then I watched as Little Pete and Carlos, and the other Mexicans, poured out onto the porch staring at the spectacle being staged in the light of the lantern. I didn't dare to hope that they would help. If they tried, I was certain that one or all of them would end up like Mick. Headville had clearly demonstrated his disrespect for life.

In a moment, Boyd tumbled past them, buttoning his trousers, the tops of his boots holding up the cuffs of his pant legs. He hurried toward us, looking between Headville and me and a writhing Dent who lay injured between us.

"Killed Mick? I—I don't believe it!"

"I didn't ask you to believe it, Boyd," Headville hissed. "What I say, is."

"But—but," Boyd stammered, his mouth gaping. "Where is he? Where be my Mick?"

"Forget him," Headville sneered. "And if you want to keep your job, you'll listen to me and do what I tell you. Now, go to Sherlee's quarters. Get his gun and his rope."

"You're gonna hang 'em?" Boyd asked incredulously.

"Only one of them," Headville replied. "To start. Now GET ME what I asked for!"

Boyd flinched at the ferocity of the demand, then hurried past me, but not before his eyes found mine, and in them I could read that he was genuinely scared.

"Pete!"

"Yes, sir, Mr. Headville?" Little Pete asked hesitantly.

"Saddle up two horses. Yours and Boyd's."

I glanced at Pete, and I saw him gawking at Headville, unmoving.

"Don't—make me—repeat myself—BOY!"

At once, the big man Oleander had nicknamed Ox bailed from the porch of the bunkhouse.

"You," Headville said nodding to the remaining men who had gathered outside. "Carlos, take your men and bring Mick here," he ordered, gesturing in the direction of the place where Mick lay dead. "He's there in the old soddy."

Carlos turned to his comrades, seemingly comprehending Headville's instructions, and barked a few words of Spanish. Within a matter of seconds, the four of them were trotting away.

From behind me, I heard Boyd shuffling toward us, and I saw that he was unhappily laden with the items Headville had sent him to retrieve.

"Give the gun to Sherlee, then help him tie JT."

Movement caught my eye, and I saw Dent struggling to get his knees beneath him. Then without warning, Headville ruthlessly buried the sharp toe of his boot into Dent's side. A muffled pop sounded in the air as the blow flipped him over onto his back, stealing his breath and smothering any cry of agony. Headville had just fractured a rib, or two. I had once heard the same sickening sound during a football game where there had been more injuries than touchdowns.

"Leave him alone!" I shouted. Immediately, Sherlee lifted me painfully higher.

"Ahhh!!" I cried out, tears burning my eyes. Then I felt the rope being wrapped and knotted around my bent wrists.

"JT!"

I heard Kate scream my name and I turned to see her standing upon the veranda, a silhouette in the light of the doorway, a nightgown clinging to her shape. In that moment, she looked to be a dream. An innocent. A bystander thrust into witnessing my astonishing terror. Then Isaiah appeared beside her.

"Boyd! Get her inside! Isaiah, lock her in her room!"

"JT!" Kate called again, and I glanced to see Isaiah pulling her away, as Boyd clambered onto the veranda taking her in his arms and lifting her across the threshold. Behind them, I caught a glimpse of Beverly just before the door slammed shut.

With an unexpected jolt to the middle of my back, Sherlee pushed me to the ground. I landed upon my knees, avoiding a faceplant into the hard, unforgiving earth. I ducked my head, the sweat of my anguish dripping from my face. I tried to focus. To think. Was Headville really going to hang Dent? Or me? What would he gain? He wanted the talisman above anything else, I was sure of it. Yet I could not dismiss the fear that tore at my throat. Frustrated and afraid, I mentally brainstormed for some way out of this nightmare. I needed to think of some unassailable tactic to save me and my brother from the rage of a psychopath. But only one thought hammered against my panic-driven mind: I had to tell Headville the truth.

What choice did I have?

"Headville," I called out, glaring at him through the sweat-soaked strands of my hair.

"Shut up!" He snapped at me. "I'll let you know when you can open your deceitful mouth. Otherwise, your next word will be paid for by your faggot-assed brother."

Hate emanated from Headville, and its authenticity was infectious. In that moment, I had never despised another human being more than I did Culver Headville. Seething, I sealed my lips and waited. Within the next minute, Boyd returned from the house, as Pete exited the barn leading two horses, both saddled and ready.

Then the vaqueros appeared from around the corral, the grim foursome carrying Mick upon a makeshift gurney. Carlos and Ramon were gripping the corners of the blanket nearest the dead cowboy's head, the others holding onto the corners supporting the weight of his legs, and from both sides, Mick's upper limbs dangled listlessly. They tenderly eased him down upon the ground just yards away from where I knelt, and his head lobbed sideways, his lifeless eyes hauntingly aimed in my direction. I turned away and vomited.

"Gawddamn!" I heard Boyd whisper, his voice aching with sorrow. "My Mick—no—no, no, no—" And then he choked back a sob and I prayed he knew that neither Dent nor I was responsible for the atrocity of the gentle cowboy's death.

"Boyd, take Pete and ride into town," Headville growled, dismissing the foreman's grief. "Bring back our deputy and that schoolteacher, Blaine. I want them here by daylight. Do you understand?"

"Yes—yes, sir," Boyd replied softly. Then, within moments he and Pete were mounted and riding away into the darkness.

"Carlos, get a shovel from the barn," I heard Headville tell him. "Bury him over there, behind the bunkhouse." I listened as their footfalls shuffled, and then faded away.

"Sherlee, bring me that brown gelding Dent Tescott thinks is a horse. No saddle."

I raised my eyes just high enough to see Sherlee pass by Dent's prostrate form, striding toward the barn like the obedient hitman he had been created to be. Then Headville crossed to confront me, squatting on the heels of his boots, and lifting my chin with the barrel of the pistol that was an hour earlier little more than a sentimental paperweight displayed harmlessly on a desk in a library.

But it was not so innocuous now.

"Are you feeling well enough to negotiate, JT?"

I stared at him, trying hard not show him how despicably evil I knew him to be.

"I'll tell you where it is," I said to him, my face melting, my eyes growing moist from the admission of my defeat.

"I knew I could count on you. So where is it?"

"Lost," I told him, before quickly expounding the details of my answer. "In the river, on my family's ranch. Not far from the keyhole."

Headville's discriminating gaze shifted right, then left, and back again, studying my face, analyzing my eyes. If he truly believed himself to be a man who could read the truth in people, he would know I was not lying to him. Instantly, his hand shot forward, snaring my face with a merciless grasp of his fingers.

"DON'T ever insult my intelligence again, J—T—Tescott," Headville hissed, proving his narcissism had no limitations.

"I'm telling you the truth—"

Then a burst of light burned into my eyes, and for an instant I felt an explosion of pain in my head.

"... come on Germ, let's go light these suckers!"
"I don't know ... those are kinda dangerous. They're black cats!"
"Yeah, big bangers!"
"But we don't have a punk."
"So? I've got matches!"
"Matches? Dent, we aren't supposed to play with matches!"
"We ain't playin' with 'em. We're just gonna use 'em to blow up these firecrackers."
"I don't know ..."
"... it's easy. I'll show ya ..."
A match with its end aflame flew into the grass ... the sizzling firecracker remained mistakenly clutched by his fingertips! No time to warn him ...
BANG!

I opened my eyes, awakened by a dream. It was one I had often experienced, though the recurring vision was really a reboot of a story

Mom had shared with my brother and I about a time when as a kid, she had nervously lit a firecracker with a match, throwing the match and holding on to the firecracker. There had been a moral to her story, but as I roused from my unconsciousness, my head was throbbing too much to remember what it was.

Aware, now, that I had been sleeping, I realized I had no memory of lying down for the night. Then the surface beneath me further muddled my mind and I wondered how long I had been curled upon the cold December ground. A few seconds passed before my eyes began to focus, and when clarity registered, I found that my face was pointed in the direction of the giant cottonwood tree that occupied the center of the ranch yard, its multitude of bare limbs stretching out into a sky that was illuminated by the circle of a bluish moon.

Beneath the tree, stood a horse, with a shirtless figure propped upon its back, and there was a rope tethered from the man's head to a branch above him. It took me a moment to process the scene, then at once I remembered what was going on, and I knew who had been poised for execution. I shivered, not just because I was freezing, but primarily due to the horror of the macabre stage that had been set during the term of my stolen cognizance.

"Dent," I called out, my voice a hoarse whisper.

"JT," I heard a distant voice echo, though I was aware enough to know it did not belong to my brother. "For a while, I thought I'd killed you," the voice spoke again, reverberating in tandem with a ringing in my ears. "And that would not have worked out well for either of us."

I turned my head, and through the dimmed blur of my vision I could discern the image of a man wrapped in a heavy coat, sitting on a chair smoking a cigar, a lantern, and an empty glass beside him on a small table. The scene was surreal.

"What … have you done to my brother?"

"Nothing," Headville replied, "Yet. What happens to him, JT, depends entirely on you."

"Headville!" Dent called out suddenly, his voice curbed by pain. "Let me talk to my brother."

"And why would I let you do that, Dent?"

"Because I'm the only one alive—who can talk sense into him," he replied, his breathing labored, his words edged with undertones of agony and discomfort. "You want that talisman? Then let me convince JT to give the damn thing to you."

Silence held the moment hostage and with each passing second the fog in my head slowly began to lift.

But an immense ache pulsed inside my skull.

Fierce and unrelenting.

By sheer will, I forced myself to roll to my side, and though my arms were bound behind me, I pushed myself up onto my elbow, and looked again at where my brother sat upon the bare back of his brown bay gelding. As I stared at his unclothed torso, my focus began to sharpen and I saw that Dent was actually facing away from me, his posture and that of the horse looking like they were bracing against the chill of a fierce northerly wind.

"Well?" Dent asked, and I realized his manner was without contempt or anger. He was uncharacteristically pleading.

Headville sighed. "No tricks," he warned, then mockingly added, "if Mick could talk, he'd remind you that Sherlee is an impeccable marksman." After a pause, I heard an additional order. "Help him up."

Hands found their way under my arms, and I was lifted to my feet. For a moment, I wobbled, my knees weak. Then I realized that Carlos and the snaggle-toothed vaquero, Ramon, were holding me up. I stood and waited for a minimal degree of equilibrium to return before attempting to walk. Taking a deep breath, I advanced a step forward, then a second step.

Then adrenaline kicked in and I moved with increased certainty. When I reached Dent, I saw that his hands, like mine, were tied behind his back. And then I noticed that Sherlee was there, concealed by the bulk of the horse, gripping its leather halter, and holding the animal stationary. I stepped next to the horse, Dent's left leg dangling beside me, and I rested my forehead upon his thigh.

In an instant, I was overwhelmed with emotion.

"Dent," I sobbed, my voice shuddering.

"Brother, you gotta be tough right now. For both of us."

I looked up at him, blinking against the blur of my tears, and saw that he was staring down at me, his mouth firm and determined, his eyes serious.

"Alone!" Dent called out suddenly. "Please."

"It's your funeral if this horse of yours moves," Sherlee informed him.

"He won't," Dent replied.

"Leave them," Headville spoke from behind me. Then after several seconds had clicked by Sherlee stepped away and strode past me, his heavy bootsteps fading until his movement ceased to make any sound at all. I glanced to where he had gone and observed him standing next to the seated Headville, both watching us as if we were the main attraction at circus freak show.

"JT," Dent said, speaking softly. I looked up at him. "I wanted to—," Dent hesitated, his chin wrinkled and quavering, his eyes glistening. "So many times, I wanted to tell you. But—"

"I don't care about any of that," I whispered, shaking my head. "I just care about you. And getting you out of this. Somehow."

"Laurie—," Dent murmured, "and the other girls … they—"

"It's all right … I understand," I quietly told him, pressing my shoulder against his thigh. "So, I have a gay brother … How cool is that?"

Through his tears, he smiled at me. "You … you would say that, wouldn't you?"

"Bet your ass, I would. And will."

"JT," Dent whispered, "the fighting—my anger—it wasn't you. It had nothing to do with you or Morgan. I was just pissed at myself … Ashamed of my own secret. But I was making you pay for it … I'm sorry, little brother," he said, his eyes begging for my forgiveness. "I'm so damn sorry about everything."

"Don't!" I begged him, my own voice restricted to a whisper. "You don't have anything to be sorry about. We've been fighting since we were old enough to crawl, so big deal. But let me be clear about one thing, Dent. You are my brother. No—matter—what."

He quietly studied me, and for a second, I thought he was about to display that killer smile of his, but suddenly he looked scared and worried. "Do you think Dad—do you think he'll still—if he knew?"

"Dad's always gonna love you, Dent. Him and Mom. Sure, he'll shit his pants at first, but he'll stand by you, you'll see."

Dent grudgingly erupted with a gusty laugh, though it promptly crippled into a sob.

"But what Dad wouldn't want is for you to be ashamed of who you are."

"But that's exactly how I feel, JT," Dent cried softly. "That, and weak. And I hate that feeling."

"Dent Tescott. You are the toughest dude I know. And the brother I know is damn sure strong enough to love who he chooses. And I'll be the first to whup the ass of anyone who tries to tell him otherwise."

Dent tried to smile, but like always, he was determined to win any argument with me.

"I wish I could be—strong—like that brother you think you have."

"Fine. Then I'll be strong *with* you. Both of us. Together. Hell, in a few years, we're going to laugh at all of this. Laugh at ourselves for being—well, for being pussies," I said, giving him a grin that I hoped would signal he had my support one hundred percent.

Dent coughed a gentle laugh, then tears pooled in the recesses of his blue eyes, and he began to shake his head.

"Mick's dead because of me," he whispered, his words strangled by heartache.

"No," I corrected him. "Not because of you. This is all on Headville. All of it!"

"When you get back home, you tell them—Mom and Dad—tell them that I loved them. That I was thinking about them—every day."

"Tell them yourself. We're both getting out of here."

"No," Dent said, his head again wavering, "You're going to have go on now—without me."

"Dent, I'm not leaving you. I've told him. I've told Headville it's lost. That the talisman is in the river."

"What?! Why?! Why would you do that?!"

"Doesn't matter. He didn't believe me. But I'll take the asshole to it, I'll take him to the place. I'm not letting him do this to you."

"JT, listen to me, goddammit!" Dent cursed, his moist eyes adamant, almost threatening. "We both know if Headville gets his hands on that thing, neither of us will ever get back home. You will never get back home. Don't you do that to Mom! You can't do that to her," he added, shaking his head. "She's gotta get one of us back, JT. Promise me! Promise me you'll get back home."

Tears stung my eyes, then slid like burning streams of liquid fire down my cheeks, mingling with the mucus that seeped from my nose. I wiped my face with the back of my hand and glared at him with obstinance. "I can't go back without you. I won't do it. Not while there's still a chance!"

"Listen, Wild Bill," Dent whispered with earnest, "you're daydreaming again. He ain't gonna let me live, we both know that. I only wish I could be there when … when you hand that sumbitch his ticket to hell."

"Dent—," I said, my mind dimming, my head pounding in alarm. "I can't beat him … maybe we can, but I can't—"

"Little brother, we're a team, right?" With a flicker of hope, I nodded. "I'm the header, you're the heeler. My lasso has landed. I've got that devil by horns. I did my job. It's your turn to throw the rope and bring that bastard down."

I stared at him, wondering *what the hell?*

"Those things," Dent murmured, "those Burmano dudes … will they take me … like they did Sam?"

"Nobody's taking you anywhere," I promised, my throat growing thick, my vision blurring.

"Ain't gonna lie … they scare me a little. But—but I gotta—," breathed my brother, the fear in is voice palatable. "I gotta cowboy-up."

"Okay, boys, you've had long enough," Headville called out, interrupting us. "What's it going to be, JT? The truth or the consequence? It's up to you."

"You're wrong," Dent hissed loudly, turning his cheek toward Headville. "You maggot-eating piece of murdering chickenshit. I'm the one making this decision, not JT!"

I shot my eyes up at Dent, alarmed by the rashness of his words and his timing.

"Get home to Mom. I'm counting on you, Germ." Then he turned his eyes away and looked up into the branches above him. At once I realized what he intended to do.

"NO!" I cried out as Dent simultaneously let loose with a blood-curdling yell and kicked his heels sharply into the flanks of his horse.

Startled, the gelding leapt forward, leaving Dent dangling behind him, his legs twitching in the air, his neck kinked and strangled.

Instinctively, I dove toward him. But with my arms tied behind my back, I was rendered virtually helpless. I bent forward desperately trying to get beneath his legs so that I might possibly raise him upon my shoulders and lift him up.

Then suddenly I was ripped away with such brutality that I stumbled backwards onto the ground. I looked up and saw Sherlee glaring at me. Then in the next instant he, again, had me captured by my hair and was dragging me away. But my eyes returned to my brother, and I watched in horror as Dent's legs relaxed, knowing in that instant he had become garroted by the lethal potency of the noose.

"NOOOOO!" I screamed, fiercely fighting against Sherlee, using my head and my shoulders and my legs to wrench free of the man's grasp. But his brute strength kept pulling me further and further away.

"Noooo," I cried out softly, tears and spit and snot spilling from me, my eyes pinned to the lifeless body of my big brother.

And then from nowhere a shadow passed by him. Then another. And in seconds a cloud swarmed around him, leaving me with nothing but a few intermittent glimpses of Dent hanging in the air.

"DENTON DEAN! Don't you leave me!"

But the alien swirl of the ghostly Burmano-Ku-Partika grew even more dense until my brother was fully engulfed by them, their alien forms veiling him from my eyes, just as they had done months earlier when they had taken Sam.

"DENT!" I screamed again.

Then at once, the cloud of wisping grey beings began to swiftly evaporate. And just as suddenly as they had appeared, they and Dent vanished into thin air. All that remained was an empty noose swaying from the limb of the tree.

"Right on time," I heard Headville speak plaintively.

Then I listened to a dash of feet scrambling away, as exclamations of Spanish spouted randomly across the night air. Then I felt Sherlee's fingers loosen their hold on my scalp and I dropped forward and wept. During the haze of several minutes, I perceived little other than my own impassioned cries, and the perplexing gallop of hooves racing away. Then an eerie quiet descended, though the silence didn't last for long.

"That foolish brother of yours. We can't deny he had balls."

"Go to hell," I hissed.

Then a fierce blow hammered the back of my head, propelling me into an instant darkness …

CHAPTER 54

My consciousness flickered.

I sensed I was being shaken, and I felt cold. Painfully cold.

And I could hear my breath panting sporadically. Moments passed before I realized I wasn't being touched by anyone. I was just shivering. Violently.

Then the sight of an aged and worn wooden floor appeared before me, its length unfurling beneath my cheek, the rows of weathered boards leading to a wall with a door and a single window. I had awakened to find myself lying on my side, my arms crossing my chest, my fingers digging into my shoulders, the cold surface beneath me resolutely soaking into my flesh. I rolled my eyes, examining my surroundings. I did not know where I was. Nor could I remember how I had gotten to this unfamiliar place.

I moved my hands as I instinctively began to rub against the bitter chill that had settled into my arms. Then I drew up my legs, but something caught at my right ankle. I pulled again and heard the clinking of metal scraping the floor. In the grey light of the room, I looked toward my feet, and realized I was without boots and socks, and discovered that my right foot was bound by a shackle of some kind, fastened with a heavy lock and tethered by a chain that anchored me to a weighty cast iron potbelly stove standing upon a bed of limestone bricks. At once, I realized I had been constrained and jailed. But why? Then without warning, the memory hit me, and, in an instant, I was weeping.

Dent was gone.

And Culver Headville was responsible.

I sobbed until I was spent. When I awoke again, nothing was different. I was still unbearably cold. I was still a prisoner to the shackle, a thing that had undoubtably been worn by others before me. And I was still filled with anger, and inconsolably broken-hearted.

My brother was dead, and I felt the all-too familiar tears returning.

Get off your ass, dipshit.

Hearing Dent's voice, I threw my eyes wide open. As quickly as I could manage, I mustered the strength of my limbs and sat myself upright on the floor, looking around, searching every shadow of the small room.

But I was alone.

I shook my head, clearing it of the cobweb of a hallucination. A trick played by my mind. A knock on the door of my instinctive subconsciousness, reminding me that I was expected to survive. Or at least to attempt to live.

I glanced around the room and noticed sticks of firewood stacked near the stove. I folded and twisted my body as I pessimistically searched for matches, discovering a box of them sitting on the floor, barely within my reach. I rolled to my knees and crawled to the stove. I opened its curved door and inside were the remnants of ashes, but arranged in their midst was an ample mix of bark and dry grass and twigs.

Someone had left a kindling for a fire.

Hindered by a chain that was barely long enough, I reached for the wood stack and began to take several of the dried logs and fed them into the belly of the stove. Then I retrieved the matches, and with shaking hands, I struck one into the magic of a flame and held it to the kindling. Within a few minutes, I had a fire that was growing inside the stove, and the heat of its flames embraced my hands with instantaneous warmth.

Squatting and balancing on the toes and balls of my bare feet, I held my hands toward the fire, noticing that my wrists were red and raw, and I remembered that I had been restrained with rope. Unfortunately, I remembered too much.

I stared into the fire. Ten minutes passed, and I sensed my body becoming invigorated, responding to the heat, but more importantly my mind was also beginning to recover.

An hour passed, and the room had grown relatively warm and tolerable even though I was without a coat or a blanket, having in my possession just the two layers of clothes on my back, but with no sign anywhere of my socks and boots, or cowboy hat for that matter. And I was hungry. But thirst was my primary yearning.

For now, I had no choice but to ignore the essentials of which I craved. So, I shifted my focus to the environment of my captivity. The place was a simple square shack, meagerly appointed with a bed in one corner that was too far away to be reached because of my metal tether. The only other furnishings were a tiny table under a singular small window, flanked by a pair of old wooden stools. And lying upon the table was an object that immediately captured my attention. Impulsively, I checked the pockets of my pants.

Empty.

Presumably then, the item was, as I suspected, a postcard.

With writing on it.

And written in my hand, though I could not get close enough to tell for certain. But for a month I had been secretly carrying the postcard I had purchased at the R.W. Evans grocery, an 1878 version of a convenience store.

Obviously, I had been searched. And equally evident was that Headville had incarcerated me here in whatever place this was. And since he had not killed me, I expected to see him at some point.

Eventually.

At whatever time suited him. Though for now, I was a prisoner.

But I was alive. And also, alone.

"Dent," I whispered, my voice hoarse and raspy.

I pushed from my mind the horrific vision of his last moments, and instead thought about his words, his requests, his wisdom. Dent had been right. Returning home was at least possible so long as there was a chance of locating the talisman. But if Headville somehow found it instead, there would be no way to get back to our time.

My time, now.

And I would be robbed of the possibility of seeing Mom and Dad again.

Headville could not be trusted with the power and abilities of the talisman. I was fully aware of that premise, but Dent had been even more perceptive of that danger. And my brother knew I would take Headville there to the place in the river if I believed that action might save his life. The difference was that Dent had understood that he was as good as dead no matter what. Headville was malicious. Evil. Without regard or respect for life. Dent had kept sight of those facts. He was a realist.

I was an optimist.

A foolish optimist.

As I sat near the stove, the heat permeating my body, I thought of Dent's bravery. With an impulsive spring into action, he had heroically done what I would not have been brave enough to do. He had voluntarily given up his life, but he had not acted with cowardice. What he had done had taken great courage. If I lived to be one hundred years old, I would never know anyone as fearless as my brother Dent. But it broke my heart that he, in his last moments, felt so shamefully apologetic for who he was. Then suddenly my mind threw salt into the wound of my heart, an echo of regret.

I had failed to tell my brother that I loved him.

Good intentions mattered little, especially now that it was too late.

"Dammit!" I called out to him, wiping away another salty expulsion of my grief, wondering how I could possibly have any tears left to shed.

Then suddenly I felt angry with Dent for choosing to abandon me. But I was more furious with myself. Out of fear for my brother, I had given up. I had been willing to let Headville win. And Dent had seen that in me. I was the one who should feel ashamed.

And for certain, guilt did weigh heavily upon me. In the solitude of this strange place, I rationalized that the loss of my brother was as much my fault as it was Headville's. And my best friend, Sam—he and Dent both ultimately died because I had lost my temper. If I could, I would roll the clock back, or more appropriately wind it forward, and reset that evening of my eighteenth birthday. Then I would do things differently. I would keep my anger in check. I would not lash out at Dad, instead I would hug him. I would not argue with Laurie, instead she and I would go see the movie as we had planned. And I sure as hell would not go to the party at the Pyramids and summon the Burmano-Ku-Partika.

Beneath the weight of this burden, I wondered if it was possible to redo a moment of my own experience. Morgan would know. But would he help me accomplish the rewriting of that fateful day? But if I manipulated those changes, then I would never meet Kate.

I then realized I could not have it both ways. And to be honest with myself, I doubted that I could change anything. Then, as I sat on the cold floor of this place in which I had been imprisoned, I decided I would not let Dent's sacrifice be in vain. I would die before I would tell Headville another word about the talisman.

In the next half hour, I found myself thinking of Kate, curiously wondering if she had been a regrettable witness to what had unfolded in the darkness of the ranch yard. I prayed that she had not. And if not, what then would she believe had happened to me? And to Dent? And Mick?

I stoked the fire with another stick of wood. I would have to be frugal. The supply was limited. And December promised more days of cold temperatures. I sat staring at the stove, the heavy thing that held me within a perimeter of six feet of its center. I had tried earlier to lift the stove, thinking I might move it enough to slide the chain from its base, but it was too heavy, and my muscles were too weak. But then, I had never been exceptionally strong. Not like my brother.

After a moment, my eyes moved upward following the circular pipe that fed the smoke through an opening in the vaulted roof above me and I imagined the tendrils of grey lifting and swirling in the air. Would anyone see it? Would anyone be curiously moved to investigate?

Then at once, I was reminded of the Burmano-Ku-Partika. I had seen them again, for a second time as an outsider, their actions impersonal, as though my presence was intended to be ignored. I had been merely a bystander watching as they managed their task of taking Dent away, just as they had done with Sam. I sat for a while quietly deliberating, but I came to no logical conclusion as to why the un-worldly beings were so compelled to confiscate the bodies of the dead. Save one supposition, but it was not an especially convincing rationale.

Dust to dust.

That is what I had heard spoken at the funeral services of my grandparents. Perhaps the Burmano-Ku-Partika were simply tasked to keep the dust of one time separate from the dust of another time, whether a time past or time of the future. And then I began to think about the very essence of being a time traveler. The incredibility of being defined as such a person. The incomprehensible prospect that had been essentially limited to the imagination of science fiction advocates. And yet, I was a living and breathing example of its legitimate existence. Perhaps I should feel blessed to have been given the opportunity. I had, after all, met my great-great-grandfather, a cherished moment that otherwise would have never happened.

But I had also lost my brother because of this misadventure through an abstract wormhole of shifting time. And I had lost my best friend, Sam. Actually, gone now were both of my best friends.

How long I sat there thinking and pondering, I had no idea, but it occurred to me that the room had grown brighter during my latest session of introspection. Harsh sunlight was streaming in through the small quad-paned window of the tiny structure. Wherever I was, it was not a home. At least not one that was recently inhabited.

And then the sound of hoofbeats touched my ears. I listened as they drew nearer until they were clearly falling just outside the door. Then they stopped and I listened to the creak of a saddle as its rider dismounted, and I waited, daring to breathe as bootsteps crushed lightly upon the ground. I stared at the entrance, with nauseous anticipation.

The door pushed open, and Culver Headville filled its void. In an instant, I was reeling with hatred.

"I hope you were not expecting Santa Claus," he said, smiling wickedly.

I just stared at him, saying nothing. I would not give the executioner the satisfaction.

Headville stepped inside, and I glanced behind him and in the distance, I recognized the circular top of a windmill. Then at once, I realized where I was being held captive. This place was the range hut. The shack that I had ridden past in the northern portion of the ranch several times before but had never entered. It was a logical place for Headville to hide someone. To be stowed out of sight. Yet convenient.

"Ah, nice and toasty," he said, closing the door behind him and nodding at the stove beside me. "I had hoped you would be sensible enough to start a fire. To be honest, when I put you here, I was not inclined to do all the work for you, but still, I didn't want you to freeze to death. You're far too valuable to me to be lost that way."

With nonchalance, I remained silent. We both knew he was speaking the truth. I was worth more to him alive than dead. And he was a greedy man. That was the only reason he was keeping me around.

"Hungry?" he asked, setting a leather-tied knapsack upon the table.

I looked at the bag, wondering about its contents. Yes, I was hungry. Famished. And thirsty. But he would not get any of those confessions from me.

"Not talking, are we?" Headville said, stating the obvious. Then he opened the food sack and took out a small loaf of bread and a miniature jar of what appeared to be honey. "Fit for a king," he added. Then he lifted a second jar from the bag. It was larger and filled with water. And I wanted to drink it. Badly.

"Today is Christmas, you know," Headville said conversationally as he thoughtfully moved one of the primitive chairs before me. He sat down, positioning himself a safe distance from my reach, not that I possessed the strength or the stupidity to initiate an attack in my feeble condition. Leaning forward, he clasped his hands together, his fingertips tapping against each other. "I came yesterday, but you were still … sleeping. Briefly, I had regretted kicking you in the ole noggin, but alas, you survived. You have a hard head, don't you JT? In more ways than one, I might add."

I listened to him, processing his words, wondering if he was speaking the truth. Could I have been unconscious for more than twenty-four hours? I knew that the night I had joined Headville at his house had been the twenty-third, Dent's death later in the early hours of the next day. But I could think of no reason for Headville to exaggerate the date of the calendar.

"Really? Nothing? No comment?" Headville asked, almost jovially. "Oh, well, I hadn't planned to come here and entertain you, but I suddenly feel inspired to tell you a story. Your silence reminds me of quiet little half-breed I once knew. A boy. My son, actually. Taken from me by his mother. A thief. A betrayer."

Headville had said as much earlier, two days ago—allegedly. He had called Kival's mother a betrayer then. He had implied that she was, in his estimation, nothing less than an unscrupulous pickpocket.

He glared at me, though I did not perceive that it was my face he was seeing, but hers.

"You've probably been wondering how the talisman came to be in my possession. Well, I'll tell you. It was a gift. And like the gift of the pistol from my friend the Colonel, I valued it not only for the power of its design, but also because of whom had thoughtfully given it to me," he paused for a moment, his mind seemingly distracted for an instant. "I so hated that you had used that pistol to slay Mick just because you had found him in a compromising situation with your brother. That is, incidentally, the story I told to Deputy Oleander, and corroborated by Sherlee, you know, in case you were wondering."

I glared at him, my hate raw and gnawing. If he hoped to provoke me into defending my brother, I was glad to disappoint him.

"Anyway … the talisman," Headville spoke, resuming the floor and continuing his monologue.

"It came to me as a gift from a revered Kiowa Indian Chief called Set'tainte, a name interpreted by the English as White Bear. He's currently in a penitentiary in Texas somewhere, last I heard. When I met him, it was during a negotiation with the Plains Indian tribes and the U.S. Government. An orator for the Kiowa, Set'tainte had impressed me as a complicated savage, as much a diplomat as he was a murderer. But I would be remiss if I did not also acknowledge his wisdom. And his inheritance. The talisman, to be specific."

"I had noticed it right away, prominently braided within the feathers and beads of his chieftain headdress. Sitting inside an army tent with him, I had been charged by my commanding officer to remove the bonnet from his head, and when I did, I noticed that there was a decoration that was extraordinarily out of place. It was round and flat, with a trio of small holes separating clusters of simple, though imaginably symbolic markings. But most intriguing was its center. Black. Ominous. Massless. How others had not noticed the thing still baffles me. I had begun to look at it more closely when Set'tainte reacted to my curiosity, attempting to recover his prize. In his eyes, I had read the intensity of his desire to have it back. I could sense he was being protective, but more than that he was incomparably possessive."

"But, I haven't the time for details, and I wouldn't want to bore you with a long story when you have more to do with your precious time than listen to me."

I watched him stand and cross three steps before kneeling to check the latch of my shackle. "I will tell you this much. Ultimately, I befriended Set'tainte and when I learned that he had a daughter whom he had regretfully bargained away in a treaty with the Cheyenne, I took advantage of his remorse, and I promised him I would free his daughter provided he told me why he so coveted the thing I would come to call the talisman. And through an interpreter, he reluctantly spoke of a sacredness bestowed upon the object, that it had a soul and a power to cross between worlds, though he, nor his father, or his father before him, had ever experienced its wonder. I was intrigued, to say the least. And when he had confessed that he had passed this secret knowledge to his only living child, I knew then, that I would in fact rescue the Kiowa maiden."

Headville then returned to the table and plucked the loaf and the jar from where he had seductively displayed them, then moved back to the stool and sat. He fished a knife from his pocket and cut into the crust of the bread and removed its soft heart. Methodically, he dipped the point of the knife into the honey and began to spread it generously, its thick viscosity dripping from the edges of the bread and falling onto the floor next to the toe of his boot.

It was then I noticed the mark on the floor.

A smudge of black.

Innocuous.

But I wondered.

I lifted my eyes and watched Headville feed the sweetened tidbit into his mouth, eyeing me as he teased my ravished gullet. "So, I took the talisman from his headdress and off I went, scouring the plains for this Indian princess. When I found her, she wasn't exactly the noble beauty of fairy tales, but she was pretty enough. But when I showed her the gift I had obtained from her father, she became putty in my hand. I named her Kitty, which was near enough to the pronunciation of her Indian name, but it suited her better. Within days, she had become my pet, my property. And soon, we became partners. I taught her English, and she taught me things about the talisman. Things she had learned from her father. And then once, purely by chance as we journeyed across the plains, we came across the landforms. The towering sediment escarpments that those of your century would name Monument Rocks. And when she saw the Keyhole, she became excited," Headville said with a wink and a hint of glee in his voice.

Then, for dramatic effect, I suppose, he took a second, more liberal bite of the bread, leaving a remnant of it pinched between his fingers. Then he flicked the morsel toward me, as though he were benevolently donating the scrap of unwanted food to a starving rat. I watched it sail past me, landing somewhere beyond my back.

"It was then," Headville continued, "I learned of the specific place where the power of the talisman could be activated and allegedly able to be used to cross into another world. And so, we camped there at that place, spending a week at the end of the year 1857, but ultimately waiting through the first days of the new calendar. Then, on the eleventh morning of our stay, in that place sacred to the Kiowa, Kitty and I, by some miracle, experienced a life-changing moment."

He looked at me and smiled. "Just like you, JT. Life-changing. Wouldn't you say?"

I gave him nothing, but it didn't matter. He was on a roll.

"Suddenly, I was thrust into the future. The year, as I soon learned, was 1959. A place with automobiles and airplanes. And air-conditioning of all things. And telephones and televisions. And on and on and on. Miraculous inventions. Things, you have probably taken for granted your entire short and dismally uneventful life."

"And the knowledge! That, my young friend, was what I relished most about that era. And it was there, everywhere, literally within reach of any direction or from any place. And knowledge, I had learned in my own youth, was power."

"So, Kitty and I, we assimilated into our new environs, but my first objective was to learn why that particular day in early January had been specifically instrumental in our time transport. My gut told me it was scientifically connected. And with little effort I learned that the day had coincided with the earth's perihelion, which of course you are already aware of, I'm sure," Headville added, the corners of his mouth twitching. "So, there you have it. My story. I'd love to hear yours. Especially how you came to be in possession of my talisman."

I stared blankly at him. Yes, I had been enthralled by his story. Amazed, to be honest. How had a man, in that time, under those conditions, been so fortunate to piece it all together?

Destiny.

I hated to think it, but there it was. And I could buy it because nothing was logical when it came to destiny. But still, the man was begrudgingly brilliant. And utterly determined. But also damned lucky.

At least, until Morgan had taken his precious talisman from him. And Kitty with it.

Then as though he had telepathically read my mind, he scorched me with his eyes.

"Did you steal the talisman from Kitty? Or was it a gift, an ignorant gesture of that bastard child of hers. He would be about your age."

For chrissakes, I thought. It was no wonder Kival's mother had wanted to escape from this man who had fathered her child. A sociopath who considered his own son to be a cur, a cull, an embarrassment.

"Damn, you are stubborn, JT," Headville scowled, then stepped to the miniature table. "Perhaps tomorrow you'll feel more like talking." Then he removed the lid from the jar of water and drank deeply from it. I watched as he wiped his mouth with the back of his hand, then he crossed and opened the door of the stove and sloshed water into the embers. The hissing of steam sounded next to me, and I silently cursed the man. When he stepped back, I saw that there was still some liquid remaining, a quarter cup or so, pooled at the bottom of the jar. Headville began to empty the container onto the floor in front of me but changed his mind.

"JT," he sighed. "I'm not as bad as you think I am." And then he sat the jar on the seat of the stool upon which he had been sitting, baiting me, knowing I would not be able to reach it with my hands. "Tomorrow, then," Headville promised, then he re-wrapped the leftover bread and with the knapsack in his clutch, he left, closing the door behind him.

I waited until after the sound of the horse cantering away faded to quiet, then I moved. Quickly, I scrambled searching for the piece of bread that had been flicked past me and I found it just beyond the few sticks of firewood that remained for the heating of my stove. I picked it up and hungrily placed it into my mouth. But I wanted the water more. But it would have to wait.

My first priority was to resuscitate the fire.

CHAPTER 55

Headville returned the next day as promised. But little did he know that in his absence, I had developed a plan to escape. However, I would need time. Three days if I could deceivingly convince him to give them to me. And I needed nourishment, for my scheme would require every ounce of strength and endurance I could muster.

"Good afternoon, my friend," Headville greeted as he stepped inside the range shack that had been my home for two days and two nights. He studied me for a moment, ascertaining that I had remained shackled and was unquestionably still his prisoner. Though finding me here should have been enough evidence to warrant that conclusion. If I had managed to free myself from the shackle, I would have been long gone.

He had returned with the same knapsack, and I assumed that packed inside were more edible items he would attempt to use to bargain with me. I would give him an inch today. But only enough to encourage him to feed and water me.

Then his eyes went to the broken jar that lay at the foot of the stool, and beside it the stick of firewood I had used to try and reach the glass container, hoping to have been able to tip it gently onto the floor without it spilling or breaking. But that had not worked out as I had hoped. He stooped and gathered the damaged jar and the larger fragments of glass. "It's a good thing I used chain and not rope. Otherwise, you might have managed to cut yourself free."

If you had used rope, I said to myself, *I would have used fire to burn through it, asshole*. But I assumed he had already thought of that scenario beforehand, so there was no rational need to explain it to him. Plus, I would gain nothing by calling him names. Sticks and stones, those things gave me a better chance.

"Not so warm in here today," he observed. "That log could have been put to better use, could it not? But I have brought you more wood. Can't have you freezing to death." Then he stepped outside and in a moment, he returned with an armful of split wood, though not nearly enough to get me through another night in toasty comfort. "There's more," he said. "I'll decide later if I leave it with you as well."

I stared at him, seeing that his expression was one of expectation, as though to presume I would be moved to throw him a bone of gratitude.

"I brought lunch!" he beamed, and then produced a pair of biscuits and a chunk of meat that looked like the remains of a small pot roast that had been drying out for a day or two. And probably had been. He had likely had it with him upon his visit the prior day. "Here's the deal. You talk, you eat. Pretty simple. What do you say?"

I said nothing.

"I will wear you down, I promise you that. But first, that all important question of the day. Where, JT, is my talisman?"

I looked away from him, enforcing my disinterest in the subject of his inquiry.

"I expected as much. Well, since you were so willingly captivated by my storytelling yesterday, I might as well indulge your curiosity a while longer. What else would you like to know about me?" he asked but did not wait for the reply he knew was not coming. "If I were in your shoes, I would probably be wondering what on God's green earth makes Culver Headville tick? That would be a reasonable inquiry. I know that I would want to have a better understanding of the mentality of my antagonist. Though, it's probably not an intelligent stratagem to share that with you, but I am nothing if not conceited."

I agreed with him, but only with my eyes.

"You know," Headville continued, as he sat down upon the stool, making himself as comfortable as he could, considering the simplicity of the furnishing, "I had developed a hunch when I first explored your century. Since I had traveled forward into time with the day of the perihelion, I theorized that I might go back into time by way of its opposite, the aphelion. And my intuition had been right, though I had no idea if the reversal would be framed by the same number of years. Luckily, it had been. And as a result, I had achieved an understanding of how to regularly use this spectacular mode of time exploration."

"The only real drawback was the involvement of those hideous things that seemed to disassemble me tooth and nail. But if that were the price, I was glad to endure it. But I also had dues to pay. Variables to experience and learn from. I had actually failed on my second attempt to travel to your time. I had concluded that I had missed the window of opportunity by mere hours, having not arrived at the keyhole in the daylight. Trial and error. That is the way of the scientist, but difficult to accept for a visionary such as myself," he explained, his conceit fully exposed.

"Regardless, I had been eager to learn what year I might travel to if I left my own time with the aphelion instead of returning by it. As I expected, I went into the past. Seventeen Fifty-eight was the year. One-hundred-one years backward from my time."

With those words of revelation, I was suddenly very interested in his story.

"Ugh! A horrendous time to be thrust into, especially out here in the middle of God-forsaken Indian country. It was nothing less than divine intervention that I was captured by a Kiowa hunting party. And to be honest, it was more of a rescue than a detention. For months, I lived with them. Learned from them. They treated me with respect and dignity, especially their chief, Pa'otank."

I listened with astonishment that this man who, by his own words, had at one time been happily co-existing with a native race of people, but would later fight against them, and imprison members of a subsequent generation as slave labor. But power changed people. One had only to look at politics to be reminded of that.

"Then one night I caught a glimpse of a surprisingly familiar trinket. A small, round, metallic thing woven into a braid of Pa'otank's hair. It was my talisman! Or one just like it. So, I showed him mine," then he paused for a moment. "A stupid thing to do, I realized too late. At first, the old Indian had panicked, sure that I had used white man magic to steal the talisman from his hair. It was only after he realized it remained in his possession as a hair accessory, that he calmed down. And so, we compared them to each other, inspecting their similarities and finding absolutely no differences. They were identical. I concluded then that his talisman and mine were one and the same."

"It was extraordinary! I remember thinking that two would surely be better than one, but if I took it, then it would not later be in the possession of Chief Set'tainte a hundred years into the future, and if that were the case, would I still have my own talisman once I returned to my time? Or would it have just vanished? And if it were to be gone, then would the second one, the earlier version of the talisman, also be missing once I returned? It was a puzzling dilemma, but also a risk I was not willing to take. Even now, years later, the concept perplexes me."

"But three days later, Pa'otank abandoned me. An old Indian woman, wrinkled and weathered by the passing of more moons than hairs on my head, had convinced the chief that I was bad medicine. Me!" Headville exclaimed. "Ha! Well, I did get the last laugh, when it was all said and done."

"Ultimately, I managed to relocate to a frontier outpost that was slightly more civilized, but mortally dangerous, as it turned out. But, even from that experience, I learned things."

"Regardless, on my second launch forward into your time, JT, I came alone, leaving my kitten behind. I was less spontaneous, more methodical, intent to wisely take full advantage of my limited resource of six-months' time. I did more research, and what I found, or I should say, what I didn't find, alarmed me," Headville said, toying with an attempt to sound dramatic.

"What I learned was that one-hundred years into the future, I was nobody. I had found nothing but entries in census ledgers that spelled out my name. Nothing about who I was, or who I had been. I had expired from the world in my natural time, and no one remembered me. I had left no significant mark in the annals of history. Well, as you can imagine, that didn't at all suit my ego."

And Headville was right, I could imagine. I had personally witnessed his inflated sense of importance. But consequently, I considered him pathetic. He could not see value in living a simple life where friendship and servitude were more meaningful aspirations than finding fame or fortune.

"So, I devised a plan to make a name for myself in connection with the growing popularity of Quarter Horses. I had already developed an obsession for them, having acquired breeding stock carrying the progeny of the famous Steel Dust sire. And by coincidence, I learned of the existence of a fraternity of like-minded breeders, and I knew immediately I had found the place where my name could endure. Cole Blake, and Dan Casement, and Coke T. Roberds, they had been pioneers in the development of the Quarter Horse. Not just for racing, but for quality and show. I found mention of them often in equine magazines of your era. I was deeply envious. I wanted my name, Culver Headville, to be historically associated with those renown horsemen. I desired to be equally revered, if not ultimately elevated above them. And surprise, surprise, I realized I possessed the ability to achieve that prominence."

"You cheated."

"Ah, he talks!" Headville exclaimed. "Progress! And here," he added, tossing me one of Isaiah's biscuits. "I keep my word, JT. Remember that."

I wasted no time with proper manners or acceptable etiquette. I bit into the bread, chewing it quickly, eager to get something into my nauseous and emaciated belly.

"Cheated, you say? Well, I prefer to call it an acceleration of the inevitable. But yes, my acquisition of Doc-Bar was paramount to my success. What a prize he had been. And is still, after seventeen years! I admit, JT, that when I read about that fabulous horse, when I saw his picture, I immediately coveted him. So, when I embarked on my next time-travel expedition the following year, I made that horse my priority. I was eager to return with him and get started with the infusion of his genetic perfection."

"You stole him," I said, knowing Dent had made the same accusation. I sat there, waiting to see if he would answer me truthfully, though I could barely tolerate looking at the man. My heart ached and seethed with an abundance of hate for this devil whose malignant actions directly led to the death of my brother.

He shrugged. "I've stolen worse. Or better, depends on your point of view."

Kate.

In his cryptic way, I believed he had just admitted to me that he had kidnapped her. And I was stunned by his guile confession.

"Ah, nothing gets past you, does it, JT? Nor I, for that matter. I can read your mind," he added laughing. "But just between the two of us, it wasn't until Kate was eleven, maybe twelve years old when it occurred to me that she was destined to develop into a beautiful young woman. One who would make an ideal mother to bear my own superior prodigy."

Clearly Headville was goading me. But I had to ignore the temptation to debate with him which of the two of us was more likely to father Kate's children. Besides, I needed additional sustenance, and I doubted I would get it if I didn't learn when to keep my mouth shut.

"But let's not entwine the two programs of propagation," he smiled deviously. "So, with Doc arriving through the time portal as unscathed as I, we set out upon a shorter journey to a little farm in Illinois owned by my father. I had already endeavored to selectively breed the daughters of Steel Dust with the best available sires of the time. And it was there on the family farm where the bloodline of Doc enjoyed an extraordinary head start. With Doc, I knew I would make unprecedented leaps and bounds, surpassing the accomplishments of Casement or Roberds, or any other twentieth century breeder. Unfortunately, the farm was inconvenient relative to the keyhole, and I had plans for even more lucrative travel. However, I needed money. And lots of it."

And then Headville diverted to another of his passions. "I wanted a ranch that was massive in size and innovative in design, a place worthy of a revolutionary line of the fledgling Quarter Horse breed. So, with the help of the talisman, I brought back a fortune in gold. Do you have any idea of what an ounce of gold is worth here in 1878 compared to its value in 1961? Not as much as you might think. But still, the gold I brought with me was worth double in my time."

"A gold thief, too," I said.

"You are paying attention," Headville said, pointing a finger at me and winking.

"Only because I want another biscuit. And some water."

He smiled, then obliged me.

"You are incorrect, JT. I did not double my money by theft. I acted as a shrewd investor. It helped though, taking six-thousand dollars of gold with me on my second adventure into the future, then banking it and returning with the same weight in gold worth twelve-thousand dollars in terms of my economy," he continued, crossing to the window, and peering outward. "Two additional time-forward expeditions and I had accumulated enough to take full advantage of Lincoln's Homestead Act and paid for most of this 25,000-acre ranch with gold on the barrel head."

"Congratulations. Most people have to work to get what you have."

"Oh, JT, I did work for it. I worked with my brain. Besides, I'm not like most people. But surely by now, you've figured that out."

"Why tell me all this?" I asked him, then took a deep swallow from the new jar of water.

"Why ask me that question, when there are a hundred better ones to test me with?"

I moved the jar away from my lips, my tongue capturing a fugitive droplet poised at the corner of my mouth. *Waste not, want not.* "Because I want what's left there on the table. I'm hungry."

Headville laughed. "Again, JT, your candor delights me. Here," he said, tossing me the chunk of meat. I caught it. And at once I felt myself salivating.

"The reason I'm being forthright with you, JT, is that I want you to have a complete and thorough understanding of why the talisman is so very important to me. Why I will do anything to get it back," Headville said, gathering the knapsack before taking from me the jar I had emptied as I had listened to him.

"Remember that, JT," he added, crossing to the door as he prepared to leave. Then I saw his head pivot toward the table. "Oh, dear," he said, then stepped across and picked up the postcard that he had obviously laid there days ago just to bait me. "I had intended to drop this in the post for you," he began, then lifted the card to scrutinize it more closely.

"Dear Mom," he spoke, reading my words, "I've met someone … etcetera, etcetera. Touching." Then Headville turned and stabbed me with his eyes. "Too bad she's already spoken for," he declared with a counterfeit smile, before returning the card to the surface of the table. "By your own hand, I know how intimately important Kate is to you. It would be unfortunate if something unpleasant would befall her." Then Headville closed the door behind him, and I listened as he ominously rode away.

It had been a silly, impulsive notion. When I bought the postcard, I knew then I would use it to write to my mother as if I were simply away at college or exploring the world on some distant trip. I wanted to tell her that I often thought about her, and Dad, knowing that if I dropped it in the post, it would just be returned with *Address Unknown* scrawled across its face. Still, I was compelled to pretend that Mom would read my note telling her about Kate, a girl who had stolen my heart and whose act of thievery would cost her a life-long sentence living happily-ever-after as my wife.

Unexpectedly, the penning of the make-believe correspondence had been therapeutic, as if by writing those words I felt sure the universe would faithfully cause them to come true. But now, the results of that impetuous action had landed in the hands of Culver Headville. And obviously, he intended to use that knowledge to his advantage.

But would he really harm Kate?

Probably, if he thought it would get him what he wanted. I just had to make sure neither of those things happened.

On schedule, Headville visited me for a third day, arriving again with a few morsels of food, and another jar of water.

And more firewood.

Only the air had been warmer, making the stove fuel less important than the nourishment of a meal and a drink. And as I had done the day before, I indulged him in conversation, but not until our prerequisite dialog was settled first.

"Any chance you've remembered the location of my talisman, JT?"

"Nope."

"I thought not," he said with a perfunctory nod, as though he had decided his efforts to extract that information from me would at some point not be a waste of his time. But I knew otherwise.

He later slyly attempted to pick at the tender wound that had been festering for three days, but I did not take the bait. Dent was one subject I would not discuss with him. Ever.

Case closed.

Eventually, Headville began to talk of other things, his commentary boastful and vain. Onerously, I listened to him as he proudly informed me that it had been he who conceived and designed the horse stables, and the layout of the central corral, and the blueprints of his grand home, and on and on. But his arrogance was not to my benefit. I knew he did not care what I thought. I had decided his soliloquy had been verbalized simply because he liked the sound of his own voice.

At one point, he elaborated upon his project of developing a higher and more suitable class of cattle that would deliver a superior and unparalleled quality of steak to the dinner tables of Americans across the country. I did not bother pointing out that the Angus breed of cattle he claimed to be advancing had nothing to do with his personal intervention, because he knew that already. His aim was purely another attempt to fleece the work and determination of someone else. But I couldn't resist asking him a relevant and very pointed question.

"Did you kill the Scot? The man who actually introduced the Angus to America?"

"No, I did not," Headville said with a shrug. "I can see how it would appear that way to you, but no. His death was entirely God's own doing. I simply capitalized on it. But honestly, I had thought about it. I'm not exactly an angel."

No, I thought. You, Culver Headville, are no angel.

"Anything else you care to ask me before I go?"

"Yes."

"Fire away."

"The other night when you had Mick murdered—

"Uh-uh," Headville interrupted me. "By my testimony, it was Dent who shot Mick. Or maybe it was you. Either way, it's your word against mine. But let's play nice, shall we? Try again."

"The other night—in your library, when you were telling me about meeting my dad, you said you had Kate with you."

"I did! An uncanny coincidence. To think, you actually met her for the first time when the two of you were little more than babes."

"You as much as admitted you kidnapped her, didn't you? Brought her back with you through the keyhole."

"Of that, I am guilty. But I prefer to think that I saved her from a mediocre life with mediocre parents. If only the two of them had not been so rude. I had merely tried to get a peek at their little one, but the mother had to make a scene there in the restaurant, and that dolt of a father thought it was his right to assault me with an arrogantly feeble twist of my arm," Headville elaborated, then shook his head and added, "I wanted to snap his neck and roast him for my supper."

I studied Headville's eyes, and believed he was not exaggerating the dramatic.

"Instead," Headville shrugged, "I backed away. Then, by coincidence, the little family had rented a room next to mine and were preparing to depart from the motel at the same time as I. Stupid of them to leave the little girl in the car unattended. I imagined that long before they realized she was missing, I was already out of town, traveling along the highway, minutes from exiting onto the obscurity of a country road that led to the place where I would catch my ride back home."

"Risky," I said plaintively, believing that soon I would be telling Kate the truth about who she was and in what time she truly belonged.

"Sure, I could have been caught. The same with Kennedy. But the adrenaline rush from tempting fate is exceedingly addictive."

"Why did you shoot him? JFK?"

"Not for political reasons, I assure you. Call it big-game hunting. I did it for the fun of it. To see if I could make a sensational headline and get away with it."

"You could have been caught. Executed."

"Hmm, perhaps. But I had life insurance."

I looked at him quizzically. What the hell was he alluding to?

"Interesting," Headville mused as a basilisk grin spread across his face. "You don't know."

"Know what?"

"My dear boy," Headville grinned. "There are more things in heaven and earth, than are dreamt of in your philosophy."

I had read that phrase before. It was from Hamlet. "Shakespeare," I said. "What exactly does that have to do with the recklessness of your time travel?"

"You tell me your secret and I'll tell you mine."

He was good. The suggestive enigma, itself, had piqued my intellectual curiosity, but the renown Shakespearean quote had been dangled as a carrot to lure my hunger for enlightenment. But he would not get a confession from me that easily.

"Pass."

Headville shrugged. "I had to try."

After he had left, I stoked the fire, then I lay back upon the floor. Headville's bantering had exhausted me. But my placation of him had rewarded me with food and water. Next, I would rest. Already, I was feeling stronger. But I would be even better in two days' time.

The following day, when Headville stepped inside the range hut, he did not find me sitting and waiting. Upon hearing the approach of his horse, I took my place on the stage I had prepared and pretended to be stoking the fire with my back toward him when he entered.

"Beautifully mild outside today," Headville informed me as I heard him sitting the usual items of negotiation onto the table.

In the previous two days, he had not appeared to have noticed that I had managed to edge his chair ever nearer toward the stove, closer in proximity to my usual station. Not by much, just inches each of the three days since I had first noticed the mark on the floor. I had wondered then if he had purposefully placed it there having made the prior determination that it was at that spot where he could be intimidatingly nearest to me without making himself vulnerable to the scope of my grasp.

The morning that I had regrettably broken the jar after having stretched myself flatly onto the floor reaching for the stool with the aid of a smooth stick of firewood, I had later decided I could take advantage of that misfortune. I had removed my shirt and wrapped a sleeve around the end of the log, then I had moistened the cloth-covered end with my saliva. Using my unconventional cleaning tool, I had dabbed and rubbed on that suspiciously premeditated smudge. Ultimately, the mark faded enough to be relatively unnoticeable.

Then with the advantage of my shirt, I had wrung it into a lengthy twisted wad, the sleeves especially helpful in my assimilation of a makeshift rope. I had knotted the cuffs, inserting a smaller stick of wood, with the idea that I could toss the apparatus in such a way as to snare some part of the stool, or at least coax it into wrapping itself around a leg with the twig boomeranging back toward me.

Prostrated upon the floor, my ankle persistently testing the restraint of the chain, my sixth attempt had been nearly successful. That had given me faith that my idea would be rewarded. I had then tried again. And again. Counting each toss. Twenty-three throws later, I arced the angle of my pitch an extra degree and the knotted end of the shirt sleeve wrapped around the leg of the chair, the twig pointing toward me.

It had finally come within reach of my fingertips.

Gently, I had eased the chair forward until I was able to manipulate it into an unnoticeably new position. With a charred ember from the stove, I had then duplicated the original mark, only it would be made four inches closer to me than the one Headville had first contrived. Now, three days later, Headville would sit down on the stool the full length of a ruler closer to me. Within my reach. Or at least within the range of my weapon.

I prayed Headville would not, in this last moment, notice what I had accomplished. I had decided I could not wait another day to attempt my escape. I was sick of listening to his bullshit.

"You won't need to worry about a fire, today, JT," he informed me. "It is unseasonably warm out there. Two days running now."

I had hoped I could count on him to talk about the weather.

"Like my dad used to say," I said to him over my shoulder, listening to the sound of his body perching itself upon the creaky wooden stool, "if you don't like the weather in Kansas, wait a few days and it'll change." And then, as if I had been thrown a pitch across home plate, I moved quickly and unexpectedly, swinging at his head with a heavy stick of firewood I had been saving for just this moment.

The blunt edge of the hard, dried piece of cottonwood smashed across his face, breaking from the impact, splinters and fragments of wood flying through the air, leaving six inches of the remaining log clinched tightly in my hand. The wood had not been as solid as I had thought it would be, but still the blow had sent Headville backwards onto the floor.

CHAPTER 56

The assault had been choreographed and rehearsed. A pivot. Two long, quick strides. And a swing of my bat. A homerun was what I had hoped to achieve.

Immediately, I analyzed his silent, motionless form. If I had not killed Headville, at least I had shut him up. But if alive, he might only be unconscious for a while, so I wasted no time. I grabbed him by his boots and pulled him into the perimeter of my metal tether and began to search through his pockets. Inside the second one, I found what I was looking for.

A key.

I tested it and was relieved that it fit the lock of my shackle.

I freed myself of the chain, then quickly I performed a cursory check of his vital signs, my diagnosis revealing that he was, unfortunately, still breathing.

"Piss!"

I rearmed myself with a second stick of firewood, determined to follow through with my plan to kill the man who had made the last hours of my brother's life a living hell. I towered over Headville, cocked my weapon, then closed my eyes, mentally visualizing the aftereffects of his crushed skull and the pattern of his blood splatter.

I should have kept my eyes open.

I sensed the spring-like tension of my uplifted arm dissolve as though someone had relieved me of the weight of the log. I decided, instead, that my macabre imagination had sent an alarm to my conscience, and it had been the intervention. Having previously convinced myself that my smartest move was to kill the man, I could not do it. I could not blatantly murder him in cold blood.

Headville had been wrong. He and I were nothing alike.

I tossed my weapon aside and stripped Headville of his boots and pulled them onto my own feet, relieved that they fit surprisingly well. Quickly, I removed his coat and picked up his black hat that had fallen inches from where he had landed. In less than a minute I was outside, stepping into the saddle. Seconds later, Doc-Bar and I were racing away. Behind me was a man who would hang me for stealing his horse. But he would have to catch me first. But when he woke up, the ungodly rancher would have to first free himself of the shackle he had used on me, and then would have to make his pursuit as a posse of one, without boots and horseless.

With part A of my plan behind me, I headed stealthily for the heart of the Headville ranch, sticking to the lower rills and ravines of the landscape. Because I did not know of Sherlee's whereabouts, there was a chance I might unexpectedly cross his path. But if he did catch a glimpse of me, I hoped that my masquerade would fool him from a distance.

And distance was, for now, my best ally.

In a few miles, I was nearly to my destination, so I skirted westerly, stopping briefly to dismount and scamper to the ridge of a low knoll that overlooked the feeding grounds. As I suspected, the task of haying the livestock was underway. Three men were at work.

Boyd and Pete, and Sherlee.

A diminished staff had forced the wrangler to contribute to the care of the cattle. But I felt no pity for the man who carried his share of blame for the shortage of labor. He had murdered Mick. And had done nothing to save my brother. And the vaqueros had fled, much like the Dog Soldiers had done, I assumed because Dent had supernaturally vanished right before their eyes.

I eased my way back to Doc and remounted. Then I reined him directly for the roadway that led to the pasture gate. If my plan of deception was going to work, I had to act the part. From the corner of my eye, I glanced in the direction of the workers. The three of them were at least two hundred yards away, twice the measurement between the goal lines of a football field. I was confident I could not be recognized from that distance. But I preferred to pass by unnoticed. Once I had arrived at the gate, I looked back and saw the men working without distraction.

So far, so good.

But I had to hurry. They would soon be returning to the barn for more hay.

I rode Doc to the stable that stood nearest the house, the barn that was his refuge, and tied him to a rail that ran the length of his exterior pen, then I eased my way toward the house. The ranch yard was quiet. Weirdly tranquil. No one else seemed to be around. Boldly, I stepped onto the veranda of the Headville home and opened the heavy door. I peered through the gap and confirmed that no threat awaited me on the other side. With a deep breath of courage, I slipped inside.

For a moment I listened, and then the announcement of footsteps sounded from the end of the hallway and Isaiah appeared, wiping his hands upon an apron tied around his waist. He looked at me, stunned.

I raised my hand to my face, and placed my finger to my lips, my eyes begging him to keep my presence a secret. Isaiah compliantly made no sound, then turned and tiptoed back from where he had come. I gently closed the door behind me, and stepping forward, I glanced into the library, but a sharp gasp pulled my attention into the opposite room. I turned and found Kate gawking at me as she sat with Beverly upon a settee, a book in her hands. And across from them, bound to a chair, sat Blaine with a rag stuffed into his mouth.

"JT!" Kate exclaimed as she leapt to her feet before rushing toward me. In the next second, we were enveloped in each other's arms.

CLICK

I heard the sound. It was so damn close I felt the hair rise on the back of my neck.

"Hands up, pussy."

Oleander Sedgwick.

I had failed to consider his presence here. Or Blaine's for that matter. At once, I felt inconsolably stupid.

I did as I was told, raising my hands after Kate had wisely let go of me. I turned to face him.

"Oleander," I said softly, "please, put the gun down."

"Sure," he replied. "Just as soon as hell freezes over."

"There will be no shooting in the house!"

It was Isaiah who had issued the proclamation, and I glanced to see that he had returned, and was standing defiantly in the foyer.

"I don't take orders from little nigga-men," Oleander spat.

"Not my order, sir," Isaiah replied. "Mister Headville's rule."

I looked at Oleander and watched him scowl at the resident man-of-many-hats. Then using the pistol, he motioned for me to enter the parlor. I stepped into the well-appointed room, with Kate following me. I glanced again at Blaine, his eyes meeting mine, surprisingly clear and calm, though conspicuously imploring me to act the same. But then, he didn't have much choice gagged as he was, and with coils of rope looped around him. That, I was sure, had been Oleander's work.

"Sit down," Oleander barked, and I went and sat in a chair next to Blaine. "You, too, blondie."

"And if I don't?" Kate challenged.

"Kate, please, sit down," Beverly told her, her advice both wise and firm.

Reluctantly, Kate returned to her place beside her tutor, then I watched as Oleander closed the pair of pocket doors that divided the room from the foyer. Then he crossed and shut a smaller door that assumingly led to what functioned as a secondary hallway, segregating the five of us from the remainder of the house.

"If any of you moves, I'm gonna shoot somebody. I don't give a shit about the rules," Oleander added with contempt, though I wasn't convinced he was as sincere as he wanted us to believe. But he did have a gun. And he was hot-headed and stupid enough to use it. Then he crossed to one of the windows and looked out upon the ranch yard. "Where's Mr. Headville?"

"Haven't seen him," I said, knowing Oleander's question had been directed at me. "Listen, Oleander. Let us go, please. Headville is a murderer. Him and Sherlee, they—"

"Bullshit!" Oleander pivoted to look at me with an air of doubt. "Mr. Headville said Double D shot and killed Mick. That's why your chickenshit brother ran off. Why he's hiding."

"Headville lied," I stated. "Sherlee shot Mick. I saw it with my own eyes."

"Why would Sherlee do that?" Oleander scoffed.

I glared at him. But I had no intention of telling him the reason. Instead, I countered. "Why would Dent kill Mick? Have you thought of that?"

"I know why. Mr. Headville told me. That fudge-packer tried to lay one on your brother. I would have shot that limp-wristed pussy, too, if he'd tried that on me. I don't blame Double D for that."

"You are so damn gullible."

Oleander ignored my insult. "So, where ya been, Worm? Hiding out with Dent somewhere? You know, I've gotta take him in, bad as I hate to. But after all, I am the law now," he added, tapping his badge.

"Dent is dead," I said to him, frowning hard, determined not to let my emotions take control of me. "Headville hung him—out there," I gestured to the window that displayed a view of the fateful tree, my throat constricting with anger and angst. I heard Kate gasp and looked to see Beverly wrap her arm around the shoulders of the girl with whom I had fallen in love. Then I turned to Blaine and nodded and saw in his eyes that he believed me. And in an instant, his face began to melt with grief. He quickly looked away, facing the wall. He and my brother had fought together on the gridiron. But they had been more than athletic compatriots. They had often seemed as close as brothers. Just as I and Sam had been.

"Bullshit," Oleander hissed. "You'd say anything to save your own hide."

"Why is Blaine here?" I asked.

"He's a guest," he replied with a cocky roll of his head. "Like me. Been here for about three days. We've been waitin' for ya. Headville's out somewhere now looking for your ass."

"No, he isn't looking for me. In fact, we've been spending a lot of time together," I informed him. "Truthfully, I've been his prisoner," I added, but that statement was for the benefit of Kate.

"Pfffst," Oleander scoffed. "If that's true, then you've obviously escaped. Pretty dumb of you to tell me that." I said nothing. Oleander wasn't smart, but I was sure he could put two and two together and come up with the right answer all on his own. Eventually.

Suddenly, he crossed to Kate, took her by the arm and lifted her from the settee. "One move from you, Worm, and I'll pistol-whip this little bitch." Then in the next moment, he crossed the room taking Kate with him. He slid open one half of the set of parlor doors, stepped into the foyer, the two of them disappearing around the corner. Then I listened as the front door swayed on his hinges.

BANG! ... BANG! ... BANG!

Instinctively, I leapt to my feet, preparing to rush in and do something. Then immediately, I remembered Oleander's threat and quickly I sat back down. Kate was fine, I had to believe that. Oleander could not be that brazen or so foolish to harm her. Then I realized in the next second that the gunshots had been a signal.

Shit!

Sherlee would undoubtably be here in minutes.

Oleander stepped back into the room with Kate remaining caught in his grasp. He was smiling. "Fooled ya, didn't I?" Then he let go of her, and I watched as she spun toward him and slapped him across the face. He reacted with the same assault, but had surprisingly refrained from hitting her too hard, just enough to send her back to Beverly, her face red, her eyes welled with tears.

But I was pissed. Oleander had gone too far. He would pay for that.

Quickly, he closed the parlor doors and turned around, gloating with satisfaction. Then he waved the pistol at me. "I'll have back-up in a few minutes."

We didn't have to wait long. The warning shots had worked. Sherlee arrived, bursting into the house, throwing open the parlor doors, his own revolver cocked and ready.

"You?" Sherlee coughed, studying me head to toe, seeing at once that I was wearing items that belonged to Headville. Unlike Oleander, Sherlee connected dots much quicker. If anyone knew where Headville had stashed me, it would be him. He turned and swiftly left the house.

Inside the parlor, we waited, all of us, except Isaiah, imprisoned by the closure of all doors leading into the room.

Across from me, a mantel clock ticked. Slowly, thirty-three minutes passed.

I could make a run for it. The thought had crossed my mind. But what would be the point? I wouldn't be able to take Kate with me. And I could not leave Blaine behind. So, I sat there, watching the clock. I was, I believed, a man on death row. When Headville returned, he would at least be fuming. Explosive at worst. Either way, he'd also have a hell of a headache.

"Is that still necessary?" I heard Kate ask, her question causing my eyes to leave the clock. When I looked at her, I saw that she was speaking to Oleander.

"What?"

"His gag," she said, gesturing to Blaine. "It's not like there's anyone for him to yell for. Unless you're just afraid of him?"

"Right," Oleander said with an arrogant shrug, then he crossed and relieved Blaine of the vocal torniquet. "One word, Hollywood, and it's back on. Comprendo?"

Blaine nodded, then glanced at me as Oleander returned to his watch post at the window.

None of us, me, Kate, Beverly, or Blaine spoke. But we attempted a silent conversation with our eyes. It was a wordless, yet expressive mix of dread, fear, worry, and anxiety. But in Kate, I saw hope, which was something I had let slip through my fingers. I had been naive to think that my plan would play out letter-perfect.

Another half-hour passed, then I heard the sound of hooves tapping the ground, growing louder by the second. Then I detected the creaking of a saddle, followed by boots scraping across the veranda. I listened as the front door opened and closed. My heart was beating fast and heavy. Fight or flight was building inside of me. Then Sherlee's voice echoed through the set of oak doors calling for Isaiah. Moments later, a mumble of whispers and muffled words touched my ears. But the speakers were still identifiable: Sherlee, Isaiah, and Culver Headville.

After a moment, one side of the parlor door slid open, and the ranch's horse wrangler walked in and sized up the room. Without a word, Sherlee stood staring at me. His gaze seemed to challenge me to make a move, daring me to try to run for freedom. And for extra effect, he had with him his lariat, coiled, and hung over a broad shoulder.

The clock ticked for almost twenty minutes before the sound of boots clomping down the flight of stairs put me on the edge of my seat, warning me that Headville was moments from making a grand appearance. But when he arrived, no one was more surprised than I. Headville paused, glancing about the room, smiling.

"Well, this is practically a reunion, isn't it?" He said, looking from Oleander to Blaine, then finally settling his eyes upon me.

I had expected him to enter with the storm of a Tasmanian Devil. Wild, loud, and angry. But instead, his posture and mood were just the opposite. He was almost a picture of refinement, dressed and cleaned up as though he were preparing to entertain all of us as guests around his elegant dinner table. Only the swelling of what had to be a broken nose, and a small bandage affixed upon his forehead above his left eye offered any evidence that he was anything other than an ordinarily pleasant host. He was incredibly composed. And that fact was frightening as hell.

The man was at least one chromosome away from being something other than human.

Headville stepped toward me, and intuitively I rose as though I was merely greeting His Graciousness with my own display of good manners. He paused within reach of me, then clapped his hands, a trio of slow, deliberate applause.

"Score one for you, my young, innovative adversary," he announced, then he plucked from my head his black Stetson. "You may keep the boots," Headville stated with his signature fraudulent smile, then added, "for now." Then his eyes shifted to Kate, and I saw his expression change immediately. He crossed to her and took her chin in his hand and lifted her face, examining her.

"Your cheek, my little bird, is red. Did someone strike you?"

I saw Kate glance away from Headville's stare, though she silently sent her gaze to rest upon Oleander. With just a look, she had named the one who had assaulted her. Headville ducked his head slightly, cocking his chin to the right. He knew who was standing where Kate had looked. Headville turned around and stepping past me, he crossed to Oleander. The sound of a vicious slap echoed in the room. I didn't want to look. I knew Oleander would not be taking the man's discipline well.

"What the hell?!"

"You hit her again, and it will be the last thing you do."

"Hey, I was just taking control of the situation. That's what you asked me to do, right?"

"Shut up, you loathsome fool," Headville snapped. I had thought the same thing. "Nothing in my instructions gave you permission to touch my Kate."

I listened to Headville. At least he had defended her. Perhaps I had unnecessarily feared for her safety.

"For now, anyway," Headville said, coyly countering his own statement. Then he circled around in front of me, "and only because Miss Carneiro has assured me that Kate remains *unspoiled,*" he added, his egotistical eyes piercing mine, seeking the acknowledgement of my understanding of the term, but also expressing his narcissistic appreciation. "Therefore, my home is her home if she knows what is best for her."

And just that quick, his true colors were flying high and loud. Kate was not safe. And she never would be as long as Headville kept her within his reach.

"JT, I really am in no hurry, but look around you. Your stubbornness is holding these good people hostage. Why prolong the inevitable? Just tell me where you've hidden the talisman and I'll set you free."

I stared back at him, obstinate and determined.

"Come, now, JT, I'd hate for something tragic to happen to someone else you care about. Your friend, Blaine, for example," Headville threatened. "I've grown tired of the violence. Really, I have," he added as he began to walk and weave his way among us. "It's one thing to bear witness to the senseless death of someone you don't like, but it's a horse of a different color when someone you're fond of loses his life. And I am fond of you, JT. But I know you know. There is no one else. There were only the four of you who came through the keyhole. Your brother, I'm sure, did not hide the talisman. I've interrogated Blaine, and I'm convinced he knows nothing about it. And of course, our esteemed deputy has been wisely excluded from knowing about the talisman, isn't that right, Oleander?"

"I don't know nothin' about no talisman, sir," Oleander agreed. "But …"

"But?" Headville asked, and I saw him pause and stare across the room at Oleander.

"Well, sir, I just remembered something."

Don't, Oleander! I silently begged him.

"What, exactly, have you remembered?" Headville asked.

"Well, there was actually five of us, sir."

"Yes, I know. You've told me that already. That Sam person, the one who died when you lost your finger."

"No, not him. There was another one of us—"

"Oleander!" I called out, my tone pleading. But I knew at this juncture, he had already untied the bag. It would now be just a matter of time before Headville would shake the cat loose.

"There were *six* of you?" Headville asked, his tone incredulous. "Why in the hell have you not mentioned him before now?"

"He's a weirdo. I've only seen him once the whole time I've been here."

"A weirdo, you say. What else? What does he look like, Oleander? I need his description."

"No problemo," Oleander spoke, and because of his conciliatory attitude I knew of his motivation. He desired to regain membership into the unholy fold of the man who had put him into his minor position of police power. "The dude looks a lot like an Indian. Black hair, darkish skin. But he's got blue eyes. Eyes like yours, sir."

Dammit.

Oleander's descriptive words had just condemned Kival.

"David," Headville whispered. "The prodigal son has returned." At once, Headville crossed and stood in front of me. "I'll give you this, JT Tescott. I now believe you. You don't know where my talisman is hidden. But my son knows. And I'm going to find him."

"I dunno about your son, sir," Oleander interrupted, "but the dude's name is Kival. It ain't no David."

Headville strode to Oleander, his eyes cold, his voice even more frigid. "If you were not standing upon a rare and expensive carpet, I would spill your guts here and now." Then I watched Headville seize the front of Oleander's shirt before shaking him violently. "Tell me, WHERE is this Kival?! WHERE did you see him last?!"

"In town—a while back—a month ago maybe!" Oleander replied, waffling his words. "He was with a girl, and—and a baby, I think. They, uh, they were in a wagon. But he'd cut his hair—he looked like them damn stinking Germans you see in town all the time."

"I've seen him," Sherlee volunteered. "He was with the widow girl. You know," he added. Headville nodded, clearly understanding the implication, as had I.

"Sherlee, saddle their horses," Headville said, releasing Oleander. "These three boys are leaving with us." Then he turned to me, smiling at my defeat. "We have business to attend to in Schoenchen."

CHAPTER 57

At Headville's command, Isaiah appeared bearing my own pair of boots with clean socks laundered and tucked inside one of them. He also presented to me my coat, buttoned up and folded with my cowboy hat perched upon it. It was then I remembered I had left my Stetson in Isaiah's hands the night of the dinner party. The night Mick and my brother had lost their lives. The night I had been chained and sequestered miles away. Why the contemptuous rancher had collected and then stowed my personal items inside his home was a curious move, but I guessed all mad men had their quirks. Headville would be no exception.

Refitted in my own attire and mounted on my own horse, I left the ranch in the company of Blaine, both of us escorted by Sherlee and Oleander, and fearfully led by the conceitedly confident Culver Headville. At a speed barely below a full gallop, we rode south, our destination more than twenty miles away. Headville was eager. He had caught a scent, and he was hungry to sink his teeth into the opportunity he had spent years awaiting its development.

Though before I had mounted Viento, Headville addressed me, gloating.

"For now, JT, you are merely insurance. But once I get what I want, and I will get it, I'm going to personally castrate you. Afterward you will die, like your brother, choking," Headville had said, grinning. "But not because of a rope. No, no, I'm going to strangle you with your own balls."

On horseback, I followed Headville, who rode upon his sleek black stallion, Ulysses, piloting his contingent with an exhilarating thirst for blood and appearing much like I had imagined Custer had looked when riding into the throws of the Battle of Little Bighorn. For Kival's sake, and my own, I hoped that Headville would experience a similar fate before either of us met our untimely end, a finale personally designed by the malicious would-be general. But that wish was an extreme longshot. However, I wasn't too particular. I would settle for a bullet in his head regardless of who pulled the trigger.

Twelve miles later, we entered Hays City and paraded down the main corridor. Oleander had taken my place behind Headville, and by all accounts, I was a fugitive under his arrest. And people had noticed, some pointing, others whispering to one another. As we passed by John White's barbershop, I noticed from the corner of my eye that the kind proprietor stood in the doorway. I could not bear to look at him, fearing that he might inadvertently read the distress in my eyes and be compelled to do something to help me. But I did not want his help, and I would not risk getting him involved.

With Sherlee riding guard beside Blaine and Buck, they were at the end of the show, I was the headliner. No doubt, word had somehow spread that a killing had taken place on the Headville ranch, and I was a desperado whose mug might as well be advertised on a nefarious wanted poster.

Headville led our motley group to the jailhouse where I had last visited as an awed spectator of a stellar performance by Jermyn Thomas, my great-great-grandfather. Promptly, Oleander dismounted, then drew his gun and cast his eyes on me. I had expected an expression of arrogance paired with his signature sneer, but instead there was something else, something that seemed distracted and apologetic. "Get off the horse, you piece of shit."

Or not.

"Lock up the schoolteacher. But not JT," Headville snapped, as I began to submit to the Oleander's command. "I've changed my mind. Cassanova is coming with us."

Oleander nodded then pointed his gun at Blaine. "You heard the man." Blaine stepped down from Buck and tied his reins to the hitching rail. Then the interim deputy moved behind his prisoner and gave him a shove. Blaine stumbled forward, crossing beneath the porch awning, and of his own volition, he opened the door and stepped into the confinement of the square building. Oleander followed him inside.

Filled with dread, I sat quietly upon Viento, my eyes pointed at the ground, my heroism having been abandoned miles behind me. Neither were Headville and Sherlee motivated to fill the silence, though I imagined that if I were to look, I would find them both pompously grinning at my defeat. A minute passed by as the three of us waited for Oleander.

"What the hell is taking you so long, deputy?!" Headville called out impatiently. "Get your groveling ass moving!"

In my mind, I counted through five Mississippi's before Oleander tumbled from the building and loudly closed the door behind him. Then the four of us left town, heading due south. Distantly ahead of us on the road, I noticed a rider, his horse kicking up a plume of dust as he hurriedly traveled in our same southerly direction. But I was certainly in no such hurry. My stomach churned with apprehension. Someone, several perhaps, might die before this evening ran its course.

Headville, with the vanity of a British Field Marshall, had demanded we spur our horses into a canter, but still, it would be almost dark before we would arrive at the settlement of Schoenchen.

I had time to think. But nothing came to mind. I was without an alternative plan B.

In seven days, the passageway could be opened.

The four of us 1878 horsemen forded the shallow crossing of the Smoky Hill River and entered the quaint little Volga-German community. With Headville cautiously in the lead, Viento and I had been booked between him and the riders behind me, Sherlee and Oleander paired like defensive gridiron safeties. As we rode through the village, my eyes scanned the shadowy silhouettes of the homes and businesses, and right away I realized that something did not feel right. Something was different. In spite of the dusk, it was too early for everyone to be missing from the narrow lattice of streets. But no one was in sight.

Within moments, we were passing by the church where Kival and Anja had been married four months earlier. That place of worship, too, was as silent as the other structures flanking the primary traffic artery of Schoenchen.

A short ride further and our ominous assembly would amble around a building that doubled as a home and as a blacksmith's workshop, and beyond it was the Beilman Farm: Helmut and Ruta's house, their dairy barn, and the original soddy where Kival and Anja, and their baby would be gathering for a pleasant supper. Special moments spent laughing, and talking, and planning for tomorrow. And a time to look forward to the blessings of a lifetime of days to come.

But not if Headville intervened.

When we reined our horses around the corner of the smithy, immediately before my eyes was the answer explaining why we had not yet seen anyone on the streets. Arranged in rows, one line after another, was a human barricade.

Headville stopped his horse. He had no choice. And neither did the other three of us. Standing elbow to elbow were the Volga German townspeople and fellow farmers and friends of the Beilmans, armed with pitchforks and shovels and scythes. Then I noticed that a few of the women held rolling pins and frying pans.

All of them were prepared.

"You'll not be getting past us!" a deep masculine voice sounded from the crowd, his English heavy with an accent of Russo-German. "No without we take a piece of you first."

Headville sat quietly, staring at the crowd. He nudged Ulysses forward a step. The front line responded and moved toward him. Restraining Ulysses, he waited a moment before speaking.

"Big. Mistake."

Then Headville reined his horse around, and we followed him back through the abandoned streets of Schoenchen.

Headville had been forced to retreat. Something I doubted he had ever experienced before. He would be seething. But there had been no calculably successful alternative. Even I could read their determination. They were going to protect their own. Not like last time when Sherlee had shot and killed young Ernst Beilman, a newlywed who should have had a full life ahead of him. Justice had failed them. So now, they appeared to be willing to take matters into their own hands.

In silence, we rode along the same road that would return us to Hays City, though now, in darkness, the pace of our horses was limited to a steady, fast walk. Headville had not uttered a word, but I knew he would not give in or give up. That much was certain. Behind us in that little German community was someone he wanted. And that someone was Kival, his alleged son known to him as David. A bastard child who Headville believed to have exclusionary custody of the thing he most desired.

I thought for a moment to tell Headville that I had not lied about the talisman. It was lost. Kival did not have it—of that I was certain. Morgan had performed a thorough search, and Kival's possessive reaction to Morgan's reveal of his own talisman was convincing enough for me. But if I said as much to Headville, I knew he would not believe me.

It was dark, the road barely visible in the weak light of a starry night. But we trekked northward. When we had traveled maybe halfway to town, Headville stopped and in the dark, he calmly hailed Oleander.

"Yes, sir?" I heard Oleander ask.

"You're fired," Headville replied.

BANG!

The sound of the unexpected gunshot exploded in the darkness.

The horses had been as startled as I was, and they churned and sidestepped in the road, and then I witnessed the shadowy form of Oleander's horse trotting away, the saddle empty. I looked about, searching the ground, and for second I caught a glimpse of a body lying prostrate upon his back. Then there was a phantom of movement. And then a hint of a nebulous thing swarming.

And then another. And in the darkness, I detected a swirling greyish mass of unworldly matter. I watched and stared, unable to see even the vaguest of details in the weak light of the stars. But within a few moments the shroud of anxiety passed, Viento fell calm, and I sensed that *they*, the indefinable Burmano-Ku-Partika, were gone. And with them, Oleander.

Murdered in cold blood.

This time, in the inky obscurity of the late hour, I sensed that Headville had been the one to pull the trigger. Though it could have been Sherlee who had fired the weapon putting a bullet into my wayward companion's back. Either way, the two men were homicidal cowards.

Suddenly, I was angry. But not just with the duo of unconscientious assassins, but I was also fuming at myself. Impulsively, my first thought was that Oleander had finally gotten what he deserved. He had struck Kate. It was his big mouth that had outed Kival's identity. It was his own failure to be compassionate that had brought him to this end. But then I felt a twinge of woe. Even though Oleander Sedgwick and I had never been on friendly terms, like it or not, he was one of us.

Another had fallen.

Sam.

Dent.

And now, Oleander.

A mile outside of town, we caught up with the runaway horse. Sherlee secured a hold on the loose reins, then we rode on into Hays City, not stopping until we had reached the fallen deputy's headquarters.

"Sherlee, lock JT in a cell. We have vigilantes to recruit."

Headville waited as Sherlee pulled me down from Viento and shoved me toward the darkened building.

"In there. Now," the unconscionable collaborator ordered me, and I walked through the doorway and waited for him. He lit a lantern and light flared inside the outer room. I looked at Blaine, who stood against the bars of his cell, his arms spread out in front of him, his hands grasping the vertical rods that imprisoned him, his face sliced by sharp, distinct shadows.

"Where's Oleander?" he whispered.

I shook my head.

"Damn it," I heard Sherlee curse, as he rifled through the drawers of the desk. Then he stomped a few steps and spoke through the space of the exterior door. "Boss, I can't find the keys. The damn kid must have had them on him."

"Sonofabitch!" Headville said, sharing the wrangler's irritation. "Here," I heard him say. "Tie him up."

Sherlee found me waiting next to Blaine, a wall of bars dividing us. He grabbed me by the scruff of my coat and shoved me to the opposite end of the row of cells, separating me from Blaine with as much distance as was possible. With barely enough light from the indirect glow of the lantern to guide him, Sherlee stood with his back to my inmate and with the rope given to him by Headville, he bound me tightly to the exterior bars of the adjacent cell, far from Blaine's reach. Once he left, I knew I would not have to tug to test the knots. They would be thoroughly cinched and expertly drawn. I said nothing, but instead I listened to the closing of the outer door, then overheard an important detail pertaining to Headville and Sherlee's anticipated return.

"Meet me back here in two hours, with no less than twelve loyal men," Headville commanded. Then their horses moved swiftly away, retreating in opposing directions. Where they would go to find vigilantes, I had no idea. But if the sort were around, both of them would know where to look.

A minute passed before I turned to look at Blaine, his face striped with shadows. Based on the angle of his jaw and the concentration in his eyes, he appeared to be listening just as I had been doing. Then he cocked his head and showed me an upward turn of one side of his mouth.

"What are you smiling about?" I asked him, wondering if he had lost his mind.

"We have a visitor."

Then I heard the echo of a faint shuffle come from behind Blaine, and I looked to see a figure roll from beneath the cot that had been used as his hiding place.

"Kival!" I exclaimed. "How the hell did you get locked up in here with Blaine?!"

"He's not exactly locked up," Blaine volunteered. "He was just about to let me out when we heard you guys ride up."

"Didn't have time to consider a better place to hide," Kival added.

"And of course, you have the missing cell keys."

"Right," he said, then he produced them and reaching through the bars, he unlocked the door.

"Guess it was a lucky break that Oleander didn't have the keys on him," I sighed with relief.

"Well, just so you know, JT," Blaine began, "Oleander tossed me the keys."

"What?" I asked, disbelieving.

"He did, I swear," he assured me. "It was a reckless, hurried pitch—only thing was, I didn't catch them. The ring hit the bars and bounced away. Too far out of my reach."

"Weren't you supposed to be some sort of star wide receiver?" Kival asked, as he stepped behind Blaine and knelt on the cold floor and fished his hand under the cot. When he returned to his feet, he had his souvenir hat in his hands, his fingers flicking particles of dirt from the rim of the black derby.

"Running back," Blaine countered with a smile, crossing the threshold with Kival on his heels. "But even the professionals drop a ball now and then."

But the coping mechanism of their humor fumbled with me. I was too busy processing the abnormal behavior of my life-long nemesis.

Oleander Sedgwick had tried to help.

Sullenly, I visualized his action of mutiny against Culver Headville, and instantly I felt grieved. And guilty. Then my eyes began to burn from the sting of tears. Oleander was right. I was a pussy.

I listened as Blaine verbally filled in details of the picture I had painted in my head. "After Oleander locked me in here, he was about halfway to the door when he stopped. Next thing I know, he turns around and looks at me, then at the keys, then at me, again. But then Headville yelled at him, and he got that crazed look in his eyes like he'd get when a squad of linebackers were targeting him for a sack. He panicked and threw the keys toward me and dashed out."

Leave it to Blaine to use football as his analogy.

"Where is Oleander?" Kival interrupted.

"Dead," I said. "Headville shot him. Just before we got back into town."

"Shit," Blaine whispered. "What happened?"

"I'll explain later. But Kival, what I'd like to know is how the hell did you get here so fast?" I asked him, still perplexed by his appearance.

"Let's get out of here first, then we'll share explanations."

Swiftly, my two friends pulled at the knots of my rope binding, and in little more than a minute they had me untied. "Let's go," Kival said, and quickly and quietly we slipped from the building and crossed to where Viento and Buck stood leisurely at the hitching post in front of the jail. We promptly untied them, and circuitously led the horses into the darkest shadows we could find.

We paused for a moment and surveyed our surroundings.

"Where's your horse?" Blaine asked Kival.

"Nearby. But I don't want to risk going there yet. Not until we have a plan."

"Should we hide them? I mean, JT's horse stands out like a movie star around here."

I smiled at him. "Takes one to know one."

"Whatever."

"Look, I could be wrong. But I don't think Headville is going to worry much about you Blaine, or me for that matter. He wants Kival. He won't waste his time on us. I say we keep them close."

"There's a place nearby," Kival said. "We can stash the horses in the back. There's a small corral there with a tree. I don't think anyone will notice them. Considering ..." he tacked on, leaving the ambiguous suggestion dangling without explanation.

"Then what?" Blaine asked.

"The corral, it's right behind a place where we can talk. Privately."

"Then let's go," I said. In three minutes, we were tying Buck and Viento inside the pen Kival had suggested. Four other horses were there. That was helpful. Our steeds would likely blend in among the others and be less noticeable to an unwitting passerby.

I closed the gate and turned to find Kival tapping at the back door of the building. I glanced around. Suddenly recognition struck me. We were behind the Sporting Palace, a place that catered to adult entertainment.

"Are you sure about this, Kival?" I asked him, wondering if he hadn't knocked on the wrong door.

"Positive. Trust me, she's a friend."

Then the door opened, and a woman stood there, her eyes and face painted in bright colors, her long red hair piled loosely atop her head, but her ample bosom was her most prominent feature, mostly because there was cleavage enough to completely hide a wallet, maybe even a small purse. Like the building, I recognized her instantly.

"K!" the woman exclaimed.

"Hello Ettie," Kival replied. "These are friends of mine. We need a room. Just for a while."

"Of course, K. All my rooms are just for a while," Ettie cooed. "They need company?"

"No, sorry."

"I'm just kiddin' ya, K," she said with a laugh, "Come on in. You can take these stairs. First door on the right. Number seven. It's mine." The three of us filed inside and she closed the door behind us. Kival and Blaine passed by her taking the stairs, but as I began to step around her, she stopped me with the tips of her fingers against my chest. "Hey there, cowboy, I think I've seen you before, haven't I?"

I glanced at Kival and Blaine, both of whom turned around to look at me. "Well, actually, um, a few months back, my—my brother and I happened to see you sitting up front on your balcony," I stuttered.

"That's it! I remember. Two little cutie pies. A dark-haired young man, your brother, I remember he waved at me."

"Yes, I think he did," I said to her, though I knew for a fact that he had.

"I thought maybe I would have gotten acquainted with the two of you long before now. Winter's half over!"

Knowing what I knew now, about Dent, he would not likely have paid her a visit. But I didn't have the heart to tell her that. Nor was I inclined to tell her he had died. "Another time, maybe," I said, and joined my friends on the stairs. We slipped into the room labeled with a painted seven, glad that Ettie had not followed us, and relieved even more that the room was empty. Kival closed the door behind us.

"And just how do you know her?" Blaine asked.

"Long story," Kival replied then he turned to me. "Blaine told me about Dent. I'm sorry. I liked him."

"Thanks," I said, but I could not bear to talk about my brother. Besides, I had questions. "How did you get away from Schoenchen so quickly?"

"I wasn't there. Anja and I and the baby, we were already here in town. And then when I saw the five of you guys riding in, I could tell something was up. I took Anja and Elsa to stay with a family. German friends. They sent their son, Wilhelm, to warn the Beilmans, just in case. Later, and purely by accident, I discovered Buck tied in front of the jail."

"So, you weren't even there when we got to Schoenchen?"

"Nope."

With that explained, I told him and Blaine about the gathering of the townspeople who had made a stand against Headville. I watched as Kival's eyes watered.

"They are good people," he said, nodding. "That's one reason why I have decided to leave. I realized it was getting too dangerous, what with my father so close."

"So, have you always known he was your father?"

"As a man called Culver Headville, no. But it didn't take me long to figure it out."

"What?" Blaine asked, "You mean, it's true? I thought that was just talk. But—but how?"

"I'll explain the birds and bees to you later," Kival said, and it made me smile. "JT knows. He can explain it to you, but not right now. We don't have the time."

"You said you were leaving," I reminded Kival. "Where are you planning to go?"

"Home."

I stared at him, unsure of where he meant. "You moved into town?"

"No. I'm talking Custer. I'm talking 1979. Nineteen-eighty technically."

"But how?"

Kival stared at me, his eyes glazing apologetically.

"JT, I lied to you. I never lost the talisman. I hid it."

CHAPTER 58

I sat down on the edge of the bed, shocked and speechless. "My mother had warned me to trust no one. I had to honor her wishes. But now, I have my own family. And they're not safe here. Not with my father around. I've told Anja where we can go. And how and what it will take to get there. She's confused. But she trusts me. I'm sorry, JT, that I did not trust you."

At once, I was overwhelmed, once again, with grief.

A couple of weeks.

If Dent could have held on for just two more weeks. The date of perihelion was only days away. January third, according to Morgan.

"I was going to tell you, when you were here a month ago, before Oleander surprised us. That's why I was in town today. I was coming to see you. I was coming to take you guys back with me."

I nodded and looked at him through teary eyes. I was grateful. I appreciated the truth. But I understood. Headville was too dangerous. The fewer who knew the truth, the better.

"If Dent died," Kival whispered, his head shaking, "because of me—"

"No," I said firmly. "It's not your fault. He's gone because of Headville. End of story."

Then Kival hugged me. It was the first brotherly contact we had shared. And then I felt Blaine's arms surround us both. We held on to each other for a moment, and I was thankful that at least three of us had a chance to make it back home. Back to our own time.

The talisman was not lost.

That was a game-changer.

"Where is it?" I asked pulling away.

"Buried," Kival replied without hesitation. "I buried it at the Pyramids. On top, above that big hole."

I listened to him, and instantly I pictured the place. Dent and I had referred to it as the Window. It was a hole, the size of a dinette table, carved high into one of the landforms that faced north, on the opposite end from the arch. "You did the right thing, Kival. Hiding it. And keeping it secret." I paused, then added, "we have a week to get there. Plenty of time."

"Right," Kival replied. "But my father will realize that will go there. Especially when he finds out I've left Schoechen and the Beilmans."

I cursed. Kival was right. That's exactly what Headville would surmise. He wouldn't even have to catch up with us. He would only have to arrive early and wait.

"What choice do we have, Kival? It's either now, or we wait until next year, or the next."

"No. We're doing it now. Here's what I'm thinking," he said, and shared with Blaine and me his plan.

"I'm in," I announced, believing Kival's proposal was promising.

"But I won't be able to travel as fast with Anja and the baby," he added. "So, I'm taking my family and leaving tonight. Under the cover of darkness. I hope to be half-way there before Headville even guesses that we've gone."

"Makes sense," I said. "But just so you know, I'm bringing someone with me, too." And I told him about Kate.

Kival smiled. "My sister. I thought she was dead."

"What?" I asked him, my comprehension stalling.

"T'on P'ee. We talked about her with Morgan, remember?"

"I remember," I said, catching up with him. "But Morgan said she died."

"Morgan called her a casualty. He didn't admit that she was dead. I made that assumption."

"And he wouldn't tell you," I added, recalling our conversation with him there inside the sod house of the Beilman farm.

"No. He only said that Headville had intervened. What he didn't tell us was that my father somehow managed to get to T'on P'ee before me and my mother could pass through the rift with her."

"Apparently Morgan didn't tell us a lot of things," I suggested. "But Headville himself has made up for that. I've learned tons from him."

"Such as?"

"For one, Kate, your T'on P'ee, is from the future. Headville kidnapped her from my time. And Blaine's," I added, not wanting to leave him out of the conversation.

"Man, you guys have stuck me out in left field. I had no idea so much was going on under my nose."

"Sorry, Blaine."

"Don't worry about. I get it. But it will probably give me a headache sorting out what you guys are talking about."

I laughed, appreciating his comic relief. "I'll make it up to you, I promise. When we get home, pizza is on me."

"We'll see," Blaine replied with a mysterious look in his eyes.

"Kate," Kival politely interrupted. "Have you told her? Does she know she's from the future?"

I shook my head. "Not yet, but I'll tell her on our way to the Pyramids."

Then Kival departed, leaving Blaine and I alone to work out our own exodus to the west. But that plan did not even reach step one.

"I've met someone, JT."

I looked at Blaine, expectantly. "Well, tell me."

Blaine smiled. "Do you remember that rule I told you about that said I could court two nights a week as long as I went to church?"

"I remember."

"Well, I hadn't really met anyone at first, but I thought why not be prepared, you know? So, I found this little Presbyterian church, and that's where I met her. Her name is Sue. Sue Krueger. Her dad owns a mercantile."

"I've met him. Nice man."

"Yeah, and he seems to like me, too. He's like, well, he treats me like a son," Blaine said, nodding his head. "A new feeling for me, I can tell you that."

"I get it," I told him, knowing how his own father had deprived Blaine of even an ounce of affection.

"Anyway, I've asked him for permission to marry his daughter. He said yes."

"Of course, he did! He's probably counting on a dozen good-looking grandkids that'll take after you."

"Ha!" Blaine said, then actually chuckled. "Maybe. Having kids has been on my mind lately. I mean, I know I'm not even twenty years old, but things are different here." I knew what he meant. Age was only relative.

"People grow up faster … here … I think."

"True," Blaine agreed. Then for a few moments he was silent, but I sensed he was wanting to tell me something.

"You know, you can bring Sue with us. It'll make a hell of story to tell our own grandkids how the three of us had to travel back into time just to find a wives."

He laughed again, and I joined him. We sat for a couple of moments longer.

"I'm not going, JT. I'm not going back with you and Kival."

"What?"

"There's no one there for me," Blaine said, shaking his head solemnly. "Nothing I want to go back to. I'm happy here. Happier than I've been my entire life. I can't leave that. I'm sorry."

Again, my heart began to turn soft. "No," I said, wrapping my arm around his shoulder. "You don't ever apologize for being happy." I thought of Dent. I hoped he had not died believing his love for Mick was wrong. "And never be sorry for loving someone. I wish my brother would have believed that."

"About Dent," Blaine said, turning to look at me. "I want you know—well, I loved him like a brother. But that was all."

I looked at him, his choice of words was intriguing.

Blaine reciprocated, looking me in the eye. "I think you know, now, that he was gay, right?"

I nodded. "Yes. Now."

"The night of prom, Dent made a pass at me. I knew he was serious because he hadn't starting drinking yet."

"I see. And that's why—why you two fell out of sorts."

"Yeah, but not because of anything I did. I want you to know that. It's just that, holy cow, he didn't take my rejection well. I think he was really, really embarrassed by what he tried. I told him it was okay. No big deal. But he got angry. And he punched me."

I laughed, then cried. For a moment I was engulfed again with grief. Quickly, I pulled it together. "That—that sounds like him," I said, thinking of Dent's temper, my head bobbling like a dashboard toy.

"We made up though. Out there," Blaine gestured with a nod of his head. "After the Indians. After Sam."

"Good," I said. I had noticed their reconciliation. I was glad they had patched things up. And now I knew what had happened between them. I understood why my brother had avoided telling me the truth.

"I don't know how—" I blubbered, "how—I'm gonna make it without him."

"There's always something to live for. Remember that JT. You live for him, that's how you make it."

We stayed another fifteen minutes in that room, talking about his plans with Sue, and of mine with Kate. Then we said our good-byes. I was going to miss Blaine. More than I admitted to him. This place and time; both had been cruel to me, but the here and now had brought Blaine hope and joy. That's what I would take back with me. His joy.

And I would be taking Kate with me, too.

I rode northeast, secreted by the night. It would be very late by the time I arrived at my destination. Or very early. Either way, I would have to approach the ranch with caution. I had no idea where Headville would be, but I imagined he was busy bargaining with the devil for the successful return of his talisman. I just hoped that Headville would not harm Ruta or Helmut, or any of the Schoenchen townsfolk.

Kival had informed me that their stance had been staged to buy him and Anja time. He assured me though, that once Headville returned to Schoenchen to extract him from the farm, he would find a different place. He would be shown, without contest, that Kival was no longer there. But would Headville still try to punish them? Probably. But probably not until he had Kival first.

I rode Viento through the wide entrance gate, though it was too dark to read, I could visualize the signage floating above me, proclaiming the CH Quarter Horse Ranch. I was now just over a mile away from the ranch yard, and I worried about what could go wrong in the next half-hour.

My palms were sweating, my nerves were raw. If things went well, I would soon have Kate riding with me from the ranch. I intended first to slip into the barn and saddle Mister Brown, hoping he was still there. If not, Kate and I would ride double. We certainly would not be stealing one of Headville's horses. Either way, we were not returning to Hays City. We would embark westward.

Then rendezvous with Kival, Anja, and baby Elsa.

I left Viento hidden within the edge of the line of trees that grew near the path that led to the gate of the daytime pasture where the stallion and the other cowboy steads had grazed when the grass was green and growing. Then I slinked around the bunkhouse, passing through the trees between it and the swimming pond, and finally emerging on the far side of the massive barn where I hustled to the far end of the central building and eased through the gap of the north doorway. Inside, the barn was pitch black, but I heard a stomp of a singular hoof. But it could be any of the four horses I expected to find there. So carefully, I felt my way along the wall of rails that defined the holding pens, knowing the first gate I would come to would be where Dent's horse had routinely been stabled.

I found the gate, lifted the latch, and stepped quietly inside. A soft muzzle touched my arm. My hand found the animal's nose, then I felt his cheek, and rubbed his ears. I sighed with relief. The brown bay gelding was still present. Getting away just got a lot easier.

In the dark, I found Dent's saddle, and saddle blanket, and bridle, all where they were normally stowed, then I fitted the horse for riding. In five minutes, I was leading Mister Brown out the same door which I had entered, and we traced our way back to where I had hidden Viento. Tying the gelding next to my stallion, I headed for the house.

At the back door, I tested the knob. It turned. Lucky or not, no one locked their doors in this day and age. I stepped inside, and to my right I saw the door to Isaiah's closet-sized sleeping room, and along the bottom was a glow of dim candlelight. I crossed to it and pushed it forward. Inside, Isaiah lay sleeping, his melting nightlight safely perched on a shelf. I moved to him and clamped my hand tightly over his mouth.

At once, his eyes were open and wide.

"It's me, Isaiah, JT," I whispered. "I'm sorry to scare you. Please, please don't yell."

He nodded, looking at me as though he were relieved to see me. I took my hand away.

"Jay-Tee, why are you here?!"

"I've come for Kate."

He stared at me for a moment, then smiled. "Good," he told me, and I could see he meant it.

"Is Headville here?" Isaiah answered me with a shake of his head. "Sherlee?"

"No. Neither have come back. Boyd and Pete are at the bunkhouse. But only the three of us here inside. Me, Miss Kate, and Miss Carneiro."

I nodded. "Can you take me to Kate's room?"

He swung his bare feet to the floor. "Follow me."

He stopped and fiddled with something for a moment, then in the next instant he struck a match and was lighting a lantern. Then he took it, and we passed through the kitchen and ascended the back stairway and down a long hall that accessed the west wing of bedrooms. We stopped at the door of the second room and Isaiah eased it open and I stepped past him. Before I crossed halfway to the bed, Kate sat up.

"JT!" she whispered, and then she was crying. I sat down on the edge of the bed next to her, embracing her and stroking her hair. "I didn't think I'd ever see you again!"

"I know. I didn't expect you would either. But we're getting out of here. Now."

She did not wait for an explanation, instead she jumped from the bed, and I turned away while she dressed. Glancing toward the hallway, I found that Isaiah was gone. Probably just waiting around the corner, protecting Kate's modesty.

"Okay," she told me, and I turned around to find her ready for riding, dressed in trousers, and shirt and coat. "All I need is my boots," she said, then she opened an armoire and retrieved the necessary footwear, then sat on the edge of the thick mattress and hurriedly fitted her feet. She looked at me, smiling, then accepting the offer of my hand, I pulled her up from the bed. Without warning, she kissed me. If nothing else, Kate knew how to surprise me.

After a moment, I pulled away from her. "There will be plenty of time for that later, I promise." Then we headed for the door.

"Wait!" Kate whispered, stopping me. She turned and hurried to the bed and threw back the covers. Toto sat up, then stood, her tail wagging. Then Kate swept the little dog up into her arms. "I'm not leaving without her."

"Of course not," I whispered, then we turned to leave.

But the doorway was blocked.

CHAPTER 59

Beverly Carneiro stood between us and our way out. She was posed with her hands on her hips, her dark eyes wide but it was her lips that startled me. She was smiling.

"Go!" she told us as she stepped aside.

We hurried down the stairs and found Isaiah waiting for us. He handed me a bulging knapsack and the lantern.

"Take care of Miss Kate, Jay-Tee."

"I will."

Kate quickly moved to Isaiah and kissed him on the cheek. "Good-bye old friend. I'll never forget you."

Then the two of us crossed the kitchen and slipped outside. We were steps away from leaping over the first hurdle of several more to come, but this was a big one, and I savored it. I took her hand, and together we hustled discreetly along the rear of the house and turned the corner.

"Eloping, are you?"

Kate cried out and I stepped protectively between her and Culver Headville. In the light of the lantern, it was clear that he was livid, though his voice had sounded deceitfully casual.

His eyes bore into me like fiery cannons of a war ship. But I was less afraid than I was stunned. I had been far too confident. I had reached for the stars, and then tripped over the moon.

With lightning speed, he struck my face with the back of his hand, spinning me away from him, my hat flying from my head. Then in the next instant I felt his hard, powerful fist land against the back of my skull, knocking me to the ground. Through short blades of dry, brown grass, I saw his boots move past me. Clearly, there was another he intended to punish.

I released the things I still had clutched in my hands and pushed myself up onto my elbows and knees and watched as Headville stalked toward Kate, backing her away from the wall of the two-story house. I launched myself forward, just as I had often done from the starting blocks of a fifty-yard dash. I dove, colliding into him inches above the fold of his knees. The effect of my tackle flipped him from his feet and sent him into a backward fall that landed him heavily upon the length of my body. For a second, we were both down, back-to-back.

Quickly I scrambled from beneath him.

I moved toward Kate, and from the corner of my eye, I saw Isaiah and Beverly clutching one another in the doorway of the house. But then I felt something snag my boot and I was down on my stomach for a third time, my face planted into the ground. I lifted my head and spit bits of grass and dry dirt from my mouth. Then the heavy weight of Culver Headville landed upon my lower back, his legs straddling me, the fingers of both hands grabbing me by the hair on both sides of my scalp. With a quick, fierce move, he lifted my head, wrenching my neck backward before sending my face brutally into the ground.

Fireworks exploded in my head.

During the next several moments, time seemed to have come to a full halt. I was aware, but my mind felt foggy, my brain concussed. I could see shapes and movement, though my perspective was seemingly aerial, as though I was undergoing an out-of-body experience. Then my vision settled into focus, and from what I perceived as a view from overhead, I watched as Headville pushed off from me, and vaulted toward Kate, his motion slow, but clearly defined by the light shining from my fallen lantern.

I heard her cry out, and saw her stumble backwards onto the porch of her childhood playhouse, losing her hold on Toto. Tumbling to the ground, the frightened little dog scurried away just as Headville captured his prey. Impulsively, Kate began to fight back in a flurry of fists and fingers. I commanded my body to move, to rise onto my feet and defend her. But I seemed paralyzed, helpless, detached. At once, darkness clouded my eyes, but I heard voices, pleading.

Beverly. Isaiah.

Momentarily, I lost consciousness, but when I opened my eyes, the hallucination of floating skyward had dissipated and I was again inhabiting the shell of my own body. Still lying prostrate on the cold ground, I looked around and my eyes found Headville fumbling with something at the door of the miniature house. And then I heard the sound of hands pounding against a wall.

"Let us out!" I heard Kate cry. Then Headville stepped away from the little building and with a wild swing of his arm, he appeared to have thrown something into the dark void beyond. Then my eyes moved suspiciously to the door where he had been so focused, and I saw that there was a latch and a lock. And where there had once been windows neighboring each side of the door, planks of wood now covered the glass.

None of those things had been there before. Not on that day when I had sat with Kate talking about her first dog, listening to her Bible stories, and dreaming of cities. Headville had obviously been preparing for this eventuality. The range shack had been my prison. But he had redesigned the playhouse as a cage for his little bird.

The man was mad.

"Mister Headville! Please, sir!" I heard Isaiah pleading. Then other voices sounded from behind me.

"What the hell be goin' on?!"

It was Boyd.

"RETRIBUTION!"

Headville's angry scream filled my ears. Then I felt arms lifting me, and turning my cheek I met the fearful eyes of Little Pete.

"Help them!" I heard Isaiah call out. "Help Miss Kate! The Mister, he's gone crazy, crazy man!"

Then the cries of feminine voices lifted and melded with the incessant pounding of hands and fists against a wooden door.

"Culver!" Boyd cried out, and through eyes that had suddenly begun to reveal images that were doubled, I saw the foreman rush to Headville, the white of his undergarments appearing ghostly in the glow of the fallen lantern. "Culver!" I heard him repeat, then I saw Boyd grab the shirt of a man dressed in black who had uncharacteristically lost complete emotional control. "What ya doin'?! The girl be soundin' scared to death?!"

His breathing heavy and labored, Headville said nothing.

Then through a blur, I watched Boyd clamber upon the porch discovering that the door to the playhouse was bolted and locked. He turned. "Why there be a damn lock?!"

But Headville ignored him. He was already heading in my direction, moving deliriously as though he were a Western Frankenstein monster. I felt profoundly faint, my eyes struggling to focus, my knees repeatedly folding. I did not have the cognizance to defend myself. If Pete had not been at my side, I would have been on the ground.

"Pete," Headville snarled, his dazed eyes fastened upon me, spittle dripping from the corner of his mouth. "Ride—into town. Find Sherlee. Bring him back—with you."

Apart from the muffled sound of soft, desperate crying, there was a silence around me, save for the heavy breath of Headville as he waited for Pete to move.

"I said—"

"I heard you," Pete spat. "Go find the bastard yourself."

The movement of his fist was rapid and unmistakably powerful, clipping Pete squarely beneath his chin, cracking his teeth together. He stumbled backward from the steeled blow, losing his grip on me. I staggered aside and watched as Headville hurled himself at the over-sized ranch hand.

"AAGGGGHHHHH!" Headville cried out in fury. With malevolence, he grabbed the dazed young cowboy by the front of his undershirt and threw his hulking body backwards against the stone wall of the imposing house. I heard the sickening sound of a skull pop against the limestone bricks. Then through my vaporous vision, I watched as Pete slid down to the ground, groaning.

In the fog of my thoughts, I sensed I would be next. But when I looked, Headville was picking up the lantern from the ground. Then he aimed his glazed eyes at me, smiling maniacally. And in that moment, I believed it was his consuming desire to burn me alive.

Behind me, wails of distress and trepidation surged from inside the little playhouse. Then Headville was moving toward me, stealing part of my attention.

Instinctively, I began to back away from the stalking assailant, my feet dragging, my mind scrambling to think of some way to stop him from launching the oil-filled lantern. But neither my brain nor my body was properly functioning, and within seconds I had run out of time and space. Helplessly, I watched as he lifted the incendiary weapon, but suddenly my bootheel caught upon something buried in the surface of the ground. It might have been a rock, a pebble, or tiny stick, or nothing at all, but I felt myself falling backwards as the lantern sailed past my head. I heard it shatter against a wall, the sound of metal and glass ricocheting into the night.

And I heard the splash of kerosene.

Then a masculine cry rose from behind me, and I rolled over to see flames billowing from the fuel-soaked sleeve of Boyd's undershirt as he stumbled from the tiny porch, fighting the ignited garment with his bare hands. Then my eyes went to Kate's childhood playhouse. Its frontage was blanketed in fire, with flames roiling and devouring the kerosene from the broken lantern.

"KATE!" I shouted, and then I scrambled to my knees, crawling to where she was trapped. Then I felt hands clutch the back of my coat as Headville pulled me away. Seemingly empowered with adrenaline-laced hate, he forcefully lifted me upright onto my knees and with a savage grip he callously turned my face toward the fire.

"THIS IS ALL YOUR DOING, YOU GODDAMNED LITTLE BASTARD! LIVE WITH—"

I heard the sound of a sharp, but heavy whack, then we both fell forward. I rolled over and found Isaiah standing behind us, a thick kitchen cutting board clutched in his dark hands. And then he dropped the unlikely weapon and scurried past me.

Screams of terror continued to rise loudly into the night air. And I was aware enough to know that I had to act. I had to save her. But when I stood, before me was an inferno.

"NOOOOOO!" I cried out, horrorstruck.

I stumbled to the burning building, the repelling heat of the flames urging me to yield. I hurled myself against the door, but I was weak and lacked the power to force it open. Then Isaiah was next to me, and together we struck our shoulders against the locked barricade. Then again. Then again. And again.

Then I saw that my coat was on fire.

But I didn't care.

Trembling, I cried out again as I feebly pushed against the fortified door. Then at once the harrowing sound of the screaming was replaced by uncontrollable bouts of coughing and gagging. Then nightmarish moments later, there was only a heavy silence, save for the billowing sound of the fire. Then I felt myself being pulled away.

Away from the flames. Away from the scorching heat. Away from the girl I loved but could not save. Shock and disbelief paralyzed me. Then hands were on me, pulling at my coat, ripping the burning jacket from my back.

"Son, come away," I heard a voice, its tenor defeated and consumed with grief. But I couldn't move. Didn't want to move. Then I felt hands lifting me and tugging me backward, the distance widening between me and the horror that roared before my eyes. Violent sobs erupted from my throat, my heart and mind unable to bear the scene that had savagely unfolded before me. Around me I felt arms, then I dropped my eyes, and I could see hands. Two with skin the color of rich chocolate, two more that were red and blistered.

Isaiah and Boyd huddled with me, and I heard the faint sounds of their sorrow and anguish muffled by my own shuddering wails. In that moment, I didn't care about a talisman. It did not matter to me if I ever got home again. I possessed no fear of dying, no wish to even live.

But I felt hate. Hate as intense as the murderous fire that blazed near me. In that moment of immense loss, I vowed to kill the man responsible. God Himself would not be able to stop me.

But He did.

At least for now.

Because Headville had disappeared.

In the dawn of a new morning, I found myself surrounded by Boyd and Pete and Isaiah, each of us bearing bandages that covered some degree of injury. We were a band of emotionally broken men. All of us weighted heavily by the loss of life that had been sacrificed hours earlier.

Kate was gone. And with her, Beverly.

It had taken just an hour for the fire to reduce the structure to a heap of embers. However, there had not been enough combustible material to turn the playhouse into a crematory. And because of some sense of dutiful responsibility, Boyd had felt someone should check, to make sure.

I knew most victims of fires succumbed first to the smoke, but even with that knowledge I could not fathom the thought of looking. I did not want to see what had been so beautiful and so full of life, now rendered horrifically unrecognizable.

Obliging the older man, Pete had hesitantly edged toward the smoldering remains, and I watched him bravely attempt a cursory sighting of any evidence that might be visible. But his confirmation had lasted but a second before he looked quickly away, his head nodding, his face ashen and bereft.

He had done more than I could have managed.

Seated now at the dining table in the bunkhouse, I stared silently into the nothingness of my mind. And then Headville, again, entered the theatre of my head and sat in the front row.

I did not know for certain if Headville had intended to kill them. He had, after all, seemed to have been aiming his wrath toward me when he had thrown the lantern. In my mind, it was because of him that they were dead. But I, also, felt partly to blame. I had come to get Kate, to take her with me. If I had stayed away, she would still be alive. I was a failed knight without a glimmer of shine upon my armor.

Boyd had spent the last hour trying his best to persuade me that I was not at fault. And I heard and understood the sense of his words. But it was not enough to rid me of my guilt. I did, however, appreciate his concern. I hugged the old man, knowing that he, too, was grieving. As were Isaiah and Pete.

Ultimately, the three of them had made a unanimous decision. They would be leaving the ranch. Their loyalty to Culver Headville had likewise perished in the fire.

I had been invited to go with them. But I had only one place I could go. I would meet Kival as planned. I would help him and his family escape from the lunacy that was Headville's creation. But, for now, it mattered little to me if I made it back home. There, like here, I would not have Kate. I would not have my brother.

I felt numb. I was, for now, exhausted of all emotion.

By the time the apex of the sun had peeked over the horizon, I was ready to leave. Twice, I had attempted to go to Kate, to retrieve and bury her scorched body. But I had failed. I was not man enough, yet, to do what needed to be done. Then Boyd promised me that he would take care of her.

Pete had found Viento and Dent's gelding in the place where I had hidden them, and he now had the two horses tethered before the bunkhouse, waiting for me. I had been inside, packing my bedroll, clearing out the few possessions that had been mine, adding them to those things I had retrieved from the Indian bunkhouse that had belonged to my brother. For now, I could not bear to throw anything away, not a shirt or even a pair of socks. Then Boyd had offered me the dime novel that had been Mick's, the one with the cover that featured Kit Carson. I did not really want it, not at first. But then I changed my mind, and I took it from him. I would keep it as a reminder of who my brother had found the courage to love.

My eyes fell to my wrist where the bracelet Kate had made for me remained tied in place. I, too, had fallen in love. But as of now, I doubted I could endure a life without her.

I donned my cowboy hat, rescued by Boyd from wherever I had lost it, and I stepped outside, and climbed onto the back of my grullo stallion. Then I turned to the young man whom Oleander had nicknamed Ox, who held what I had wanted that had been Kate's. I nodded at Pete, and he offered me the little pup, Toto. Then Boyd gave me the rope that tethered Dent's horse and I tied the end to my saddle horn. Then a movement caught my eye, and I found Isaiah hurrying toward us from the house. With him he carried a package, and on tiptoes, he stuffed the cloth-wrapped bundle into the pocket of the saddle bag. His signature biscuits, a parting gift to me.

He then tapped my leg, and I looked down to see his dark face smiling at me, his eyes moist.

There were no good-byes.

None were needed.

With Toto tucked under my arm, I reined Viento away, and then I, and a dog, and two horses trotted away, leaving behind a place that held both wonderful and gruesome memories.

Without looking back, we left the Culver Headville Quarter Horse Ranch, and I charted a path westward. I would camp somewhere along the way and hoped to arrive at Karl and Abelard's place by this time tomorrow.

That is, if I didn't find Headville first. Or if he found me.

CHAPTER 60

It was Saturday, the twenty-nineth of December. The year was 1878. If all went according to plan, in three days, I would advance into a new year. And two days after that, I would take a 101-year trip forward into a new century.

Returning to my time.

1980.

Unless I changed my mind.

It was mid-morning when I approached the farmstead where months earlier, I had learned to manually cut thin stalks of wheat before tying them into sheaves, and ultimately assembling the bundles as stooks in the field. But my approach had not been direct. I had first stayed close to the river, riding on the far south side, using the breadth of the waterway as a defensive tactic should someone other than a friend spy me from the refuge of the embanked home and decide to pursue me forthwith.

That someone, of course, being Culver Headville.

I paused, me with the two horses and the little dog, and studied the place where Kival and I had chosen as our meeting point. Nothing looked out of the ordinary, except for the reddish gelding that Morgan had given to Kival. The sorrel stood leisurely inside the small pen next to the dug-out abode, and loitering with him was the brethren's large, clunky draft horse. Since my friend's horse was present at this place, it was logical to expect that Kival was also here, waiting for me.

I wanted to embrace that positive expectation. But in the last week I had learned that shit happens.

The brawny Abelard and his brother, Karl, were outside tending to the chore of splitting firewood in the bare yard near the front door. There was nothing alarming about their actions, or their moods, they were going about their business as though it was just a normal day at the end of a chilly December.

Arriving here was hurdle number two, though my plan had included Kate being at my side. I hoped this leap of faith would not coincide with other innocent fatalities. I had been too optimistic then. I was paranoid, now.

I hesitated to call out to the German brothers, fearing that a trap may have been set, and they were the bait. So, I waited, hoping they might glance my way and perhaps communicate to me that all was safe, or conversely, signal to me to run like hell. But I did not have to wait long. The tall, skinny brother looked up and spied me watching them from across the river. With perhaps a distance of less than 500 feet from where I waited, I knew that Viento would be easily recognizable, even if I were not. And as I surmised, I was proven correct. Karl began to wave, enthusiastically urging me to come to him. And then I saw the stockier Abelard set down a long-handled axe, and he, too, waved at me. And then I heard them both chattering excitedly.

In the next moment, the simple planked door residing within the face of the stunted wall of the dug-out opened, and a tall, lanky young man wearing a black derby hat stepped outside.

Kival.

I sighed, relieved to see him.

I reined Viento into the shallow stream of water, and my humble party of four crossed the width of the river that was no more than the breadth of a two-lane highway with decent sized shoulders. By the time I was inside the area of the yard, Anja had appeared and with her the baby I had met just barely a month earlier. At least my co-collaborator had been successful with his part of our plan.

Kival looked at me, his eyes concerned and apprehensive.

"Kate?" he asked.

I shook my head, and then the dam broke again.

Inside the home, Anja and Kival did their best to console me as I told them what had happened. They were compassionately shocked. Themselves, stunned into tears, especially Anja. Outside, Karl and Abelard tended to my horses, and I had left Toto in their care, giving her a chance to scamper about and stretch her legs.

When I had sufficiently collected and rebottled my emotions, I told them about Blaine's decision to stay, and then we discussed our next move.

"What about the horses? If Headville passes by here, he'll see them. Recognize them," Kival said, expressing a concern that I had also been wrestling with.

"Well, obviously I know nothing for certain, but we're five days out from our launch date," I said. "I don't think Headville would try to get to the arch any earlier than necessary. He knows of the date, I'm sure of it. And knows we can't leave from this time any earlier than the third of January. So, I think we've got a couple days, at least, before we risk being found."

"And Headville, he will be coming."

"Hell, yeah."

Later that night, we sat at the table with Abelard and Karl, and discussed contingencies with them. Communication was easier this time. Anja had learned enough English from Kival to function as an adequate interpreter. Not to mention, Kival himself had mastered a number of the more common words and phrases of the Volga-German language.

Deciding that we were only second-guessing what Headville might do, we opted to be proactive but cautionary, beginning first thing the next morning. During the daylight hours, we four men would rotate as lookouts, keeping watch for Headville, and probably Sherlee. Likely both would be riding together, but we could not rule out a split march between them. Knowing when they were nearby was prudent. But we would need only minutes to secret ourselves away. Abelard had insisted we practice hiding. We did not argue with him. When animals were involved, you just never knew.

Luckily, the place where the brothers had built their homestead, the ground was slightly elevated and in addition there was a knoll that was less than 200 yards away toward the east that made for an ideal place to keep an eye on the open prairie that drifted for miles away in all directions. Two full days had passed, both quiet and uneventful, and at the end of that second day, the year 1878 ended.

Again.

On the first day of the new year, I sat upon the peak of the low hill, hidden securely behind thick clumps of sage brush, scouring the landscape, my eyes continuously sweeping north to south, studying the land for any sign of a horse and rider. Behind me, roughly forty miles west, stood Monument Rocks, the landforms the locals of my community had christened the Smoky Hill Pyramids.

Months earlier, it had taken two days to journey from there to here, on foot. By horseback, the distance could be traversed easily in a day and half, or less, if we were hurried. But there would be a baby traveling with us, and her young mother. Most, if not all, of the trip would have to be done at the pace of a horse's brisk walk.

Tomorrow morning, we would need to leave. At the crack of dawn, or slightly beforehand, if we decided to take advantage of the sky-glow of the impeding sunrise. Traveling in the dark was impractical and too risky given the circumstance of baby Elsa. We would need to camp overnight, ideally within a six-to-seven-hour ride from the Pyramids. That would give us plenty of time to still catch the daylight of the late afternoon of our presumed extra-terrestrial transport.

I had been at my post for several hours, often my thoughts returning again and again to my brother, Dent, and to Kate. I grieved for both of them, praying that time might eventually bring me a token of peace. For now, though, my sense of loss was still raw, especially for Kate and the life I had begun to imagine sharing with her.

I had anticipated that we would have children, that we would get to watch them learn and play, that we would hold them in times of joy as well as in those special moments when they would need us to kiss their boo-boos and shoo away the monsters hiding beneath their beds. I had imagined their little faces surrounded by locks of golden hair, miniature replicas of their mother. But that would never be.

Not now.

Distracted by my daydreaming, Kival appeared at my side, startling me as he had done on each occasion when he had come to relieve me.

"Shit!" I exclaimed. "You gave me a heart attack. Again. I don't know how you manage to sneak up on me so quietly."

"Genetics," Kival replied rationally, as though it were reasonable to accept that his Indian heritage had ordained in him an inherent ability to be stealth.

"Must be," I agreed, reluctantly.

"Anything?"

"Nothing. But any minute now could be the time," I replied. The clock that was ticking for Headville was also ticking for us.

I left Kival and returned to the dug-out. Karl had breakfast waiting for me, and I did not need to be invited twice to sit down and eat. Anja lay on the lower of the set of bunked beds, nursing baby Elsa, so I ate quickly, feeling like a creepy voyeur, even though I did not once glance their way.

Then I stepped outside where the brothers had staged for a third day in a row, a scene of wood chopping and stacking, despite a supply of fuel enough to last a month had already been gathered and stowed out of sight. I patted Abelard on the back and smiled at him, then I thanked Karl for the meal, before bending over to pet the little pup that pranced around my feet.

Suddenly Abelard called out some German word that was clearly a tone of warning. Instantly, I looked up and saw Kival running toward us. We did not have to wait for him to discern the obvious. His urgency told us it was time to get into place. Hopefully, our dress rehearsals would pay dividends.

By the time Kival reached the dug-out, the three of us had already moved the visiting three horses inside the primitive home, crowding them into one end of the open room. Anja retreated with the baby into the far corner of the small bed, and I quickly hurried outside and gathered Toto and brought her in and sat her down beside the mother and child. When I turned around, Kival entered, his breath panting, and he closed the door behind him. In the next moment, he surveyed the room. It was just as we practiced. And for now, both the humans and the horses were calm. I glanced at Kival and caught his eyes and nodded. There was little else he and I could do. Neither of us had a gun.

I crossed and peeked through a dusty pane of the window glass and watched as the brothers quickly and thoroughly swept and camouflaged the tracks of our horses. Then at once, they resumed the charade with the wood and the axe and cart.

Silently, I counted to sixty. Then sixty again. Then twice more. Nothing.

One-thousand-one I started again and had reached the two decimal place count of thirty-seven when I heard Karl's low whistle. I looked past him, searching. Then I saw a movement.

Two men on horseback were sauntering along, following the edge of the river, both staring our way. More often than I could count, I had observed these two men. I knew their size, their postures, their characteristic movements. And I certainly recognized their horses. Especially the black stallion with socks of white.

I watched, my breath trapped in my lungs, as Headville and Sherlee pushed onward. Their interest in Karl and Abelard appeared to be too minimal to waste their time. Nor were they baited by anything that would cast suspicion or unduly draw their attention. There would have been a dozen or more other homesteads dotted along the river from whence they had traveled. I doubted they would have searched each one. And why would they?

Our enemies knew where they would ultimately find us.

I watched as the two men rode another twenty, then thirty yards further, but suddenly they stopped, and again they looked our way.

"Shit," I whispered and glanced at Kival.

"What is it?" he whispered back.

I shook my head and held a finger to my lips. When I turned back toward the window, Sherlee was loping his horse toward us, leaving Headville at the river's edge. Cautiously I eased back into the shadowed side of the window, and watched the scene, comfortably knowing that I could not be viewed from the outside.

Boldly, the henchman rode into the perimeter of the yard with a speed that was at best inconsiderate. Then with a quick tug of the reins he pulled the horse to a stop just yards away from where the brothers worked.

"You see anybody pass by here lately?" I heard Sherlee question. Then I watched as Abelard's shoulders raised an inch, before replying something in German. Then Sherlee spit on the ground and glanced around. "I mighta known. Damn farmers."

Then Abelard spoke again, his tone congenial.

Behind me, Toto began to whimper, and I turned to see Kival cross and kneel at the bed, cupping the pup's nose into the palms of his hands, then he pressed his face into the makeshift wind tunnel and softly blew into it, quieting the dog.

Sherlee cursed.

For an instant, I feared the pup had given us away.

"How about you?" Sherlee asked, his gaze pointing at Karl. "I'm lookin' for a young man, black hair, Injun half-breed, maybe with a woman and baby? Or another kid, light hair, bruised up a little?"

Karl replied with a pair of brief Germanic sentences, also shrugging his shoulders.

Sherlee cursed again, and after another glance around, he reined his horse and galloped away.

I expelled my breath. Then turned to Kival and gave him a thumbs up. I watched through the window as Sherlee rejoined Headville, where a recitation of Sherlee's investigation was apparently being reported to the bossman. Then the riders put their horses in second gear and trotted away, fading westward.

We waited inside, while Abelard strolled down to the river, his eyes studying the western landscape. When he returned, we learned that he had glimpsed the two men far in the distance. But we stayed hidden for another hour, just to be safe.

The encounter had been carefully prepared for, and I was relieved that we had managed to put it behind us unscathed. But tomorrow there would be no place to hide. And the next day, we would require the help of celestial guardians to get ourselves into position at the arch.

I knew of at least two angels who I believed would have my back. God willing.

In eighteen hours, the passageway could be entered.

The next morning, we said good-bye to the German brothers. I could not help but envy them. They still had each other. And I hoped they would not take that for granted.

We snaked our way westward, keeping the river in sight, going to it only when thirst began to pull the horses in the direction of the water. We were a caravan of three mounted riders, plus the priceless baggage of a baby and a sentimental keepsake named Toto. Though we were now ironically followers instead of leaders, we remained vigilant. Ahead of us lay both sanctuary and danger. Though we would probably not experience the first without enduring the second condition beforehand.

At dusk, we stopped for the night, secreting ourselves on the south side of the river, finding a shallow ravine in which to shield ourselves. Not only did we want to avoid being discovered and routed by Headville and Company, but neither did we want to expose ourselves to Indians, though there was at least one less Dog Soldier to be feared, thanks to the retaliation of Oleander.

The night passed quietly, and when the sun rose on the morning of the perihelion, we were just hours away from the Pyramids.

The passageway was ready. The escorts could be summoned.

We wasted no time getting back into the saddle, and though we were as close as twenty miles to the landmark that was our destination, my heart pounded heavily with anticipation.

I thought of Morgan. In my mind, I replayed his many cryptic phrases, as well as his words of advice and experience. Months earlier, when I had finally accepted the fact that Morgan knew me from my future, it had been easy to assume that I would eventually return to my own time. But then he had dropped a life-altering bomb on me, telling me that history was a fallacy. That the deeds of other time travelers who lacked the respect or the discipline to act only as observers when crossing into alternate dimensions of time, could easily change the trajectory of future events.

Headville had intentionally done just that. For one, he had traveled forward into my era and had assassinated a President, a man who in Morgan's time did not die on a street in Dallas but lived to win a consecutive presidential term. But neither had I been an innocent bystander. I had gotten involved and had helped orchestrate things here that perhaps I should have just left alone. And who knew what implications might unfold with Blaine's decision to remain behind and weave himself into the fabric of a previous history.

It was entirely possible that despite my twenty-first century association with Morgan, my current version of time might ultimately be the only life I would know going forward. Yet, odds were in my favor that at least my body would be escorted from this present-time by the Burmano-Ku-Partika. Just like Sam and Dent, and Oleander.

I carried with me no expectation that I would make it through the day alive. I had but one motive. And that was to make sure Kival and Anja and the baby girl, Elsa, made their arrival into the time that waited on the other side of the archway portal. I had not conceived of an alternative idea other than being a distraction, a decoy. How else could Kival retrieve the talisman? How else would there be time to gather inside the arch and summon the Burmano-Ku-Partika without Headville intervening?

I had not told Kival of my intentions. What worried me was that he planned to sacrifice himself as well, to save his wife and child. Or to save me, for that matter. But I no longer needed his sacrifice. With any circumstance of adversity there had to be priorities. And as far as I was concerned, I was last among the four of us. The bottom of the list.

Besides, life was hardly worth living when you had nothing to live for.

But I was wrong to think that way. Blaine had advised me otherwise. And I could imagine hearing Kate telling me to let her go and to seek happiness in a life without her. And my brother, he would certainly be saying the same thing, plus smacking me on the head as a reminder that he had placed his faith in me to return to our mother.

Mom and Dad.

I could not deny I owed it to them to at least try and step thru the arch with Kival and his family.

CHAPTER 61

The day was cold, as was expected in January on the High Plains of Kansas, and its frigid air tingled my nostrils. Huddled within the leathered bowl of our saddles, we trekked onward, already weary, but equally wary. We had decided that our best odds of success lay in the strategy of splitting up shortly before the last leg of our approach to Monument Rocks.

When we had come within an estimated distance of six or seven miles from the Pyramids, Kival and Anja and the baby left the path of the river and charted a course to the northwest. They would route their way through the lowlands that were cut by gullies and ravines, and would ultimately approach ground zero from due north, waiting to change direction once they were within sight of the lone chalk rock pilon, Old Chief Smoky. If found safe to do so, Anja and the baby and the horses would conceal themselves behind the signature rock, while Kival would steal his way to the northern face of the towering formation that was home to the Window.

My route would be a steady passage following the river, with the last segment of my approach striking from the south, a bearing that would be most direct, and most expected, and fully out in the open.

Intentionally.

I was meant to be an allurement. A distraction. A minnow to bait a ravenously dangerous fish.

I reined Viento to a stop next to the southernmost landform of the chalk pyramids that I had often referred to as Hitchhiker Rock. I sat upon the grullo stallion with Toto cradled between my lap and the swell and horn of the saddle, all of us relatively cloaked in the late afternoon shadow of the geological formation. With shifting eyes, I studied the second and most compact cluster of Monument Rocks rising from the prairie a quarter of a mile north of where I waited and watched.

But the shadow of my weak hiding spot was not as sharply defined as I had hoped. An enormous and heavy cloud bank had moved into the Western Kansas sky, blotting out the sun. And as a result, my surroundings had grown both picturesque and ominous. But there was still time for the sun to reappear. It would surely have to shine. Its light was needed.

Morgan had said as much. It was the fourth condition necessary for this mode of time travel, the one Morgan had initially forgotten to tell me.

Daylight is important ... absolutely necessary.

Those had been his words in the hotel room the day he had boarded the east-bound train. Mentally, I itemized the stipulations: The day of the perihelion, the place of the arch, the possession of the talisman, and the power of sunlight. All four of these conditions were required to call forth the Burmano-Ku-Partika.

If Morgan was correct, the perihelion, that day when the earth was at its closest to the sun, was currently on the clock. The talisman, no longer known by me as an object lost, lay hidden and buried just a short distance away. The arch, too, was nearby. That natural occurring aperture that had been created within an ancient geological formation by the forces of wind erosion over the course of a millennia of time. However, that place which had been inexplicably chosen as a doorway separating a 101-year division of time, was guarded.

Or watched.

Culver Headville also knew of its contribution toward the process of transporting those who trespassed from one's legitimate existence of time to the unnatural reality of a different age. And he was nearby. He had to be.

He also had to stop us.

And then, with a blink of my eye, the man confirmed his presence.

From the relative obscurity of where I had been conducting my surveillance, I had a point-to-point line of sight between me and the rock that boasted the arch, the Keyhole, the passageway. However, because of the less-than idyllic angle of my alignment, I did not have an unobstructed view of the physical cleft in the rock, but I knew exactly where the opening was. And Headville had just seconds earlier passed through it.

He sat astride his black stallion, posing just yards away from where I knew the super-natural aperture to be, unconcerned that I or anyone else might see him.

But then, that was probably what he wanted. Either that, or he didn't care.

In his mind, I'm sure he considered himself in possession of the proverbial upper hand. But from my perspective, I had the advantage. Or so I hoped. Yet, the truth of the matter was both of us had underestimated the other. The game was not over. No one had waved a white flag. The fat lady had yet to sing.

It was time to step forward, boldly, with confidence.

Hoping for an element of surprise, I nudged Viento, and we started moving directly toward my nemesis. One-hundred yards later, crossing the non-descript terrain at a point where, in my time, there would be a gravel road, a movement in the peripheral vision of my right eye caused me to glance in its direction. Sherlee had extracted himself from a covert space between the pillars of the southern cluster of the tall rock formations, riding leisurely upon his favored sorrel mare, aiming to intercept me.

I decided to make it easy for him. I reined Viento to a stop and waited for Sherlee. His appearance was, after all, anticipated.

He rode up to me, positioning his horse and himself in front my stallion, his gun drawn, as though he thought I would try and maneuver around him. I failed to understand why he might think I would attempt such a move, considering I had just given him an easy opportunity to join me. I stared at the henchman; my curiosity piqued.

"Mr. Headville wants to talk to you."

"No kidding," I said. "But I thought by now, he would have gotten bored of my company."

"I want to know what happened. Exactly." Sherlee demanded solemnly.

I studied Sherlee's countenance, spending a long moment reading the intensity of his round, beady eyes. "I don't know what you mean," I said, and I genuinely didn't have a clue.

"Kate."

I shrugged and glanced away for a moment to hide from him the instant grief that surged through me upon hearing her name. I looked back at him after anger had overruled my sorrow. "I don't know what he's told you, but if you think for a second that I would ever hurt her, you are dead wrong."

Sherlee stared hard into my eyes, evaluating my integrity, as if he were looking for a sign that would tell him I was lying. But he wouldn't find one. I had not been the maniac who had trapped Kate and Beverly inside the little house. I had not been the villain who had thrown the lantern. I had not been the coward who had vanished, leaving without attempting a remorseful rescue.

Someone else had done those things.

"Who did it?"

I gawked at him. "Really? You can't figure that out on your own?" Then I let up on the reins and nudged Viento with the heels of my boots and proceeded onward leaving Sherlee to contemplate the truth.

Despite his gruff demeanor, I believe he had been fond of Kate. He had seemed protective of her, especially where I was concerned. But just as likely, he could have been guarding her interests because of orders that had come down from the top. Sherlee had demonstrated more times than once that he was at Headville's command. Why he was so viciously loyal, I hadn't a clue. But I suspected Sherlee was as inherently mean and ruthless as was the man he worked for.

Seconds later, Sherlee's horse was clomping along behind me as I held Viento to a causal advance. Ahead of me, Headville sat regally upon the black stallion, holding to a place that was just a few feet away from the space of the arch. He gave me the impression that if I somehow managed to get past him and was able to trigger the talisman, he was going to make damn sure he was close enough to travel with me.

But if that was his assumption, there were two things that were fundamentally wrong with the idea. One, there was, at present, no sunlight. Two, I did not have the talisman. It lay hidden beyond him, atop the flat and elevated surface of the relatively near, but northernmost jagged row of eroded chalk-rock pillars. From beneath the canopy of my Stetson, I furtively glanced upward in that direction, barely discerning the elevated ridge where Kival would soon be operating a mission to recover the prize which Headville dearly coveted. In another thirty yards, I would be too close to see over the nearer row of the pyramid rocks. But then, neither would Headville be able to make the same observation.

I aimed Viento to a specific point I had decided would be my preferred position to engage in conversation with Headville, neither too close to him, nor too far away. When I arrived at the spot, I reined my horse and faced the maliciously seasoned time-traveler as though he and I were opponents in a jousting match. In front of me, Headville and Ulysses were framed within the keyhole of the fateful archway that rose behind them.

"That half-breed whelp of mine. I know he came with you. Where is he?"

"Who?" I asked.

"Stubborn to the end, aren't you JT?"

"Somebody's end." I agreed.

"You are not surprised I'm here, are you?"

"Where else would you be? You're not stupid. But unquestionably, I've also proven that you're not as smart as you think you are."

He looked across at me, his face indifferent. A mask, I surmised. I felt sure I had just given him a verbal right hook. Then he laughed. Hard. "Damn, JT, you do amuse me! I will regret putting a bullet in your head."

"You mean, Sherlee," I corrected him. "He's the weapon you use to do the dirty work, right?"

The corner of his mouth noticably twitched. "Not all the time," he replied sardonically.

"Oh, my mistake. You did murder Kate all on your own."

I watched as his countenance flipped from disdain to acute vehemence. He was seconds away from losing his shit.

Again.

I fully expected him to draw his beloved Custer-gifted pistol and shoot me where he had promised. But, if his intelligence managed to override his emotion, he would keep it together. For now, he needed me.

"You have no sense of morality, do you, Headville? No conscience?"

"Neither. Morality is overrated. If I were to allow you to live long enough, you'd learn as I have that a conscience is a dull and boring companion. Best to cut it loose and live your life without it."

"You are pathetic."

"You are right about one thing. I could have Sherlee kill you right where you sit. But you've persuaded me to do it myself."

"Then do it," I said, hedging my bet. "No skin off my teeth to disappear in front of you, taking the talisman with me."

"You don't have the talisman."

"Sure about that?"

He could not be certain. Both of us knew that.

"You are either more brave than I have given you credit, or you are even more foolish than your brother, or that nine-fingered idiot Oleander."

"Fifty-fifty," I told him.

"Meaning what, exactly," Headville asked, glaring across at me.

"Half brave, half foolish. Right now, I don't really give a shit if I live or die. You've taken my future away from me."

"Kate?!" he scoffed. "You, JT, have a pitifully inept understanding of what, or who, might be waiting for you in the future."

I studied him for a moment, judiciously processing his words. I had for months carried a thought with me, though I had not dared to pin much hope on it. Even Morgan had issued me a warning, though I had wondered then if he knew. That was also fifty-fifty.

"Do you really want to forfeit that life?" Headville asked. "It's really not that bad living here in my era of time," he added, and I sensed he was attempting to correct the implication of his prior statement.

"Kate was my future," I replied, deciding I preferred to give him a pointed piece of my mind, rather than be seduced by his cloak-and-dagger words. "She and I, we were planning a life together. But you couldn't live with that, could you? Your bastardly ego wouldn't let your little bird fly away with me, so, you caged her. And it wasn't a spontaneous decision. You had already guessed and had prepared her prison in advance. The lock on that door. It was not there before. You had already decided to punish her. To show Kate that loving me, instead of you, would cost her freedom."

From the short distance between us, I could see him seething. I had not planned to be so stupidly brave or so daringly foolish. My goal was simply to distract. I needed to stick to the plan. To give Kival time. But suddenly I sensed that I may have pushed Headville too hard.

"Kate was collateral damage," Headville sneered. "I would have made her my wife!" he added, his voice crescendoing with a penetrating tone of resentment. "By her loins, I would have sired heirs worthy of my blood and my name! Don't you dare think her loss is yours alone!"

Instantly, I was incensed that Kate had meant nothing more to him than just another species of breeding stock.

"She hated you, Culver Headville."

"SHOOT HIM!" Headville raged.

BANG!

CHAPTER 62

The gunshot fired from behind me, and I flinched from the repercussion and saw that Headville had also recoiled. Then, he slumped, and fell from the saddle, his cowboy hat falling from his head, a boot catching in a stirrup. Shied by the unexpected commotion, the black stallion reared back upon his hind legs, his rider dangling within the space around his hooves. Nervously, the horse side-stepped his way through the arch, then panicked, he spun around and trotted fearfully westward, dragging Headville with him, not stopping until he had moved a good fifty yards away.

Through the frame of the archway, I stared at the fallen man, wondering how the hell Sherlee had missed shooting me and had instead put a bullet into Headville. I turned around to face the man that was both wrangler and assassin, preparing myself for a second attempt on my life.

But Sherlee had holstered his firearm.

I looked at him, my eyes filled with suspicious wonder.

"If that bastard is not dead, tell him I quit."

Then Sherlee reined his horse around and kicked his heels into the animal's flanks and with a slow gallop, the horse carried his atoned rider away disappearing over a knoll and entering the openness of the eastern prairie. I watched him ride off, stunned by the unexpected re-write of the script. Then I turned to check my back, to reestablish Headville into my line of sight. But he and the horse were gone.

Damn it!

Had Headville just been winged? That had been my initial thought. But internally, I argued with myself that he had been knocked from the saddle! Or had the horse simply taken off again, frightened once more by his rider's abnormal position? Impulsively, I heeled Viento sharply, reining him through the arch, then caution struck me suddenly, and I pulled my horse to an abrupt stop. If Headville were still alive, he was surely armed. And Sherlee had not been certain he had killed him.

A quick glance to my left proved that the horse and its rider had not fled south, but to my right was a labyrinth of eighty-foot-tall rocky towers and outcroppings that formed ninety percent of the northern cluster of the chalk pyramids. I knew from my boyhood explorations, that there were multiple pockets and corners and niches easy enough to conceal a man. Several of which lay at the bottom of the landform containing the hole the Tescott brothers had named the Window: The place where Kival would be climbing toward if he had not already gotten there.

I dismounted, taking the pup and sitting her on the ground just around the corner of the archway, hiding her there on the east side.

"Sit," I said to her, and she complied. I had known that Kate had been teaching her things. "Stay," I ordered, hoping Toto would also obey that command. She looked up at me, her doe eyes bright with a desire to please. Then knowing that I was a far better target on horseback than I was on foot, I took Viento by his bridle and lead him past the obedient dog, walking him several yards along the wall of rock. I quickly untied the knot of the two reins and dropped them to the ground. I did not need to tell him to stay. Viento knew what it meant to be theoretically ground tied.

I slipped back through the arch and scanned both directions. Then I rushed to the western pinnacle of the nearest latitudinal row of the jagged rock wall and eased my way around its vertical face. I peered around the corner, searching, and found part of what I was looking for.

Ulysses.

The black horse stood twenty feet away, the saddle and its stirrups empty.

I cursed.

Beyond the horse were multiple hiding places. To explore them all would take time. But with Headville assumed to be armed with the Custer pistol or some other weapon, it would also be dangerous to move through the area without being extremely cautious. My heart was pounding. Now, adrenaline had begun to course through my blood. Boldly, I moved forward.

Slowly, I worked my way through a gap that opened between the second row of the disjointed landform, keeping my back against the wall. I eased to the right, my eyes flicking around in all directions. Twenty-five yards away, I faced the last irregular line of an east-west trajectory of the pyramid cluster, and after I had shifted another three paces, a movement high upon the wall across from me caught my attention. It was a man, scaling the fallen remains of what had once been a shear vertical wall of layered Cretaceous sediment that had accumulated when during a prior millennium the area had been part of a vast inland sea. Then, a second later, he saw me.

I signaled to Kival, motioning in such a way as to warn him that I doubted that I was alone, and that he needed to be wary. He nodded, confirming he had understood. I watched for a moment as Kival resumed his climb. He was maybe twenty feet from the top, and slightly further than that from the place of the elevated surface that was directly above the Window.

Soon, he would be where he had professed to have hidden the talisman. So long as he didn't fall. And providing Headville did not interfere.

Wherever he was.

Stealthily, I made my way through the space that was constrained by natural walls on both the north and south sides, searching the quasi-cave recesses that pitted the vertical landforms.

Nothing.

I then retraced my steps, noting that Kival had halved his previous distance to the top. I eased carefully past him and investigated the eastern portion of the natural amphitheater. My quarry still eluded me. To my right was an exit and I took it and glanced around the corner and saw that eighty yards away Viento and the puppy were both where I had left them. I turned back and looked toward where I had been and I saw Kival walking carefully upon the high flat ridge of the Monument Rock that had been the secret, but temporary, vault of his ancestral talisman.

Suddenly, a large, bright shaft of sunlight fell upon him, breaking through the bank of clouds, its source far lower in the sky than I had expected. The sands of our hourglass had somehow gotten away from us. At once, I was alarmed. We were running out of time. And fast.

In twenty-seven minutes, the passageway would close.

I still had no idea where Headville had hidden himself. Or if he had perhaps succumbed to his gunshot wound. He was, I presumed, a mere mortal.

Quickly, I eased my way across the exit gap and began a swift skirt along the north face of the eroded sedimentary wall. There was no sign of Headville there either. Somehow, I had missed him. Either that, or he had circled around behind me. That move was more plausible, for it would put him into closer proximity to the arch.

I looked northward to where Old Chief Smoky solitarily reigned a quarter mile away. The distance was less than one lap around a conventional running track, but the landscape was much, much rougher.

I headed that way; the countdown of the sun had made it imperative that I gather Anja and baby Elsa and get them swiftly back to Kival and to the arch. At first, I walked, covering a distance that thirty paces would take me. But I feared discovery by Headville, and the last thing I wanted was to tip him off that something of value was hidden behind the rock profile. I turned to glance behind me, praying I was not being pursued, and when I looked my eyes caught Kival rising from his knees above the window in the rock wall. He held up two thumbs.

It was time to Rock 'n Roll.

I sprinted ahead.

Rounding the far side of the Indian-faced pillar, I found Anja waiting in the saddle, her baby nestled in a blanket tucked snuggly against her chest. Beneath her stood Dent's horse, Mister Brown. As planned, Kival had already unsaddled his red gelding. Neither of us wanted to abandon any of the horses with the encumbrances of riding gear.

Quickly, I unfastened the bridle from the horse, freeing it. Then I crossed to the other horse, put my foot in the stirrup and swung myself up and sat behind Anja.

"Hold on to that baby!"

And in an instant, we were riding double-saddle and galloping toward a destination that resembled a natural Stonehenge. Only now, the Pyramids were no longer beneath a cover of clouds, instead they were glowing like buttery pillars in the radiance of a setting sun. Upon our swift approach, I saw that Kival had disappeared. But that was what I hoped for. He had but minutes to meet us at the launching pad of the arch. I just prayed that Headville would not intercept him.

Riding upon the galloping brown bay gelding, we cut around the northeast corner of the rock cluster and ahead of us stood Viento cloaked in the dark shadow of the rock wall still waiting where I left him just yards from the archway. I spurred my mount with a sharp kick of my heels, and he responded, running faster, carrying the three of us forward.

I reined the horse to an abrupt stop, bailed from the saddle, then glanced around for any evidence of Headville, but found neither sign nor subject. Quickly, I helped Anja and the baby from the horse. She knew where to go.

Then with haste, I pulled the saddle and bridle from the heroic gelding and slapped his rump with the end of a rein, sending him off in a carefree canter. I turned toward Viento, planning to likewise undress him of saddle and bridle, but from the corner of my eye I realized Anja was not where I expected her to be.

On this day of the year when the earth was at its nearest to the sun, three minutes remained to open the rift and engage the passageway.

She had probably just crossed through to the west side of the arch. But I needed to know for certain.

I stepped toward the opening where golden sunlight poured through and saw then that an elongated shadow of two adults stretched across the gravelly slope of the eastern side of the arch.

Kival was there. He and Anja were together.

I sighed, believing my assumption. But when I peered around the edge of the deep aperture in the rock, I discovered I had assumed wrong.

Headville held Anja, his grip clenched around the arm of her coat, and in his other hand he held a gun pointed at the young mother as she clutched the baby to her breast, her face a mask of terror.

Headville stood just feet away from me, his face bloodied, a deep flesh-wound creasing his cheek, a torn remnant of what had been his right ear, dangling loosely at the side of his head. Then I watched as he shifted his weapon, aiming it at me.

I lifted my hands, though I didn't know why. It was just a natural response learned from watching an abundance of Western TV shows.

"Times up," Headville snarled. Then he jerked, his body stiffening, his eyes wide with shock. Then his grasp that had seized his hostage came loose and he fell forward onto the ground, the pistol still in his hand, the hilt of a knife sticking from his back, its blade mortally embedded. Kival stood behind where Headville lay, gasping for breath. Then Anja rushed to him and Kival embraced his wife and daughter.

I looked past them and saw a sliver of the setting sun.

In less than two minutes, the passageway would close.

"Kival!" I yelled, gesturing behind him. He looked, then stepping around Headville's body, he quickly brought Anja and the baby into the heart of the archway. Then Kival reached for his neck and withdrew a chain that held the talisman. He began to turn toward the light.

"Wait!" I yelled again, stopping him. Then I brushed past him and grabbed the dead man by his hands and began to drag Headville's body away.

"What are doing?!" Kival exclaimed.

"We're not taking this asshole with us!" I fired back. I pulled hard on Headville's arms, until I had him beyond the distance where I believed Oleander's truck had been parked on that fateful evening six months earlier.

"Hurry!" Kival called out to me.

I dashed forward and wrapped my arms around the three of them, bracing for what I anticipated would be an explosion of blinding white light. Kival turned facing westward but there was no sunlight in his eyes. He broke the chain loose from his neck and lifted the talisman up toward the sky.

Nothing.

I glanced upward and saw that neither was there any sunlight on his hand. Yet only inches above his outstretched arm, I saw the moving line that separated day from night crawling upward along the wall of the archway.

"Shit!" I cursed. Then instantly I remembered Viento. I pulled away from the others, hurried around the corner, caught a rein, and stepped into the saddle. I spurred Viento into the archway and stood up in the stirrups and lifted my hand. My palm glowed in the golden beams of the last rays of the day's sun, as though I had the magic of the Midas touch. I looked down at Kival, his eyes fixed on my hand.

"Kival! Give it to me!"

He looked at me, hesitating.

"Kival, you gotta trust me," I whispered, my voice sincere and urgent.

He nodded and tossed me the talisman. I began to reach for the sky when I remembered the dog.

"Toto! Come!"

The little red and white speckled pup appeared around the corner. I smiled and lifted the talisman into the last beam of sunlight.

An explosion of bright, white light engulfed us, forcing shut the lids of my eyes.

CHAPTER 63

The intensity of a powerful brightness glowed through the thin skin of my eyelids, and I could feel its enveloping heat as if it were a thick blanket of suffocating August air. I squeezed my eyes tighter, guarding them against what I had feared the first time, a threat of irreversible blindness.

In a moment of ambiguous lucidity, I felt keenly aware that I was embarking on a journey that presumably required a molecular disassembly of my flesh and I visualized myself in the transport room of the Enterprise having just ordered Scottie to beam me up. But then in the next second an instantaneous iciness affronted the barrier of the cocoon that was my skin, biting with teeth razor sharp.

I felt myself shudder, then an abrupt weightlessness overwhelmed me.

And then I felt an unsettling presence in my midst and the intimate touch of hands fluttering upon me, and the gray matter of my brain reminded me of who they were.

The Burmano-Ku-Partika.

Touching me. Caressing me. Seeming to analytically scan my anatomy as though I were being x-rayed by an energy that pulsed from their fingertips. Hundreds of points of contact moved simultaneously across my head and face, over my torso and groin, and along my limbs. Though I had experienced this once before, I felt myself tremble from the sensation, the rational side of my mind screaming that something unnatural was upon me. Then at once, I felt the familiar, intensely agonizing pain, as though my very flesh was being stripped from my bone, and the remains of my skeleton being pulverized into hot granules.

I screamed as a chorus of cries, male and female, joined me, our wails of fear and helplessness catatonically diminishing from the realm of my consciousness.

Then darkness devoured me.

With the last light of the perihelion, the passageway closed.

A lambent consciousness floated from my mind, leaving me with a guarded desire to regain an awareness of my surroundings. I lay motionless and recumbent, curled up like a fetus at home in his mother's womb, except I felt as though I were frozen in place, unable to stir or shift.

Or perhaps I was simply afraid and skeptical of a painless movement.

Minutes passed. Perhaps even hours had lapsed as I quietly listened to the resonating sound of my breathing that felt barely shallow, let alone effectively reverberant. Then slowly a cognizance of my heart beating deeply within my core grew stronger, willfully taking command of my attention. Then, a high-pitched ringing sounded in my ears just moments before I aggressively began to shiver and quake, sensing the coldness that had immobilized me was fading and fading fast.

A sense of tranquility wrapped its invisible breath around me, and I felt a tingling, pleasurable warmth pulse through my veins, gradually and steadily intensifying. Then a vague memory ignited a perception in me that I had lived through this experience before, and in a subconscious corner of my mind I believed I was in a state of thawing.

Suspended in unmeasurable time, I was content to lay quiet, and unmoving, though I felt the shifting of my eyes behind my closed lids. As the neurons of my brain steadily networked and reconnected, I discerned that I had recently suffered through an unfathomable torment, but I had no concept if it had been an episode from years ago, or just a mere tick of a few seconds past. Or if the recollection was only a part of a dream.

For a while, time seemed to have stalled, held in place, as if the earth had paused spinning upon its axis. Then suddenly I consciously recognized the presence of others, that I was again among those with whom I had previously acquired an unfathomable familiarity.

I opened my eyes, and the sensation of excitement instantly consumed me. I was surrounded by dozens of weightless and spirited forms swirling about as if they were worker bees in the presence of their hive.

Then, as before, one of the Burmano-Ku-Partika floated toward me, appearing for a moment to have morphed into a physical body real enough to touch. I watched as the unworldly-being paused to stare into my eyes with a kind, intelligent face. I was, in that moment, both astonished and grateful. In my mind, I knew they had brought me home.

I closed my eyes, overwhelmed by exhaustion.

When I awakened, I found myself lying upon my back, a deep and seemingly impenetrable blackness surrounding me, though vestiges of the constellation of Orion were pinned onto the dark sky above me, its full image partly obscured by a suspended bridge of stone.

The arch.

I was back where I belonged. Or was I? Time would tell, but patience might be required.

I hoped to have been escorted and introduced to the year 1980, a round-trip journey that challenged the construct of a continuum of time. If so, I could hardly wait to see my mom. And my dad. Though I dreaded that I would have to break their hearts. To tell them that their son, Dent, had perished.

As I had sensed before, my journey back had taken far longer than just minutes. It had taken hours. At least hours as measured by the world of humans. Either way, I was anxious to know of my current time. I folded my stomach and sat up. Pivoting my head in an arc of 180 degrees, I blinked my eyes again and again, struggling to bring into view something, anything. But my veiled sight revealed nothing.

Perhaps this time, I had been rendered blind.

However, my hearing was as sharp as a cactus needle. That functioning sense easily discerning the sound of a large animal hefting itself upon its rigid hooves. Then a whimper lifted nearby.

"Toto?!" I whispered, relieved that I had command of my voice. "Come girl!" The light padding of her paws sounded upon the ground as she made her way to me and crawled into my lap. I picked her up and she licked my face. Then another stirring, closer to me ambushed my attention.

"Kival?" I spoke.

"It is me, Anja," was the reply, then, still unable to see, the soft cry of an awakening baby touched my ears and I smiled.

"Kival?" I asked again, and I reached out and found him next to me. I sat the pup down and rolled onto my knees and knelt beside him, feeling for his face, and finding it. I tilted my cheek and held it an inch above his mouth. Instantly, I felt the invisible push of a breath.

We had made it through. All of us.

In my hand I realized I held the talisman. But I did not need it anymore, nor was it mine to keep. I reached and found my unconscious friend's arm and traced its length to his hand and there I placed the talisman into his palm and closed his fingers over it.

Behind me Viento snorted a greeting, letting me know that he was also alive and well. At least no matter what year we were experiencing, be it a time with or without automobiles, Anja and the baby would not have to walk.

Then, as if I had conjured by simply thinking it, a set of bright lights flashed on, their beams hitting me squarely in the eyes, forcing me to duck my head. As though I were in the frames of a slow-motion movie, I lifted Toto into my arms and stood up facing the lights, one hand shielding my view, filtering the intense glare. Then I heard the sound of a pickup door opening and the soft crush of boots stepping along the ground, then a body moved in front of the lamp of the driver's side and formed a silhouette within the artificial light. And then, in the context of a few seconds, I realized just how similar in shape and carriage was my brother compared to my dad.

With a fierce expulsion of breath, I immediately wept at the sight of him. Tears of pure happiness streaked down my cheeks as a joyful laugh stuttered from my throat.

"About damn time!" Dent called out to me, and in my mind, I could see him grinning ear to ear.

That idea … that concept … that almost unthinkable possibility had proven to be true. It had been with me for a long time, since that first day when Sam had noticed that my injuries had healed. However, I had not died. And that was the difference. That was what had kept me from believing it possible. But now, I realized that it was not just the dust-to-dust hypothesis I had thought it might be. Conceptually, it appeared that one could not perish in a time that was not their own. The Burmano-Ku-Partika could not only repair injuries, but they could also restore life.

"You jackass!" I screamed at my brother. I broke my knees just enough to return Toto to the ground, then I ran to him unabated. Dent met me half-way, and we threw our arms around each other, embracing as though we had not seen each other in years.

"Long time no see, JT," Dent's voice chimed as he patted my back with exalted merriment. And he was right, it had been a long time. One-hundred-one years had separated us.

"Don't you ever do that to me again," I scolded him, then I pulled away and cupped his clean-shaven face in my hands and poured out my affection for him through the tears in my eyes. But I also had words for him. Words I had thought often but had never said. "I love you, big brother," I told him. He grinned and nodded, then we embraced a second time.

"Welcome home, little brother," Dent whispered in my ear.

Then a second set of pickup lights flicked on, and at once I could hear Waylon Jennings and Willie Nelson singing *Mamas Don't Let Your Babies Grow Up to Be Cowboys*. Throughout my time in 1878,

I had accepted his fate, I had dared not to hope. But now, I believed differently. I was certain the audio of that song would only be from a specific 8-track cassette, one which had been played for me months earlier. I turned to see another male figure approaching us. In the reflective illumination of headlights, Sam materialized, his compelling face dominated by an enormous and bone fide smile.

I sobbed again. I couldn't help it. I had already reconciled with the fact that I was the most overly sensitive Tescott, or Thomas, to have ever been hatched along the lines of my family tree. And in this moment, I was totally fine with that ranking. I motioned to Sam to join me and my brother and when he was just feet away, I stepped toward him and pulled my childhood friend back into my life.

I held on to Sam, my eyes on the edge of a second meltdown. Then I felt Dent's arm settle around my shoulder. In that moment, I was at peace. Perhaps because the three of us were in the protection of God's own hand.

Then I thought of Kate.

If my present soaring hunch was right, then there was hope.

And hope was good enough. It was all I needed.

For now.

EPILOGUE

MAY 1988

I spent the night and half of the next morning at the county courthouse. There had been no sleep for me, just an occasional five-minute bathroom break between interrogations conducted by the Chief of Police and the District Attorney, though the latter referred to our chats as interviews. Both elected officials, as well as their respective right-hand counterparts, had all relentlessly questioned me regarding the disappearance of a three-member family who had inexplicably vanished from a hospital room that had been blocked and barricaded by, well, by me.

Despite being arrested with a 9mm Glock in my possession, without bodies, or because of the absence of even a spec of blood as evidence of foul play, the team of law enforcement had nothing to present to Custer's presiding judge that would warrant an extended stay at police headquarters. So, with my attorney at my side, I left, leaving a group of intelligent men and women scratching their collective heads. I had been party to a similar scene eight years and four months earlier. Only it was different this time.

Today, there were witnesses who had made sworn statements of testimony that I had been with the missing man and wife, and their eight-year-old child, who likewise had mysteriously disappeared from her deathbed.

Before, I had simply been a teenage adult who had returned six months after his sudden and baffling disappearance, reuniting with his parents and his brother. Naturally, there had been questions then, too. But Dent, and Sam, and Kival and I had remained resolute in our mutual conviction that we had no memory of anything, though my parents knew differently. Dent had told them everything, and his explanation had given them the hope they had needed to believe that I, too, would make it back home.

And I had learned then, eight years ago, that my parents had found Sam, weak but alert, when he had knocked on the back door of our ranch home in an early dawn hour of July 6, two days after my eighteenth birthday. Dent, on the other hand, had been discovered half-naked more than five months later by a rancher's wife who had been roused from her sleep by the incessant barking of the family dog. She, Edith Morton, had compassionately welcomed a bewildered Dent into the warm comfort of her modest home while her husband, Robert, contacted the local authorities of Ellis County.

To this day, on the anniversary of December 24th, Mom and Dad would personally deliver to the Mortons a gift of their appreciation. In them, my parents found unexpected friendship, and made frequent visits to their Charolais Cattle Ranch, a modest twelve-hundred acre spread that hugs the spring waters of Sweetwater Creek. I have never gone with them. I am too fearful that I might see the ghost of a man I would sooner forget. But Mom has shown me pictures. The structures of the Morton ranch are less grand and more practical than those I had become acquainted with while a cowboy in the employ of a historically forgotten man named Culver Headville. Accordingly, Mother Nature had also erased the evidence of Headville's extravagance with the destructive power of a monstrous tornado in the spring of 1896.

One place, though, was still the same. An 1862 homestead dug-out faced with limestone rock. Dent had told me of its existence after having made a pilgrimage there that first summer after our return. He had taken with him the book that had belonged to Mick that featured a cover drawing and story about the legendary Kit Carson: The dime novel I had brought back with me through the perihelion portal of 1879. Dent confessed that in the quiet of that lonely place, he had read aloud the featured story found in its pages. But my brother had left the book there, a gesture of his affection for the young man whom he needed to let go.

The disappearance of six teens from a small town in Kansas had made national headlines, though there had been an undercurrent of speculation that we had been merely runaways. Local news people, who knew us better, attributed the disappearance of the six of us Custer High graduates as victims of a bizarre plot involving a potential routing of a narcotics ring. They reasoned that we had accidentally discovered a criminal lair and had subsequently been drugged thus explaining the theft of our memories, even though the results of a battery of tests had been negative. Except for the one who had apparently escaped, his blood test proved positive for marijuana.

Perry Hutchinson had been found wondering aimlessly seven miles south of the Pyramids in the early hours of the following day, July 5th. Known to be a pothead, his bizarre story of a spaceship landing was decidedly rejected by both the local law enforcement and the Kansas Bureau of Investigation.

However, one popular tabloid, whose conspiratorially minded editor had gotten wind of our disappearance, had headlined the six of us as casualties of a government cover-up for what he proposed to have been an astonishing alien abduction.

But two aspects remained to be explained to the satisfaction of the authorities, and by extension, the press.

Paul Blaine Wallace, Jr. was still listed as a missing person.

And Oleander Sedgwick was dead. He had been the victim of a baffling pedestrian accident on US Highway 183 south of Hays, Kansas where the drivers of two different automobiles claimed the young man had just materialized out of nowhere. Tragically, one of them had been unable to avoid rolling over his prostrate body, the force of the car's tires inflicting mortal internal injuries and a concussion. Oleander died at a hospital two days later without ever regaining consciousness.

There had been no report that Oleander had suffered a gunshot wound. But what I had come to realize was that Oleander's body had been healed and his life restored by the Burmano-Ku-Partika, just as they had done for Sam and Dent. The difference was location. He had departed from a remote locality in 1878 but had been returned to the same coordinate that was, in 1979, a relatively high-traffic thoroughfare. Culver Headville's assassination of Oleander had put our comrade in the wrong place at the wrong time. The Burmano-Ku-Partika had their own rules to follow. I, for one, would not question them.

As I had also been accosted by media reporters and news cameramen during a cold January week in 1980, there was today, on an unusually rainy afternoon in May, a second swarm of them set to pounce once I left the building.

And swarm they did.

But just as I had responded to the officials who had been trying to pry a sliver of information from me, I said as much to the folks who shook microphones at my head and pointed cameras into my face.

"No comment."

My attorney, who had escorted me down the courthouse steps, ushered me to a car he had waiting with a driver ready to whisk me away from the eyes of the curious and the damning. He opened the door and I slid into the back seat, and waiting there for me was my wife, Kate.

Yes, my Kate: The one who had stolen my heart in the year 1878.

We kissed and hugged and then held hands as we were chauffeured away, heading for my parents' ranch where our two little blonde-headed boys waited for their mommy and daddy. A heavy tear slipped down my cheek as I thought of the life we were about to leave behind. I felt tremendously grieved for my decision to temporarily distance my little family from my mom and my dad, but I would especially miss my brother. And my kids would, in no time flat, long for their playful Uncle Dent, as well as their new Uncle Trevor.

Kate and I, and our little boys, were withdrawing from the scrutiny of others. Relocating to some place quieter and more private. Because of the disappearances at the hospital of Kival, Anja, and Elsa, the inevitability of starting over had caught up with us sooner than expected. But we had planned ahead, and a new home awaited the six of us, including Viento and Toto, neither of which we could leave behind.

And in an unknown place and time, I knew there was a friend waiting to meet me.

A man called Morgan.

ABOUT THE AUTHOR

Gary Stapp is an established playwright with nearly twenty titles licensed and represented by various play publishing companies. His scripts have been frequently staged throughout the United States and Canada. Two of his titles have been translated into other languages and ultimately produced by theatre companies in Europe. As a recognized winner of a mini fellowship for playwriting sponsored by the Kansas Arts Commission, Gary has deep roots in the Sunflower State, having been born and raised in Southwest Kansas. His hometown of Satanta, the enchanting state landmark of Monument Rocks, and a sprawling ranch north of Hays founded in the 1870s by his wife's great-great-grandfather, have inspired both fictional settings and real locales for his debut novel. Currently residing in Texas, he is either working on, or dreaming about his next story.